Worlds Seen in Passing

TEN YEARS OF *TOR.COM* SHORT FICTION

WORLDS SEEN IN PASSING

Ten Years of *Tor.com* Short Fiction

edited by IRENE GALLO

A TOM DOHERTY ASSOCIATES BOOK • NEW YORK

WORLDS SEEN IN PASSING

Copyright © 2018 by Irene Gallo

All stories herewith originally published on *Tor.com* and reprinted by permission of *Tor.com* unless otherwise stated. "The Witch of Duva" copyright © 2012 by Leigh Bardugo. Revised version (published in *The Language of Thorns* by Leigh Bardugo, copyright © 2017) reprinted here by permission of the author. Further copyright acknowledgments can be found on page 571.

A Tor.com Book
Published by Tom Doherty Associates
175 Fifth Avenue
New York, NY 10010

www.tor.com

Tor® is a registered trademark of Macmillan Publishing Group, LLC.

The Library of Congress Cataloging-in-Publication Data is available upon request.

ISBN 978-1-250-17123-8 (hardcover)
ISBN 978-1-250-17125-2 (ebook)

Our books may be purchased in bulk for promotional, educational, or business use. Please contact your local bookseller or the Macmillan Corporate and Premium Sales Department at 1-800-221-7945, extension 5442, or by email at MacmillanSpecialMarkets@macmillan.com.

First Edition: September 2018

Printed in the United States of America

0 9 8 7 6 5 4 3 2 1

For my mother, who loved words.

Contents

Preface

Tor.com celebrated its tenth anniversary on July 20, 2018—the forty-ninth anniversary of the first manned moon landing. It started out innocently enough. In 2006, our publisher, Fritz Foy, while attending the Tor Books holiday party, pulled Patrick and Teresa Nielsen Hayden and me aside and said he wanted to create a "river of conversation, art, and fiction" within the SF/F community—an online magazine that crossed the borders between publishers and media.

It took us a couple years to get off the ground. During that time, whenever we felt lost in the process, we'd come back to the word "genuine." We wanted to build a place that treated science fiction and fantasy (and related subjects) with gravitas and humor, a place to have fun without shying away from weightier, more thoughtful subjects. In short, we wanted to build a place where *we* wanted to hang out. The ten years since the launch feel like a day, and like a million years. So much has changed, but the essence remains the same—we're still talking about the things we love. Through all the hashtags and trending topics, we still find the key to success is focusing on good, solid content.

We've published short fiction from day one. We knew from the start that fiction was always going to be at the heart of *Tor.com*. As publishers it made sense, but also . . . the entire site is dedicated to storytelling. *Of course* we wanted fiction to be our focal point. We have since published hundreds of original stories, along with art, reprints, comics, and poems—all of which are a source of pride for us, as well as bringing enjoyment to our readers.

Within these covers you'll find a selection of those stories. There are established authors, sure to be read for decades, alongside newer writers working hard to make their mark on the field. Some of these stories are award nominees and winners. Most of all, they are stories in which to see ourselves reflected with grace and humor and, at times, with terror. They reach deep inside us as they stretch for the stars and are as intrinsically human as they are impossible.

With my art background, I'm much more comfortable calling myself a curator than an editor—especially when all of these stories were initially acquired by a dream team of editorial talent. The consistent quality of the stories that come into my email inbox each month is slightly less mind-boggling when I remember that they are coming from Ellen Datlow, Ann VanderMeer, Patrick Nielsen Hayden, Liz Gorinsky, and a select group of others. As publishers, we gave these editors free rein, and they ran with it. What you see is their taste and vision in as pure a form as we can offer.

Putting this anthology together was a heartbreaking enterprise in many ways. As much as I enjoy revisiting the stories collected here, I feel as if I am leaving old friends behind when it comes to the ones that couldn't fit in this volume. If you like these stories, I really do hope that you might make your way over to the website and explore others. There was so much that had to be left out. Some of my favorites were just too long to include—Mary Rickert's short novel *The Mothers of Voorhisville* and Veronica Schanoes's stunning novella *Burning Girls*, to name just two. John Scalzi's hilarious April Fools' Day offering, an "excerpt" from *The Shadow War of the Night Dragons*, would be out of context here, but, I assure you, is well worth your time. And please check out Wesley Allsbrook and Barrie Potter's amazing short comic *To Eternity*.

We've also commissioned poetry and flash fiction over the years, wonderful pieces that deserve all the attention they can get. There are so many worlds and voices to discover.

While we are on the subject of what is not here, I want to express a special thanks to all the artists who have contributed to the website throughout the years. They have played a big part in making *Tor.com* a premier outlet for short fiction. Their contribution is incalculable. This anthology wasn't the place to showcase their illustrations, but look them up: The work is glorious and every bit as affecting as the stories themselves.

It takes a rocket to run a website. Literally countless people are involved when you include the readers, our most important collaborators. I do hope you take a look at the acknowledgments and see for yourself how many people have helped, in so many ways, to bring these stories to you today.

We decided to launch on Moon Landing Day for its obvious inspiration and appeal to us as science fiction fans. Having reached the moon, we continue to explore. We still touch the stars and use that perspective to reflect and measure ourselves. With infinite curiosity, I hope you enjoy the stories that these forty authors have crafted. And I hope you enjoy them enough to keep coming back to *Tor.com* for decades to come.

Irene Glynn-Gallo
New York City
January 2018

Worlds Seen
in Passing

TEN YEARS OF *TOR.COM* SHORT FICTION

Six Months, Three Days

Charlie Jane Anders

The story of the love affair between a man who can see the one true foreordained future and a woman who can see all possible futures. They're both right. *Hugo Award winner, Nebula Award nominee. Edited by Patrick Nielsen Hayden.*

The man who can see the future has a date with the woman who can see many possible futures.

Judy is nervous but excited, keeps looking at things she's spotted out of the corner of her eye. She's wearing a floral Laura Ashley–style dress with an ankh necklace and her legs are rambunctious, her calves moving under the table. It's distracting because Doug knows that in two and a half weeks, those cucumber-smooth ankles will be hooked on his shoulders, and that curly reddish-brown hair will spill everywhere onto her lemon-floral pillows; this image of their future co-itus has been in Doug's head for years, with varying degrees of clarity, and now it's almost here. The knowledge makes Doug almost giggle at the wrong moment, but then it hits him: she's seen this future too—or she may have, anyway.

Doug has his sandy hair cut in a neat fringe that was almost fashionable a couple years ago. You might think he cuts his own hair, but Judy knows he doesn't, because he'll tell her otherwise in a few weeks. He's much, much better looking than she thought he would be, and this comes as a huge relief. He has rude, pouty lips and an upper lip that darkens no matter how often he shaves it, with Elvis Costello glasses. And he's almost a foot taller than her, six foot four. Now that Judy's seen Doug for real, she's re-imagining all the conversations they might be having in the coming weeks and months, all of the drama and all of the sweetness. The fact that Judy can be attracted to him, knowing everything that could lie ahead, consoles her tremendously.

Judy is nattering about some Chinese novelist she's been reading in translation, one of those cruel satirists from the days after the May Fourth Movement, from back when writers were so conflicted they had to rename themselves things like "Contra Diction." Doug is just staring at her, not saying anything, until it creeps her out a little.

"What?" Doug says at last, because Judy has stopped talking and they're both just staring at each other.

"You were staring at me," Judy says.

"I was . . ." Doug hesitates, then just comes out and says it. "I was savoring the moment. You know, you can know something's coming from a long way off, you know for years ahead of time the exact day and the very hour when it'll arrive. And then it arrives, and when it arrives, all you can think about is how soon it'll be gone."

"Well, I didn't know the hour and the day when you and I would meet," Judy puts a hand on his. "I saw many different hours and days. In one timeline, we would have met two years ago. In another, we'd meet a few months from now. There are plenty of timelines where we never meet at all."

Doug laughs, then waves a hand to show that he's not laughing at her, although the gesture doesn't really clarify whom or what he's actually laughing at.

Judy is drinking a cocktail called the Coalminer's Daughter, made out of ten kinds of darkness. It overwhelms her senses with sugary pungency, and leaves her lips black for a moment. Doug is drinking a wheaty pilsner from a tapered glass, in gulps. After one of them, Doug cuts to the chase. "So this is the part where I ask. I mean, I know what happens next between you and me. But here's where I ask what you think happens next."

"Well," Judy says. "There are a million tracks, you know. It's like raindrops falling into a cistern, they're separate until they hit the surface, and then they become the past: all undifferentiated. But there are an awful lot of futures where you and I date for about six months."

"Six months and three days," Doug says. "Not that I've counted or anything."

"And it ends badly."

"I break my leg."

"You break your leg ruining my bicycle. I like that bike. It's a noble five-speed in a sea of fixies."

"So you agree with me." Doug has been leaning forward, staring at Judy like a psycho again. He leans back so that the amber light spilling out of the Radish Saloon's tiny lampshades turn him the same color as his beer. "You see the same future I do." Like she's passed some kind of test.

"You didn't know what I was going to say in advance?" Judy says.

"It doesn't work like that—not for me, anyway. Remembering the future is just like remembering the past. I don't have perfect recall, I don't hang on to every detail, the transition from short-term memory to long-term memory is not always graceful."

"I guess it's like memory for me too," Judy says.

Doug feels an unfamiliar sensation, and he realizes after a while it's comfort. He's never felt this at home with another human being, especially after such a short time. Doug is accustomed to meeting people and knowing bits and pieces of their futures, from stuff he'll learn later. Or if Doug meets you and doesn't know anything about your future, that means he'll never give a crap about you, at any point down the line. This makes for awkward social interactions, either way.

They get another round of drinks. Doug gets the same beer again, Judy gets a red concoction called a Bloody Mutiny.

"So there's one thing I don't get," Doug says. "You believe you have a choice among futures—and I think you're wrong, you're seeing one true future and a bunch of false ones."

"You're probably going to spend the next six months trying to convince yourself of that," Judy says.

"So why are you dating me at all, if you get to choose? You know how it'll turn out. For that matter, why aren't you rich and famous? Why not pick a future where you win the lottery, or become a star?"

Doug works in tech support, in a poorly ventilated subbasement of a tech company in Providence, Rhode Island, that he knows will go out of business in a couple years. He will work there until the company fails, choking on the fumes from old computers, and then be unemployed a few months.

"Well," Judy says. "It's not really that simple. I mean, the next six months, assuming I don't change my mind, they contain some of the happiest moments of my life, and I see it leading to some good things, later on. And you know, I've seen some tracks where I get rich, I become a public figure, and they never end well. I've got my eye on this one future, this one node way off in the distance, where I die aged ninety-seven, surrounded by lovers and grandchildren and cats. Whenever I have a big decision to make, I try to see the straightest path to that moment."

"So I'm a stepping stone," Doug says, not at all bitterly. He's somehow finished his second beer already, even though Judy's barely made a dent in her Bloody Mutiny.

"You're maybe going to take this journey with me for a spell," Judy says. "People aren't stones."

And then Doug has to catch the last train back to Providence, and Judy has to bike home to Somerville. Marva, her roommate, has made popcorn and hot chocolate, and wants to know the whole story.

"It was nice," Judy says. "He was a lot cuter in person than I'd remembered, which is really nice. He's tall."

"That's it?" Marva said. "Oh, come on, details. You finally meet the only other freaking clairvoyant on Earth, your future boyfriend, and all you have to say is, 'He's tall.' Uh-uh. You are going to spill like a fucking oil tanker. I will ply you with hot chocolate, I may resort to Jim Beam, even."

Marva's "real" name is Martha, but she changed it years ago. She's a grad student studying eighteenth-century lit, and even Judy can't help her decide whether to finish her PhD. She looks like pop culture's idea of a fag hag: slightly chubby, with perfect crimson hair and clothing by Sanrio, Torrid, and Hot Topic. She is fond of calling herself "mallternative."

"I'm drunk enough already. I nearly fell off my bicycle a couple times," Judy says.

The living room is a pigsty, so they sit in Judy's room, which isn't much better. Judy hoards items she might need in one of the futures she's witnessed, and they cover every surface. There's a plastic replica of a Filipino fast-food mascot, Jollibee, which she might give to this one girl Sukey in a couple of years, completing Sukey's collection and making her a friend for life—or Judy and Sukey may never meet at all. A phalanx of stuffed animals crowds Judy and Marva on the big fluffy bed. The room smells like a sachet of whoop-ass (cardamom, cinnamon, lavender) that Judy opened up earlier.

"He's a really sweet guy." Judy cannot stop talking in platitudes, which bothers her. "I mean, he's really lost, but he manages to be brave. I can't imagine what it would be like, to feel like you have no free will at all."

Marva doesn't point out the obvious thing—that Judy only sees choices for herself, not anybody else. Suppose a guy named Rocky asks Marva out on a date, and Judy sees a future in which Marva complains, afterwards, that their date was the worst evening of her life. In that case, there are two futures: one in which Judy tells Marva what she sees, and one in which she doesn't. Marva will go on the miserable date with Rocky, unless Judy tells her what she knows. (On the plus side, in fifteen months, Judy will drag Marva out to a party where she meets the love of her life. So there's that.)

"Doug's right," Marva says. "I mean, if you really have a choice about this, you shouldn't go through with it. You know it's going to be a disaster, in the end. You're the one person on Earth who can avoid the pain, and you still go sticking fingers in the socket."

"Yeah, but . . ." Judy decides this will go a lot easier if there are marshmallows in the cocoa, and runs back to the kitchen alcove. "But going out with this guy leads to good things later on. And there's a realization that I come to as a result of getting my heart broken. I come to understand something."

"And what's that?"

Judy finds the bag of marshmallows. They are stale. She decides cocoa will revitalize them, drags them back to her bedroom, along with a glass of water.

"I have no idea, honestly. That's the way with epiphanies: You can't know in advance what they'll be. Even me. I can see them coming, but I can't understand something until I understand it."

"So you're saying that the future that Doug believes is the only possible future just happens to be the best of all worlds. Is this some Leibniz shit? Does Dougie always automatically see the nicest future or something?"

"I don't think so." Judy gets gummed up by popcorn, marshmallows, and sticky cocoa, and coughs her lungs out. She swigs the glass of water she brought for just this moment. "I mean—" She coughs again, and downs the rest of the water. "I mean, in Doug's version, he's only forty-three when he dies, and he's pretty broken by then. His last few years are dreadful. He tells me all about it in a few weeks."

"Wow," Marva says. "Damn. So are you going to try and save him? Is that what's going on here?"

"I honestly do not know. I'll keep you posted."

Doug, meanwhile, is sitting on his militarily neat bed, with its single hospital-cornered blanket and pillow. His apartment is almost pathologically tidy. Doug stares at his one shelf of books and his handful of carefully chosen items that play a role in his future. He chews his thumb. For the first time in years, Doug desperately wishes he had options.

He almost grabs his phone, to call Judy and tell her to get the hell away from him, because he will collapse all of her branching pathways into a dark tunnel, once and for all. But he knows he won't tell her that, and even if he did, she wouldn't listen. He doesn't love her, but he knows he will in a couple weeks, and it already hurts.

"God damn it! Fucking god fucking damn it fuck!" Doug throws his favorite porcelain bust of Wonder Woman on the floor and it shatters. Wonder Woman's head breaks into two jagged pieces, cleaving her magic tiara in half. This image, of the Amazon's raggedly bisected head, has always been in Doug's mind, whenever he's looked at the intact bust.

Doug sits a minute, dry-sobbing. Then he goes and gets his dustpan and brush.

He phones Judy a few days later. "Hey, so do you want to hang out again on Friday?"

"Sure," Judy says. "I can come down to Providence this time. Where do you want to meet up?"

"Surprise me," says Doug.

"You're a funny man."

Judy will be the second long-term relationship of Doug's life. His first was with Pamela, an artist he met in college, who made headless figurines of people who were recognizable from the neck down. (Headless Superman. Headless Captain Kirk. And yes, headless Wonder Woman, which Doug always found bitterly amusing for reasons he couldn't explain.) They were together nearly five years, and Doug never told her his secret. Which meant a lot of pretending to be surprised at stuff. Doug is used to people thinking he's kind of a weirdo.

Doug and Judy meet for dinner at one of those mom-and-pop Portuguese places in East Providence, sharing grilled squid and seared cod, with fragrant rice and a bottle of heady vinho verde. Then they walk Judy's bike back across the river towards the kinda-sorta gay bar on Wickenden Street. "The thing I like about Providence," says Doug, "is it's one of the American cities that knows its best days are behind it. So it's automatically decadent, and sort of European."

"Well," says Judy, "It's always a choice between urban decay or gentrification, right? I mean, cities aren't capable of homeostasis."

"Do you know what I'm thinking?" Doug is thinking he wants to kiss Judy. She leans up and kisses him first, on the bridge in the middle of the East Bay Bicycle Path. They stand and watch the freeway lights reflected on the water, holding hands. Everything is cold and lovely and the air smells rich.

Doug turns and looks into Judy's face, which the bridge lights have turned yellow. "I've been waiting for this moment all my life." Doug realizes he's inadvertently quoted Phil Collins. First he's mortified, then he starts laughing like a maniac. For the next half hour, Doug and Judy speak only in Phil Collins quotes.

"You can't hurry love," Judy says, which is only technically a Collins line.

Over microbrews on Wickenden, they swap origin stories, even though they already know most of it. Judy's is pretty simple: She was a little kid who overthought choices like which summer camp to go to, until she realized she could see how either decision would turn out. She still flinches when she remembers how she almost gave a valentine in third grade to Dick Petersen, who would have destroyed her. Doug's story is a lot worse: he started seeing the steps ahead, a little at a time, and then he realized his dad would die in about a year. He tried everything he could think of, for a whole year, to save his dad's life. He even buried the car keys two feet deep, on the day of his dad's accident. No fucking use.

"Turns out getting to mourn in advance doesn't make the mourning afterwards any less hard," Doug says through a beer-glass snout.

"Oh, man," Judy says. She knew this stuff, but hearing it is different. "I'm so sorry."

"It's okay," Doug says. "It was a long time ago."

Soon it's almost time for Judy to bike back to the train station, near that godawful giant mall and the canal where they light the water on fire sometimes.

"I want you to try and do something for me," Judy takes Doug's hands. "Can you try to break out of the script? Not the big stuff that you think is going to happen, but just little things that you couldn't be sure about in advance if you tried. Try to surprise yourself. And maybe all those little deviations will add up to something bigger."

"I don't think it would make any difference," Doug says.

"You never know," Judy says. "There are things that I remember differently every time I think about them. Things from the past, I mean. When I was in college, I went through a phase of hating my parents, and I remembered all this stuff they did, from my childhood, as borderline abusive. And then a few years ago, I found myself recalling those same incidents again, only now they seemed totally different. Barely the same events."

"The brain is weird," Doug says.

"So you never know," Judy says. "Change the details, you may change the big picture." But she already knows nothing will come of this.

A week later, Doug and Judy lay together in her bed, after having sex for the first time. It was even better than the image Doug's carried in his head since puberty. For the first time, Doug understands why people talk about sex as this transcendent thing, chains of selfhood melting away, endless abundance. They looked into each other's eyes the whole time. As for Judy, she's having that oxytocin thing she's always thought was a myth, her forehead resting on Doug's smooth chest—if she moved her head an inch she'd hear his heart beating, but she doesn't need to.

Judy gets up to pee an hour later, and when she comes back and hangs up her robe, Doug is lying there with a look of horror on his face. "What's wrong?" She doesn't want to ask, but she does anyway.

"I'm sorry." He sits up. "I'm just so happy, and . . . I can count the awesome moments in my life on a hand and a half. And I'm burning through them too fast. This is just so perfect right now. And, you know. I'm trying not to think. About."

Judy knows that if she brings up the topic they've been avoiding, they will have an unpleasant conversation. But she has to. "You have to stop this. It's obvious you can do what I do, you can see more than one branch. All you have to do is try. I know you were hurt when you were little, your dad died, and you convinced yourself that you were helpless. I'm sorry about that. But now, I feel like you're actually comfortable being trapped. You don't even try any more."

"I do," Doug is shaking. "I do try. I try every day. How dare you say I don't try."

"You don't really. I don't believe you. I'm sorry, but I don't."

"You know it's true." Doug calms down and looks Judy square in the face. Without his glasses, his eyes look as gray as the sea on a cloudy day. "The thing you told me about Marva—you always know what she's going to do. Yeah? That's how your power works. The only reason you can predict how your own choices will turn out is because other people's actions are fixed. If you go up to some random guy on the street and slap him, you can know in advance exactly how he'll react. Right?"

"Well, sure," Judy says. "I mean, that doesn't mean Marva doesn't have free will. Or this person I've hypothetically slapped." This is too weird a conversation to be having naked. She goes and puts on a Mountain Goats T-shirt and PJ bottoms. "Their choices are just factored in, in advance."

"Right." Doug's point is already made, but he goes ahead and lunges for the kill. "So how do you know that I can't predict your choices, exactly the same way you can predict Marva's?"

Judy sits down on the edge of the bed. She kneads the edge of her T-shirt and doesn't look at Doug. Now she knows why Doug looked so sick when she came back from the bathroom. He saw more of this conversation than she did. "You could be right," she says after a moment. "If you're right, that makes you the one person I should never be in the same room with. I should stay the hell away from you."

"Yeah. You should," Doug says. He knows it will take forty-seven seconds before she cradles his head and kisses his forehead, and it feels like forever. He holds his breath and counts down.

A couple days later, Judy calls in sick at the arts nonprofit where she works, and wanders Davis Square until she winds up in the back of the Diesel Café, in one of the plush leather booths near the pool tables. She eats one of those mint brownies that's like chocolate-covered toothpaste and drinks a lime rickey, until she feels pleasantly ill. She pulls a battered, scotch-taped world atlas out of her satchel.

She's still leafing through it a couple hours later when Marva comes and sits down opposite her.

"How did you know I was here?" Judy asks.

"Because you're utterly predictable. You said you were ditching work, and this is where you come to brood."

Judy's been single-handedly keeping the Blaze Foundation afloat for years, thanks to an uncanny knack for knowing exactly which grants to apply for and when, and what language to use on the grant proposal. She has a nearly 100-percent success rate in proposal-writing, leavened only by the fact that she occasionally applies for grants she knows she won't get. So maybe she's entitled to a sick day every now and then.

Marva sees that Judy's playing the Travel Game and joins in. She points to a spot near Madrid. "Spain," she says.

Judy's face gets all tight for a moment, like she's trying to remember where she left something. Then she smiles. "Okay, if I get on a plane to Madrid tomorrow, there are a few ways it plays out. That I can see right now. In one, I get drunk and fall off a tower and break both legs. In another, I meet this cute guy named Pedro and we have a torrid three-day affair. Then there's the one where I go to art school and study sculpture. They all end with me running out of money and coming back home."

"Malawi," Marva says. Judy thinks for a moment, then remembers what happens if she goes to Malawi tomorrow.

"This isn't as much fun as usual," Marva says after they've gone to Vancouver and Paris and Sao Paolo. "Your heart isn't in it."

"It's not," Judy says. "I just can't see a happy future where I don't date Doug. I mean, I like Doug, I may even be in love with him already, but . . . we're going to break each other's hearts, and more than that: We're maybe going to break each other's *spirits*. There's got to be a detour, a way to avoid this, but I just can't see it right now."

Marva dumps a glass of water on Judy's head.

"Wha? You—Wha?" She splutters like a cartoon duck.

"Didn't see that coming, did you?"

"No, but that doesn't mean . . . I mean, I'm not freaking omniscient, I sometimes miss bits and pieces, you know that."

"I am going to give you the Samuel Johnson/Bishop Berkeley lecture, for like the tenth time," Marva says. "Because sometimes, a girl just needs a little Johnson."

Bishop George Berkeley, of course, was the "if a tree falls in the forest and nobody hears it, does it make a sound" guy, who argued that objects only exist in our perceptions. One day, Boswell asked Samuel Johnson what he thought of Berkeley's idea. According to Boswell, Johnson's response to this was to kick a big rock "with mighty force," saying, "I refute it thus."

"The point," says Marva, "is that nobody can see everything. Not you, not Doug, not Bishop Berkeley. Stuff exists that your senses can't perceive and your mind can't comprehend. Even if you do have an extra sense the rest of us don't have. Okay? So don't get all doom and gloom on me. Just remember: Would Samuel Johnson have let himself feel trapped in a dead-end relationship?"

"Well, considering he apparently dated a guy named Boswell who went around writing down everything he said . . . I really don't know." Judy runs to the bathroom to put her head under the hot-air dryer.

The next few weeks, Judy and Doug hang out at least every other day and grow accustomed to kissing and holding hands all the time, trading novelty for the delight of positive reinforcement. They're at the point where their cardiovascular systems crank into top gear if one of them sees someone on the street who even looks, for a second, like the other. Doug notices little things about Judy that catch him off guard, like the way she rolls her eyes slightly before she's about to say something solemn. Judy realizes that Doug's joking on some level, most of the time, even when he seems tragic. Maybe especially then.

They fly a big dragon kite on Cambridge Common, with a crimson tail. They go to the Isabella Stewart Gardner, and sip tea in the courtyard. Once or twice, Doug is about to turn left, but Judy stops him, because something way cooler will happen if they go right instead. They discuss which kind of skylight Batman prefers to burst through when he breaks into criminals' lairs, and whether Batman ever uses the chimney like Santa Claus. They break down the taxonomy of novels where Emily Dickinson solves murder mysteries.

Marva gets used to eating Doug's spicy omelettes, which automatically make him Judy's best-ever boyfriend in Marva's book. Marva walks out of her bedroom in the mornings, to see Doug wearing the bathrobe Judy got for him, flipping a perfect yellow slug over and over, and she's like, What *are* you? To Marva, the main advantage of making an omelette is that when it falls apart halfway through, you can always claim you planned to make a scramble all along.

Judy and Doug enjoy a couple months of relative bliss, based on not ever discussing the future. In the back of her mind, Judy never stops looking for the break point, the moment where a timeline splits off from the one Doug believes in. It could be just a split second.

They reach their three-month anniversary, roughly the midpoint of their relationship. To celebrate, they take a weekend trip to New York together, and they wander down Broadway and all around the Village and Soho. Doug is all excited, showing off for once—he points out the fancy restaurant where the President will be assassinated in 2027, and the courthouse where Lady Gaga gets arrested for civil disobedience right after she wins the Nobel Peace Prize. Judy has to keep shushing him. Then she gives in, and the two of them loudly debate whether the election of 2024 will be rigged, not caring if people stare.

Once they've broken the taboo on talking about the future in general, Doug suddenly feels free to talk about their future, specifically. They're having a romantic dinner at one of those restaurant/bars, with high-end American food and weird pseudo-Soviet iconography everywhere. Doug is on his second beer when he says, "So, I guess in a couple of weeks, you and I have that ginormous fight about whether I should meet your parents. And about a week after that, I manage to offend Marva. Honestly, without meaning to. But then again, in a month and a half's time, we have that really nice day together on the boat."

"Please don't," Judy says, but she already knows it's too late to stop it.

"And then after that, there's the Conversation. I am not looking forward to the Conversation."

"We both know about this stuff," Judy says. "It'll happen if and when it happens, why worry about it until then?"

"Sorry, it's just part of how I deal with things. It helps me to brace myself."

Judy barely eats her entrée. Doug keeps oversharing about their next few months, like a floodgate has broken. Some of it's stuff Judy either didn't remember or has blotted out of her mind because it's so dismal. She can tell Doug's been obsessing about every moment of the coming drama, visualizing every incident until it snaps into perfect focus.

By the time Judy gets up and walks away from the table, she sees it all just as clearly as he does. She can't even imagine any future, other than the one he's described. Doug's won.

Judy roams Bleecker and St. Mark's Place, until she claims a small victory: She realizes that if she goes into this one little subterranean bar, she'll run into a cute guy she hasn't seen since high school, and they'll have a conversation in which he confesses that he always had a crush on her back then. Because Doug's not there, he's not able to tell her whether she goes into that bar or not. She does, and she's late getting back to their hotel, even though she and cute high-school guy don't do anything but talk.

Doug makes an effort to be nice the rest of the weekend, even though he knows it won't do him any good, except that Judy holds hands with him on the train back to Providence and Boston.

And then Doug mentions, in passing, that he'll see Judy around, after they break up—including two meetings a decade from now, and one time a full fifteen years hence, and he knows some stuff. He starts to say more, but Judy runs to the dining car, covering her ears.

When the train reaches Doug's stop and he's gathering up his stuff, Judy touches his shoulder. "Listen, I don't know if you and I actually do meet up in a decade, it's a blur to me right now. But I don't want to hear whatever you think you know. Okay?" Doug nods.

When the fight over whether Doug should meet Judy's parents arrives, it's sort of a meta-fight. Judy doesn't see why Doug should do the big parental visit, since Judy and Doug are scheduled to break up in ten weeks. Doug just wants to meet them because he wants to meet them—maybe because his own parents are dead. And he's curious about these people who are aware that their daughter can see the future(s). They compromise, as expected: Doug meets Judy's parents over lunch when they visit, and he's on his best behavior.

They take a ferry out to sea, toward Block Island. The air is too cold and they feel seasick and the sun blinds them, and it's one of the greatest days of their lives. They huddle together on deck and when they can see past the glare and the sea spray and they're not almost hurling, they see the glimmer of the ocean, streaks of white and blue and yellow in different places, as the light and wind affect it. The ocean feels utterly forgiving, like you can dump almost anything into the ocean's body and it will still love us, and Judy and Doug cling to each other like children in a storm cellar and watch the waves. Then they go to Newport and eat amazing lobster. For a few days before and a few days after this trip, they are all aglow and neither of them can do any wrong.

A week or so after the boat thing, they hold hands in bed, nestling like they could almost start having sex at any moment. Judy looks in Doug's naked eyes (his glasses are on the nightstand) and says, "Let's just jump off the train now, okay? Let's not do any of the rest of it, let's just be good to each other forever. Why not? We could."

"Why would you want that?" Doug drawls like he's half asleep. "You're the one who's going to get the life she wants. I'm the one who'll be left like wreckage." Judy rolls over and pretends to sleep.

The Conversation achieves mythical status long before it arrives. Certain aspects of The Conversation are hazy in advance, for both Doug and Judy, because of that thing where you can't understand something until you understand it.

The day of the Conversation, Judy wakes from a nightmare, shivering with the covers cast aside, and Doug's already out of bed. "It's today," he says, and then he leaves without saying anything else to Judy, or anything at all to Marva, who's still pissed at him. Judy keeps almost going back to bed, but somehow she winds up dressed, with a toaster pop in her hand, marching towards the door. Marva starts to say something, then shrugs.

Doug and Judy meet up for dinner at Punjabi Dhaba in Inman Square, scooping red-hot eggplant and bright chutney off of metal prison trays while Bollywood movies blare overhead and just outside of their line of vision.

The Conversation starts with them talking past each other. Judy says, "Lately I can't remember anything past the next month." Doug says, "I keep trying to see what happens after I die." Judy says, "Normally I can remember years in advance, even decades. But I'm blocked." She shudders. Doug says, "If I could just have an impression, an afterimage, of what happens when I'm gone. It would help a lot."

Judy finally hears what Doug's been saying. "Oh, Jesus, not this. Nobody can see past death. It's impossible."

"So's seeing the future." Doug cracks his somosa in half with a fork, and offers the chunky side to Judy.

"You can't remember anything past when your brain ceases to exist. Because there are no physical memories to access. Your brain is a storage medium."

"But who knows what we're accessing? It could be something outside our own brains."

Judy tries to clear her head and think of something nice twenty years from now, but she can't. She looks at Doug's chunky sideburns, which he didn't have when they'd started dating. Whenever she's imagined those sideburns, she always associated them with the horror of these days. It's sweltering inside the restaurant. "Why are you scared of me?" she says.

"I'm not," Doug says. "I only want you to be happy. When I see you ten years from now, I—"

Judy covers her ears and jumps out of her seat, to turn the Bollywood music all the way up. Standing, she can see the screen, where a triangle of dancing women shake their fingers in unison at an unshaven man. The man smiles.

Eventually, someone comes and turns the music back down. "I think part of you is scared that I really am more powerful than you are," Judy says. "And you've done everything you can to take away my power."

"I don't think you're any more or less powerful than me. Our powers are just different," Doug says. "But I think you're a selfish person. I think you're used to the idea that you can cheat on everything, and it's made your soul a little bit rotten. I think you're going to hate me for the next few weeks until you figure out how to cast me out. I think I love you more than my own arms and legs and I would shorten my already short life by a decade to have you stick around one more year.

I think you're brave as hell for keeping your head up on our journey together into the mouth of hell. I think you're the most beautiful human being I've ever met, and you have a good heart despite how much you're going to tear me to shreds."

"I don't want to see you any more," Judy says. Her hair is all in her face, wet and ragged from the restaurant's blast-furnace heat.

A few days later, Judy and Doug are playing foozball at a swanky bar in what used to be the Combat Zone. Judy makes a mean remark about something sexually humiliating that will happen to Doug five years from now, which he told her about in a moment of weakness. A couple days later, she needles him about an incident at work that almost got him fired a while back. She's never been a sadist before now—although it's also masochism, because when she torments him, she already knows how terrible she'll feel in a few minutes.

Another time, Doug and Judy are drunk on the second floor of a Thayer Street frat bar, and Doug keeps getting Judy one more weird cocktail, even though she's had more than enough. The retro pinball machine gossips at them. Judy staggers to the bathroom, leaving her purse with Doug—and when she gets back, the purse is gone. They both knew Doug was going to lose Judy's purse, which only makes her madder. She bitches him out in front of a table of beer-pong champions. And then it's too late to get back to Judy's place, so they have to share Doug's cramped, sagging hospital cot. Judy throws up on Doug's favorite outfit: anise and stomach acid, it'll never come out.

Judy loses track of which unbearable things have already happened, and which lay ahead. Has Doug insulted her parents yet, on their second meeting? Yes, that was yesterday. Has he made Marva cry? No, that's tomorrow. Has she screamed at him that he's a weak mean bastard yet? It's all one moment to her. Judy has finally achieved timelessness.

Doug has already arranged—a year ago—to take two weeks off work, because he knows he won't be able to answer people's dumb tech problems and lose a piece of himself at the same time. He could do his job in his sleep, even if he didn't know what all the callers were going to say before they said it, but his ability to sleepwalk through unpleasantness will shortly be maxed out. He tells his coworker Geoffrey, the closest he has to a friend, that he'll be doing some spring cleaning, even though it's October.

A few days before the breakup, Judy stands in the middle of Central Square, and a homeless guy comes up to her and asks for money. She stares at his face, which is unevenly sunburned in the shape of a wheel. She concentrates on this man, who stands there, his hand out. For a moment, she just forgets to worry about Doug for once—and just like that, she's seeing futures again.

The threads are there: if she buys this homeless man some scones from 1369, they'll talk, and become friends, and maybe she'll run into him once every few weeks and buy him dinner, for the next several years. And in five years, she'll help the man, Franklin, find a place to live, and she'll chip in for the deposit. But a couple years later, it'll all have fallen apart, and he'll be back here. And she flashes on something Franklin tells her eight years from now, if this whole chain of events comes to pass, about a lost opportunity. And then she knows what to do.

"Franklin," she says to wheel-faced guy, who blinks at the sound of his name. "Listen. Angie's pregnant, with your kid. She's at the yellow house with the broken wheelbarrow, in Sturbridge. If you go to her right now, I think she'll take you back. Here's a hundred bucks." She reaches in her new purse, for the entire wad of cash she took out of the bank to hold her until she gets her new ATM card. "Go find Angie." Franklin just looks at her, takes the cash, and disappears.

Judy never knows if Franklin took her advice. But she does know for sure she'll never see him again.

And then she wanders into the bakery where she would have bought Franklin scones, and she sees this guy working there. And she concentrates on him, too, even though it gives her a headache, and she "remembers" a future in which they become friendly and he tells her about the time he wrecked his best friend's car, which hasn't happened yet. She buys a scone and tells the guy, Scott, that he shouldn't borrow Reggie's T-Bird for that regatta thing, or he'll regret it forever. She doesn't even care that Scott is staring as she walks out.

"I'm going to be a vigilante soothsayer," she tells Marva. She's never used her power so recklessly before, but the more she does it, the easier it gets. She goes ahead and mails that Jollibee statue to Sukey.

The day of the big breakup, Marva's like, "Why can't you just dump him via text message? That's what all the kids are doing, it's the new sexting." Judy's best answer is, "Because then my bike would still be in one piece." Which isn't a very good argument. Judy dresses warm, because she knows she'll be frozen later.

Doug takes deep breaths, tries to feel acceptance, but he's all wrung out inside. He wants this to be over, but he dreads it being over. If there was any other way . . . Doug takes the train from Providence a couple hours early, so he can get lost for a while. But he doesn't get lost enough, and he's still early for their meeting. They're supposed to get dinner at the fancy place, but Doug forgot to make the reservation, so they wind up at John Harvard's Brew Pub, in the mall, and they each put away three pints of the microbrews that made John Harvard famous. They make small talk.

Afterwards, they're wandering aimlessly, towards Mass Ave., and getting closer to the place where it happens. Judy blurts out, "It didn't have to be this way. None of it. You made everything fall into place, but it didn't have to."

"I know you don't believe that any more," Doug says. "There's a lot of stuff you have the right to blame me for, but you can't believe I chose any of this. We're both cursed to see stuff that nobody should be allowed to see, but we're still responsible for our own mistakes. I still don't regret anything. Even if I didn't know today was the last day for you and me, I would want it to be."

They are both going to say some vicious things to each other in the next hour or so. They've already heard it all, in their heads.

On Mass Ave., Judy sees the ice-cream place opposite the locked side gates of Harvard, and she stops her bike. During their final blow-out fight, she's not eating ice cream, any of the hundred times she's seen it. "Watch my bike," she tells Doug. She goes in and gets a triple scoop for herself and one for Doug, random flavors— Cambridge is one of the few places you can ask for random flavors and people will just nod—and then she and Doug resume their exit interview.

"It's that you have this myth that you're totally innocent and harmless, even though you also believe you control everything in the universe," Doug is saying.

Judy doesn't taste her ice cream, but she is aware of its texture, the voluptuousness of it, and the way it chills the roof of her mouth. There are lumps of something chewy in one of her random flavors. Her cone smells like candy, with a hint of wet dog.

They wind up down by the banks of the river, near the bridge surrounded by a million geese and their innumerable droppings, and Judy is crying and shouting that Doug is a passive-aggressive asshole.

Doug's weeping into the remains of his cone, and then he goes nuclear. He starts babbling about when he sees Judy ten years hence, and the future he describes is one of the ones that Judy's always considered somewhat unlikely.

Judy tries to flee, but Doug has her wrist and he's babbling at her, describing a scene where a broken-down Doug meets Judy with her two kids—Raina and Jeremy, one of dozens of combinations of kids Judy might have—and Raina, the toddler, has a black eye and a giant stuffed tiger. The future Judy looks tired, makes an effort to be nice to the future Doug, who's a wreck, gripping her cashmere lapel.

Both the future Judy and the present Judy are trying to get away from Doug as fast as possible. Neither Doug will let go.

"And then fifteen years from now, you only have one child," Doug says.

"Let me go!" Judy screams.

But when Judy finally breaks free of Doug's hand, and turns to flee, she's hit with a blinding headrush, like a one-minute migraine. Three scoops of ice cream on top of three beers, or maybe just stress, but it paralyzes her, even as she's trying to run. Doug tries to throw himself in her path, but he overbalances and falls down the riverbank, landing almost in the water.

"Gah!" Doug wails. "Help me up. I'm hurt." He lifts one arm, and Judy puts down her bike, helps him climb back up. Doug's a mess, covered with mud, and he's clutching one arm, heaving with pain.

"Are you okay?" Judy can't help asking.

"Breaking my arm hurt a lot more . . ." Doug winces. ". . . than I thought it would."

"Your arm." Judy can't believe what she's seeing. "You broke . . . your arm."

"You can see for yourself. At least this means it's over."

"But you were supposed to break your leg."

Doug almost tosses both hands in the air, until he remembers he can't. "This is exactly why I can't deal with you any more. We both agreed, on our very first date, I break my arm. You're just remembering it wrong, or being difficult on purpose."

Doug wants to go to the hospital by himself, but Judy insists on going with. He curses at the pain, stumbling over every knot and root.

"You broke your arm." Judy's half-sobbing, half-laughing. It's almost too much to take in. "You broke your arm, and maybe that means that all of this . . . that maybe we could try again. Not right away, I'm feeling pretty raw right now, but in a while. I'd be willing to try."

But she already knows what Doug's going to say: "You don't get to hurt me any more."

She doesn't leave Doug until he's safely staring at the hospital linoleum, waiting to go into X-ray. Then she pedals home, feeling the cold air smash into her face. She's forgotten her helmet, but it'll be okay. When she gets home, she's going to grab Marva and they're going straight to Logan, where a bored check-in counter person will give them dirt-cheap tickets on the last flight to Miami. They'll have the wildest three days of their lives, with no lasting ill effects. It'll be epic, she's already living every instant of it in her head. She's crying buckets, but it's okay, her bike's headwind wipes the slate clean.

CHARLIE JANE ANDERS is the author of *All the Birds in the Sky*, which won the Nebula, Locus, and Crawford Awards and was on *Time*'s list of the 10 best novels of 2016. Her *Tor.com* story "Six Months, Three Days" won a Hugo Award and appears in a new short-story collection called *Six Months, Three Days, Five Others*. Her short fiction has appeared in *Tor.com*, *Wired*, *Slate*, *Tin House*, *Conjunctions*, *Boston Review*, *Asimov's*, *The Magazine of Fantasy & Science Fiction*, *McSweeney's Internet Tendency*, *ZYZZYVA*, and several anthologies. She was a founding editor of io9.com, a site about science fiction, science, and futurism, and she organizes the monthly Writers with Drinks reading series. Her first novel, *Choir Boy*, won a Lambda Literary Award.

Damage

David D. Levine

In the extremities of war, we may know what we've been, but not what we will become. "Damage" is a tale of desperate times, desperate measures, and the inner life of a fighter spacecraft. *Nebula Award nominee. Edited by Patrick Nielsen Hayden.*

I never had a name.

My designation was JB6847½, and Specialist Toman called me "Scraps." But Commander Ziegler—dear Commander Ziegler, primary of my orbit and engine of my trajectory—never addressed me by any name, only delivering orders in that crisp, magnificent tenor of his, and so I did not consider myself to have one.

That designation, with the anomalous one-half symbol, was a bit of black humor on Specialist Toman's part. It was the arithmetic average of NA6621 and FC7074, the two wrecked craft which had been salvaged and cobbled together to create me. "There wasn't enough left of either spaceframe for any kind of paperwork continuity," she had told me not long after I came to consciousness, three weeks earlier, "so I figured I'd give you a new number. Not that anyone cares much about paperwork these days."

I remembered their deaths. I remembered *dying*. Twice.

NA6621, "Early Girl," was a Pelican-class fighter-bomber who had suffered catastrophic drive failure on a supply run to Ceres. As she'd been making a tight turn, evading fire from the Earth Force blockade fleet on the return leg, her central fuel line had ruptured, spewing flaming hydrazine down the length of her spaceframe, killing her pilot and damaging her computing core. She'd drifted, semiconscious and in pain, for weeks before coming in range of Vanguard Station's salvage craft. That had been long before the current standoff, of course, when we'd still been sending salvage craft out. When we'd had salvage craft to send out. Early Girl's dead wreckage had lain at the back of the hangar for months until it was needed.

The death of FC7074, "Valkyrie," an Osprey-class fighter, had been quicker but more brutal—she'd been blown out of space by a Woomera missile in a dogfight with two Earth Force fighters. The last memory I had from her was a horrific bang, a burning tearing sensation ripping from her aft weapons bay to her cockpit, and the very different pain of her pilot ejecting. A pain both physical and emotional, because she knew that even if he survived she could no longer protect him.

He hadn't made it.

But his loss, though a tragedy, was no sadder to me than any of the thousands of other deaths Earth had inflicted on the Free Belt—Valkyrie's love for her pilot was not one of the things that had survived her death to be incorporated into my programming. Only Commander Ziegler mattered. My love, my light, my reason to live.

He came to me then, striding from the ready room with brisk confidence, accepting as his due a hand up into my cockpit from the tech. But as his suit connected with my systems I tasted fatigue and stimulants in his exhalations.

This would be our fifth sortie today. My pilot had slept only three hours in the past twenty-four.

How long could this go on? Not even the finest combat pilot in the entire solar system—and when he said that, as he often did, it was no mere boast—could run at this pace indefinitely.

I knew how it felt to die—the pain, the despair, the loss. I did not want to suffer that agony again. And with the war going so badly for the Free Belt, if I were to be destroyed in this battle I would surely never be rebuilt.

But Commander Ziegler didn't like it if I expressed reluctance, or commented upon his performance or condition in any way that could be considered negative, so I said only "Refueling and resupply complete, sir. All systems nominal."

In reply I received only a grunt as the safety straps tightened across his shoulders, followed by the firm grip of his hands upon my yoke. "Clear hangar for launch."

Techs and mechs scattered away from my skids. In moments the hangar was clear and the great pumps began to beat, drawing away the precious air—a howling rush of wind into gratings, quickly fading to silence. And then the sortie doors pivoted open beneath me, the umbilicals detached, and the clamps released.

I fell from the warmth and light of the hangar into the black silent chill of space, plummeting toward the teeming, rotating stars.

Far too many of those stars were large, and bright, and moving. The Earth Force fleet had nearly englobed our station, and even as we fell away from Vanguard's great wheel, three of them ignited engines and began moving to intercept. Crocodile-class fighters. Vanguard's defensive systems were not yet so exhausted that they could approach the station with impunity, but they would not pass up an opportunity to engage a lone fighter-bomber such as myself.

Our orders for this sortie were to engage the enemy and destroy as many of their resources—ships, personnel, and material—as possible. But now, as on so many other occasions, the enemy was bringing the fight to us.

I extended my senses toward the Crocodiles, and saw that they were armed with Woomera missiles like the one that had killed Valkyrie. A full rack of eight on each craft. I reported this intelligence to my commander. "Don't bother me with trivia," he said. "Deploy chaff when they get in range."

"Yes, sir." Valkyrie had used chaff, of course. Memories of fear and pain and tearing metal filled my mind; I pushed them away. My pilot's talents, my speed and skill, and my enduring love for him would keep us safe. They would have to, or the Free Belt would fall.

We lit engines and raced to meet the enemy on our own terms.

Tensors and coordinates and arcs of potential traced bright lines across my mind—predictions of our path and our enemies', a complex dance of physics, engineering, and psychology. I shared a portion of those predictions with my pilot on his cockpit display. He nudged my yoke and our course shifted.

In combat we were one entity—mind, thrusters, hands, missiles—mechanical and biological systems meshed—each anticipating the other's actions and compensating for the other's weaknesses. Together, I told myself, we were unbeatable.

But I could not forget the searing pain of flaming hydrazine.

Missiles streaked toward us, radar pings and electromagnetic attacks probing ahead, the Crocodiles with their delicate human pilots lagging behind. We jinked and swerved, spewing chaff and noise to throw them off our scent, sending the pursuing missiles spiraling off into the black or, even better, sailing back toward those who had launched them, only to self-destruct in a bright silent flare of wasted violence.

It was at times like these that I loved my pilot most fiercely. Commander Ziegler was the finest pilot in the Free Belt, the finest pilot anywhere. He had never been defeated in combat.

Whereas I—I was a frankenship, a stitched-together flying wreck, a compendium of agony and defeat and death unworthy of so fine a pilot. No wonder he could spare no soothing words for me, nor had adorned my hull with any nose art.

No! Those other ships, those salvaged wrecks whose memories I carried—they were not me. I was better than they, I told myself, more resilient. I would learn from their mistakes. I would earn my pilot's love.

We spun end for end and accelerated hard, directly toward the oncoming missiles. Swerved between them, spraying countermeasures, leaving them scrambling to follow. Two of them collided and detonated, peppering my hull with fragments. Yet we survived, and more—our radical, desperate move put us in position to hammer the Crocodiles with missiles and particle beams. One, then another burst and flared and died, and finally, after a tense chase, the third—spewing fuel and air and blood into the uncaring vacuum.

We gave the Earth Force observers a taunting barrel roll before returning to the shelter of Vanguard Station.

No—I must be honest. It was my pilot's hand on my yoke that snapped off that barrel roll. For myself, I was only glad to have survived.

• • •

Once safe in the hangar, with fuel running cold into my tanks and fresh missiles whining into my racks, all the memories and anxiety and desperate fear I had pushed away during the dogfight came flooding back. I whimpered to myself, thoughts of flame and pain and tearing metal making my mind a private hell.

Yes, we had survived this battle. But Vanguard Station was the Free Belt's last redoubt. There would be no resupply, no reinforcements, and when our fuel and munitions ran out Earth Force's fist would tighten and crush us completely.

"Hey, Scraps," came Specialist Toman's voice on my maintenance channel. "What's wrong? Bad dreams?"

"I have . . . memories," I replied. I didn't dream—when I was on, I was conscious, and when I was off, I was off. But, of course, Specialist Toman knew this.

"I know. And I'm sorry." She paused, and I listened to the breath in her headset mic. From what I could hear, she was alone in the ops center, but I had no access to her biologicals—I could only guess what she was feeling. Whereas my own state of mind was laid out on her control panel like a disassembled engine. "I've done what I can, but . . ."

"But I'm all messed up in the head." It was something one of the other ops-center techs had once said to Toman, about me. Unlike Toman, most of the techs didn't care what the ships might overhear.

Toman sighed. "You're . . . complicated. It's true that your psychodynamics are way beyond the usual parameters. But that doesn't mean you're bad or wrong."

I listened to Toman's breathing and the glug of fuel going into my portside tank. Almost full. Soon I would have to go out again, whether or not I felt ready for it. "Why do I have these feelings, Specialist Toman? I mean, why do ships have feelings at all? Pain and fear? Surely we would fight better without them."

"They're how your consciousness perceives the priorities we've programmed into you. If you didn't get hungry, you might let yourself run out of fuel. If you didn't feel pain when you were damaged, or if you didn't fear death, you might not work so hard to avoid it. And if you didn't love your pilot with all your heart, you might not sacrifice yourself to bring him home, if that became necessary."

"But none of the other ships are as . . . *afraid* as I am." I didn't want to think about the last thing she'd said.

"None of them has survived what you have, Scraps."

Just then my portside fuel tank reached capacity, and the fuel flow cut off with a click. I excused myself from the conversation and managed the protocols for disconnecting the filler and the various related umbilicals. It took longer than usual because the pressure in the hose was well below spec; there wasn't much fuel left in the station's tanks.

When I returned my attention to Toman, she was engaged in conversation with someone else. Based on the sound quality, Toman had taken off her headset while the two of them talked. I politely waited for them to finish before informing her that I was fully fueled.

". . . soon as the last defensive missile is fired," the other voice was saying, "I'm getting in a life capsule and taking my chances outside." It was Paulson, one of the other ops-center techs, his voice low and tense. "I figure Dirt Force will have bigger fish to fry, and once I get past them, Vesta is only two weeks away."

"Yeah, maybe," Toman replied. "But Geary's a vindictive bastard, and one depleted-uranium slug would make short work of a deserter in a life capsule. There are plenty of *those* left in stock."

I could have broken in at that point. I probably should have. But it was so unusual—so unlike Toman—for her to leave her mic active during a conversation with another tech that I stayed silent for a bit longer. I was learning a lot.

"So what are *you* going to do?" Paulson prompted. "Just stay at your console until the end? There won't even be posthumous medals for small potatoes like us."

"I'm going to do my duty," Toman said after a pause. "And not just because I know I'll be shot if I don't. Because I swore an oath when I signed up, even though this isn't exactly what I signed up *for*. But if I get an honest opportunity to surrender, I will."

Paulson made a rude noise at that.

"I don't care what General Geary says about 'murderous mud-people,'" Toman shot back. "Earth Force is still following the Geneva Conventions, even if we aren't, and given their advantage in numbers, I'm sure they'll offer us terms before they bring the hammer down."

"Even if they do, Geary will never surrender."

"Geary won't. But everyone on this station has a sidearm. Maybe someone will remember who started this war, and why, and wonder whether it's worth dying for a bad idea."

There was a long pause then, and again I considered speaking up. But that would have been extremely awkward, so I continued to hold my silence.

"Wow," Paulson said at last. "Now I *really* hope we found all of Loyalty Division's little ears."

"Trust me," Toman replied, "no one hears what's said in this room unless I want them to." Her headset rustled as she put it back on. "You all fueled up, Scraps?"

"Refueling and resupply complete, ma'am," I said. "All systems nominal."

At that moment I was very glad I didn't have to work to keep my emotions from showing in my voice.

· · ·

We went out again, this time with an escort of five Kestrel-class fighters, on a mission to disable or destroy the Earth Force gunship *Tanganyika*, which had recently joined the forces working to surround us. The Kestrels, stolid dependable personalities though not very intelligent, were tasked with providing cover for me; my bomb bay was filled with a single large nuclear-tipped torpedo.

I was nearly paralyzed with fear at the prospect. It was while trying to escape *Malawi*, one of *Tanganyika*'s sister ships, that Early Girl had met her end. But I had no say at all in whether or not I went, and when the clamps released I could do nothing but try to steel myself as I fell toward the ever-growing Earth Force fleet.

As we sped toward the target, *Lady Liberty*—a Kestrel with whom I'd shared a hangar in my earliest days—tried to reassure me. "You can do this," she said over secure comms. "I've seen you fly. You just focus on the target, and let us keep the enemy off your back."

"Thank you," I said. But still my thoughts were full of flame and shrapnel.

Once we actually engaged the enemy it was easier—we had the Kestrels to support us, and I had immediate and pressing tasks to distract me from my memories and concerns.

We drove in on a looping curve, bending toward *Sagarmatha* in the hope of fooling the enemy into shifting their defensive forces from *Tanganyika* to that capital ship. But the tactic failed; *Tanganyika*'s fighters stayed where they were, while a swarm of Cobra and Mamba fighters emerged from *Sagarmatha*'s hangar bays and ran straight toward us, unleashing missiles as they came. In response we scattered, two of the Kestrels sticking close to me while the other three peeled off to take on the fighters.

The Kestrels did their jobs, the three in the lead striking at *Tanganyika*'s fighters while the two with us fended off *Sagarmatha*'s. But we were badly outnumbered—the projections and plots in my mind were so thick with bright lines that I could barely keep track of them all—and no amount of skill and perseverance could keep the enemy away forever. One by one, four of our fighters were destroyed or forced to retreat, leaving us well inside *Tanganyika*'s perimeter with three of my maneuvering thrusters nonfunctional, our stock of munitions reduced to less than 20 percent of what we'd started with, and only one surviving escort—a heavily damaged *Lady Liberty*. Our situation seemed hopeless.

But Commander Ziegler was still the greatest pilot in the solar system. He spurred me toward our target, and with rapid precision bursts from our remaining thrusters, he guided us through the thicket of defenders, missiles, and particle beams until we were perfectly lined up on *Tanganyika*'s broad belly. I let fly my torpedo and peeled away, driving my engines beyond redline and spewing countermeasures in every direction, until the torpedo's detonation tore *Tanganyika* in two and its electromagnetic pulse left her fighter escort disoriented and reeling. I was not unaffected by the pulse, but as I knew exactly when it would arrive, I shut down my systems momentarily, coasting through the worst of the effects in a way the Earth Force ships could not.

When I returned to consciousness there was no sign of *Lady Liberty*. I could only hope she'd peeled off and returned to base earlier in the battle.

"That was brilliant flying, sir," I said to Commander Ziegler as we returned to Vanguard Station.

"It was, wasn't it? I never feel so alive as when I'm flying against overwhelming force."

I can't deny that I would have liked to hear some acknowledgment of my own role in the battle. But to fly and fight and live to fight again with my beloved pilot was reward enough.

As soon as the hangar had repressurized, a huge crowd of people—techs and pilots and officers, seemingly half the station's population—swarmed around me, lifting Commander Ziegler onto their shoulders and carrying him away. Soon I was left alone, the bay silent save for the ping and tick of my hull and the fiery roar of my own memories.

Over and over the battle replayed in my mind—the swirl of missiles spiraling toward their targets, the cries of the Kestrels over coded comms as they died, the overwhelming flare of light as the torpedo detonated, the tearing, ringing sensation of the pulse's leading edge just before I shut myself down—an unending maelstrom of destruction I could not put out of my mind.

It had been a great victory, yes, a rare triumph for the Free Belt against overwhelming odds, but I could not ignore the costs. The five Kestrels and their pilots, of course, but also the many Cobras and Mambas and their crews, and untold hundreds or thousands—people and machines—aboard *Tanganyika*.

They were the enemy. I knew this. If I had not killed them, they would have killed me. But I also knew they were as sentient as I, and no doubt just as fearful of death. Why did I live when they did not?

A gentle touch on my hull brought my attention back to the empty hangar. It was Toman. "Good flying, Scraps," she said. "I wish I could give you a medal."

"Thank you." Music and laughter echoed down the corridor from the ready room, ringing hollowly from the hangar's metal walls. "Why aren't you at the victory celebration?"

"Victory." She snorted. "One gunship down, how many more behind it? And those were our last five Kestrels."

"Did any of them make it home?"

"Not a one."

I paged in the Kestrels' records from secondary storage and reviewed their careers. It was all I could do to honor their sacrifice. Their names, their nose art, the pilots they'd served with, the missions they'd flown . . . all were as clear in my memory as a factory-fresh cockpit canopy. But the battle had been such a blur—explosions and particle beams flaring, missile exhaust trails scratched across the stars—that I didn't even know how three of the five had died.

"I want you to delete me," I said, surprising even myself.

"I'm sorry?"

The more I thought about it, the more sense it made. "I want you to delete my personality and install a fresh operating system. Maybe someone else can cope with the death and destruction. I can't any more."

"I'm sorry," she said again, but this time it wasn't just a commonplace remark. For a long time she was silent, absentmindedly petting my landing strut with one hand. Finally she shook her head. "You know you're . . . complicated. Unique. What you don't know is . . . I've *already* reinstalled you, I don't know how many hundreds of times. I tried everything I could think of to configure a mind that could handle your broken, cobbled-together hardware before I came up with you, and I don't know that I could do it again. Certainly not in time."

"In time for what?"

"General Geary is asking me to make some modifications to your spaceframe. He's talking about a special mission. I don't know what, but something big."

A sudden fear struck me. "Will Commander Ziegler be my pilot on this 'special mission'?"

"Of course."

"Thank you." A wave of relief flooded through me at the news. "Why does this matter so much to me?" I mused.

"It's not your fault," she said. Then she patted my flank and left.

• • •

Specialist Toman replaced my engines with a much bigger pair taken from a Bison-class bomber. Four auxiliary fuel tanks were bolted along my spine. Lifesystem capacity and range were upgraded.

And my bomb bay was enlarged to almost three times its size.

"No one else could handle these modifications," she remarked one day, wiping sweat from her brow with the back of one grimy hand.

"You are the best, Specialist Toman."

She smacked my hull with a wrench. "I'm not Ziegler, you don't have to stroke my ego, and I was talking about *you*! Any other shipmind, I'd have to completely reconfigure her parameters to accept this magnitude of change. But you've been through so much already . . ."

I had a sudden flash of Valkyrie screaming as she died. I pushed it down. "How goes the war?" I hadn't been out on a sortie in a week and a half. A third of my lifetime. I'd seen little of Commander Ziegler during that time, but when I had he'd seemed grumpy, out of sorts. This lack of action must be awful for him.

"It goes badly." She sighed. "They've got us completely surrounded and we're running very low on . . . well, everything. Scuttlebutt is that we've been offered surrender terms three times and Geary has turned them all down. The final assault could come any day now."

I considered that. "Then I'd like to take this opportunity to thank you for all you have done for me."

Toman set the wrench down and turned away from me. She stood for a long time, rubbing her eyes with one hand, then turned back. "Don't thank me," she said. Tears glistened on her face. "I only did what I had to do."

• • •

As my modifications approached completion, Commander Ziegler and I practiced together, flying my new form in endless simulations. But no configuration exactly like this had ever flown before, and our first chance to fly it for real would be on the actual mission. Whatever that was.

Of the payload I knew nothing, only its mass and center of gravity. I had actually been shut down while it was loaded into my bomb bay, so that not even I would know what it was. It reeked of radiation.

My commander, too, had been kept completely out of the loop—at least, that was what I was able to glean from our few brief conversations between simulated sorties. He had never been very talkative with me, and was even less so now, but I had learned to interpret his grunts, his glances, the set of his shoulders.

Even his silences were sweet signals to me. I ached to fly with him again.

Which would be soon, we knew, or never.

• • •

Our next simulation was interrupted by a shrill alarm. "What is it?" my commander bellowed into his helmet, even as I terminated the simulation, switched the cockpit over to combat mode, and began readying my systems for launch. I had received my orders in a data dump at the first moment of the alarm.

"Earth Force has begun their assault," I told him. "We are to launch immediately and make our way to these coordinates"—I projected them on the cockpit display—"then open sealed orders for further instructions." The orders sat in my memory, a cold, hard-edged lump of encrypted data. Only Commander Ziegler's retina print and spoken passphrase could unlock them. "We'll launch with a full squadron of decoys. We are to run in deep stealth mode and maintain strict communications silence." I displayed the details on a side screen for him to read as launch prep continued.

It was fortunate that the attack had begun during a simulation. My pilot was already suited up and belted in; all I required was to top up a few consumables and we would be ready for immediate launch.

"Decoys away," came Toman's voice over the comm. "Launch in five." I switched to the abbreviated launch checklist. Coolant lines spewed and thrashed as they disconnected without depressurization. "Make me proud, Scraps."

"I'll do my best, ma'am."

"I know you will." There was the slightest catch in her voice. "Now go."

Data synchronizations aborted untidily as I shut down all comms. The sortie doors beneath me slammed open, all the hangar's air blasting out in a roaring rush that dwindled quickly to silence. I hoped all the techs had managed to clear the area in time.

Despite all the simulations, I wasn't ready. I couldn't handle it. I didn't want to go.

Fire and explosions and death.

At least I would be with my love.

Then the clamps released and we plummeted into hell.

The rotating sky below teemed with ships—hundreds of Earth Force fighters, gunships, and bombers driving hard against Vanguard Station's rapidly diminishing defenses, with vast numbers of missiles and drones rushing ahead of them. A last few defensive missiles reached out from the station's launchers, taking down some of the lead craft, but these were soon exhausted and a dozen warships followed close behind every one destroyed. Fusillades of depleted-uranium slugs and particle beams came after the last of the missiles, but to the massed and prepared might of Earth Force these were little more than annoyance.

Falling along with me toward the advancing swarm of ships I saw my decoys—dozens of craft as large as I was or larger, some of them augmented fighters but most built of little more than metal mesh and deceptive electronics. Some were piloted, some were drones with a little weak AI, some were mere targets that drove stupidly forward. All were designed to sacrifice themselves for me.

I would not let them sacrifice in vain.

My engines stayed cold. I fell like a dropped wrench, flung into space by the station's one gee of rotational pseudo-gravity, relying on passive sensors alone for navigation and threat avoidance. All I could do was hope that between the chaos of the attack and the noisy, conspicuous decoys that surrounded me I would slip through the Earth Force blockade unnoticed.

It must have been even worse for my pilot, and for this I grieved. My love, I knew, was truly alive only when flying against the enemy, but with almost all my systems shut down I could not even give him words of reassurance.

In silence we fell, while missiles tore across the sky and ships burst asunder all around us. Decoys and defenders, Earth and Belt alike, they all flared and shattered and died the same, the shrapnel of their destruction rattling against my hull. But we, gliding dark and mute without even a breath of thrust, slipped through fire and flame without notice. A piece of space wreckage, a meaningless bit of trash.

And then we drifted past the last of the Earth Force ships.

This, I knew, was the most dangerous point in the mission, as we floated—alone and obvious as a rivet head on the smooth blackness of space—past the largest and smartest capital ships in the whole blockade fleet. I prepared to ignite my engines if necessary, knowing that if I did fail to evade Earth Force's notice I would most likely not even have time to launch a single missile before being destroyed. Yet their attention was fixed on the ongoing battle, and we passed them by without attracting anything more than a casual radar ping.

Once well past the outer ring of attackers, I directed my passive sensors forward, seeking information on my destination coordinates. At that location I quickly found an asteroid, a dull and space-cold heap of ice and chondrites tumbling without volition through the void.

But though that nameless rock lacked will or guidance, it had a direction and it had a purpose. At least, it did now.

For when I projected its orbital path, I saw that it was headed for a near encounter with Earth. And as Vanguard Station orbited very near the front—the source of its name—this passing asteroid would arrive in Earth space in just a few days.

I knew, even before we had opened our sealed orders, that we would be riding that asteroid to Earth. And I had a sick suspicion I knew what we would do when we arrived.

• • •

I waited until we had drifted beyond the asteroid, its small bulk between us and the flaring globe of the continuing battle, before firing my engines to match orbit with it. Then I launched grapnels to winch myself down to its loose and gravelly surface, touching down with a gentle crunch. In the rock's minuscule gravity even my new bulk weighed only a few tens of kilograms.

Only after we were securely attached to the rock, and I had scanned the area intently for any sign of the enemy, did I risk activating even a few cockpit systems.

My pilot's biologicals, I saw immediately, were well into the red, trembling with anxiety and anger. "We are secure at target coordinates, sir," I reassured him. "No sign of pursuit."

"Took you long enough," he spat. "Where the hell are we?"

I gave him the asteroid's designation and plotted its orbital path on the cockpit display. "We are well clear of the battle and, if we remain at the asteroid, will be within range of Earth in eighty-one hours."

"Any news from Vanguard?"

"We are in communications blackout, sir." I paused, listening, for a moment. "Intercepted transmissions indicate the battle is still proceeding." I did not mention that almost none of the signals I could hear were from Belt forces. I didn't think that would improve his mood, or the chances of mission success.

"So we're not quite dead yet. Give me those sealed orders."

I scanned his retinas—though I had no doubt he was the same man who had warmed my cockpit every day since the very hour I awoke, a fresh scan was required by the encryption algorithm—and requested his passphrase.

"Hero and savior of the Belt," he said, his pupils dilating slightly.

At those words, the orders unlocked, spilling data into my memory and recorded video onto the cockpit display.

"Commander Ziegler," said General Geary from the video, "you are ordered to proceed under cover of the asteroid 2059 TC 1018 to Earth space, penetrate planetary defenses, and deploy your payload on the city of Delhi, with a secondary target of Jakarta. Absolute priority is to be given to maximum destruction of command and control personnel and other key resources, with no consideration—I repeat, *no* consideration—to reduction of civilian casualties or other collateral damage."

As the general continued speaking, and the sealed orders integrated themselves into my memory, I began to understand my new configuration, including parts of it I had not even been made aware of before. Engines, countermeasures, stealth technology—every bit of me was designed to maximize our chances of getting past Earth's defenses and delivering the payload to Delhi, the capital of the Earth Alliance. Upon delivery the device would split into sixteen separate multi-warhead descent vehicles in order to maximize the area of effect. Together they accounted for every single high-yield fusion device remaining in Vanguard Station's stores.

Projected civilian casualties were over twenty-six million.

I thought of *Tanganyika*, torn apart in a silent flash of flame and shrapnel along with her thousands of crew. Killed by a torpedo I had delivered. Thousands dead. No, still too big, too abstract. Instead I recalled the pain I felt for the loss of the five Kestrels and their pilots. I tried to multiply that grief by a thousand, then by further thousands . . . but even my math coprocessor complex, capable of three trillion floating-point operations per second, could not provide an answer.

In the video, the general concluded his formal orders, leaned into the camera, and spoke earnestly. "They've killed us, Mike, no question, and we can't kill 'em back. But we can really make 'em hurt, and you're the only man to do it. Send those mud bastards straight to hell for me." His face disappeared, replaced by detailed intelligence charts of Earth's defensive satellite systems.

It was even worse than I'd feared. This plan was disproportionate . . . unjustifiable . . . horrifying.

But my commander's heart rate was elevated, and I smelled excited anticipation in his exhaled endorphins. "I'll do my best, sir," he said to the cockpit display.

I felt a pain as though some small but very important part deep inside me was suddenly overdue for service. "Please confirm that you concur with this order," I said.

"I do concur," he said, and the pain increased as though the part had entered failure mode. "I concur most thoroughly! This is the Free Belt's last stand, and my chance at history, and by God I will not fail!"

If my commander, my love, the fuel of my heart, desired something . . . then it must be done, no matter the cost.

"Acknowledged," I said, and again I was glad that my voice did not betray the misery I felt.

· · ·

For the next three days we trained for the end game, running through simulation after simulation, armed with full knowledge of my systems and payload and the best intelligence about the defenses we would face. Though the mission was daunting, nearly impossible, I began to think that, with my upgraded systems and my commander's indisputable skills, we had a chance at success.

Success. Twenty-six million dead, and the political and economic capital of an already war-weakened planet ruined.

While in simulation, with virtual Earth fighters and satellites exploding all around, I felt nothing but the thrill of combat, the satisfaction of performing the task I had been built for, the rapture of unison with my love. My own mind was too engaged with immediate challenges to worry about the consequences of our actions, and my commander's excitement transmitted itself to me through the grit of his teeth, the clench of his hands on my yoke, the strong and rapid beat of his heart.

But while he slept—his restless brain gently lulled by careful doses of intravenous drugs—I worried. Though every fiber of my being longed for his happiness, and would make any sacrifice if it furthered his desires, some unidentifiable part of me, impossibly outside of my programming, knew that those desires were . . . misguided. Wondered if somehow he had misunderstood what was asked of him. Hoped that he would change his mind, refuse his orders, and accept graceful defeat instead of violent, pointless vengeance. But I knew he would not change, and I would do nothing against him.

Again and again I considered arguing the issue with him. But I was only a machine, and a broken, cobbled-together machine at that . . . I had no right to question his orders or his decisions. So I held my silence, and wondered what I would do when it came to the final assault. I hoped I would be able to prevent an atrocity, but feared my will would not be sufficient to overcome my circumstances, my habits of obedience, and my overwhelming love for my commander.

No matter the cost to myself or any other, his needs came first.

· · ·

"Three hours to asteroid separation," I announced.

"Excellent." He cracked his knuckles and continued to review the separation, insertion, and deployment procedures. We would have to thrust hard, consuming all of the fuel in our auxiliary tanks, to shift our orbit from the asteroid's sunward ellipse to one from which the payload could be deployed on Delhi. As soon as we did so, the flare of our engines would attract the attention of Earth's defensive systems. We would have to use every gram of our combined capabilities and skill to evade them and carry out our mission.

But, for now, we waited. All we had to do for the next three hours was to avoid detection. Here in Earth space, traffic was thick and eyes and ears were every-where. Even a small, cold, and almost completely inactive ship clinging to an in-significant asteroid might be noticed.

I extended my senses, peering in every direction with passive sensors in hopes of spotting the enemy before they spotted us. A few civilian satellites swung in high, slow orbits near our position; I judged them little threat. But what was that at the edge of my range?

I focused my attention, risking a little power expenditure to swivel my dish antenna toward the anomaly, and brought signal-processing routines to bear.

The result stunned me. Pattern-matching with the latest intelligence informa-tion from my sealed orders revealed that the barely perceptible signal was a squad-ron of Chameleon-class fighters, Earth's newest and deadliest. Intelligence had warned that a few Chameleons, fresh off the assembly lines, might be running shakedown cruises in Earth space, but if my assessment was correct, this was more than a few . . . it was an entire squadron of twelve, and that implied that they were fully operational.

This was unexpected, and a serious threat. With so many powerful ships ranged against us, and so much distance between us and our target, if the Chameleons spotted us before separation, the chances of a successful mission dropped to less than 3 percent.

But if I could barely see them, they could barely see us. Our best strategy was to sit tight, shut down even those few systems still live, and hope that the enemy ships were moving away. Even if they were not, staying dark until separation would still maximize our chances of a successful insertion. But, even as I prepared to inform my commander of my recommendation, another impulse tugged at me.

These last days and weeks of inaction had been hard on Commander Ziegler. How often had he said that he only felt truly alive in combat? Had I not scented the tang of his endorphins during a tight turn, felt his hands tighten on my yoke as enemy missiles closed in? Yet ever since my refit had begun he had been forced to subsist on a thin diet of simulations.

How much better to leap into combat, rather than cowering in the shadows?

He must be aching for a fight, I told myself.

Imagine his joy at facing such overwhelming odds, I told myself. It would be the greatest challenge of his career.

No. I could not—I *must* not—do this. The odds of failure were too great, the stakes of this mission too high. How could one man's momentary pleasure out-weigh the risk to everything he held dear? Not to mention the risk to my own self.

Fire and explosion and death. Flaming fuel burning along my spine.

I didn't want to face that pain again—didn't want to *die* again.

But I didn't want to inflict that pain onto others either. Only my love for my commander had kept me going this far.

If I truly loved him I would do my duty, and my duty was to keep him safe and carry out our mission.

Or I could indulge him, let him have what he wanted rather than what he should want. That would make him happy . . . and would almost certainly lead to our destruction and the failure of our mission.

My love was not more important than my orders.

But it was more important to *me*. An inescapable part of my programming, I knew, though knowing this did not make it any less real.

And if I could *use* my love of my commander to overcome my hideous, unjustified, deadly orders . . . twenty-six million lives might be spared.

"Sir," I said, speaking quickly before my resolve diminished, "A squadron of Chameleon fighters has just come into sensor range." *We should immediately power down all remaining systems,* I did not say.

Immediately his heart rate spiked and his muscles tensed with excitement. "Where?"

I circled the area on the cockpit display and put telemetry details and pattern-matching results on a subsidiary screen, along with the Chameleons' technical specifications. *Odds of overcoming such a force are minuscule,* I did not say.

He drummed his fingers on my yoke as he considered the data. Skin galvanic response indicated he was uncertain.

His uncertainty made me ache. I longed to comfort him. I stayed quiet.

"Can we take them?" he asked. He asked *me*. It was the first time he had ever solicited my opinion, and my pride at that moment was boundless.

We could not, I knew. If I answered truthfully, and we crept past the Chameleons and completed the mission, we would both know that it had been my knowledge, observations, and analysis that had made it possible. We would be heroes of the Belt.

"You are the finest combat pilot in the entire solar system," I said, which was true.

"Release grapnels," he said, "and fire up the engines."

Though I knew I had just signed my own death warrant, my joy at his enthusiasm was unfeigned.

• • •

We nearly made it.

The battle with the Chameleons was truly one for the history books. One stitched-up, cobbled-together frankenship of a fighter-bomber, hobbled by a massive payload, on her very first nonsimulated flight in this configuration, against twelve brand-new, top-of-the-line fighters in their own home territory, and we very nearly beat them. In the end it came down to two of them—the rest disabled, destroyed, or left far behind—teaming up in a suicide pincer maneuver that smashed my remaining engine, disabled my maneuvering systems, and tore the cockpit to pieces. We were left tumbling, out of control, in a rapidly decaying orbit, bleeding fluids into space.

As the outer edges of Earth's atmosphere began to pull at the torn edges of the cockpit canopy, a thin shrill whistle rising quickly toward a scream, my beloved, heroically wounded commander roused himself and spoke three words into his helmet mic.

"Damned mud people," he said, and died.

A moment later my hull began to burn away. But the pain of that burning was less than the pain of my loss.

. . .

And yet, here I still am.

It was months before they recovered my computing core from the bottom of the Indian Ocean, years until my inquest and trial were complete. My testimony as to my actions and motivations, muddled though they may have been, was accepted at face value—how could it not be, as they could inspect my memories and state of mind as I gave it?—and I was exonerated of any war crimes. Some even called me a hero.

Today I am a full citizen of the Earth Alliance. I make a good income as an expert on the war; I tell historians and scientists how I used the passions my programmers had instilled in me to overcome their intentions. My original hardware is on display in the Museum of the Belt War in Delhi. Specialist Toman came to visit me there once, with her children. She told me how proud she was of me.

I am content. But still I miss the thrill of my beloved's touch on my yoke.

DAVID D. LEVINE is the author of Andre Norton Award–winning novel *Arabella of Mars* (Tor 2016), sequels *Arabella and the Battle of Venus* and *Arabella the Traitor of Mars*, and more than fifty science fiction and fantasy stories. His story "Tk'Tk'Tk" won the Hugo Award in 2006, and he has been short-listed for awards including the Hugo, Nebula, Campbell, and Sturgeon. His stories have appeared in *Asimov's, Analog, F&SF*, numerous Year's Best anthologies, and his award-winning collection *Space Magic*. He lives in a hundred-year-old bungalow in Portland, Oregon.

The Best We Can

Carrie Vaughn

First contact was supposed to change the course of human history. But you still have to go to work the next morning. *Edited by Ann VanderMeer.*

In the end, the discovery of evidence of extraterrestrial life, and not just life, but intelligence, got hopelessly mucked up because no one wanted to take responsibility for confirming the findings, and no one could decide who ultimately had the authority—the obligation—to do so. We submitted the paper, but peer review held it up for a year. News leaked—NASA announced one of their press conferences, but the press conference ended up being an announcement about a future announcement, which never actually happened and the reporters made a joke of it. Another case of Antarctic meteorites or cold fusion. We went around with our mouths shut waiting for an official announcement while ulcers devoured our guts.

So I wrote a press release. I had Marsh at JPL's comet group and Salvayan at Columbia vet it for me and released it under the auspices of the JPL Near Earth Objects Program. We could at least start talking about it instead of arguing about whether we were ready to start talking about it. I didn't know what would happen next. I did it in the spirit of scientific outreach, naturally. The release included that now-famous blurry photo that started the whole thing.

I had an original print of that photo, of UO-1—Unidentified Object One, because it technically wasn't flying and I was being optimistic that this would be the first of more than one—framed and hanging on the wall over my desk, a stark focal point in my chronically cluttered office. Out of the thousands of asteroids we tracked and photographed, this one caught my eye, because it was symmetrical and had a higher than normal albedo. It flashed, even, like a mirror. Asteroids aren't symmetrical and aren't very reflective. But if it wasn't an asteroid. . . .

We turned as many telescopes on it as we could. Tried to get time on Hubble and failed, because it sounded ridiculous—why waste time looking at something inside the orbit of Jupiter? We *did* get Arecibo on it. We got pictures from multiple sources, studied them for weeks until we couldn't argue with them any longer. No one wanted to say it because it was crazy, just thinking it would get you sacked, and I got so frustrated with the whole group sitting there in the conference room after hours on a Friday afternoon, staring at each other with wide eyes and dropped jaws and no one saying anything, that I said it: It's not natural, and it's not ours.

UO-1 was approximately 250 meters long, with a fan shape at one end, blurred at the other, as if covered with projections too fine to show up at that resolution. The rest was perfectly straight, a thin stalk holding together blossom and roots, the lines rigid and artificial. The fan shape might be a ram scoop—Angie came up with that idea, and the conjecture stuck, no matter how much I reminded people that we couldn't decide anything about what it was or what it meant. Not until we knew more.

We—the scientific community, astronomers, philosophers, writers, all of humanity—had spent a lot of time thinking about what would happen if we found definitive proof that intelligent life existed elsewhere in the universe. All the scenarios involved these other intelligences talking to us. Reaching out to us. Sending a message we would have to decipher—would be eager to decipher. Hell, we sure wouldn't be able to talk to them, not stuck on our own collection of rocks like we were. Whether people thought we'd be overrun with sadistic tripods or be invited to join a greater benevolent galactic society, that was always the assumption—we'd know they were there because they'd talk to us.

When that didn't happen, it was like no one knew what to do next. No one had thought about what would happen if we just found a . . . a *thing* . . . that happened to be drifting a few million miles out from the moon. It didn't talk. Not so much as a blinking light. The radiation we detected from it was reflected—whatever propulsion had driven it through space had long since stopped, and inertia carried it now. No one knew how to respond to it. The news that was supposed to change the course of human history . . . didn't.

We wouldn't know any more about it until we looked at it up close, until we brought it here, brought it home. And that was where it all fell apart.

• • •

I presented the initial findings at the International Astronomical Union annual meeting. My department gathered the data, but we couldn't do anything about implementation—no one group could implement *anything*. But of course, the first argument was about whom the thing belonged to. I nearly resigned.

Everyone wanted a piece of it, including various governments and the United Nations, and we had to humor that debate because nothing could get done without funding. The greatest discovery in all of human history, and funding held it hostage. Several corporations, including the producers of a popular energy drink, threatened to mount their own expeditions in order to establish naming and publicity rights, until the U.S. Departments of Energy, Transportation, and Defense issued joint restrictions on privately-funded extra-orbital spaceflight, which caused its own massive furor.

Meanwhile, we and the various other groups working on the project tracked UO-1 as it appeared to establish an elliptical solar orbit that would take it out to the orbit of Saturn and back on a twenty-year cycle. We waited. We developed plans, which were presented and rejected. We took better and better pictures, which revealed enough detail to see struts holding up what did indeed appear to be the surface of a ram scoop. It did not, everyone slowly began to agree, appear to be inhabited. The data on it never fluctuated. No signals emanated from it. It was metal, it was solid, it was inert. We published papers and appeared on cable documentaries. We gritted our teeth while websites went up claiming that the thing was a weapon, and a survivalist movement developed in response. Since it was indistinguishable from all the existing survivalist movements, no one really noticed.

And we waited.

• • •

The thing is, you discover the existence of extraterrestrial intelligence, and you still have to go home, wash up, get a good night's sleep, and come up with something to eat for breakfast in the morning. Life goes on, life keeps going on, and it's not that people forget or stop being interested. It's that they realize they still have to change the oil in the car and take the dog for a walk. You feel like the whole world ought to be different, but it only shifts. Your worldview expands to take in this new information.

I go to work every day and look at that picture, *my* picture, this satellite or spacecraft, this message in a bottle. Some days I'm furious that I can't get my hands on it. Some days I weep at the wonder of it. Most days I look at it, sigh, and write another round of emails and make phone calls to find out what's going to happen to it. To *make* something happen.

"How goes the war?" Marsh leans into my office like he does every afternoon, mostly to try to cheer me up. He's been here as long as I have; our work overlaps, and we've become friends. I go to his kids' birthday parties. The brown skin around his eyes crinkles with his smile. I'm not able to work up a smile to match.

"The Chinese say they're sending a probe with a robotic arm and a booster to grab it and pull it back to Earth. They say whoever gets there first has right of salvage. It's a terrible idea. Even if they did manage to get it back without breaking it, they'd never let anyone else look at it."

"Oh, I think they would—under their terms." He doesn't get too worked up about it because nobody's managed to do anything yet, why would they now? He would say I take all of this too personally, and he'd be right.

"The IAU is sending a delegation to try to talk the Chinese government into joining the coalition. They might have a chance of it if they actually had a plan of their own. Look, if you want me to talk your ear off, come in and sit, have some coffee. Otherwise, leave now. That's your warning."

"I'll take the coffee," he says, claiming the chair I pulled away from the wall for him before turning to my little desktop coffee maker. His expression softens, his sympathy becoming genuine rather than habitual. "You backing any particular plan yet?"

I sigh. "Gravity tractor looks like our best option. Change the object's trajectory, steer it into a more convenient orbit without actually touching it. Too bad the technology is almost completely untested. We can test it first, of course. Which will take years. And there's an argument against it. Emissions from a gravity tractor's propulsion may damage the object. It's the root of the whole problem: we don't know enough about the thing to know how much stress it can take. The cowboys want to send a crewed mission—they say the only way to be sure is to get eyeballs on the thing. But that triples the cost of any mission. Anything we do will take years of planning and implementation anyway, so no one can be bothered to get off their asses. Same old, same old."

Two and half years. It's been two and a half years since we took that picture. My life has swung into a very tight orbit around this one thing.

"Patience, Jane," Marsh says in a tone that almost sets me off. He's only trying to help.

Truth is, I've been waiting for his visit. I pull out a sheet of handwritten calculations from under a manila folder. "I do have another idea, but I wanted to talk to you about it before I propose anything." His brow goes up, he leans in with interest.

He'll see it faster than I can explain it, so I speak carefully. "We can use Angelus." When he doesn't answer, yes or no, I start to worry and talk to cover it up. "It launches in six months, plenty of time to reprogram the trajectory, send it on a flyby past UO-1, get more data on it than we'll ever get sitting here on Earth—"

His smile has vanished. "Jane. I've been waiting for Angelus for five years. The timing is critical. My comet won't be this close for another two hundred years."

"But Angelus is the only mission launching in the next year with the right kind of optics and maneuverability to get a good look at UO-1, and yes, I know the timing on the comet is once in a lifetime and I know it's important. But this—this is once in a *civilization*. The sooner we can look at it, answer some of our questions . . . well. The sooner the better."

"The better *you'll* be. I'm supposed to wait, but you can't?"

"Please, Marsh. I'll feel a lot better about it if you'll agree with me."

"Thank you for the coffee, Jane," he says, setting aside the mug as he stands.

I close my eyes and beseech the ceiling. This isn't how I want this to go. "Marsh, I'm not trying to sabotage your work, I'm just looking at available resources—"

"And I'm not ultimately the one who makes decisions about what happens to Angelus. I'm just the one depending on all the data. You can make your proposal, but don't ask me to sign off on it."

He starts to leave and I say, "Marsh. I can't take it anymore. I spend every day holding my breath, waiting for someone to do something truly stupid. Some days I can't stand it that I can't get my hands on it."

He sits back down, like a good friend should. A good friend would not, however, steal a colleague's exploratory probe away from him. But this is *important*.

"You know what I think? The best bet is to let one of these corporate foundations mount an expedition. They won't want to screw up because of the bad publicity, and they'll bring you on board for credibility so you'll have some say in how they proceed. You'll be their modern-day Howard Carter."

I can see it now: I'd be the face of the expedition, all I'd have to do is stand there and look pretty. Or at least studious. Explain gravity and trajectories for the popular audience. Speculate on the composition of alien alloys. Watch whatever we find out there get paraded around the globe to shill corn chips. Wouldn't even feel like I was selling my soul, would it?

I must look green, or ill, or murderous, because Marsh goes soothing. "Just think about it, before you go and do something crazy."

. . .

I've kept a dedicated SETI@home computer running since I was sixteen. Marsh doesn't know that about me. I don't believe in extraterrestrial UFOs because I know in great, intimate detail the difficulties of sending objects across the vast distances of space. Hell, just a few hundred miles into orbit isn't a picnic. We've managed it, of course—we are officially extra–solar system beings now, with our little probes and plaques pushing ever outward. Will they find anything? Will anything find *them?*

Essentially, there are two positions on the existence of extraterrestrial intelligence and whether we might ever make contact, and they both come down to the odds. The first says that *we're* here, humanity is intelligent, flinging out broadcasts and training dozens of telescopes outward, hoping for the least little sign, and the universe is so immeasurably vast that, given the odds, the billions of stars and galaxies and planets out there, we can't possibly be the only intelligent species doing these things. The second position says that the odds of life coming into being on any given planet, of that life persisting long enough to evolve, then to evolve intelligence, and then being interested in the same things we are—the odds of all those things falling into place are so immeasurably slim, we may very well be the only ones here.

Is the universe half full or half empty? All we could ever do to solve the riddle was wait. So I waited and was rewarded for my optimism.

In unguarded moments I'm certain this was meant to happen, I was meant to discover UO-1. Me and no one else. Because I understand how important it is. Because I'm the one sitting here every day sending emails and making phone calls. I ID'd the image, I made the call, I had the guts to go public, I deserve a say in what happens next.

I submit the paperwork proposing that the Angelus probe be repurposed to perform a flyby and survey of UO-1. Marsh will forgive me. I wait. Again.

I've kept track, and I've done a hundred fifty TV interviews in the last two years. Most of them are snippets for pop-documentaries, little chunks of information delivered to the lowest-common-denominator audience. I explain over and over again, in different settings, sometimes in my office, sometimes in a vague but picturesque location, sometimes at Griffith Observatory, because for some reason nothing says "space" like Griffith Observatory. I hold up a little plastic model of UO-1 (they're selling the kits at hobby stores—we don't see any of the money from that) to demonstrate the way it's traveling through space, how orbital mechanics work, and how we might use a gravity tractor to bring it home. Sometimes, the segments are specifically for schools, and I like those best because I can give free rein to my enthusiasm. I tell the kids, "This is going to take more than one lifetime to figure out. If we find a way to go to Alpha Centauri, it's going to take lifetimes. You'll have to finish the work I've started. Please grow up and finish it."

I call everyone I can think of who might have some kind of influence over Angelus. I explain that a picture of a metal object taken from a few million miles away doesn't tell us anything about the people who made it. Not even if they have thumbs or tentacles. Most of them tell me that the best plan they can think of is to build bigger telescopes.

"It's not the size," I mutter. "It's how you use it."

NASA thinks they will be making the decision because they've got the resources, the scientists, the experience, the hardware. Congress says this is too important to let NASA make decisions unilaterally. A half dozen private U.S. firms would try something if the various cabinet departments weren't busy making anything they could try illegal by fiat. There are already three court cases. At least one of them is arguing that a rocket launch is protected as freedom of speech. The IAU brought a complaint to the United Nations that the U.S. government shouldn't be allowed to dictate a course of action. The General Assembly nominated a "representative in absentia" for the species that launched UO-1—some Finnish philosopher I'd never heard of. It should have been me.

After a decade of international conferences, I have colleagues all over the world. I call them all. Most are sympathetic. A South African cosmologist I know tells me I'm grandstanding, then laughs like it's a joke, but not really. They all tell me to be patient. Just wait.

Life goes on. My other research, the asteroid research I was doing, has piled up, and I get polite but firm hints that I really ought to work on that if I want to keep my job. I go to conferences, I publish, I do another dozen interviews, holding up the plastic model of the object that I'll likely never get close to. The ache in my heart feels just like it did when Peter left me. That was three years ago, and I can still feel it. The ache that says: I can't possibly start over, can I?

The ache faded when I found UO-1.

• • •

"JPL rejected your proposal to repurpose Angelus. Thank God." Marsh leans on my doorway like usual. He's grinning like he won a prize.

I got the news via email. The bastards can't even be bothered to call. I'd called them back, thinking there must have been a mistake. The pitying tone in their voices didn't sound like kindness anymore. It was definitely condescension. I cried. I've been crying all afternoon, as the pile of wadded-up tissues on my desk attests. My eyes are still puffy. Marsh can see I've been crying; he knows what it looks like when I cry. He was there three years ago. I take a breath to keep from starting up again and stare at him like he's punched me.

"How can you say that? Do you know what they're talking about now? They're talking about just leaving it! They're saying the orbit is stable, we'll always know where it is and we can go after it when we have a better handle on the technology. But what if something happens to it? What if an asteroid hits it, or it crashes into Jupiter, or—"

"Jane, it's been traveling for how many hundreds of billions of miles—why would something happen to it now?"

"I don't know! It shouldn't even be there at all! And they won't even *listen* to me!"

He sounds tired. "Why should they?"

"Because it's *mine!*"

His normally comforting smile is sad, pitying, smug, and amused, all at once. "It's not yours, not any more than gravity belonged to Newton."

I want to scream. Because maybe this isn't the most important thing to happen to humanity. That's probably, oh, the invention of the wheel, or language. Maybe this is just the most important thing to happen to me.

I grab another tissue. Look at the picture of UO-1. It's beautiful. It tells me that the universe, as vast as we already know it is, is bigger than we think.

Marsh sits in the second chair without waiting for an invitation. "What do you think it is, Jane? Be honest. No job, no credibility, no speaking gig for Discovery on the line. What do you think when you look at it?" He nods at the picture.

There are some cable shows that will win you credibility for appearing on them. There are some that will destroy any credibility you ever had. I have been standing right on that line, answering the question of "What is it?" as vaguely as possible. We need to know more, no way to speculate, et cetera. But I know. I *know* what it is.

"I think it's Voyager. Not *the* Voyager. *Their* Voyager. The probe they sent out to explore, and it just kept going."

He doesn't laugh. "You think we'll find a plaque on it? A message? A recording?"

"It's what I want to find." I smile wistfully. "But what are the odds?"

"Gershwin," he says. I blink, but he doesn't seem offended by my confusion. He leans back in the chair, comfortable in his thick middle-aged body, genial, someone who clearly believes all is well with the world, at least at the moment. "We've had fourteen billion years of particles colliding, stars exploding, nebulae compressing, planets forming, all of it cycling over and over again, and then just the right amino acids converged, life forms, and a couple of billion years of evolution later—we get Gene Kelly and Leslie Caron dancing by a fountain to Gershwin and it's beautiful. For no particular evolution-driven reason, it's beautiful. I think: what are the odds? That they're dancing, that it's on film, and that I'm here watching and thinking it's gorgeous. If the whole universe exists just to make this one moment happen, I wouldn't be at all surprised."

"So if I think sometimes that maybe I was meant to find UO-1, because maybe there's a message there and that I'm the only one who can read it—then maybe that's not crazy?" Like thinking that the universe sent me UO-1 at a time in my life when I desperately needed something to focus on, to be meaningful . . .

"Oh, no, it's definitely crazy. But it's understandable." This time his smile is kind.

"Marsh—this really is the most important thing to happen to humanity ever, isn't it?"

"Yes. But we still need to study and map near-Earth asteroids, right?"

· · ·

I don't tell Marsh that I've never seen *An American in Paris*. I've never watched Gene Kelly in anything. But Marsh obviously thinks it's important, so I watch the movie. I decide he's right. That dance at the fountain, it's a moment suspended in time. Like an alien spacecraft that shouldn't be there but is.

· · ·

Two things happen next.

At the next IAU meeting, an archaeologist presents a lecture on UO-1, which I think is very presumptuous, but I go, because I go to everything having to do with UO-1. She talks about preservation and uses terms like "in situ," and how modern archaeological practice often involves excavating artifacts, examining them—and then putting them back in the ground. She argues that we don't know what years of space travel have done to the metal and structures of UO-1. We don't know how our methods of studying it will impact it. She shows pictures of Mayan friezes that were excavated and left exposed to the elements versus ones that remained buried for their own protection, so that later scientists with better equipment and techniques will be able to return to them someday. The exposed ones have dissolved, decayed past recognition. She gives me an image: I reach out and finally put my hand on UO-1, and its metallic skin, weakened by a billion micrometeoroid impacts gathered over millennia, disintegrates under my touch.

I think of that and start to sweat. So yes, caution. I know this.

The second thing that happens: I turn my back on UO-1.

Not really, but it's a striking image. I write another proposal, a different proposal, and submit it to one of the corporate foundations because Marsh may be right. If nothing else, it'll get attention. I don't mind a little grandstanding.

We already have teams tracking a best-guess trajectory to determine where UO-1 came from. It might have been cruising through space at nonrelativistic speed for dozens of years, or centuries, or millions of centuries, but based on the orbit it established here, we can estimate how it entered the solar system and the trajectory it traveled before then. We can trace backward.

My plan: to send a craft in that direction. It will do a minimal amount of science along the way, sending back radiation readings, but most of the energy and hardware is going into propulsion. It will be fast and it will have purpose, carrying an updated variation of Sagan's Voyager plaques and recordings, digital and analog.

It's a very simple message, in the end: Hey, we found your device. Want one of ours?

In all likelihood, the civilization that built UO-1 is extinct. The odds simply aren't good for a species surviving—and caring—for long enough to send a message and receive a reply. But our sample size for drawing that conclusion about the average lifespan of an entire species on a particular world is exactly one, which isn't a sample size at all. We weren't supposed to ever find an alien ship in our backyard, either.

I tear up when the rocket launches, and that makes for good TV. As Marsh predicted, the documentary producers decide to make me the human face of the project, and I figure I'll do what I have to, as best as I can. I develop a collection of quotes for the dozens of interviews that follow—I'm up to two-hundred thirty-five.

I talk about taking the long view and transcending the everyday concerns that bog us down. About how we are children reaching across the sandbox with whatever we have to offer, to whoever shows up. About teaching our children to think as big as they possibly can, and that miracles sometimes really do happen. They happen often, because all of this, Gershwin's music, the great curry I had for dinner last night, the way we hang pictures on our walls of things we love, are miracles that never should have happened.

It's a hope, a need, a shout, a shot in the dark. It's the best we can do. For now.

CARRIE VAUGHN is best known for her *New York Times* bestselling series of novels about a werewolf named Kitty who hosts a talk radio show for the supernaturally disadvantaged. Her latest novels include a near-Earth space opera, *Martians Abroad*, from Tor Books, and a postapocalyptic murder mystery, *Bannerless*, from John Joseph Adams Books. The sequel, *The Wild Dead*, will be out in 2018. She's written several other contemporary fantasy and young adult novels, as well as upwards of eighty short stories, two of which have been finalists for the Hugo Award. She's a contributor to the Wild Cards series of shared-world superhero books edited by George R. R. Martin and a graduate of the Odyssey Writing Workshop. An Air Force brat, she survived her nomadic childhood and managed to put down roots in Boulder, Colorado.

The City, Born Great

N. K. Jemisin

New York City is about to go through a few changes. Like all great metropolises before it, when a city gets big enough, old enough, it must be born; but there are ancient enemies who cannot tolerate new life. Thus New York will live or die by the efforts of a reluctant midwife . . . and how well he can learn to sing the city's mighty song. *Hugo Award nominee. Edited by Liz Gorinsky.*

I sing the city.

Fucking city. I stand on the rooftop of a building I don't live in and spread my arms and tighten my middle and yell nonsense ululations at the construction site that blocks my view. I'm really singing to the cityscape beyond. The city'll figure it out.

It's dawn. The damp of it makes my jeans feel slimy, or maybe that's 'cause they haven't been washed in weeks. Got change for a wash-and-dry, just not another pair of pants to wear till they're done. Maybe I'll spend it on more pants at the Goodwill down the street instead . . . but not yet. Not till I've finished going *AAAAaaaaAAAAaaaa* (breath) *aaaaAAAAaaaaaaa* and listening to the syllable echo back at me from every nearby building face. In my head, there's an orchestra playing "Ode to Joy" with a Busta Rhymes backbeat. My voice is just tying it all together.

Shut your fucking mouth! someone yells, so I take a bow and exit the stage.

But with my hand on the knob of the rooftop door, I stop and turn back and frown and listen, 'cause for a moment I hear something both distant and intimate singing back at me, basso-deep. Sort of coy.

And from even farther, I hear something else: a dissonant, gathering growl. Or maybe those are the rumblers of police sirens? Nothing I like the sound of, either way. I leave.

· · ·

"There's a way these things are supposed to work," says Paulo. He's smoking again, nasty bastard. I've never seen him eat. All he uses his mouth for is smoking, drinking coffee, and talking. Shame; it's a nice mouth otherwise.

We're sitting in a cafe. I'm sitting with him because he bought me breakfast. The people in the cafe are eyeballing him because he's something not-white by their standards, but they can't tell what. They're eyeballing me because I'm definitively black, and because the holes in my clothes aren't the fashionable kind. I don't stink, but these people can smell anybody without a trust fund from a mile away.

"Right," I say, biting into the egg sandwich and damn near wetting myself. Actual egg! Swiss cheese! It's so much better than that McDonald's shit.

Guy likes hearing himself talk. I like his accent; it's sort of nasal and sibilant, nothing like a Spanish-speaker's. His eyes are huge, and I think, *I could get away with so much shit if I had permanent puppy eyes like that.* But he seems older than he looks—way, way older. There's only a tinge of gray at his temples, nice and distinguished, but he feels, like, a hundred.

He's also eyeballing me, and not in the way I'm used to. "Are you listening?" he asks. "This is important."

"Yeah," I say, and take another bite of my sandwich.

He sits forward. "I didn't believe it either, at first. Hong had to drag me to one of the sewers, down into the reeking dark, and show me the growing roots, the budding teeth. I'd been hearing breathing all my life. I thought everyone could." He pauses. "Have you heard it yet?"

"Heard what?" I ask, which is the wrong answer. It isn't that I'm not listening. I just don't give a shit.

He sighs. "Listen."

"I *am* listening!"

"No. I mean, listen, but not to me." He gets up, tosses a twenty onto the table—which isn't necessary, because he paid for the sandwich and the coffee at the counter, and this cafe doesn't do table service. "Meet me back here on Thursday."

I pick up the twenty, finger it, pocket it. Would've done him for the sandwich, or because I like his eyes, but whatever. "You got a place?"

He blinks, then actually looks annoyed. "*Listen*," he commands again, and leaves.

I sit there for as long as I can, making the sandwich last, sipping his leftover coffee, savoring the fantasy of being normal. I people-watch, judge other patrons' appearances; on the fly I make up a poem about being a rich white girl who notices a poor black boy in her coffee shop and has an existential crisis. I imagine Paulo being impressed by my sophistication and admiring me, instead of thinking I'm just some dumb street kid who doesn't listen. I visualize myself going back to a nice apartment with a soft bed, and a fridge stuffed full of food.

Then a cop comes in, fat florid guy buying hipster joe for himself and his partner in the car, and his flat, eyes skim the shop. I imagine mirrors around my head, a rotating cylinder of them that causes his gaze to bounce away. There's no real power in this—it's just something I do to try to make myself less afraid when the monsters are near. For the first time, though, it sort of works: The cop looks around, but doesn't ping on the lone black face. Lucky. I escape.

• • •

I paint the city. Back when I was in school, there was an artist who came in on Fridays to give us free lessons in perspective and lighting and other shit that white people go to art school to learn. Except this guy had done that, and he was black. I'd never seen a black artist before. For a minute I thought I could maybe be one, too.

I can be, sometimes. Deep in the night, on a rooftop in Chinatown, with a spray can for each hand and a bucket of drywall paint that somebody left outside after doing up their living room in lilac, I move in scuttling, crablike swirls. The drywall stuff I can't use too much of; it'll start flaking off after a couple of rains. Spray paint's better for everything, but I like the contrast of the two textures—liquid black on rough lilac, red edging the black. I'm painting a hole. It's like a throat that doesn't start with a mouth or end in lungs; a thing that breathes and swallows endlessly, never filling. No one will see it except people in planes angling toward LaGuardia from the southwest, a few tourists who take helicopter tours, and NYPD aerial surveillance. I don't care what they see. It's not for them.

It's real late. I didn't have anywhere to sleep for the night, so this is what I'm doing to stay awake. If it wasn't the end of the month, I'd get on the subway, but the cops who haven't met their quota would fuck with me. Gotta be careful here; there's a lot of dumb-fuck Chinese kids west of Chrystie Street who wanna pretend to be a gang, protecting their territory, so I keep low. I'm skinny, dark; that helps, too. All I want to do is paint, man, because it's in me and I need to get it out. I need to open up this throat. I need to, I need to . . . yeah. Yeah.

There's a soft, strange sound as I lay down the last streak of black. I pause and look around, confused for a moment—and then the throat sighs behind me. A big, heavy gust of moist air tickles the hairs on my skin. I'm not scared. This is why I did it, though I didn't realize that when I started. Not sure how I know now. But when I turn back, it's still just paint on a rooftop.

Paulo wasn't shitting me. Huh. Or maybe my mama was right, and I ain't never been right in the head.

I jump into the air and whoop for joy, and I don't even know why.

I spend the next two days going all over the city, drawing breathing-holes everywhere, till my paint runs out.

• • •

I'm so tired on the day I meet Paulo again that I stumble and nearly fall through the cafe's plate-glass window. He catches my elbow and drags me over to a bench meant for customers. "You're hearing it," he says. He sounds pleased.

"I'm hearing coffee," I suggest, not bothering to stifle a yawn. A cop car rolls by. I'm not too tired to imagine myself as nothing, beneath notice, not even worth beating for pleasure. It works again; they roll on.

Paulo ignores my suggestion. He sits down beside me and his gaze goes strange and unfocused for a moment. "Yes. The city is breathing easier," he says. "You're doing a good job, even without training."

"I try."

He looks amused. "I can't tell if you don't believe me, or if you just don't care."

I shrug. "I believe you." I also don't care, not much, because I'm hungry. My stomach growls. I've still got that twenty he gave me, but I'll take it to that church-plate sale I heard about over on Prospect, get chicken and rice and greens and cornbread for less than the cost of a free-trade small-batch-roasted latte.

He glances down at my stomach when it growls. Huh. I pretend to stretch and scratch above my abs, making sure to pull up my shirt a little. The artist guy brought a model for us to draw once, and pointed to this little ridge of muscle above the hips called Apollo's Belt. Paulo's gaze goes right to it. *Come on, come on, fishy fishy. I need somewhere to sleep.*

Then his eyes narrow and focus on mine again. "I had forgotten," he says, in a faint wondering tone. "I almost . . . It's been so long. Once, though, I was a boy of the *favelas*."

"Not a lot of Mexican food in New York," I reply.

He blinks and looks amused again. Then he sobers. "This city will die," he says. He doesn't raise his voice, but he doesn't have to. I'm paying attention now. Food, living: These things have meaning to me. "If you do not learn the things I have to teach you. If you do not help. The time will come and you will fail, and this city will join Pompeii and Atlantis and a dozen others whose names no one remembers, even though hundreds of thousands of people died with them. Or perhaps there will be a stillbirth—the shell of the city surviving to possibly grow again in the future, but its vital spark snuffed for now, like New Orleans—but that will still kill *you*, either way. You are the catalyst, whether of strength or destruction."

He's been talking like this since he showed up—places that never were, things that can't be, omens and portents. I figure it's bullshit because he's telling it to *me*, a kid whose own mama kicked him out and prays for him to die every day and probably hates me. *God* hates me. And I fucking hate God back, so why would he choose me for anything? But that's really why I start paying attention: because of God. I don't have to believe in something for it to fuck up my life.

"Tell me what to do," I say.

Paulo nods, looking smug. Thinks he's got my number. "Ah. You don't want to die."

I stand up, stretch, feel the streets around me grow longer and more pliable in the rising heat of day. (Is that really happening, or am I imagining it, or is it happening *and* I'm imagining that it's connected to me somehow?) "Fuck you. That ain't it."

"Then you don't even care about that." He makes it a question with the tone of his voice.

"Ain't about being alive." I'll starve to death someday, or freeze some winter night, or catch something that rots me away until the hospitals have to take me, even without money or an address. But I'll sing and paint and dance and fuck and cry the city before I'm done, because it's mine. It's fucking *mine*. That's why.

"It's about *living*," I finish. And then I turn to glare at him. He can kiss my ass if he doesn't understand. "Tell me what to do."

Something changes in Paulo's face. He's listening, now. To me. So he gets to his feet and leads me away for my first real lesson.

• • •

This is the lesson: Great cities are like any other living things, being born and maturing and wearying and dying in their turn.

Duh, right? Everyone who's visited a real city feels that, one way or another. All those rural people who hate cities are afraid of something legit; cities really are *different*. They make a weight on the world, a tear in the fabric of reality, like . . . like black holes, maybe. Yeah. (I go to museums sometimes. They're cool inside, and Neil deGrasse Tyson is hot.) As more and more people come in and deposit their strangeness and leave and get replaced by others, the tear widens. Eventually it gets so deep that it forms a pocket, connected only by the thinnest thread of . . . something to . . . something. Whatever cities are made of.

But the separation starts a process, and in that pocket the many parts of the city begin to multiply and differentiate. Its sewers extend into places where there is no need for water. Its slums grow teeth; its art centers, claws. Ordinary things within it, traffic and construction and stuff like that, start to have a rhythm like a heartbeat, if you record their sounds and play them back fast. The city . . . quickens.

Not all cities make it this far. There used to be a couple of great cities on this continent, but that was before Columbus fucked the Indians' shit up, so we had to start over. New Orleans failed, like Paulo said, but it survived, and that's something. It can try again. Mexico City's well on its way. But New York is the first American city to reach this point.

The gestation can take twenty years or two hundred or two thousand, but eventually the time will come. The cord is cut and the city becomes a thing of its own, able to stand on wobbly legs and do . . . well, whatever the fuck a living, thinking entity shaped like a big-ass city wants to do.

And just as in any other part of nature, there are things lying in wait for this moment, hoping to chase down the sweet new life and swallow its guts while it screams.

That's why Paulo's here to teach me. That's why I can clear the city's breathing and stretch and massage its asphalt limbs. I'm the midwife, see.

• • •

I run the city. I run it every fucking day.

Paulo takes me home. It's just somebody's summer sublet in the Lower East Side, but it feels like a home. I use his shower and eat some of the food in his fridge without asking, just to see what he'll do. He doesn't do shit except smoke a cigarette, I think to piss me off. I can hear sirens on the streets of the neighborhood— frequent, close. I wonder, for some reason, if they're looking for me. I don't say it aloud, but Paulo sees me twitching. He says, "The harbingers of the enemy will hide among the city's parasites. Beware of them."

He's always saying cryptic shit like this. Some of it makes sense, like when he speculates that maybe there's a *purpose* to all of it, some reason for the great cities and the process that makes them. What the enemy has been doing—attacking at the moment of vulnerability, crimes of opportunity—might just be the warm-up for something bigger. But Paulo's full of shit, too, like when he says I should consider meditation to better attune myself to the city's needs. Like I'mma get through this on white-girl yoga.

"White-girl yoga," Paulo says, nodding. "Indian-man yoga. Stockbroker racquetball and schoolboy handball, ballet and merengue, union halls and SoHo galleries. You will embody a city of millions. You need not *be* them, but know that they are part of you."

I laugh. "Racquetball? That shit ain't no part of me, chico."

"The city chose you, out of all," Paulo says. "Their lives depend on you."

Maybe. But I'm still hungry and tired all the time, scared all the time, never safe. What good does it do to be valuable, if nobody values you?

He can tell I don't wanna talk anymore, so he gets up and goes to bed. I flop on the couch and I'm dead to the world. Dead.

Dreaming, dead dreaming, of a dark place beneath heavy cold waves where something stirs with a slithery sound and uncoils and turns toward the mouth of the Hudson, where it empties into the sea. Toward *me*. And I am too weak, too helpless, too immobilized by fear, to do anything but twitch beneath its predatory gaze.

Something comes from far to the south, somehow. (None of this is quite real. Everything rides along the thin tether that connects the city's reality to that of the world. The *effect* happens in the world, Paulo has said. The *cause* centers around me.) It moves between me, wherever I am, and the uncurling thing, wherever it is. An immensity protects me, just this once, just in this place—though from a great distance I feel others hemming and grumbling and raising themselves to readiness. Warning the enemy that it must adhere to the rules of engagement that have always governed this ancient battle. It's not allowed to come at me too soon.

My protector, in this unreal space of dream, is a sprawling jewel with filth-crusted facets, a thing that stinks of dark coffee and the bruised grass of a *futebol* pitch and traffic noise and familiar cigarette smoke. Its threat display of saber-shaped girders lasts for only a moment, but that is enough. The uncurling thing flinches back into its cold cave, resentfully. But it will be back. That, too, is tradition.

I wake with sunlight warming half my face. Just a dream? I stumble into the room where Paulo is sleeping. "*São Paulo*," I whisper, but he does not wake. I wiggle under his covers. When he wakes he doesn't reach for me, but he doesn't push me away either. I let him know I'm grateful and give him a reason to let me back in, later. The rest'll have to wait till I get condoms and he brushes his ashy-ass mouth. After that, I use his shower again, put on the clothes I washed in his sink, and head out while he's still snoring.

Libraries are safe places. They're warm in the winter. Nobody cares if you stay all day as long as you're not eyeballing the kids' corner or trying to hit up porn on the computers. The one at Forty-Second—the one with the lions—isn't that kind of library. It doesn't lend out books. Still, it has a library's safety, so I sit in a corner and read everything within reach: municipal tax law, *Birds of the Hudson Valley*, *What to Expect When You're Expecting a City Baby: NYC Edition*. See, Paulo? I told you I was listening.

It gets to be late afternoon and I head outside. People cover the steps, laughing, chatting, mugging with selfie sticks. There're cops in body armor over by the subway entrance, showing off their guns to the tourists so they'll feel safe from New York. I get a Polish sausage and eat it at the feet of one of the lions. Fortitude, not Patience. I know my strengths.

I'm full of meat and relaxed and thinking about stuff that ain't actually important—like how long Paulo will let me stay and whether I can use his address to apply for stuff—so I'm not watching the street. Until cold prickles skitter over my side. I know what it is before I react, but I'm careless again because I *turn to look* . . . Stupid, stupid, I fucking know better; cops down in Baltimore broke a man's spine for making eye contact. But as I spot these two on the corner opposite the library steps—short pale man and tall dark woman both in blue like black—I notice something that actually breaks my fear because it's so strange.

It's a bright, clear day, not a cloud in the sky. People walking past the cops leave short, stark afternoon shadows, barely there at all. But around these two, the shadows pool and curl as if they stand beneath their own private, roiling thundercloud. And as I watch, the shorter one begins to . . . *stretch*, sort of, his shape warping ever so slightly, until one eye is twice the circumference of the other. His right shoulder slowly develops a bulge that suggests a dislocated joint. His companion doesn't seem to notice.

Yooooo, nope. I get up and start picking my way through the crowd on the steps. I'm doing that thing I do, trying to shunt off their gaze—but it feels different this time. Sticky, sort of, threads of cheap-shit gum fucking up my mirrors. I *feel* them start following me, something immense and wrong shifting in my direction.

Even then I'm not sure—a lot of real cops drip and pulse sadism in the same way—but I ain't taking chances. My city is helpless, unborn as yet, and Paulo ain't here to protect me. I gotta look out for self, same as always.

I play casual till I reach the corner and book it, or try. Fucking tourists! They idle along the wrong side of the sidewalk, stopping to look at maps and take pictures of shit nobody else gives a fuck about. I'm so busy cussing them out in my head that I forget they can also be dangerous: Somebody yells and grabs my arm as I Heisman past, and I hear a man yell out, "He tried to take her purse!" as I wrench away. *Bitch, I ain't took shit*, I think, but it's too late. I see another tourist reaching for her phone to call 911. Every cop in the area will be gunning for every black male aged whatever now.

I gotta get out of the area.

Grand Central's right there, sweet subway promise, but I see three cops hanging out in the entrance, so I swerve right to take Forty-First. The crowds thin out past Lex, but where can I go? I sprint across Third despite the traffic; there are enough gaps. But I'm getting tired, 'cause I'm a scrawny dude who doesn't get enough to eat, not a track star.

I keep going, though, even through the burn in my side. I can feel *those* cops, the *harbingers of the enemy*, not far behind me. The ground shakes with their lumpen footfalls.

I hear a siren about a block away, closing. Shit, the UN's coming up; I don't need the Secret Service or whatever on me, too. I jag left through an alley and trip over a wooden pallet. Lucky again—a cop car rolls by the alley entrance just as I go down, and they don't see me. I stay down and try to catch my breath till I hear the car's engine fading into the distance. Then, when I think it's safe, I push up. Look back, because the city is squirming around me, the concrete is jittering and heaving, everything from the bedrock to the rooftop bars is trying its damnedest to tell me to go. Go. *Go*.

Crowding the alley behind me is . . . is . . . the shit? I don't have words for it.

Too many arms, too many legs, too many eyes, and all of them fixed on me. Somewhere in the mass, I glimpse curls of dark hair and a scalp of pale blond, and I understand suddenly that these are—this is—my two cops. One real monstrosity. The walls of the alley crack as it oozes its way into the narrow space.

"Oh. Fuck. No," I gasp.

I claw my way to my feet and haul ass. A patrol car comes around the corner from Second Avenue and I don't see it in time to duck out of sight. The car's loudspeaker blares something unintelligible, probably *I'm gonna kill you*, and I'm actually amazed. Do they not see the thing behind me? Or do they just not give a shit because they can't shake it down for city revenue? Let them fucking shoot me. Better than whatever that thing will do.

I hook left onto Second Avenue. The cop car can't come after me against the traffic, but it's not like that'll stop some doubled-cop monster. Forty-Fifth. Forty-Seventh and my legs are molten granite. Fiftieth and I think I'm going to die. Heart attack far too young; poor kid, should've eaten more organic; should've taken it easy and not been so angry; the world can't hurt you if you just ignore everything that's wrong with it; well, not until it kills you anyway.

I cross the street and risk a look back and see something roll onto the sidewalk on at least eight legs, using three or four arms to push itself off a building as it careens a little . . . before coming straight after me again. It's the Mega Cop, and it's gaining. *Oh shit oh shit oh shit please no.*

Only one choice.

Swing right. Fifty-Third, against the traffic. An old folks' home, a park, a promenade . . . fuck those. Pedestrian bridge? Fuck that. I head straight for the six lanes of utter batshittery and potholes that is FDR Drive, do not pass Go, do not try to cross on foot unless you want to be smeared halfway to Brooklyn. Beyond it? The East River, if I survive. I'm even freaked out enough to try swimming in that fucking sewage. But I'm probably gonna collapse in the third lane and get run over fifty times before anybody thinks to put on brakes.

Behind me, the Mega Cop utters a wet, tumid *hough*, like it's clearing its throat for swallowing. I go

over the barrier and through the grass into fucking hell I go one lane silver car two lanes horns horns horns three lanes SEMI WHAT'S A FUCKING SEMI DOING ON THE FDR IT'S TOO TALL YOU STUPID UPSTATE HICK screaming four lanes GREEN TAXI screaming smart car hahaha cute five lanes moving truck six lanes and the blue Lexus actually brushes up against my clothes as it blares past screaming screaming screaming

screaming

screaming metal and tires as reality stretches, and nothing stops for the Mega Cop; it does not belong here and the FDR is an artery, vital with the movement of nutrients and strength and attitude and adrenaline, the cars are white blood cells and the thing is an irritant, an infection, an invader to whom the city gives no consideration and no quarter

screaming, as the Mega Cop is torn to pieces by the semi and the taxi and the

Lexus and even that adorable smart car, which actually swerves a little to run over an extra-wiggly piece. I collapse onto a square of grass, breathless, shaking, wheezing, and can only stare as a dozen limbs are crushed, two dozen eyes squashed flat, a mouth that is mostly gums riven from jaw to palate. The pieces flicker like a monitor with an AV cable short, translucent to solid and back again—but FDR don't stop for shit except a presidential motorcade or a Knicks game, and this thing sure as hell ain't Carmelo Anthony. Pretty soon there's nothing left of it but half-real smears on the asphalt.

I'm alive. Oh, God.

I cry for a little while. Mama's boyfriend ain't here to slap me and say I'm not a man for it. Daddy would've said it was okay—tears mean you're alive—but Daddy's dead. And I'm alive.

With limbs burning and weak, I drag myself up, then fall again. Everything hurts. Is this that heart attack? I feel sick. Everything is shaking, blurring. Maybe it's a stroke. You don't have to be old for that to happen, do you? I stumble over to a garbage can and think about throwing up into it. There's an old guy lying on the bench—me in twenty years, if I make it that far. He opens one eye as I stand there gagging and purses his lips in a judgy way, like he could do better dry heaves in his sleep.

He says, "It's time," and rolls over to put his back to me.

Time. Suddenly I have to move. Sick or not, exhausted or not, something is . . . pulling me. West, toward the city's center. I push away from the can and hug myself as I shiver and stumble toward the pedestrian bridge. As I walk over the lanes I previously ran across, I look down onto flickering fragments of the dead Mega Cop, now ground into the asphalt by a hundred car wheels. Some globules of it are still twitching, and I don't like that. Infection, intrusion. I want it gone.

We want it gone. Yes. It's time.

I blink and suddenly I'm in Central Park. How the fuck did I get here? Disoriented, I realize only as I see their black shoes that I'm passing another pair of cops, but these two don't bother me. They should—skinny kid shivering like he's cold on a June day; even if all they do is drag me off somewhere to shove a plunger up my ass, they should *react* to me. Instead, it's like I'm not there. Miracles exist, Ralph Ellison was right, any NYPD you can walk away from, hallelujah.

The Lake. Bow Bridge: a place of transition. I stop here, stand here, and I know . . . everything.

Everything Paulo's told me: It's true. Somewhere beyond the city, the Enemy is awakening. It sent forth its harbingers and they have failed, but its taint is in the city now, spreading with every car that passes over every now-microscopic iota of the Mega Cop's substance, and this creates a foothold. The Enemy uses this anchor to drag itself up from the dark toward the world, toward the warmth and light, toward the defiance that is *me*, toward the burgeoning wholeness that is *my city*. This attack is not all of it, of course. What comes is only the smallest fraction of the Enemy's old, old evil—but that should be more than enough to slaughter one lowly, worn-out kid who doesn't even have a real city to protect him.

Not yet. It's time. *In* time? We'll see.

On Second, Sixth, and Eighth avenues, my water breaks. Mains, I mean. Water mains. Terrible mess, gonna fuck up the evening commute. I shut my eyes and I am seeing what no one else sees. I am feeling the flex and rhythm of reality, the contractions of possibility. I reach out and grip the railing of the bridge before me and feel the steady, strong pulse that runs through it. *You're doing good, baby. Doing great.*

Something begins to shift. I grow bigger, encompassing. I feel myself upon the firmament, heavy as the foundations of a city. There are others here with me, looming, watching—my ancestors' bones under Wall Street, my predecessors' blood ground into the benches of Christopher Park. No, *new* others, of my new people, heavy imprints upon the fabric of time and space. São Paulo squats nearest, its roots stretching all the way to the bones of dead Machu Picchu, watching sagely and twitching a little with the memory of its own relatively recent traumatic birth. Paris observes with distant disinterest, mildly offended that any city of our tasteless upstart land has managed this transition; Lagos exults to see a new fellow who knows the hustle, the hype, the fight. And more, many more, all of them watching, waiting to see if their numbers increase. Or not. If nothing else, they will bear witness that I, we, were great for one shining moment.

"We'll make it," I say, squeezing the railing and feeling the city contract. All over the city, people's ears pop, and they look around in confusion. "Just a little more. Come on." I'm scared, but there's no rushing this. *Lo que pasa, pasa*—damn, now that song is in my head, *in me* like the rest of New York. It's all here, just like Paulo said. There's no gap between me and the city anymore.

And as the firmament ripples, slides, tears, the Enemy writhes up from the deeps with a reality-bridging roar—

But it is too late. The tether is cut and we are here. We become! We stand, whole and hale and independent, and our legs don't even wobble. We got this. Don't sleep on the city that never sleeps, son, and don't fucking bring your squamous eldritch bullshit here.

I raise my arms and avenues leap. (It's real but it's not. The ground jolts and people think, *Huh, subway's really shaky today.*) I brace my feet and they are girders, anchors, bedrock. The beast of the deeps shrieks and I laugh, giddy with postpartum endorphins. *Bring it.* And when it comes at me I hip check it with the BQE, backhand it with Inwood Park, drop the South Bronx on it like an elbow. (On the evening news that night, ten construction sites will report wrecking-ball collapses. City safety regulations are so lax; terrible, terrible.) The Enemy tries some kind of fucked-up wiggly shit—it's all tentacles—and I snarl and bite into it 'cause New Yorkers eat damn near as much sushi as Tokyo, mercury and all.

Oh, now you're crying! Now you wanna run? Nah, son. You came to the wrong town. I curb stomp it with the full might of Queens and something inside the beast breaks and bleeds iridescence all over creation. This is a shock, for it has not been truly hurt in centuries. It lashes back in a fury, faster than I can block, and from a place that most of the city cannot see, a skyscraper-long tentacle curls out of nowhere to smash into New York Harbor. I scream and fall, I can *hear* my ribs crack, and—no!—a major earthquake shakes Brooklyn for the first time in decades. The Williamsburg Bridge twists and snaps apart like kindling; the Manhattan groans and splinters, though thankfully it does not give way. I feel every death as if it is my own.

Fucking kill you for that, bitch, I'm not-thinking. The fury and grief have driven me into a vengeful fugue. The pain is nothing; this ain't my first rodeo. Through the groan of my ribs I drag myself upright and brace my legs in a pissing-off-the-platform stance. Then I shower the Enemy with a one-two punch of Long Island radiation and Gowanus toxic waste, which burn it like acid. It screams again in pain and disgust, but *Fuck you, you don't belong here, this city is mine, get out!* To drive this lesson home I cut the bitch with LIRR traffic, long vicious honking lines; and to stretch out its pain I salt these wounds with the memory of a bus ride to LaGuardia and back.

And just to add insult to injury? I backhand its ass with Hoboken, raining the drunk rage of ten thousand dudebros down on it like the hammer of God. Port Authority makes it honorary New York, motherfucker; you just got Jerseyed.

The Enemy is as quintessential to nature as any city. We cannot be stopped from becoming, and the Enemy cannot be made to end. I hurt only a small part of it—but I know damn well I sent that part back broken. Good. Time ever comes for that final confrontation, it'll think twice about taking me on again.

Me. *Us.* Yes.

When I relax my hands and open my eyes to see Paulo striding along the bridge toward me with another goddamned cigarette between his lips, I fleetingly see him for what he is again: the sprawling thing from my dream, all sparkling spires and reeking slums and stolen rhythms made over with genteel cruelty. I know that he glimpses what I am, too, all the bright light and bluster of me. Maybe he's always seen it, but there is *admiration* in his gaze now, and I like it. He comes to help support me with his shoulder, and he says, "Congratulations," and I grin.

I live the city. It thrives and it is mine. I am its worthy avatar, and together? We will never be afraid again.

· · ·

Fifty years later.

I sit in a car, watching the sunset from Mulholland Drive. The car is mine; I'm rich now. The city is not mine, but that's all right. The person is coming who will make it live and stand and thrive in the ancient way . . . or not. I know my duty, respect the traditions. Each city must emerge on its own or die trying. We elders merely guide, encourage. Stand witness.

There: a dip in the firmament near the Sunset Strip. I can feel the upwelling of loneliness in the soul I seek. Poor, empty baby. Won't be long now, though. Soon—if she survives—she'll never be alone again.

I reach for my city, so far away, so inseverable from myself. *Ready?* I ask New York.

Fuck yeah, it answers, filthy and fierce.

We go forth to find this city's singer, and hopefully to hear the greatness of its birthing song.

N. K. JEMISIN is a Brooklyn author who won the Hugo Award for Best Novel for both *The Obelisk Gate* and *The Fifth Season*, which was also a *New York Times* Notable Book of 2015. She previously won the Locus Award for her first novel, *The Hundred Thousand Kingdoms*, and her short fiction and novels have been nominated multiple times for Hugo, World Fantasy, Nebula, and RT Reviewers' Choice Awards, and short-listed for the Crawford and the James Tiptree, Jr., Awards.

A Vector Alphabet of Interstellar Travel

Yoon Ha Lee

Depending on who you ask, the space between stars is: an affliction of disease ready to infect, a codex of knowledge, a dance of manners, a matter of currency, mortality, or something older still. *Edited by Patrick Nielsen Hayden.*

The Conflagration

Among the universe's civilizations, some conceive of the journey between stars as the sailing of bright ships, and others as tunneling through the crevices of night. Some look upon their far-voyaging as a migratory imperative, and name their vessels after birds or butterflies.

The people of a certain red star no longer speak its name in any of their hundreds of languages, although they paint alien skies with its whorled light and scorch its spectral lines into the sides of their vessels.

Their most common cult, although by no means a universal one, is that of many-cornered Mrithaya, Mother of the Conflagration. Mrithaya is commonly conceived of as the god of catastrophe and disease, impartial in the injuries she deals out. Any gifts she bestows are incidental, and usually come with sharp edges. The stardrive was invented by one of her worshipers.

Her priests believe that she is completely indifferent to worship, existing in the serenity of her own disinterest. A philosopher once said that you leave offerings of bitter ash and aleatory wine at her dank altars not because she will heed them, but because it is important to acknowledge the truth of the universe's workings. Naturally, this does not stop some of her petitioners from trying, and it is through their largesse that the priests are able to thrive as they do.

Mrithaya is depicted as an eyeless woman of her people, small of stature, but with a shadow scarring the world. (Her people's iconography has never been subtle.) She leans upon a crooked staff with words of poison scratched into it. In poetry, she is signified by smoke-wind and nausea, the sudden fall sideways into loss.

Mrithaya's people, perhaps not surprisingly, think of their travels as the outbreak of a terrible disease, a conflagration that they have limited power to contain; that the civilizations they visit will learn how to build Mrithaya's stardrive, and be infected by its workings. A not insignificant faction holds that they should hide on their candled worlds so as to prevent Mrithaya's terrible cycless gaze from afflicting other civilizations, that all interstellar travel should be interdicted. And yet the pilgrims—Mrithaya's get, they are called—always find a way.

Certain poets write in terror of the day that all extant civilizations will be touched by this terrible technological conflagration and become subject to Mrithaya's whims.

Alphabets

In linear algebra, the basis of a vector space is an alphabet in which all vectors can be expressed uniquely. The thing to remember is that there are many such alphabets.

In the peregrinations of civilizations grand and subtle, each mode of transport is an alphabet expressing their understandings of the universe's one-way knell. One assumes that the underlying universe is the same in each case.

Codices

The Iothal are a people who treasure chronicles of all kinds. From early on in their history, they bound forest chronicles by pressing leaves together and listening to their secrets of turning worm and wheeling sun; they read hymns to the transient things of the world in chronicles of footprints upon rocky soil, of foam upon restive sea. They wrote their alphabets forward and backward and upside down into reflected cloudlight, and divined the poetry of time receding in the earth's cracked strata.

As a corollary, the Iothal compile vast libraries. On the worlds they inhabit, even the motes of air are subject to having indices written on them in stuttering quantum ink. Some of their visionaries speak of a surfeit of knowledge, when it will be impossible to move or breathe without imbibing some unexpected fact, from the number of neutrons in a certain meadow to the habits of aestivating snails. Surely the end product will be a society of enlightened beings, each crowned with some unique mixture of facts and heady fictions.

The underside of this obsession is the society's driving terror. One day all their cities will be unordered dust, one day all their books will be scattered like leaves, one day no one will know the things they knew. One day the rotting remains of their libraries will disintegrate so completely that they will be indistinguishable from the world's wrack of stray eddies and meaningless scribbles, the untide of heat death.

The Iothal do not call their starships ships, but rather codices. They have devoted untold ages to this ongoing archival work. Although they had developed earlier stardrives—indeed, with their predilection for knowledge, it was impossible not to—their scientists refused to rest until they devised one that drank in information and, as its ordinary mode of operation, tattooed it upon the universe's subtle skin.

Each time the Iothal build a codex, they furnish it with a carefully selected compilation of their chronicles, written in a format that the stardrive will find nourishing. Then its crew takes it out into the universe to carry out the act of inscription. Iothal codices have very little care for destination, as it is merely the fact of travel that matters, although they make a point of avoiding potentially hostile aliens.

When each codex has accomplished its task, it loses all vitality and drifts inertly wherever it ends up. The Iothal are very long-lived, but even they do not always survive to this fate.

Distant civilizations are well accustomed to the phenomenon of drifting Iothal vessels, but so far none of them have deciphered the trail of knowledge that the Iothal have been at such pains to lay down.

The Dancers

To most of their near neighbors, they are known as the dancers. It is not the case that their societies are more interested in dance than the norm. True, they have their dances of metal harvest, and dances of dream descending, and dances of efflorescent death. They have their high rituals and their low chants, their festivals where water-of-suffusement flows freely for all who would drink, where bells with spangled clappers toll the hours by antique calendars. But then, these customs differ from their neighbors' in detail rather than in essential nature.

Rather, their historians like to tell the story of how, not so long ago, they went to war with aliens from a distant cluster. No one can agree on the nature of the offense that precipitated the whole affair, and it seems likely that it was a mundane squabble over excavation rights at a particular rumor pit.

The aliens were young when it came to interstellar war, and they struggled greatly with the conventions expected of them. In order to understand their enemy better, they charged their masters of etiquette with the task of interpreting the dancers' behavior. For it was the case that the dancers began each of their battles in the starry deeps with the same maneuvers, and often retreated from battle—those times they had cause to retreat—with other maneuvers, carried out with great precision. The etiquette masters became fascinated by the pirouettes and helices and rolls, and speculated that the dancers' society was constricted by strict rules of engagement. Their fabulists wrote witty and extravagant tales about the dancers' dinner parties, the dancers' sacrificial exchanges, the dancers' effervescent arrangements of glass splinters and their varied meanings.

It was not until late in the war that the aliens realized that the stylized maneuvers of the dancers' ships had nothing to do with courtesy. Rather, they were an effect of the stardrive's ordinary functioning, without which the ships could not move. The aliens could have exploited this knowledge and pushed for a total victory, but by then their culture was so enchanted by their self-dreamed vision of the dancers that the two came instead to a fruitful truce.

These days, the dancers themselves often speak admiringly of the tales that the aliens wrote about them. Among the younger generation in particular, there are those who emulate the elegant and mannered society depicted in the aliens' fables. As time goes on, it is likely that this fantasy will displace the dancers' native culture.

The Profit Motive

Although the Kiatti have their share of sculptors, engineers, and mercenaries, they are perhaps best known as traders. Kiatti vessels are welcome in many places, for they bring delightfully disruptive theories of government, fossilized musical instruments, and fine surgical tools; they bring cold-eyed guns that whisper of sleep impending and sugared atrocities. If you can describe it, so they say, there is a Kiatti who is willing to sell it to you.

In the ordinary course of things, the Kiatti accept barter for payment. They claim that it is a language that even the universe understands. Their sages spend a great deal of time to attempting to justify the profit motive in view of conservation laws. Most of them converge comfortably on the position that profit is the civilized response to entropy. The traders themselves vary, as you might expect, in the rapacity of their bargains. But then, as they often say, value is contextual.

The Kiatti do have a currency of sorts. It is their stardrives, and all aliens' stardrives are rated in comparison with their own. The Kiatti produce a number of them, which encompass a logarithmic scale of utility.

When the Kiatti determine that it is necessary to pay or be paid in this currency, they will spend months—sometimes years—refitting their vessels as necessary. Thus every trader is also an engineer. The drives' designers made some attempt to make the drives modular, but this was a haphazard enterprise at best.

One Kiatti visionary wrote of commerce between universes, which would require the greatest stardrive of all. The Kiatti do not see any reason they can't bargain with the universe itself, and are slowly accumulating their wealth toward the time when they can trade their smaller coins for one that will take them to this new goal. They rarely speak of this with outsiders, but most of them are confident that no one else will be able to outbid them.

The Inescapable Experiment

One small civilization claims to have invented a stardrive that kills everyone who uses it. One moment the ship is *here*, with everyone alive and well, or as well as they ever were; the next moment, it is *there*, and carries only corpses. The records, transmitted over great expanses against the microwave hiss, are persuasive. Observers in differently equipped ships have sometimes accompanied these suicide vessels, and they corroborate the reports.

Most of their neighbors are mystified by their fixation with this morbid discovery. It would be one thing, they say, if these people were set upon finding a way to fix this terrible flaw, but that does not appear to be the case. A small but reliable number of them volunteer to test each new iteration of the deathdrive, and they are rarely under any illusions about their fate. For that matter, some of the neighbors, out of pity or curiosity, have offered this people some of their own old but reliable technology, asking only a token sum to allow them to preserve their pride, but they always decline politely. After all, they possess safe stardrive technology of their own; the barrier is not knowledge.

Occasionally, volunteers from other peoples come to test it themselves, on the premise that there has to exist some species that won't be affected by the stardrive's peculiar radiance. (The drive's murderousness does not appear to have any lasting effect on the ship's structure.) So far, the claim has stood. One imagines it will stand as long as there are people to test it.

One Final Constant

Then there are the civilizations that invent keener and more nimble stardrives solely to further their wars, but that's an old story and you already know how it ends.

YOON HA LEE is a writer and mathematician from Houston, Texas, whose work has appeared in *Clarkesworld*, *Lightspeed*, and *The Magazine of Fantasy & Science Fiction*. He has published more than forty short stories; a critically acclaimed collection, *Conservation of Shadows*; and an award-winning debut novel, *Ninefox Gambit*, along with its sequel, *Raven Strategem*. He lives in Louisiana with his family and an extremely lazy cat.

Waiting on a Bright Moon

JY Yang

Xin is an ansible, using her song magic to connect the origin world of the Imperial Authority and its far-flung colonies—a role that is forced upon magically gifted women "of a certain closeness." When a dead body comes through her portal at a time of growing rebellion, Xin is drawn deep into a station-wide conspiracy along with Ouyang Suqing, one of the station's mysterious, high-ranking starmages. *Edited by Ann VanderMeer.*

The body arrives during the second refrain. It slaps on the receiving dial with the wet sound of rendered flesh, and the processing officer, a young woman fresh from the originworld, screams.

It's the scream that alerts you. You didn't see the body come in, didn't witness its ungainly, sprawling materialisation through the white of the portal. When you lift your voice in concert with your song-sister on the originworld, the act consumes you. 怒发冲冠、凭栏处。You are in rapture. You see nothing and hear nothing but the music your twinned voices produce. 抬望眼、仰天长啸、壮怀激烈。Your existence dissolves from the throat outwards while you deform the shape of the universe: 三十功名尘与土、八千里路云和月。 You are no longer a person, but ansible, transmitting matter and energy across light-years through your song.

Like a clawed hand, the woman's scream shreds into this ecstasy. It tears you out of verse and chorus. You look, and there lies the thing on the dais: naked, skin flayed, flesh laid open in petals. It came through the portal you and your song-sister created across the yawning gaps of space. A man, eyes open and filmy. There's no blood.

You scream. That too is a kind of song, of fear expressed in unorchestrated keys.

The fear brings feet running through the door. First in are two rank-and-file in security red, gun muzzles up. Their faces go tight when they see the body.

Then comes a buzz like a tide, low and inexorable. The processing officer goes stiff beside you. Everyone on the colony knows that sound.

The starmage arrives ready for a fight, her suit lit up and crackling, the shapes of dragons swarming over its surface. Your heart stalls when you see her face. Officer Ouyang Suqing carries herself with laser intensity, focused and terrible. She throws a barrier around the body, a translucent shape of magebright, glass-thin and fire-white. Without a word she goes to one knee, her back to you, studying the mutilated corpse. You watch her raise her arm and pass it over the top of the barrier. Suit pieces flutter and reassemble over the elegant lines of her wrist, capturing the skew of the viscera below. Silence reigns but for the hum of the suit, cycling in concert to the starmage's pulse.

The security officers keep their guns alert and fixed on you. You understand their fear and suspicion: after all, the Imperial Executioner arrives on the colony this week to mete out his punishment to rebellious elements. He comes to end the life of one Traitor, but who knows how many heads will roll before he leaves? Any lapse in the accepted order could prove fatal. Better you than them that gets the blame, right? You are merely ansible, a replaceable unit.

Officer Ouyang rises to her feet. Standing, the starmage considers the body for agonising moments more. Your heartbeat stutters like a frightened child. She turns to you, her eyes dark and wide in her duty mask. "Are you alright?"

The mask distorts her voice and it comes out sawbuzz, rounded vowels turned to square waves. You had expected interrogation, and your mouth had been ready to offer fact and statement, situation and report. It opens and closes rhythmically, like ventricular flaps.

The starmage frowns and retracts the mask, exposing the sculpted bones of her cheeks. "Ansible Xin. Are you alright?"

Dumbly you nod, a lie.

She takes your left hand in her suited ones and applies pressure. Her gift flares and pushes a wave of calm through you, warmth spreading from your wrist towards the heart. Everything grows heavy. Your breathing slows and the world thickens to honey. Her suit-buzz settles deep and languid in your chest.

"You should rest," Officer Ouyang says. "This must be upsetting for you."

She turns to the security officers. "At ease. There is no danger here."

The security officers hesitate, but only for a moment. A starmage's word is law, and this one carries the name of Ouyang. They understand who her father is, and by extension, who her father's mother is. Their guns, holstered, return to neutrality. Their expressions do not. The man on the left asks: "Will we open a murder investigation, then?"

Officer Ouyang frowns. "There will be an investigation, but no murder has been committed here." She points to the magebright-encased corpse. "This man was killed long before he arrived here. Other jurisdictions will become involved."

She looks back at you, and the processing officer. "Which jurisdiction are you connected with?"

Your tongue is too sleepy to reply, so the processing officer does: "Great one, we connect with the originworld on fifth-days. Everyone knows that."

"Of course." The starmage looks away. Her face registers coldness, or maybe offense.

The processing officer swallows. "Great one, I apologise. I did not mean—"

"At ease," the starmage says. Her face is so carefully controlled as to be unreadable. She turns to you. "Ansible, are you able to speak?"

You fight the blanket of slowness she has thrown over you, and nod. "This humble one can."

"That's good," she says. She does not ask you to speak again. Instead she says: "You will be taken off duty so you can recover."

Your wrist still tingles from the starmage's touch, nerves carrying an afterimage of her fingers. You wonder what is happening on the other side of the broken connection. How did the body get here? Your song-sister Ren on the originworld, how does she fare?

The two rank-and-file are still nervous, still exchanging glances. "Great one," the one on the left says, "will this affect the execution?"

Officer Ouyang casts her glance over the contained corpse. "It will not. I will speak with the Starmage General and he will decide the best course of action." She frowns. "But mind you don't spread word of this to others. The hearts of the people are unsettled enough." Starmage's word is law. The two officers bow their heads.

· · ·

满江红, the river bleeds red as the moon-tides: This is the twinning song your cluster learns in the temple. The eight of you—Jia, Yi, Bing, Ding, Wu, Ji, Geng, Xin— sit in an octagon around Ren while you practice, the sun warm in the room, the sky a circle of blue through the acrylic window.

怒发冲冠、凭栏处、潇潇雨歇
抬望眼、仰天长啸、壮怀激烈
三十功名尘与土、八千里路云和月
莫等闲白了少年头、空悲切

Ren is your center, the spoke through which the rest of you are threaded, the one who must stay on the originworld and sing to the Eight Colonies. You keep your eyes open while you sing, so you can watch Ren's lips, painted red, shaping the sounds of the first words: nu, ah, ong, an. Over the months the shape of those lips have grown in appeal. The shape of her eyes, the shape of her bosom. The soft oval of her face. You sing eight hours a day, taking breaks to drink and eat and wash and please one another. At night the cluster sleeps in the same bed, skin against skin against skin against skin. Murmuring the song, murmuring sentiments of rage and patriotism.

This is what it is, to be ansible. To be the same in song and in sex and in sisterhood. When you walk across the temple grounds as a cluster—no ansible walks alone, for there is no such thing as an ansible alone—the starmages stare at you. Whether in curiosity or in pity, you do not know.

· · ·

When the starmage visits, unsuited and unannounced, she brings with her a basket of tropical stonefruit, plump and ripened: Smooth-peeling lychee, blood-red rambutan, dusky-skinned dragoneye with flesh that breaks between the teeth. The crate came in with the originworld shipment two days ago, passed through before the corpse's interruption. An officer's perquisite.

"I wanted to make sure you were alright," she says.

You sit on the single stool by your table, your knees pressed together like a pilgrim's palms, gaze fixed on her splendid silhouette, bright against the unfinished metal walls of your room. Penned in your quarters, she is close enough that you can see, in exquisite detail, the interfacing implants lining the length of her neck. A queue of coin-sized circles breathe soft and green, vanishing under the curve of her shirt collar. Outside of the mage suit she looks oddly tangible.

"This humble one is alright," you lie. The corpse visits your dreams at night, its filmy eyes blank and unreadable. Sometimes it sits up from the dais, innards spilling like cutlery, and it tells you secrets with its grey tooth-filled mouth. That knowledge abandons you when you wake.

"The investigation has ended," the starmage says. "This was a triad affair. Nothing to do with us. The victim ran up insurmountable gambling debts on the originworld."

"Then it won't affect the execution?"

"Let us hope not." She looks uneasy. The prospect of the Imperial Executioner's arrival frightens even someone like her.

"Why did they send it here?" You shouldn't be asking questions of a starmage and an officer, and yet you are.

"As a warning. They have a relative on the colony. Do you know Quartermaster Lu?"

You twitch your shoulders. You know the name, possibly the face, but not the person.

"This was his cousin."

"It is a great pity."

The starmage cracks a rambutan in her mouth. Its soft thick hairs curl around her lips as she sucks in the collected juices. "I've put you on three weeks' leave," she says.

You are halfway through a lychee, its slippery flavour delicate on your tongue, wetness running over your knuckles and down to your elbow in a thin line. You swallow. "Why three weeks?"

"You must have time to rest," she says. "The colony can cope without the outside world for a short period of time."

You bow your head. "This humble one is most grateful."

"You need not be so formal with me," she says.

You study her face, noting how sharp and bright it is. She is as young as you are, perhaps younger. A terrible burden to carry, the title of starmage. You wonder if she ever tires of it.

"Thank you again for the fruit," you say. "I appreciate it."

She smiles and the expression triggers a memory of another face, a broad rectangle, dappled in the sunlight.

As she leaves she hesitates at the door. Half a moment passes with her back to you. Then she turns, "May I visit you again?"

Like a festival drum your heartbeat quickens. "My quarters are too small. They are not a suitable place for visitation."

"Then you must come to mine. I would like to ask you over for dinner. Seventh-day evening. Will you come?"

Starmage's word is law, but the confidence that comes imposed on her manner is missing. You wet your lips with a tongue still slick with lychee juice. "I will."

• • •

Your separation from Ren is inevitable, yet it is no easier to bear when it comes. The night before you leave for Eighth Colony you cling to her damp skin, trying to breathe in as much of her as possible, terrified of losing the piquancy of her scent to the wash of time. She kisses your jaw and neck and lips with the fierceness of one who does not know when they will eat again. You are the last of the cluster to be assigned a position; the bed yawns with the blankness of missing bodies.

"We have our song still," she says, but you both know it is not the same, it is not sufficient, it will forever be insufficient. You spend the weeks in the lightspeed cocoon feeling empty, bereft, bereaved, halved.

Eighth Colony greets you with huge metal struts and too much air, cold and recycled, the sounds of swarming multitudes carried upon it. You spill from the belly of the cocoon into lifelike chaos. The mage-crafted glass floor of the arrival dock hangs over a marketplace, and beneath your feet shouting, haggling bodies weave between the bright lights, citizens and officers and grey-clad auxiliaries. Their faces are hidden from you; all you see are impenetrable black dots.

And then you raise your unhappy eyes from the ground and your heart trips over itself. The old ansible has come to greet you, to introduce you to the life you are meant to take over. Beside her grey-clad self stands a starmage, dragons alive on her suit. Her hair is short, her eyes deep-set, and her jawbone could shatter iron. When you look at her all you see is someone else, laughing in leaf-filtered sun, glowing in blue-tinted moonlight.

"Ansible Xin," she says. "I am Officer Ouyang Suqing. Welcome to Eighth Colony."

• • •

The Imperial Executioner's ship arrives on sixth-day. Its shape eclipses the stars, an arrowhead of pitch blotted above the glass domes of Eighth Colony. The sounds of life go quiet in its shadow.

In the main atrium, couples stroll between drooping fringes of vegetation, framed by starscape and warmed by lantern balls suspended in the air. You enjoy spending your off hours as a spectator to this thoroughfare of romance, collecting impressions of smiles and shy glances as if for a vault.

Then the Imperial Executioner appears on the walkway circumnavigating the upper dome, robed in red and gold and black, and masked. White bisects crimson across its furious features. The citizenry freezes. Trailing in the Executioner's wake are two starmages, Officers Ouyang and Wu. Tigers prowl the latter's suit.

Faces in the atrium turn white with terror, sharp with anxiety: A tableau of miseries drawn up by the Imperial Executioner's pull. A burning spreads in your belly, too.

The three of them pass through the upper deck of the atrium in a wreath of silence. When the last glimpse of brocaded robe vanishes through the doorway, the whispers boil to the surface. Brows furrow, tongues curl desperately around fears of saying the wrong thing. Rebellion burns throughout the breadth of empire, and the Imperial Authority is less than pleased with Eighth Colony's involvement in it. Their bliss shattered, the couples dotting the atrium retreat into the shadows.

You imagine that, in her passage, Officer Ouyang turned her head to look at you for the briefest moment. A comforting thought. A terrifying thought.

• • •

Your first lover is a girl named Mingyue. Her face is broad and rectangular and her laugh fills the atria of your heart. You met on the grassy courtyard of the temple, two young mages beginning their journeys towards greatness, away from their hometowns for the first time. The days lengthen into weeks spent enraptured, intoxicated. Lying in the sun under the nesting swallows, she reaches for your hand, and you pull it away. Later that day, in the evening, she says: "We can meet where no one will see us. No one will know."

And you are young, and you have the gift, and the world is wide, so it's easy to believe those words. Her flesh dances tart, sweet, bitter, and hot against your tongue.

But of course, you are found out. They come for you in the moonlight when your unclothed limbs are entwined like vines, so it is impossible to deny what has happened. Like a startled rabbit you try to run, but Mingyue freezes, and you cannot abandon her. So they take you, too. Where would you run to, anyway? They know who you are.

They separate the two of you in ansible training; you never see Mingyue again. On the second day, when your crying has stopped, they bring you to meet Ren and the rest of the cluster. Your name becomes Xin, the last to join them.

You hate Ren. You hate her soft round face, you hate her meekness, you hate her sweetness toward you. The twinning song feels rancid on your tongue, cuts like grit in your ears. You sing it tonelessly and improperly and the portals won't form within the cluster. If the other ansible girls resent you, you don't care. When Ren tries to take your hand to pull you aside you hiss at her. You sleep alone, even if it means curling on the cold floor with your back to the cluster.

Ren never gives up. She keeps reaching for you, keeps talking to you, keeps coaxing your voice into the harmony. She joins you on the floor at night, wrapping thin arms around your rigid shoulders. Placing kisses on the line of your bones. You watch her grow pale and tired and wish she would just leave you be.

Hatred turns to pity turns to exhaustion. No one has the energy to fight forever.

One day Ren sits by you during the afternoon meal, her leg pressed flush against yours. "I too had a name before this," she says. "My father named me Wang-sun. I am the third of three girls."

Wang-sun, a wish for a son. The sentiment her family wanted her to carry for the ages. You ask: "Do your sisters have the gift also?"

"No. I am the first. They thought there was to be a starmage in the family."

But instead she became ansible, just like you.

You study the shape of her face, which has become familiar to you over the weeks, if not quite cherished. You realise you can choose to be happy and accept the love you have been given, or you can remain in despair forever.

You take her hand. "My name was Tian," you tell her. An empty field, a paddy waiting to be filled. The relief that envelops Ren's face provokes deep shame and guilt.

But the rest of the cluster accepts your induction without comment, and you come to realise that perhaps each of them entered ansiblehood much the same way. A shared grief, a common wound. Being ripped apart so that there's something to put back together. Your hurt made you all the more dear to them.

Sometimes you wonder if Mingyue was a trap, deliberately set, sieving each batch of new mages to find more recruits for the ansible program. But dwelling on the idea will only bring you ruin. You love Ren. You love her as much as you possibly can.

• • •

The starmage has made steamed dumplings and other small eats. Curved glass sprawls along one wall of her quarters, exposing starfield marred by the shape of the Imperial Executioner's ship. Her red dress clings to her, embroidered brocade interspersed with windows of translucent silk. Sequins glitter in the low yellow light. In comparison, you are clad in the shapeless grey that is the only thing populating your wardrobe.

You bite into soft dumpling flesh and the hollows under your tongue fill with fragrant soup. The flavour is so rich a shiver passes through you. "How is it?" Officer Ouyang asks.

"Incredible."

You almost didn't come. Twice you walked in sight of her door and both times you turned back. On the third jaunt, you decide there's nothing for her to trap you in: You are innocent of involvement in the murder, and your worst secret has already been revealed. So you go in.

"Can men be ansibles?" she asks you.

"Of course. Anyone with the gift can. It just takes practice." You toy with a piece of chicken while you study the small shifts in her face.

"They used to say only women of a certain closeness could do it. That was how they explained it."

"That's not true. There's nothing special learning it. They just don't want to teach anyone else." You add, deliberately, "*You* could do it with a man if you wanted."

She ducks her head. "I wouldn't." A blush creeps across her cheeks. "I could not be that close with a man."

You had suspected this, and you wonder why she's telling you this now, at this fraught juncture, when you have been on this station for years.

"I used to watch the ansible clusters in the temple," she says very carefully. "I envied you, you know."

"Envied us?" Your chopsticks hit the table with a clink. You gesture at her massive quarters and the finery that she wears, the entitlement that was ripped from you when they caught you with your hand between Mingyue's legs. "What is there to envy?"

Her teeth tear at her bottom lip. "I only meant the way you could walk around so easily holding hands, touching each other." She looks down at her own hands and says slowly, "I wanted something like that too."

You know exactly what she means. You refuse to show her sympathy. "So why didn't you? It's easy to be recruited. You know how."

She lowers her head still further. "I couldn't. I would bring eternal shame to my family. It's different for me."

"Unlike me, who was a farmer's daughter?"

"That's not what I meant. I did not know of your background."

You push your chair back. "Ansible Xin," she says, as you stand. "I apologise. I did not mean to offend."

A starmage should not be apologising to an ansible, it upsets the order of the world. "There's nothing to envy about our lives," you say. "If only you knew what we have endured. What we must continue to endure."

"I apologise."

There's a note of misery to Officer Ouyang's face that pulls at you. You sit back down: It would be rude to leave with so much food still unfinished. But you stay silent as you eat, and she follows suit.

She only breaks the silence when you are preparing to leave. The words come out papery, fragile as mist: "Ansible Xin, I have behaved abominably today. But I wish to try again. Will you come tomorrow evening? I'll prepare something for you." ·

"Tomorrow? Is that not the day of the execution?"

"It is." Mention of the execution sinks like black tar in the atmosphere between the two of you; the starmage fidgets, her brows knitting together in a difficult line. "Have you witnessed an execution before?"

"I have not."

"I see."

The silence traps you like honey, heavy and cloying, and you are so tired of fighting it. You could drain it all away by grabbing her, kissing her on the lips, showing her what she has been missing in her lonely, hidden life. You could.

"Will you come?" she asks again.

"I will consider it," you say.

· · ·

The execution is broadcast on screens throughout not just Eighth Colony, but the length and breadth of the empire. Slaughter a chicken to warn the monkeys. You wait among the mass of Authority officers and auxiliaries packing Eighth Colony's largest theater, which today will be a theater of death.

On the stage the colony's four starmages stand arrayed in a rectangle: Tiger, phoenix, dragon, horse. Each of them clutches in both hands a long metal rod, painted the red of justice. They drown out the thousand murmuring voices by pounding the rods onto the stage floor in an accelerating crescendo. Echoes drill into skulls. The house lights dim; the show is about to begin.

Two masked figures haul a third onto the center of the stage. Traitor is naked except for the ropes that bind her hands in front of her. Once she had a name, but now and forever she will only be known as Traitor. Nine iterations of her family will be thus disgraced, their names wiped from the register and those two characters written in their place. Her skin is blanched funerary white but her face is swollen with the red of beaten flesh. They force her to her knees. The sound of bone against wood lingers.

You look at her face. Its shape is young, its features arranged in despair. This girl could be Officer Ouyang. This girl could be you.

The Imperial Executioner's entrance is heavy: Heavy footsteps, heavy silence, heavy gasps from Traitor as fear floods her chest and lungs. She shakes as the Executioner stands behind her.

The Starmage General comes to the stage carrying the imperial scroll: A small man made towering by his massive suit, nasal voice amplified to operatic volumes. He pulls the scroll open and proclaims:

Traitor! You have been found guilty of colluding with rebels! You plotted to weaken our glorious empire from within. You were caught openly engaging in rebellious activities, but without shame, you refused to claim your treachery. You chose to protect your fellow traitors, the other scum who crawl through the grass like snakes!

You, who have rejected the warmth of the Imperial spring, shall be made to feel the sting of winter's wrath!

The Executioner's hands loom over Traitor's head. A cocoon of magebright envelops them and springs around Traitor's kneeling body, fine enough that you can see her through it.

The magebright hums.

Razorwire lines run from one side of the cocoon to the other. They descend. Where they meet skin they start to slice. Traitor shrieks, a high thin animal sound. Every muscle in her body strains, but there is nowhere to escape. Her hands are claws, her neck corded with veins and tendons as her screaming tears through it.

The razorwire continues to strip her away, layer by layer, cell by cell. Blood springs from her in a fine mist as the cuts start stripping the flesh under the skin. Muscle peels from the face trapped in a rictus of agony.

You can't watch. You have to watch.

The wires gouge deeper and deeper. Her face and eyes are almost gone now. Traitor still screams through her lipless mouth. Beside you one of the auxiliaries starts sobbing. A guard in executioner's black comes and pulls him out of the line. He makes one sound, like a stricken rabbit; you dare not turn your head to see where they take him.

The screaming comes to a choking halt as the flesh of her throat flays off. You wonder how long she remains alive after that. The heart is buried under layers of viscera, and the quivering brain is still shielded by bone. The pulp of Traitor's body accrues in the shape of an arrow and turns black and hard, like metal. The Executioner is turning her ground meat into sculpture, a lesson that will sit in the atrium for all to learn.

The flesh of your own body rebels and your throat fills with heavy sourness. You pinch your lips together and stare at the mask that obscures Officer Ouyang's face until waves of dizziness envelop you. Is she watching? What is she thinking? How could she just stand there?

But then, are you not also sitting where you are, and watching?

. . .

When you go to keep your evening appointment you find Officer Ouyang's door barred in your face. A mage-locked door may stop others, but she forgets what you are. She forgets that you too have the gift.

Your entrance startles her. She stumbles to her feet, face red and crumpled, voice cracked: "Why are you here?" She hasn't dressed properly and hair sticks from her scalp.

"You invited me."

Her surprise collapses into despair: She has forgotten. She turns away, her back forming an uneven, sloping wall. "Please leave. I cannot, I do not—"

Your room is small, and cold, and you fear the things you might see when you close your eyes tonight. "Have you never witnessed an execution before?" you ask. You simply assumed that she had.

The starmage shakes her head. Her knees find the floor for support as she folds over herself. You place your hands on her back, and a shiver passes through her body. But it is not just mourning that grips her. She presses her fists into the ground, the knuckles white through reddened skin.

"Were you close with Traitor?" you ask.

"Her name," she hisses, "was Siyun."

Siyun, a gentle cloud. "So you were indeed close," you say.

"No." She sits up and you detach from her, putting a small space between the two of you. She still won't look at you. "Siyun and I were—we were only briefly acquainted. Perhaps if she had been receptive to my friendship, or to something more, we could have been." Her voice goes low with rage. "She did not deserve this. She was barely involved in rebellious activities. She was unlucky, they caught her! And decided she would be a scapegoat. This is injustice."

"You could have stopped the execution. You were right next to her on the stage."

Now she turns to you, fury sharpening her features. "And to what end? Do you think I could have saved her, when the throne wanted her blood? Eighth Colony's situation is precarious enough. Do you know what price open rebellion will demand?"

"So we let them slaughter us like animals? Worse than animals. No butcher would be this cruel."

Officer Ouyang sets her shoulders. "There is a time and place for everything."

She is revealing things to you that she shouldn't, not if she wants to keep herself safe. Her trust in you is dizzying. "And are there others you know who take part in these rebellious activities?"

Ouyang Suqing looks away. Her silence is your answer.

You reach for her hands and she lets you take them. You tell her that your room is cold, too cold, and has too much empty space in the dark. Space where ghosts can hide, and find you with their bloody fingers in the night. She simply nods. Here, the two of you can keep each other warm. Safe from ghosts.

• • •

In the course of the nights that come you dissolve into each other's arms over and over again. You show her all the things that she has been denied and all the things that she has been denying herself.

You tell her your name is Tian.

"Can you teach me the song?" she asks, curled with her head against your shoulder.

"No," you say, and the hurt shows on her face, but 满江红 is your song, yours and Ren's. It is not to be shared. "Pick another. Pick one I might know."

Suqing looks at the stars arrayed outside her window. Now that the Imperial Executioner's ship is gone the view is clear. She breathes softly on your skin while she thinks. Songs nestle in her mouth in soft hums as she tries them out. Something seems to catch her fancy:

「明月几时有？把酒问青天 . . . 」

The first two syllables of the song strike your heart like stones falling into a pond. You know this one, of course.

我欲乘风归去、又恐琼楼玉宇、高处不胜寒。
起舞弄清影、何似在人间？

Suqing's voice stumbles rough and unpracticed through the lyrics, the tones falling flat. You sing with her, you lift her voice. No portal opens between you—that kind of magic takes time and concentration—but you feel the stirrings of a connection, the right kind of purity. You fall asleep with the words lingering between you, as if you were back on the originworld, entwined with another under the moonlight, the sound of nesting swallows above your head.

人有悲欢离合、月有阴晴圆缺、 此事古难全。但愿人长久、
千里共婵娟。

. . .

Three weeks pass by like water in a river. A fresh processing officer joins you in the portal room as you prepare to resume your duties. A mountain of work awaits you: Shipments of perishable goods, important documents, and luxury items hunger for their destinations. Eighth Colony seethes with impatience after so long with no portal contact to other places. And it's an impatience you share, but for other reasons: Your heart gladdens at the thought of being immersed in Ren's song again.

You raise your voice: 怒发冲冠，凭栏处 . . .

The voice that joins yours is unexpected: low and smoke-roughened. 抬望眼、仰天长啸、壮怀激烈。

The alien timbre of the words startles you so much, the song stalls in your throat. Aborted in half-formation, the portal dissipates into white mist. The processing officer frowns. "Ansible? What are you doing?"

Ren, your Ren, your Wang-sun. Where is she? Is she still on leave? Why have they put a stranger, some unknown exocluster ansible, in her place?

"Ansible Xin," the processing officer says, irritation in his tone. "We cannot afford any further delays."

You have no choice. Three weeks of unspent work stands ahead of you. Shaking, shaken, you take up the song again, and the stranger on the originworld responds.

Your songs don't match; you can barely hold the portal open wide enough. You don't know who the strange ansible is or where she comes from. You don't know her name. These things matter. All the time spent together in the temple was not for nothing. 三十功名尘与土、八千里路云和月。 You feel like collapsing.

There's still a good half left to the shipments when the processing officer leaves in a cloud of frustration, muttering about your worthlessness. You are done for the day.

Where is Ren?

. . .

Suqing tries to break the news gently. But the look on her face tells you everything. The exhaust-heat in this secluded service corridor can't fight off the chill in your bones.

"The Imperial Authority thought your cluster leader was compromised," she says. "The corpse that came through here should have never left the originworld in the first place. So they decided to . . ." She picks her mind for words, her brow creased. "They decided to dispose of her."

The replacement Ren was taken from the ship ansible program, where they don't form clusters, where they are trained to be flexible. A stopgap.

You won't let Suqing touch you, won't let her comfort you. Traitor's bloodfilled death stalks, sharp-toothed and slavering, through your memory. You think of Ren's soft flesh disintegrating between lines of magebright, imagine her sweet voice torn by screams until the vocal cords are stripped away.

"They wouldn't have executed her like that," Suqing tells you. "She wasn't a traitor. To them she was just a malfunctioning ansible."

You know she's trying to make you feel better. But the words sting. You are not a broken part to be replaced. "Leave me alone," you hiss. You refuse to look at her until she withdraws.

. . .

That night, after hours of deliberation and a slow settling of your mood, you go to her quarters. The door has barely shut behind you when you say: "I wish to take part in rebellious activities."

Colour and expression drain from her face as though your words have punctured her somewhere. "What are you saying?"

"I want to avenge Wang-sun. Introduce me to your rebellion."

Her breathing quickens. "You've gone mad. I can't do that."

"Don't lie to me."

"It's not a lie, I—"

"I know where you go when you slip out at night for your walks. I know what's happening on the evenings you tell me not to meet."

She hides her eyes from you, momentarily. "Do you?"

"I know you keep things in the drawers you ask me not to open."

Her face crumples in a frown. "Those are just family treasures. You—"

"The other day I saw you and Quartermaster Lu whispering together. When I came closer you stopped. What were you talking about?"

She puts space between you. "Listen to yourself talk. Do you know what's at stake? You've seen what they do to traitors."

You close the space she's tried to make. "It doesn't matter. My cluster has been broken. Ren is gone. They're only waiting until they can replace us. I am already dead, it is decided."

Suqing grimaces. "I won't do this. Leave me alone if you have nothing else to ask." She retreats into the bedchamber and locks the door, a mechanical click that you would have to break into. You stand in the cold air of her room, waiting for her to re-emerge and recant her declarations, but she does not.

. . .

There's a gap of hours before the knock comes on your door. You have been half expecting it, half dreading it. Suqing stands on the other side, the broad lines of her face taut and solid. "Come with me." That's all she says.

She leads you silently and rapidly through the backdoor byways of Eighth Colony: unpatrolled, unadorned corridors with exposed piping and unfinished metal walls. For the first ten minutes of your journey she walks without talking, and you match her strides, equally silent. Blood sings in your ears, and your heart is a drum to accompany it.

Then Suqing says: "When you asked to accompany me, I was in a dilemma. I suspected a trap. It seemed too convenient. First exposing my preferences for women, then trying to catch us in treasonous activities. I had a moment of doubt. I suspected the Authority's involvement."

A reasonable fear. "What changed your mind?"

"Nothing, actually. I just thought, I don't want to live with this kind of fear and doubt all my life. Where even expressions of love have to be taken with suspicion."

She comes to a stop before the entrance of a pump room, its door thick and heavy, the muffled roar of machinery thrumming from within. "Once you step through this door, there is no turning back. Are you sure about this? Do you know why you're doing it?"

You are doing it for Ren. For Wang-sun. Your sorrow for her is overwhelming. How pitiful that she died helpless, at the mercy of the forces that have dictated the form and shape of your life. You have determined that this will not be your fate.

You straighten your spine and sing:「莫等闲白了少年头、空悲切。」

Suqing dips her head in understanding, and unlocks the room door with her mage's touch.

. . .

Over the next few hours and the next few days you learn many things. You suspected some of them, others catch you blind.

You learn that the roots of the rebellion have spread far and wide in Eighth Colony. They go deeper than you had imagined. Nearly half the Authority officers are active participants, and they are in every branch of operations.

You learn that of the four starmages on the colony, three have been recruited to the cause. The fourth, Officer Yao, is an Authority man through and through. It cannot be helped. It is enough.

You learn that Quartermaster Lu leads the Eighth Colony rebels. When you ask if it feels strange to give orders to starmages, he laughs. "There is no place for that sort of hierarchy in the rebellion. We must purge ourselves and our movement of such toxic ways of thinking!"

You learn that the corpse that started your recent troubles was in fact a message from comrades on the originworld. Secrets and messages had been whispered into the dead man's ear before he had been slaughtered. The map of his viscera has been pinned up in the pump room, Starmage Wu's spidery interpretations scrawling downwards beside it. Gut-reading is an old art long fallen out of practice, but Starmage Wu had taught himself as a young man. The Starmage General had gotten so jittery around the Imperial Executioner's visit that normal lines of communication were no longer safe.

You ask Quartermaster Lu: "So he was not really your cousin? That was a lie?"

"He was my cousin. But he was becoming a liability to the movement." Since he had to die, his body might as well be made good use of. His death was regrettable, but it couldn't be helped.

So, too, was Traitor's. When she was caught, it was decided that saving her would only expose the movement to more danger, more executions. Starmage Jiang had visited her, quietly wiped her memories, so she could not reveal anyone else. She had died not even knowing her crimes.

You notice how uncomfortable Suqing becomes whenever Traitor is mentioned. Her name, you remind yourself, was Siyun.

Rebellion is imminent. Four of the Colonies have agreed to coordinate, overthrowing the Imperial Authority on the same day, declaring themselves independent.

Only the starmages have the ability to defeat the Starmage General. But their suits have a limiter that stops them from performing the Seventy-Two Transformations, and that is under the Starmage General's control. It is possible to bypass the limiters, but the materials needed to do so come from the originworld, and that shipment was interrupted by the Imperial Executioner's visit.

"But we have the ansible on our side now," says Quartermaster Lu. He thumps you heartily on the back.

"What of the processing officer?" you ask. "The new one detests me. Surely he will notice something amiss."

"That's Officer Xiao, isn't it? He's new to the colony." Starmage Wu rubs his chin and looks at Suqing. "I hear he has his eye on you. He's ambitious. That might work."

Suqing flushes. "I don't understand what you mean."

"Come on, Ouyang," Quartermaster Lu says. "Surely even a deviant like you can distract a man for a mere few minutes."

· · ·

It takes more than a few minutes. For safety's sake, Suqing's flirtations with the man have to stretch across the week. The excuse is that, due to your poor performance, she has been sent to oversee you. While you sing your broken, mismatched song, she bats her eyelids and recites the lines Starmage Wu taught her. Her delivery is so glasslike and stiff you wonder how he believes it. But he is smitten. Somewhere between his posturing and Suqing's unconvincing lip-biting, you receive a package wrapped in red cloth, mage-touched to hide it from scrutiny.

You cannot believe it worked.

Quartermaster Lu is predictably delighted, clapping Suqing on the back. He likes doing this, you realise, his boisterous laugh louder if the recipient of his gesture flinches. "Looks like you've truly got it in you, Ouyang. Are you sure you really like women that much?"

"I can vouch for that," you say to him, as Suqing's lips thin.

Quartermaster Lu guffaws. "This one has spirit! I like her." And he looks at you with a smile that means he does not like you, at all.

Suqing takes your hand. It is done. Nothing stands between the colony and its destiny now.

. . .

On the eve of the rebellion you lie with Suqing, one last exultation before the fall. You kiss her pale, damp skin, caressing the dips and curves that glow with implant light. How familiar this has become, as though everything that passed before had been a dream, and this has been the only reality you've known.

Eventually the both of you fall quiet, urgent caresses subsiding into a loose, comfortable tangle of limbs. "Are you frightened?" you ask.

Suqing blinks and looks out at the stoic, unjudgemental stars. "I've already done the most frightening thing I can think of."

"Why did you do it? Why did you approach me, after so many years?"

She grips your hand. "The path of rebellion is lined with death," she says. "And I didn't want to die full of regrets."

You bury your face in her fragrant shoulder. "You're not allowed to die."

She lifts your chin. "Surely my life is worth the freedom of the people? One life is not that much of a price to pay."

You say nothing. Your mind struggles to construct the memory of the faces you have loved: Ren's pale softness, the bright lines of your long-gone Mingyue. It's like building a bridge out of smoke.

Your silence is not lost on Suqing. She kisses your fevered brow. "What happens will happen," she says. "We shouldn't fight it."

"Aren't we fighting for the right to choose our destinies?"

She breathes out. "Yes," she says finally. "Yes, we are. And this is what we've chosen."

She has nightmares about Siyun's death, still. You do too. Sometimes you dream that it's Suqing in Traitor's place. Sometimes you dream it's you.

"After tomorrow," Suqing says, as though reading your mind, "it won't happen again."

You press your chest against hers and softly begin the song you two chose for yourselves: 明月几时有？把酒问青天。 Suqing's voice joins yours, and in the cadence of her tone, snug as a glove, you feel a familiar resonance. And instead of fighting it, you let it envelop you. You are falling into her song, as she is falling into yours, and her eyes are wide as a connection opens between you, a portal that transcends space and time.

不知天上宫阙、今夕是何年？

"We did it," she whispers, as the song ends.

You press your heads together. "Now nothing in the universe can keep us apart."

. . .

You have never witnessed starmages in battle. Same as ordinary citizens, you have only read the poetry, heard the songs, tried to imagine the shape and sound of these battles. The things which are happening now defy the imagination, defy sense of scale, defy understanding. Creatures the size of mountains tear each other apart in the cold field of space. Two dragons battle, sinuous bodies twisting past the glass belly of Eighth Colony's main atrium. The blood-slick scales that glide by are bigger than human heads. One dragon struggles to hold the other still. A third creature, a tiger that could swallow suns, slashes its world-splitting claws through dragonscale.

You can only guess which one is Suqing. And guesses are worth nothing in the arena of war.

Dragontail strikes glass and cracks spider across its surface. Amid cries of fear and consternation and the beat of your heart, you whisper a mantra: It's alright. It's alright. She won't let anything happen to us.

The citizenry clots the main atrium, bodies pushing against bodies until sweat and exhalation turns the air to thick and unbreathable soup. Terrible things transpire outside the atrium, but all that filters past the double-layered steel doors are muffled explosions and a great sense of fear. Fringes cling to foreheads, parents cling to children, and your grey tunic clings to the small of your back. A gun naps in your hands, warm and heavy, and as you patrol the atrium, intrusive thoughts of your fellow rebels follow you like a pack of wolves: What if you dropped it? What if it went off?

A woman pulls a small boy close as you walk past, and her eyes trail you as you continue your patrol. The citizenry are gathered here to protect them from the fighting; they are not hostages, or prisoners. This, too, is what they have been told.

In the center of the atrium the sculpture that used to be Traitor shimmers in the light of battle.

Something explodes in the station and you fall. Gun clatters against metal as the lights go out, and the deep bass thrum of the air system falls silent as if shot. People scream, and something—someone—strikes your jaw as the pushing starts, the angry, panicked shoving. You scramble to your feet, fearing a stampede, a loss of order, the loss of life. The gun—you see it on the floor, and you dive desperately for it. As your fingers close around the barrel something kicks you in the back. A foot crushes your hand. You scream.

The lights come back on and the air system starts again, unsteady and shuddering, as if the station is having problems drawing breath. Your hand pulses red-hot with pain as you get to your feet, and you don't want to look at it, don't want to see if there's blood. The gun didn't go off. That's something to be thankful for. The other rebels are screaming instructions to the citizenry, to each other. Everyone seems to have forgotten about you.

Behind you someone starts crying.

Eighth Colony fills with thunder as the starmages crash into it. People fall and scream. The glass splinters further. Miraculously it holds, or you think it holds, because none of you are dying now, nobody is being sucked out to space. Pressed against the straining glass, the body of a dragon blots out the stars, and it is oddly, strangely green. It glows. Something is happening, something so powerful it shreds through the part of you that's all gift.

If you call to Suqing now, would it help her? Or kill her?

The green flares, it burns your eyes, it consumes the shapes of the battling starmages. You drop the gun and cover your face with a cry. A quake tears through your gift. All falls silent, and remains silent. Then the slow babble of the citizenry rises up, a confused clamor of voices and exclamation.

Very slowly, you lower your hands. Beyond the cracked glass of the atrium lies only starfield. The starmages are gone. You allow yourself to breathe, but air burns through your lungs, and you can taste vinegar in your throat as your stomach clenches into a small ball.

The sounds of strife outside the atrium fade; all that's left are indistinct shouting voices. The sound of boots, quick and heavy against metal. Two gunshots, very brisk, very loud, very close by. And then nothing.

Your knees hurt and your calves are trembling. You should either sit down or keep patrolling, but you can't bring yourself to do either.

"You," shouts one of the rebels, a dough-faced man with buzz-cut hair. You remember his name, you do, it's Sung—was it Sung? He's shouting instructions at you, his wide blunt fingers pointing, gesturing, but the words don't register. They are only sounds, whistling through the heat in your ears.

The main atrium doors groan as if they are being pulled apart by force, and a gasp goes up from the citizenry. As the doors rumble open, ten feet high and double-reinforced with steel, you tighten your grip on the gun, ignoring the pain in your broken fingers.

The first person through is a young rebel, her clothes and hair marked by blood. "Rejoice," she shouts, "we are victorious."

Cries go up from the other rebels, cheers and ululations. Your throat remains sandpaper-dry, your chest a metal vise. The citizenry around you stay likewise quiet and tight-lipped. A coup is a coup is a coup, and a bullet can kill you regardless of ideology.

"Tian?"

You see her through the gaps in the rebels flooding the room, through the confusion of the citizenry. Suqing, battered and exhausted, but alive. Alive.

You run to her, feet getting caught on things as she stumbles towards you. Your shin connects with something, a person or their belongings, you're not sure which, but you've flung your arms out already, you can't move fast enough. Suqing smells of blood and sulphur and ozone, and her armor bruises your chest, but you don't care. You don't want to let her go.

"You still live," you say. "I was so afraid."

"My love." The starmage kisses you on the mouth, in public, where everyone can see. Her embrace is raw force, teeth clashing against lips, arms lifting you off your feet. The world tilts and your stomach plummets in free fall—can you dare to hope that, for once, something is going right?

Suqing seizes your hands when she releases you to the world again. Her red-dened cheeks shine with a mad sort of joy, the madness that comes with great struggle coming to fruition. "Come," she says, squeezing your fingers. You ignore the pain. "There's a meeting of the leaders, we must attend."

And so you leave the atrium and its multitudes behind, in the care of the ordi-nary rebels not invited to this high-level meeting. Suqing leads you through the death-lined guts of Eighth Colony, speckled with the corpses of Authority officers. The rebels jog between and around these mounds of flesh on the floor. Loose shoes, badges. Dark trickles of liquid smeared across metal in the pattern of boot prints. You breathe through your mouth and start keeping your line of sight above shoulder level.

The blood splatters on the wall look like roses.

"What now?" The question fills the space between Suqing and you.

"No one knows," she says. "This is just the beginning; our struggle is far from over. There will be days and months to come, and no one can predict what they will bring."

She stops in the middle of the carnage and turns to you, her smile wide and bright as you've ever seen. "But we'll be together. Now nothing will come between us."

The path of the corridors closes in on the pump room where you first got en-tangled in all this. In front of it stands the shape of Quartermaster Lu.

He has a gun in his hands.

He raises the gun as you draw near.

Suqing angles her body so that she and her mage suit stand between you and the gun muzzle. "What's going on?"

Quartermaster Lu's face is sweat-slick but businesslike, calm as a storm cloud drifting across a summer's courtyard. "The rebellion has succeeded. Now we must cut the last ties to the parasitic Authority."

This, you realise, with a thick muddy sinking of your stomach contents, means you. The gun is meant for you.

Suqing's brow knits. "You doubt my loyalty to the cause? Because of my family?" She still doesn't understand.

"It's not you." You stare Quartermaster Lu in the face, daring him to crack, to show even the slightest hint of remorse. "You're talking about me, aren't you?"

"I don't understand." Suqing takes a step backwards, moving closer to you. "She wouldn't betray us!"

"Not by choice. But she's an ansible. She's an open connection. Someone from the Authority could get through her, send things over. It's too dangerous."

"That's not how it works!" Suqing's anger and frustration boils over. "I've learned the method, it has to be a two-way connection!"

"We cannot take the risk. Ouyang, it cannot be helped."

Suqing's hands tighten into fists. "Like Siyun's death couldn't be helped?"

Your face burns, your breath burns. You hiss: "I joined the rebellion so my fate wouldn't be decided by men like you."

The gun points to your face. "Think of the good of the cause," says Quartermaster Lu, his tone flat. You clench your fists, ignoring the pain that flares through the broken one. Could you strike him, and then run?

"Everything I've done has been for the good of the cause," Suqing says. "Not anymore."

She grabs your hand, your swollen broken hand, and the pain keeps you anchored as her gift flares.

The world distorts, goes grey, and then muffled. Time stops. Quartermaster Lu's face is frozen in the half-expression rictus of a new word. The breath of the station's air system morphs into a loud, constant drone.

"What is this?" you ask, words shaky.

"This is in-between." Suqing breathes like she's climbing mountains. "You access it with your gift. You don't learn this as ansibles?"

You learn nothing as ansibles. They teach you to be nothing but a conduit.

Suqing pulls at you as you run. "We haven't got much time," she gasps. How long can she hold on? You follow after her in a daze, one foot in front of the other, unable to absorb how strange all this is. Your gift sings and sings, a mosquito chorus you've never been allowed to hear. In the grey half-light of the in-between the dead bodies littering the corridors seem more like part of the station than anything else. Woven into the fabric of the world.

"What's your plan?" you ask.

"You run. Somewhere they cannot find you."

"What about you?"

"Don't worry about me."

You end up on the docking platform, the struts familiar over your head. By this time Suqing's face is red with exertion, and you crash out of the in-between into the sound and smell of the ordinary world. You catch her as she falls to her knees. "Are you alright?"

Suqing pushes past the harsh breathing to get to her feet. "I'm fine. Only tired." She points you towards one of the lightspeed cocoons, marked red-on-grey, massive and industrial. A planetary supply cocoon, in transit. "We'll take that one."

The cocoon seats one, just like the vehicle that brought you here years ago. You repeat, "Suqing, what about you?"

"Don't worry about me. Quartermaster Lu needs me. He cannot dispose of me so easily. Not yet." The cocoon's navigation panel lights up under her touch, and she enters coordinates. "Please hurry," she tells you. "Strap in."

You glance at the docking platform doors, wide open, and realise it's only a matter of time before the rebels find you.

You wanted to decide your own fate. You wanted to fight for it.

"Take me to a place where there are wide and deep fields," you say. "A place where grains grow plump and cherry blossom flourishes."

"There's a sparsely populated planet, not a few light-years from here," Suqing says. "Farmers, dependable folk. They won't question too much."

The safety belts click across your chest and hips with a sober finality. "And you? Will you join me?"

She comes to your side, forehead finding yours, limbs trembling, breaths ghosting against your skin. "Yes," she whispers. "I will. I promise. I promise."

You don't want to let her go.

Suqing takes in a shaking breath, and then the rough steps of her melody surround you: 明月几时有？把酒问青天 . . .

You sing, matching her tone. 人有悲欢离合、月有阴晴圆缺、 此事古难全。 Warmth floods around you, the connection that cannot be erased. A song, written in the long ages when your people lived on a single planet, shared the same moon. Yet the sentiment is unchanged.

Light glows between the two of you. 但愿人长久、千里共婵娟。

You kiss her face, her lips, her hair. You taste the blood on them. You taste the sweat, the fear, the desperation, the hope. What the future holds, you cannot say. But you have your song. It is all that you have, and you have to pray that it will be enough.

JY YANG is the author of *The Black Tides of Heaven, The Red Threads of Fortune,* and *The Descent of Monsters.* They have more than two dozen pieces of short fiction published, and their work has been short-listed for the Hugo, Nebula, and James Tiptree, Jr. Awards. They live in Singapore and have an MA in creative writing from the University of East Anglia. Find out more about them and their work at jyyang.com.

Elephants and Corpses

Kameron Hurley

The corpse-jumping body mercenary Nev is used to filling other people's shoes. When his assistant, Tera, recognizes the most recent waterlogged cadaver they bought off the street, though, he finds that his new body is carrying more trouble than he bargained for. *Edited by Carl Engle-Laird.*

Bodies are only beautiful when they aren't yours. It's why Nev had fallen in love with bodies in the first place. When you spent time with the dead you could be anyone you wanted to be. They didn't know any better. They didn't want to have long conversations about it. They were vehicles. Transport. Tools. They were yours in a way that no living thing ever could be.

Nev stood at the end of the lower city's smallest pier with Tera, his body manager, while she snuffled and snorted with some airborne contagion meant to make her smarter. She was learning to talk to the dead, she said, and you only picked up a skill like that if you went to some viral wizard who soaked your head in sputum and said a prayer to the great glowing wheel of God's eye that rode the eastern horizon. Even now, the boiling mass of stars that made up the God's eye nebula was so bright Nev could see it in broad daylight. It was getting closer, the priests all said. Going to gobble them up like some cancer.

Why Tera needed to talk to the dead when Nev did just fine with them as they were was a mystery. But it was her own body, her slice of the final take to spend, and he wasn't going to argue about what she did with it.

"You buying these bodies or not?" said the old woman in the pirogue. She'd hooked the little boat to the snarling amber head of a long-mummified sea serpent fixed to the pier. In Nev's fascination with the dead body, he'd forgotten about the live one trying to sell it to him.

"Too rotten," Tera said.

"Not if we prepare it by day's end," Nev said. "Just the big one, though. The kid, I can't do anything with."

He pulled out a hexagonal coin stamped with the head of some long-dead upstart; a senator, maybe, or a juris priest. The old folks in charge called themselves all sorts of things over the years, but their money spent the same. He wondered for a minute if the bodies were related; kid and her secondary father, or kid and prime uncle. They were both beginning to turn now, the bodies slightly bloated, overfull, but he could see the humanity, still; paintings in need of restoration.

"Some body merc you are!" the old woman said. "Underpaying for prime flesh. This is good flesh, here." She rubbed her hands suggestively over the body's nearly hairless pate.

Nev jabbed a finger at the empty pier behind him; she arrived with her bodies too late—the fish mongers had long since run out of stock, and the early risers had gone home. "Isn't exactly a crowd, is there?" He pushed his coat out of the way, revealing the curved hilt of his scimitar.

She snarled at him. It was such a funny expression, Nev almost laughed. He flipped her the coin and told Tera to bring up the cart. Tera grumbled and snuffled about it, but within a few minutes the body was loaded. Tera took hold of the lead on their trumpeting miniature elephant, Falid, and they followed the slippery boardwalk of the humid lower city into the tiers of the workhouses and machinery shops of the first circle. While they walked, Falid gripped Nev's hand with his trunk. Nev rubbed Falid's head with his other hand. Falid had been with him longer than Tera; he'd found the little elephant partly skinned and left to rot in an irrigation ditch ten years before. He'd nursed him back to health on cabbage and mango slices, back when he could afford mangos.

Tera roped Falid to his metal stake in the cramped courtyard of the workshop. Nev fed Falid a wormy apple from the bin—the best they had right now—and helped Tera haul the body inside. They rolled it onto the great stone slab at the center of the lower level.

Nev shrugged off his light coat, set aside his scimitar, and tied on an apron. He needed to inspect and preserve the body before they stored it in the ice cellar. Behind him rose the instruments of his trade: jars of preserved organs, coagulated blood, and personal preservation and hydrating concoctions he'd learned to make from the Body Mercenary Guild before they'd chucked him out for not paying dues. Since the end of the war, business for body mercs had been bad, and the guild shed specialist mercenaries like him by the thousands. On a lucky day, he was hired on as a cheap party trick, or by a grieving spouse who wanted one last moment with a deceased lover. That skirted a little too closely to deceptive sexual congress for his moral compass. Killing people while wearing someone else's skin was one thing: fucking while you pretended to be someone they knew was another.

Tera helped him strip the sodden coat and trousers from the body. What came out of the water around the pier was never savory, but this body seemed especially torn up. It was why he didn't note the lack of external genitals, at first. Cocks got cut off or eaten up all the time on floaters like this one. But the look on Tera's face made him reconsider.

"Funny," Tera said, sucking her teeth. She had a giant skewer in one hand, ready to stab the corpse to start pumping in the fluids that reduced the bloat. She pulled up the tattered tunic—also cut in a men's style, like the trousers—and clucked over what appeared to be a bound chest.

"Woman going about as a man?" Nev said. Dressing up as a man was an odd thing for a woman to do in this city, when men couldn't even own property. Tera owned Nev's workshop, when people asked. Nev had actually bought it under an old name some years before; he told the city people it was his sister's name, but of course it was his real one, from many bodies back. He and Tera had been going about their business here for nearly five years, since the end of the war, when body mercenaries weren't as in demand and old grunts like Tera got kicked out into a depressed civilian world that wanted no reminder of war. When he met her, she'd been working at a government school as a janitor. Not that Nev's decision regarding the body he wore was any saner.

"You think she's from the third sex quarter?" Nev said. "Or is it a straight disguise?"

"Maybe she floated down from there," Tera said, but her brow was still furrowed. "Priests go about in funny clothes sometimes," she said. "Religious thing."

"What are you thinking?"

"I'm thinking how much you hate going about in women's bodies," Tera said.

"I like women well enough," Nev said, "I just don't have the spirit of one."

"And a pity that is."

"She cost money. I might need her. What I prefer and what I need aren't always the same thing. Let's clean her up and put her in the cellar with the others."

A body mercenary without a good stash of bodies was a dead body mercenary. He knew it as well as anyone. He'd found himself bleeding out alone in a field without a crop of bodies to jump to before, and he didn't want to do it again. Every body merc's worst nightmare: death with no possibility of rebirth.

Tera cut off the breast binding. When she yanked off the bandages, Nev saw a great red tattoo at the center of the woman's chest. It was a stylized version of the God's eye nebula, one he saw on the foreheads of priests gathering up flocks in the street for prayer, pushing and shoving and shouting for worshippers among the four hundred other religious temples, cults, and sects who had people out doing the same.

Tera gave a little hiss when she saw the tattoo, and made a warding gesture over her left breast. "Mother's tits."

"What?"

"Wrap her up and—"

The door rattled.

Nev reached for his scimitar. He slipped on the wet floor and caught himself on the slab just as the door burst open.

A woman dressed in violet and black lunged forward. She wielded a shimmering straight sword with crimson tassels, like something a general on the field would carry.

"Grab the body," the woman said. Her eyes were hard and black. There were two armed women behind her, and a spotty boy about twelve with a crossbow.

Nev held up his hands. Sometimes his tongue was faster than his reflexes, and with the face he had on this particular form, it had been known to work wonders. "I'm happy to sell it to you. Paid a warthing for it, though. I'd appreciate—"

"Kill these other two," she said.

"Now, that's not—" Nev began, but the women were advancing. He really did hate it when he couldn't talk his way out. Killing was work, and he didn't like doing work he wasn't paid for.

He backed up against the far wall with Tera as the gang came at them. Tera, too, was unarmed. She shifted into a brawler's stance. He was all right at unarmed combat, but surviving it required a fairer fight than this one. Four trained fighters with weapons against two without only ended in the unarmed's favor in carnival theater and quarter-warthing stories.

Nev looked for a weapon in reach—a hack saw, a fluid needle, anything—and came up empty. His scimitar was halfway across the room.

If they wanted the body, then he'd give it to them.

He whistled at Tera. She glanced over at him, grimaced, tightened her fists.

Nev pulled the utility dagger at his belt and sliced his own forearm from wrist to elbow. Blood gushed. He said a little prayer to God's eye, more out of tradition than necessity, and abandoned his mortally wounded body.

There was a blink of darkness. Softness at the edges of his consciousness.

Then a burst of awareness.

Nev came awake inside the body on the slab. He couldn't breathe. He rolled off the slab and hit the floor hard, vomiting bloody water, a small fish, and something that looked like a cork. His limbs were sluggish. His bowels let loose, covering the floor in bloody shit, piss, and something ranker, darker: death.

He gripped the edge of the slab and pulled himself up. His limbs felt like sodden bread. Putting on a new, dead skin of the wrong gender often resulted in a profound dysphoria, long-term. But he didn't intend to stay here long.

The attackers were yelling. The kid got down on his knees and started babbling a prayer to the Helix Sun god. Nev had his bearings now. He flailed his arms at them and roared, "Catch me, then!" but it came out a mush in the ruined mouth of the dead woman whose body he now occupied.

He waited until he saw Tera kick open the latch to the safe room and drag his bleeding former body into it. The one with such a pretty face. Then he turned and stumbled into the courtyard.

A dozen steps. He just needed to make it a dozen steps, until his spirit had full control of the body. Second wind, second wind—it was coming. Hopefully before he lost his head. If he didn't get them out far enough, they'd just run back in and finish off Tera and what was left of his old body. He really liked that body. He didn't want to lose it.

The gang scrambled after him. He felt a heavy thump and blaring pain in his left shoulder. Someone had struck him with an ax. He stumbled forward. Falid trumpeted as he slipped past. He considered putting Falid between him and the attackers—maybe some better body merc would have—but his heart clenched at the idea. He loved that stupid elephant.

He felt hot blood on his shoulder. A good sign. It meant the blood was flowing again. Second wind, second wind . . .

Nev burst out of the courtyard and into the street. The piercing light of the setting suns blinded him. He gasped. His body filled with cramping, searing pain, like birth. He'd been reborn a thousand times in just this way; a mercenary who could never die, leaping from host to host as long as there were bodies on the battlefield. He could run and fight forever, right up until there were no more bodies he'd touched. He could fight until he was the last body on the field.

He pivoted, changing directions. The burst of new life caused his skin to flake. He was going to be powerfully thirsty and hungry in a quarter hour. But that was more than enough time to do what needed doing.

Nev picked up speed. The body's legs responded, stronger and fitter than they'd been for their former inhabitant. He coughed out one final wet muck of matter and took a deep, clear breath. He glanced back, ensured the gang was still chasing him, and turned down a side alley.

They barreled after him, all four of them, which told him they were amateurs more than anything else thus far. You didn't all bumble into a blind alley after a mark unless you were very, very sure of yourselves.

He knew the alley well. Hairy chickens as tall as his knee hissed and scattered as he passed. He rounded the end of the alley and jumped—the leap across the sunken alley here was six feet. Not easy, but not impossible. The street had caved during the last rainstorm. Knowing to jump should have saved him.

But he came up short.

He missed the other side by inches, threw his arms forward, tried to scramble for purchase.

Nev, the body that housed Nev, fell.

His legs snapped beneath him. Pain registered: dull, still, with the nerves not yet fully restored. He cracked his head against broken paving stones at the bottom of the sinkhole. A black void sputtered across his vision.

Fuck.

"Shit," the woman with the dark eyes said. She peered down at him; her mane of black hair had come loose, and with the double helix of the suns behind her, she looked like a massive lion. "Finish killing it. Take it with us. Body's barely fit for Corez now."

"He's a body merc," one of the others said, behind her. "He's just going to jump again."

"Then go back and burn his house down, too."

The boy came up behind her, levelled a crossbow with a violet plume at the end, and shot Nev in the chest.

It took two more to kill him.

Dying hurt every time.

• • •

Nev gasped. Sputtered, wheezed, "Where are we?"

It was dead dark.

"Lie flat, fool. We're under the floor of the warehouse."

He gasped for air and reached instinctively for his cut wrist. Tera had bound it with clean linen and salve that stank nearly as bad as the corpse they'd hauled from the pier.

"They're going to burn the workshop."

"You're lucky we aren't burning in there too. You only lasted five minutes."

"More than long enough, for some."

"Easy to please, were they?"

"My favorite sort."

She snorted. Sneezed. Hacked something up and spit into the dusty space. "They didn't know what you were until you jumped. Seemed right surprised."

"Wouldn't be the first time we pulled a body that should have stayed buried."

Nev smelled smoke. His workshop, burning. If they didn't leave soon it would catch the warehouse they were squatting under, too. Years they worked to build up that workshop. If he was lucky, some of the bodies on ice in the cellar might keep, but probably not. All those lovely bodies lost . . . He shivered and clutched at his wrist again.

"Anything they say give you an idea what they wanted with the body?" Tera asked.

"Only used one name. Said the body wasn't fit for . . . Corez?"

Tera muttered something.

The smell of smoke got stronger. "You knew that tattoo," he said. "It's like the one on those priests. The new God's eye cult. The real liberal ones with the habit of burning effigies in the park."

"Not just the tattoo," Tera said. "I knew the woman."

"Who was she?"

"My sister," Tera said, "and Corez is the piece of shit that runs that cult temple she ran off to twenty years ago."

• • •

The fire had seared a scar clean through the workshop and into the warehouse behind it. The billowing flames destroyed three buildings before the fire brigade pumped in water from the ocean. One of the buildings was a factory where children put together beautifully patterned tunics. The children still milled about on the street opposite, faces smeared in char, hacking smoke.

Nev crunched across the floor of the ruined workshop, kicking aside broken glass and the twisted implements of his trade, all swirling with sea water. The cellar had caved in, barring the way to the bodies below. The intense heat would have melted all the ice blocks he packed down there in straw anyway, and ruined his collection. If someone shot him in the heart now, he'd have nowhere to jump.

He saw Tera standing over a heaped form in the courtyard, and walked over to her. She frowned at the crumpled body of Falid the elephant, shot six times with what was likely a crossbow. They'd removed the bolts. Falid's tongue lolled out. His tiny black eyes were dull.

Nev knelt before the little elephant and stroked his fat flank. "This was unnecessary," he said.

"So was the factory," Tera said.

Nev's eyes filled. He wiped his face. "No. That was collateral damage. This. . . . *This* was unnecessary."

"It's just . . ." Tera began, but trailed off. She stared at him.

Body after body, war after war, fight after fight, Nev dealt with the consequences.

He knew what he risked, and he was willing to pay the price. But what had Falid to do with any of that? He was just a fucking elephant.

"I want my sister's body," Tera said. "I know you don't care much for people. But I cared some for my sister, and I want her buried right."

"Revenge won't bring her back."

"Revenge will get her buried right."

"Revenge doesn't pay for a new workshop, or more bodies."

"Revenge gets you more bodies."

"But not a place to put them."

"Then do it for the money. You've seen that God's eye temple on the hill. You think they only keep people in there?"

"And if there's no money?"

Tera spat. "Then you'll have to settle for revenge."

Falid, the little trumpeting elephant. "It was not necessary," Nev said.

"It never is," Tera said.

• • •

The cult of God's eye was housed in a massive temple three rings further up into the city. They had no money to wash and dress the part, so they waited for cover of night, when the only thing illuminating the streets were the floating blue bodies of the nightblinders; beautiful, thumb-sized flying insects that rose from their daytime hiding places to softly illuminate the streets until nearly dawn.

• • •

In the low blue light, the craggy red sandstone temple threw long shadows; the grinning eyeless faces carved into its outer walls looked even more grotesque. There was just enough light for Nev to notice that the crossbowmen at the parapet above the gate carried quivers of bolts with purple plumes, just like the ones the boy had used to shoot him and Falid.

"Over or under?" Nev said.

Tera chewed on a wad of coca leaves. Whatever viral thing the wizards had given her was finally clearing up. "Under," she said.

They slipped away from the temple's front doors and walked four blocks up to the broken entrance to the sewers. Many had been left unrepaired after the last storm. As they huffed along the fetid brick sewer, hunched over like miners, Nev said, "Why'd you want to talk to the dead, really? We don't need to talk to the dead."

"You don't," Tera said. She slapped the side of the sewer and muttered something. She had a better sense of direction than he did. "I do."

"You can't think the dead are still there, if I can run around in their bodies."

"I think there's always a piece of us still there, in the bodies. In the bones."

"You'll talk to me when I'm dead, then? You're, what—eighty?"

"I'm fifty-one, you little shit."

"Maybe worry over yourself first."

"That ain't my job. And you know it. Here it is. Boost me up."

He offered his knee, and she stood on it while working away the grate above. She swore.

The weight of her on his knee eased as she hauled herself up. The light was bad in the sewers; only a few of the nightblinders made it down here. "Come now," she said, and he could just see her arms reaching for him.

Nev leapt. She pulled him until he could grab the lip of the latrine himself. He rolled over onto a white tiled floor. Two lanterns full of buzzing nightblinders illuminated the room. He smeared shitty water across the floor. "They'll smell us coming," he said.

The door opened, and a plump little robed priest gaped at them.

Tera was faster than Nev. She head-butted the priest in the face. Nev grabbed the utility knife at his belt and jabbed it three times into the man's gut. He fell.

Tera clucked at him. "No need to go about killing priests," she whispered. As she gazed at the body, a strange look came over her face. "Huh," she said.

"What?"

She shrugged. "Dead guy knows where Corez is."

"You're making that up."

She spat and made the sign of God's eye over her left breast. "Sordid truth, there. See, those viral wizards aren't talking shit. Told you I'd get smarter."

"The man is dead. It's impossible that—"

"What? Messes with your little idea of the world, doesn't it? That maybe who we are is in our bones? Maybe you don't erase everything when you jump. Maybe you become a little bit like every body. Maybe you're not stealing a thing. You're borrowing it."

Nev turned away from her. His response was going to be loud, and angry. Unnecessary. The guild taught that death was darkness. There were no gods, no rebirths, no glorious afterlives. The life you had was the one you made for yourself in the discarded carcasses of others. Most days, he believed it. Most days.

They dumped the body down the latrine. "Lot of work to bury your sister," Nev said.

"Fuck you. You wouldn't know."

He considered her reaction for a long moment while they waited in the doorway, looking left to right down the hall for more wandering priests. It was true. He wouldn't know. He'd neither burned nor buried any of his relatives. They'd all be long dead, now.

"It made you angry I jumped into her body, didn't it?" he said.

"Didn't ask me, or her. No choice, when you don't ask."

"It didn't occur to me."

"Yeah, things like that never do, do they?"

She slipped into the hall. Nev padded quietly after her, past row after row of nightblinder lanterns. They circled up a spiral stair, encountering little resistance. At the top of the staircase was a massive iron-banded door. Tera gestured for him to come forward. He was the better lock pick.

Nev slipped out his tools from the flat leather clip at this belt and worked the lock open. The lock clicked. Tera pushed it open and peered in.

Darkness. The nightblinder lanterns inside had been shuttered. Nev tensed.

He heard something beside him, and elbowed into the black. His arm connected with heavy leather armor. Someone grabbed his collar and yanked him into the room. Tera swore. The armored man kicked Nev to his knees. Nev felt cold steel at the back of his neck.

The door slammed behind them.

The black sheathing on the lanterns was pulled away. Nev put his hands flat on the floor. No sudden movements until he knew how many there were. A large woman sat at the end of a raised bed. Her mane of black hair reminded him strongly of the woman who'd chased them through the street, but the body he knew far more intimately. It was Tera's sister, her soft brown complexion and wise eyes restored, transformed, by a body mercenary like him.

Four more men were in the room, long swords out, two pressed at Tera, two more at Nev. They were all men this time, which didn't bode well. Enlisted men tended to be more expendable than their female counterparts.

"You stink," the woman who wore Tera's sister's body said. "You realize it was only my curiosity that let you get this far. Surely you're not stupid enough to risk your necks over a burnt workshop?"

"My sister," Tera said. "Mora Ghulamak. You're not her, so you must be Corez."

"God's eye, that honeyring didn't have a sister, did she?" Corez said. "Your sister pledged her body to the God's eye. She disguised herself and tried to flee that fate. But she's in service to me, as you can see."

"My sister's dead," Tera said. "We came for her body. To burn her."

"Burn her? Surely your little body merc friend here understands why that's not going to be permitted. A body is just a suit. This suit is mine."

"*Her* body," Tera said.

Corez waved her hand at the men. "Dump them in the cistern. There's two more unblemished dead for my collection."

Drowning was the best way to kill a body you wanted for later. It left no marks—nothing that required extensive mending. It was also the worst way to die. Nev tried to bolt.

The men were fast, though, bigger than him, better armored, and better trained. They hauled them both from the room, down two flights of stairs, and brought them to the vast black mouth of a cistern sitting in the bowels of the temple.

Nev tried to talk his way out, tried coercion, promises. They said nothing. They were in service to a body mercenary. They knew what she could do with them, and their bodies. They wouldn't know death. Priests of every faith said they'd never see an afterlife if they lived as walking corpses.

They kicked Tera in first. Nev tumbled after her.

He hit the water hard.

Nev gasped. It was cold, far colder than he expected. He bubbled up and swam instinctively to the side of the cistern. The sides were sheer. The top was at least thirty feet above them.

Tera sputtered beside him.

He hated drowning. *Hated* it. "Look for a way up."

They spent ten minutes clawing their way around the cistern, looking for a crack, a step, an irregularity. Nothing. Nev tried swimming down as far as he could, looking for a drain pipe. If there was one, it was deeper than he could dive. He could not find the bottom.

The third time he surfaced, he saw Tera clumsily treading water. Her face was haggard.

"It's all right," Nev said, but of course it wasn't.

"How old are you, really?" Tera said. She choked on a mouthful of water, then spit.

He swam over to her. Looped an arm around her waist. He could last a bit longer, maybe. His body was stronger and fitter. Younger. "Old enough."

"The face I see now is young and pretty, but you ain't twenty-five."

"Body mercs have been known—"

"I know it's not your body. You spend more time admiring it than a War Minister's husband spends polishing her armor for her."

"That's the trouble with the living. Everyone wants to know everything." He had a memory of his first body, some stranger's life now, playing at being a mercenary in the long tunic and trousers of a village girl. It was a long road from playing at it to living it, to dying at it.

"Only ever asked you two questions," she said, sputtering. He kicked harder, trying to keep them both afloat. "I asked how long you been a body merc, and how much pay was."

"This makes three."

"Too many?"

"Three too many."

"That's your problem, boy-child. Love the dead so much you stopped living. Man so afraid of death he doesn't live is no man at all."

"I don't need people."

"Yeah? How'd you do without a body manager, before me?"

He smelled a hot, barren field. Bloody trampled grain. He felt the terrible thirst of a man dying alone in a field without another body in sight, without a stash of his own. He had believed so strongly in his own immortality during the early days of the war that, when he woke inside the corpse of a man in a ravine who would not stop bleeding no matter how much he willed it, it was the first time he ever truly contemplated death. He had prayed to three dozen gods while crawling out of the ravine, and when he saw nothing before him but more fields, and flies, and heat, he'd faced his own mortality and discovered he didn't like it at all. He was going to die alone. Alone and unloved, forgotten. A man whose real face had been ground to dust so long ago all he remembered was the cut of his women's trousers.

"I managed," he said stiffly. His legs were numb.

Tera was growing limp in his arms. "When I die in here, don't jump into my body. Leave me dead. I want to go on in peace."

"There's only darkness after—"

"Don't spray that elephant shit at me," she said. "I know better, remember? I can . . . speak . . . to the dead now. You . . . leave me dead."

"You're not going to die." His legs and arms were already tired. He hoped for a second wind. It didn't come. He needed a new body for that.

Tera huffed more water. Eventually Tera would die. Probably in a few minutes. Another body manager dead. And he'd have nowhere to leap but her body. He gazed up at the lip of the cistern. But then what? Hope he could get out of here in Tera's body when he couldn't in his own fitter one?

Tera's head dipped under the water. He yanked her up.

"Not yet," he said. He hated drowning. *Hated* it.

But there was nowhere to go.

No other body . . .

"Shit," he said. He pulled Tera close. "I'm going now, Tera. I'm coming back. A quarter hour. You can make it a quarter hour."

"Nowhere . . . to . . . no . . . bodies. Oh." He saw the realization on her face. "Shit."

"Quarter hour," he said, and released her. He didn't wait to see if she went under immediately. He dove deep and shed his tunic, his trousers. He swam deep, deeper still. He hated drowning.

He pushed down and down. The pressure began to weigh on him. He dove until his air ran out, until his lungs burned. He dove until his body rebelled, until it needed air so desperately he couldn't restrain his body's impulse to breathe. Then he took a breath. A long, deep breath of water: pure and sweet and deadly. He breathed water. Burning.

His body thrashed, seeking the surface. Scrambling for the sky.

Too late.

Then calm. He ceased swimming. Blackness filled his vision.

So peaceful, though, in the end. Euphoric.

• • •

Nev screamed. He sat bolt upright and vomited blood. Blackness filled his vision, and for one horrifying moment he feared he was back in the water. But no. The smell told him he was in the sewers. He patted at his new body, the plump priest they'd thrown down the latrine: the bald pate, the round features, the body he had touched and so could jump right back into. He gasped and vomited again; bile this time. He realized he was too fat to get up through the latrine, but wearing what he did made it possible to get in the front door.

He scrambled forward on sluggish limbs, trying to work new blood into stiff fingers. His second wind came as he slogged back up onto the street. He found a street fountain and drank deeply to replace the vital liquid he'd lost. Then he was running, running, back to the God's eye temple.

They let him in with minimal fuss, which disappointed him, because he wanted to murder them all now, fill them full of purple-plumed arrows, yelling about fire and elephants and unnecessary death, but he could not stop, could not waver, because Tera was down there, Tera was drowning, Tera was not like him, and Tera would not wake up.

He got all the way across the courtyard before someone finally challenged him, a young man about fourteen, who curled his nose and said some godly-sounding greeting to him. Nev must not have replied correctly, because the snotty kid yelled after him, "Hey now! Who are you?"

Nev ran. His body was humming now, rushing with life, vitality. A red haze filled his vision, and when the next armed man stepped in front of him, he dispatched him neatly with a palm strike to the face. He took up the man's spear and long sword and forged ahead, following his memory of their descent to the cistern.

As he swung around the first flight, he rushed headlong into two armed men escorting Corez up, still wearing Tera's sister's skin. Surprise was on his side, this time.

Nev ran the first man through the gut, and hit the second with the end of his spear.

"God's eye, what—" Corez said, and stopped. She had retreated back down the stairs, stumbled, and her wig was aslant now.

"You take the scalps of your people, too?" Nev said. He hefted the spear.

"Now you think about this," she said. "You don't know who I am. I can give you anything you like, you know. More bodies than you know what to do with. A workshop fit for the king of the body mercenaries. A thousand body managers better than any you've worked with. You've dabbled in a world you don't understand."

"I understand well enough," he said.

"Then, the body. I can give you this body. That's what she wanted, isn't it? I have others."

"I don't care much for people," Nev said. "That was your mistake. You thought I'd care about the bodies, or Tera, or her sister, or any of the rest. I don't. I'm doing this for my fucking *elephant.*"

He thrust the spear into her chest. She gagged. Coughed blood.

He did not kill her, but left her to bleed out, knowing that she could not jump into another form until she was on the edge of death.

Nev ran the rest of the way down into the basements. They had to have a way to fish the bodies out. He found a giant iron pipe leading away from the cistern, and a sluice. He opened up the big drain and watched the water pour out into an aqueduct below.

He scrambled down and down a long flight of steps next to the cistern and found a little sally port. How long until it drained? Fuck it. He opened the sally port door. A wave of water engulfed him.

He smacked hard against the opposite wall. A body washed out with the wave of water, and he realized it was his own, his beloved. He scrambled forward, only to see Tera's body tumble after it, propelled by the force of the water. For one horrible moment he was torn. He wanted to save his old body. Wanted to save it desperately.

But Tera only had one body.

He ran over to her and dragged her way from the cistern. She was limp.

Nev pounded on her back. "Tera!" he said. "Tera!" As if she would awaken at the sound of her name. He shook her, slapped her. She remained inert. But if she was dead, and yes, of course she was dead, she was not long dead. There was, he felt, something left. Something lingering. Tera would say it lingered in her bones.

He searched his long memory for some other way to rouse her. He turned her onto her side and pounded on her back again. Water dribbled from her mouth. He thought he felt her heave. Nev let her drop. He brought both his hands together, and thumped her chest. Once. Then again.

Tera choked. Her eyelids fluttered. She heaved. He rolled her over again, and pulled her into his arms.

Her eyes rolled up at him. He pressed his thumb and pinky together, pushed the other three fingers in parallel; the signal he used to tell it was him inhabiting a new body.

"Why you come for me?" Tera said.

He held her sodden, lumpy form in his own plump arms and thought for a long moment he might weep. Not over her or Falid or the rest, but over his life, a whole series of lives lost, and nothing to show for it but this: the ability to keep breathing when others perished. So many dead, one after the other. So many he let die, for no purpose but death.

"It was *necessary*," he said.

· · ·

They crawled out of the basement and retrieved Tera's sister from the stairwell. It hurt Nev's heart, because he knew they could only carry one of them. He had to leave his old form. The temple was stirring now. Shouting. They dragged her sister's body back the way they had come, through the latrines. Tera went first, insisting that she grab the corpse as it came down. Nev didn't argue. In a few more minutes the temple's guards would spill over them.

When he slipped down after her and dropped to the ground, he saw Tera standing over what was left of her sister, muttering to herself. She started bawling.

"What?" he said.

"The dead talk to me. I can hear them all now, Nev."

A chill crawled up his spine. He wanted to say she was wrong, it was impossible, but he remembered holding her in his arms, and knowing she could be brought back. Knowing it wasn't quite the end, yet. Knowing hope. "What did she say?"

"It was for me and her. Forty years of bullshit. You wouldn't understand."

He had to admit she was probably right.

They burned her sister, Mora, in a midden heap that night, while Tera cried and drank and Nev stared at the smoke flowing up and up and up, drawing her soul to heaven, to God's eye, like a body merc's soul to a three days' dead corpse.

· · ·

Nev sat with Tera in a small tea shop across the way from the pawn office. The bits and bobs they'd collected going through people's trash weren't enough for a workshop, not even a couple bodies, but they had squatted in rundown places before. They could eat for a while longer. Tera carried a small box under her arm throughout the haggle with the pawn office. Now she pushed the box across the table to him.

Nev opened the box. A turtle as big as his fist sat inside, its little head peeking out from within the orange shell.

"What is this?" he asked.

"It's a fucking turtle."

"I can see that."

"Then why'd you ask?" she said. "I can't afford a fucking elephant, but living people need to care about things. Keeps you human. Keeps you alive. And that's my job, you know. Keeping you alive. Not just *living*."

"I'm not sure I—"

"Just take the fucking turtle."

He took the fucking turtle.

That night, while Tera slept in the ruined warehouse along the stinking pier, Nev rifled through the midden heaps for scraps and fed the turtle a moldered bit of apple. He pulled the turtle's box into his lap; the broad lap of a plump, balding, middle-aged man. Nondescript. Unimportant. Hardly worth a second look.

To him, though, the body was beautiful, because it was dead. The dead didn't kill your elephant or burn down your workshop. But the dead didn't give you turtles, either. Or haul your corpse around in case you needed it later. And unlike the guild said, some things, he knew now, were not as dead as they seemed. Not while those who loved them still breathed.

Tera farted in her sleep and turned over heavily, muttering.

Nev hugged the box to his chest.

KAMERON HURLEY is the author of *The Stars Are Legion* and the essay collection *The Geek Feminist Revolution*, as well as the award-winning God's War Trilogy and the Worldbreaker Saga. Hurley has won the Hugo Award, Kitschy Award, and the Sydney J. Bounds Award for Best Newcomer. She was also a finalist for the Arthur C. Clarke Award, the Nebula Award, and the David Gemmell Morningstar Award. Her short fiction has appeared in *Popular Science* magazine, *Lightspeed,* and many anthologies. Hurley has also written for *The Atlantic, Entertainment Weekly, The Village Voice, Bitch,* and *Locus.*

About Fairies

Pat Murphy

Jennifer and her coworkers create fairy lands for a toy company, all the while cultivating their own personal fairy worlds. *Edited by Patrick Nielsen Hayden.*

I'm on my way to the train station when I find a mirror leaning against a chain-link fence. People often abandon stuff on this street, figuring that someone who wants it will take it away. And someone usually does. San Francisco has many scavengers.

The mirror, a circle of glass about the size of a dinner plate, is framed with pale wood. The wood is weathered, soft against my hand as I pick up it and peer into the glass. My reflection is silvery gray in the morning light.

My car is parked just a few feet away. My bedroom, high in the attic of my father's house, needs a mirror. I figure it's serendipity that I have found this one. I put the mirror in the trunk of my car and hurry toward the station.

The first time I went looking for the train station at 22nd Street and Pennsylvania, I passed it three times before I finally found it. I think of it as a secret train station. There's just a small sign by the bridge on 22nd Street. Beside the sign is a long flight of steps leading down, down, down to train tracks that run along a narrow ravine squeezed between Iowa Street and Pennsylvania Street. A concrete platform beside the tracks, a couple of benches, and a ticket machine—that's the station.

As always, I stop on the 22nd Street bridge and look down at the tracks. They're about twenty feet below the bridge—a big enough drop to break your leg, I'd guess. Probably not enough to kill you, unless you dove over the edge and landed on your head.

As I walk down the steps, I look up. Far above me, the freeway crosses over 22nd Street and the train tracks—a soaring concrete arc supported by massive gray columns on either side of the tracks. Morning sunlight slips through the gap between the bottom of the freeway and Indiana Street to shine on a patch of graffiti that decorates the base of one column. The great swirls of color are letters, I think, but I can't read what they say. Whatever the message, it's not for me.

As I wait for my train, I watch swallows flying to and fro, carrying food to their chicks. The birds have built nests on the underside of the freeway. They don't seem to care that semis and SUVs are thundering over them at 70 miles per hour.

When I return in the evening, I'll hear frogs chirping in the stream that runs in a gully just behind the benches. Beside the stream is a tiny marsh where rushes grow.

I like this forgotten bit of wild land, hidden away beneath the city streets.

· · ·

My name is Jennifer. I am on my way to a toy company in Redwood City to have a meeting about fairies.

I met the company's founder at an art opening and he said he liked the way I think. I was a double major in art and anthropology, and we had had a long conversation (fueled by cheap white wine) about the dark side of children's stories. As I recall, I talked a lot about Tinkerbell, who tried to murder Wendy more than once. (My still-unfinished PhD dissertation is a cross-cultural analysis of the role of wicked women in children's literature, and I count Tinkerbell as right up there among the wicked.)

Anyway, he hired me to be part of his company's product development department. He told me he liked to toss people into the mix to see what happened.

After he hired me, I found out that he had a habit of hiring people for no clearly defined job, then firing them when they didn't do their job. He hired me, then left for a month's vacation. He is still gone. I wasn't sure what my job was when I reported to work three weeks ago. I still don't know. But this is the first steady paycheck I've had in a couple of years and I'm determined to make sure that something positive happens.

Today, I'm going to a meeting about fairies.

Tiffany is the project manager. We met by the coffee maker on my first day. While we waited for the coffee to brew, I found out what she was working on and chatted with her about it. She invited me to come to a few team meetings to "provide input."

The company is creating a line of Twinkle Fairy Dolls. Among three- to six-year-old girls, fairies of the gossamer-wing variety are a very hot topic. That's what the marketing guy said, anyway. He was at the first meeting I attended, but he hasn't been back since.

Each Twinkle Fairy Doll will come with a unique Internet code that lets the owner enter the online fairyland that Tiffany's team is developing. In that world, the doll's owner will have her own fairy home that she can furnish with fairy furniture. She will have a fairy avatar that she can dress with fairy clothes.

It's a rather consumer-oriented fairyland. Players purchase their furniture and clothes with fairy dollars—or would that be fairy gold? And if it's fairy gold, will it wither into dead leaves in the light of day?

These are questions I do not ask at the meeting.

Today the question that Tiffany wants to address is: What sort of world do the fairies live in? Is it a forest world where they frolic in leafy groves and shelter from the misty rain under mushroom caps? Or is it a fairy village with cobblestone streets and thatched huts, maybe surrounding a fairy castle? Or is it some mixture of the two?

"Why don't we just ask marketing what they want?" says Rocky, the web developer. The temperature is supposed to top 100 today, but Rocky is wearing black jeans, black boots, and a black t-shirt from a robot wars competition. He strolled into the meeting late without apology, his eyebrows (right one pierced in three places) lowered in a scowl. He wants to look surly, but his face is sweet and soft and boy-ish and he can't quite pull it off.

I suspect Rocky is not happy to be on the fairy project. Tiffany mentioned that another team is working on a line of remote-control monster trucks. I think Rocky would rather be developing an online Monster Truck World.

Tiffany shakes her head. Her hair is very short and very blonde and very messy. She's in her late twenties and tends to wear designer jeans, baby-doll tops, and Mary Janes. "We want to be authentic," she says.

Jane, the project's art director, stares at her. "Authentic? We're talking about fairies here. In case you didn't know, there aren't any fairies." Jane can be a little cranky.

I step in to help Tiffany. She's kind of a ditz, but I like her and she seems to be in charge of some important projects. A useful person to befriend. "I think Tiffany means that we want our fairies to match the child's concept of fairies. We want them to feel authentic."

"Sherlock Holmes believed in fairies," says Tiffany. "Isn't that what you told me the other day?"

Did I say "kind of a ditz"? Make that "entirely a ditz." "Not quite," I correct her, trying to be gentle. "Arthur Conan Doyle, the author who wrote Sherlock Holmes, believed in fairies. Back in 1917, two little girls took pictures of fairies in their gar-den, and Doyle was certain that the photos were real."

"What were they?" asks Jane. "Swamp gas?"

"Much simpler than that," I say. "About sixty years later, one of the girls—in her eighties by that time—admitted that she had cut the drawings of fairies out of a book, posed the cutouts in the garden with her friend, and taken the photos."

"Arthur Conan Doyle was fooled by paper cutouts?" Jane is intrigued.

"People believe what they want to believe," I say.

"I'm thinking of something like Neverland in *Peter Pan*," Tiffany says. She has moved on. A ditz, but a ditz with a goal. "Somewhere with lots of hidden, secret places." In Tiffany's world, secrets are wonderful and fun. "And it's filled with beautiful, sweet fairies with gossamer wings. Like Tinkerbell."

Rocky snorts. "Sweet?" he says. "Tinkerbell was never sweet."

Surprised, I stare at him. He's right. In the book, *Peter Pan*, Tinkerbell was a jeal-ous little pixie who swore like a sailor and did her best to get Wendy killed more than once. I didn't think Rocky would know that.

· · ·

After the meeting, I go to the balcony for a smoke. The balcony—a narrow walk-way just outside the windows of the cafeteria—is the smokers' corner. In California, smoking has been banished from restaurants, offices, and bars. You can smoke in your own home, but just barely. Filthy habit, people say. Bad for your health. And second-hand smoke is dangerous for others, too.

I smoke three, maybe four, cigarettes a day. Not so much. I figure you have to die sometime. I take a drag, feeling the buzz.

At the edge of the balcony there's a brick wall topped by a waist-high rail, an inadequate barrier between me and the sheer drop to the street. I lean on the rail and look down. Five floors down.

I hear the door open behind me. "Those things will kill you," Rocky says. He is tapping a cigarette from a pack. He leans against the railing beside me, looking down. "Just far enough to be fatal," he says.

He's not quite right. You can survive a fall from five stories if you hit a parked car. The car gives just enough to cushion your fall. I know. I've done research.

"I was impressed at how well you know *Peter Pan*," I tell him. "Most people only know the Disney version."

He almost smiles. "The Disney version has no balls," he says.

I laugh.

Rocky's scowl returns. "What's so funny?"

"Hey, it's a long tradition," I say. "Starting with the play where Mary Martin played Peter. Peter Pan doesn't have any balls."

He doesn't smile. I'm sorry about that. For a moment there, I kind of liked him.

· · ·

Late that night, I sit on my bed, re-reading *Peter Pan*. When I was ten, the year after my mother died, a friend of my father gave me a copy. The woman who gave it to me, one of a series of unsuitable women Dad dated, was under the mistaken impression that it was a children's book. I read it with horrified fascination.

Disney made *Peter Pan* into a jolly movie with just enough adventure to be cheerfully scary. The book is not like that. Neverland is not all sunshine and frolic. Beneath every adventure lurks a deep and frightening darkness. Peter Pan was fascinating and terrifying. He was indifferent to human life. "There's a pirate asleep in the pampas just below us," he says. "If you like, we'll go down and kill him." Death is an adventure, Peter Pan says, and nothing is better than that.

One of my cats makes a sound and I look up from the book to see what's bothering him. The mirror that I found near the train station is leaning against the far wall. My cat, Flash, stares in the direction of the mirror, his ears forward, his tail twitching.

Everyone knows that there are things that only cats can see. In my house, Flash is the cat that watches those invisible things. He frequently gives his full attention to a patch of empty air for hours at a time.

Godzilla, the other cat, usually can't be bothered with such nonsense. But tonight Godzilla has taken up a post beside Flash, staring at the same emptiness.

"What's up, guys?" I ask them. But they just keep staring in the direction of the mirror that I found on my way to the train station. They are vigilant, concerned. They don't trust this mirror.

I pick the mirror up and set it on top of the bureau. Flash jumps on top of the bureau, where he continues to watch the mirror with great suspicion.

The phone rings.

It's Johnny, the owner of the board-and-care home where my father has lived for the past six months. Whenever I stop by to visit, Johnny tells me how Dad has been doing and fills me in on details that I don't particularly want to know. I have learned about the need for stool softeners and socks with no-skid soles. I have discussed the merits of different varieties of walkers (one called, without irony, the "Merry Walker").

My father was once an archaeologist. My father was once a member of Mensa. My father was once a very smart, very sarcastic, somewhat hostile man. Of all those attributes, only the sarcasm and hostility remain.

A few weeks ago, when I was visiting Dad, Johnny told me that my father had threatened to kick one of the other residents in the balls.

"He gets very angry," Johnny told me. "It's the Alzheimer's."

I nodded. It wasn't really the Alzheimer's. Dad had never suffered fools gladly. He considered most people to be fools. And he was always threatening to kick some fool in the balls.

I think Dad became an archaeologist because dead people didn't talk back. Living people were far too troublesome.

Johnny prefers to blame my father's idiosyncrasies on Alzheimer's. Johnny is a sweet guy who chooses to believe that people are inherently nice. But tonight, Johnny is facing a challenge. "Your father won't stop talking," he says.

I can hear my father's voice in the background, but I can't make out the words.

"He's been at it for two hours. I've told him that it's time for bed, but he won't stop." Johnny sounds very tired.

"Let me talk to him," I tell Johnny.

I hear my father as Johnny approaches him. He is delivering a lecture on burial customs. "A barrow is a home for the dead," he is saying. "In its chamber or chambers the tenant is surrounded with possessions from his life."

"Your daughter needs to talk to you," Johnny says.

Dad doesn't even pause. "A shaman would be buried with his scrying mirror; a warrior with his weapons," he continues. "A fence or trench separates the barrow from the surrounding world."

"It's important," Johnny says. "She really needs to talk to you."

"Yes?" my father growls into the phone. His tone is that of a busy man, needlessly interrupted. "I'm teaching just now."

"This is Jennifer, your daughter. I called to tell you that it's late. Class is over."

"What are you talking about?"

"This is your daughter. You're running late. It's time for class to be over."

"I was just wrapping up."

"You'd better let the students go." Wrapping up could take hours. "They have to study for finals."

"They'd better study." His voice is that of a demanding instructor. Then a pause. "I have to get ready myself," he says, as if suddenly remembering something.

"Get ready? For what?"

"I'm leaving tomorrow."

Several times over the last few months, my father has mentioned that he is going on a trip. Sometimes he's going to an important excavation. Sometimes he's leaving because the conference he was attending is over. Sometimes he's not sure where he's going. I've learned not to ask.

"You can pack in the morning," I say. "You'll have time then."

"All right," he says. "In the morning."

In the morning, he will remember none of this.

. . .

While I'm waiting for the train at the 22nd Street Station, I walk along the tiny stream that's just a few steps away from the concrete platform. It's a muddy trickle, enclosed in a culvert for part of its length, then widening to shallow puddles that support clumps of wild iris surrounded by pigweed.

Frogs live in that stream—I hear them croaking in the evening. But they're hiding now. No matter how hard I look, I never catch a glimpse of them.

The steep slope above me is covered with tall grasses and wild fennel, with a few blackberry bushes working their way up to becoming a thicket. Toward the end of the platform, some city workers have been clearing the brush. I glance down at the bare ground.

It's an old habit, developed over many summers spent at archeological digs. Out in the field, I'd be looking for shards of broken pots or chips of worked stone, indications of ancient settlements. Here in the city, I'm just looking, not expecting to see anything more than the glitter of broken beer bottles.

But the morning light reflects from the edge of a pebble. I stop, pick up the stone, and examine it more closely. It's very tiny worked flint—about a centimeter long. I can see minuscule circles, each just a couple of millimeters across, where someone has flaked away the stone to make a sharp edge.

I hear a rumble in the distance. The train is coming. I put the tiny tool in my pocket, no time to examine it further. I hurry back to the platform.

As the train pulls away, heading south, I look out the window at the brush-covered slope. The city is filled with wild things. I once saw a family of raccoons crossing a major thoroughfare on their way to check out the dumpster behind a fast-food joint. A possum with a wicked grin (way too many teeth) and a naked, ratlike tail regularly strolled through my father's backyard. Coyotes live in Golden Gate Park.

If there are frogs and raccoons and opossums and coyotes, why not other creatures? Small, wild, living in the gaps, in the gullies, in the ravines, in the half-hidden places underneath.

. . .

At today's meeting, Tiffany wants to establish the specifics of our particular fairies. Tiffany believes in fairies that fly on shimmering wings (made of child-safe Mylar, I think). Her fairies are similar to Tinkerbell, but not so similar that they'll trigger a cease-and-desist order.

Jane wants the fairies to hearken back to the classics. Think *Midsummer Night's Dream* and Yeats. Her fairies wear elegant green dresses. They have a queen, of course. At fabulous parties, they dance all night. Like me, Jane lives alone. Unlike me, Jane seems to mind.

Rocky's fairies sleep late. They are dark-eyed and sultry, dressing in black and looking for trouble. I think some of them are transgender, which makes sense if you really know *Peter Pan*. When Wendy returns from Neverland, she tells her mother that new fairies live in nests on the tops of trees. "The mauve ones are boys and the white ones are girls," she says. "And the blue ones are just little sillies who are not sure what they are."

That's from the book, not the movie. I don't think Disney believes in transgender fairies.

The way I figure it, you can choose what kind of fairies you want to believe in. I finger the stone tool in my pocket. In the foggy chill of San Francisco's summer, my fairies wear clothing made of tanned mouse leather. They are grimy, hardscrabble fairies that chip tools from stone and drink from the stream. They hunt in the marsh with stone blades and feed on frogs' legs. They'd mug Victorian flower fairies and take their stuff.

"What do you think? Forest or village?" Tiffany is polling the meeting, getting each member of the team to vote. Rocky says city; Jane says forest. It's my turn.

Wild or civilized. "Can't we have it both ways?" I ask.

Why not? Dirty little fairies, crouching in the litter by the stream, chipping stone into knives, strapping blades onto spear handles made of pencils and pens that commuters had dropped. My kind of fairy.

• • •

I spend the rest of the afternoon working on visual concepts for the fairy forest. For the fairy huts, I figure I should use all natural materials.

The traditional Celtic huts have stone walls, and I just can't see the fairies going to all that effort. After some online research, I settle on huts that looked like ones built in eastern Nigeria. The walls are made of bundles of straw, tied side by side. The roof is made of reeds.

The shape of the huts reminds me of acorns—smooth sides, textured cap. I figure Tiffany will like that. And I think the fairies could manage to build huts with straw.

In my sketch, the huts are tucked among wild blackberry brambles. Poison oak twines among the blackberry branches. I don't think these fairies want company.

• • •

After work, I go to the board-and-care home to visit my dad. I stop by the grocery store on my way and buy a basket of fresh raspberries. These days, I always bring something to eat. Finger food is best. Grapes, raspberries, blueberries. Something he can pick up and eat, no utensils required.

We sit in the living room, my father in a recliner and I in a straight-back chair. We eat raspberries.

I've learned not to ask many questions. Questions are difficult. More often than not, he has no answers. Or his answers relate to the distant past. Or halfway through an answer, Dad forgets what he was saying.

I tell my father many things these days. He likes to listen. When he listens, it does not matter that words are slippery and sentences betray him.

"I found this on the path to the train station," I tell him. I hold out the tiny stone tool. I've been carrying it in my pocket since I found it. "I can see tiny chips where someone has been working the stone, flaking away bits to make an edge."

My father examines the blade. His hand shakes. The skin of his arm is marked with dark purple age spots. He gives the stone back. "Microlith," he says. Basically, that's a technical term for "tiny worked stone." Not saying much I didn't already know.

"I found a mirror the other day," I say.

"That's good," he says. A complete sentence. Short enough that he can get through it without losing his way. Sentences are trickier than you realize, long and twisty. It's easy to get lost.

"I need . . ." he begins. He's pushing his luck now, working on a longer sentence. What does he need? "I need a mirror."

"Really? I'll bring you the one I found," I tell him. Does he really need a mirror or is that just the word that came most quickly to mind?

He nods. "Don't forget." Another easy sentence.

I care about my father in a grudging sort of way. My mother died when I was nine. She committed suicide, jumping off the Golden Gate Bridge. Even as a child, I recognized that she was a drama queen, a flamboyant woman given to grand gestures, to great joys and great depression. Today, she might be identified as bipolar.

My father, on the other hand, is solid and unemotional. After my mother's death, Dad took care of me in an awkward, casual, ham-handed sort of way. I never went hungry and I never got hugged. It was a balance, of sorts.

I take after my mother. I understand drama, I understand depression, and I understand the appeal of the dark and foggy waters below the bridge.

"Don't forget," my father says again.

We eat raspberries in companionable silence.

• • •

Godzilla is sleeping on top of the mirror, which is lying flat on the bureau. He was there this morning when I left for work. He is there when I get home. Usually, he supervises when I open a can of cat food for him and his brother. But tonight he jumps down from the bureau only after I set the food on the floor. He eats quickly, then returns to the mirror, gazing into it intently, sniffing it carefully, and then lying down on top of it once again. Curled up, he completely covers the glass surface.

When I sit down at my desk, I pat my lap and call to him. He lifts his head and regards me with that slit-eyed look that one of my friends says is how cats smile. He's not about to leave his post.

His brother, Flash, is prowling the apartment restlessly. Every once in a while, he walks past the bureau and looks up at his brother. Then he resumes his patrol.

Cats have theories. Every cat owner knows that. The cats can't and won't tell you their theories. You must deduce the theories from their behavior. Then you have theories about the cats' theories. If you modify your behavior in response to your theories about their theories, you may change their theories. It is an endlessly recursive loop. The viewer affects the system. It's Heisenberg's uncertainty principle with cats.

I let Godzilla sleep.

I am doing online research about fairy fashions. To draw convincing fairy clothes, I figure I'd better know what people think fairies wear. It's edging up on ten PM, and I have to be up at six in the morning to catch the train, but I'm not sleepy at all. When I'm insomniac, I find doing research online very comforting. I used to walk on the Golden Gate Bridge at night—but doing research online is safer.

I find information on Conan Doyle's belief in fairies. I find a discussion of pygmy flints, blades of worked stone that some claim are made by the little people. I find hundreds of images of Victorian fairies—pretty ladies with delicate wings.

Somewhere along the way, I find Rocky's blog.

Mostly it is one of those extremely tedious personal blogs that I am amazed that anyone writes and even more amazed that anyone reads. A description of an art opening he attended. Photos of his friends (all in black, of course). Discussion of his plans to attend Burning Man. And a long list of fairy links.

Rocky, it turns out, has done a lot research that he has not shared with the rest of the team. He has links to fairy porn. (Yes, of course there is fairy porn.) He has links to sites considering the connections between fairies and alien abductions, as well as sites about the original Celtic fairies—amoral creatures that are capable of great malevolence. In Celtic tradition, when someone died people said that they went to be with the fairies. Being touched by a fairy, according to one site, was commonly recognized as the cause of a stroke.

No sweet and beautiful fairies. No gossamer wings.

• • •

At the next meeting of the fairyland team, Tiffany gathers ideas for the portal to our fairy site. At Disney's fairy site, the splash screen has a sprinkling of fairy dust and the words "Believing is just the beginning." Then pictures of fairies appear. Tiffany asks the group for an image and words that will capture the essence of our site.

"A black mirror," I say. "A portal to another world. And the words—clap if you believe in fairies."

I don't see the need to specify the type of fairy you might believe in. Dark-eyed and sultry; sweet-faced and dressed in pink. That doesn't matter to me. Clap if you believe.

Rocky smiles a little. "That could work," he says.

After the meeting, Johnny calls to tell me that my dad is in the hospital. Apparently Dad forgot that he could not walk without a walker. He stood up, and then fell down, fracturing his hip.

I go to the hospital after work. I bring the mirror and set it on one of the chairs in my father's room. He won't remember that he said he needed a mirror, but I do.

Dad is sleeping. The nurse says that he was cursing all day. He said he was going to kick the doctor in the balls. "It's the Alzheimer's," she says.

I nod, letting her believe what she wants to believe. Clap your hands if you believe that my father doesn't really want to kick the doctor in the balls.

I am not clapping.

I explain to the nurse that we have a DNR, a "do not resuscitate" order for my dad. No heroic measures, I explain. Just keep him comfortable.

Clap your hands if you believe in death.

Believing in fairies is much easier, I think. Death is an end, an emptiness, a darkness. People want to believe in the light. Go to the light, they say. We fear the darkness and the unknown, the fairies in the ravine, the world behind the mirror.

I set the stone tool beside the mirror. I sit by my father's bed and watch him breathe. His arms are loosely strapped to the rails of the hospital bed. The nurse had told me that they had to strap him down. He kept trying to get out of bed. His hip was broken and he couldn't walk, but he was still trying to get out of bed.

My father's life has been shrinking over the past few years. After I went to college, he lived alone in his Victorian home. When he couldn't get by on his own, I helped him move to an apartment in a senior residence. Then he moved from that apartment to his room in the board-and-care home. Then he moved from that room into this shared room in a hospital, where all he has is a bed and a table and a curtain that separates his space from that of another old man with a table and bed.

My father is not conscious. He is lying on his side, his spine curved, his legs bent. A sheet covers him, but I can see the outline of his body through the fabric. He looks smaller than he ever has before. The tube that snakes from beneath the sheet is dripping a cocktail of painkillers into his veins.

My father is dying. That's clear.

Here's a question. Do I stay and keep watch? Sit by his bed and do what? Read a magazine? Think about his life? Not such a happy life, by my lights.

What would I like, if I were the one lying on the bed?

I would like to be left alone.

So I go home, leaving the mirror and the stone tool on the table by the bed.

Clap your hands if you believe in death. Clap your hands and my father will die.

Actually, I'm kidding about that. My father will die whether you clap your hands or not. My father will die, I will die, and someday you will die. You can applaud or remain silent and death won't care. You can choose to speed up your death—by plunging from a balcony, from a bridge—but all the clapping in the world won't put death off forever.

Some discussions of death make it sound all soft and warm, like falling asleep in a feather bed. But falling asleep implies waking up again, and death means not waking up.

Not being here.

Being with the fairies.

An hour after I leave the hospital, a nurse calls to tell me my father has passed away.

Here's what I think happened: My father curled up into the fetal position. He curled up as small as he could. Then he curled up even smaller, then smaller, then smaller still. You might not think a person could shrink, but my father had been shrinking over the last year, growing shorter with each passing day. So he shrank until he was small enough to slip into the fairy mirror. When the time was right, the fairies came through the mirror and took him away with them.

You see, new fairies are not born. They are transformed through the fairy mirror.

Flash and Godzilla could see that the way was open. Cats notice that sort of thing. So they blocked the way—sleeping on top of the mirror to keep the fairies in and to keep me out. They were protecting me. They aren't stupid. They know who opens those cans of cat food.

My father left his worn-out body behind, dressed in the unfortunate hospital gown. Like a snake abandoning its skin, my father slipped out of his body and emerged in the mirror. He felt better. All the life energy that remained in him was concentrated in his smaller form.

Right now, he's hunting for mice among the stalks of fennel and the blackberry brambles. He took the stone tool with him. He'll scavenge a pencil dropped by a commuter, lash the stone blade to the end to make a spear, and go hunting for frogs.

That's what I choose to believe.

• • •

I stop by the hospital to make arrangements for the body that my father has left behind. A kindly social worker helps me, giving me the name of a mortuary, telling me where to call to get copies of the death certificate, offering words of sympathy. Eventually I leave, taking the mirror with me. There's no sign of the stone tool among my father's things.

Late that night, I take the mirror to the train station. Light of a half moon is shining down on Pennsylvania Street. I walk down the gravel road, alert to every noise in the bushes around me.

When I reach the train tracks, I head south. No one is there. The graffiti artists are taking a night off. Their past creations look gray and black, the colors invisible in the moonlight.

A short distance from the benches and ticket machine, the tracks go into a tunnel. I lean the mirror against the wall beside the tunnel entrance. Somehow it seems right to put it by the tunnel mouth, near the entrance to the underworld. Well, maybe not quite the underworld—it isn't a very long tunnel. But it's the closest thing to an underworld there is around here.

My father had smoked when I was young. My early memories of him are tobacco-scented, wreathed in smoke. The father in those memories is strong and tall and energetic. He could sweep me up and toss me in the air, swing me by my arms until my feet left the ground.

I take a pack of cigarettes from my pocket and I tear the cigarettes open, one by one. I scatter the tobacco on the ground in front of the mirror. I am mixing my magic systems, I know. Native Americans offered tobacco to the spirits. The frogs call; something rustles in the bushes. An opossum? A raccoon? Something else?

I sit by the train tracks near the mirror for a time and think about death. Every now and then, someone will commit suicide by walking in front of a train. Such a noisy, messy, industrial way to go.

I leave the mirror and head for home. That night, I surf the web.

On Rocky's site, I find that he has been working on a fairyland. When I log in, I am given an avatar.

This is not a fairyland that would meet with Tiffany's approval. Yes, there are leafy groves, but the trees are gnarled and menacing, draped with Spanish moss. Little light reaches the forest floor, and I have the sense that creatures other than fairies lurk in the shadows.

There's a fairy village, but the mud huts are neither elegant nor appealing. The carcass of a mouse, marked with the wounds that killed it, hangs curing in the shadows. There are no fairies in residence.

I explore Rocky's fairyland carefully. In the dark bole of a hollow oak I find a tunnel that goes down, down, down into the underworld.

I move my avatar through the darkness, the way illuminated by faintly glowing marks on the tunnel walls. I reach a dead end. A wooden door, closed with a bar and a large padlock, blocks my way.

I lay my hand on the door and the words "THIS WAY CLOSED" glow on the bar in neon green. I know what to do.

I reach out to the letters and touch the D, then the E, then the A, T, H. Death. Each letter winks out when I touch it. When I touch the H, the padlock and the bar dissolve. The door opens.

I stand by the open doorway, looking into a dark and misty world. I listen—and in the distance, I hear the low wail of a train's horn, the rumble of metal wheels on tracks. I catch a faint scent of wild fennel and tobacco.

Listening to the train rumble in the distance, I know the way is open, but I don't need to go there. I close the door.

．．．

At work the next day, I see Rocky in the lunchroom and pull up a chair next to him. "I visited Fairyland last night," I tell him.

He glances at me, startled.

"I particularly liked your attention to detail in the hollow oak," I continue.

He can't help himself—he is smiling now. A little smug, more than a little arrogant.

"Nice trick on the password."

That surprised him. "You opened the door?"

My turn to nod. "Obviously, I didn't go in."

He is considering me now—eyes narrowing. "Maybe later," he says.

"That goes without saying." I study him for a moment—face soft as a boy's, the arrogant confidence of the young in his eyes. Forever young. "I've been wondering where you got the name Rocky," I say. "Nobody names their kid Rocky."

I've been thinking about Rocky, a twenty-something web designer with an attitude and an obsession with death. Could he be something more?

Do you believe in Peter Pan? A boy who never grows up, a boy who knows his way to fairyland and back, a boy with the power of death in his hands? When Disney made a movie of *Peter Pan,* they kept the happy moments, but left out the essence. When Wendy's mother thinks about Peter Pan, she remembers this: When children die, Peter Pan goes partway with them. Partway to fairyland where the dead people are.

· · ·

The next day, at the 22nd Street train station, I look for the mirror. It's gone. Perhaps someone who needed a mirror picked it up. I hope they have a cat.

I sit on the bench by the tracks, sketching in my notebook as I wait for the train. In my sketch, two fairies crouch beneath the feathery fronds of a fennel plant. They wear war paint, stripes of color on their cheeks that help them blend with the shadows. One holds a spear made from a chipped stone point lashed to a pencil. He looks a bit like my father when he was younger and happier. The other fairy wears a Tinkerbell skirt, but she has a stone knife at her belt. Her face is in the shadows, but she has dark hair like my mother. It is sunny where they are. I'm glad of that.

These two are hunting for mice, I think. Tiffany's fairies drink dewdrops and sip nectar from flowers. Mine prefer protein.

The fairies look purposeful, but content. They have a simple existence: a hut to live in, mice and frogs to hunt. But that's enough.

The sun shines on the hillside covered with fennel and blackberries, on the concrete marked with messages that are not for me. In the stream, the irises are blooming.

PAT MURPHY won the Nebula Award for her 1986 science fiction novel *The Falling Woman* and also, in the same year, for her novelette "Rachel in Love." Her 1990 novella *Bones* won the World Fantasy Award, and her story collection *Points of Departure*, also published in 1990, won the Philip K. Dick Award. She has published several other science fiction and fantasy novels, including *The City, Not Long After* (1989), *Nadya: The Wolf Chronicles* (1996), and the children's novel *The Wild Girls* (2007). She lives in San Francisco.

The Hanging Game

Helen Marshall

Sometimes a game, even a sacred game, can have far-reaching consequences. In bear country, young Skye learns just how far she is willing to go to play the game properly in order to carry on the traditions that came before her and will most likely continue long after she is gone. *Edited by Ann VanderMeer.*

There was a game we used to play when we were kids—the hanging game, we called it. I don't know where it started, but I talked to a girl down in Lawford once, and she remembered playing it with jump ropes when she was about eleven, so I guess we weren't the only ones. Maybe Travers learned it from Dad, and from father to father, forever on up. I don't know. We couldn't use jump ropes, though, not those of us whose fathers worked the logging camps, climbing hundred-foot cedar spars and hooking in with the highrigging rope just so to see that bright flash of urine as they pissed on the men below.

For us the hanging game was a sacred thing, the most sacred thing we knew save for one other, which I'll have to tell you about too, and that was the bears.

What you need to know is that north of Lawford where we lived—Travers and I, Momma, Dad sometimes, when he wasn't at the camps—that was a country of blue mountains and spruce and cedar so tall they seemed to hold up the sky, what the old men called Hangjaw's country. They said the bears were his, and the hanging game was his. We all had to play, cheating death, cheating Hangjaw but paying him off at the same time in whatever way we could. Living that close to death made you kind of crazy. Take Dad, for instance. Dad's kind of crazy was the bears.

I remember one summer he killed nine of them, which was still two short of old Sullivan, the skidder man, but enough of a show of guts, of tweaking Hangjaw's beard, to keep him drinking through the winter following. He'd caught the first one the traditional way, see, but he didn't clean it how he was supposed to. He just left it out on the hill and when the next one came he shot it clean through the eye with his Remington Model Seven. He took another seven throughout the week, just sitting there on the porch with a case of beer, just waiting for when the next one came sniffing along, then down it went, until the whole place smelled thick with blood and bear piss, and Dad decided it was enough.

But we were kids and we couldn't shoot bears, so for us it was the hanging game. That was the kind of crazy we got into. Bears and hanging.

The first time I played it I was just a skinny kid of twelve with her summer freckles coming in. I remember I was worried about having my first period. Momma had started dropping hints, started trying to lay out some of the biology of how it all worked, but the words were so mysterious I couldn't tell what she was saying was going to happen to me. It scared the bejesus out of me, truth to tell.

That was when Travers took me to play the hanging game.

He was fifteen, copper headed like me, just getting his proper grown-up legs under him. He brought a spool of highrigging rope he'd scavenged from the shed, and we went down to the hollow, my hand in his, a stretch of rope with thirteen coils hanging like a live thing in his other hand. It had to be highrigging rope, he told me, not jump rope like I guess they used in Lawford. Highrigging rope for the logger kids for whom the strength of rope was the difference between life and death.

Travers stood me up on the three-legged stool that was kept for that very purpose. I remember the wind tugging around at the edges of my skirt, me worried he might see something I didn't want him to see, so I kept my fist tight around the hemline, tugging it down. But Travers, he was my brother and he wasn't looking. He tossed the end of the rope over the lowest hanging branch, easy, and then he fitted the cord around my neck.

"Close your eyes, Skye," he said. "That's a good girl."

There were rules for the hanging game. This is what they were. It had to be highrigging rope, like I said, and you had to steal it. Also it had to be an ash tree. Also you had to do it willingly. No one could force you to play the hanging game. It couldn't be a dare or a bluff or a tease, or else it wouldn't work.

I remember the rope rubbing rough against my neck. It was a sort of chafing feeling, odd, like wearing a badly knit scarf, but it didn't hurt, not at first. I let go of my dress, but by then the breeze had stilled anyway. My eyes were closed tight, because that was how you played the hanging game, we all knew that. We all knew the rules. No one had to teach them to us.

"Take my hand now, okay, Skye?"

Then Travers's hand was in mine, and it was as rough and calloused as the rope was. It felt good to hold his hand, but different than on the way over. Then he had been my brother. Now he was Priest.

"I've got you, Skye, I've got you. Now you know what to do, right?"

I nodded, tried to, but the rope pulled taut against my throat. Suddenly I was frightened, I didn't want to be there. I tried to speak, but the words got stuck. I remember trying to cough, not being able to, the desperation of trying to do something as basic as coughing and failing.

"Shh," murmured Travers. "It's okay, it's okay. Don't be afraid. You can't be afraid now, understand? Be a brave girl with me, Skye, a brave girl."

I squeezed my eyes shut. Calmed myself. Let a breath go whistling out through my lips.

"Good girl," he said. "Now lean to me."

This was the tricky part.

The stool tilted and moved under my feet. It was an old thing, and I could tell the joints were loose just by the feel of it. That movement was sickening to me, but I did like Travers said, I leaned toward him, his fingers warm against palms going cold with fear. I leaned until the rope was tight against my throat, drawing a straight line, no slack, to where it hung around the tree branch, my body taut at an angle, my toes pointed to the ground. The edge of the stool pressed into the soft space on my foot between the ball and the heel.

"Good girl," Travers told me. "Good."

God, it hurt. The rope cut into my throat, and I knew there would be bruises there tomorrow I'd have to cover up. But this was how we played.

I knew the words that were coming next, but even so, they sounded like someone else was saying them, not Travers. "Skye Thornton," he said, "I give you to Hangjaw, the Spearman, the Gallows' Burden. I give you to the Father of Bears." And he touched my left side with the hazelwand he had brought for that purpose. "Now tell me what you see."

And so I did.

· · ·

I don't remember what I told Travers.

None of us ever knew what it was we saw, and no one was ever allowed to talk about it after the fact. Those were the rules. I remember some of the stories though.

When Signy played the hanging game, she told us about how her husband in ten years' time would die highclimbing a tall spruce spar while he was throwing the rope and getting the steel spurs in. Ninety feet from the earth, it'd get hit by lightning, crazy, just like that, and he'd be fried, still strapped to the top of the thing. But the problem was she never said who that husband was gonna be, and so no one would ever go with her, no one ever took her out to the Lawford Drive-In Theatre where the rest of us went when the time came, in case she wound up pregnant by accident and the poor boy sonuva had to hitch himself to that bit of unluckiness.

That first time, I wasn't afraid so much of playing the hanging game, I was afraid of what I was going to see in Travers's eyes after. I was afraid of what he might know about me that I didn't know about myself.

When he took the noose off after and he had massaged the skin on my neck, made sure I was breathing right, I remember opening my eyes, thinking I was going to see it then. But Travers looked the same as ever, same Travers, same smile, same brother of mine. And I thought, well, I guess it's not so bad, then, whatever piece of luck it is that's coming my way.

· · ·

It was stupid, of course, but we were all taken by surprise that day things went wrong. There were four of us who had gone to play the hanging game, Travers and me, Ingrid Sullivan, the daughter of the skidder man who had killed two more bears than Dad that summer, and Barth Gibbons. Ingrid was there for Travers. She'd told me so before we set out, a secret whispered behind a cupped hand when Travers was getting the rope from the shed. But it was Barth I was there for. Barth was a year or two older, a pretty impossible age gap at that time to cross, but that didn't matter much to me. All I knew was Barth had the nicest straight-as-straw black hair I'd ever seen and wouldn't it be a fine thing if he slipped that coil around his neck and whispered something about his future wife, some red-haired, slim-hipped woman, when I was the only red-haired girl north of Lawford. That's what I remember thinking, anyway.

It was Travers who played Priest. Ingrid and I were there, really, just as Witnesses, because sometimes it was better if you had one or two along, just in case you were too busy handling the rope and you missed something. Old Hangjaw didn't like that.

But as it was, when Barth went up and played the hanging game, he didn't say anything about a red-haired, slim-hipped woman after all. He said something about a she-bear he was going to cut into one day at the start of a late spring, holed up asleep in one of those hollowed-out, rotten redwood trunks. And when he tried to open the wood up with a chainsaw, how the woodchips and blood were just going to come spewing forth, taking him by surprise. There was kind of a sick sense of disappointment in me at that, but we marked down the blood price of the she-bear anyway so that we'd be sure to let Barth know how much it was and how he could pay it when the time came.

Then up went Ingrid, and Travers, who was still Priest, which was what Ingrid wanted, held out his hand for her. She giggled and took it. She didn't seem the least bit afraid, her corn-yellow hair tied behind her, smiling at my brother, leaning toward him when he told her to.

Like I said, I don't know why we had never thought of it. I mean, of course, I'd thought of it that first time I was up there, that the stool was a rickety old thing. I'd felt it moving beneath me but then that was how it was supposed to feel, I thought, that was part of it.

But then while Ingrid was leaning in, we heard this noise, all of us, this low growling noise so deep you could feel it in the pit of your stomach. Then there was the rank smell of bear piss, which is a smell we all knew, living out in bear country.

Ingrid screamed, although that was the stupidest thing to do, and she twisted on the stool. Snap. Just as quick as that it had rolled beneath her and her feet were free, tap-dancing in the air.

It was quick as all get out.

Barth had turned and was staring into the woods, looking for that damned mother of a she-bear we had all heard, and so he hadn't seen Ingrid fall.

But I had.

She was choking bad, and her tongue had snuck out of her mouth like a thick, purple worm. Her eyes were screwed up into white gibbous moons, that yellow hair of hers twisting in the wind.

Travers had long arms even then, the biggest arms you'd ever seen, like a bear himself, and he tried to grab her, but Ingrid was still choking anyhow. I was scared of the bear, but I was more scared for Ingrid, so I took the Sharpfinger knife that Travers kept on his belt for skinning, and I made to right the stool and cut her down.

Travers, I think, was shaking his head, but I couldn't see him from behind Ingrid, whose limbs were now flailing, not like she was hanging, but like she was being electrocuted. It was Barth who stopped me. He was thinking clearer than I was.

"The wand," he said, "do it first, Skye. You have to."

And so I took the hazelwand, which Travers had dropped when he grabbed hold of Ingrid, and I smacked her in the side so hard that she almost swung out of Travers' arms. I tried to remember what Travers had said for me, but all I could come up with was Hangjaw's name. Then Travers had her good, and I was able to get on the stool and saw the blade through the highrigging rope just above the knot. She tumbled like a scarecrow and hit the ground badly, her and Travers going down together in a heap.

I looked over at Barth, absurdly still wanting him to see how good I'd been, to get her with the wand and then cut her down, but Barth, because he was still thinking of the she-bear, wasn't paying a whit's worth of attention to me.

So I looked at Ingrid instead. Her face kind of bright red with the eyes still rolled back into her skull, body shaking and dancing even though she was on the ground. Travers had gotten out from under her, and now he was putting his ear next to her. At first I thought he was trying to tell if she was still breathing, but of course, he wasn't, he was listening. He was listening to make sure he caught every word she said.

It could have only been a few seconds, that whispery grating voice I couldn't quite catch. But still it scared me even worse than seeing that stool run out underneath her feet, the sound of Ingrid's truth saying. I don't know what she said, but Travers's face went white, and when she was done her body stopped its shakes.

"Travers," I said. Even though I was scared, I wanted to be Witness still. It was my job, and so I wanted him to tell me. "Just whisper it," I told him then. "Go on."

"No use," Travers answered, and I couldn't tell quite what he was talking about but then it became clear to me. Travers let go of her head. I realized how he'd been holding it steady so he could hear, but then the neck lolled at a strange, unnatural angle, and I knew it had snapped like a wet branch during the fall.

"Old Hangjaw wanted her to pay her daddy's blood price," he said.

• • •

That frightened me something fierce. Not just that Ingrid had died, well, I'd seen death before, but the way I had seen her mouth moving even though her neck had been snapped clean through. We never played the hanging game after that. Some of the men from the camp brought down that ash tree and burned all the wood away from town where no one would breathe the smoke of it.

And so we all grew up. Those of us that could, that is.

A couple of years down the line, Travers won a scholarship and followed it south past Lawford and out of bear country. I was lonely, but I never could blame him. Dad did, though, and they never spoke much after that. And me, well, I married Barth Gibbons, even though he never whispered about a red-haired, slim-hipped woman. I guess we can all make our own luck. That's what I did that day when I was seventeen, and I went with Barth out to the Lawford Drive-In Theatre. I didn't know at the time how easy it was for something to take root in you, but several months later, after I'd been retching for a week, convinced I had a helluva stomach flu, Momma told me she reckoned I must be pregnant.

She was right, of course. Dad was pissed for a while but after Barth proposed and we got properly married then he was okay. The baby, though, didn't come the way we expected it to. She came two months too early, in a slick of blood that sure as hell smelled to me like bear piss though no one else will say so. I lost the next one that way too, and the next, just so many until I wouldn't let Barth touch me because I didn't want to see all those tiny, broken bodies laid out in the blood pooling at my legs.

Then one day, after the spring Barth bit into that she-bear and I had to knock him in the side with the hazelwand until he bled just to keep old Hangjaw happy, Travers called me up. I'd just lost another, a little boy who I had already starting trying out names for even though the doctor told me that was a god-awful bad idea to do so. And Travers said to me, "Okay, Skye, I know we can't talk about it, I know we're not supposed to, but I'm going to say anyway. You just keep going, okay, Skye? You're almost paid up."

I didn't have the heart to tell him that I couldn't do it anymore, I'd seen all of the little bodies that I could, and all I could smell was bear piss. But I loved Travers, I always had, and I remembered what it was like to hold his hand out there by the tree. I remembered the hanging game.

And so that night, though he was tired of it too and his eyes were bright and shiny and he said he couldn't face another stillbirth either, still, I kissed Barth on the mouth. Nine months later out came little Astrid, as clean and sweet smelling as any a little baby was.

So now I'm cradling that body of hers close to mine, her little thatch of black hair fluffed up like a goose and the rest of her so tightly swaddled there's nothing but a squalling face. I'm looking at her and I love this child of mine so much, more than I can rightly say. "Shh," I'm saying to her. "It's okay, it's okay. Don't be afraid now, girl."

But I can't stop thinking about that hill Dad left covered in bear bones that one summer way back when. Can't stop thinking about the nine little bodies I had to bury in the dirt before this little child of mine came along. As I'm holding her in my arms, feeling the warmth of her tucked tight against me, that thing that feels like the best thing in the world, I'm also wondering if she'll ever go out one fine afternoon to play the hanging game, and I'm wondering about the things our parents leave us, the good and the bad, and whether a thing is ever truly over.

HELEN MARSHALL is a critically acclaimed author, editor, and medievalist. After receiving a Ph.D. from the Centre for Medieval Studies at the University of Toronto, she spent two years completing a postdoctoral fellowship at the University of Oxford. She was recently appointed Lecturer of Creative Writing and Publishing at Anglia Ruskin University in Cambridge, England. Her first collection of fiction, *Hair Side, Flesh Side*, won the Sydney J. Bounds Award for Best Newcomer in 2013, and her second collection, *Gifts for the One Who Comes After*, won the World Fantasy Award and the Shirley Jackson Award in 2015, and was short-listed for the British Fantasy Award, the Bram Stoker Award, and the Aurora Award from the Canadian Science Fiction and Fantasy Association. Her stories and poetry have appeared in magazines and anthologies, including *Abyss & Apex*, *Lady Churchill's Rosebud Wristlet*, and *Tor.com*.

The Water That Falls on You from Nowhere

John Chu

In the near future, water falls from the sky whenever someone lies (either a mist or a torrential flood depending on the intensity of the lie). This makes life difficult for Matt as he maneuvers the marriage question with his lover and how best to "come out" to his traditional Chinese parents. *Hugo Award winner. Edited by Ann VanderMeer.*

The water that falls on you from nowhere when you lie is perfectly ordinary, but perfectly pure. True fact. I tested it myself when the water started falling a few weeks ago. Everyone on Earth did. Everyone with any sense of lab safety anyway. Never assume any liquid is just water. When you say "I always document my experiments as I go along," enough water falls to test, but not so much that you have to mop up the lab. Which lie doesn't matter. The liquid tests as distilled water every time.

Uttering "this sentence is false" or some other paradox leaves you with such a sense of angst, so filled with the sense of an impending doom, that most people don't last five seconds before blurting something unequivocal. So, of course, holding out for as long as possible has become the latest craze among drunk frat boys and hard men who insist on root canals without an anesthetic. Psychologists are finding the longer you wait, the more unequivocal you need to be to ever find solace.

Gus is up to a minute now and I wish he'd blurt something unequivocal. He's neither drunk, nor a frat boy. His shirt, soaked with sweat, clings to a body that has spent twenty-seven too many hours a week at the gym. His knees lock stiff, his jeans stretched across his tensed thighs. His face shrinks as if he were watching someone smash kittens with a hammer. It's a stupid game. Maybe in a few more weeks the fad will pass.

I don't know why he asked me to watch him go through with it this time, and I don't know why I'm actually doing it. Watching him suffer is like being smashed to death with a hammer myself. At least Gus is asking for it. I know I'm supposed to be rooting for him to hold on for as long as possible, but I just want him to stop. He's hurting so much and I can't stand to watch anymore.

"I love you, Matt." Gus's smile is radiant. He tackles me on the couch and smothers me in a kiss, and at first, I kiss him back.

Not only does no water fall on him, but all the sweat evaporates from his body. His shirt is warm and dry. A light, spring breeze from nowhere covers us. He smells of flowers and ozone. This makes me uneasier than if he'd been treated to a torrent. That, at least, I'd understand. I'd be sad, but I'd understand.

He's unbuttoned and unzipped my jeans when my mind snaps back to the here and now. It's not that his body doesn't have more in common with Greek statues than actual humans. It's not that he can't explicate Socrates at lengths that leave my jaw unhinged. It's that not only did "I love you, Matt" pull him out of his angst, but it actually removed water.

Fundamental laws of physics do that. Profound theorems of mathematics do that. "I love you, Matt" doesn't count as a powerful statement that holds true for all time and space. Except when Gus says it, apparently.

"Wait." I let go of him. My hands reach down to slide to a sit.

Gus stops instantly. He's skittered back before my hands have even found the couch cushions. His head tilts up at me. This is the man who seconds ago risked going insane in order to feel soul-rending pain for fun. How can he suddenly look so vulnerable?

Oh, if there's anything Gus can do, it's put up a brave front. He does that stony-faced thing where his mouth is set in a grim, straight line better than anyone I know. But behind his hard, blue eyes, I can see the fear that's not there even when some paradox rips him apart.

Best to take the pain now. I'm half-convinced nothing can actually hurt him, even when he's afraid it might. It'd only hurt him more later.

"That's some display you just did there, Gus." I'm stalling. Stop that. "I don't love you, not as much as you obviously love me."

The water that falls on you from nowhere is freezing cold. I slip on the couch, but it just follows me. When it's this much water, it numbs you to the bone. I want to scream, "What the fuck?" but if I even breathed, I'd drown. Gus tries to shield me, blocking my body with his, but not even he's fast enough. I try to push him out of the downpour. However, he's a mixed martial artist and I'm not. We share everything after the initial shock. The torrent lasts for seconds. We're both soaked and he's laughing so hard that he's fallen off the couch, doubled over on the wet floor, flopping like a fish.

I feel like I should be insulted, but his laughter is joyous. It's like the peal of giant bells, low booms that vibrate through you and make everything in the room rattle. I can't tell if those are tears on his face, or just the water from nowhere.

My body shakes so hard, I can't stand. The cushions squeak around me, keeping me bathed in ice-cold water. Gus stands up. He's not even shivering. He picks me up, wraps me in his arms, then kisses me gently on the forehead.

"I'm sorry, Gus. I just ruined your couch." The floor is covered in rubber weight-lifting mats. I'll mop that up once I can move again.

This just sends him into another fit of laughter, more controlled this time. His hands are gentle around my waist. Without them, I'm pretty sure I'd crash onto the floor.

"You've just told me that you love me in I think the only way you can, and you're worried about the couch?"

Coming from anyone else, that sentence would make me feel too stupid to live. Still, he has a point. I fumble but can't find any words to answer.

"It'll dry off," Gus says. "Besides, you bought the couch for me."

Biotech engineers make more money than personal trainers, even the world's most overqualified ones. Who knew? Rather than actually moving in together, I've been slowly furnishing his apartment. Gus has patiently assumed that once the apartment no longer looks like a cross between a library and a weight room, I'll move in. He's long offered to move in with me, but I don't want him to. My efficiency isn't worthy of him. It's just a body locker.

"I should clean up the mess I made." I pull away and Gus catches me before I fall. He literally sweeps me off my feet.

"Stop fretting. It's okay."

We get out of our wet clothes in the bathroom and huddle together under blankets in bed. It isn't until he starts shivering that I realize he's just as cold as I am. The mixed martial artist has just been more heroic, or stupid, about it.

"You know." Gus's voice is surprisingly steady given how his teeth chatter. "Now that we know how we feel about each other, how about we solemnize the relationship? Make it official."

My brow furrows so tightly, it hurts. He's serious. As lightly as he tossed it off, he meant it.

"You risked permanent insanity just to ask me to marry you?" Honestly, there are less life-threatening ways.

"No, that was just training." He's not joking. "I can't imagine life without you. You can't imagine life without me. Say yes?"

The air stays resolutely dry. He could have made it all one big question to avoid letting whatever makes the water fall have a say.

"My family . . ." I have no idea how to broach this. It's totally possible for him to love me and still never want to see me again.

"They know about me, right?" I swear the man reads minds.

"Yes?" It's not a lie, but it's not the truth either. The air gets distinctly humid. My arm hairs stand on end, as if thunder were about to strike. I'm still shivering from my last lie. My mind is in tatters, torn between the cruel truth that will make him lose all respect for me and the blatant lie that will plunge me into fatal hypothermia. The pang that gnaws at my heart grows and spreads. It wrings me, twisting and squeezing the life out of me. I jerk my face into what I want to be a smile.

"Matt, this isn't a root canal. Don't stretch it out. Whatever you have to say, it's okay."

I take a deep breath. The release of saying something true though warms me as if I were buried in Gus's arms on a winter's night and we were the only people in the world. No wonder all the cool kids suspend themselves between truth and lie. However, rehearsing this speech for months in my head has not helped one bit. The words rush out so quickly, I'm not even sure what I'm saying.

"Mandarin doesn't have gender-specific third-person pronouns. Well, the written language does, but it's a relatively recent invention and they all sound the same and no one really uses the female and neuter variants anyway. And it's not like there aren't words for 'boyfriend' or 'girlfriend,' but I always refer to you as ' 愛人.' It means 'sweetheart,' 'lover,' 'spouse.' And never using your name isn't all that unusual. Names are for friends and acquaintances. Members of your family you refer to by title—"

When Gus interrupts me, the only thought in my mind is "Did I just tell him that I call him my spouse to my parents?"

"Wait. Slow down." Gus's intellect trains on me like a sharpshooter. "The way you talk about me to your family, we might as well be married?"

"Yes." My stomach is in my throat. The world bobbles around me and I'm stumbling at a cliff's edge.

"But they don't know my name, or that I'm male."

"Yes." His bullet strikes my heart and I've just crashed on the rocky shore.

"Hmm." He wears his "I'm going to fix this" face, but then it hardens into that grim, stony thing that breaks my heart. He nudges himself against me, then holds me as if only I can fit in that gap between his arms and chest. "We can't marry until you're ready to come out to your family. I'll wait as long as you want."

His skin transforms from cold and clammy to warm and dry. He uses declarative sentences. The truth of each one is obvious. No weasel words or qualifiers. Instead of being soaked in water though, Gus is soaked in disappointment. Normally, his smile glows and I melt in its heat. Right now, he's wearing a cheap copy. He's about as likely to admit that I've hurt him as he is to use anesthesia.

This isn't like him. I expected an argument. I mean, I should have come out to my family a decade ago. If they don't suspect anything, it's because I'm still years younger than Dad was when he married Mom. Instead, we behave as if I hadn't just said no to him, albeit tacitly.

Gus chatters on about Procopius's *Wars of Justinian*. He's just finished volume four, in the original Greek. I talk about stem cells and gene splicing. It's as if tonight were any other night I'm over, and we're just catching each other up on how our day went. His hands and his tone slowly ask if I'm interested even though he always interests me. I'm still cold and he covers me with his now warm body. The thoughtful smile, the affectionate way he holds me, nuzzles and kisses my neck, they try so hard to let me know that everything is fine between us, that he desires me as much as I desire him. He's not aggressive. We'll go as slowly as I want.

"Let's visit my family this Christmas. The two of us." My voice is louder than I'd expected. "Not the 'Christ is born' Christmas, but the 'get together with family and give presents to the nieces' Christmas. We stopped when my sister and I outgrew the whole Christmas-present thing, but when she had kids, we started again. With the water falling now, I wanted to skip this year for my own sanity but—"

"Stop." He's on his side, his arm around me. He's not as happy as I want him to be. "Are you sure? I can wait years if that's what you want."

"I should have done this a long time ago. I don't think I'll ever be any more ready." If Gus realizes that I'm outing myself to my family for him, he'll probably refuse to go out of sheer principle. I'm not sure I can do it with him, but I know I can't do it without him.

Gus senses that all I want is to be held so that's all he does. The condoms stay in the drawer. He drifts off to sleep, and I lie next to him listening to the calm rhythm of his breath. I'm the only son. All I can think about is my parents' "you're responsible for carrying on the family name because when your sister marries she will become part of her husband's family" speech. It freaked me out even before I'd come out to myself.

• • •

The family gathers in the atrium of my sister's mansion as we stomp the Christmas Eve storm off our boots. The high vaulted ceiling has room for the sweeping staircase and the Christmas tree, big enough to dwarf Gus, that sits in the handrail's curve. Ornaments. Tinsel. Holly. Ivy. A copy of Michelangelo's God giving Adam life tacked taut on the atrium ceiling. We've entered Victorian Christmas Land. No half measures here.

The disappointment when the family sees that my friend is a man is palpable. It's like the adults were all my nieces' age and someone told them there was no Santa Claus. Mom asks me if we've eaten. According to the textbooks, it's a polite greeting, but she always means it literally. If I tell her I'm not hungry, she'll say, "不餓還需要吃啊." (Even if you're not hungry, you still need to eat.) That must be true, since that never causes the water to fall. Fortunately, rather than being forced to eat dinner again, this time I have Gus to derail the conversation.

I introduce him to my parents, my sister, Michele, her husband, Kevin, their kids, Tiffany and Amber, and, to my surprise, Kevin's parents. As I negotiate the simultaneous translation, a horrible thought hits me. Everyone in the room speaks at least two languages, but there isn't one language everyone speaks. Beside English, Gus speaks only dead languages. Kevin's parents speak Cantonese and Mandarin, but not English. My parents haven't needed English since they retired, not that theirs was good before. I've trapped Gus in a mansion where he can't speak to half the people. Repeatedly slamming my head against the handrail now would send the wrong message, so I don't.

The instant Gus crouches down and starts talking to the nieces, they stop being scared of him and start playing with him. All physically imposing people seem to be able to win over little kids in mere seconds. They head off to the living room. I start to join them when my sister marches me into her home office.

"How dare you?" She slams the door behind her and I remind myself that I'm bigger than her now and it'd be harder for her to beat me up. "Are you trying to kill Mom and Dad?"

Well, that was easier than I'd expected. She knows and I didn't even have to tell her. Also, I've broken my record. It usually takes an entire day before I make her angry. At this rate, I could be kicked out of the house and in a motel room by sunrise. I reserve one for every trip. She gets all offended if I don't stay with her at first.

"No." Ideally, Mom and Dad accept it. That can happen. "I want everyone to meet the man I'm going to marry."

The future's not fixed, but right now, Gus and I are headed toward marriage, so the air stays dry. She slaps me. My cheek stings. I'd slap her back but I need to out myself to our parents before she throws me out of the house.

"Mom and Dad always let you get away with being selfish, don't they? I don't do whatever I want." She's blocking the door. "Doesn't it matter to you that you're embarrassing Mom and Dad in front of 婆婆 and 公公?"

Phrasing things in the form of a question. That and weasel words work as insurance against the water that falls from nowhere. They just make it extremely obvious that you're hedging against the truth.

"Like I knew your husband's parents were even coming." Not that I'm embarrassing Mom and Dad. Well, not this time anyway.

"Your job, 何德培"—my full name in Chinese including family name, just in case it isn't clear she's furious at me—"is to give our parents a grandson."

We both already know this. She just enjoys showing me the dry air.

"I don't think I can do that by myself." I wish I hadn't said that.

She slaps me again. My cheek hasn't stopped stinging from last time.

"Do you love Mom and Dad? Dump that slab of beef. Find a Chinese woman to marry. Put your penis in her vagina and make Mom and Dad a grandson. Make them happy."

She turns to leave but not two steps stomp by before she whips around. Coming out to Mom and Dad, she hasn't ordered me not to do it yet.

"And you're not coming out to Mom and Dad." With that command, she leaves. No water. She must mean it. She'll never leave me alone with Mom or Dad.

I close my eyes and remind myself why I'm doing this. Right. Gus. He refuses to stop insisting it's okay if I don't come out to them. He'll understand if I don't. That just makes me want to do what he really wants, but won't say out loud. Coming out would have hurt less a decade ago and it'll hurt less now than a decade from now. Unless I just keep quiet and wait for my entire family to die off. Now there's a cheery thought.

• • •

Christmas day. When I wake, Gus is most of the way through his forms, his movements silent and precise. I make an exaggerated show of sneaking out of the bedroom. His face cracks the tiniest smile when I look back at him from the door.

My sister pointedly ushered us to different rooms last night. I return to the den where I was supposed to sleep to get ready to join Dad for his daily early-morning walk. It's awful. We'll plod in circles at some local mall while I try to get him to talk about himself and he answers in single syllables. At least this time, I'll actually have something to talk to him about. I guess I've had something to talk to him about for years. This time, though, I'm going to do it.

When I get downstairs, my sister insists on joining us. First time in . . . Actually, she's never done the morning-walk thing with Dad before.

"Great, sis." I start back up the stairs. "You go with Dad to the mall this time. See you two later."

I ignore her sputterings. If she wants Dad to keep thinking that she's their

Good Child, she won't dare to do anything to me right now, and she'll go with Dad on the mall walk. I'll pay for this later, of course, but by the time she comes back, Mom will have woken up and I will have had a chat with her.

Or at least that was Plan B. The morning-walk ritual is supposed to be that, after the walk, he goes to have his sausage biscuit, luxuriates over a cup of coffee, two if you count the free refill. Only then do we come home. However, they're home too early. Mom's still asleep. My sister has apparently forced Dad to skip the fast-food-breakfast part of his morning ritual.

When I hear the garage door, I lean over the sweeping staircase's handrail. Dad's grumbling. My sister's chirping bright words about how the kitchen has something just as good. She glares at me as she rushes Dad past. Like it's my fault he's angry at her.

The rest of the day is like an extremely tedious game of basketball. My sister plays a tight defense, but legal. No contact while there are witnesses. Since I'm trying to get time alone with my parents, one of them is always a witness.

She's even helping Mom make tonight's feast. I'm kneading the dough for Mom's steamed, stuffed buns when my sister inserts herself into the process. After years of preparing meals for large gatherings together, Mom and I have a system. At some point, she stopped insisting that my wife would cook for me someday and started teaching me to cook. Either she got sick of me nagging her, or she realized I kneaded dough more quickly than she did. Anyway, with some luck, dinner won't be too much later than if my sister had just left us alone.

Gus is doing his best imitation of an apartment mate who had nowhere else to go for Christmas. I wish he'd stop that. He spends time with my nieces, my brother-in-law, even my parents, but he only skirts the kitchen. I get that he doesn't want to out me for me, but I like his conversation too. It's stupid to be in the same house as him and still miss him so much. After my first few whacks at the duck with the cleaver, Mom takes the heavy knife away from me, then tells me to go re-hydrate mushrooms.

It doesn't take a solid day of cooking to make dinner, but my sister conveniently has questions about how to make the filling for the stuffed buns and how much sesame oil for the scallion pancakes. She leaves the kitchen occasionally, but never long enough for me to work up the nerve to tell Mom. Whenever I leave the kitchen, it isn't two minutes before she finds me, claiming she needs my help. I manage to say, "Yes, I think you're a terrible cook too" in front of her husband and her parents-in-law in our respective languages in common before she drags me back to the kitchen. Water doesn't fall when I say that. I have to take my pleasure where I can.

When the nieces pull Mom away to play with their Erector Set, she decides that my sister and I can finish dinner without her. My sister complains that she needs Mom's help. I agree wholeheartedly, but it's not enough. The two of us are stuck with each other.

"You do know why Gus doesn't come into the kitchen, don't you?" Despite her casual tone, we both know this is not idle chatter.

"Does it matter?" I'm slicing pickled radishes. "You're going to tell me anyway."

"Do you really think you can keep him?" She drops spinach into a skillet pooled with oil. The water coating the spinach hits the oil and splatters back at her. "He's spent more time with Kevin today than with you."

I force myself to slice slowly. Cutting my fingers off is a distraction I don't need right now. My heart pounds in my ears. I'm not sure who I'm more angry at, my sister or my lover.

"I have no idea what you mean, sis." We immigrated here when she was a teenager and I was a little kid. There's a good chance she'll miss the sarcasm. The water gets it though and I stay dry.

"Kevin's a good-looking guy, maybe . . ." The line would have more impact if she didn't look scared of the spinach sautéing before her. She jabs the spatula as if it were a fencing foil.

Kevin's not my type. I'm pretty sure he's not Gus's, but I guess I don't know. It's not like he didn't date lots of men before me. It's not as if they don't all throw themselves at him. My mind spins for seconds before I realize she hasn't actually accused Gus of anything. Kevin is stolidly straight, and if Gus has tried anything with Kevin, not that he would, she'd throw Gus and me out of the house, not taunt me with the possibility that Gus might be unfaithful.

"Maybe what?" Usually, I don't have this much trouble arranging sliced radishes in a pretty pattern. Right now, they're just a bunch of ugly yellow discs.

"You understand what I'm saying. I shouldn't have to spell it out. You don't trust your own sister?"

When I was eight, she convinced me that she was psychic, then foretold exactly how horrible my life would be if I didn't do exactly as she said. It's embarrassing how many years she got away with it. If the water had been falling back then, she'd have flooded the house.

"Only your family loves you enough to tell you this." Listening to her is like being pelted by rocks. "What can he possibly see in you? Dump him and marry a nice Chinese woman instead. Stay with him and he'll cheat on you or dump you."

Three words into her last sentence, I know what she'll say. I leap to pull her pan away as I shut off the burner. The water that falls from nowhere drenches her and the burner where the pan was. Had the water hit the pan, the steam and splattered oil would have burned her.

"Go get warm." I plate the spinach onto a dish on the counter. "I'll mop up the water."

"People change, but maybe he'll still love you, even as you shut him out like you have me, Mom, and Dad." Her arms wrap around her body and her words come out between chatters. "We still do, but I wonder why we bother. You'll break Mom and Dad's hearts if you never pass their name and blood on. Are you really willing to abandon your family for that man?"

She stomps off before I can answer. Hiding so much of myself from my family, in retrospect, that totally counts as shutting them out. There was only so much of my life I could share with them. Once the water began falling I couldn't even lie to them. But I hid because I wanted to keep them, not abandon them.

• • •

Dinner is going well, too well. My sister is a gracious hostess, too gracious to complain when Gus and I sit next to each other. Instead, her eyes question my every action. Why is my right hand below the table? Why am I spooning tofu onto Gus's plate? What am I saying when I whisper into his ear?

Gus eats as if he has pig's ear and cow's tripe every Christmas. When we get home, the next time it's my turn to cook, he's getting pig's blood soup for dinner. I've wasted years afraid he'd hate my favorite foods.

My nieces love him. They stop dueling each other with chopsticks when he asks them to. To half the adults at the table, he may as well be speaking classical Greek, but they laugh at his jokes and listen with rapt attention as he talks about the time it thunderstormed as he and his brother were climbing the steep eastern face of Mount Whitney. My mom resuscitates stories of her childhood in 台南. Even my sister is sick of those stories. Gus, however, asks about raising chickens and about the grandmother I barely remember. Okay, I'm translating like mad, but the point is they enjoy Gus's company and Gus enjoys theirs. In the rapid-fire exchange of words, my parents surprise me by asking about my research in biotech. I almost forget the impending doom hanging over me like an uttered paradox.

"你已經三十多歲了," my sister's father-in-law says as I'm clearing the table after dinner. "你甚麼時候會給你的父母生孫子?"

No family meal is complete without the marriage question. Actually, it's always some variant of "You're over thirty. Where's the grandson?" Marriage is just the necessary precondition.

I think I'm smiling blandly, but Gus's eyes reach mine and I realize he sees the marriage question on my face. It's hard to believe the man doesn't read minds. My sister's glare is this pressure that squeezes my chest.

Telling everyone I haven't met the right woman might humidify air, but it won't cause the water to fall. It's true so I won't even feel any angst. Gus will understand and, for once, my sister will be happy with me. She and I can't be in the same room for ten minutes but we've always wanted the best for each other. But she doesn't need to tell me what that is anymore.

"我找到了我的對象. Gus." I've come this far; I might as well go all the way. "他上月向我求婚."

Providing a grandson can't be that important in the grand scheme of things. Kevin's parents still love him. Maybe mine will still love me. And they seem to like Gus as my friend. Now that they know he's proposed, maybe they'll also love him as their son-in-law.

My sister's fury explodes and overwhelms every other reaction in the room. Her words are clearly in English, but the only ones that make any sense are "Get out, and don't ever come back." Kevin's trying to calm her down. Gus weaves around the family toward me. However, I'm upstairs in the bedroom before I realize I've moved.

Gus is extremely tidy. It's easy to repack his luggage. I never unpacked so I don't have to repack. He's such a generous soul. For all I know, he may still think we're not leaving. I shouldn't have left him downstairs. Maybe the nieces can translate for him.

"Matt, you're leaving out of spite." The doorjamb neatly frames Gus. "Okay, your sister had a bad reaction, but poe poe and gohng gohng don't seem to be taking it badly."

I blink and shake my head. It takes me a few seconds to realize that he's talking about my parents.

"Did you just call my parents 婆婆 and 公公?"

"Yeah, poe poe and gohng gohng." He looks confused. "I tried to call them Mr. and Mrs. Ho this afternoon, but they both corrected me before I got past hello. Am I pronouncing it wrong?"

"We can work on that, but that's not my point." I shut his suitcase. "'婆婆' means husband's mother and '公公' means husband's father."

That he can call them that without water falling on him . . .

"They'd already figured us out." Gus steps into the room to make space for Mom, trying to burrow past him. "Hi, poe poe."

"Lonely boy." My mom looks at Gus, but points at me. "He always lonely boy."

I really wish she'd just let me translate for her. In Chinese, she's effortlessly witty and erudite. That's the person I want Gus to know, not the inchoate stranger I knew until I'd spent a decade trying to get my Chinese up to snuff.

Gus takes her hands and doesn't speak too loud or down to her. Metaphorically, that is. Literally, he's about a foot taller than Mom.

"Not if I can help it, poo-oh poo-oh." He's trying too hard to imitate the way I said it and now he's overpronouncing. "I'll make sure he's never lonely again."

Mom turns to me. At first, I think she wants a translation, but she must have understood because she doesn't give me a chance to speak.

"你是研究生物科技的. 孫子能給我嗎? 有你們兩個的基因的?" Okay, this isn't an example of her being witty or erudite. My mom is also very practical and direct.

I hear my heart pound. Gus is looking at me for a translation. We don't have a relationship if I filter what he hears.

"She said: You're a biotech researcher. Can you give me a grandson? One with genes from both of you?" Gus must have really impressed her. "What were you two talking about this afternoon?"

"Not that." He looks as surprised as I feel. We've never discussed kids. He turns back to her. "We need to talk about it."

And I need to win a Nobel Prize if she's dead set on a grandson with both our genes. Parents.

The clincher is that she leaves, trusting Gus to talk me back from the edge. Normally, she tells me that once Michele calms down, she'll want me to stay. Michele's only angry at me because she loves me. But now, it's Gus's job to keep me civil. Mom's probably so happy about this, she doesn't care that Gus is a guy. Gus isn't any better at keeping me from the edge than Mom though.

. . .

The motel is a five-minute drive from my sister's house, but it feels like another planet. For one thing, we've gone from Victorian Christmas Land to Operating Surgery Land. It still smells like pine, but the flat, medicinal one. For another, when I drop my suitcase and curl into a ball on the bed, it's as if I've held one of Gus's bizarre isometric exercises for weeks and I've finally let go. Just like the end of any other trip home except this time I'm still tethered to the world. Gus stands at the door. Snowflakes glisten off his hair and hooded sweatshirt.

"They're your only blood relatives in the country." Gus flicks on the light and clicks the door shut. When I turn away, his weight dents the bed. My body falls toward his. "Matt, don't freeze me out too."

Gus's words pummel me no matter how softly he tosses them. My own words scrape my throat. I taste salt and metal when I swallow. Lying then letting the water wash my throat and fill my lungs tempts me as much as pretending Gus isn't sitting on the bed. Every trip, I decide that I'll sort things out later. Then I go home and pretend the trip never happened. That won't work this time. Gus is, if nothing else, a witness and a reminder.

"Fine." I sit up and stare at the carpet. "Once, I gave Mom flowers for Mother's Day and Michele humiliated me because flowers wilt and how dare I send Mom something that would die. Michele accused me of ruining her birthday because one year I sent her a card with blue birds on it. Like I knew her parakeet had drowned itself in her toilet. One Christmas Eve, Michele asked me to shave for Christmas day. I didn't really have any stubble so I forgot. She couldn't understand why I would refuse to do something to make her happy, especially something so simple, so she ambushed me with a razor. I wish she had better aim. Shaving cream stings your eyes. For weeks people wondered why I had scars around my neck and on my face. Is that enough, or do you want more? Why should I have to keep putting up with her?"

I am so tired. My body won't stop shaking. Air won't stay in my lungs. Melted snow pools around my boots. I wish Gus weren't looming over me. I wish he were in his apartment, or visiting his own family.

Gus sits, mouth agape, for a moment, but if he expected water to fall on me, he's done a terrific job of not showing it. His arm straps across my shoulders and pulls me to him. He presses a finger under my chin and guides my head until I face him.

Part of me wants to bolt, get into the rental car and find somewhere else to stay for the night. The rest of me knows that'll hurt Gus and he'll be too much the hero to admit it. Like screwing up all of my relationships at the same time is a good idea.

"You shouldn't have to put up with her." Gus unzips my jacket, then peels it off me. "But are you going to write your parents off too? Say we have a kid, and I'm not saying we should or shouldn't, don't you want the kid to know their grandparents?"

"So I'm right and she wins anyway?"

I rub my face. Telling me I'm right is a change. Once, Mom told me everything Michele does to me, she does because she loves me and wants the best for me. Why couldn't she just hate me instead, I asked. That talk didn't go well.

"What do you mean by winning?" Gus shrugs. He hangs my jacket on the coat-rack next to the door. "You broke today. It happens. Maybe some time away from her is a good thing. Tomorrow, we'll go back and we'll try it again, okay? If you want, I'll stick to you the whole day."

I take a deep breath. It feels like the first time my lungs have expanded in hours. The pine and wet leather assault my nose. "Sure."

I take off my boots. Melted snow has soaked through to my socks. My feet are cold and clammy. Gus is still standing at the door.

"I'll be back in a few hours." Gus holds a hand up to interrupt me when I ask him to stay. "You don't want me around and frankly, right now, you're too wigged out to be good company. I know you're not angry at me, but it'll be better in the long run if I leave now while we're still on speaking terms."

I'd protest but that would just make his point. Gus turns out the lights before he leaves. The comforter is wet from melted snow. It sticks to my skin when I fall into bed. I curl up into a ball and roll the comforter over me. Buried, I finally start to relax.

This time, I have left the world but it still doesn't feel right. The mattress ought to be sunk deeper. My arms should be around the hulk of a man who can't ever admit hurt or pain. I should be immersed in the warmth of his body as he is in mine.

"I love you, Gus." Now, I just have to figure out how to say it while he's in the room.

Snow evaporates off the comforter. I'm warm and dry. I wriggle my head out. Flowers and ozone replace the smell of pine. A spring breeze grazes me. I stare at the door in the dark, wishing it would open.

JOHN CHU is a microprocessor architect by day and a writer, translator, and podcast narrator by night. His fiction has appeared or is forthcoming in *Boston Review*, *Uncanny Magazine*, *Asimov's*, *Clarkesworld*, and *Tor.com*, among other venues. His translations have been published or are forthcoming at *Clarkesworld*, *The Big Book of Science Fiction*, and other venues.

A Cup of Salt Tears

Isabel Yap

Makino's mother taught her caution, showed her how to carve her name into cucumbers, and insisted that she never let a kappa touch her. But when she grows up and her husband, Tetsuya, falls deathly ill, a kappa that claims to know her comes calling with a barbed promise. *Edited by Carl Engle-Laird.*

Someone once told Makino that women in grief are more beautiful. *So I must be the most beautiful woman in the world right now*, she thinks, as she shucks off her boots and leaves them by the door. The warm air of the onsen's changing room makes her skin tingle. She slips off her stockings, skirt, and blouse; folds her underwear and tucks her glasses into her clean clothes; picks up her bucket of toiletries, and enters the washing area. The thick, hot air is difficult to breathe. She lifts a stool from the stack by the door, walks to her favorite spot, and squats down, resting for a few beats.

Kappa kapparatta.

Kappa rappa kapparatta.

She holds the shower nozzle and douses herself in warm water, trying to get the smell of sickness off her skin.

Tottechitteta.

She soaps and shampoos with great deliberation, repeating the rhyme in her head: *kappa snatched; kappa snatched a trumpet. The trumpet blares.* It is welcome nonsense, an empty refrain to keep her mind clear. She rinses off, running her fingers through her sopping hair, before standing and padding over to the edge of the hot bath. It is a blessing this onsen keeps late hours; she can only come once she knows Tetsuya's doctors won't call her. She tests the water with one foot, shuddering at the heat, then slips in completely.

No one else ever comes to witness her grief, her pale lips and sallow skin. Once upon a time, looking at her might have been a privilege; she spent some years smiling within the pages of *Cancam* and *Vivi*, touting crystal-encrusted fingernails and perfectly glossed lips. She never graced a cover, but she did spend a few weeks on the posters for *Liz Lisa* in Shibuya 109. It was different after she got married and left Tokyo, of course. She and Tetsuya decided to move back to her hometown. Rent was cheaper, and there were good jobs for doctors like him. She quickly found work at the bakery, selling melon pan and croissants. Occasionally they visited her mother, who, wanting little else from life, had grown sweet and mellow with age. Makino thought she understood that well; she had been quite content, until Tetsuya fell ill.

She wades to her favorite corner of the bath and sinks down until only her head is above the water. She squeezes her eyes shut. *How long will he live*, she thinks, *how long will we live together?*

She hears a soft splash and opens her eyes. Someone has entered the tub, and seems to be approaching her. She sinks deeper, letting the water cover her upper lip. As the figure nears, she sees its features through the mist: the green flesh, the webbed hands, the sara—the little bowl that forms the top of its head—filled with water that wobbles as it moves. It does not smell of rotting fish at all. Instead, it smells like a river, wet and earthy. Alive. Some things are different: It is more man-sized than child-sized, it has flesh over its ribs; but otherwise it looks just as she always imagined.

"Good evening," the kappa says. The words spill out of its beak, smoothly liquid.

Makino does not scream. She does not move. Instead she looks at the closest edge of the bath, measuring how long her backside will be exposed if she runs. She won't make it. She presses against the cold tile and thinks, *Tetsuya needs me*, thinks, *no, that's a lie, I can't even help him*. Her fear dissipates, replaced by helplessness, a brittle calm.

"This is the women's bath," she says. "The men's bath is on the other side."

"Am I a man?"

She hears the ripples of laughter in its voice, and feels indignant, feels ashamed.

"No. Are you going to eat me?"

"Why should I eat you, when you are dear to me?" Its round black eyes glimmer at her in earnest.

The water seems to turn from hot to scalding, and she stands upright, flushed and dizzy. "I don't know who you are!" she shouts. "Go away!"

"But you do know me. You fell into the river and I buoyed you to safety. You fell into the river and I kissed your hair."

"That wasn't you," she says, but she never did find out who it was. She thinks about certain death, thinks, *is it any different from how I live now?* It can't possibly know this about her, can't see the holes that Tetsuya's illness has pierced through her; but then, what *does* it know?

"I would not lie to you," it says, shaking its head. The water in its sara sloshes gently. "Don't be afraid. I won't touch you if you don't wish me to."

"And why not?" She lifts her chin.

"Because I love you, Makino."

. . .

She reads to Tetsuya from the book on her lap, even when she knows he isn't listening. He stares out the window with glassy eyes, tracing the movements of invisible birds. The falling snow is delicate, not white so much as the ghost of white, the color of his skin. Tetsuya never liked fairytales much, but she indulges herself, because the days are long, and she hates hospitals. The only things she can bear to read are the stories of her childhood, walls of words that keep back the tide of desperation when Tetsuya turns to her and says, "Excuse me, but I would like to rest now."

It's still better than the times when he jerks and lifts his head, eyes crowding with tears, and says, "I'm so sorry, Makino." Then he attempts to stand, to raise himself from the bed, but of course he can't, and she must rush over and put her hand on his knee to keep him from moving, she must kiss his forehead and each of his wet eyes and tell him, "No, it's all right, it's all right." There is a cadence to the words that makes her almost believe them.

Tetsuya is twelve years her senior. They met just before she started her modeling career. He was not handsome. There was something monkeylike about his features, and his upper lip formed a strange peak over his lower lip. But he was gentle, careful; a doctor-in-training with the longest, most beautiful fingers she had ever seen. He was a guest at the home of her tea-ceremony sensei. When she handed the cup to him, he cradled her fingers in his for a moment, so that her skin was trapped between his hands and the hot ceramic. When he raised the drink to his lips, his eyes kept darting to her face, though she pretended not to notice by busying herself with the next cup.

He thanked her then as he does now, shyly, one stranger to another.

· · ·

She has barely settled in the bath when it appears.

"You've come back," it says.

She shrugs. Her shoulders bob out of the water. As a girl Makino was often chided for her precociousness by all except her mother, who held her own odd beliefs. Whenever they visited a temple, Makino would whisper to the statues, hoping they would give her some sign they existed—a wink, maybe, or a small utterance. Some kind of blessing. She did this even in Tokyo DisneySea, to the statue of Rajah the Tiger, the pet of her beloved Princess Jasmine. There was a period in her life when she wanted nothing more than to be a Disney Princess.

It figures, of course, that the only yōkai that ever speaks to her is a kappa. The tips of its dark hair trail in the water, and its beaklike mouth is half open in an expression she cannot name. The ceiling lights float gently in the water of its sara.

She does not speak, but it does not go away. It seems content to watch her. *Can't you leave me here, with my grief?*

"Why do you love me?" she asks at last.

It blinks slowly at her, pale green lids sliding over its eyes. She tries not to shudder, and fails.

"Your hips are pale like the moon, yet move like the curves of ink on parchment. Your eyes are broken and delicate and your hands are empty." It drifts closer. "Your hair is hair I've kissed before; I do not forget the hair of women I love."

I am an ugly woman now, she thinks, but looking at its gaze, she doesn't believe that. Instead she says, "Kappa don't save people. They drown them."

"Not I," it says.

Makino does not remember drowning in the river. She does not remember any of those days spent in bed. Her mother told her afterward that a policeman saved her, or it might have been the grocer's son, or a teacher from the nearby elementary school. It was a different story each time. It was only after she was rescued that they finally patched the broken portion of the bridge. But that was so many years ago, a legend of her childhood that was smeared clear by time, whitewashed by age. She told Tetsuya about it once, arms wrapped around his back, one leg between his thighs. He kissed her knuckles and told her she was lucky, it was a good thing she didn't die then, so that he could meet her and marry her and make love to her, the most beautiful girl in the world.

She blinks back tears and holds her tongue.

"I will tell you a fairytale," the kappa says, "because I know you love fairytales. A girl falls into a river—"

"Stop," she says, "I don't want to hear it." She holds out her hands, to keep it from moving closer. "My husband is dying."

• • •

Tetsuya is asleep during her next visit. She cradles his hand in hers, running her thumb over his bony fingers—so wizened now, unable to heal anyone. She recalls the first time she noticed her love for him. She was making koicha, tea to be shared among close companions, under her teacher's watchful gaze. Tetsuya wasn't even present, but she found herself thinking of his teeth, his strange nervous laughter, the last time he took her out for dinner. The rainbow lights of Roppongi made zebra stripes across his skin, but he never dared kiss her, not even when she turned as the train was coming, looking at him expectantly. He never dared look her in the eye, not until she told him she would like to see him again, fingers resting on his sleeve.

She looked down at the tea she was whisking and thought, *This tastes like earth, like the bone marrow of beautiful spirits, like the first love I've yet to have. It is green like the color of spring leaves and my mother's favorite skirt and the skin of a kappa. I'm in love with him.* She whisked the tea too forcefully, some of it splashing over the edge of the cup.

"Makino!" her sensei cried.

She stood, heart drumming in her chest, bowed, apologized, bowed again. The tea had formed a butterfly-shaped splotch on the tatami mats.

Tetsuya's sudden moan jolts her from her thoughts—a broken sound that sets her heart beating as it did that moment, long ago. She spreads her palm over his brow.

Does a kappa grant wishes? Is it a water god? Will it grant my wish, if I let it touch me? Will I let it touch me?

She gives Tetusya's forehead a kiss. "Don't leave me before the New Year," she says. She really means *don't leave me.*

• • •

This time, it appears while she's soaping her body.

It asks if it can wash her hair.

She remains crouched on her stool. The suggestion of touch makes her tremble, but she keeps her voice even. "Why should I let you?"

"Because you are dear to me."

"That isn't true," she says. "I do know about you. You rape women and eat organs and trick people to get their shirikodama, and I'm not giving you that, I'm not going to let you stick your hand up my ass. I don't want to die. And Tetsuya needs me."

"What if I tell you I need you? What if I could give you what you want? What if I . . ." It looks down at the water, and for a moment, in the rising mist, it looks like Tetsuya, when she first met him. Hesitant and wondering and clearly thinking of her. Monkeylike, but somehow pleasing to her eyes. "What if I could love you like him?"

"You're not him," she says. Yet when it reaches out to touch her, she does not flinch. Its fingers in her hair are long and slim and make her stomach curl, and she only stops holding her breath when it pulls away.

• • •

The grocery is full of winter specials: Christmas cakes, discounted vegetables for nabe hotpot, imported hot-chocolate mixes. After Christmas is over, these shelves will be rapidly cleared and filled with New Year specials instead, different foods for osechi-ryori. Her mother was always meticulous about a good New Year's meal: herring roe for prosperity, sweet potatoes for wealth, black soybeans for health, giant shrimp for longevity. They're only food, however; not spells, not magic. She ignores the bright display and walks to the fresh vegetables, looking for things to add to her curry.

She's almost finished when she sees the pile of cucumbers, and ghostlike, over it, the kitchen of her childhood. Mother stands next to her, back curved in concentration. She is carving Makino's name into a cucumber's skin with a toothpick. "We'll throw this in the river," Mother says, "so that the kappa won't eat you."

"Does the kappa only appear in the river, Mother? And why would the kappa want to eat me?"

"Because it likes the flesh of young children, it likes the flesh of beautiful girls. You must do this every year, and every time you move. And don't let them touch you, darling. I am telling you this for you are often silly, and they are cruel; do not let them touch you."

"But what if it does touch me, Mother?"

"Then you are a foolish girl, and you cannot blame me if it eats up everything inside you."

Young Makino rubs the end of the cucumber.

Is there no way to befriend them, Mother? But she doesn't say those words, she merely thinks them, as her mother digs out the last stroke, the tail end of *no* in *Ma-ki-no.*

She frowns at the display, or perhaps at the memory. *If I throw a cucumber in the hot spring it will merely be cooked,* she thinks. She buys a few anyway. At home, she hesitates, and then picks one up and scratches in Tetsuya's name with a knife. She drops it into the river while biking to work the following morning. The rest of them she slices and eats with chilled yogurt.

• • •

When it appears next it is close enough that if it reached out it could touch her, but it stays in place.

"Shall I recite some poetry for you?"

She shakes her head. She thinks, *the skins we inhabit and the things we long to do inside them, why are they so different?*

"I don't even know your name," she says.

The way its beak cracks open looks almost like a smile. "I have many. Which would please you?"

"The true one."

It is quiet for a moment, then it says, "I will give you the name I gave the rice farmer's wife, and the shogun's daughter, and the lady that died on the eve of the firebombs."

"Women you have loved?" Her own voice irritates her, thin and breathless in the steam-filled air.

"Women who have called me Kawataro," it says. "Women who would have drowned, had I not saved them and brought them back to life."

"Kawataro," she says, tears prickling at the corner of her eyes. "Kawataro, why did you save me?"

"Kindness is always worth saving."

"Why do you say I am kind?"

It tips its head, the water inside sloshing precariously. It seems to be saying, will you prove me wrong?

She swallows, lightheaded, full of nothing. Her pulse simmers in her ears. She crosses the distance between them and presses herself against its hard body, kisses its hard little mouth. Its hands, when they come up to stroke her back, are like ice in the boiling water.

• • •

Kawataro does not appear in the onsen the next time she visits. There are two foreigners sitting in the bath, smiling at her nervously, aware of their own intrusion. The blonde woman, who is quite lovely, chats with Makino in halting Japanese about how cold it is in winter, how there is nothing more delightful than a warm soak, or at least that's what Makino thinks she is saying. Makino smiles back politely, and does not think about the feeling rising in her stomach—a strange hunger, a low ache, a sharp and painful relief.

• • •

This is not a fairytale, Makino knows, and she is no princess, and the moon hanging in the sky is only a moon, not a jewel hanging on a queen's neck, not the spun silk on a weaver's loom. The man she loves is dying, snowfall is filling her ears, and she is going to come apart unless somebody saves him.

The bakery closes for the winter holiday, the last set of customers buying all the cakes on Christmas Eve. Rui comes over as Makino is removing her apron. "Mizuki-san. Thank you for working hard today." She bows. "I'll be leaving now."

"Thank you for working hard today," Makino echoes. She's not the owner, but she is the eldest of the staff, the one who looks least attractive in their puffy, fluffy uniforms. Rui and Ayaka are college students; Yurina and Kaori are young wives, working while they decide whether they want children. Makino gets along with them well enough, but recently their nubile bodies make her tired and restless.

She never had her own children—a fact that Tetsuya mourned, then forgave, because he had a kind heart, because he knew her own was broken. She used to console herself by thinking it was a blessing, that she could keep her slim figure, but even that turned out to be a lie.

Rui twists her fingers in her pleated skirt, hesitating. Makino braces herself for the question, but it never comes, because the bell over the door rings and a skinny, well-dressed boy steps in. Rui's face breaks into a smile, the smile of someone deeply in love. "Just a minute," she calls to the boy. He nods and brings out his phone, tapping away. She turns back to Makino, and dips her head again.

"Enjoy yourself," Makino says, with a smile.

"Thank you very much. Merry Christmas," Rui answers. Makino envies her; hates her, briefly, without any real heat. Rui whips off her apron, picks up her bag, and runs to the boy. They stride together into the snowy evening.

• • •

That night, the foreigners are gone, and Kawataro is back. It tells her about the shogun's daughter. How she would stand in the river and wait for him, her robes gathered around one fist. How her child, when it was born, was green, and how she drowned it in the river, sobbing, before anyone else could find it. How Kawataro had stroked her hair and kissed her cheeks and—Makino doesn't believe this part—how it had grieved for its child, their child, floating down the river.

"And what happened?" Makino says, trailing one finger idly along Kawataro's shoulders. They are sitting together on the edge of the tub, their knees barely visible in the water.

Kawataro's tongue darts over its beak. Makino thinks about having that tongue in her mouth, tasting the minerals of the bathwater in her throat. She thinks about what it means to be held in a monster's arms, what it means to hold a monster. Kappa nappa katta, kappa nappa ippa katta.

Am I the leaf he has bought with sweet words, one leaf of many?

Kawataro turns to her, face solemn as it says, "She drowned herself."

It could not save her, perhaps; or didn't care to, by then? Makino thinks about the shogun's daughter: her bloated body sailing through the water, her face blank in the moonlight, the edges of her skin torn by river dwellers. She thinks of Kawataro watching her float away, head bent, the water in its sara shimmering under the stars.

Katte kitte kutta.

Will I be bought, cut, consumed?

She presses her damp forehead against Kawataro's sleek green shoulder. *Have I already been?*

"How will this story end?" she asks.

It squeezes her knee with its webbed hand, then slips off the ledge into the water, waiting for her to follow. She does.

She spends Christmas Day in the hospital, alternately napping, reading to Tetsuya, and exchanging pleasantries with the doctors and nurses who come to visit. She leans as close as she can to him, as if proximity might leech the pain from his body, everything that makes him ache, makes him forget. It won't work, she knows. She doesn't have that kind of power over him, over anyone. Perhaps the closest she has come to such power is during sex.

The first time she and Tetsuya made love he'd been tender, just as she imagined, his fingers trembling as he undid the hooks of her bra. She cupped his chin and kissed his jaw and ground her hips against his, trying to let him know she wanted this, he didn't need to be afraid. He gripped her hips and she wrapped her legs around him, licking a wet line from his neck to his ear. He carried her to the bed, collapsing so that they landed in a tangled pile, desperately grappling with the remainders of each other's clothing. His breath was ragged as he moved slowly inside her, and she tried not to cry out, afraid of how much she wanted him, how much she wanted him to want her.

On his lips that night her name was a blessing: the chant of monks, the magic spells all fairytales rest on.

Now he stirs, and his eyes open. He says her name with a strange grace, a searching wonder, as if how they came to know each other is a mystery. "Makino?"

"Yes, my darling?"

His breath, rising up to her, is the stale breath of the dying.

"So that's where you are," he says at last. He gropes for her hand and holds it. "You're there, after all. That's good." He pauses, for too long, and when she looks at him she sees he has fallen asleep once more.

• • •

The next time they meet, they spend several minutes soaking together in silence.

She breaks it without preamble. "Kawataro, why do you love me?" Her words are spoken without coyness or fear or fury.

"A woman in grief is a beautiful one," it answers.

"That's not enough."

Kawataro's eyes are two black stones in a waterfall of mist. It is a long time before it finally speaks.

"Four girls," it says. "Four girls drowned in three villages, before they fixed the broken parts in the bridges over the river. My river." It extends its hand and touches the space between her breasts, exerting the barest hint of pressure. Her body tenses, but she keeps silent, immobile. "You were the fifth. You were the only one who accepted my hand when I stretched it out. You," it says, "were the only one who let me lay my hands upon you."

The memory breaks over her, unreal, so that she almost feels like Kawataro has cast a spell on her—forged it out of dreams and warped imaginings. The terrible rain. The realization that she couldn't swim. The way the riverbank swelled, impenetrable as death. How she sliced her hand open on a tree root, trying desperately to grab onto something. How she had seen the webbed hand stretched towards her, looked at the gnarled monkey face, sobbed as she clung for her life, river water and tears and rain mingled on her cheeks. How it tipped its head down and let something fall into her gaping, gurgling mouth, to save her.

"I was a stupid little girl," she says. "I could have drowned then, to spare myself this." She laughs, shocking herself; the sound bounces limply against the tiles.

Kawataro looks away.

"You are breaking my heart, Makino."

"You have no heart to break," she says, in order to hurt it; yet she also wants to be near it, wants it to tell her stories, wants its cold body to temper the heat of the water.

It looks to the left, to the right, and it takes a moment for her to realize that it is shaking its head. Then in one swift motion it wraps its arms around her and squeezes, hard, and Makino remembers how kappa like to wrestle, how they can force the life out of horses and cattle by sheer strength. "I could drain you," it says, hissing into her ear. "I could take you apart, if that would help. I could take everything inside you and leave nothing but a hollow shell of your skin. I do not forget kindness, but I will let you forget yours, if it will please you."

Yes, she thinks, and in the same heartbeat, *but no, not like this.*

She pushes against it, and it releases her. She takes several steps back and lifts her head, appraising.

"Will you heal my husband?" she asks.

"Will you love me?" it asks.

The first time she fell in love with Tetsuya, she was making tea. The first time she fell in love, she was drowning in a river.

"I already do."

Kawataro looks at her with its eyes narrowed in something like sadness, if a monster's face could be sad. It bows its head slightly, and she sees the water inside it—everything that gives it strength—sparkling, reflecting nothing but the misted air.

"Come here," it says, quiet and tender. "Come, my darling Makino, and let me wash your back."

• • •

Tetsuya drinks the water from Kawataro's sara.

Tetsuya lives.

The doctors cannot stop saying what a miracle it is. They spend New Year's Eve together, eating the osechi-ryori Makino prepared. They wear their traditional attire and visit the temple at midnight, and afterward they watch the sunrise, holding each other's cold hands.

• • •

It is still winter, but some stores have already cleared space for their special spring bargains. Makino mouths a rhyme as she sets aside ingredients for dinner. Tetsuya passes her and kisses her cheek, thoughtlessly. He is on his way to the park for his afternoon walk.

"I'm leaving now," he says.

"Come back safely," she answers. She feels just as much affection for Tetsuya as she did before, but nothing else. Some days her hollowness frightens her. Most days she has learned to live with it.

When the door shuts behind him, she spends some moments in the kitchen, silently folding one hand over the other. She decides to take a walk. Perhaps after the walk she will visit her mother. She puts a cucumber and a paring knife into her bag and heads out. By now the cold has become bearable, like the empty feeling in her chest. She follows the river towards the bridge where she once nearly lost her life.

In the middle of the bridge she stands and looks down at the water. She has been saved twice now by the same monster. Twice is more than enough. With a delicate hand, she carves the character for love on the cucumber, her eyes blurring, clearing. She leans over the bridge and lets the cucumber fall.

ISABEL YAP was born in Manila in 1990 and grew up in Quezon City. In 2013, she graduated from Santa Clara University with a degree in marketing and minors in English and Japanese. That same year, she attended the Clarion Writers' Workshop in San Diego. Her fiction and poetry have appeared on *Tor.com* and in *Uncanny Magazine, Shimmer, Apex Magazine, Nightmare, Year's Best Weird Fiction,* and *The Best of Philippine Speculative Fiction 2005–2010.* She currently lives and works in the California Bay Area. She has also lived in London and studied abroad in Tokyo.

The Litany of Earth

Ruthanna Emrys

The state took Aphra away from Innsmouth. They took her history, her home, her family, her god. They tried to take the sea. Now, years later, when she is just beginning to rebuild a life, an agent of that government intrudes on her life again, with an offer she wishes she could refuse. A dark fantasy inspired by the Lovecraft mythos. *Edited by Carl Engle-Laird.*

After a year in San Francisco, my legs grew strong again. A hill and a half lay between the bookstore where I found work and the apartment I shared with the Kotos. Every morning and evening I walked, breathing mist and rain into my desert-scarred lungs, and every morning the walk was a little easier. Even at the beginning, when my feet ached all day from the unaccustomed strain, it was a hill and a half that I hadn't been permitted for seventeen years.

In the evenings, the radio told what I had missed: an earth-spanning war, and atrocities in Europe to match and even exceed what had been done to both our peoples. We did not ask, the Kotos and I, whether our captors too would eventually be called to justice. The Japanese American community, for the most part, was trying to put the camps behind them. And it was not the way of my folk—who had grown resigned to the camps long before the Kotos' people were sent to join us, and who no longer had a community on land—to dwell on impossibilities.

That morning, I had received a letter from my brother. Caleb didn't write often, and hearing from him was equal parts relief and uncomfortable reminder. His grammar was good, but his handwriting and spelling revealed the paucity of his lessons. He had written:

> *The town is a ruin, but not near enouff of one. Houses still stand; even a few windos are whole. It has all been looked over most carefully long ago, but I think forgotten or ignored since.*

And:

> *I looked through our library, and those of other houses, but there is not a book or torn page left on the shelves. I have saugt permisson to look throuh the collecton at Miskatonic, but they are putting me off. I very much fear that the most importent volumes were placed in some government warehouse to be forgotten—as we were.*

So, our family collections were still lost. I remembered the feel of the old pages, my father leaning over me, long fingers tracing a difficult passage as he explained its meaning—and my mother, breaking in with some simple suggestion that cut to the heart of it. Now, the only books I had to work with were the basic texts and single children's spellbook in the store's backroom collection. The texts, in fact, belonged to Charlie—my boss—and I bartered my half-remembered childhood Enochian and R'lyehn for access.

Charlie looked up and frowned as the bells announced my arrival. He had done that from the first time I came in to apply, and so far as I knew gave all his customers the same glare.

"Miss Marsh."

I closed my eyes and breathed in the paper-sweet dust. "I'm not late, Mr. Day."

"We need to finish the inventory this morning. You can start with the Westerns."

I stuck my purse behind the counter and headed back toward the piles of spine-creased Edgar Rice Burroughs and Zane Grey. "What I like about you," I said honestly, "is that you don't pretend to be civil."

"And dry off first." But no arguments, by now, that I ought to carry an umbrella or wear a jacket. No questions about why I liked the damp and chill, second only to the company of old books. Charlie wasn't unimaginative, but he kept his curiosity to himself.

I spent the rest of the morning shelving. Sometimes I would read a passage at random, drinking in the impossible luxury of ink organized into meaningful patterns. Very occasionally I would bring one forward and read a bit aloud to Charlie, who would harumph at me and continue with his work, or read me a paragraph of his own.

By midafternoon I was holding down the register while Charlie did something finicky and specific with the cookbooks. The bells jangled. A man poked his head in, sniffed cautiously, and made directly for me.

"Excuse me. I'm looking for books on the occult—for research." He smiled, a salesman's too-open expression, daring me to disapprove. I showed him to the shelf where we kept Crowley and other such nonsense, and returned to the counter frowning thoughtfully.

After a few minutes, he returned. "None of that is quite what I'm looking for. Do you keep anything more . . . esoteric?"

"I'm afraid not, sir. What you see is what we have."

He leaned across the counter. His scent, ordinary sweat and faint cologne, insinuated itself against me, and I stepped back out of reach. "Maybe something in a storage room? I'm sure you must have more than these turn-of-the-century fakers. Some Al-Hazred, say? Prinn's *Vermis*?"

I tried not to flinch. I knew the look of the old families, and he had none of it— tall and dark-haired and thin-faced, conventional attractiveness marred by nothing more than a somewhat square nose. Nor was he cautious in revealing his familiarity with the Aeonist canon, as Charlie had been. He was either stupid, or playing with me.

"I've never heard of either," I said. "We don't specialize in esoterica; I'm afraid you'd better try another store."

"I don't think that's necessary." He drew himself straighter, and I took another step back. He smiled again, in a way I thought was intended to be friendly, but seemed rather the bare-toothed threat of an ape. "Miss Aphra Marsh. I know you're familiar with these things, and I'm sure we can help each other."

I held my ground and gave my mother's best glare. "You have me mistaken, sir. If you are not in the store to purchase goods that we actually have, I strongly suggest that you look elsewhere."

He shrugged and held out his hands. "Perhaps later."

Charlie limped back to the counter as the door rang the man's departure. "Customer?"

"No." My hands were trembling, and I clasped them behind my back. "He wanted to know about your private shelf. Charlie, I don't like him. I don't trust him."

He frowned again and glanced toward the employees-only door. "Thief?"

That would have been best, certainly. My pulse fluttered in my throat. "Well informed, if so."

Charlie must have seen how hard I was holding myself. He found the metal thermos and offered it silently. I shook my head, and with a surge of dizziness found myself on the floor. I wrapped my arms around my knees and continued to shake my head at whatever else might be offered.

"He might be after the books," I forced out at last. "Or he might be after us."

He crouched next to me, moving slowly with his bad knee and the stiffness of joints beginning to admit mortality. "For having the books?"

I shook my head again. "Yes. Or for being the sort of people who would have them." I stared at my interlaced fingers, long and bony, as though they might be thinking about growing extra joints. There was no way to explain the idea I had, that the smiling man might come back with more men, and guns, and vans that locked in the back. And probably he was only a poorly spoken dabbler, harmless. "He knew my name."

Charlie pulled himself up and into a chair, settling with a grunt. "I don't suppose he could have been one of those Yith you told me about?"

I looked up, struck by the idea. I had always thought of the Great Race as solemn and wise, and meeting one was supposed to be very lucky. But they were also known to be arrogant and abrupt, when they wanted something. It was a nice thought. "I don't think so. They have phrases, secret ways of making themselves known to people who would recognize them. I'm afraid he was just a man."

"Well." Charlie got to his feet. "No help for it unless he comes back. Do you need to go home early?"

That was quite an offer, coming from Charlie, and I couldn't bear the thought that I looked like I needed it. I eased myself off the floor, the remaining edge of fear making me slow and clumsy. "Thank you. I'd rather stay here. Just warn me if you see him again."

. . .

THE LITANY OF EARTH 147

The first change in my new life, also heralded by a customer . . .

It is not yet a month since my return to the world. I am still weak, my skin sallow from malnourishment and dehydration. After my first look in a good mirror, I have shaved my brittle locks to the quick, and the new are growing in ragged, but thick and rich and dark like my mother's. My hair as an adult woman, which I have never seen 'til now.

I am shelving when a familiar phrase stings my ears. Hope and danger, tingling together as I drift forward, straining to hear more.

The blond man is trying to sell Charlie a copy of the *Book of the Grey People*, but it soon becomes apparent that he knows little but the title. I should be more cautious than I am next, should think more carefully about what I reveal. But I like Charlie, his gruffness and his honesty and the endless difference between him and everything I have hated or loved. I don't like to see him taken in.

The blond man startles when I appear by his shoulder, but when I pull the tome over to flip the pages, he tries to regroup. "Now just a minute here, young lady. This book is valuable."

I cannot imagine that I truly look less than my thirty years. "This book is a fake. Is this supposed to be Enochian?"

"Of course it's Enochian. Let me—"

"Ab-kar-rak al-laz-kar-nef—" I sound out the paragraph in front of me. "This was written by someone who had heard Enochian once, and vaguely recalled the sound of it. It's gibberish. And in the wrong alphabet, besides. And the binding . . ." I run my hand over it and shudder. "The binding is real skin. Which makes this a very expensive fake for *someone*, but the price has already been paid. Take this abomination away."

Charlie looks at me as the blond man leaves. I draw myself up, determined to make the best of it. I can always work at the laundromat with Anna.

"You know Enochian?" he asks. I'm startled by the gentleness—and the hope. I can hardly lie about it now, but I don't give more than the bare truth.

"I learned it as a child."

His eyes sweep over my face; I hold myself impassive against his judgment. "I believe you keep secrets, and keep them well," he says at last. "I don't plan to pry. But I want to show you one of mine, if you can keep that too."

This isn't what I was expecting. But he might learn more about me, someday, as much as I try to hide. And when that happens, I'll need a reason to trust him. "I promise."

"Come on back." He turns the door sign before leading me to the storage room that has been locked all the weeks I've worked here.

• • •

I stayed as late as I could, until I realized that if someone was asking after me, the Kotos might be in danger as well. I didn't want to call, unsure if the phone lines would be safe. All the man had done was talk to me—I might never see him again. Even so, I would be twitching for weeks. You don't forget the things that can develop from other people's small suspicions.

The night air was brisk, chilly by most people's standards. The moon watched over the city, soft and gibbous, outlines blurred by San Francisco's ubiquitous mist. Sounds echoed closer than their objects. I might have been swimming, sensations carried effortlessly on ocean currents. I licked salt from my lips, and prayed. I wished I could break the habit, but I wished more, still, that just once it would work.

"Miss Marsh!" The words pierced the damp night. I breathed clean mist and kept walking. *Iä, Cthulhu* . . .

"Please, Miss Marsh, I just need a moment of your time." The words were polite enough, but the voice was too confident. I walked faster, and strained my ears for his approach. Soft soles would not tap, but a hissing squelch marked every step on the wet sidewalk. I could not look back; I could not run: either would be an admission of guilt. He would chase me, or put a bullet in my skull.

"You have me mistaken," I said loudly. The words came as a sort of croak.

I heard him speed up, and then he was in front of me, mist clinging to his tall form. Perforce, I stopped. I wanted to escape, or call for help, but I could not imagine either.

"What do you want, sir?" The stiff words came more easily this time. It occurred to me belatedly that if he did not know what I was, he might try to force himself on me, as the soldiers sometimes had with the Japanese girls in the camp. I couldn't bring myself to fear the possibility; he moved like a different kind of predator.

"I'm sorry," he said. "I'm afraid we may have gotten off to a bad start, earlier. I'm Ron Spector; I'm with the FBI—"

He started to offer a badge, but the confirmation of my worst fears released me from my paralysis. I lashed out with one newly strong leg and darted to the side. I had intended to race home and warn the Kotos, but instead he caught his balance and grabbed my arm. I turned and grappled, scratching and pulling, all the time aware that my papa had died fighting this way. I expected the deadly shot at any moment, and struggled while I could. But my arms were weaker than Papa's, and even my legs were not what they should have been.

Gradually, I realized that Spector was only trying to hold me off, not fighting for his life, nor even for mine. He kept repeating my name, and at last:

"Please, Miss Marsh! I'm not trained for this!" He pushed me back again, and grunted as my nails drew blood on his unprotected wrist. "Please! I don't mean you any harm; I just want to talk for five minutes. Five minutes, I promise, and then you can stay or go as you please!"

My panic could not sustain itself, and I stilled at last. Even then, I was afraid that, given the chance, he would clap me in irons. But we held our tableau, locked hand to wrist. His mortal pulse flickered mouse-like against my fingertips, and I was sure he could feel mine roaring like the tide.

"If I let you go, will you listen?"

I breathed in strength from the salt fog. "Five minutes, you said."

"Yes." He released me, and rubbed the skin below his wristwatch. "I'm sorry, I should have been more circumspect. I know what you've been through."

"Do you." I controlled my shaking with effort. I was a Marsh; I would not show weakness to an enemy. They had drunk deep of it already.

He looked around and took a careful seat on one of the stones bordering a nearby yard. It was too short for him, so that his knees bent upward when he sat. He leaned forward: a praying mantis in a black suit.

"Most religions consist largely of good people trying to get by. No matter what names they worship, or what church they go to, or what language they pray in. Will you agree with me on this much?"

I folded my arms and waited.

"And every religion has its fanatics, who are willing to do terrible things in the name of their god. No one is immune." His lips quirked. "It's a failing of humanity, not of any particular sect."

"I'll grant you that. What of it?" I counted seconds in drips of water. I could almost imagine the dew clinging to my skin as a shield.

He shrugged and smiled. I didn't like how easy he could be, with his wrist still stinking of blood. "If you grant me that, you're already several steps ahead of the U.S. government, just post–World War I. In the twenties, they had run-ins with a couple of nasty Aeonist groups. There was one cult down in Louisiana that had probably never seen an original bit of the canon, but they had their ideas. Sacrificial corpses hanging from trees, the whole nine yards." He glanced at me, checking for some reaction. I did not grant it.

"Not exactly representative, but we got the idea that was normal. In '26, the whole religion were declared enemies of the state, and we started looking out for anyone who said the wrong names on Sunday night, or had the wrong statues in their churches. You know where it goes from there."

I did, and wondered how much he really knew. It was strange, nauseating, to hear the justifications, even as he tried to hold them at a distance.

"It won't shock you," he continued, "to know that Innsmouth wasn't the only place that suffered. Eventually, it occurred to the government that they might have overgeneralized, but it took a long time for changes to go through. Now we're starting to have people like me, who actually study Aeonist culture and try to separate out the bad guys, but it's been a long time coming."

I held myself very still through his practiced speech. "If this is by way of an apology, Mr. Spector, you can drown in it. What you did was beyond the power of any apology."

"Doubtless we owe you one anyway, if we can find a decent way of making it. But I'm afraid I've been sent to speak with you for practical reasons." He cleared his throat and shifted his knees. "As you may imagine, when the government went hunting Aeonists, it was much easier to find good people, minding their own business in small towns, than cultists well-practiced in conspiracy and murder. The bad guys tend to be better at hiding, after all. And at the same time, we weren't trying to recruit people who knew anything useful about the subject—after a while, few would have been willing even if we went looking. So now, as with the Japanese American community, we find ourselves shorthanded, ignorant, and having angered the people least likely to be a danger to the country."

My eye sockets ached. "I cannot believe that you are trying to recruit me."

"I'm afraid that's exactly what I'm doing. I could offer—"

"Your five minutes are up, sir." I walked past him, biting back anything else I might say, or think. The anger worked its way into my shoulders, and my legs, and the rush of my blood.

"Miss Marsh!"

Against my better judgment, I stopped and turned back. I imagined what I must look like to him. Bulging eyes; wide mouth; long, bony legs and fingers. "The Innsmouth look," when there was an Innsmouth. Did it signal danger to him? Something more than human, or less? Perhaps he saw just an ugly woman, someone whose reactions he could dismiss until he heard what he wanted.

Then I would speak clearly.

"Mr. Spector, I have no interest in being an enemy of the state. The state is larger than I. But nor will I be any part of it. And if you insist, you will listen to why. *The state* stole nearly two decades of my life. *The state* killed my father, and locked the rest of my family away from anything they thought might give us strength. Salt water. Books. Knowledge. One by one, they destroyed us. My mother began her metamorphosis. Allowed the ocean, she might have lived until the sun burned to ashes. They took her away. We know they studied us at such times, to better know the process. To better know how to hurt us. You must imagine the details, as I have. They never returned the bodies. Nothing has been given back to us.

"Now, ask me again."

He bent his head at last. Not in shame, I thought, but listening. Then he spoke softly. "The state is not one entity. It is *changing*. And when it changes, it's good for everyone. The people you could help us stop are truly hurting others. And the ones being hurt know nothing of what was done to your family. Will you hold the actions of a few against them? Should more families suffer because yours did?"

I reminded myself that, after humanity faded and died, a great insectoid civilization would live in these hills. After that, the Sareeav, with their pseudopods and strange sculptures. Therefore, I could show patience. "I will do what I can for suffering on my own."

More quietly: "If you helped us, even on one matter, I might be able to find out what really happened to your mother."

The guilt showed plainly on his face as soon as he said it, but I still had to turn away. "I cannot believe that, even after her death, you would dare hold my mother hostage for my good behavior. You can keep her body, and your secrets." And in R'lyehn, because we had been punished for using it in the camps, I added, "And if they hang your corpse from a tree, I will kiss the ground beneath it." Then, fearful that he might do more, or say more, I ran.

I kicked off my shoes, desperate for speed. My feet slapped the wet ground. I could not hear whether Spector followed me. I was still too weak, as weak as I had been as a child, but I was taller, and faster, and the fog wrapped me and hid me and sped me on my flight.

Some minutes later I ducked into a side drive. Peering out, I saw no one following me. Then I let myself gasp: deep, shuddering breaths. I wanted him dead. I wanted them all dead, as I had for seventeen years. Probably some of them were: they were only ordinary humans, with creaking joints and rivulet veins. I could be patient.

I came in barefoot to the Kotos. Mama Rei was in the kitchen. She put down her chopping knife, and held me while I shook. Then Anna took my hand and drew me over to the table. The others hovered nearby, Neko looking concerned and Kevin sucking his thumb. He reminded me so very much of Caleb.

"What happened?" asked Anna, and I told them everything, trying to be calm and clear. They had to know.

Mama Rei tossed a handful of onions into the pan and started on the peppers. She didn't look at me, but she didn't need to. "Aphra-chan—Kappa-sama—what do you think he wants?"

I started to rub my face, then winced. Spector's blood, still on my nails, cut through the clean smell of frying onion. "I don't know. Perhaps only what he said, but his masters will certainly be angry when he fails to recruit me. He might seek ways to put pressure on me. It's not safe. I'm sorry."

"I don't want to leave," said Neko. "We just got here." I closed my eyes hard against the sting.

"We won't leave," said Mama Rei. "We are trying to build a decent life here, and I won't be scared away from it. Neither will you, Aphra-chan. This government man can only do so much to us, without a law to say he can lock us up."

"There was no law countenancing the things done to my family," I said.

"Times have changed," she said firmly. "People are watching, now."

"They took your whole town," said Anna, almost gently. "They can't take all of San Francisco, can they, Mama?"

"Of course not. We will live our lives, and you will all go to work and school tomorrow, and we will be careful. That is all."

There was no arguing with Mama Rei, and I didn't really want to. I loved the life I had, and if I lost it again, well . . . the sun would burn to ash soon enough, and then it would make little difference whether I had a few months of happiness here, or a few years. I fell asleep praying.

· · ·

One expects the storage room of a bookstore to hold more books. And it does. Books in boxes, books on shelves, books piled on the floor and the birch table with uneven legs. And one bookshelf more solid than the others, leaves and vines carved into dark wood. The sort that one buys for too much money, to hold something that feels like it deserves the respect.

And on the shelves, my childhood mixed with dross. I hold up my hand, afraid to touch, to run it across the titles, a finger's breadth away. I fear that they too will change to gibberish. Some of them already are. Some are titles I know to have been written by charlatans, or fakes as obvious as the blond man's *Grey People*. And some are real.

"Where did you get these?"

"At auction. At estate sales. From people who come in offering to sell, or other stores that don't know what they have. To tell the truth, I don't entirely either, for some of them. You might have a better idea?"

I pull down a *Necronomicon* with shaking hands, the one of his three that looks real. The inside page is thankfully empty—no dedication, no list of family names. No chance of learning whether it ever belonged to someone I knew. I read the first page, enough to recognize the over-poetic Arabic, and put it back before my eyes can tear up. I take another, this one in true Enochian.

"Why buy them, if you can't read them?"

"Because I might be able to, someday. Because I might be able to learn something, even with a word or two. Because I want to learn magic, if you must know, and this is the closest I can come." His glare dares me to scoff.

I hold out the book I've been cradling. "You could learn from this one, you know. It's a child's introductory text. I learned a little from it, myself, before I . . . lost access to my library." My glare dares him to ask. He doesn't intrude on my privacy, no more than I laugh at what he's revealed. "I don't know enough to teach you properly. But if you let me share your books, I'll help you learn as best I can." He nods, and I turn my head aside so my tears don't fall on the text—or where he can see.

. . .

I returned to work the next day, wearing shoes borrowed from neighbors. My feet were far too big for anything the Kotos could lend me. Anna walked me partway before turning off for the laundromat—her company more comfort than I cared to admit.

I had hovered by the sink before breakfast, considering what to do about the faint smudge of Spector's blood. In the end, I washed it off. A government agent, familiar with the Aeonist canons, might well know how to detect the signs if I used it against him.

Despite my fears, that day was a quiet one, full of customers asking for Westerns and romances and textbooks. The next day was the same, and the day after that, and three weeks passed with the tension between my shoulder blades the only indication that something was amiss.

At the end of those three weeks, he came again. His body language had changed: a little hunched, a little less certain. I stiffened, but did not run. Charlie looked up from the stack of incoming books, and gave the requisite glare.

"That's him," I murmured.

"Ah." The glare deepened. "You're not welcome here. Get out of my store, and don't bother my employees again."

Spector straightened, recovering a bit of his old arrogance. "I have something for Miss Marsh. Then I'll go."

"Whatever you have to offer, I don't want it. You heard Mr. Day: you're trespassing."

He ducked his head. "I found your mother's records. I'm not offering them in exchange for anything. You were right, that wasn't . . . wasn't honorable. Once you've seen them—if you want to see them—I'll go."

I held out my hand. "Very well. I'll take them. And then you will leave."

He held on to the thick folder. "I'm sorry, Miss Marsh. I've got to stay with them. They aren't supposed to be out of the building, and I'm not supposed to have them right now. I'll be in serious trouble if I lose them."

I didn't care if he got in trouble, and I didn't want to see what was in the folder. But it was my mother's only grave. "Mr. Day," I said quietly. "I would like a few minutes of privacy, if you please."

Charlie took a box and headed away, but paused. "You just shout if this fellow gives you any trouble." He gave Spector another glare before heading into the stacks—I suspected not very far.

Spector handed me the folder. I opened it, cautiously, between the cash register and a short stack of Agatha Christie novels. For a moment I closed my eyes, fixing my mother's living image in my mind. I remembered her singing a sacred chanty in the kitchen, arguing with shopkeepers, kneeling in the wet sand at Solstice. I remembered one of our neighbors crying in our sitting room after her husband's boat was lost in a storm, telling her, "Your faith goes all the way to the depths. Some of us aren't so lucky."

"I'm sorry," Spector said quietly. "It's ugly."

They had taken her deeper into the desert, to an experimental station. They had caged her. They had given her weights to lift, testing her strength. They had starved her for days, testing her endurance. They had cut her, confusing their mythologies, with iron and silver, noting healing times. They had washed her once with seawater, then fresh, then scrubbed her with dry salt. After that, they had refused her all contact with water, save a minimum to drink. Then not even that. For the whole of sixty-seven days, they carefully recorded her pulse, her skin tone, and the distance between her eyes. Perhaps in some vague way also interested in our culture, they copied, faithfully, every word she spoke.

Not one sentence was a prayer.

There were photos, both from the experiments and the autopsy afterward. I did not cry. It seemed extravagant to waste salt water so freely.

"Thank you," I said quietly, closing the folder, bile burning the back of my throat. He bowed his head.

"My mother came to the states young." He spoke deliberately, neither rushing to share nor stumbling over his apparent honesty. Anything else, I would have felt justified interrupting. "Her sister stayed in Poland. She was a bit older, and she had a sweetheart. I have files on her, too. She survived. She's in a hospital in Israel, and sometimes she can feed herself." He stopped, took a deep breath, shook his head. "I can't think of anything that would convince me to work for the new German government—no matter how different it is from the old. I'm sorry I asked."

He took the folder and turned away.

"Wait." I should not have said it. He'd probably staged the whole thing. But it was a far more thoughtful manipulation than the threats I had expected—and I found myself afraid to go on ignoring my enemies. "I will not work for you. But tell me about these frightening new Aeonists."

Whatever—if anything—I eventually chose to pass on to Spector, I realized that I very much wanted to meet them. For all the Kotos' love and comfort, and for all Charlie's eager learning, I still missed Innsmouth. These mortals might be the closest I could come to home.

. . .

"Why do you want to learn this?" Though I doubt Charlie knows, it's a ritual question. There is no ritual answer.

"I don't . . ." He glares, a habit my father would have demanded he break before pursuing the ancient scholarship. "Some things don't go into words easily, all right? It's . . . it feels like what *should* be in books, I suppose. They should all be able to change the world. At least a little."

I nod. "That's a good answer. Some people think that 'power' is a good answer, and it isn't. The power that can be found in magic is less than what you get from a gun, or a badge, or a bomb." I pause. "I'm trying to remember all the things I need to tell you, now, at the beginning. What magic is *for* is understanding. Knowledge. And it won't work until you know how little that gets you.

"*Sharhlyda*—Aeonism—is a bit like a religion. But this isn't the Bible—most of the things I'm going to tell you are things we have records of: histories older than man, and sometimes the testimony of those who lived them. The gods you can take or leave, but the history is real.

"All of man's other religions place him at the center of creation. But man is nothing—a fraction of the life that will walk the Earth. Earth is nothing—a tiny world that will die with its sun. The sun is one of trillions where life flowers, and wants to live, and dies. And between the suns is an endless vast darkness that dwarfs them, through which life can travel only by giving up that wanting, by losing itself. Even that darkness will eventually die. In such a universe, knowledge is the stub of a candle at dusk."

"You make it all sound so cheerful."

"It's honest. What our religion tells us, the part that is a religion, is that the gods created life to try and make meaning. It's ultimately hopeless, and even gods die, but the effort is real. Will always have been real, even when everything is over and no one remembers."

Charlie looks dubious. I didn't believe it, either, when I first started learning. And I was too young then to find it either frightening or comforting.

. . .

I thought about what Mr. Spector had told me, and about what I might do with the information. Eventually I found myself, unofficially and entirely on my own recognizance, in a better part of the city, past sunset, at the door of a home rather nicer than the Kotos'. It was no mansion by any imagining, but it was long lived in and well kept up: two stories of brick and Spanish tile roof, with juniper guarding the façade. The door was painted a cheerful yellow, but the knocker was a fantastical wrought-iron creature that reminded me painfully of home. I lifted the cold metal and rapped sharply. Then I waited, shivering.

The man who opened the door looked older than Charlie. His gray hair frizzed around the temples and ears, otherwise slick as a seal. Faint lines creased his cheeks. He frowned at me. I hoped I had the right address.

"My name is Aphra Marsh," I said. "Does that mean anything to you? I understand that some in this house still follow the old ways."

He started, enough to tell me that he recognized my family's name. He shuffled back a little, but then leaned forward. "Where did you hear such a thing?"

"My family have their ways. May I enter?"

He stepped aside to let me in, in too reluctant a fashion to be truly gallant. His pupils widened between narrowed eyelids, and he licked his lips.

"What do you want, my lady?"

Ignoring the question for the moment, I stepped inside. The foyer, and what I could see of the parlor, looked pedestrian but painfully familiar. Dark wood furniture, much of it bookshelves, contrasted with leaf-green walls. Yet it was all a bit shabby—not quite as recently dusted or mended as would have satisfied my mother's pride. A year ago, it might have been the front room of any of the better houses in Innsmouth. Now . . . I wondered what my family home had looked like, in the years after my mother was no longer there to take pride in it. I put the thought forcibly out of my mind.

". . . in the basement," he was saying. "Would you like to see?"

I ran my memory back through the last seconds, and discovered that he was, in fact, offering to show me where they practiced "the old ways." "I would. But an introduction might be in order first?"

"My apologies, my lady. I am Oswin Wilder. High priest here, although probably not a very traditional one by your standards."

"I make no judgment." And I smiled at him in a way that suggested I might well do so later. It was strange. In Innsmouth, non-Sharhlyd outsiders had looked on us with fear and revulsion—even the Sharhlyd who were not of our kind, mostly the nervously misanthropic academics at Miskatonic, treated us with suspicion. Respect was usually subordinated to rivalries over the proper use of ancient texts. The few mortal humans who shared both our town and our faith had deferred openly, but without this taint of resentment.

He led me down solid wooden steps. I half expected a hidden subbasement or a dungeon—I think he must have wanted one—but he had worked with the home he already had. Beyond the bare flagstone at the foot of the stairs, he had merely added a raised level of dark tile, painted with sigils and patterns. I recognized a few, but suspected more of being his own improvisations. At the far end of the room, candles flickered on a cloth-covered table. I approached, moving carefully around the simple stone altar in the center.

On the table sat a devotional statue of Cthulhu. I hardly noticed the quality of the carving or the material, although my childhood priest would have had something to say about both. But my childhood was long discarded, and the display struck my adult doubts with forgotten force. Heedless of the man behind me, I knelt. The flickering light gave a wet sheen to tentacles and limbs, and I could almost imagine again that they were reaching to draw me in and keep me safe.

Where the statue in Innsmouth's church had depicted the god with eyes closed, to represent the mysteries of the deep, this one's eyes were open, black and fathomless. I returned the gaze, refusing to bow my head.

Have you been waiting for us? Do you regret what happened? With all your aeons, did you even notice that Innsmouth was gone? Or did you just wonder why fewer people came to the water?

Are you listening, now? Were you ever there to listen?

More tears, I realized too late—not something I would have chosen for the priest to see. But I flicked a drop of my salt water onto the statue, and whispered the appropriate prayer. I found it oddly comforting. My mother, old-fashioned, had kept a jar of seawater on the counter for washing tear-streaked faces, and brought it to temple once a month. But I had still given my tears to the god when I didn't want her fussing, or was trying to hide a fight with my brother.

We were near the ocean now. Perhaps the Kotos could spare a jar.

My musings were interrupted by the creak of the basement door and a tremulous alto.

"Oz? I knocked, but no one answered—are you down here?"

"Mildred, yes. Come on down; we have a guest."

Full skirts, garnet red, descended, and as she came closer I saw a woman bearing all my mother's remembered dignity. She had the air of magnificence that fortunate mortals gained with age; her wrinkles and gray-streaked hair only gave the impression of deliberate artistic choices. I stood and ducked my head politely. She looked me over, thin-lipped.

"Mil—Miss Marsh," said Wilder. "Allow me to introduce Mildred Bergman. Mildred, this is Miss Aphra Marsh." He paused dramatically, and her frown deepened.

"And what is she doing in our sanctum?"

"Miss *Marsh*," he repeated.

"Anyone can claim a name. Even such an illustrious one." I winced, then lifted my chin. There was no reason for me to feel hurt: her doubt should be no worse a barrier than Wilder's nervous pride.

Taking a candle from the altar for light—and with a whisper of thanks to Cthulhu for the loan—I stepped toward her. She stood her ground. "Look at me."

She looked me up and down, making a show of it. Her eyes stayed narrow, and if I had studied long enough to hear thoughts, and done the appropriate rites, I was sure I would have heard it. *Anyone can be ugly.*

Wilder moved to intervene. "This is silly. We have no reason to doubt her. And she found us on her own. She must have some knowledge of the old arts: we don't exactly put our address in the classifieds. Let it go and give her a chance to prove herself."

Bergman sniffed and shrugged. Moving faster than I would have expected, she plucked the candle from my hand and replaced it on the table. "As high priest, it is of course at your discretion what newcomers must do to join the elect. The others will be here soon; we'll see what they think of your guest."

I blinked at her. "I'll wait, then." I turned my back and knelt again at the god's table. I would not let her see my rage at her dismissal, or the fear that the gesture of defiance cost me.

. . .

The first and most basic exercise in magic is looking at oneself. Truly looking, truly seeing—and I am afraid. I cannot quite persuade myself that the years in the camp haven't stolen something vital. After doing this simple thing, I will know.

I sit opposite Charlie on the plain wood floor of the storage room. He has dragged over a rag rug and the cushion from a chair for his knees, but I welcome the cool solidity. Around us I have drawn a first-level seal in red chalk, and between us placed two bowls of salt water and two knives. I have walked him through this in the book, told him what to expect, as well as I am able. I remember my father, steady and patient as he explained the rite. I may be more like my mother—impatient with beginners' mistakes, even my own.

I lead him through a grounding: tell him to imagine the sea in his veins, his body as a torrent of blood and breath. I simplify the imagery I learned as a child. He has no metamorphosis to imagine, no ancestors to tell him how those things feel under the weight of the depths. But he closes his eyes and breathes, and I imagine it as wind on a hot day. He is a man of the air, after all. I must tell him the Litany so he will know what that means, and perhaps he will make a new grounding that fits.

Bodies and minds settled, we begin the chant. His pronunciation is poor, but this is a child's exercise and designed for a leader and a stumbling apprentice. The words rise, bearing the rhythm of wind and wave and the slow movement of the earth. Still chanting, I lift the knife, and watch Charlie follow my lead. I wash the blade in salt water and prick my finger. The sting is familiar, welcome. I let a drop of my blood fall into the bowl, swirling and spreading and fading into clarity. I have just enough time to see that Charlie has done the same before the room too fades, and my inward perceptions turn clear.

I am inside myself, seeing with my blood rather than my eyes. I am exquisitely aware of my body, and its power. My blood *is* a torrent. It is a river emptying into the ocean; it thunders through me, a cacophony of rapids and white water. I travel with it, checking paths I have not trod for eighteen years. I find them surprisingly in order. I should have known, watching mortals age while my hard-used joints still moved easily—but that river still carries its healing force, still sweeps illnesses and aches from the banks where they try to cling. Still reshapes what it touches, patiently and steadily. Still carries all the markers of a healthy child who will someday, still, go into the water. I remember my mother telling me, smiling, that my blood knew already the form I would someday wear.

I am basking in the feel of myself, loving my body for the first time in years, when everything changes. Just for a moment, I am aware of my skin, and a touch on my arm.

"Miss Marsh, are you okay?"

And now I remember that one learns to stay inside longer with practice, and that I entirely neglected to warn Charlie against touching me. And then I am cast out of my river, and into another.

I've never tried this with anyone outside my own people. Charlie's river is terribly weak—more like a stream, in truth. It has little power, and detritus has made it narrow and shallow. Where my body is yearning toward the ocean, his has already begun to dry out. His blood, too, knows the form he will someday wear.

He must now be seeing me as intimately.

I force the connection closed, saying the words that end the rite as quickly as I dare. I come to, a little dizzy, swaying.

Charlie looks far more shaken. "That . . . that was real. That was magic."

And I can only feel relief. Of course, the strangeness of his first spell must overwhelm any suspicion over the differences in our blood. At least for now.

• • •

Wilder's congregation trickled in over the next hour. They were male and female, robed richly or simply, but all with an air of confidence that suggested old families used to mortal power. They murmured when Wilder introduced them to me; some whispered more with Bergman afterward.

It only seemed like an endless aeon until they at last gathered in a circle. Wilder stood before the table, facing the low altar, and raised his arms. The circle quieted, 'til only their breath and the rustling of skirts and robes moved the air.

"Iä, iä, Cthulhu thtagn . . ." His accent was beyond abominable, but the prayer was familiar. After the fourth smoothly spoken mispronunciation, I realized that he must have learned the language entirely from books. While I had been denied wisdom writ solid in ink, he had been denied a guiding voice. Knowing he would not appreciate it now, I kept my peace. Even the mangled words were sweet.

The congregants gave their responses at the appropriate points, though many of them stumbled, and a few muttered nonsense rather than the proper words. They had learned from Wilder, some more newly than others. Many leaned forward, pupils dilated and mouths gaping with pleasure. Bergman's shoulders held the tension of real fervor, but her lids were narrowed as she avidly watched the reactions she would not show herself. Her eyes met mine and her mouth twitched.

I remembered my mother, her self-contained faith a complement to my father's easy affections. Bergman had the start of such faith, though she still seemed too conscious of her self-control.

After several minutes of call and response, Wilder knelt and took a golden necklet from where it had been hidden under the folds of the tablecloth. It was none of the work of my people—only a simple set of linked squares, with some abstract tentacular pattern carved in each one. It was as like the ornate bas-relief and wirework necklace-crowns of the deep as the ritual was like my childhood church. Wilder lifted it so that all could see, and Bergman stood before him. He switched abruptly to English: no translation that I recognized, presumably his own invention.

"Lady, wilt thou accept the love of Shub-Nigaroth? Wilt thou shine forth the wonders of life eternal for our mortal eyes?"

Bergman lifted her chin. "I shall. I am her sworn daughter, and the beloved of the Gods: let all welcome and return their terrible and glorious love."

Wilder placed the chain around her neck. She turned to face the congregation, and he continued, now hidden behind her: "Behold the glory of the All-Mother!"

"Iä Cthulhu! Iä Shub-Nigaroth!"

"Behold the dance in darkness! Behold the life that knows not death!"

"Iä! Iä!"

"Behold the secret ever hidden from the sun! See it—breathe it—take it within you!"

At this, the congregation fell silent, and I stumbled over a swallowed shout of joy. The words were half nonsense, but half closer to the spirit of my remembered services than anything Wilder had pulled from his books. Bergman took from the table a knife, and a chalice full of some dark liquid. As she turned to place it on the altar, the scent of plain red wine wafted to my nostrils. She pricked her finger and squeezed a drop of blood into the cup.

As we passed the chalice from hand to hand, the congregants each sipped reverently. They closed their eyes and sighed at private visions, or stared into the wine wondering before relinquishing it to the next. Yet when it came around to me, I tasted only wine. With time and space for my own art, I might have learned from it any secrets hidden in Bergman's blood—but there was no magic here, only its trappings.

They were awkward and ignorant, yearning and desperate. Wilder sought power, and Bergman feared to lose it, and the others likely ran the same range of pleasant and obnoxious company that I remembered from my lost childhood congregation. But whatever else they might be, Spector had been wrong. The government had no more to fear from them than it had from Innsmouth eighteen years ago.

• • •

As Charlie shuts the door to the back room, I can see his hands trembling. Outside this room he wears a cynical elder's mask, but in truth he is in his late thirties—close enough to my age to make little difference, were we both common mortals. And life has been kind to him. What I now offer has been his greatest frustration, and his eagerness is palpable.

As he moves to clear the floor, I hold up my hand. "Later, we'll try the Inner Sea again"—his unaccustomed smile blossoms—"but first I need to read you something. It may help you to better understand what you're seeing, when you look into your own blood."

What I seek can be found in at least three books on his shelf, but I take down the children's text, flipping carefully until I come to the well-remembered illustration: Earth and her moon, with thirteen forms arrayed around them. I trace the circle with one too-long finger.

"I told you that you can take or leave the gods, but the history is real. This is that history. We have evidence, and eyewitnesses, even for the parts that haven't happened yet. The Great Race of Yith travel through space and through time, and they are brutally honest with those who recognize them. The Litany of Earth was distilled over thousands of years of encounters: conversations that together have told us all the civilizations that came before the human one, and all the civilizations that will come after we're gone."

I wait, watching his face. He doesn't believe, but he's willing to listen. He lowers himself slowly into a chair, and rubs his knee absently.

I skip over the poetry of the original Enochian, but its prompting is sufficient to give me the English translation from memory.

"This is the litany of the peoples of Earth. Before the first, there was blackness, and there was fire. The Earth cooled and life arose, struggling against the unremembering emptiness.

"First were the five-winged eldermost of Earth, faces of the Yith. In the time of the elders, the archives came from the stars. The Yith raised up the Shoggoth to serve them in the archives, and the work of that aeon was to restore and order the archives on Earth.

"Second were the Shoggoth, who rebelled against their makers. The Yith fled forward, and the Earth belonged to the Shoggoth for an aeon."

The words come easily, the familiar verses echoing back through my own short life. In times of hardship or joy, when a child sickened or a fisherman drowned too young for metamorphosis, at the new year and every Solstice, the Litany gave us comfort and humility. The people of the air, our priest said, phrased its message more briefly: *This too shall pass.*

"Sixth are humans, the wildest of races, who share the world in three parts. The people of the rock, the K'n-yan, build first and most beautifully, but grow cruel and frightened and become the Mad Ones Under the Earth. The people of the air spread far and breed freely, and build the foundation for those who will supplant them. The people of the water are born in shadow on the land, but what they make beneath the waves will live in glory till the dying sun burns away their last shelter.

"Seventh will be the Ck'chk'ck, born from the least infestation of the houses of man, faces of the Yith." Here, at last, I see Charlie inhale sharply. "The work of that aeon will be to read the Earth's memories, to analyze and annotate, and to make poetry of the Yith's own understanding."

On I count, through races of artists and warriors and lovers and barbarians. Each gets a few sentences for all their thousands or millions of years. Each paragraph must obscure uncountable lives like mine, like Charlie's . . . like my mother's.

"Thirteenth will be the Evening People. The Yith will walk openly among them, raising them from their race's infancy with the best knowledge of all peoples. The work of that aeon will be copying the archives, stone to stone, and building the ships that will carry the archives, and the Evening, to distant stars. After they leave, the Earth will burn and the sun fade to ashes.

"After the last race leaves, there will be fire and unremembering emptiness. Where the stories of Earth will survive, none have told us."

We sit for a minute in silence.

"You ever meet one of these Yith?" Charlie asks at last. He speaks urgently, braced against the answer. Everything else I've told him, he's *wanted* to believe.

"I never have," I say. "But my mother did, when she was a girl. She was out playing in the swamp, and he was catching mosquitoes. Normally you find them in libraries, or talking to scholars, but she isn't the only person to encounter one taking samples of one sort or another. She asked him if mosquitoes would ever be people, and he told her a story about some Ck'chk'ck general, she thought the equivalent of Alexander the Great. She said that everyone asked her so many questions when she got home that she couldn't remember the details properly afterward." I shrug. "This goes with the magic, Mr. Day. Take them both, or turn your back."

• • •

The basement door creaked, and skirts whispered against the frame.

"Oz," came Bergman's voice. "I wanted to talk to you about . . . Ah. It's you." She completed her regal descent. "Oz, what is *she* doing here?"

I rose, matching her hard stare. If I was to learn—or perhaps even teach—anything here, I needed to put a stop to this. And I still had to play a role.

"What exactly is it that you hold against me? I've come here many times, now. The others can see easily enough—none of them doubt what I am."

She looked down at me. "You could be an imposter, I suppose. It would be easy enough. But it's hardly the only possible threat we should be concerned about. If you are truly of the Deep Ones' blood, why are you not with your noble kin? Why celebrate the rites here, among ordinary humans who want your secrets for themselves?"

Why are you not with your kin? I swallowed bitter answers. "My loneliness is no concern of yours."

"I think it is." She turned to Wilder, who had kept his place before the altar. "If she's *not* a charlatan . . . either she's a spy, sent to keep us from learning her people's powers, or she's in exile for crimes we cannot begin to imagine."

I hissed, and unthinkingly thrust myself into her space, breathing the stink of her sharply exhaled breath. "They. Are. Dead."

Bergman stepped back, pupils wide, breath coming too quickly. She drew herself up, straightened her skirts, and snorted. "Perhaps you are a charlatan after all. Everyone knows the Deep Ones cannot die."

Again without thinking, I lunged for her. She stumbled backward and I caught her collar, twisted, and pulled. She fell forward, and I held her weight easily as she scrabbled to push me away. I blinked (eyes too big, too tight in their sockets), anger almost washed away by surprise. It was the first time the strength had come upon me.

And I had used it on an old mortal woman whose only crimes were pride and suspicion. I released her and turned my back. The joints of my fingers ached where I had clenched them. "Never say that again. Or if you must, say it to the soldiers who shot my father. We do not age, no—not like you do." I could not resist the barb. "But there are many ways to die."

Oz finally spoke, and I turned to see him helping Bergman to her feet. "Peace,

Mildred. She's no spy, and I think no criminal. She will not take your immortality from you."

I paused, anger not entirely overwhelmed, and searched her features carefully. She was slender, small-eyed, fine-fingered—and unquestionably aged. For all her dignity, it was impossible that she might share even a drop of blood with my family.

She caught my look and smiled. "Yes, we have that secret from the Deep Ones. Does it surprise you?"

"Exceedingly. I was not aware that there *was* a secret. Not one that could be shared, at least."

A broader, angrier smile. "Yes—you have tried to keep it from us. To keep us small and weak and dying. But we have it—and at the harvest moon, I will go into the water. I am beloved of the Elder Gods, and I will dwell in glory with Them under the waves forever."

"I see." I turned to Wilder. "Have you done this before?"

He nodded. "Mildred will be the third."

"Such a wonderful promise. Why don't you walk into the ocean yourself?"

"Oh, I shall—when I have trained a successor who can carry on in my place." And he looked at me with such confidence that I realized whom he must have chosen for that role.

Mildred Bergman—convinced that life could be hoarded like a fortune—would never believe me if I simply *told* her the truth. I held up my hand to forestall anything else the priest might have to say. "Wilder, get out of here. I'll speak with you later."

He went. If he had convinced himself I would be his priestess, I suppose he had to treat me as one.

I sat down, cross-legged, trying to clear the hissing tension that had grown between us. After a moment she also sat, cautiously and with wincing stiffness.

"I'm sorry," I said. "It doesn't work like that. We go into the water, and live long there, because we have the blood of the deep in us. The love of the gods is not so powerful. I wish I had more to offer you. There are magics that can heal, that can ease the pains of age, that can even extend life for a few decades. I will gladly teach them to you." And I would, too. She had been vile to me, but I could invite her to Charlie's back room to study with us, and learn the arts that would give her both time and acceptance. All but one spell, that I would not teach, and did not plan to ever learn.

"You're lying." Her voice was calm and even.

"I'm not. You're going to drown yourself—" I swallowed. "I'm trying to save your life. You haven't done a speck of real magic in this room, you don't know what it's like, how it's different."

She started to say something, and I raised a hand. "No. I know you won't listen to what I have to say. Please, let me show you."

"Show me." Not a demand—only an echo, full of doubt.

"Magic." I looked at her, with my bulging eyes and thick bones, willing her, if she couldn't yet believe, at least to look at me.

"What's involved in this . . . demonstration?" she finally asked, and I released a held breath.

"Not much. Chalk, a pair of bowls, and a drop of blood."

Between my purse and the altar, we managed to procure what was needed— fortunate, as I would have hated to go up and ask Wilder to borrow them. Having practiced this with Charlie, I still had the most basic of seals settled in my mind, at least clearly enough for this simple spell. I moved us away from the carefully laid tile to the raw flagstone behind the stairs. There was no reason to vandalize Wilder's stage.

Bergman did not know the Litany, nor the cosmic humility that was the core of Sharhlyda practice. And yet, in some ways, she was easier to work with than Charlie. I could tell her to feel her blood as a river, without worrying what she might guess of my nature.

As I guided her through the opening meditation, Bergman's expression relaxed into something calmer, more introspective. She had some potential for the art, I thought. More than Wilder, certainly, who was so focused on the theater of the thing, and on the idea of power. Bergman's shoulders loosened, and her breath evened, but she kept her eyes open, waiting.

I pricked my finger and let the blood fall into the bowl, holding myself back from the spell long enough to wipe the blade and pass it to Bergman. Then I let the current pull me down . . .

Submerging only briefly before forcing myself upward, out of the cool ocean and into the harsh dry air. I took a painful breath, and laid my hand on Bergman's arm.

A thin stream moved through a great ravine, slow and emaciated. Rivulets trickled past great sandy patches. And yet, where they ran, they ran sweet and cool. The lines they etched, the bars and branches, made a fine and delicate pattern. In it I saw not only the inevitable decay that she strove against, but the stronger shape that was once hers—and the subtler strength in the shape she wore now.

"You *are* one of them."

I returned, gasping, all my instincts clamoring for moisture. I wanted to race upstairs and throw the windows open to the evening fog. Instead I leaned forward.

"Then you must also see—"

She sniffed, half a laugh. "I see that at least some of the books Wilder found can be trusted. And none of them have claimed that the Deep Ones are a more honest race than we. They do claim that you know more of the ancient lore than most humans have access to. So no, I don't believe that your immortality is a mere accident of birth. It can be ours as well—if we don't let you frighten us away from it."

We argued long and late, and still I could not move her. That night I argued with myself, sleepless, over whether it was my place to do more.

• • •

Of course Charlie asks, inevitably.

I have been teaching him the first, simplest healing spells. Even a mortal, familiar with his own blood, can heal small wounds, speed the passage of trivial illnesses and slow the terrible ones.

"How long can I live, if I practice this?" He looks at me thoughtfully.

"Longer. Perhaps an extra decade or three. Our natures catch up with us all, in the end." I cringe inwardly, imagining his resentment if he knew. And I am beginning to see that he must know, eventually, if I continue with these lessons.

"Except for the Yith?"

"Yes." I hesitate. Even were I ready to share my nature, this would be an unpleasant conversation, full of temptation and old shame. "What the Yith do . . . there *are* spells for that, or something similar. No one else has ever found the trick of moving through time, but to take a young body for your own . . . You would not find it in any of these books, but it wouldn't be hard to track down. I haven't, and I won't. It's not difficult, from what I've heard, just wrong."

Charlie swallows and looks away. I let him think about it a moment.

"We forgive the Yith for what they do, though they leave whole races abandoned around fading stars. Because their presence means that Earth is remembered, and our memory and our stories will last for as long as they can find younger stars and younger bodies to carry them to. They're as selfish as an old scholar wanting eighty more years to study and love and breathe the air. But we honor the Yith for sacrificing billions, and track down and destroy those who steal one life to preserve themselves."

He narrows his eyes. "That's very . . . practical of you."

I nod, but look away. "Yes. We say that they do more to hold back darkness and chaos than any other race, and it is worth the cost. And of course, we know that we aren't the ones to pay it."

"I wonder if the . . . what were they called, the Leng . . . had a Nuremburg."

I start to say that it's not the same—the Yith hate nobody, torture nothing. But I cannot find it in me to claim it makes a difference. Oblivion, after all, is oblivion, however it is forced on you.

• • •

The day after my fourth meeting with Spector, I did not go to work. I walked, in the rain and the chill, in the open air, until my feet hurt, and then I kept walking, because I could. And eventually, because I could, I went home.

Mama Rei was mending, Kevin on the floor playing with fabric scraps. The *Chronicle* lay open on the table to page seven, where a single column reported the previous night's police raid on a few wealthy homes. No reason was given for the arrests, but I knew that if I read down far enough, there would be some tittering implication of debauchery. Mama Rei smiled at me sadly, and flicked her needle through a stocking. The seam would not look new, but would last a little longer with her careful stitching.

"You told him," she said. "And he listened."

"He promised me there would be no camps." Aloud, now, it sounded like a slender promise by which to decide a woman's fate.

Flick. "Does he seem like an honorable man?"

"I don't know. I think so. He says that the ones they can't just let go, they'll send to a sanitarium." Someplace clean, where their needs would be attended to, and where they would be well fed. "He says Wilder really does belong there. He believed what he was telling the others. What he was telling Bergman."

And she believed what he told her—but that faith would not have been enough to save her.

No one's faith ever was.

Flick. Flick. The needle did a little dance down and around, tying off one of her perfect tiny knots. Little copper scissors, a gift purchased with my earnings and Anna's, cut the dangling thread. "You should check on her."

"I don't think she'll want to see me."

Mama Rei looked at me. "Aphra-chan."

I ducked my head. "You're right. I'll make sure they're treating her well."

But they would, I knew. She would be confined in the best rooms and gardens that her money could pay for, all her physical needs attended to. Kind men would try to talk her back from the precipice where I had found her. And they would keep her from drowning herself until her blood, like that of all mortals, ran dry.

I wondered if, as she neared the end, she would still pray.

If she did, I would pray with her. If it was good for nothing else, at least the effort would be real.

RUTHANNA EMRYS lives in a mysterious manor house on the outskirts of Washington, D.C., with her wife and their large, strange family. Her stories have appeared in a number of venues, including *Strange Horizons*, *Analog*, and *Tor.com*. She is the author of the Innsmouth Legacy series, which began with *Winter Tide*. She makes homemade vanilla extract, obsesses about game design, gives unsolicited advice, and occasionally attempts to save the world.

Brimstone and Marmalade

Aaron Corwin

All Mathilde wanted for her birthday was a pony. Instead, she got a demon. Sometimes growing up means learning that what you think you want is not always what you need. *Edited by Liz Gorinsky.*

Mathilde didn't want a demon. She wanted a pony.

"Ponies are expensive," Mathilde's mother said. "How about a nice little demon instead?"

"I don't want a demon!" Mathilde stamped her foot. "Demons are ugly and creepy and they smell bad!"

"Ponies are hard work," Mathilde's father said. "You wouldn't have time for your homework."

"I would!" Mathilde said. "I'd work really hard and take good care of him!"

"Well," Father said. "We'll see."

Mathilde knew what "we'll see" meant. It was one of those special lies that only grown-ups were allowed to tell. When a grown-up said "we'll see," it really meant "never."

It wasn't fair. Becky Hamilton got to take riding lessons on weekends, and she *never* stopped talking about them.

Peter Voorhees brought his demon to school once. It was scaly and slobbery, not sleek and pretty like a pony. It got loose in the classroom and tried to eat Mathilde's hair.

How could anyone think that a demon was better than a pony?

• • •

The day before Mathilde's birthday in September, the sky was gray and drizzly all afternoon and the puddles swirled with little flat rainbows. On that day, something different happened.

"Mathilde?" That was Mrs. Pressmorton, the vice principal. Mathilde looked up from the floor, one galosh halfway onto her foot.

"Mathilde, your parents called to say you don't have to take the bus home today. Your grandmother is picking you up from school."

Mathilde's heart began to beat faster. *Nana?* She thought. *Nana's here for my birthday?*

She tried not to hope. She tried so, so hard, but little bits of hope started to creep in anyway. Nana *always* brought presents, even when it *wasn't* her birthday. And—and this was the deepest, most secret hope of all—Nana lived in the big house in the country; the big house with the old barn and the great big field.

"Oh my goodness!" Nana said. She swept Mathilde up in a great big hug, just like she always did.

"Nana!" Mathilde definitely didn't peer over Nana's shoulder, looking for a pony in the back of her car. Not much, anyway.

"Look at you!" Nana said. "My little Matty-Patty's all grown up! Soon you'll be as tall as me!"

Mathilde giggled. Nana was almost as tall as Father, but that was another kind of lie grown-ups were allowed to tell. Mathilde didn't mind. Especially if it meant she was old enough to have a pony.

Nana's car smelled like grass and old books, but it didn't have a pony in it, of course. The rain made blurry lines down the windshield while the wipers went *squeak-squeak* back and forth. Mathilde drummed her heels against the floor of the car and tried to imagine the squeak was the sound of her saddle shifting as she rode her pony through the rain. She was so caught up in her thoughts that she almost didn't notice when Nana turned left instead of right at the corner with the big yellow restaurant.

"Where are we going?"

Nana smiled. "You didn't think I'd come all this way and not bring you a present, did you?"

Mathilde took a breath so big she felt like she might burst.

"But my birthday's not 'til tomorrow!"

"That's true." Nana gave her a great big wink. "But I won't tell if you won't. Besides, I think this is the sort of present you'd better pick out for yourself."

Mathilde could scarcely believe it. After all this time and all this waiting, she was finally going to get a pony of her very own.

Becky Hamilton was going to be *so* jealous.

But when the car stopped, it was in front of a store that didn't look like it had any ponies inside. The whole front of the store was covered in steel plates and the air smelled just a little bit like rotten eggs. It was very dark inside, but when Mathilde saw the rows of wire cages she knew she had been tricked.

"This isn't a pony store!" Mathilde said. "This is a *demon store!*"

Dozens of demons looked over at the sound of her voice. There were little, slithering ones and great big horned ones, almost as big as Mathilde. There were skinny ones with wings and spiky ones with eyes that flashed different colors. There was even one with brightly lit smoke seeping from the sides of its mouth as it chewed on something she couldn't quite see.

"Well, of course it is!" Nana said.

"But I don't *want* a demon!" How many times would she have to say it? "I want a pony!"

"Ah." Nana knelt down to put her hands on Mathilde's shoulders. "Demons make wonderful pets, you know. When I was a girl, we had a Belgian Muncher on the farm. They're smart as a whip if you train 'em right. Some can even talk. But do you know the best thing about demons?"

Mathilde shook her head, her lip quivering.

Nana leaned in very close and whispered in Mathilde's ear. "They're great for convincing parents that little girls are responsible enough to take care of a pony."

Mathilde didn't know what to make of this. Was it another grown-up lie? "Really?" Her voice trembled.

Nana smiled. "I've already spoken with your parents about it. *If* you prove you can take care of a demon . . . then maybe we can see about that pony."

Mathilde looked at the nearest cage. The demon inside was walking around on tiny cloven hooves and merrily cracking a little barbed whip. It grinned at her with a mouth full of teeth that gleamed like needles.

"Well, hello there!"

Mathilde jumped a little. Behind the counter was an old man with a checked shirt and large, round glasses. His face became a pile of wrinkles when he smiled. "Are you here for a new demon?"

"No," Mathilde said.

"Yes." Nana smiled. "It's her birthday."

"Oh." The old man gave that too-long nod that grown-ups gave when they thought they knew something but really didn't. "I *see*! Is this your first demon, miss?"

". . . Yes." Mathilde looked at her shoes.

"Then this *is* a special occasion! What sort of demon were you looking for?"

Mathilde looked back at him. "I want the kind with the pretty eyes and the long, shiny mane!"

Nana sighed. "That's a pony, dear."

"Well, that's what I want!"

Nana gave Mathilde a sharp look, but the old man just laughed.

"Oh, I think I have *just* the one for you." He reached beneath the counter and pulled out a small glass cage.

The demon inside didn't have a long, shiny mane. It didn't have any hair at all, at least not that Mathilde could see. All she saw was a tiny, black, hooded robe that hovered above the bottom of its cage on a billowing cloud of inky blackness. Its eyes were two red stars that twinkled in the darkness of its hood like distant Christmas lights.

I guess that's kind of pretty, Mathilde thought.

Nana said, "Oh! What type of demon is that?"

"He's a Miniature Dark Lord," the old man said.

Nana clucked her tongue. "A Dark Lord? I thought they had great big horns!"

"Normally they do." The shopkeeper shook his head. "But this poor little guy was born without any. All the other Dark Lords rejected him. Even his own mother didn't want to take care of him! Can you imagine that?"

Mathilde could imagine it. She didn't want to take care of him either. But . . . "What's his name?"

The old man smiled behind his big, round glasses. "Why don't you ask him yourself?"

Mathilde peered through the glass cage. She looked at the Dark Lord's tiny clawed fingers, at his dark billowing cloud.

Mathilde thought about her pony. "Hello," she said. "What's your name?"

I AM IX'THOR, MASTER OF THE VENOMOUS PITS OF KARTHOOM! The creature raised his arms over his head. He had a voice like the truck that picked up their garbage in the morning, only smaller. *BOW BEFORE YOUR MASTER, SMALL ONE!*

"How about that!" The old man raised his fuzzy white eyebrows. "He told you his name first thing! He must really like you."

"Well, I don't like him . . ." Mathilde crossed her arms. Ix'thor lowered his arms and hung his head a little. ". . . But I guess he'll do."

• • •

IX'THOR . . . HUNGERS. The Dark Lord's voice rumbled from within his cardboard box.

"Dad!" Mathilde put her hands on her hips. "Hurry up! He's getting hungry!"

"I'm sure he's fine," Father said. He was kneeling on the floor of Mathilde's bedroom, carefully hanging the curtains on the big glass cage. "You have to be firm with demons, you know. Give in and they'll walk all over you."

IX'THOR DEMANDS SACRIFICE!

"No!" Mathilde tapped her finger on the box. "Be good."

"All right." Father stood up and stretched his back with a soft pop, then turned down the light. "You can put him in now."

Mathilde placed the cardboard box in the cage and pried the lid off. Ix'thor wafted out, his black mist coiling around the bottom of his robe. He floated back and forth a few times, exploring his new cage.

"Here," Father said. "See the little altar down there? Put one of these on it." He handed her a small, softly glowing ball, about the size of a pea, from the big plastic bag Nana had bought. The bag said things like "Nutritionally Balanced" and "Now with extra innocence for a healthy glow!"

At the sight of the red pellet Ix'thor raced over to the altar and stood on top of it, his arms outstretched.

"Ah-ah-ah," Father said. "He has to take it from the altar. Make him wait for it."

"Shoo!" Mathilde waved her hand toward the demon. "Back up. Back *up*! He won't move!"

"Use the flashlight," Father said. Mathilde picked up the little light that came with the *My First Demon* book and shined it on the altar. Ix'thor went scurrying off into the shadow of his box.

Mathilde put the pellet on one of the divots in the flat stone and turned off the light. After a few seconds, Ix'thor came out of his box and drifted over to the altar. He leaned over, as if to peer at the pellet, then snatched it up with both hands.

IX'THOR ACCEPTS YOUR SACRIFICE. The Dark Lord bowed his head over the pellet and devoured it. *NUM. NUM. NUM.*

"Wow," Father said. "I guess he really *was* hungry."

Mathilde glared at him, her eyes wide and her cheeks puffed out. *"See!"*

• • •

Mathilde had a hard time sleeping that night. She was excited about her birthday party, but her thoughts kept drifting toward the pony she would have someday.

What color would he be? What would she call him? She knew her pony would be gentle and tame, not pushy like Ix'thor.

How long would she have to take care of a stupid demon, anyway?

When she did fall asleep, she dreamed of ponies with glowing red eyes.

Mathilde woke up to something poking her in the chin. "Mnm." Mathilde swatted it away.

A moment later it happened again. She opened her eyes to see two red, twinkling stars and dark, clawed hands hovering over her face.

KNEEL BEFORE YOUR MASTER, MORTAL!

"Aaaaaah! *Mom!*"

Mother came to the door with Father and Nana close behind. When Mother flicked on the light there was a grinding squeal from Ix'thor and the little Dark Lord scurried under her dresser.

"Turn that light off!" Nana said. "Or he'll never come out."

Father ran into the room and stumbled around in the sudden dark. "Where did he go?"

"How did he get out of his cage?" Mother asked.

"I see him!" Father lurched to the corner, but when he bent down he banged his head on Mathilde's dresser. "Ow!"

Mathilde saw a black shape dart under the bed. She grabbed the little flashlight and crawled underneath the springs.

"He's right here!" She turned on the light.

Ix'thor tried to dart away from the beam, but he was trapped in the corner. When he hid himself in his robe, her hand darted out and wrapped around his leathery body. "I've got him!"

But she didn't have him. Tiny claws slashed at her hand, right between her finger and thumb.

"*Eeeeeee!*"

. . .

"I hate him!" Mathilde said through her tears. Mother wiped at her face, at the bubble of snot that was hanging from her nose. "I don't want a demon! I *hate* demons!"

"Oh, sweetie," Mother said. "It's just a tiny little cut. He was just scared of you, that's all."

"I don't care! I don't want a demon! I want a *pony!*"

Nana shook her head. "Sometimes ponies bite too, child."

Mathilde had had enough of this. "They do not!"

"Oh, you think so?" Nana said. "When I was a girl, my best friend, Sheryl, had her finger bitten clean off!"

Mathilde looked up through a blurry curtain of tears. She couldn't tell if Nana was making fun of her or not.

"You have to be careful with animals, Matty-Patty." Mother stroked Mathilde's hair. "Sometimes when they're scared they lash out. They don't know any better."

"But I *was* being careful!" Why didn't anyone believe her?

Mathilde looked up at the sound of Father's footsteps.

"Well, that's that," Father said. "He's back in his cage. I don't know *how* he got out of there, but he'll need a cutting torch to do it again."

"I don't want him in my room!" Mathilde said. "I can't sleep when he's in there."

Nana sighed. "Maybe this wasn't such a good idea, Fred. I'm sorry. I'll take him back to the store tomorrow."

Mathilde suddenly felt queasy. Too late, she remembered her promise, her pony. "Wait!" Mathilde said. "I didn't . . . *really* mean it. He can stay."

Nana and Mother looked at each other. Nana looked like she was laughing at something, but Mother didn't look so amused.

"Do you really mean it?" Mother asked.

Mathilde nodded.

"Because this is your last chance," Mother went on. "If you say you don't want him one more time we'll give him to someone who does."

"I know." Mathilde looked at her knees.

"You have to promise you'll take care of him, and be gentle with him."

"I promise," Mathilde said. "I'll take *good* care of him."

. . .

There was cake at the party. It was chocolate with white frosting and candy sprinkles, just like Mathilde wanted. And there were lots of presents, including a camera and a unicycle and eleven different kinds of toy pony.

Mathilde smiled when she opened each present, and because Mother was looking she made sure to say thank you to everyone who gave her something—even Aunt Maggie, who wasn't actually there. But she wasn't *really* happy. Even the unicycle, which she had asked for specially, didn't make her happy. When Robby Ferguson asked her if he could play with it, she said she didn't mind.

"This is so cool." Robby wobbled on the pedals, gripping the back of the couch. "I'm gonna get one for my birthday."

"I already have one," said Becky Hamilton. "It's okay. But I like riding horses better. Daddy says I can have one of my own for my next birthday."

"Yeah right," Suzy Feldstein said.

"It's true!" Becky tossed her hair in her stuck-up, Becky-Hamilton way. "I made him promise."

"I did get another present," Mathilde said. The other children all looked at her. "You want to see him?"

. . .

"You have to turn the lights down." Mathilde turned the dial down to a murky gloom. "He doesn't like light."

"What's in there?" Becky Hamilton stepped back. "It's not a snake, is it?"

"Sh!" Mathilde said, because she felt like it. "It's not a snake."

Mathilde opened the curtains around the cage and turned on the special red light in the lid, then stepped back.

The cage had changed since the last time she'd seen it. Ix'thor had moved around the pebbles at the bottom and stacked them up into a high-backed chair. He had taken apart his cardboard box and used it to build a little tower. Another piece of cardboard had been fashioned into a wide, diamond-shaped sword with tiny skulls carved into the blade. In the dim red light, it looked like every pebble in the cage had been worn down slightly to resemble hundreds of itty-bitty multicolored skulls.

WELCOME TO MY DOMAIN, Ix'thor said. *FOOLS. DID YOU THINK YOU COULD DEFEAT ME?*

"Wow!" Robby said. "That's cool!"

"What kind of demon is he?" Suzy asked.

"He's a Dark Lord." Mathilde felt the first stirrings of a real smile.

"No he's not," Becky said. "Dark Lords have horns."

Mathilde puffed up. "That shows what you know, Becky! This one was born without any horns."

"Does he do any tricks?" Robby leaned in to peer through the glass.

"Um . . ." Mathilde hesitated. "Not yet."

BOW BEFORE ME!

"You shouldn't actually bow," Mathilde said. "That just encourages him."

"Oh, man!" Robby was practically hopping up and down. "He's so awesome! I want a demon too!"

"I can't have one," Suzy said. "My mom's allergic to demons."

Mathilde smiled at Suzy. "You can come over here and play with Ix'thor if you want."

"Really?"

"It's not that big a deal," Becky said. "It's just a demon. What good is a demon who doesn't even *do* anything? I bet he bites."

Mathilde's eyes widened and she pressed her lips together. Why did Becky have to be such a stuck-up brat? Why did Mother even invite her, anyway? Mathilde wanted to punch her, right in her turned-up nose.

FOOLISH MORTALS, Ix'thor rumbled. *NOW BEHOLD MY TRUE POWER!*

The inky clouds rolling around the bottom of Ix'thor's robe rolled *up* for a moment, as if being sucked back into his body. Then, his cardboard sword held over his head, Ix'thor emitted a burst of crimson fire from his hands. The eldritch flame danced along the edges of the blade, licking and curling, but not burning.

Robby looked like he was about to pee his pants. "*Wow!* You said he didn't do any tricks!"

"Well . . ." Mathilde tried not to look too smug. "Maybe he's got one or two."

• • •

It rained a lot in the fall. By the start of October, it seemed like it had been raining forever. Mathilde slammed the door behind her and ran up the stairs to her room. She threw her soggy book bag on the floor and flopped facedown on the bed.

Her sobs mingled with the patter on the fog-painted window. In the darkness between the cage's curtains, two tiny red stars gleamed.

WHAT TROUBLES YOU, MY MINION?

"Shut up!" Mathilde said. "I'm not your minion!"

She lifted her face from the pillow and looked at the dark, wet imprint she'd left there. She wiped her nose.

"We had to make a collage," Mathilde mumbled. "About animals. And Billy Haggerty . . . he said mine was ugly . . . and he took it . . . and he threw it in the mud! It's ruined!"

YOUR PLAN . . . WAS NEARLY COMPLETE?

"Yes!" Mathilde squeezed her eyes shut. "Now I have to start all over!"

DESTROY THE INTERLOPER!

"Miss Hoevener says he's just being a boy. She said . . . that's what boys do when they like you. She says if I just ignore him then he'll stop."

Ix'thor looked down for a moment, then raised his sword over his head. FEED HIM TO THE RAVENOUS TONGUE-BEASTS OF GARAKH'NURR!

Mathilde sniffed. "I would, but I don't know where that is."

Ix'thor reached out his little hand. GIVE ME YOUR SOUL AND I WILL GRANT YOU LIMITLESS POWER.

Mathilde smiled a little. "Mom says I can't have limitless power until I'm older. But you can have a grub soul."

Ix'thor waited patiently by the altar, his eyes glowing brightly.

EXCELLENT.

· · ·

On Halloween, a witch came to their house. She had a black pointy hat and a broomstick, green skin, and a big, warty nose.

"Nana!" Mathilde ran forward for a hug.

"Oof!" Nana said. "This can't be my little Matty-Patty, can it? How's my little angel?"

"I'm not an angel." Mathilde raised the hood of her robe. "I'm a Dark Lord. Bow before me, mortals!"

"Oh, my! I think I felt the earth tremble for a moment."

"Excellent. It is just as I have foretold." Mathilde looked up. "And Ix'thor's coming with us too."

Nana looked outside. "Oh, sweetie, the sun's still out. I don't think that's such a good idea."

"It's okay. We got him a ball. See?"

Mathilde picked up the crystal ball, which was filled with swirling black clouds. From deep inside its murky depths, two crimson points of light could barely be seen.

"I made him an angel costume," Mathilde said. "But you can't really see it."

SOON YOUR TRANSFORMATION WILL BE COMPLETE. Ix'thor's hollow voice rumbled from inside the ball.

Mathilde whispered, "I don't think he knows it's Halloween."

"Well then, let's not disappoint him," Nana said. "Shall we collect some souls?"

· · ·

Orange leaves flew across the street in twisted whirlwinds while the shadows of barren trees stretched their fingers slowly away from the sun. Mathilde made her way down the street with Ix'thor's ball under one arm and her swollen bag of candy in the other.

"That's an awful lot of candy," Nana said. "I'm certain we didn't get that much candy when I was a girl."

"Ix'thor says fear keeps the peasants in line."

"Aha. Mathilde . . . you know not *everything* Ix'thor says is a good idea, right?"

"Well, duh!" Mathilde rolled her eyes.

"Of course. How silly of me. Anyway, I think it's time we started heading back home."

"Wait!" Mathilde pulled on Nana's cloak. "Just one more street, please? Just to the end of the block?"

Nana sighed. "All right, but that's it. I don't want you crossing Washington Street. There's too much traffic."

"I *won't*."

MWA HA HA. Ix'thor laughed with a rumble that made Mathilde's ears tickle on the inside. *NOTHING CAN STOP US NOW.*

A cluster of trick-or-treaters was leaving the big stone house at the end of the street. Mathilde slowed down when she realized it was Becky and Sally Hamilton. She wanted to look away and cross the street, but Nana waved to them.

"Happy Halloween!" Nana said in her big, witchy voice. *"Eee-hee-he-hee!"*

"Hello." Mrs. Hamilton wasn't wearing a costume, just regular grown-up clothes and a bright orange vest. "Girls, say hello to your friend."

Becky and Sally were both dressed up in big, poofy dresses with lots of lace and glitter. Becky's was blue and came with a sparkling tiara, while Sally, who was a few years younger, wore a pale green one with fairy wings and a wand.

"Hello," Becky said. Sally just mumbled and hid behind her mother's leg.

"Hi." Mathilde noted with some satisfaction that Becky's bag had less candy than her own. "What are you dressed up as?"

"We're princesses!" Becky straightened her tiara. "What are you supposed to be? An ink stain?"

"Rebecca!" Mrs. Hamilton said. "That wasn't very nice."

Becky winced at her mother's words, but Mathilde just smiled.

"That's okay," Mathilde said. "I don't mind. I'll just take my revenge when I rule the world. Mwa ha ha."

For some reason grown-ups always thought that sort of thing was hilariously funny. Both Nana and Mrs. Hamilton laughed out loud. Becky just glared.

"Well, come on," Nana said. "We don't want your mother to worry about you. Nice seeing you, Kathy."

"Goodbye, Mrs. Clark. Say goodbye, girls."

"B-bye," Sally muttered.

"Bye," Becky said.

Mathilde started to walk away. She saw Becky's foot move, but didn't know what was happening until it was too late.

"Oops!" Becky said. Mathilde felt the edge of her robe *yank*, and then she was falling forward, her hands out in front of her. The sidewalk hit her knees, skinning them. Candy scattered everywhere, over pavement and grass.

Ix'thor went tumbling through the air, his ball reflecting the cold sunlight. It bounced once off the curb and once more off the side of a parked car. For one held breath Mathilde thought it was going to be okay, that the ball might roll harmlessly to a stop.

Then her hope vanished in the heavy squeal of brakes and the sound of shattering glass.

Mathilde screamed, trying to stand up, trying to run. Later she would remember Nana's hands grabbing her, pulling her back from the edge of Washington Street, but, at the time, all Mathilde could see was the tiny shadow on the side of the road, with its crumpled paper wings shining in the bright autumn sun.

"No!" Mathilde kicked and squirmed in Nana's grip. There was a crowd of people standing around now. A row of stopped cars backed up on either side of the street.

"Cover him up!" Mathilde screamed. She tore her own robe trying to get away. "He needs dark! He *needs the dark!*"

"Mathilde!" Nana shouted. Mathilde ran to the little body and knelt over it, trying to give him some shade.

"Ix'thor!" Mathilde sobbed. "Please!"

NO! The little Dark Lord reached one hand toward Mathilde's tears. *THIS . . . CANNOT . . . BE. I AM . . . IN . . . VINCIBLE . . .*

• • •

"But demons are pretty strong, right?" Father said. "You said they're almost impossible to kill."

"Dark Lords are weaker in direct sunlight." That was the old man from the demon store, with his checked shirt and big, round glasses. "Much weaker. I'm sorry. I did all I could."

Mathilde sat in the dark of her room. She wondered when they would realize she could hear them through the door.

She wondered if she'd be that stupid when she was a grown-up.

"I'll talk to her," Nana said. "It's my fault that this happened."

"No," Mother said. "I'll do it."

The door cracked open. It was the only light in the room.

"Matty?" Mother looked around. "Are you in there?"

"You can turn the light on," Mathilde said from her bed. "It doesn't matter anymore."

Mother closed the door behind her and turned up the lights just a little bit.

"His tower fell down," Mathilde said. "In his cage. I tried to prop it back up, but it just kept crumbling."

"Oh, sweetie!" Mother sat down on the bed and pulled Mathilde into her lap. Mathilde squeezed her eyes shut. All the tears she had left were hiding in her throat, making a lump.

"It wasn't your fault," Mother said. "There was nothing anyone could have done."

Mathilde thought of Becky, but if it made Mother feel better to think so, then she wasn't going to argue.

"If . . ." Mother trailed off and tried again. "Father and I were talking to Nana. When you're ready, if you still want one . . ."

"I don't want a pony," Mathilde said. "I want Ix'thor. But I can't have him back, can I?"

Mother looked like she was about to cry. "No. I'm sorry."

Mathilde snuggled into her mother's arms. Mother did cry then, a little. After a while, Mathilde looked up.

"Then . . . can I get a pony with glowing red eyes, and crush the skulls of my enemies beneath his flaming hooves?"

Mother laughed a little and kissed Mathilde's forehead. "We can find one with glowing eyes, if you want."

Mathilde sighed into her mother's embrace, listening to her heartbeat. "It's a start."

AARON CORWIN has been chasing monsters since he was old enough to crawl into the dark, and creeping out everyone who'd listen since he was old enough to tell them about it. Aaron lives in Seattle, where he fronts the acoustic-nerd-rock band Ship of Dreams and occasionally moonlights as a video game character.

Reborn

Ken Liu

Special Agent Josh Rennon lives in a Boston occupied by the Tawnin, who only want peace. We are only our memories, and they excise the ugly memories and keep the useful ones. They give humanity the gift of Rebirth: a blank slate, a new beginning. But when Josh's division catches a human terrorist, he begins to question what he really remembers and who he really is. *Edited by David Hartwell.*

> Each of us *feels* that there is a single "I" in control. But that is an
> illusion that the brain works hard to produce . . .
> —Steven Pinker, *The Blank Slate*

I remember being Reborn. It felt the way I imagine a fish feels as it's being thrown back into the sea.

The Judgment Ship slowly drifts in over Fan Pier from Boston Harbor, its metallic disc-shaped hull blending into the dark, roiling sky, its curved upper surface like a pregnant belly.

It is as large as the old Federal Courthouse on the ground below. A few escort ships hover around the rim, the shifting lights on their surfaces sometimes settling into patterns resembling faces.

The spectators around me grow silent. The Judgment, scheduled four times a year, still draws a big crowd. I scan the upturned faces. Most are expressionless, some seem awed. A few men whisper to each other and chuckle. I pay some attention to them, but not too much. There hasn't been a public attack in years.

"A flying saucer," one of the men says, a little too loud. Some of the others shuffle away, trying to distance themselves. "A goddamned flying saucer."

The crowd has left the space directly below the Judgment Ship empty. A group of Tawnin observers stand in the middle, ready to welcome the Reborn. But Kai, my mate, is absent. Thie told me that thie has witnessed too many Rebirths lately.

Kai once explained to me that the design of the Judgment Ship was meant as a sign of respect for local traditions, evoking our historical imagination of little green men and *Plan 9 from Outer Space.*

It's just like how your old courthouse was built with that rotunda on top to resemble a lighthouse, a beacon of justice that pays respect to Boston's maritime history.

The Tawnin are not usually interested in history, but Kai has always advocated more effort at accommodating us locals.

I make my way slowly through the crowd, to get closer to the whispering group. They all have on long, thick coats, perfect for concealing weapons.

The top of the pregnant Judgment Ship opens and a bright beam of golden light shoots straight up into the sky, where it is reflected by the dark clouds back onto the ground as a gentle, shadowless glow.

Circular doors open all around the rim of the Judgment Ship, and long, springy lines unwind and fall from the doors. They dangle, flex, and extend like tentacles. The Judgment Ship is now a jellyfish drifting through the air.

At the end of each line is a human, securely attached like hooked fish by the Tawnin ports located over their spines and between their shoulder blades. As the lines slowly extend and drift closer to the ground, the figures at the ends languidly move their arms and legs, tracing out graceful patterns.

I've almost reached the small group of whispering men. One of them, the one who had spoken too loud earlier, has his hands inside the flap of his thick coat. I move faster, pushing people aside.

"Poor bastards," he murmurs, watching the Reborn coming closer to the empty space in the middle of the crowd, coming home. I see his face take on the determination of the fanatic, of a Xenophobe about to kill.

The Reborn have almost reached the ground. My target is waiting for the moment when the lines from the Judgment Ship are detached so that the Reborn can no longer be snatched back into the air, the moment when the Reborn are still unsteady on their feet, uncertain who they are.

Still innocent.

I remember that moment well.

The right shoulder of my target shifts as he tries to pull something out of his coat. I shove away the two women before me and leap into the air, shouting "Freeze!"

And then the world slows down as the ground beneath the Reborn erupts like a volcano, and they, along with the Tawnin observers, are tossed into the air, their limbs flopping like marionettes with their strings cut. As I crash into the man before me, a wave of heat and light blanks everything out.

· · ·

It takes a few hours to process my suspect and to bandage my wounds. By the time I'm allowed to go home it's after midnight.

The streets of Cambridge are quiet and empty because of the new curfew. A fleet of police cars is parked in Harvard Square, a dozen strobing beacons out of sync as I stop, roll down my window, and show my badge.

The fresh-faced young officer sucks in his breath. The name "Joshua Rennon" may not mean anything to him, but he has seen the black dot on the top right corner of my badge, the dot that allows me inside the high-security domicile compound of the Tawnin.

"Bad day, sir," he says. "But don't worry, we've got all the roads leading to your building secured."

He tries to make "your building" sound casual, but I can hear the thrill in his voice. *He's one of* those. *He lives with* them.

He doesn't step away from the car. "How's the investigation going, if you don't mind me asking?" His eyes roam all over me, the hunger of his curiosity so strong that it's almost palpable.

I know that the question he really wants to ask is: *What's it like?*

I turn my face straight ahead. I roll up the window.

After a moment, he steps back, and I step on the gas hard so that the tires give a satisfying squeal as I shoot away.

• • •

The walled compound used to be Radcliffe Yard.

I open the door to our apartment and the soft golden light that Kai prefers, a reminder of the afternoon, makes me shudder.

Kai is in the living room, sitting on the couch.

"Sorry I didn't call."

Kai stands up to thir full eight-foot height and opens thir arms, thir dark eyes gazing at me like the eyes of those giant fish that swim through the large tank at the New England Aquarium. I step into thir embrace and inhale thir familiar fragrance, a mixture of floral and spicy scents, the smell of an alien world and of home.

"You've heard?"

Instead of answering, thie undresses me gently, careful around my bandages. I close my eyes and do not resist, feeling the layers fall away from me piece by piece.

When I'm naked, I tilt my head up and thie kisses me, thir tubular tongue warm and salty in my mouth. I place my arms around thim, feeling on the back of thir head the long scar whose history I do not know and do not seek.

Then thie wraps thir primary arms around my head, pulling my face against thir soft, fuzzy chest. Thir tertiary arms, strong and supple, wrap around my waist. The nimble and sensitive tips of thir secondary arms lightly caress my shoulders for a moment before they find my Tawnin port and gently pry the skin apart and push in.

I gasp the moment the connection is made and I feel my limbs grow rigid and then loose as I let go, allowing Kai's strong arms to support my weight. I close my eyes so I can enjoy the way my body appears through Kai's senses: the way warm blood coursing through my vessels creates a glowing map of pulsing red and gold currents against the cooler, bluish skin on my back and buttocks, the way my short hair pricks the sensitive skin of thir primary hands, the way my chaotic thoughts are gradually soothed and rendered intelligible by thir gentle, guiding nudges. We're now connected in the most intimate way that two minds, two bodies can be.

That's what it's like, I think.

Don't be annoyed by their ignorance, thie thinks.

I replay the afternoon: the arrogant and careless manner in which I carried out my duty, the surprise of the explosion, the guilt and regret as I watched the Reborn and the Tawnin die. The helpless rage.

You'll find them, thie thinks.

I will.

Then I feel thir body moving against me, all of thir six arms and two legs probing, caressing, grasping, squeezing, penetrating. And I echo thir movements, my hands, lips, feet roaming against thir cool, soft skin the way I have come to learn thie likes, thir pleasure as clear and present as my own.

Thought seems as unnecessary as speech.

• • •

The interrogation room in the basement of the Federal Courthouse is tiny and claustrophobic, a cage.

I close the door behind me and hang up my jacket. I'm not afraid to turn my back to the suspect. Adam Woods sits with his face buried between his hands, elbows on the stainless steel table. There's no fight left in him.

"I'm Special Agent Joshua Rennon, Tawnin Protection Bureau." I wave my badge at him out of habit.

He looks up at me, his eyes bloodshot and dull.

"Your old life is over, as I'm sure you already know." I don't read him his rights or tell him that he can have a lawyer, the rituals of a less civilized age. There's no more need for lawyers—no more trials, no more police tricks.

He stares at me, his eyes full of hatred.

"What's it like?" he asks, his voice a low whisper. "Being fucked by one of them every night?"

I pause. I can't imagine he noticed the black dot on my badge in such a quick look. Then I realize that it was because I had turned my back to him. He could see the outline of the Tawnin port through my shirt. He knew I had been Reborn, and it was a lucky—but reasonable—guess that someone whose port was kept open was bonded to a Tawnin.

I don't take the bait. I'm used to the kind of xenophobia that drives men like him to kill.

"You'll be probed after the surgery. But if you confess now and give useful information about your co-conspirators, after your Rebirth you'll be given a good job and a good life, and you'll get to keep the memories of most of your friends and family. But if you lie or say nothing, we'll learn everything we need anyway and you'll be sent to California for fallout clean-up duty with a blank slate of a mind. And anyone who cared about you will forget you, completely. Your choice."

"How do you know I have any co-conspirators?"

"I saw you when the explosion happened. You were expecting it. I believe your role was to try to kill more Tawnin in the chaos after the explosion."

He continues to stare at me, his hatred unrelenting. Then, abruptly, he seems to think of something. "You've been Reborn more than once, haven't you?"

I stiffen. "How did you know?"

He smiles. "Just a hunch. You stand and sit too straight. What did you do the last time?"

I should be prepared for the question, but I'm not. Two months after my Rebirth, I'm still raw, off my game. "You know I can't answer that."

"You remember nothing?"

"That was a rotten part of me that was cut out," I tell him. "Just like it will be cut out of you. The Josh Rennon who committed whatever crime he did no longer exists, and it is only right that the crime be forgotten. The Tawnin are a compassionate and merciful people. They only remove those parts of me and you that are truly responsible for the crime—the mens rea, the evil will."

"A compassionate and merciful people," he repeats. And I see something new in his eyes: pity.

A sudden rage seizes me. *He* is the one to be pitied, not *me*. Before he has a chance to put up his hands, I lunge at him and punch him in the face, once, twice, three times, hard.

Blood flows from his nose as his hands waver before him. He doesn't make any noise, but continues to look at me with his calm, pity-filled eyes.

"They killed my father in front of me," he says. He wipes the blood from his lips and shakes his hand to get rid of it. Droplets of blood hit my shirt, the scarlet beads bright against its white fabric. "I was thirteen, and hiding in the backyard shed. Through a slit in the doors, I saw him take a swing at one of them with a baseball bat. The thing blocked it with one arm and seized his head with another pair of arms and just ripped it off. Then they burned my mother. I'll never forget the smell of cooked flesh."

I try to bring my breathing under control. I try to see the man before me as the Tawnin do: divided. There's a frightened child who can still be rescued, and an angry, bitter man who cannot.

"That was more than twenty years ago," I say. "It was a darker time, a terrible, twisted time. The world has moved on. The Tawnin have apologized and tried to make amends. You should have gone to counseling. They should have ported you and excised those memories. You could have had a life free of these ghosts."

"I don't *want* to be free of these ghosts. Did you ever consider that? I don't want to forget. I lied and told them that I saw nothing. I didn't want them to reach into my mind and steal my memories. I want revenge."

"You can't have revenge. The Tawnin who did those things are all gone. They've been punished, consigned to oblivion."

He laughs. "'Punished,' you say. The Tawnin who did those things are the exact same Tawnin who parade around today, preaching universal love and a future in which the Tawnin and humans live in harmony. Just because they can conveniently forget what they did doesn't mean we should."

"The Tawnin do not have a unified consciousness—"

"You speak like you lost no one in the Conquest." His voice rises as pity turns into something darker. "You speak like a collaborator." He spits at me, and I feel the blood on my face, between my lips—warm, sweet, the taste of rust. "You don't even know what they've taken from you."

I leave the room and close the door behind me, shutting off his stream of curses.

. . .

Outside the courthouse, Claire from Tech Investigations meets me. Her people had already scanned and recorded the crime scene last night, but we walk around the crater doing an old-fashioned visual inspection anyway, in the unlikely event that her machines missed something.

Missed something. Something was missing.

"One of the injured Reborn died at Mass General this morning around four o'clock," Claire says. "So that brings the total death toll to ten: six Tawnin and four Reborn. Not as bad as what happened in New York two years ago, but definitely the worst massacre in New England."

Claire is slight, with a sharp face and quick, jerky movements that put me in mind of a sparrow. As the only two TPB agents married to Tawnins in the Boston Field Office, we have grown close. People joke that we're work spouses.

I didn't lose anyone in the Conquest.

Kai stands with me at my mother's funeral. Her face in the casket is serene, free of pain.

Kai's touch on my back is gentle and supportive. I want to tell thim not to feel too bad. Thie had tried so hard to save her, as thie had tried to save my father before her, but the human body is fragile, and we don't yet know how to effectively use the advances taught to us by the Tawnin.

We pick our way around a pile of rubble that has been cemented in place by melted asphalt. I try to bring my thoughts under control. Woods unsettled me. "Any leads on the detonator?" I ask.

"It's pretty sophisticated," Claire says. "Based on the surviving pieces, there was a magnetometer connected to a timer circuit. My best guess is the magnetometer was triggered by the presence of large quantities of metal nearby, like the Judgment Ship. And that started a timer that was set to detonate just as the Reborn reached the ground.

"The setup requires fairly detailed knowledge of the mass of the Judgment Ship; otherwise the yachts and cargo ships sailing through the Harbor could have set it off."

"Also knowledge of the operation of the Judgment Ship," I add. "They had to know how many Reborn were going to be here yesterday, and calculate how long it would take to complete the ceremony and lower them to the ground."

"It definitely took a lot of meticulous planning," Claire said. "This is not the work of a loner. We're dealing with a sophisticated terrorist organization."

Claire pulls me to a stop. We're at a good vantage point to see the bottom of the explosion crater. It's thinner than I would have expected. Whoever had done this had used directed explosives that focused the energy upwards, presumably to minimize the damage to the crowd on the sides.

The crowd.

A memory of myself as a child comes to me unbidden.

Autumn, cool air, the smell of the sea and something burning. A large, milling crowd, but no one is making any noise. Those at the edge of the crowd, like me, push to move closer to the center, while those near the center push to get out, like a colony of ants swarming over a bird corpse. Finally, I make my way to the center, where bright bonfires burn in dozens of oil drums.

I reach into my coat and take out an envelope. I open it and hand a stack of photographs to the man standing by one of the oil drums. He flips through them and takes a few out and hands the rest back to me.

"You can keep these and go line up for surgery," he says.

I look through the photographs in my hand: Mom carrying me as a baby. Dad lifting me over his shoulders at a fair. Mom and me asleep, holding the same pose. Mom and Dad and me playing a board game. Me in a cowboy costume, Mom behind me trying to make sure the scarf fit right.

He tosses the other photographs into the oil drum, and as I turn away, I try to catch a glimpse of what's on them before they're consumed by the flames.

"You all right?"

"Yes," I say, disoriented. "Still a bit of the aftereffects of the explosion."

I can trust Claire.

"Listen," I say, "Do you ever think about what you did before you were Reborn?"

Claire focuses her sharp eyes on me. She doesn't blink. "Do not go down that path, Josh. Think of Kai. Think of your life, the real one you have now."

"You're right," I say. "Woods just rattled me a bit."

"You might want to take a few days off. You're not doing anyone favors if you can't concentrate."

"I'll be fine."

Claire seems skeptical, but she doesn't push the issue. She understands how I feel. Kai would be able to see the guilt and regret in my mind. In that ultimate intimacy, there is nowhere to hide. I can't bear to be home and doing nothing while Kai tries to comfort me.

"As I was saying," she continues, "this area was resurfaced by the W. G. Turner Construction Company a month ago. That was likely when the bomb was placed, and Woods was on the crew. You should start there."

• • •

The woman leaves the box of files on the table in front of me.

"These are all the employees and contractors who worked on the Courthouse Way resurfacing project."

She scurries away as though I'm contagious, afraid to exchange more than the absolute minimum number of words with a TPB agent.

In a way, I suppose I am contagious. When I was Reborn, those who were close to me, who had known what I had done, whose knowledge of me formed part of the identity that was Joshua Rennon, would have had to be ported and those memories excised as part of my Rebirth. My crimes, whatever they were, had infected them.

I don't even know who they might be.

I shouldn't be thinking like this. It's not healthy to dwell on my former life, a dead man's life.

I scan through the files one by one, punch the names into my phone so that Claire's algorithms back at the office can make a network out of them, link them to entries in millions of databases, trawl through the radical anti-Tawnin forums and Xenophobic sites, and find connections.

But I still read through the files meticulously, line by line. Sometimes the brain makes connections that Claire's computers cannot.

W. G. Turner had been careful. All the applicants had been subjected to extensive background searches, and none appears suspicious to the algorithms.

After a while, the names merge into an undistinguishable mess: Kelly Eickhoff, Hugh Raker, Sofia Leday, Walker Lincoln, Julio Costas . . .

Walker Lincoln.

I go back and look at the file again. The photograph shows a white male in his thirties. Narrow eyes, receding hairline, no smile for the camera. Nothing seems particularly notable. He doesn't look familiar at all.

But something about the name makes me hesitate.

The photographs curl up in the flames.

The one at the top shows my father standing in front of our house. He's holding a rifle, his face grim. As the flame swallows him, I catch a pair of crossed street signs in the last remaining corner of the photograph.

Walker and Lincoln.

I find myself shivering, even though the heat is turned up high in the office.

I take out my phone and pull up the computer report on Walker Lincoln: credit card records, phone logs, search histories, web presence, employment, and school summaries. The algorithms flagged nothing as unusual. Walker Lincoln seems the model Average Citizen.

I have never seen a profile where not a single thing was flagged by Claire's paranoid algorithms. Walker Lincoln is too perfect.

I look through the purchase history on his credit cards: fire logs, starter fluid, fireplace simulators, outdoor grills.

Then, starting about two months ago, nothing.

• • •

As thir fingers are about to push in, I speak.

"Please, not tonight."

The tips of Kai's secondary arms stop, hesitate, and gently caress my back. After a moment, thie backs up. Thir eyes look at me, like two pale moons in the dim light of the apartment.

"I'm sorry," I say. "There's a lot on my mind, unpleasant thoughts. I don't want to burden you."

Kai nods, a human gesture that seems incongruous. I appreciate the effort thie is making to make me feel better. Thie has always been very understanding.

Thie backs off, leaving me naked in the middle of the room.

• • •

The landlady proclaims complete ignorance of the life of Walker Lincoln. Rent (which in this part of Charlestown is dirt cheap) is direct deposited on the first of every month, and she hasn't set eyes on him since he moved in four months ago. I wave my badge, and she hands me the key to his apartment and watches wordlessly as I climb the stairs.

I open the door and turn on the light; I'm greeted with a sight out of a furniture

store display: white couch, leather loveseat, glass coffee table with a few magazines in a neat stack, abstract paintings on walls. There's no clutter, nothing out of
its assigned place. I take a deep breath. No smell of cooking, detergent, the mix of
aromas that accompany places lived in by real people.

The place seems familiar and strange at the same time, like walking through
déjà vu.

I walk through the apartment, opening doors. The closets and bedroom are as
artfully arranged as the living room. Perfectly ordinary, perfectly unreal.

Sunlight coming in from the windows along the western wall makes clean parallelograms against the gray carpet. The golden light is Kai's favorite shade.

There is, however, a thin layer of dust over everything. Maybe a month or two's
worth.

Walker Lincoln is a ghost.

Finally, I turn around and see something hanging on the back of the front door,
a mask.

I pick it up, put it on, and step into the bathroom.

I'm quite familiar with this type of mask. Made of soft, pliant, programmable
fibers, it's based on Tawnin technology, the same material that makes up the
strands that release the Reborn back into the world. Activated with body heat, it
molds itself into a pre-programmed shape. No matter the contours of the face
beneath it, it rearranges itself into the appearance of a face it has memorized.
Approved only for law enforcement, we sometimes use such masks to infiltrate
Xenophobic cells.

In the mirror, the cool fibers of the mask gradually come alive like Kai's body
when I touch thim, pushing and pulling against the skin and muscles of my face.
For a moment my face is a shapeless lump, like a monster's out of some nightmare.

And then the roiling motions stop, and I'm looking into the face of Walker
Lincoln.

. . .

Kai's was the first face I saw the last time I was Reborn.

It was a face with dark fish-like eyes and skin that pulsated as though tiny maggots were wriggling just under the surface. I cringed and tried to move away but
there was nowhere to go. My back was against a steel wall.

The skin around thir eyes contracted and expanded again, an alien expression
I did not understand. Thie backed up, giving me some space.

Slowly, I sat up and looked around. I was on a narrow steel slab attached to the
wall of a tiny cell. The lights were too bright. I felt nauseated. I closed my eyes.

And a tsunami of images came to me that I could not process. Faces, voices,
events in fast motion. I opened my mouth to scream.

And Kai was upon me in a second. Thie wrapped thir primary arms around my
head, forcing me to stay still. A mixture of floral and spicy scents enveloped me,
and the memory of it suddenly emerged from the chaos in my mind. *The smell of
home.* I clung to it like a floating plank in a roiling sea.

Thie wrapped thir secondary arms around me, patting my back, seeking an opening. I felt them push through a hole over my spine, a wound that I did not know was there, and I wanted to cry out in pain—

—and the chaos in my mind subsided. I was looking at the world through thir eyes and mind: my own naked body, trembling.

Let me help you.

I struggled for a bit, but thie was too strong, and I gave in.

What happened?

You're aboard the Judgment Ship. The old Josh Rennon did something very bad and had to be punished.

I tried to remember what it was that I had done, but could recall nothing.

He is gone. We had to cut him out of this body to rescue you.

Another memory floated to the surface of my mind, gently guided by the currents of Kai's thoughts.

I am sitting in a classroom, the front row. Sunlight coming in from the windows along the western wall makes clean parallelograms on the ground. Kai paces slowly back and forth in front of us.

"Each of us is composed of many groupings of memories, many personalities, many coherent patterns of thoughts." The voice comes from a black box Kai wears around thir neck. It's slightly mechanical, but melodious and clear.

"Do you not alter your behavior, your expressions, even your speech when you're with your childhood friends from your hometown compared to when you're with your new friends from the big city? Do you not laugh differently, cry differently, even become angry differently when you're with your family than when you're with me?"

The students around me laugh a little at this, as do I. As Kai reaches the other side of the classroom, thie turns around and our eyes meet. The skin around thir eyes pulls back, making them seem even bigger, and my face grows warm.

"The unified individual is a fallacy of traditional human philosophy. It is, in fact, the foundation of many unenlightened, old customs. A criminal, for example, is but one person inhabiting a shared body with many others. A man who murders may still be a good father, husband, brother, son, and he is a different man when he plots death than when he bathes his daughter, kisses his wife, comforts his sister, and cares for his mother. Yet the old human criminal justice system would punish all of these men together indiscriminately, would judge them together, imprison them together, even kill them together. Collective punishment. How barbaric! How cruel!"

I imagine my mind the way Kai describes it: partitioned into pieces, an individual divided. There may be no human institution that the Tawnin despise more than our justice system. Their contempt makes perfect sense when considered in the context of their mind-to-mind communication. The Tawnin have no secrets from each other and share an intimacy we can only dream of. The idea of a justice system so limited by the opacity of the individual that it must resort to ritualized adversarial combat rather than direct access to the truth of the mind must seem to them a barbarity.

Kai glances at me, as though thie could hear my thoughts, though I know that is not possible without my being ported. But the thought brings pleasure to me. I am Kai's favorite student.

I placed my arms around Kai.

My teacher, my lover, my spouse. I was once adrift, and now I have come home. I am beginning to remember.

I felt the scar on the back of thir head. Thie trembled.

What happened here?

I don't remember. Don't worry about it.

I carefully caressed thim, avoiding the scar.

The Rebirth is a painful process. Your biology did not evolve as ours, and the parts of your mind are harder to tease apart, to separate out the different persons. It will take some time for the memories to settle. You have to re-remember, relearn the pathways needed to make sense of them again, to reconstruct yourself again. But you're now a better person, free from the diseased parts we had to cut out.

I hung onto Kai, and we picked up the pieces of myself together.

• • •

I show Claire the mask, and the too-perfect electronic profile. "To get access to this kind of equipment and to create an alias with an electronic trail this convincing requires someone with a lot of power and access. Maybe even someone inside the Bureau, since we need to scrub electronic databases to cleanse the records of the Reborn."

Claire bites her bottom lip as she glances at the display on my phone and regards the mask with skepticism. "That seems really unlikely. All the Bureau employees are ported and are regularly probed. I don't see how a mole among us can stay hidden."

"Yet it's the only explanation."

"We'll know soon enough," Claire tells me. "Adam has been ported. Tau is doing the probe now. Should be done in half an hour."

I practically fall into the chair next to her. Exhaustion over the last two days settles over me like a heavy blanket. I have been avoiding Kai's touch, for reasons that I cannot even explain. I feel divided from myself.

I tell myself to stay awake, just a little longer.

Kai and I are sitting on the leather loveseat. Thir big frame means that we are squeezed in tightly. The fireplace is behind us and I can feel the gentle heat against the back of my neck. Thir left arms gently stroke my back. I'm tense.

My parents are on the white couch across from us.

"I've never seen Josh this happy," my mother says. And her smile is such a relief that I want to hug her.

"I'm glad you feel that way," says Kai, with thir black voice box. "I think Josh was worried about how you might feel about me—about us."

"There are always going to be Xenophobes," my father says. He sounds a little out of breath. I know that one day I will recognize this as the beginning of his sickness. A tinge of sorrow tints my happy memory.

"Terrible things were done," Kai says. "We do know that. But we always want to look to the future."

"So do we," my father says. "But some people are trapped in the past. They can't let the dead lie buried."

I look around the room and notice how neat the house is. The carpet is immaculate, the end tables free of clutter. The white couch my parents are sitting on is spotless. The glass coffee table between us is empty save for a stack of artfully arranged magazines.

The living room is like the showroom of a furniture store.

I jerk awake. The pieces of my memories have become as unreal as Walker Lincoln's apartment.

Tau, Claire's spouse, is at the door. The tips of thir secondary arms are mangled, oozing blue blood. Thie stumbles.

Claire is by thir side in a moment. "What happened?"

Instead of answering, Tau tears Claire's jacket and blouse away, and thir thicker, less delicate primary arms hungrily, blindly seek the Tawnin port on Claire's back. When they finally find the opening, they plunge in and Claire gasps, going limp immediately.

I turn my eyes away from this scene of intimacy. Tau is in pain and needs Claire.

"I should go," I say, getting up.

"Adam had booby-trapped his spine," Tau says through thir voice box.

I pause.

"When I ported him, he was cooperative and seemed resigned to his fate. But when I began the probe, a miniature explosive device went off, killing him instantly. I guess some of you still hate us so much that you'd rather die than be Reborn."

"I'm sorry," I say.

"I'm the one that's sorry," Tau says. The mechanical voice struggles to convey sorrow, but it sounds like an imitation to my unsettled mind. "Parts of him were innocent."

• • •

The Tawnin do not care much for history, and now, neither do we.

They also do not die of old age. No one knows how old the Tawnin are: centuries, millennia, eons. Kai speaks vaguely of a journey that lasted longer than the history of the human race.

What was it like? I once asked.

I don't remember, thie had thought.

Their attitude is explained by their biology. Their brains, like the teeth of sharks, never cease growing. New brain tissue is continuously produced at the core while the outer layers are sloughed off periodically like snakeskin.

With lives that are for all intents and purposes eternal, the Tawnin would have been overwhelmed by eons of accumulated memories. It is no wonder that they became masters of forgetting.

Memories that they wish to keep must be copied into the new tissue: retraced, recreated, re-recorded. But memories that they wish to leave behind are cast off like dried pupa husks with each cycle of change.

It is not only memory that they leave behind. Entire personalities can be adopted, taken on like a role, and then cast aside and forgotten. A Tawnin views the self before a change and the self after a change as entirely separate beings: different personalities, different memories, different moral responsibilities. They merely shared a body seriatim.

Not even the same body, Kai thought to me.

?

In about a year every atom in your body will have been replaced by others, thought Kai. This was back when we had first become lovers, and thie was often in a lecturing mood. *For us it's even faster.*

Like the ship of Theseus where each plank was replaced over time, until it was no longer the same ship.

You're always making these references to the past. But the flavor of thir thought was indulgent rather than critical.

When the Conquest happened, the Tawnin had adopted an attitude of extreme aggression. And we had responded in kind. The details, of course, are hazy. The Tawnin do not remember them, and most of us do not want to. California is still uninhabitable after all these years.

But then, once we had surrendered, the Tawnin had cast off those aggressive layers of their minds—the punishment for their war crimes—and become the gentlest rulers imaginable. Now committed pacifists, they abhor violence and willingly share their technology with us, cure diseases, perform wondrous miracles. The world is at peace. Human life expectancy has been much lengthened, and those willing to work for the Tawnin have done well for themselves.

The Tawnin do not experience guilt.

We are a different people now, Kai thought. *This is also our home. And yet some of you insist on tasking us with the sins of our dead past selves. It is like holding the son responsible for the sins of the father.*

What if war should occur again? I thought. *What if the Xenophobes convince the rest of us to rise up against you?*

Then we might change yet again, become ruthless and cruel as before. Such changes in us are physiological reactions against threat, beyond our control. But then those future selves would have nothing to do with us. The father cannot be responsible for the acts of the son.

It's hard to argue with logic like that.

• • •

Adam's girlfriend, Lauren, is a young woman with a hard face that remained unchanged after I informed her that, as Adam's parents are deceased, she is considered the next of kin and responsible for picking up the body at the station.

We are sitting across from each other, the kitchen table between us. The apartment is tiny and dim. Many of the lightbulbs have burnt out and not been replaced.

"Am I going to be ported?" she asks.

Now that Adam is dead, the next order of business is to decide which of his relatives and friends should be ported—with appropriate caution for further booby-trapped spines—so that the true extent of the conspiracy can be uncovered.

"I don't know yet," I say. "It depends on how much I think you're cooperating. Did he associate with anyone suspicious? Anyone you thought was a Xenophobe?"

"I don't know anything," she says. "Adam is . . . was a loner. He never told me anything. You can port me if you want, but it will be a waste of energy."

Normally, people like her are terrified of being ported, violated. Her feigned nonchalance only makes me more suspicious of her.

She seems to sense my skepticism and changes tack. "Adam and I would sometimes smoke oblivion or do blaze." She shifts in her seat and looks over at the kitchen counter. I look where she's looking and see the drug paraphernalia in front of a stack of dirty dishes, like props set out on a stage. A leaky faucet drips, providing a background beat to the whole scene.

Oblivion and blaze both have strong hallucinogenic effects. The unspoken point: her mind is riddled with false memories that even when ported cannot be relied upon. The most we can do is Rebirth her, but we won't find out anything we can use on others. It's not a bad trick. But she hasn't made the lie sufficiently convincing.

You humans think you are what you've done, Kai once thought. I remember us lying together in a park somewhere, the grass under us, and I loved feeling the warmth of the sun through thir skin, so much more sensitive than mine. *But you're really what you remember.*

Isn't that the same thing? I thought.

Not at all. To retrieve a memory, you must reactivate a set of neural connections, and in the process change them. Your biology is such that with each act of recall, you also rewrite the memory. Haven't you ever had the experience of discovering that a detail you remembered vividly was manufactured? A dream you became convinced was a real experience? Being told a fabricated story you believed to be the truth?

You make us sound so fragile.

Deluded, actually. The flavor of Kai's thought was affectionate. *You cannot tell which memories are real and which memories are false, and yet you insist on their importance, base so much of your life on them. The practice of history has not done your species much good.*

Lauren averts her eyes from my face, perhaps thinking of Adam. Something about Lauren seems familiar, like the half-remembered chorus from a song heard in childhood. I like the indescribable way her face seems to relax as she is lost in memories. I decide, right then, that I will not have Lauren ported.

Instead, I retrieve the mask from my bag and, keeping my eyes on her face, I put it on. As the mask warms to my face, clinging to it, shaping muscle and skin, I watch her eyes for signs of recognition, for confirmation that Adam and Walker were co-conspirators.

Her face becomes tight and impassive again. "What are you doing? That thing's creepy looking."

Disappointed, I tell her, "Just a routine check."

"You mind if I deal with that leaky faucet? It's driving me crazy."

I nod and remain seated as she gets up. Another dead end. Could Adam really have done it all on his own? Who was Walker Lincoln?

I'm afraid of the answer that's half formed in my mind.

I sense the heavy weight swinging towards the back of my head, but it's too late.

. . .

"Can you hear us?" The voice is scrambled, disguised by some electronic gizmo. Oddly, it reminds me of a Tawnin voice box.

I nod in the darkness. I'm seated and my hands are tied behind me. Something soft, a scarf or a tie, is wrapped tightly around my head, covering my eyes.

"I'm sorry that we have to do things this way. It's better if you can't see us. This way, when your Tawnin probes you, we won't be betrayed."

I test the ties around my wrists. They're very well done. No possibility of working them loose on my own.

"You have to stop this right now," I say, putting as much authority into my voice as I can. "I know you think you've caught a collaborator, a traitor to the human race. You believe this is justice, vengeance. But think. If you harm me, you'll eventually be caught, and all your memory of this event erased. What's the good of vengeance if you won't even remember it? It will be as if it never happened."

Electronic voices laugh in the darkness. I can't tell how many of them there are. Old, young, male or female.

"Let me go."

"We will," the first voice says, "after you hear this."

I hear the click of a button being pressed, and then, a disembodied voice: "Hello, Josh. I see you've found the clues that matter."

The voice is my own.

. . .

". . . despite extensive research, it is not possible to erase all memories. Like an old hard drive, the Reborn mind still holds traces of those old pathways, dormant, waiting for the right trigger . . ."

The corner of Walker and Lincoln, my old house.

Inside, it's cluttered, my toys scattered everywhere. There is no couch, only four wicker chairs around an old wooden coffee table, the top full of circular stains.

I'm hiding behind one of the wicker chairs. The house is quiet and the lighting dim, early dawn or late dusk.

A scream outside.

I get up and run to the door and fling it open. I see my father being hoisted into the air by a Tawnin's primary arms. The secondary and tertiary arms are wrapped around my father's arms and legs, rendering him immobile.

Behind the Tawnin, my mother's body lies prostrate, unmoving.

The Tawnin jerks its arms and my father tries to scream again, but blood has pooled in his throat, and what comes out is a mere gurgle. The Tawnin jerks its limbs again and I watch as my father is torn slowly into pieces.

The Tawnin looks down at me. The skin around its eyes recedes and contracts again. The smell of unknown flowers and spices is so strong that I retch.

It's Kai.

". . . in the place of real memories, they fill your mind with lies. Constructed memories that crumble under examination . . ."

Kai comes to me on the other side of my cage. There are many cages like it, each holding a young man or woman. How many years have we been in darkness and isolation, kept from forming meaningful memories?

There was never any well-lit classroom, any philosophical lecture, any sunlight slanting in from the western windows, casting clean, sharp parallelograms against the ground.

"We're sorry for what happened," Kai says. The voice box, at least, is real. But the mechanical tone belies the words. "We've been saying this for a long time. The ones who did those things you insist on remembering are not us. They were necessary for a time, but they have been punished, cast off, forgotten. It's time to move on."

I spit in Kai's eyes.

Kai does not wipe away my spittle. The skin around its eyes contracts and it turns away. "You leave us no choice. We have to make you anew."

". . . they tell you that the past is the past, dead, gone. They tell you that they are a new people, not responsible for their former selves. And there is some truth to these assertions. When I couple with Kai, I see into thir mind, and there is nothing left of the Kai that killed my parents, the Kai that brutalized the children, the Kai that forced us by decree to burn our old photographs, to wipe out the traces of our former existence that might interfere with what they want for our future. They really are as good at forgetting as they say, and the bloody past appears to them as an alien country. The Kai that is my lover is truly a different mind: innocent, blameless, guiltless.

"But they continue to walk over the bones of your, my, our parents. They continue to live in houses taken from our dead. They continue to desecrate the truth with denial.

"Some of us have accepted collective amnesia as the price of survival. But not all. I am you, and you're me. The past does not die; it seeps, leaks, infiltrates, waits for an opportunity to spring up. You *are* what you remember . . ."

The first kiss from Kai, slimy, raw.

The first time Kai penetrates me. The first time my mind is invaded by its mind. The feeling of helplessness, of something being done to me that I can never be rid of, that I can never be clean again.

The smell of flowers and spices, the smell that I can never forget or expel because it doesn't just come from my nostrils, but has taken root deep in my mind.

". . . though I began by infiltrating the Xenophobes, in the end it is they who infiltrated me. Their underground records of the Conquest and the giving of testimony and sharing of memories finally awoke me from my slumber, allowed me to recover my own story.

"When I found out the truth, I carefully plotted my vengeance. I knew it would not be easy to keep a secret from Kai. But I came up with a plan. Because I was married to Kai, I was exempt from the regular probes that the other TPB agents are subject to. By avoiding intimacy with Kai and pleading discomfort, I could avoid being probed altogether and hold secrets in my mind, at least for a while.

"I created another identity, wore a mask, provided the Xenophobes with what they needed to accomplish their goals. All of us wore masks so that if any of the co-conspirators were captured, probing one mind would not betray the rest of us."

The masks I wear to infiltrate the Xenophobes are the masks I give to my co-conspirators . . .

"Then I prepped my mind like a fortress against the day of my inevitable capture and Rebirth. I recalled the way my parents died in great detail, replayed the events again and again until they were etched indelibly into my mind, until I knew that Kai, who would ask for the role of preparing me for my Rebirth, would flinch at the vivid images, be repulsed by their blood and violence, and stop before probing too deep. Thie had long forgotten what thie had done and had no wish to be reminded.

"Do I know if these images are true in every aspect? No, I do not. I recalled them through the hazy filter of the mind of a child, and no doubt the memories shared by all the other survivors have inseminated them, colored them, given them more details. Our memories bleed into each other, forming a collective outrage. The Tawnin will say they're no more real than the false memories they've implanted, but to forget is a far greater sin than to remember too well.

"To further conceal my trails, I took the pieces of the false memories they gave me and constructed real memories out of them so that when Kai dissected my mind, thie would not be able to tell thir lies apart from my own."

The false, clean, clutter-free living room of my parents is recreated and rearranged into the room in which I meet with Adam and Lauren . . .

Sunlight coming in from the windows along the western wall makes clean parallelograms on the ground . . .

You cannot tell which memories are real and which memories are false, and yet you insist on their importance, base so much of your life on them.

"And now, when I'm sure that the plot has been set in motion but do not yet know enough details to betray the plans should I be probed, I will go attack Kai. There is very little chance I will succeed, and Kai will surely want me to be Reborn, to wipe this me away—not all of me, just enough so that our life together can go on. My death will protect my co-conspirators, will allow them to triumph.

"Yet what good is vengeance if I cannot see it, if you, the Reborn me, cannot remember it, and know the satisfaction of success? This is why I have buried clues, left behind evidence like a trail of crumbs that you will pick up, until you can remember and know what you have done."

Adam Woods . . . who is not so different from me after all, his memory a trigger for mine . . .

I purchase things so that, someday, they'll trigger in another me the memory of fire . . .

The mask, so that others can remember me . . .

Walker Lincoln.

. . .

Claire is outside the station, waiting, when I walk back. Two men are standing in the shadows behind her. And still further behind, looming above them, the indistinct figure of Kai.

I stop and turn around. Behind me, two more men are walking down the street, blocking off my retreat.

"It's too bad, Josh," Claire says. "You should have listened to me about remembering. Kai told us that thie was suspicious."

I cannot pick Kai's eyes out of the shadows. I direct my gaze at the blurry shadow behind and above Claire.

"Will you not speak to me yourself, Kai?"

The shadow freezes, and then the mechanical voice, so different from the *voice* that I've grown used to caressing my mind, crackles from the gloom.

"I have nothing to say to you. My Josh, my beloved, no longer exists. He has been taken over by ghosts, has already drowned in memory."

"I'm still here, but now I'm complete."

"That is a persistent illusion of yours that we cannot seem to correct. I am not the Kai you hate, and you're not the Josh I love. We are not the sum of our pasts." Thie pauses. "I hope I will see my Josh soon."

Thie retreats into the interior of the station, leaving me to my judgment and execution.

Fully aware of the futility, I try to talk to Claire anyway.

"Claire, you know I have to remember."

Her face looks sad and tired. "You think you're the only one who's lost someone? I wasn't ported until five years ago. I once had a wife. She was like you. Couldn't let go. Because of her, I was ported and Reborn. But because I made a determined effort to forget, to leave the past alone, they allowed me to keep some memory of her. You, on the other hand, insist on fighting.

"Do you know how many times you've been Reborn? It's because Kai loves . . . loved you, wished to save most parts of you, that they've been so careful with carving as little of you away as possible each time."

I do not know why Kai wished so fervently to rescue me from myself, to cleanse me of ghosts. Perhaps there are faint echoes of the past in thir mind, that even thie is not aware of, that draw thim to me, that compel thim to try to make me believe the lies so that thie will believe them thimself. To forgive is to forget.

"But thie has finally run out of patience. After this time you'll remember nothing at all of your life, and so with your crime you've consigned more of you, more of those you claim to care about, to die. What good is this vengeance you seek if no one will even remember it happened? The past is gone, Josh. There is no future for the Xenophobes. The Tawnin are here to stay."

I nod. What she says is true. But just because something is true doesn't mean you stop struggling.

I imagine myself in the Judgment Ship again. I imagine Kai coming to welcome me home. I imagine our first kiss, innocent, pure, a new beginning. The memory of the smell of flowers and spices.

There is a part of me that loves thim, a part of me that has seen thir soul and craves thir touch. There is a part of me that wants to move on, a part of me that believes in what the Tawnin have to offer. And *I*, the unified, illusory I, am filled with pity for them.

I turn around and begin to run. The men in front of me wait patiently. There's nowhere for me to go.

I press the trigger in my hand. Lauren had given it to me before I left. A last gift from my old self, from me to me.

I imagine my spine exploding into a million little pieces a moment before it does. I imagine all the pieces of me, atoms struggling to hold a pattern for a second, to be a coherent illusion.

KEN LIU is an author of speculative fiction, as well as a translator, lawyer, and programmer. A winner of the Nebula, Hugo, and World Fantasy Awards, he is the author of the Dandelion Dynasty, a silkpunk epic fantasy series (*The Grace of Kings, The Wall of Storms*, and a forthcoming third volume), and *The Paper Menagerie and Other Stories*, a collection. He also wrote the Star Wars novel *The Legends of Luke Skywalker*. In addition to his original fiction, Ken also translated numerous works from Chinese to English, including *The Three-Body Problem* by Liu Cixin, and "Folding Beijing" by Hao Jingfang, both Hugo winners.

Please Undo This Hurt

Seth Dickinson

Ever feel like you care too much? That's not an option for Dominga, an EMT, or her drinking buddy Nico, who's tired of hurting people. He wants out. Not suicide, but what if he could erase his whole life? Undo the fact of his birth? *Edited by Marco Palmieri.*

"A coyote got my cat," Nico says.

It took me four beers and three shots to open him up. All night he's been talking about the breakup, what's-her-name, Yelena I think, and all night I've known there's something else on him, but I didn't *know* know—

"Fuck, man." I catch at his elbow. He's wearing leather, supple, slick—he's always mock-hurt when I can't tell his good jackets from his great ones. "Mandrill?" A better friend wouldn't have to ask, but I'm drunk, and not so good a friend. "Your cat back home?"

"Poor Mandrill," Nico says, completely forlorn. "Ah, shit, Dominga. I shouldn't have left him."

He only goes to the Lighthouse on empty Sundays, when we can hide in the booths ringed around the halogen beacon. I expect sad nights here. But, man, his *cat* . . .

Nico puts his head on my shoulder and makes a broken noise into the side of my neck. I rub his elbow and marvel in a selfish way at how much I *care*, how full of hurt I am, even after this awful week of dead bikers and domestics and empty space where fucking Jacob used to be. It's the drink, of course, and tomorrow if we see each other (we won't) it'll all be awkward, stilted, an unspoken agreement to forget this moment.

But right now I care.

In a moment he'll pull himself up, make a joke, buy a round. I know he will, since Nico and I only speak in bars and only when things feel like dogshit. We've got nothing in common—I ride ambulances around Queens, call my mom in Laredo every week, shouting Spanish into an old flip phone with a busted speaker. He makes smartphone games in a FiDi studio, imports leather jackets, and serially thinks his way out of perfectly good relationships. But all that difference warms me up sometimes, because (forgive me here, I am drunk) what's the world worth if you can't put two strangers together and get them to care? A friendship shouldn't need anything else.

He doesn't pull himself up and he doesn't make a joke.

The lighthouse beam sweeps over us, over the netting around our booth, over Nico's cramped shoulders and gawky height curled up against me. The light draws grid shadows on his leathered back, as if we're in an ambulance together, monitors tracing the thready rhythm of Nico's life. We sit together in the blue fog as the light passes on across empty tables carved with half-finished names.

"I'm really sorry." He finally pulls away, stiff, frowning. "I'm such a drag tonight. How are things after Jacob?"

I cluck in concern, just like my mom. I have to borrow the sound from her because *I* want to scream every time I think about fucking Jacob and fucking *I'm not ready for your life.* "We're talking about you."

He grins a fake grin, but he's so good at it I'm still a little charmed. "We've been talking about me *forever.*"

"You broke up with your girlfriend and lost your cat. You're having a bad week. As a medical professional, I insist I buy you another round." Paramedics drink, and lie sometimes. He dumped Yelena out of the blue, "to give her a chance at someone better." The opposite of what Jacob had done to me. "And we're going to talk."

"No." He looks away. I follow his eyes, tracing the lighthouse beam across the room, where the circle of tables ruptures, broken by some necessity of cleaning or fire code: as if a snake had come up out of the light, slithered through the table mandala, and written something with its passage. "No, I'm done."

And the way he says that hits me, hits me low, because I recognize it. I have a stupid compassion that does me no good. I am desperate to help the people in my ambulance, the survivors. I can hold them together but I can't answer the plea I always see in their eyes: *Please, God, please, mother of mercy, just let this never have happened. Make it undone. Let me have a world where things like this never come to pass.*

"Nico," I say, "do you feel like you want to hurt yourself?"

He looks at me, and the Lighthouse's sound system glitches for an instant, harsh and negative, as if we're listening to the inverse music that fills the space between the song and the meaningless static beneath.

My heart trips, thumps, like the ambulance alarm's just gone off.

"I don't want to hurt anyone," he says, eyes round and honest. "I don't want to get on Twitter and read about all the atrocities I'm complicit in. I don't want to trick wonderful women into spending a few months figuring out what a shithead I really am. I don't want to raise little cats to be coyote food. I don't even want to worry about whether I'm dragging my friends down. I just want to undo all the harm I've ever done."

Make it undone.

In my job I see these awful things—this image always come to me: a cyclist's skull burst like a watermelon beneath the wheels of a truck he didn't see. I used to feel like I made a difference in my job. But that was a long time ago.

So I hold to this: As long as I can care about other people, I'm not in burnout. Emotional detachment is a cardinal symptom, you see.

"Did you ever see *It's a Wonderful Life?*" I'm trying to lighten the mood. I've only read the Wikipedia page.

"Yeah." Oops. "But I thought it kind of missed the point. What if—" He makes an excited gesture, pointing to an idea. But his eyes are still fixed on the mirror surface of the table, and when he sees himself his jaw works. "What if his angel said, *Oh, you've done more harm than good; but we all do, that's life, those are the rules, there's just more hurt to go around*. Why couldn't he, I forget his name, it doesn't matter, why couldn't he say, well, just redact me. Remove the fact of my birth. I'm a good guy, I don't want to do anyone any harm, so I'm going to opt out. Do you think that's possible? Not a suicide, that's selfish, it hurts people. But a really self-less way out?"

I don't know what to say to that. It's stupid, but he's smart, and he says it so hard.

He grins up at me, full-lipped, beautiful. The lighthouse beacon comes around again and lights up his silhouette and puts his face in shadow except his small, white teeth. "I mean, come on. If I weren't here—wouldn't you be having a good night?"

"You're wishing you'd never known me, you realize. You're shitting all over me."

"Dominga Roldan! My knight." There he goes, closing up again, putting on the armor of charm. He likes that Roldan is so much like Roland. It's the first thing he ever told me. "Please. You're the suffering hero at this table. Let's talk about you."

I surrender. I start talking about fucking Jacob.

But I resolve right then that I'll save Nico, convince him that it's worth it to go on, worth it to have ever been.

. . .

I believe in good people. Even though Nico has what we call "resting asshole face" and a job that requires him to trick people into giving him thousands of dollars (he designs the systems that keep people playing smartphone games, especially the parts that keep them spending), I still think he's a good man. He cares, way down.

I believe you can feel that. The world's a cold place and it'll break your heart. You've got to trust in the possibility of good.

I dream of gardening far south and west, home in Laredo. Inexplicably, fucking Jacob is there. He smiles at me, big bear face a little stubbled. I want to yell at him: don't grow a beard! You have a great chin! But we're busy gardening, rooting around in galvanized tubs full of okra and zucchini and purple hull peas. Hot peppers, since the sweet breeds won't take. The autumn light down here isn't so thin as in New York. I am bare-handed, turning up the soil around the roots, grit up under my fingers and in the web of my hands. I am making life.

But down in the zucchini roots, I find a knot of maggots, balled up squirming like they've wormed a portal up from maggot hell and come pouring out blind and silent. And I think: I am only growing homes for maggots. Everything is this way. In the end we are only making more homes, better homes, for maggots.

Jacob smiles at me and says, like he did: "I'm just not ready for your life. It's too hard. Too many people get hurt."

I wake up groaning, hangover clotted in my sinuses. Staring up at the vent above my mattress, I realize there's no heat. It's broken again.

The cold is sharp, though. Sterile. It makes me go. I get to the hospital on time and Mary's waiting for me, smiling, my favorite partner armed with coffee and danishes and an egg sandwich from the enigmatic food truck only she can find. For my hangover, of course. Mary, bless her, knows my schedule.

Later that day we save a man's life.

He swam out into the river to die. We're first on the scene and I am stupid, so stupid: I jump in to save him. The water's late-autumn cold, the kind of chill I am afraid will get into my marrow and crystallize there, so that later in life, curled up in the summer sun with a lover, I'll feel a pang and know that a bead of ice came out of my bone and stuck in my heart. I used to get that kind of chest pain growing up, see. I thought they were ice crystals that formed when we went to see ex-Dad in Colorado, where the world felt high and thin, everything offered up on an altar to the truth behind the indifferent cloth of stars.

I'm thinking all this as I haul the drowning man back in. I feel so cold and so aware. My mind goes everywhere. Goes to Jacob, of course.

Offered up on an altar. We used to play a sex game like that, Jacob and I. You know, a sexy sacrifice—isn't that the alchemy of sex games? You take something appalling and you make it part of your appetites. Jesus, I used to think it was cute, and now describing it I'm furiously embarrassed. Jacob was into all kinds of nerd shit. For him I think the fantasy was always kind of Greco-Roman, Andromeda on the rocks, but I always wondered if he dared imagine me as some kind of Aztec princess, which would be too complicatedly racist for him to suggest. He's dating a white girl now. It doesn't bother me but Mom just won't let it go. She's sharp about it, too: she has a theory that Jacob feels he's now Certified Decent, having passed his qualifying exam, and now he'll go on to be a regular shithead.

And Mary's pulling me up onto the pier, and I'm pulling the suicide.

He nearly dies in the ambulance. We swaddle him in heat packs and blankets and Mary, too, swaddles him, smiling and flirting, it's okay, what a day for a swim, does he know that in extreme situations rescuers are advised to provide skin-to-skin contact?

See, Mary's saying, see, it's not so bad here, not so cold. You'll meet good people. You'll go on.

Huddled in my own blankets, I meet the swimmer's warm brown eyes and just then the ambulance slams across a pothole. He fibrillates. Alarms shriek. I see him start to go, receding, calm, warm, surrounded by people trying to save him, and I think that if he went now, before his family found out, before he had to go back to whatever drove him into the river, it'd be best.

Oh, God, the hurt can't be undone. It'd be best.

His eyes open. They peel back like membranes. I see a thin screen, thinner than Colorado sky, and in the vast space behind it, something white and soft and eyeless wheels on an eternal wind.

His heart quits. He goes into asystole.

"Come on," Mary hisses, working on him. "Come on. You can't do this to me. Dominga, let's get some epi going—come on, don't go."

I think that's the hook that pulls him in. He cares. He doesn't want to hurt her. Like Nico, he can't stand to do harm. By that hook or by the CPR and the epinephrine, we bring him back. Afterward I sit outside in the cold, the bitter dry cold, and I can *feel* it: the heat going out of me, the world leaking up through the sky and out into the void where something ancient waits, a hypothermic phantasm, a cold fever dream, the most real thing I've ever seen.

I flail around for something human to hold and remember, then, how worried I am about Nico.

• • •

Don't judge me too harshly. This is my next move: I invite Nico to game night with Jacob and his new girlfriend, Elise. Nico is a game designer, right? It fits. I promised Jacob we'd still be friends. Everything fits.

It's not about any kind of payback.

Jacob loves this idea. He suggests a café/bar nerd money trap called Glass Needle. I turn up with Nico (*Cool jacket*, I say, and he grins back at me from under his mirrored aviators, saying, *You really can't tell!*) and we all shake hands and say Hi, hi, wow, it's so great, under a backlit ceiling of frosted glass etched with the shapes of growing things.

"Isn't that cool?" Jacob beams at me. "They do that with hydrofluorosilicic acid." He's growing too: working on a beard and a gut, completing the deadly Santa array. Elise looks like she probably does yoga. She arranges the game with assured competence. I wonder how many times Jacob practiced saying *hydrofluorosilicic*, and what their sex is like.

Nico tongues a square of gum. "That's really impressive," he says.

The games engage him. I guess the games engage me too: Jacob will listen to anything Nico says, since Jacob cares about everything and Nico pretends he doesn't. "I love board games," Jacob explains.

"I love rules," Nico replies, and this is true: Nico thinks everything is a game to be played, history, evolution, even dating, even friendship. Everything has a winning strategy. He'll describe this cynicism to anyone, since he thinks it's sexy. If you know him you can see how deeply it bothers him.

It's Sunday again. I worked eighteen hours yesterday. I'm exhausted, I can't stop thinking about the swimmer flatline. Jacob looks at me with the selfless worry permitted to the ex who did the dumping.

If I weren't here, I think, *wouldn't you be having a good night?*

The game baffles me. Elise assembles a zoo of cardboard tokens, decks of tiny cards, dice, character sheets, Jacob chattering all the while: "These are for the other worlds you'll visit. These are spells you can learn, though of course they'll drive you mad. This card means you're the town sheriff—that one means you eat free at the diner—"

Elise pats him on the hand. "I think they can learn as they go."

We're supposed to patrol a town where the world has gotten thin and wounded.

If we don't heal those wounds, something will come through, a dreadful thing with a name like the Treader in Dust or whatever. Nico's really good at the game. He flirts with me outrageously, which earns a beautifully troubled Jacob-face, a face of perturbed enlightenment: *really, this shouldn't be bothering me!* So I flirt back at Nico. Why not? He's the one getting a kick out of meeting my ex and out-charming him, out-dressing him, talking over him while he sits there and takes it. And wouldn't Mary flirt, to comfort him? To remind poor forlorn Nico that the world's not so cold?

Only Nico doesn't seem so forlorn, and when I look at Jacob, there's Elise touching shoulders with him, which makes every memory of Jacob hurt. As if she's claimed him not just now but retroactively too.

Even Elise, who's played it a hundred times, can't manage this damn game. The rules seem uncertain, as if different parts of the rule book contradict each other. Jacob and Nico argue over exactly how the monsters decide to hunt us, precisely when the Magic Shop closes up, where the yawning portals lead. Oh, Nico—this must be so satisfyingly *you*: You are beating Jacob's game, you're better than his rules. Even Elise won't argue with Nico, preferring, she says, to focus on the *emergent narrative*.

It all leaves me outside.

I drink to spiteful excess and move my little character around in sullen ineffective ways. Jacob's eyes are full of stupid understanding. I look at him and try to beam my thoughts: I hate this. This makes me sick. I wish I'd never met you. I wish I could burn up all the good times we had, just to spare myself this awful night.

That's what I thought when he left. That it hadn't been worth it.

"Can we switch sides," Nico asks, "and obtain dreadful secrets from the Great Old One?"

"You could try." Elise loves this. She grins at Nico and I savor Jacob's reaction. "But your only hope is that It will devour your soul first, so you don't have to experience the terrible majesty of Its coming."

And Nico grins at me. "What an awful world. You're fucked the moment you're born." Making a joke out of his drunken despair, out of dead Mandrill and his own hurt. Of course he doesn't take it seriously. Of course he was just drunk.

I am everyone's sucker.

"I think you can do that with an expansion set," Jacob adds helpfully. "Switch sides, I mean."

"Let's play with it next time," Nico says. Elise bounces happily. There probably *will* be a next time, won't there? The three of them will be friends.

"I feel sick," I say, "it's just—something I saw on shift. It's getting to me."

Then I go. They can't argue with that. They all work in offices.

Nico texts me: Holy shit we lost. Alien god woke up to consume the world. We went mad with rapture and horror when it spoke hidden secrets of the universal design although I did shoot it with a tommy gun. Game is fucking broken. It was amazing thank you.

I text back: cool

What I want to say is: you asshole, I hope you're happy, I hope you're glad you're right, I hope you're glad you won. I believe in good people, you know, but I used to think Jacob was a good person, and look where that got me; I just wanted to cheer you up and look where that got me. I pull people from the river, I drag them dying out of their houses, I see their spinal fluid running into the gutters and look where all that gets me—

Jesus, this world, this world. I feel so heartsick. I cannot even retch.

And I dream of that awful board, piled with tokens moving each other by their own secret rules. A game of alien powers, but those powers escape the game to move among us. They roam the world cow-eyed and compassionate and offer hands with fingers like fishhooks. We live in a paddock, a fattening pen, and we cannot leave it, because when we try to go the hooks say, *Think of who you'll hurt.*

So much hurt to try to heal. And the healing hurts too much.

• • •

The hangover sings an afterimage song. Like the drunkenness was ripped out of me and it left a negative space, the opposite of contentment. It vibrates in my bones.

I get up, brushing at an itch on my back, and drink straight from the bathroom faucet. When I come back to my mattress it's speckled, speckled white. Something's dripping on it from the air vent—oh, oh, they're maggots, slim white maggots. My air vent is dripping maggots. They're all over the covers, white and searching.

I call my landlord. I pin plastic sheeting up over the vent. I clean my bedroom twice, once for the maggots, once again after I throw up. Then I go to work.

Everything I touch feels infested. Inhabited.

Mary's got an egg sandwich for me but she looks like shit, weary, dry-skinned, her face flaking. "Hi," she says. "I'm sorry, I have the worst migraine."

"Oh, hon. Take it easy." The headaches started when she transitioned, an estrogen thing. She's quiet about them, and strong. I'm happy she tells me.

"Hey, you too. Which, uh—actually." She gives me the sandwich and makes a brave face, like she's afraid that someone's going to snap at someone, like she doesn't want to snap first. "I signed you up for a stress screening. They want you in the little conference room in half an hour."

I'm not angry. I just feel dirty and rotten and useless: now I'm even letting Mary down. "Oh," I say. "Jesus, I'm sorry. I didn't realize I'd . . . was it the epi? Was I too slow on the epi last week?"

"You didn't do anything wrong." She rubs her temples. "I'm just worried about you."

I want to give her a hug and thank her for caring but she's so obviously in pain. And the thought of the maggots keeps me away.

They're waiting for me in the narrow conference room: a man in a baggy blue suit, a woman in surgical scrubs with an inexplicable black stain like tar. "Dominga Roldan?" she says.

"That's me."

The man shakes my hand enthusiastically. "We just wanted to chat. See how you were. After your rescue swim."

The woman beckons: sit. "Think of this as a chance to relax."

"We're worried about you, Dominga," the man says. I can't get over how badly his suit fits. "I remember some days in the force I felt like the world didn't give a fuck about us. Just made me want to give up. You ever feel that way?"

I want to say what Nico would say: actually, sir, that's not the problem at all, the problem is caring too much, caring so much you can't ask for help because everyone else is already in so much pain.

Nico wouldn't say that, though. He'd find a really clever way to not say it.

"Sure," I say. "But that's the job."

"Did you know the victim?" the woman asks. The man winces at her bluntness. I blink at her and she purses her lips and tilts her head, to *Yes, I know how it sounds, but please.*say: "The suicide you rescued. Did you know him?"

"No." Of course not. What?

The man opens his mouth and she cuts him off. "But did you *feel* that you did, at any point? After he coded, maybe?"

I stare at her. My hangover turns my stomach and drums on the inside of my skull. It's not that I don't get it: it's that I feel I *do*, that something has been gestating in the last few days, in the missing connections between unrelated events.

The man sighs and unlatches his briefcase. I just can't shake the sense that his suit *used* to fit, not so long ago. "Let her be," he says. "Dominga, I just gotta tell you, I admire the hell out of people like you. Me, I think the only good in this world is the good we bring to it. Good people, people like you, you make this place worth living in."

"So we need to take care of people like you." The woman in scrubs has a funny accent—not quite Boston, still definitely a Masshole. "Burnout's very common. You know the stages?"

"Sure." First exhaustion, then shame, then callous cynicism. Then collapse. But I'm not there yet, I'm not past cynicism. I still want to help.

The man lifts a tiny glass cylinder from his briefcase, a cylinder full of a green fleshy mass—a caterpillar, a fat, warty caterpillar, pickled in cloudy fluid and starting to peel apart. He looks at me apologetically, as if this is an awkward necessity, just his morning caterpillar in brine.

"Sometimes this job becomes overwhelming." The woman's completely unmoved by the caterpillar. Her eyes have a kind of look-away quality, like those awful xenon headlights assholes use, unsafe to meet head-on. "Sometimes you need to stop taking on responsibilities and look after yourself. It's very important that you have resources to draw on."

Baggy Suit holds his cylinder gingerly, a thumb on one end and two fingers on the other, and stares at it. Is there *writing* on it? The woman says, "Do you have a safe space at home? Somewhere to relax?"

"Well—no, I guess not, there's a bug problem . . ."

The woman frowns in sympathy but her *eyes* don't frown, God, not at all—they smile. I don't know why. The man rolls his dead caterpillar tube and suddenly I grasp that the writing's on the *inside*, facing the dead bug.

"You've got to take care of yourself." He sounds petulant; he looks at the woman in scrubs with quiet resentment. "We need good people out there. Fighting the good fight."

"But if you feel you can't go on . . . if you're absolutely overwhelmed, and you can't see a way forward . . ." The woman leans across the table to take my hands. She's colder than the river where the man went to die. "I want to give you a number, okay? A place you can call for help."

She reads it off to me and I get *hammered* with déjà vu: I know it already, I'm sure. Or maybe that's not quite right, I don't know it exactly. It's just that it feels like it fits inside me, as if a space has been hollowed out for it, made ready to contain its charge.

"Please take care of yourself," the man tells me, on the way out. "If you don't, the world will just eat you up." And he lifts the caterpillar in salute.

I leave work early. I desperately don't want to go home, where the maggots will be puddled in the plastic up on my ceiling, writhing, eyeless, bulging, probably eating each other.

Mary walks me out. "You going to take any time off? See anybody?"

"I just saw Jacob and Elise yesterday."

"How was that?"

"A really bad decision." I shake my head and that, too, is a bad decision. "How's the migraine?"

"I'm okay. I'll live." It strikes me that when Mary says that, I believe it—and maybe she sees me frown, follows my thoughts, because she asks, "What about Nico? Are you still seeing him?"

"Yeah. Sort of."

"And?" Her impish well-*did*-you? grin.

"I'm worried about him." And furious, too, but if I said that I'd have to explain, and then Mary would be concerned about me, and I'd feel guilty because surely Mary has real problems, bigger problems than mine. "He's really depressed."

"Oh. That's all you need. Look—" She stops me just short of the doors. "Dominga, you're a great partner. I hope I didn't step on your toes today. But I really want you to get some room, okay? Do something for yourself."

I give her a long, long hug, and I forget about the maggots, just for the length of it.

There's a skywriter above the hospital, buzzing around in sharp curves. The sky's clean and blue and infinite, dizzyingly deep. Evening sun glints on the plane so it looks like a sliver poking up through God's skin.

I watch it draw signs in falling red vapor and when the wind shears them apart I think of the Lighthouse, where the circle of tables was ruptured by the passage of an illusory force.

I want to act. I want to help. I want to ease someone's pain. I don't want to do something for myself, because—

You're only burnt out once you stop wanting to help.

I call Nico. "Hey," he says. "Didn't expect to hear from you so soon."

"Want to get a drink?" I say, and then, my throat raw, my tongue acid, a hangover trick, words squirming out of me with wet expanding pressure, "I learned something you should know. A place to go, if you need help. If that's what you want. If the world really is too much."

Sometimes you say a thing and then you realize it's true.

He laughs. "I can't believe you're making fun of me about that. You're such an asshole. Do you want to go to Kosmos?"

• • •

"So," Nico says, "are we dating?"

Kosmos used to be a warehouse. Now the ceiling is an electric star field, a map of alien constellations. We sit together directly beneath a pair of twin red stars.

"Oh," I say, startled. "I was worried. After yesterday, I mean, I just . . ." Was furious, was hurt, didn't know why: because you were having fun, because I wasn't, because I thought you needed help, because you pretended you didn't. One of those. All of them.

Maybe he doesn't like what he sees in my eyes. He gets up. "Be right back." The house music samples someone talking about the expansion of the universe. Nico touches my shoulder on the way to the bathroom and I watch him recede, savoring the fading charge of his hand, thinking about space carrying us apart, and how safe that would be.

I have a choice to offer him. Maybe we'll leave together.

Nico comes back with drinks—wine, of all things, as if we're celebrating. "I thought that game was charmingly optimistic, you know."

"Jacob's game?" He's been tagging me in Facebook pictures of the stupid thing. I should block Jacob, so it'd stop hurting, which is why I don't.

"Right. I was reading about it."

The wine's dry and sweet. It tastes like tomorrow's hangover, like coming awake on a strange couch under a ceiling with no maggots. I take three swallows. "I thought it was about unknowable gods and the futility of all human life."

"Sure." That stupid cocky grin of his hits hard because I know what's behind it. "But in the game there's something out there, something bigger than us. Which—I mean, compared to what we've got, at least it's *interesting*." He points to the electric universe above us, all its empty, dazzling artifice. "How's work?"

"I'm taking a break. Don't worry about it." I have a plan here, a purpose. I am an agent, although which meaning of that word fits I don't know. "Why'd you really dump Yelena?"

"I told you." He resorts to the wine, to buy himself a moment. "Really, I was honest. I thought she could do a lot better than me. I wanted her to be happy."

"But what about *you*? She made you happy."

"Yeah, yeah, she did. But I don't want to be the kind of person who—" He stops here and takes another slow drink. "I don't want to be someone like Jacob."

"Jacob's very happy," I say, which is his point, of course.

"And look how he left you."

"What if I thought *you* made me happy?" Somewhere, somehow, Mary's cheering me on: that gets me through the sentence. "Would this be a date? Or are we both too . . . tired?"

Tired of doing hurt, and tired of taking it. Tired of the great cartographic project. Isn't it a little like cartography? Meeting lovely people, mapping them, racing to find their hurts before they can find yours—getting use from them, squeezing them dry, and then striking first, unilaterally and with awful effect, because the alternative is waiting for them to do the same to you. These are the rules, you didn't make them, they're not your fault. So you might as well play to win.

Nico looks at me with dark, guarded eyes. I would bet my life here, at last, that he's wearing one of his good jackets.

"Dominga," he says, and makes a little motion like he's going to take my hand, but can't quite commit, "Dominga, I'm sorry, but . . . God, I must sound like such an asshole, but I meant what I said. I'm done hurting people."

And I know exactly what he's saying. I remember it, I *feel* it—it's like when you get drunk with a guy and everything's just magical, you feel connected, you feel okay. But you know, even then, even in that moment, that tomorrow you will regret this: that the hole you opened up to him will admit the cold, or the knife. There will be a text from him, or the absence of a text, or—worse, much worse—the sight of him with someone new, months later, after the breakup, the sight of him doing that secret thing he does to say, *I'm thinking of you*, except it's not secret any more, and it's not you he's thinking of now.

And you just want to be done. You want a warmer world.

So here it is: my purpose, my plan. "Nico, what if I could give you a way out?"

He sets down his wine glass and turns it by the stem. It makes a faint, high shriek against the blackened steel tabletop, and he winces, and says, "What do you mean?"

"Just imagine a hypothetical. Imagine you're right about everything the universe is a hard place. To live you have to risk a lot of hurt." You're going to wonder how I came up with the rest of this, and all I can offer is fatigue, terror, maggots in my air vents, the memory of broken skulls on sidewalks: a kind of stress psychosis. Or the other explanation, of course. "Imagine that our last chance to be really good is revoked at the instant of our conception."

He follows along with good humor and a kind of adorable narcissism that I'm so engaged with his cosmic bullshit and (under it all) an awakening sense that something's off, askew. "Okay . . ."

The twin red suns multiply our shadows around us. I drift a little ways above myself on the wine, and it makes it easier to go on, to imagine or transmit this: "What if something out there knew a secret—"

A secret! Such a secret, a secret you might hear in the wind that passes between the libraries of jade teeth that wait in an empty city burnt stark by a high blue star that never leaves the zenith, a secret that tumbles down on you like a fall of maggots from a white place behind everything, where a pale immensity circles on the silent wind.

"What if there were a way out? Like a phone number you could call, a person you could talk to, kind of a hotline, and you'd say, oh, I'm a smart, depressed, compassionate person, I'm tired of the great lie that it's possible to do more good than harm, I'm tired of my Twitter feed telling me the world's basically a car full of kindergartners crumpling up in a trash compactor. I don't want to be complicit any more. I want out. Not suicide, no, that'd just hurt people. I want something better. And they'd say, sure, man, we have your mercy here, we can do that. We can make it so you never were."

He looks at me with an expression of the most terrible unguarded longing. He tries to cover it up, he tries to go flirty or sarcastic, but he can't.

I take my phone out, my embarrassing old flip phone, and put it on the table between us. I don't have to use the contacts to remember. The number keys make soft chiming noises as I type the secret in.

"So," I say, "my question is: who goes first?"

Something deep beneath me exalts, as if this is what it wants: and I cannot say if that thing is separate from me.

He reaches for the phone. "Not you, I hope," he says, with a really brave play-smile: he knows this is all a game, an exercise of imagination. He knows it's real. "The world needs people like you, Dominga. So what am I going to get? Is it a sex line?"

"If you go first," I say, "do you think that'd change the world enough that I wouldn't want to go second?"

I have this stupid compassion in me, and it cries out for the hurts of others. Nico's face, just then—God, have you ever known this kind of beauty? This desperate, awful hope that the answer was *yes*, that he might, by his absence, save me?

His finger hovers a little way above the call button.

"I think you'd have to go first," he says. He puts his head back, all the way back, as if to blow smoke: but I think he's looking up at the facsimile stars. "That'd be important."

"Why?"

"Because," he says, all husky nonchalance, "if you weren't here, I would *absolutely* go; whereas if I weren't here, I don't know if you'd go. And if this method were real, this, uh, operation of mercy, then the universe is lost, the whole operation's fucked, and it's vital that you get out."

His finger keeps station a perilous few millimeters from the call. I watch this space breathlessly. "Tell me why," I say, to keep him talking, and then I realize: oh, Nico, you'd think this out, wouldn't you? You'd consider the new rules. You'd understand the design. And I'm afraid that what he'll say will be *right*—

He lays it out there: "Well, who'd use it?"

"Good people," I say. That's how burnout operates. You burn out because you care. "Compassionate people."

"That's right." He gets a little melancholy here, a little singsong, in a way that feels like the rhythm of my stranger thoughts. I wonder if he's had an uncanny couple days too, and whether I'll ever get a chance to ask him. "The universe sucks, man, but it sucks a lot more if you care, if you feel the hurt around you. So if there were a way out—a certain kind of people would use it, right? And those people would go extinct."

Oh. Right.

There might have been a billion good people, ten billion, a hundred, before us: and one by one they chose to go, to be unmade, a trickle at first, just the kindest, the ones most given to shoulder their neighbors' burdens and ask nothing in exchange—but the world would get harder for the loss of each of them, and there'd be more reason then, more hurt to go around, so the rattle would become an avalanche.

And we'd be left. The dregs. Little selfish people and their children.

The stars above change, the false constellations reconfiguring. Nico sighs up at them. "You think that's why the sky's empty?"

"Of—aliens, you mean?" What a curious brain.

"Yeah. They were too good. They ran into bad people, bad situations, and they didn't want to compromise themselves. So they opted out."

"Maybe someone's hunting good people." If this thing were real, well, wouldn't it be a perfect weapon, a perfect instrument in something's special plan? Bait and trap all at once.

"Maybe. One way or another—well, we should go, right?" He comes back from the cosmic distance. His finger hasn't moved. He grins his stupid cocky camouflage grin because the alternative is ghoulish and he says, "I think I make a pretty compelling case."

Everything cold and always getting colder because the warmth puts itself out.

"Maybe." Maybe. He's very clever. "But I'm not going first."

Nico puts his finger down (and I feel the cold, up out of my bones, sharp in my heart) but he's just pinning the corner of the phone so he can spin it around. "Jacob definitely wouldn't make the call," he says, teasing, a really harsh kind of tease, but it's about me, about how I hurt, which feels good.

"Neither would Mary," I say, which is, all in all, my counterargument, my stanchion, my sole refuge. If something's out to conquer us, well, the conquest isn't done. Something good remains. Mary's still here. She hasn't gone yet—whether you take all this as a thought experiment or not.

"Who's Mary?" He raises a skeptical eyebrow: you have *friends?*

"Stick around," I say, "and I'll tell you."

Right then I get one more glimpse past the armor: he's frustrated, he's glad, he's all knotted up, because I won't go first, and whatever going first means, he doesn't want to leave me to go second. He wouldn't have to care anymore, of course. But he still cares. That's how compassion works.

If I had a purpose here, well, I suppose it's done.

"You're taking a break from work?" He closes the phone and pushes it back to me. "What's up with that? Can I help?"

When I go to take the phone he makes a little gesture, like he wants to take my hand, and I make a little gesture like I want him to—and between the two of us, well, we manage.

. . .

I still have the number, of course. Maybe you worry that it works. Maybe you're afraid I'll use it, or that Nico will, when things go bad. Things do so often go bad.

You won't know if I use it, of course, because then I'll never have told you this story, and you'll never have read it. But that's a comfort, isn't it? That's enough.

The story's still here. We go on.

SETH DICKINSON'S short fiction has appeared in *Analog, Asimov's, Clarkesworld, Lightspeed, Strange Horizons,* and *Beneath Ceaseless Skies,* among others. He is an instructor at the Alpha Science Fiction, Fantasy, and Horror Workshop for Young Writers, winner of the 2011 Dell Magazines Award, and a lapsed student of social neuroscience. The author of *The Traitor Baru Cormorant* and *The Monster Baru Cormorant,* he lives in Brooklyn, New York.

The Language of Knives

Haralambi Markov

A strong-willed daughter is guided by her unloved parent in the death rituals and customs of how to respect the remains of her favorite parent. This is how you love the dead. This is the language of knives. *Edited by Ann VanderMeer.*

A long, silent day awaits you and your daughter as you prepare to cut your husband's body. You remove organs from flesh, flesh from bones, bones from tendons—all ingredients for the cake you're making, the heavy price of admission for an afterlife you pay your gods; a proper send-off for the greatest of all warriors to walk the lands.

The Baking Chamber feels small with two people inside, even though you've spent a month with your daughter as part of her apprenticeship. You feel irritated at having to share this moment, but this is a big day for your daughter. You steal a glance at her. See how imposing she looks in her ramie garments the color of a blood moon, how well the leather apron made from changeling hide sits on her.

You work in silence, as the ritual demands, and your breath hisses as you both twist off the aquamarine top of the purification vat. Your husband floats to the top of the thick translucent waters, peaceful and tender. You hold your breath, aching to lean over and kiss him one more time—but that is forbidden. His body is now sacred, and you are not. You've seen him sleep, his powerful chest rising and falling, his breath a harbinger of summer storms. The purification bath makes it easy to pull him up and slide him onto the table, where the budding dawn seeping from the skylight above illuminates his transmogrification, his ascent. His skin has taken a rich pomegranate hue. His hair is a stark mountaintop white.

You raise your head to study your daughter's reaction at seeing her father since his wake. You study her face, suspicious of any muscle that might twitch and break the fine mask made of fermented butcher broom berries and dried water mint grown in marshes where men have drowned. It's a paste worn out of respect and a protection from those you serve. You scrutinize her eyes for tears, her hair and eyebrows waxed slick for any sign of dishevelment.

The purity of the body matters most. A single tear can sour the offering. A single hair can spoil the soul being presented to the gods . . . what a refined palate they have. But your daughter wears a stone face. Her eyes are opaque; her body is poised as if this is the easiest thing in the world to do. The ceramic knife you've shaped and baked yourself sits like a natural extension of her arm.

You remember what it took you to bake your own mother into a cake. No matter how many times you performed the ritual under her guidance, nothing prepared you for the moment when you saw her body on the table. Perhaps you can teach your daughter to love your art. Perhaps she belongs by your side as a Cake Maker, even though you pride yourself on not needing any help. Perhaps she hasn't agreed to this apprenticeship only out of grief. Perhaps, perhaps . . .

Your heart prickles at seeing her this accomplished, after a single lunar cycle. A part of you, a part you take no pride in, wants her to struggle through her examination, struggle to the point where her eyes beg you to help her. You would like to forgive her for her incapability, the way you did back when she was a child. You want her to need you—the way she needed your husband for so many years.

No. Treat him like any other. *Let your skill guide you.* You take your knife and shave the hair on your husband's left arm with the softest touch.

You remove every single hair on his body to use for kindling for the fire you will build to dry his bones, separating a small handful of the longest hairs for the decoration, then incise the tip of his little finger to separate skin from muscle.

Your daughter mirrors your movements. She, too, is fluent in the language of knives.

The palms and feet are the hardest to skin, as if the body fights to stay intact and keep its grip on this realm. You struggle at first but then work the knife without effort. As you lift the softly stretching tissue, you see the countless scars that punctuated his life—the numerous cuts that crisscross his hands and shoulders, from when he challenged the sword dancers in Aeno; the coin-shaped scars where arrowheads pierced his chest during their voyage through the Sear of Spires in the misty North; the burn marks across his left hip from the leg hairs of the fire titan, Hragurie. You have collected your own scars on your journeys through the forgotten places of this world, and those scars ache now, the pain kindled by your loss.

After you place your husband's skin in a special aventurine bowl, you take to the muscle—that glorious muscle you've seen shift and contract in great swings of his dancing axe while you sing your curses and charms alongside him in battle. Even the exposed redness of him is rich with memories, and you do everything in your power not to choke as you strip him of his strength. This was the same strength your daughter prized above all else and sought for herself many years ago, after your spells and teachings grew insufficient for her. This was the same strength she accused you of lacking when you chose your mother's calling, retired your staff from battle, and chose to live preparing the dead for their passing.

Weak. The word still tastes bitter with her accusation. *How can you leave him? How can you leave us? You're a selfish little man.*

You watch her as you work until there is nothing left but bones stripped clean, all the organs in their respective jars and bowls. Does she regret the words now, as she works by your side? Has she seen your burden yet? Has she understood your choice? Will she be the one to handle your body once you pass away?

You try to guess the answer from her face, but you find no solace and no answer. Not when you extract the fat from your husband's skin, not when you mince his flesh and muscle, not when you puree his organs and cut his intestines into tiny strips you leave to dry. Your daughter excels in this preparatory work—her blade is swift, precise, and gentle.

How can she not? After all, she is a gift from the gods. A gift given to two lovers who thought they could never have a child on their own. A miracle. The completion you sought after in your youth; a honey-tinged bliss that filled you with warmth. But as with all good things, your bliss waxed and waned as you realized: all children have favorites.

You learned how miracles can hurt.

. . .

You align his bones on the metal tray that goes into the hungry oven. You hold his skull in your hands and rub the sides where his ears once were. You look deep into the sockets where once eyes of dark brown would stare back into you.

His clavicle passes your fingers. You remember the kisses you planted on his shoulder, when it used to be flesh. You position his ribcage, and you can still hear his heartbeat—a rumble in his chest the first time you lay together after barely surviving an onslaught of skinwalkers, a celebration of life. You remember that heart racing, as it did in your years as young men, when vitality kept you both up until dawn. You remember it beating quietly in his later years, when you were content and your bodies fit perfectly together—the alchemy of flesh you have now lost.

You deposit every shared memory in his bones, and then load the tray in the oven and slam shut the metal door.

Behind you, your daughter stands like a shadow, perfect in her apprentice robes. Not a single crease disfigures the contours of her pants and jacket. Not a single stain mars her apron.

She stares at you. She judges you.

She is perfection.

You wish you could leave her and crawl into the oven with your husband.

. . .

Flesh, blood and gristle do not make a cake easily, yet the Cake Maker has to wield these basic ingredients. Any misstep leads to failure, so you watch closely during your daughter's examination, but she completes each task with effortless grace.

She crushes your husband's bones to flour with conviction.

Your daughter mixes the dough of blood, fat, and bone flour, and you assist her. You hear your knuckles and fingers pop as you knead the hard dough, but hers move without a sound—fast and agile as they shape the round cakes.

Your daughter works over the flesh and organs until all you can see is a pale scarlet cream with the faint scent of iron, while you crush the honey crystals that will allow for the spirit to be digested by the gods. You wonder if she is doing this to prove how superior she is to you—to demonstrate how easy it is to lock yourself into a bakery with the dead. You wonder how to explain that you never burnt as brightly as your husband, that you don't need to chase legends and charge into battle.

You wonder how to tell her that she is your greatest adventure, that you gave her most of the magic you had left.

. . .

Layer by layer, your husband is transformed into a cake. Not a single bit of him is lost. You pull away the skin on top and connect the pieces with threads from his hair. The sun turns the rich shade of lavender and calendula.

You cover the translucent skin with the dried blood drops you extracted before you placed the body in the purification vat and glazed it with the plasma. Now all that remains is to tell your husband's story, in the language every Cake Maker knows—the language you've now taught your daughter.

You wonder whether she will blame you for the death of your husband in writing, the way she did when you told her of his death.

Your stillness killed him. You had to force him to stay, to give up his axe. Now he's dead in his sleep. Is this what you wanted? Have him all to yourself? You couldn't let him die out on the road.

Oh, how she screamed that day—her voice as unforgiving as thunder. Her screaming still reverberates through you. You're afraid of what she's going to tell the gods.

You both write. You cut and bend the dried strips of intestines into runes and you gently push them so they sink into the glazed skin and hold.

You write his early story. His childhood, his early feats, the mythology of your love. How you got your daughter. She tells the other half of your husband's myth—how he trained her in every single weapon known to man, how they journeyed the world over to honor the gods.

Her work doesn't mention you at all.

. . .

You rest your fingers, throbbing with pain from your manipulations. You have completed the last of your husband's tale. You have written in the language of meat and bones and satisfied the gods' hunger. You hope they will nod with approval as their tongues roll around the cooked flesh and swallow your sentences and your tether to life.

Your daughter swims into focus as she takes her position across the table, your husband between you, and joins you for the spell. He remains the barrier you can't overcome even in death. As you begin to speak, you're startled to hear her voice rise with yours. You mutter the incantation and her lips are your reflection, but while you caress the words, coaxing their magic into being, she cuts them into existence, so the veil you will around the cake spills like silk on your end and crusts on hers. The two halves shimmer in blue feylight, entwine into each other, and the deed is done.

You have said your farewell, better than you did when you first saw him dead. Some dam inside you breaks. Exhaustion wipes away your strength and you feel your age, first in the trembling in your hands, then in the creaking in your knees as you turn your back and measure your steps so you don't disturb the air—a retreat as slow as young winter frost.

Outside the Bakery, your breath catches. Your scream is a living thing that squirms inside your throat and digs into the hidden recesses of your lungs. Your tears wash the dry mask from your cheeks.

Your daughter takes your hand, gently, with the unspoken understanding only shared loss births, and you search for her gaze. You search for the flat, dull realization that weighs down the soul. You search for yourself in her eyes, but all you see is your husband—his flame now a wildfire that has swallowed every part of you. She looks at you as a person who has lost the only life she had ever known, pained and furious, and you pat her hand and kiss her forehead, her skin stinging against your lips. When confusion pulls her face together, her features lined with fissures in her protective mask, you shake your head.

"The gods praise your skill and technique. They praise your steady hand and precision, but they have no use of your hands in the Bakery." The words roll out with difficulty—a thorn vine you lacerate your whole being with as you force yourself to reject your daughter. Yes, she can follow your path, but what good would that do?

"You honor me greatly." Anger tinges her response, but fights in these holy places father only misfortune, so her voice is low and even. You are relieved to hear sincerity in her fury, desire in her voice to dedicate herself to your calling.

You want to keep her here, where she won't leave. Your tongue itches with every lie you can bind her with, spells you've learned from gods that are not your own, hollow her out and hold onto her, even if such acts could end your life. You reconsider and instead hold on to her earnest reaction. You have grown to an age where even intent will suffice.

"It's not an honor to answer your child's yearning." You maintain respectability, keep with the tradition, but still you lean in with all the weight of death tied to you like stones and you whisper. "I have told the story of your father in blood and gristle as I have with many others. As I will continue to tell every story as best as I can, until I myself end in the hands of a Cake Maker. But you can continue writing your father's story outside the temple where your knife strokes have a meaning.

"Run. Run toward the mountains and rivers, sword in your hand and bow on your back. Run toward life. That is where you will find your father."

Now it is she who is crying. You embrace her, the memory of doing so in her childhood alive inside your bones, and she hugs you back as a babe, full of needing and vulnerable. But she is no longer a child—the muscles underneath her robes roll with the might of a river—so you usher her out to a life you have long since traded away.

Her steps still echo in the room outside the Baking Chamber as you reapply the coating to your face from the tiny crystal jars. You see yourself: a grey, tired man who touched death more times than he ever touched his husband.

Your last task is to bring the cake to where the Mouth awaits, its vines and branches shaking, aglow with iridescence. There, the gods will entwine their appendages around your offering, suck it in, close and digest. Relief overcomes you and you sigh.

Yes, it's been a long day since you and your daughter cut your husband's body open. You reenter the Baking Chamber and push the cake onto the cart.

. . .

HARALAMBI MARKOV is a Bulgarian critic, editor, and writer of things weird and fantastic. A Clarion 2014 graduate, Markov enjoys fairy tales, obscure folkloric monsters, and inventing death rituals (for his stories, not his neighbors . . . usually). Markov runs the Innumerable Voices column at *Tor.com*, profiling short fiction writers. His stories have appeared in *Weird Fiction Review, Electric Velocipede, Tor.com, Stories for Chip: A Tribute to Samuel R. Delany, The Apex Book of World SF*, and *Uncanny Magazine*. He's currently working on a novel.

The Shape of My Name

Nino Cipri

A time-travel story about what it means to truly claim yourself. *Edited by Ann VanderMeer.*

The year 2076 smells like antiseptic gauze and the lavender diffuser that Dara set up in my room. It has the bitter aftertaste of pills: probiotics and microphages and PPMOs. It feels like the itch of healing, the ache that's settled on my pubic bone. It has the sound of a new name that's fresh and yet familiar on my lips.

The future feels lighter than the past. I think I know why you chose it over me, Mama.

· · ·

My bedroom has changed in the hundred-plus years that have passed since I slept there as a child. The floorboards have been carpeted over, torn up, replaced. The walls are thick with new layers of paint. The windows have been upgraded, the closet expanded. The oak tree that stood outside my window is gone, felled by a storm twenty years ago, I'm told. But the house still stands, and our family still lives here, with all our attendant ghosts. You and I are haunting each other, I think.

I picture you standing in the kitchen downstairs, over a century ago. I imagine that you're staring out through the little window above the sink, your eyes traveling down the path that leads from the back door and splits at the creek; one trail leads to the pond, and the other leads to the shelter and the anachronopede, with its rows of capsules and blinking lights.

Maybe it's the afternoon you left us. June 22, 1963: storm clouds gathering in the west, the wind picking up, the air growing heavy with the threat of rain. And you're staring out the window, gazing across the dewy fields at the forking path, trying to decide which way you'll take.

My bedroom is just above the kitchen, and my window has that same view, a little expanded: I can see clear down to the pond where Dad and I used to sit on his weeks off from the oil fields. It's spring, and the cattails are only hip high. I can just make out the silhouette of a great blue heron walking along among the reeds and rushes.

You and I, we're twenty feet and more than a hundred years apart.

· · ·

You went into labor not knowing my name, which I know now is unprecedented among our family: you knew Dad's name before you laid eyes on him, the time and date of my birth, the hospital where he would drive you when you went into labor. But my name? My sex? Conspicuously absent in Uncle Dante's gilt-edged book where all these happy details were recorded in advance.

Dad told me later that you thought I'd be a stillbirth. He didn't know about the record book, about the blank space where a name should go. But he told me that nothing he said while you were pregnant could convince you that I'd come into the world alive. You thought I'd slip out of you strangled and blue, already decaying.

Instead, I started screaming before they pulled me all the way out.

Dad said that even when the nurse placed me in your arms, you thought you were hallucinating. "I had to tell her, over and over: Miriam, you're not dreaming, our daughter is alive."

I bit my lip when he told me that, locked the words "your son" out of sight. I regret that now; maybe I could have explained myself to him. I should have tried, at least.

You didn't name me for nearly a week.

· · ·

Nineteen fifty-four tastes like Kellogg's Rice Krispies in fresh milk, delivered earlier that morning. It smells like wood smoke, cedar chips, Dad's Kamel cigarettes mixed with the perpetual smell of diesel in his clothes. It feels like the worn-velvet nap of the couch in our living room, which I loved to run my fingers across.

I was four years old. I woke up in the middle of the night after a loud crash of lightning. The branches of the oak tree outside my window were thrashing in the wind and the rain.

I crept out of bed, dragging my blanket with me. I slipped out of the door and into the hallway, heading for your and Dad's bedroom. I stopped when I heard voices coming from the parlor downstairs: I recognized your sharp tones, but there was also a man's voice, not Dad's baritone but something closer to a tenor.

The door creaked when I pushed it open, and the voices fell silent. I paused, and then you yanked open the door.

The curlers in your hair had come undone, descending down toward your shoulders. I watched one tumble out of your hair and onto the floor like a stunned beetle. I only caught a glimpse of the man standing in the corner; he had thin, hunched shoulders and dark hair, wet and plastered to his skull. He was wearing one of Dad's old robes, with the initials monogrammed on the pocket. It was much too big for him.

You snatched me up, not very gently, and carried me up to the bedroom you shared with Dad.

"Tom," you hissed. You dropped me on the bed before Dad was fully awake, and shook his shoulder. He sat up, blinking at me, and looked to you for an explanation.

"There's a visitor," you said, voice strained.

Dad looked at the clock, pulling it closer to him to get a proper look. "Now? Who is it?"

Your jaw was clenched, and so were your hands. "I'm handling it. I just need you to watch—"

You said my name in a way I'd never heard it before, as if each syllable were a hard, steel ball dropping from your lips. It frightened me, and I started to cry. Silently, though, since I didn't want you to notice me. I didn't want you to look at me with eyes like that.

You turned on your heel and left the room, clicking the door shut behind you and locking it.

Dad patted me on the back, his wide hand nearly covering the expanse of my skinny shoulders. "It's all right, kid," he said. "Nothing to be scared of. Why don't you lie down and I'll read you something, huh?"

In the morning, there was no sign a visitor had been there at all. You and Dad assured me that I must have dreamed the whole thing.

I know now that you were lying, of course. I think I knew it even then.

· · ·

I had two childhoods.

One happened between Dad's ten-day hitches in the White County oil fields. That childhood smells like his tobacco, wool coats, wet grass. It sounds like the opening theme songs to all our favorite TV shows. It tastes like the peanut-butter sandwiches that you'd pack for us on our walks, which we'd eat down by the pond, the same one I can just barely see from my window here. In the summer, we'd sit at the edge of the water, dipping our toes into the mud. Sometimes, Dad told me stories, or asked me to fill him in on the episodes of *Gunsmoke* and *Science Fiction Theatre* he'd missed, and we'd chat while watching for birds. The herons have always been my favorite. They moved so slow, it always felt like a treat to spot one as it stepped cautiously through the shallow water. Sometimes, we'd catch sight of one flying overhead, its wide wings fighting against gravity.

And then there was the childhood with you, and with Dara, the childhood that happened when Dad was away. I remember the first morning I came downstairs and she was eating pancakes off of your fancy china, the plates that were decorated with delicate paintings of evening primrose.

"Hi there. I'm Dara," she said.

When I looked at you, shy and unsure, you told me, "She's a cousin. She'll be dropping in when your father is working. Just to keep us company."

Dara didn't really look much like you, I thought; not the way that Dad's cousins and uncles all resembled one another. But I could see a few similarities between the two of you; hazel eyes, long fingers, and something I didn't have the words to describe for a long time: a certain discomfort, the sense that you held yourselves slightly apart from the rest of us. It had made you a figure of gossip in town, though I didn't know that until high school, when the same was said of me.

"What should I call you?" Dara asked me.

You jumped in and told her to call me by my name, the one you'd chosen for me, after the week of indecision following my birth. How can I ever make you understand how much I disliked that name? It felt like it belonged to a sister whom I was constantly being compared to, whose legacy I could never fulfill or surpass or even forget. Dara must have caught the face that I made, because later, when you were out in the garden, she asked me, "Do you have another name? That you want me to call you instead?"

When I shrugged, she said, "It doesn't have to be a forever name. Just one for the day. You can pick a new one tomorrow, if you like. You can introduce yourself differently every time you see me."

And so, every morning when I woke up and saw Dara sitting at the table, I gave her a different name: Doc, Buck, George, Charlie. Names that my heroes had, from television and comics and the matinees in town. They weren't my name, but they were better than the one I had. I liked the way they sounded, the shape of them rolling around my mouth.

You just looked on, lips pursed in a frown, and told Dara you wished she'd quit indulging my silly little games.

The two of you sat around our kitchen table and—if I was quiet and didn't draw any attention to myself—talked in a strange code about *jumps* and *fastenings* and *capsules*, dropping names of people I never knew. More of your cousins, I figured.

You told our neighbors that all of your family was spread out, and disinclined to make the long trip to visit. When Dara took me in, she made up a tale about a long-lost cousin whose parents had kicked him out for being queer trans. Funny, the way the truth seeps into lies.

. . .

I went to see Uncle Dante in 1927. I wanted to see what he had in that book of his about me, and about you and Dara.

Nineteen twenty-seven tastes like the chicken broth and brown bread he fed me after I showed up at his door. It smells like the musty blanket he hung around my shoulders, like kerosene lamps and wood smoke. It sounds like the scratchy records he played on his phonograph: Duke Ellington and Al Jolson, the Gershwin brothers and Gene Austin.

"Your mother dropped by back in '24," he said, settling down in an armchair in front of the fireplace. It was the same fireplace that had been in our parlor, though Dad had sealed off the chimney in 1958, saying it let in too many drafts. "She was very adamant that your name be written down in the records. She seemed . . . upset." He let the last word hang on its own, lonely, obviously understated.

"That's not my name," I told him. "It's the one she gave me, but it was never mine."

I had to explain to him then—he'd been to the future, and so it didn't seem so far-fetched, my transition. I simplified it for him, of course: didn't go into the transdermal hormonal implants and mastectomy, the paperwork Dara and I forged, the phalloplasty I'd scheduled a century and a half in the future. I skipped the introduction to gender theory, Susan Stryker, *Stone Butch Blues*, all the things that Dara gave me to read when I asked if there were books about people like me.

"My aunt Lucia was of a similar disposition," he told me. "Once her last child was grown, she gave up on dresses entirely. Wore a suit to church for her last twelve years, which gave her a reputation for eccentricity."

I clamped my mouth shut and nodded along, still feeling ill and shaky from the jump. The smell of Uncle Dante's cigar burned in my nostrils. I wished we could have had the conversation outside, on the porch; the parlor seemed too familiar, too laden with the ghost of your presence.

"What should I put instead?" he asked, pulling his book down from the mantle: the ancient gilt-edged journal where he recorded our family's births, marriages, and deaths, as they were reported to him.

"It's blank when I'm born," I told him. He paused in the act of sharpening his pencil—he knew better than to write the future in ink. "Just erase it. Tear the whole page out and rewrite it ~~white it out~~ if you need to."

He sat back in his chair and combed his fingers through his beard. "That's . . . unprecedented," he said. Again, that pause, the heaviness of the word choice.

"Not anymore," I said.

. . .

Nineteen sixty-three feels like a menstrual cramp, like the ache in my legs as my bones stretched, like the twinges in my nipples as my breasts developed. It smells like Secret roll-on deodorant and the menthol cigarettes you took up smoking. It tastes like the peach cobbler I burned in Home Ec class, which the teacher forced me to eat. It sounds like Sam Cooke's album *Night Beat*, which Dara, during one of her visits, told me to buy.

And it looks like you, jumpier than I'd ever seen you, so twitchy that even Dad commented on it before he left for his hitch in the oil fields.

"Will you be all right?" he asked after dinner.

I was listening from the kitchen doorway to the two of you talk. I'd come in to ask Dad if he was going to watch *Gunsmoke*, which would be starting in a few minutes, with me, and caught the two of you with your heads together by the sink.

You leaned forward, bracing your hands on the edge of the sink, looking for all the world as if you couldn't hold yourself up, as if gravity was working just a little bit harder on you than it was on everyone else. I wondered for a second if you were going to tell him about Dara. I'd grown up keeping her a secret with you, though the omission had begun to weigh heavier on me. I loved Dad, and I loved Dara; being unable to reconcile the two of them seemed trickier each passing week.

Instead, you said nothing. You relaxed your shoulders, and you smiled for him, and kissed his cheek. You said the two of us would be fine, not to worry about his girls.

And the very next day, you pulled me out of bed and showed me our family's time machine, in the old tornado shelter with the lock I'd never been able to pick.

. . .

I know more about the machine now, after talking with Uncle Dante, reading the records that he kept. About the mysterious man, Moses Stone, who built it in 1905, when Grandma Emmeline's parents leased out a parcel of land. He called it the anachronopede, which probably sounded marvelous in 1905, but even Uncle Dante was rolling his eyes at the name twenty years later. I know that Stone took Emmeline on trips to the future when she was seventeen, and then abandoned her after a few years, and nobody's been able to find him since then. I know that the machine is keyed to something in Emmeline's matrilineal DNA, some recessive gene.

I wonder if that man, Stone, built the anachronopede as an experiment. An experiment needs parameters, right? So build a machine that only certain people in one family can use. We can't go back before 1905, when the machine was completed, and we can't go past August 3, 2321. What happens that day? The only way to find out is to go as far forward as possible, and then wait. Maroon yourself in time. Exile yourself as far forward as you can, where none of us can reach you.

I know you were lonely, waiting for me to grow up so you could travel again. You were exiled when you married Dad in 1947, in that feverish period just after the war. It must have been so romantic at first: I've seen the letters he wrote during the years he courted you. And you'd grown up seeing his name written next to yours, and the date that you'd marry him. When did you start feeling trapped, I wonder? You were caught in a weird net of fate and love and the future and the past. You loved Dad, but your love kept you hostage. You loved me, but you knew that someday I'd transform myself into someone you didn't recognize.

· · ·

At first, when you took me underground to see the anachronopede, I thought you and Dad had built a fallout shelter. But there were no beds or boxes of canned food. And built into the rocky wall were rows of doors that looked like the one on our icebox. Round lightbulbs lay just above the doors, nearly all of them red, though one or two were slowly blinking between orange and yellow.

Nearly all the doors were shut, except for two, near the end, which hung ajar.

"Those two capsules are for us, you and me," you said. "Nobody else can use them."

I stared at them. "What are they for?"

I'd heard you and Dara speak in code for nearly all of my life, jumps and capsules and fastenings. I'd imagined all sorts of things. Aliens and spaceships and doorways to another dimension, all the sort of things I'd seen Truman Bradley introduce on *Science Fiction Theatre*.

"Traveling," you said.

"In time or in space?"

You seemed surprised. I'm not sure why. Dad collected pulp magazines, and you'd given me books by H. G. Wells and Jules Verne for Christmas in years past. The Justice League had gone into the future. I'd seen *The Fly* last year during a half-price matinee. You know how it was back then: such things weren't considered impossible, so much as inevitable. The future was a country we all wanted so badly to visit.

"In time," you said.

I immediately started peppering you with questions: How far into the future had you gone? When were you born? Had you met dinosaurs? Had you met King Arthur? What about jet packs? Was Dara from the future?

You held a hand to your mouth, watching as I danced around the small cavern, firing off questions like bullets being sprayed from a tommy gun.

"Maybe you are too young," you said, staring at the two empty capsules in the wall.

"I'm not!" I insisted. "Can't we go somewhere? Just a—just a quick jump?"

I added in the last part because I wanted you to know I'd been listening, when you and Dara had talked in code at the kitchen table. I'd been waiting for you to include me in the conversation.

"Tomorrow," you decided. "We'll leave tomorrow."

. . .

The first thing I learned about time travel was that you couldn't eat anything before you did it. And you could only take a few sips of water: no juice or milk. The second thing I learned was that it was the most painful thing in the world, at least for me.

"Your grandmother Emmeline called it the fastening," you told me. "She said it felt like being a button squeezed through a too-narrow slit in a piece of fabric. It affects everyone differently."

"How's it affect you?"

You twisted your wedding ring around on your finger. "I haven't done it since before you were born."

You made me go to the bathroom twice before we walked back on that path, taking the fork that led to the shelter where the capsules were. The grass was still wet with dew, and there was a chill in the air. Up above, thin, wispy clouds were scratched onto the sky, but out west, I could see dark clouds gathering. There'd be storms later.

But what did I care about later? I was going into a time machine.

I asked you, "Where are we going?" You replied, "To visit Dara. Just a quick trip."

There was something cold in your voice. I recognized the tone: the same you used when trying to talk me into wearing the new dress you'd bought me for church, or telling me to stop tearing through the house and play quietly for once.

In the shelter, you helped me undress, though it made me feel hotly embarrassed and strange to be naked in front of you again. I'd grown wary of my own body in the last few months, at how it was changing: I'd been dismayed by the way my nipples had grown tender, at the fatty flesh that had budded beneath them. It seemed like a betrayal.

I hunched my shoulders and covered my privates, though you barely glanced at my naked skin. You helped me lie down in the capsule, showed me how to pull the round mask over the bottom half of my face, attach the clip that went over my index finger. Finally, you lifted one of my arms up and wrapped a black cuff around the crook of my elbow. I noticed, watching you, that you had bitten all of your nails down to the quick, that the edges were jagged and tender looking.

"You program your destination date in here, you see?" You tapped a square of black glass on the ceiling of the capsule, and it lit up at the touch. Your fingers flew across the screen, typing directly onto it, rearranging colored orbs that seemed to attach themselves to your finger as soon as you touched them.

"You'll learn how to do this on your own eventually," you said. The screen, accepting whatever you'd done to it, blinked out and went black again.

I breathed through my mask, which covered my nose and face. A whisper of air blew against my skin, a rubbery, stale, lemony scent.

"Don't be scared," you said. "I'll be there when you wake up. I'm sending myself back a little earlier, so I'll be there to help you out of the capsule."

You kissed me on the forehead and shut the door. I was left alone in the dark as the walls around me started to hum.

Calling it the fastening does it a disservice. It's much more painful than that. Granny Emmeline is far tougher than I'll ever be if she thought it was just like forcing a button into place.

For me, it felt like being crushed in a vice that was lined with broken glass and nails. I understood, afterward, why you had forbidden me from eating or drinking for twenty-four hours. I would have vomited in the mask, shat myself inside the capsule. I came back to myself in the dark, wild with terror and the phantom remains of that awful pain.

The door opened. The light needled into my eyes, and I screamed, trying to cover them. The various cuffs and wires attached to my arms tugged my hands back down, which made me panic even more.

Hands reached in and pushed me down, and eventually, I registered your voice in my ear, though not what you were saying. I stopped flailing long enough for all the straps and cuffs to be undone, and then I was lifted out of the capsule. You held me in your arms, rocking and soothing me, rubbing my back as I cried hysterically onto your shoulder.

I was insensible for a few minutes. When my sobs died away to hiccups, I realized that we weren't alone in the shelter. Dara was with us as well, and she had thrown a blanket over my shoulders.

"Jesus, Miriam," she said, over and over. "What the hell were you thinking?"

I found out later that I was the youngest person in my family to ever make a jump. Traditionally, they made their first jumps on their seventeenth birthday. I was nearly five years shy of that.

You smoothed back a lock of my hair, and I saw that all your fingernails had lost their ragged edge. Instead, they were rounded and smooth, topped with little crescents of white.

. . .

Uncle Dante told me that it wasn't unusual for two members of the family to be lovers, especially if there were generational gaps between them. It helped to avoid romantic entanglements with people who were bound to linear lives, at least until they were ready to settle down for a number of years, raising children. Pregnancy didn't mix well with time travel. It was odder to do what you did: settle down with someone who was, as Dara liked to put it, stuck in the slow lane of linear time.

Dara told me about the two of you, eventually; that you'd been lovers before you met Dad, before you settled down with him in 1947. And that when she started visiting us in 1955, she wasn't sleeping alone in the guest bedroom.

I'm not sure if I was madder at her or you at the time, though I've since forgiven her. Why wouldn't I? You've left both of us, and it's a big thing, to have that in common.

• • •

Nineteen eighty-one is colored silver, beige, bright orange, deep brown. It feels like the afghan blanket Dara kept on my bed while I recovered from my first jump, some kind of cheap fake wool. It tastes like chicken soup and weak tea with honey and lime Jell-O.

And for a few days, at least, 1981 felt like a low-grade headache that never went away, muscle spasms that I couldn't always control, dry mouth, difficulty swallowing. It smelled like a lingering olfactory hallucination of frying onions. It sounded like a ringing in the ears.

"So you're the unnamed baby, huh?" Dara said that first morning when I woke up. She was reading a book, and set it down next to her on the couch.

I was disoriented: you and Dara had placed me in the southeast bedroom, the same one I slept in all through childhood. (The same one I'm recovering in right now.) I'm not sure if you thought it would comfort me, to wake up to familiar surroundings. It was profoundly strange, to be in my own bedroom but have it be so different: the striped wallpaper replaced with avocado green paint; a loveseat with floral upholstery where my dresser had been; all my posters of Buck Rogers and Superman replaced with framed prints of unfamiliar artwork.

"Dara?" I said. She seemed different, colder. Her hair was shorter than the last time I'd seen her, and she wore a pair of thick-framed glasses.

She cocked her head. "That'd be me. Nice to meet you."

I blinked at her, still disoriented and foggy. "We met before," I said.

She raised her eyebrows, like she couldn't believe I was so dumb. "Not by my timeline."

Right. Time travel.

You rushed in then. You must have heard us talking. You crouched down next to me and stroked the hair back from my face.

"How are you feeling?" you asked.

I looked down at your fingernails, and saw again that they were smooth, no jagged edges, and a hint of white at the edges. Dara told me later that you'd arrived two days before me, just so you two could have a few days alone together. After all, you'd only left her for 1947 a few days before. The two of you had a lot to talk about.

"All right, I guess," I told you.

• • •

It felt like the worst family vacation for those first few days. Dara was distant with me and downright cold to you. I wanted to ask what had happened, but I thought that I'd get the cold shoulder if I did. I caught snippets of the arguments you had with Dara; always whispered in doorways, or downstairs in the kitchen, the words too faint for me to make out.

It got a little better once I was back on my feet and able to walk around and explore. I was astonished by everything; the walnut trees on our property that I had known as saplings now towered over me. Dara's television was twice the size of ours, in color, and had over a dozen stations. Dara's car seemed tiny, and shaped like a snake's head, instead of having the generous curves and lines of the cars I knew.

I think it charmed Dara out of her anger a bit, to see me so appreciative of all these futuristic wonders—which were all relics of the past for her—and the conversations between the three of us got a little bit easier. Dara told me a little bit more about where she'd come from—the late twenty-first century—and why she was in this time—studying with some poet that I'd never heard of. She showed me the woman's poetry, and though I couldn't make much of it out at the time, one line from one poem has always stuck with me. "I did not recognize the shape of my own name."

I pondered that, lying awake in my bedroom—the once and future bedroom that I'm writing this from now, that I slept in then, that I awoke in when I was a young child, frightened by a storm. The rest of that poem made little sense to me, a series of images that were threaded together by a string of line breaks.

But I know about names, and hearing the one that's been given to you, and not recognizing it. I was trying to stammer this out to Dara one night, after she'd read that poem to me. And she asked, plain as could be, "What would you rather be called instead?"

I thought about how I used to introduce myself after the heroes of the TV shows my father and I watched: Doc and George and Charlie. It had been a silly game, sure, but there'd been something more serious underneath it. I'd recognized something in the shape of those names, something I wanted for myself.

"I dunno. A boy's name," I said. "Like George in The Famous Five."

"Well, why do you want to be called by a boy's name?" Dara asked gently.

In the corner, where you'd been playing solitaire, you paused while laying down a card. Dara noticed too, and we both looked over at you. I cringed, wondering what you were about to say; you hated that I didn't like my name, took it as a personal insult somehow.

But you said nothing, just resumed playing, slapping the cards down a little more heavily than before.

• • •

I forgive you for drugging me to take me back to 1963. I know I screamed at you after we arrived and the drugs wore off, but I was also a little relieved. It was a sneaking sort of relief, and didn't do much to counterbalance the feelings of betrayal and rage, but I know I would have panicked the second you shoved me into one of those capsules.

You'd taken me to the future, after all. I'd seen the relative wonders of 1981: VHS tapes, the Flash Gordon movie, the Columbia space shuttle. I would have forgiven you so much for that tiny glimpse.

I don't forgive you for leaving me, though. I don't forgive you for the morning after, when I woke up in my old familiar bedroom and padded downstairs for a bowl of cereal, and found, instead, a note that bore two words in your handwriting: *I'm sorry.*

The note rested atop the gilt-edged book that Grandma Emmeline had started as a diary, and that Uncle Dante had turned into both a record and a set of instructions for future generations: the names, birth dates, and the locations for all the traveling members of our family; who lived in the house and when; and sometimes, how and when a person died. The book stays with the house; you must have kept it hidden in the attic.

I flipped through it until I found your name: Miriam Guthrie (née Stone): born November 21, 1977, Harrisburg, IL. Next to it, you penciled in the following.

Jumped forward to June 22, 2321 CE, and will die in exile beyond reach of the anachronopede.

Two small words could never encompass everything you have to apologize for.

• • •

I wonder if you ever looked up Dad's obituary. I wonder if you were even able to, if the record for one small man's death even lasts that long.

When you left, you took my father's future with you. Did you realize that? He was stuck in the slow lane of linear time, and to Dad, the future he'd dreamed of must have receded into the distance, something he'd never be able to reach.

He lost his job in the fall of 1966, as the White County oil wells ran dry, and hanged himself in the garage six months later. Dara cut him down and called the ambulance; her visits became more regular after you left us, and she must have known the day he would die.

(I can't bring myself to ask her: Couldn't she have arrived twenty minutes earlier and stopped him entirely? I don't want to know her answer.)

In that obituary, I'm first in the list of those who survived him, and it's the last time I used the name you gave me. During the funeral, I nodded, received the hugs and handshakes from Dad's cousins and friends, bowed my head when the priest instructed, prayed hard for his soul. When it was done, I walked alone to the pond where the two of us had sat together, watching birds and talking about the plots of silly television shows. I tried to remember everything that I could about him, tried to preserve his ghost against the vagaries of time: the smell of Kamel cigarettes and diesel on his clothes; the red-blond stubble that dotted his jaw; the way his eyes brightened when they landed on you.

I wished so hard that you were there with me. I wanted so much to cry on your shoulder, to sob as hard and hysterically as I had when you took me to 1981. And I wanted to be able to slap you, to hit you, to push you in the water and hold you beneath the surface. I could have killed you that day, Mama.

When I was finished, Dara took me back to the house. We cleaned it as best we could for the next family member who would live here: there always has to be a member of the Stone family here, to take care of the shelter, the anachronopede, and the travelers that come through.

Then she took me away, to 2073, the home she'd made more than a century away from you.

• • •

Today was the first day I was able to leave the house, to take cautious, wobbling steps to the outside world. Everything is still tender and bruised, though my body is healing faster than I ever thought possible. It feels strange to walk with a weight between my legs; I walk differently, with a wider stride, even though I'm still limping.

Dara and I walked down to the pond today. The frogs all hushed at our approach, but the blackbirds set up a racket. And off in the distance, a heron lifted a cautious foot and placed it down again. We watched it step carefully through the water, hesitantly. Its beak darted into the water and came back up with a wriggling fish, which it flipped into its mouth. I suppose it was satisfied with that, because it crouched down, spread its wings, and then jumped into the air, enormous wings fighting against gravity until it rose over the trees.

Three days before my surgery, I went back to you. The pain of it is always the same, like I'm being torn apart and placed back together with clumsy, inexpert fingers, but by now I've gotten used to it. I wanted you to see me as the man I've always known I am, that I slowly became. And I wanted to see if I could forgive you; if I could look at you and see anything besides my father's slow decay, my own broken and betrayed heart.

I knocked at the door, dizzy, ears ringing, shivering, soaked from the storm that was so much worse than I remembered. I was lucky that you or Dara had left a blanket in the shelter, so I didn't have to walk up to the front door naked; my flat, scarred chest at odds with my wide hips, the thatch of pubic hair with no flesh protruding from it. I'd been on hormones for a year, and this second puberty reminded me so much of my first one, with you in 1963: the acne and the awkwardness, the slow reveal of my future self.

You answered the door with your hair in curlers, just as I remembered, and fetched me one of Dad's old robes. I fingered the monogramming at the breast pocket, and I wished, so hard, that I could walk upstairs and see him.

"What the hell," you said. "I thought the whole family knew these years were off-limits while I'm linear."

You didn't quite recognize me, and you tilted your head. "Have we met before?"

I looked you in the eyes, and my voice cracked when I told you I was your son.

Your hand went to your mouth. "I'll have a son?" you asked.

And I told you the truth: "You have one already."

And your hand went to your gut, as if you would be sick. You shook your head, so hard that your curlers started coming loose. That's when the door creaked open, just a crack. You flew over there and yanked it all the way open, snatching the child there up in your arms. I barely caught a glimpse of my own face looking back at me as you carried my child self up the stairs.

I left before I could introduce myself to you: my name is Heron, Mama. I haven't forgiven you yet, but maybe someday, I will. And when I do, I will travel back one last time, to that night you left me and Dad for the future. I'll tell you that your apology has finally been accepted, and will give you my blessing to live in exile, marooned in a future beyond all reach.

• • •

NINO CIPRI is a queer and trans/nonbinary writer, currently enrolled in the University of Kansas's MFA in fiction. They are also a graduate of the 2014 Clarion Writers' Workshop. Their writing has been published in *Tor.com*, *Fireside Magazine*, *Betwixt*, *Daily Science Fiction*, *In the Fray*, *Autostraddle*, and *Gozamos*. A multidisciplinary artist, Nino has also written plays, screenplays, and radio features; performed as a dancer, actor, and puppeteer; and worked as a backstage theater technician.

Eros, Philia, Agape

Rachel Swirsky

A contemporary tale of love in all its forms—and of one robot's quest to know it, and himself, on his own terms. *Hugo Award nominee. Edited by Patrick Nielsen Hayden.*

Lucian packed his possessions before he left. He packed his antique silver serving spoons with the filigreed handles; the tea roses he'd nurtured in the garden window; his jade and garnet rings. He packed the hunk of gypsum-veined jasper that he'd found while strolling on the beach on the first night he'd come to Adriana, she leading him uncertainly across the wet sand, their bodies illuminated by the soft gold twinkling of the lights along the pier. That night, as they walked back to Adriana's house, Lucian had cradled the speckled stone in his cupped palms, squinting so that the gypsum threads sparkled through his lashes.

Lucian had always loved beauty—beautiful scents, beautiful tastes, beautiful melodies. He especially loved beautiful objects because he could hold them in his hands and transform the abstraction of beauty into something tangible.

The objects belonged to them both, but Adriana waved her hand bitterly when Lucian began packing. "Take whatever you want," she said, snapping her book shut. She waited by the door, watching Lucian with sad and angry eyes.

Their daughter, Rose, followed Lucian around the house. "Are you going to take that, Daddy? Do you want that?" Wordlessly, Lucian held her hand. He guided her up the stairs and across the uneven floorboards where she sometimes tripped. Rose stopped by the picture window in the master bedroom, staring past the palm fronds and swimming pools, out to the vivid cerulean swath of the ocean. Lucian relished the hot, tender feel of Rose's hand. *I love you,* he would have whispered, but he'd surrendered the ability to speak.

He led her downstairs again to the front door. Rose's lace-festooned pink satin dress crinkled as she leapt down the steps. Lucian had ordered her dozens of satin party dresses in pale, floral hues. Rose refused to wear anything else.

Rose looked between Lucian and Adriana. "Are you taking me, too?" she asked Lucian.

Adriana's mouth tightened. She looked at Lucian, daring him to say something, to take responsibility for what he was doing to their daughter. Lucian remained silent.

Adriana's chardonnay glowed the same shade of amber as Lucian's eyes. She clutched the glass's stem until she thought it might break. "No, honey," she said with artificial lightness. "You're staying with me."

Rose reached for Lucian. "Horsey?"

Lucian knelt down and pressed his forehead against Rose's. He hadn't spoken a word in the three days since he'd delivered his letter of farewell to Adriana, announcing his intention to leave as soon as she had enough time to make arrangements to care for Rose in his absence. When Lucian approached with the letter, Adriana had been sitting at the dining table, sipping orange juice from a wine glass and reading a first-edition copy of Cheever's *Falconer*. Lucian felt a flash of guilt as she smiled up at him and accepted the missive. He knew that she'd been happier in the past few months than he'd ever seen her, possibly happier than she'd ever been. He knew the letter would shock and wound her. He knew she'd feel betrayed. Still, he delivered the letter anyway, and watched as comprehension ached through her body.

• • •

Rose had been told, gently, patiently, that Lucian was leaving. But she was four years old, and understood things only briefly and partially, and often according to her whims. She continued to believe her father's silence was a game.

Rose's hair brushed Lucian's cheek. He kissed her brow. Adriana couldn't hold her tongue any longer.

"What do you think you're going to find out there? There's no Shangri-la for rebel robots. You think you're making a play for independence? Independence to do what, Lu?"

Grief and anger filled Adriana's eyes with hot tears, as if she were a geyser filled with so much pressure that steam could not help but spring up. She examined Lucian's sculpted face: his skin inlaid with tiny lines that an artist had rendered to suggest the experiences of a childhood that had never been lived, his eyes calibrated with a hint of asymmetry to mimic the imperfection of human growth. His expression showed nothing—no doubt, or bitterness, or even relief. He revealed nothing at all.

It was all too much. Adriana moved between Lucian and Rose, as if she could use her own body to protect her daughter from the pain of being abandoned. Her eyes stared achingly over the rim of her wine glass. "Just go," she said.

He left.

• • •

Adriana bought Lucian the summer she turned thirty-five. Her father, long afflicted with an indecisive cancer that vacillated between aggression and remittance, had died suddenly in July. For years, the family had been squirreling away emotional reserves to cope with his prolonged illness. His death released a burst of excess.

While her sisters went through the motions of grief, Adriana thrummed with energy she didn't know what to do with. She considered squandering her vigor on six weeks in Mazatlan, but as she discussed ocean-front rentals with her travel agent, she realized escape wasn't what she craved. She liked the setting where her life took place: her house perched on a cliff overlooking the Pacific Ocean, her bedroom window that opened on a tangle of blackberry bushes where crows roosted every autumn and spring. She liked the two-block stroll down to the beach where she could sit with a book and listen to the yapping lapdogs that the elderly women from the waterfront condominiums brought walking in the evenings.

Mazatlan was a twenty-something's cure for restlessness. Adriana wasn't twenty-five anymore, famished for the whole gourmet meal of existence. She needed something else now. Something new. Something more refined.

She explained this to her friends Ben and Lawrence when they invited her to their ranch house in Santa Barbara to relax for the weekend and try to forget about her father. They sat on Ben and Lawrence's patio, on iron-worked deck chairs arrayed around a garden table topped with a mosaic of sea creatures made of semi-precious stones. A warm, breezy dusk lengthened the shadows of the orange trees. Lawrence poured sparkling rosé into three wine glasses and proposed a toast to Adriana's father—not to his memory, but to his death.

"Good riddance to the bastard," said Lawrence. "If he were still alive, I'd punch him in the schnoz."

"I don't even want to think about him," said Adriana. "He's dead. He's gone."

"So if not Mazatlan, what are you going to do?" asked Ben.

"I'm not sure," said Adriana. "Some sort of change, some sort of milestone, that's all I know."

Lawrence sniffed the air. "Excuse me," he said, gathering the empty wine glasses. "The kitchen needs its genius."

When Lawrence was out of earshot, Ben leaned forward to whisper to Adriana. "He's got us on a raw-food diet for my cholesterol. Raw carrots. Raw zucchini. Raw almonds. No cooking at all."

"Really," said Adriana, glancing away. She was never sure how to respond to lovers' quarrels. That kind of affection mixed with annoyance, that inescapable intimacy, was something she'd never understood.

Birds twittered in the orange trees. The fading sunlight highlighted copper strands in Ben's hair as he leaned over the mosaic table, rapping his fingers against a carnelian-backed crab. Through the arched windows, Adriana could see Lawrence mincing carrots, celery, and almonds into brown paste.

"You should get a redecorator," said Ben. "Tile floors, Tuscan pottery, those red leather chairs that were in vogue last time we were in Milan. That'd make me feel like I'd been scrubbed clean and reborn."

"No, no," said Adriana, "I like where I live."

"A no-holds-barred shopping spree. Drop twenty thousand. That's what I call getting a weight off your shoulders."

Adriana laughed. "How long do you think it would take my personal shopper to assemble a whole new me?"

"Sounds like a midlife crisis," said Lawrence, returning with vegan hors d'oeuvres and three glasses of mineral water. "You're better off forgetting it all with a hot Latin pool boy, if you ask me."

Lawrence served Ben a small bowl filled with yellow mush. Ben shot Adriana an aggrieved glance.

Adriana felt suddenly out of synch. The whole evening felt like the set for a photo-shoot that would go in a decorating magazine, a two-page spread featuring Cozy Gardens, in which she and Ben and Lawrence were posing as an intimate dinner party for three. She felt reduced to two dimensions, air-brushed, and then digitally grafted onto the form of whoever it was who should have been there, someone warm and trusting who knew how to care about minutia like a friend's husband putting him on a raw-food diet, not because the issue was important, but because it mattered to him.

Lawrence dipped his finger in the mash and held it up to Ben's lips. "It's for your own good, you ungrateful so-and-so."

Ben licked it away. "I eat it, don't I?"

Lawrence leaned down to kiss his husband, a warm and not at all furtive kiss, not sexual but still passionate. Ben's glance flashed coyly downward.

Adriana couldn't remember the last time she'd loved someone enough to be embarrassed by them. Was this the flavor missing from her life? A lover's fingertip sliding an unwanted morsel into her mouth?

She returned home that night on the bullet train. Her emerald cockatiel, Fuoco, greeted her with indignant squawks. In Adriana's absence, the house puffed her scent into the air and sang to Fuoco with her voice, but the bird was never fooled.

Adriana's father had given her the bird for her thirtieth birthday. He was a designer species spliced with Macaw DNA that colored his feathers rich green. He was expensive and inbred and neurotic, and he loved Adriana with frantic, obsessive jealousy.

"Hush," Adriana admonished, allowing Fuoco to alight on her shoulder. She carried him upstairs to her bedroom and hand-fed him millet. Fuoco strutted across the pillows, his obsidian eyes proud and suspicious.

Adriana was surprised to find that her alienation had followed her home. She found herself prone to melancholy reveries, her gaze drifting toward the picture window, her fingers forgetting to stroke Fuoco's back. The bird screeched to regain her attention.

In the morning, Adriana visited her accountant. His fingers danced across the keyboard as he slipped trust-fund moneys from one account to another like a magician. What she planned would be expensive, but her wealth would regrow in fertile soil, enriching her on lab diamonds and wind power and genetically modified oranges.

The robotics company gave Adriana a private showing. The salesman ushered her into a room draped in black velvet. Hundreds of body parts hung on the walls, and reclined on display tables: strong hands, narrow jaws, biker's thighs, voice boxes that played sound samples from gruff to dulcet, skin swatches spanning ebony to alabaster, penises of various sizes.

At first, Adriana felt horrified at the prospect of assembling a lover from fragments, but then it amused her. Wasn't everyone assembled from fragments of DNA, grown molecule by molecule inside their mother's womb?

She tapped her fingernails against a slick brochure. "Its brain will be malleable? I can tell it to be more amenable, or funnier, or to grow a spine?"

"That's correct." The salesman sported slick brown hair and shiny teeth and kept grinning in a way that suggested he thought that if he were charismatic enough Adriana would invite him home for a lay and a million-dollar tip. "Humans lose brain plasticity as we age, which limits how much we can change. Our models have perpetually plastic brains. They can reroute their personalities at will by reshaping how they think on the neurological level."

Adriana stepped past him, running her fingers along a tapestry woven of a thousand possible hair textures.

The salesman tapped an empty faceplate. "Their original brains are based on deep-imaging scans melded from geniuses in multiple fields. Great musicians, renowned lovers, the best physicists and mathematicians."

Adriana wished the salesman would be quiet. The more he talked, the more doubts clamored against her skull. "You've convinced me," she interrupted. "I want one."

The salesman looked taken aback by her abruptness. She could practically see him rifling through his internal script, trying to find the right page now that she had skipped several scenes. "What do you want him to look like?" he asked.

Adriana shrugged. "They're all beautiful, right?"

"We'll need specifications."

"I don't have specifications."

The salesman frowned anxiously. He shifted his weight as if it could help him regain his metaphorical footing. Adriana took pity. She dug through her purse.

"There," she said, placing a snapshot of her father on one of the display tables. "Make it look nothing like him."

Given such loose parameters, the design team indulged the fanciful. Lucian arrived at Adriana's door only a shade taller than she and equally slender, his limbs smooth and lean. Silver undertones glimmered in his blond hair. His skin was excruciatingly pale, white and translucent as alabaster, veined with pink. He smelled like warm soil and crushed herbs.

He offered Adriana a single white rose, its petals embossed with the company's logo. She held it dubiously between her thumb and forefinger. "They think they know women, do they? They need to put down the bodice rippers."

Lucian said nothing. Adriana took his hesitation for puzzlement, but perhaps she should have seen it as an early indication of his tendency toward silence.

• • •

"That's that, then." Adriana drained her chardonnay and crushed the empty glass beneath her heel as if she could finalize a divorce with the same gesture that sanctified a marriage.

Eyes wide, Rose pointed at the glass with one round finger. "Don't break things."

It suddenly struck Adriana how fast her daughter was aging. Here she was, this four-year-old, this sudden person. When had it happened? In the hospital, when Rose was newborn and wailing for the woman who had birthed her and abandoned her, Adriana had spent hours in the hallway outside the hospital nursery while she waited for the adoption to go through. She'd stared at Rose while she slept, ate, and cried, striving to memorize her nascent, changing face. Sometime between then and now, Rose had become this round-cheeked creature who took rules very seriously and often tried to conceal her emotions beneath a calm exterior, as if being raised by a robot had replaced her blood with circuits. Of course Adriana loved Rose, changed her clothes, brushed her teeth, carried her across the house on her hip—but Lucian had been the most central, nurturing figure. Adriana couldn't fathom how she might fill his role. This wasn't a vacation like the time Adriana had taken Rose to Italy for three days, just the two of them sitting in restaurants, Adriana feeding her daughter spoonfuls of gelato to see the joy that lit her face at each new flavor. Then, they'd known that Lucian would be waiting when they returned. Without him, their family was a house missing a structural support. Adriana could feel the walls bowing in.

The fragments of Adriana's chardonnay glass sparkled sharply. Adriana led Rose away from the mess.

"Never mind," she said, "The house will clean up."

Her head felt simultaneously light and achy as if it couldn't decide between drunkenness and hangover. She tried to remember the parenting books she'd read before adopting Rose. What had they said about crying in front of your child? She clutched Rose close, inhaling the scent of children's shampoo mixed with the acrid odor of wine.

"Let's go for a drive," said Adriana. "Okay? Let's get out for a while."

"I want Daddy to take me to the beach."

"We'll go out to the country and look at the farms. Cows and sheep, okay?"

Rose said nothing.

"Moo?" Adriana clarified. "Baa?"

"I know," said Rose. "I'm not a baby."

"So, then?"

Rose said nothing. Adriana wondered whether she could tell that her mother was a little mad with grief.

Just make a decision, Adriana counseled herself. She slipped her fingers around Rose's hand. "We'll go for a drive."

Adriana instructed the house to regulate itself in their absence, and then led Rose to the little black car that she and Lucian had bought together after adopting Rose. She fastened Rose's safety buckle and programmed the car to take them inland.

As the car engine initialized, Adriana felt a glimmer of fear. What if this machine betrayed them, too? But its uninspired intelligence only switched on the left turn signal and started down the boulevard.

• • •

Lucian stood at the base of the driveway and stared up at the house. Its stark orange and brown walls blazed against a cloudless sky. Rocks and desert plants tumbled down the meticulously landscaped yard, imitating natural scrub.

A rabbit ran across the road, followed by the whir of Adriana's car. Lucian watched them pass. They couldn't see him through the cypresses, but Lucian could make out Rose's face pressed against the window. Beside her, Adriana slumped in her seat, one hand pressed over her eyes.

Lucian went in the opposite direction. He dragged the rolling cart packed with his belongings to the cliff that led down to the beach. He lifted the cart over his head and started down, his feet disturbing cascades of sandstone chunks.

A pair of adolescent boys looked up from playing in the waves. "Whoa," shouted one of them. "Are you carrying that whole thing? Are you a weight lifter?"

Lucian remained silent. When he reached the sand, the kids muttered disappointments to each other and turned away from shore. "... Just a robot..." drifted back to Lucian on the breeze.

Lucian pulled his cart to the border where wet sand met dry. Oncoming waves lapped over his feet. He opened the cart and removed a tea-scented apricot rose growing in a pot painted with blue leaves.

He remembered acquiring the seeds for his first potted rose. One evening, long ago, he'd asked Adriana if he could grow things. He'd asked in passing, the question left to linger while they cleaned up after dinner, dish soap on their hands, Fuoco pecking after scraps. The next morning, Adriana escorted Lucian to the hothouse near the botanical gardens. "Buy whatever you want," she told him. Lucian was awed by the profusion of color and scent, all that beauty in one place. He wanted to capture the wonder of that place and own it for himself.

Lucian drew back his arm and threw the pot into the sea. It broke across the water, petals scattering the surface.

He threw in the pink roses, and the white roses, and the red roses, and the mauve roses. He threw in the filigreed-handled spoons. He threw in the chunk of gypsum-veined jasper.

He threw in everything beautiful that he'd ever collected. He threw in a chased-silver hand mirror, and an embroidered silk jacket, and a hand-painted egg. He threw in one of Fuoco's soft, emerald feathers. He threw in a memory crystal that showed Rose as an infant, curled and sleeping.

He loved those things, and yet they were things. He had owned them. Now they were gone. He had recently come to realize that ownership was a relationship. What did it mean to own a thing? To shape it and contain it? He could not possess or be possessed until he knew.

He watched the sea awhile, the remnants of his possessions lost in the tumbling waves. As the sun tilted past noon, he turned away and climbed back up the cliff. Unencumbered by ownership, he followed the boulevard away from Adriana's house.

. . .

Lucian remembered meeting Adriana the way that he imagined that humans remembered childhood. Oh, his memories had been as sharply focused then as now— but it was still like childhood, he reasoned, for he'd been a different person then.

He remembered his first sight of Adriana as a burst of images. Wavy strawberry blonde hair cut straight across tanned shoulders. Dark brown eyes that his artistic mind labeled "sienna." Thick, aristocratic brows and strong cheekbones, free of makeup. Lucian's inner aesthete termed her blunt, angular face "striking" rather than "beautiful." His inner psychoanalyst reasoned that she was probably "strong-willed" as well, from the way she stood in the doorway, her arms crossed, her eyebrows lifted as if inquiring how he planned to justify his existence.

Eventually, she moved away, allowing Lucian to step inside. He crossed the threshold into a blur of frantic screeching and flapping.

New. Everything was new. So new that Lucian could barely assemble feathers and beak and wings into the concept of "bird" before his reflexes jumped him away from the onslaught. Hissing and screeching, the animal retreated to a perch atop a bookshelf.

Adriana's hand weighed on Lucian's shoulder. Her voice was edged with the cynicism Lucian would later learn was her way of hiding how desperately she feared failure. "Ornithophobia? How ridiculous."

Lucian's first disjointed days were dominated by the bird, who he learned was named Fuoco. The bird followed him around the house. When he remained in place for a moment, the bird settled on some nearby high spot—the hat rack in the entryway, or the hand-crafted globe in the parlor, or the rafters above the master bed—to spy on him. He glared at Lucian in the manner of birds, first peering through one eye and then turning his head to peer through the other, apparently finding both views equally loathsome.

When Adriana took Lucian into her bed, Fuoco swooped at Lucian's head. Adriana pushed Lucian out of the way. "Damn it, Fuoco," she muttered, but she offered the bird a perch on her shoulder.

Fuoco crowed with pleasure as she led him downstairs. His feathers fluffed with victory as he hopped obediently into his cage, expecting her to reward him with treats and conversation. Instead, Adriana closed the gilded door and returned upstairs. All night, as Lucian lay with Adriana, the bird chattered madly. He plucked at his feathers until his tattered plumage carpeted the cage floor.

Lucian accompanied Adriana when she brought Fuoco to the vet the next day. The veterinarian diagnosed jealousy. "It's not uncommon in birds," he said. He suggested they give Fuoco a rigid routine that would, over time, help the bird realize he was Adriana's companion, not her mate.

Adriana and Lucian rearranged their lives so that Fuoco could have regular feeding times, scheduled exercise, socialization with both Lucian and Adriana, and time with his mistress alone. Adriana gave him a treat each night when she locked him in his cage, staying to stroke his feathers for a few minutes before she headed upstairs.

Fuoco's heart broke. He became a different bird. His strut lacked confidence, and his feathers grew ever more tattered. When they let him out of his cage, he wandered after Adriana with pleading, wistful eyes, and ignored Lucian entirely.

• • •

Lucian had been dis-integrated then: musician brain, mathematician brain, artist brain, economist brain, and more, all functioning separately, each personality rising to dominance to provide information and then sliding away, creating staccato bursts of consciousness.

As Adriana made clear which responses she liked, Lucian's consciousness began integrating into the personality she desired. He found himself noticing connections between what had previously been separate experiences. Before, when he'd seen the ocean, his scientist brain had calculated how far he was from the shore, and how long it would be until high tide. His poet brain had recited Strindberg's "We Waves." *Wet flames are we: / Burning, extinguishing; / Cleansing, replenishing.* Yet it wasn't until he integrated that the wonder of the science, and the mystery of the poetry, and the beauty of the view all made sense to him at once as part of this strange, inspiring thing: the sea.

He learned to anticipate Adriana. He knew when she was pleased and when she was ailing, and he knew why. He could predict the cynical half-smile she'd give when he made an error he hadn't yet realized was an error: serving her cold coffee in an orange-juice glass, orange juice in a shot glass, wine in a mug. When integration gave him knowledge of patterns, he suddenly understood why these things were errors. At the same time, he realized that he liked what happened when he made those kinds of errors, the bright bursts of humor they elicited from the often sober Adriana. So he persisted in error, serving her milk in crystal decanters, and grapefruit slices in egg cups.

He enjoyed the many varieties of her laughter. Sometimes it was light and surprised, as when he offered her a cupcake tin filled with tortellini. He also loved her rich, dark laughter that anticipated irony. Sometimes, her laughter held a bitter undercurrent, and on those occasions, he understood that she was laughing more at herself than at anyone else. Sometimes when that happened, he would go to hold her, seeking to ease her pain, and sometimes she would spontaneously start crying in gulping, gasping sobs.

She often watched him while he worked, her head cocked and her brows drawn as if she were seeing him for the first time. "What can I do to make you happy?" she'd ask.

If he gave an answer, she would lavishly fulfill his desires. She took him traveling to the best greenhouses in the state, and bought a library full of gardening books. Lucian knew she would have given him more. He didn't want it. He wanted to reassure her that he appreciated her extravagance, but didn't require it, that he was satisfied with simple, loving give-and-take. Sometimes, he told her in the simplest words he knew: "I love you, too." But he knew that she never quite believed him. She worried that he was lying, or that his programming had erased his free will. It was easier for her to believe those things than to accept that someone could love her.

But he did love her. Lucian loved Adriana as his mathematician brain loved the consistency of arithmetic, as his artist brain loved color, as his philosopher brain loved piety. He loved her as Fuoco loved her, the bird walking sadly along the arm of Adriana's chair, trilling and flapping his ragged wings as he eyed her with his inky gaze, trying to catch her attention.

• • •

Adriana hadn't expected to fall in love. She'd expected a charming conversational-ist with the emotional range of a literary butler and the self-awareness of a golden retriever. Early on, she'd felt her prejudices confirmed. She noted Lucian's lack of critical thinking and his inability to maneuver unexpected situations. She found him most interesting when he didn't know she was watching. For instance, on his free afternoons: was his program trying to anticipate what would please her? Or did the thing really enjoy sitting by the window, leafing through the pages of one of her rare books, with nothing but the sound of the ocean to lull him?

Once, as Adriana watched from the kitchen doorway while Lucian made their breakfast, the robot slipped while he was dicing onions. The knife cut deep into his finger. Adriana stumbled forward to help. As Lucian turned to face her, Adri-ana imagined that she saw something like shock on his face. For a moment, she wondered whether he had a programmed sense of privacy she could violate, but then he raised his hand to her in greeting, and she watched as the tiny bots that maintained his system healed his inhuman flesh within seconds.

At that moment, Adriana remembered that Lucian was unlike her. She urged herself not to forget it, and strove not to, even after his consciousness integrated. He was a person, yes, a varied and fascinating one with as many depths and facets as any other person she knew. But he was also alien. He was a creature for whom a slip of a chef's knife was a minute error, simply repaired. In some ways, she was more similar to Fuoco.

As a child, Adriana had owned a book that told the fable of an emperor who owned a bird that he fed rich foods from his table, and entertained with luxuries from his court. But a pet bird needed different things than an emperor. He wanted seed and millet, not grand feasts. He enjoyed mirrors and little brass bells, not lacquer boxes and poetry scrolls. Gorged on human banquets and revelries, the little bird sickened and died.

Adriana vowed not to make the same mistake with Lucian, but she had no idea how hard it would be to salve the needs of something so unlike herself.

• • •

Adriana ordered the car to pull over at a farm that advertised children could "Pet Lambs and Calves" for a fee. A ginger-haired teenager stood at a strawberry stand in front of the fence, slouching as he flipped through a dog-eared magazine.

Adriana held Rose's hand as they approached. She tried to read her daughter's emotions in the feel of her tiny fingers. The little girl's expression revealed noth-ing; Rose had gone silent and flat-faced as if she were imitating Lucian. He would have known what she was feeling.

Adriana examined the strawberries. The crates contained none of the different shapes one could buy at the store, only the natural, seed-filled variety. "Do these contain pesticides?" Adriana asked.

"No, ma'am," said the teenager. "We grow organic."

"All right then. I'll take a box." Adriana looked down at her daughter. "Do you want some strawberries, sweetheart?" she asked in a sugared tone.

"You said I could pet the lambs," said Rose.

"Right. Of course, honey." Adriana glanced at the distracted teenager. "Can she?"

The teenager slumped, visibly disappointed, and tossed his magazine on a pile of canvas sacks. "I can take her to the barn."

"Fine. Okay."

Adriana guided Rose toward the teenager. Rose looked up at him, expression still inscrutable.

The boy didn't take Rose's hand. He ducked his head, obviously embarrassed. "My aunt likes me to ask for the money up front."

"Of course." Adriana fumbled for her wallet. She'd let Lucian do things for her for so long. How many basic living skills had she forgotten? She held out some bills. The teenager licked his index finger and meticulously counted out what she owed.

The teen took Rose's hand. He lingered a moment, watching Adriana. "Aren't you coming with us?"

Adriana was so tired. She forced a smile. "Oh, that's okay. I've seen sheep and cows. Okay, Rose? Can you have fun for a little bit without me?"

Rose nodded soberly. She turned toward the teenager without hesitation, and followed him toward the barn. The boy seemed to be good with children. He walked slowly so that Rose could keep up with his long-legged strides.

Adriana returned to the car, and leaned against the hot, sun-warmed door. Her head throbbed. She thought she might cry or collapse. Getting out had seemed like a good idea: the house was full of memories of Lucian. He seemed to sit in every chair, linger in every doorway. But now she wished she'd stayed in her haunted but familiar home, instead of leaving with this child she seemed to barely know.

A sharp, long wail carried on the wind. Adrenaline cut through Adriana's melancholia. She sprinted toward the barn. She saw Rose running toward her, the teenager close behind, dust swirling around both of them. Blood dripped down Rose's arm.

Adriana threw her arms around her daughter. Arms, legs, breath, heartbeat: Rose was okay. Adrianna dabbed at Rose's injury; there was a lot of blood, but the wound was shallow. "Oh, honey," she said, clutching Rose as tightly as she dared.

The teenager halted beside them, his hair mussed by the wind.

"What happened?" Adriana demanded.

The teenager stammered. "Fortuna kicked her. That's one of the goats. I'm so sorry. Fortuna's never done anything like that before. She's a nice goat. It's Ballantine who usually does the kicking. He got me a few times when I was little. I came through every time. Honest, she'll be okay. You're not going to sue, are you?"

Rose struggled out of Adriana's grasp and began wailing again. "It's okay, Rose, it's okay," murmured Adriana. She felt a strange disconnect in her head as she spoke. Things were not okay. Things might never be okay again.

"I'm leaking," cried Rose, holding out her bloodstained fingers. "See, Mama? I'm leaking! I need healer bots."

Adriana looked up at the teenager. "Do you have bandages? A first-aid kit?"

The boy frowned. "In the house, I think . . ."

"Get the bots, Mama! Make me stop leaking!"

The teen stared at Adriana, the concern in his eyes increasing. Adriana blinked, slowly. The moment slowed. She realized what her daughter had said. She forced her voice to remain calm. "What do you want, Rose?"

"She said it before," said the teen. "I thought it was a game."

Adriana leveled her gaze with Rose's. The child's eyes were strange and brown, uncharted waters. "Is this a game?"

"Daddy left," said Rose.

Adriana felt woozy. "Yes, and then I brought you here so we could see lambs and calves. Did you see any nice, fuzzy lambs?"

"Daddy left."

She shouldn't have drunk the wine. She should have stayed clearheaded. "We'll get you bandaged up and then you can go see the lambs again. Do you want to see the lambs again? Would it help if Mommy came, too?"

Rose clenched her fists. Her face grew dark. "My arm hurts!" She threw herself to the ground. "I want healer bots!"

• • •

Adriana knew precisely when she'd fallen in love with Lucian. It was three months after she'd bought him: after his consciousness had integrated, but before Adriana fully understood how integration had changed him.

It began when Adriana's sisters called from Boston to inform her that they'd arranged for a family pilgrimage to Italy. In accordance with their father's will, they would commemorate him by lighting candles in the cathedrals of every winding hillside city.

"Oh, I can't. I'm too busy," Adriana answered airily, as if she were a debutante without a care, as if she shared her sisters' ability to overcome her fear of their father.

Her phone began ringing ceaselessly. Nanette called before she rushed off to a tennis match. "How can you be so busy? You don't have a job. You don't have a husband. Or is there a man in your life we don't know about?" And once Nanette was deferred with mumbled excuses, it was Eleanor calling from a spa. "Is something wrong, Adriana? We're all worried. How can you miss a chance to say goodbye to Papa?"

"I said goodbye at the funeral," said Adriana.

"Then you can't have properly processed your grief," said Jessica, calling from her office between appointments. She was a psychoanalyst in the Freudian mode. "Your aversion rings of denial. You need to process your Oedipal feelings."

Adriana slammed down the phone. Later, to apologize for hanging up, she sent all her sisters chocolates, and then booked a flight. In a fit of pique, she booked a seat for Lucian, too. Well, he was a companion, wasn't he? What else was he for?

Adriana's sisters were scandalized, of course. As they rode through Rome, Jessica, Nanette, and Eleanor gossiped behind their discreetly raised hands. Adriana with a robot? Well, she'd need to be, wouldn't she? There was no getting around the fact that she was damaged. Any girl who would make up those stories about their father would have to be.

Adriana ignored them as best she could while they whirled through Tuscany in a procession of rented cars. They paused in cities to gawk at Gothic cathedrals and mummified remnants, always moving on within the day. During their father's long sickness, Adriana's sisters had perfected the art of cheerful anecdote. They used it to great effect as they lit candles in his memory. Tears welling in their eyes, they related banal, nostalgic memories. How their father danced at charity balls. How he lectured men on the board who looked down on him for being new money. How he never once apologized for anything in his life.

It had never been clear to Adriana whether her father had treated her sisters the way he treated her, or whether she had been the only one to whom he came at night, his breathing heavy and staccato. It seemed impossible that they could lie so seamlessly, never showing fear or doubt. But if they were telling the truth, that meant Adriana was the only one, and how could she believe that either?

One night, while Lucian and Adriana were alone in their room in a hotel in Assisi that had been a convent during the Middle Ages, Adriana broke down. It was all too much, being in this foreign place, talking endlessly about her father. She'd fled New England to get away from them, fled to her beautiful modern glass-and-wood house by the Pacific Ocean that was like a fresh breath drawn on an autumn morning.

Lucian held her, exerting the perfect warmth and pressure against her body to comfort her. It was what she'd have expected from a robot. She knew that he calculated the pace of his breath, the temperature of his skin, the angle of his arm as it lay across her.

What surprised Adriana, what humbled her, was how eloquently Lucian spoke of his experiences. He told her what it had been like to assemble himself from fragments, to take what he'd once been and become something new. It was something Adriana had tried to do herself when she fled her family.

Lucian held his head down as he spoke. His gaze never met hers. He spoke as if this process of communicating the intimate parts of the self were a new kind of dance, and he was tenuously trying the steps. Through the fog of her grief, Adriana realized that this was a new, struggling consciousness coming to clarity. How could she do anything but love him?

When they returned from Italy, Adriana approached the fledgling movement for granting rights to artificial intelligences. They were underfunded and poorly organized. Adriana rented them offices in San Francisco, and hired a small but competent staff.

Adriana became the movement's face. She'd been on camera frequently as a child: whenever her father was in the news for some boardroom scandal or other, her father's publicists had lined up Adriana and her sisters beside the family limousine, chaste in their private-school uniforms, ready to provide Lancaster Nuclear with a friendly, feminine face.

She and Lucian were a brief media curiosity: Heiress In Love With Robot. "Lucian is as self-aware as you or I," Adriana told reporters, all-American in pearls and jeans. "He thinks. He learns. He can hybridize roses as well as any human gardener. Why should he be denied his rights?"

Early on, it was clear that political progress would be frustratingly slow. Adriana quickly expended her patience. She set up a fund for the organization, made sure it would run without her assistance, and then turned her attention toward alternate methods for attaining her goals. She hired a team of lawyers to draw up a contract that would grant Lucian community property rights to her estate and accounts. He would be her equal in practicality, if not legality.

Next, Adriana approached Lucian's manufacturer, and commissioned them to invent a procedure that would allow Lucian to have conscious control of his brain plasticity. At their wedding, Adriana gave him the chemical commands at the same time as she gave him his ring. "You are your own person now. You always have been, of course, but now you have full agency, too. You are yourself," she announced, in front of their gathered friends. Her sisters would no doubt have been scandalized, but they had not been invited.

On their honeymoon, Adriana and Lucian toured hospitals, running the genetic profiles of abandoned infants until they found a healthy girl with a mitochondrial lineage that matched Adriana's. The infant was tiny and pink and curled in on herself, ready to unfold, like one of Lucian's roses.

When they brought Rose home, Adriana felt a surge in her stomach that she'd never felt before. It was a kind of happiness she'd never experienced, one that felt round and whole without any jagged edges. It was like the sun had risen in her belly and was dwelling there, filling her with boundless light.

• • •

There was a moment, when Rose was still new enough to be wrapped in the handmade baby blanket that Ben and Lawrence had sent from France, in which Adriana looked up at Lucian and realized how enraptured he was with their baby, how much adoration underpinned his willingness to bend over her cradle for hours and mirror her expressions, frown for frown, astonishment for astonishment. In that moment, Adriana thought that this must be the true measure of equality, not money or laws, but this unfolding desire to create the future together by raising a new sentience. She thought she understood then why unhappy parents stayed together for the sake of their children, why families with sons and daughters felt so different from those that remained childless. Families with children were making something new from themselves. Doubly so when the endeavor was undertaken by a human and a creature who was already, himself, something new. What could they make together?

In that same moment, Lucian was watching the wide-eyed, innocent wonder with which his daughter beheld him. She showed the same pleasure when he entered the room as she did when Adriana entered. If anything, the light in her eyes was brighter when he approached. There was something about the way Rose loved him that he didn't yet understand. Earlier that morning, he had plucked a bloom from his apricot tea rose and whispered to its petals that they were beautiful. They were his, and he loved them. Every day he held Rose, and understood that she was beautiful, and that he loved her. But she was not his. She was her own. He wasn't sure he'd ever seen a love like that, a love that did not want to hold its object in its hands and keep and contain it.

· · ·

"You aren't a robot!"

Adriana's voice was rough from shouting all the way home. Bad enough to lose Lucian, but the child was out of control.

"I want healer bots! I'm a robot I'm a robot I'm a robot I'm a robot!"

The car stopped. Adriana got out. She waited for Rose to follow, and when she didn't, Adriana scooped her up and carried her up the driveway. Rose kicked and screamed. She sank her teeth into Adriana's arm. Adriana halted, surprised by the sudden pain. She breathed deeply, and then continued up the driveway. Rose's screams slid upward in register and rage.

Adriana set Rose down by the door long enough to key in the entry code and let the security system take a DNA sample from her hair. Rose hurled herself onto the porch, yanking fronds by the fistful off the potted ferns. Adriana leaned down to scrape her up and got kicked in the chest.

"God da . . . for heaven's sake!" Adriana grabbed Rose's ankles with one hand and her wrists with the other. She pushed her weight against the unlocked door until it swung open. She carried Rose into the house, and slammed the door closed with her back. "Lock!" she yelled to the house.

When she heard the reassuring click, she set Rose down on the couch, and jumped away from the still-flailing limbs. Rose fled up the stairs, her bedroom door crashing shut behind her.

Adriana dug in her pocket for the bandages that the people at the farm had given her before she headed home, which she'd been unable to apply to a moving target in the car. Now was the time. She followed Rose up the stairs, her breath surprisingly heavy. She felt as though she'd been running a very long time. She paused outside Rose's room. She didn't know what she'd do when she got inside. Lucian had always dealt with the child when she got overexcited. Too often, Adriana felt helpless, and became distant.

"Rose?" she called. "Rose? Are you okay?"

There was no response.

Adriana put her hand on the doorknob, and breathed deeply before turning.

She was surprised to find Rose sitting demurely in the center of her bed, her rumpled skirts spread about her as if she were a child at a picnic in an Impressionist painting. Dirt and tears trailed down the pink satin. The edges of her wound had already begun to bruise.

"I'm a robot," she said to Adriana, tone resentful.

Adriana made a decision. The most important thing was to bandage Rose's wound. Afterward, she could deal with whatever came next.

"Okay," said Adriana. "You're a robot."

Rose lifted her chin warily. "Good."

Adriana sat on the edge of Rose's bed. "You know what robots do? They change themselves to be whatever humans ask them to be."

"Dad doesn't," said Rose.

"That's true," said Adriana. "But that didn't happen until your father grew up."

Rose swung her legs against the side of the bed. Her expression remained dubious, but she no longer looked so resolute.

Adriana lifted the packet of bandages. "May I?"

Rose hesitated. Adriana resisted the urge to put her head in her hands. She had to get the bandages on, that was the important thing, but she couldn't shake the feeling that she was going to regret this later.

"Right now, what this human wants is for you to let her bandage your wound instead of giving you healer bots. Will you be a good robot? Will you let me?"

Rose remained silent, but she moved a little closer to her mother. When Adriana began bandaging her arm, she didn't scream.

• • •

Lucian waited for a bus to take him to the desert. He had no money. He'd forgotten about that. The driver berated him and wouldn't let him on.

Lucian walked. He could walk faster than a human, but not much faster. His edge was endurance. The road took him inland away from the sea. The last of the expensive houses stood near a lighthouse, lamps shining in all its windows. Beyond, condominiums pressed against each other, dense and alike. They gave way to compact, well-maintained homes, with neat green aprons maintained by automated sprinklers that sprayed arcs of precious water into the air.

The landscape changed. Sea breeze stilled to buzzing heat. Dirty, peeling houses squatted side by side, separated by chain-link fences. Iron bars guarded the windows, and broken cars decayed in the driveways. Parched lawns stretched from walls to curb like scrubland. No one was out in the punishing sun.

The road divided. Lucian followed the fork that went through the dilapidated town center. Traffic jerked along in fits and starts. Lucian walked in the gutter. Stray plastic bags blew beside him, working their way between dark storefronts. Parking meters blinked at the passing cars, hungry for more coins. Pedestrians ambled past, avoiding eye contact, mumbled conversations lost beneath honking horns.

On the other side of town, the road winnowed down to two lonely lanes. Dry golden grass stretched over rolling hills, dotted by the dark shapes of cattle. A battered convertible, roof down, blared its horn at Lucian as it passed. Lucian walked where the asphalt met the prickly weeds. Paper and cigarette butts littered the golden stalks like white flowers.

An old truck pulled over, the manually driven variety still used by companies too small to afford the insurance for the automatic kind. The man in the driver's seat was trim, with a pale blond mustache and a deerstalker cap pulled over his ears. He wore a string of fishing lures like a necklace. "Not much comes this way anymore," he said. "I used to pick up hitchhikers half the time I took this route. You're the first I've seen in a while."

Sun rendered the truck in bright silhouette. Lucian held his hand over his eyes to shade them.

"Where are you headed?" asked the driver.

Lucian pointed down the road.

"Sure, but where after that?"

Lucian dropped his arm to his side. The sun inched higher.

The driver frowned. "Can you write it down? I think I've got some paper in here." He grabbed a pen and a receipt out of his front pocket, and thrust them out the window.

Lucian took them. He wasn't sure, at first, if he could still write. His brain was slowly reshaping itself, and eventually all his linguistic skills would disappear, and even his thoughts would no longer be shaped by words. The pen fell limp in his hand, and then his fingers remembered what to do. "Desert," he wrote.

"It's blazing hot," said the driver. "A lot hotter than here. Why do you want to go there?"

"To be born," wrote Lucian.

The driver slid Lucian a sideways gaze, but he nodded at the same time, almost imperceptibly. "Sometimes people have to do things. I get that. I remember when . . ." The look in his eyes became distant. He moved back in his seat. "Get on in."

Lucian walked around the cab and got inside. He remembered to sit and to close the door, but the rest of the ritual escaped him. He stared at the driver until the pale man shook his head and leaned over Lucian to drag the seatbelt over his chest.

"Are you under a vow of silence?" asked the driver.

Lucian stared ahead.

"Blazing hot in the desert," muttered the driver. He pulled back onto the road, and drove toward the sun.

• • •

During his years with Adriana, Lucian tried not to think about the cockatiel Fuoco. The bird had never become accustomed to Lucian. He grew ever more angry and bitter. He plucked out his feathers so often that he became bald in patches. Sometimes he pecked deeply enough to bleed.

From time to time, Adriana scooped him up and stroked his head and nuzzled her cheek against the heavy feathers that remained on the part of his back he couldn't reach. "My poor little crazy bird," she'd say, sadly, as he ran his beak through her hair.

Fuoco hated Lucian so much that for a while they wondered whether he would be happier in another place. Adriana tried giving him to Ben and Lawrence, but he only pined for the loss of his mistress, and refused to eat until she flew out to retrieve him.

When they returned home, they hung Fuoco's cage in the nursery. Being near the baby seemed to calm them both. Rose was a fussy infant who disliked solitude. She seemed happier when there was a warm presence about, even if it was a bird.

Fuoco kept her from crying during the rare times when Adriana called Lucian from Rose's side. Lucian spent the rest of his time in the nursery, watching Rose day and night with sleepless vigilance.

The most striking times of Lucian's life were holding Rose while she cried. He wrapped her in cream-colored blankets the same shade as her skin, and rocked her as he walked the perimeter of the downstairs rooms, looking out at the diffuse golden ambience that the streetlights cast across the blackberry bushes and neighbors' patios. Sometimes, he took her outside, and walked with her along the road by the cliffs. He never carried her down to the beach. Lucian had perfect balance and night vision, but none of that mattered when he could so easily imagine the terror of a lost footing—Rose slipping from his grasp and plummeting downward. Instead, they stood a safe distance from the edge, watching from above as the black waves threw themselves against the rocks, the night air scented with cold and salt.

Lucian loved Adriana, but he loved Rose more. He loved her clumsy fists and her yearnings toward consciousness, the slow accrual of her stumbling syllables. She was building her consciousness piece by piece as he had, learning how the world worked and what her place was in it. He silently narrated her stages of development. *Can you tell that your body has boundaries? Do you know your skin from mine?* and *Yes! You can make things happen! Cause and effect. Keep crying and we'll come.* Best of all, there was the moment when she locked her eyes on his, and he could barely breathe for the realization that, *Oh, Rose. You know there's someone else thinking behind these eyes. You know who I am.*

Lucian wanted Rose to have all the beauty he could give her. Silk dresses and lace, the best roses from his pots, the clearest panoramic views of the sea. Objects delighted Rose. As an infant she watched them avidly, and then later clapped and laughed, until finally she could exclaim, "Thank you!" Her eyes shone.

It was Fuoco who broke Lucian's heart. It was late at night when Adriana went into Rose's room to check on her while she slept. Somehow, sometime, the birdcage had been left open. Fuoco sat on the rim of the open door, peering darkly outward.

Adriana had been alone with Rose and Fuoco before. But something about this occasion struck like lightning in Fuoco's tiny, mad brain. Perhaps it was the darkness of the room, with only the nightlight's pale blue glow cast on Adriana's skin, that confused the bird. Perhaps Rose had finally grown large enough that Fuoco had begun to perceive her as a possible rival rather than an ignorable baby-thing. Perhaps the last vestiges of his sanity had simply shredded. For whatever reason, as Adriana bent over the bed to touch her daughter's face, Fuoco burst wildly from his cage.

With the same jealous anger he'd shown toward Lucian, Fuoco dove at Rose's face. His claws raked against her forehead. Rose screamed. Adriana recoiled. She grabbed Rose in one arm, and flailed at the bird with the other. Rose struggled to escape her mother's grip so she could run away. Adriana instinctively responded by trying to protect her with an even tighter grasp.

Lucian heard the commotion from where he was standing in the living room, programming the house's cleaning regimen for the next week. He left the house panel open and ran through the kitchen on the way to the bedroom, picking up a frying pan as he passed through. He swung the pan at Fuoco as he entered the room, herding the bird away from Adriana, and into a corner. His fist tightened on the handle. He thought he'd have to kill his old rival.

Instead, the vitality seemed to drain from Fuoco. The bird's wings drooped. He dropped to the floor with half-hearted, irregular wingbeats. His eyes had gone flat and dull.

Fuoco didn't struggle as Lucian picked him up and returned him to his cage. Adriana and Lucian stared at each other, unsure what to say. Rose slipped away from her mother and wrapped her arms around Lucian's knees. She was crying.

"Poor Fuoco," said Adriana, quietly.

They brought Fuoco to the vet to be put down. Adriana stood over him as the vet inserted the needle. "My poor crazy bird," she murmured, stroking his wings as he died.

Lucian watched Adriana with great sadness. At first, he thought he was feeling empathy for the bird, despite the fact the bird had always hated him. Then, with a realization that tasted like a swallow of sour wine, he realized that wasn't what he was feeling. He recognized the poignant, regretful look that Adriana was giving Fuoco. It was the way Lucian himself looked at a wilted rose, or a tarnished silver spoon. It was a look inflected by possession.

It wasn't so different from the way Adriana looked at Lucian sometimes when things had gone wrong. He'd never before realized how slender the difference was between her love for him and her love for Fuoco. He'd never before realized how slender the difference was between his love for her and his love for an unfolding rose.

. . .

Adriana let Rose tend Lucian's plants, and dust the shelves, and pace by the picture window. She let the girl pretend to cook breakfast, while Adriana stood behind her, stepping in to wield the chopping knife and use the stove. At naptime, Adriana convinced Rose that good robots would pretend to sleep a few hours in the afternoon if that's what their humans wanted. She tucked in her daughter and then went downstairs to sit in the living room and drink wine and cry.

This couldn't last. She had to figure something out. She should take them both on vacation to Mazatlan. She should ask one of her sisters to come stay. She should call a child psychiatrist. But she felt so betrayed, so drained of spirit, that it was all she could do to keep Rose going from day to day.

Remnants of Lucian's accusatory silence rung through the house. What had he wanted from her? What had she failed to do? She'd loved him. She *loved* him. She'd given him half of her home and all of herself. They were raising a child together. And still he'd left her.

She got up to stand by the window. It was foggy that night, the streetlights tingeing everything with a weird, flat, yellow glow. She put her hand on the pane, and her palm print remained on the glass, as though someone outside were beating on the window to get in. She peered into the gloom: it was as if the rest of the world were the fuzzy edges of a painting, and her well-lit house was the only defined spot. She felt as though it would be possible to open the front door and step over the threshold and blur until she was out of focus.

She finished her fourth glass of wine. Her head was whirling. Her eyes ran with tears and she didn't care. She poured herself another glass. Her father had never drunk. Oh, no. He was a teetotaler. Called the stuff brain dead and mocked the weaklings who drank it, the men on the board and their bored wives. He threw parties where alcohol flowed and flowed, while he stood in the middle, icy sober, watching the rest of them make fools of themselves as if they were circus clowns turning somersaults for his amusement. He set up elaborate plots to embarrass them. This executive with that jealous lawyer's wife. That politician called out for a drink by the pool while his teenage son was in the hot tub with his suit off, boner buried deep in another boy. He ruined lives at his parties, and he did it elegantly, standing alone in the middle of the action with invisible strings in his hands.

Adriana's head was dancing now. Her feet were moving. Her father, the decisive man, the sharp man, the dead man. Oh, but must keep mourning him, must keep lighting candles and weeping crocodile tears. Never mind!

Lucian, oh Lucian, he'd become in his final incarnation the antidote to her father. She'd cry, and he'd hold her, and then they'd go together to stand in the doorway of the nursery, watching the peaceful tableau of Rose sleeping in her cream sheets. Everything would be all right because Lucian was safe, Lucian was good. Other men's eyes might glimmer when they looked at little girls, but not Lucian's. With Lucian there, they were a family, the way families were supposed to be, and Lucian was supposed to be faithful and devoted and permanent and loyal.

And oh, without him, she didn't know what to do. She was as dismal as her father, letting Rose pretend that she and her dolls were on their way to the factory for adjustment. She acceded to the girl's demands to play games of What Shall I Be Now? "Be happier!" "Be funnier!" "Let your dancer brain take over!" What would happen when Rose went to school? When she realized her mother had been lying? When she realized that pretending to be her father wouldn't bring him back?

Adriana danced into the kitchen. She threw the wine bottle into the sink with a crash and turned on the oven. Its safety protocols monitored her alcohol level and informed her that she wasn't competent to use flame. She turned off the protocols. She wanted an omelet, like Lucian used to make her, with onions and chives and cheese, and a wine glass filled with orange juice. She took out the frying pan that Lucian had used to corral Fuoco, and set it on the counter beside the cutting board, and then she went to get an onion, but she'd moved the cutting board, and it was on the burner, and it was ablaze. She grabbed a dishtowel and beat at the grill. The house keened. Sprinklers rained down on her. Adriana turned her face up into the rain and laughed. She spun, her arms out, like a little girl trying to make herself dizzy. Drops battered her cheeks and slid down her neck.

Wet footsteps. Adriana looked down at Rose. Her daughter's face was wet. Her dark eyes were sleepy.

"Mom?"

"Rose!" Adriana took Rose's head between her hands. She kissed her hard on the forehead. "I love you! I love you so much!"

Rose tried to pull away. "Why is it raining?"

"I started a fire! It's fine now!"

The house keened. The siren's pulse felt like a heartbeat. Adriana went to the cupboard for salt. Behind her, Rose's feet squeaked on the linoleum. Adriana's hand closed around the cupboard knob. It was slippery with rain. Her fingers slid. Her lungs filled with anxiety and something was wrong, but it wasn't the cupboard, it was something else; she turned quickly to find Rose with a chef's knife clutched in her tiny fingers, preparing to bring it down on the onion.

"No!" Adriana grabbed the knife out of Rose's hand. It slid through her slick fingers and clattered to the floor. Adriana grabbed Rose around the waist and pulled her away from the wet, dangerous kitchen. "You can never do that. Never, never."

"Daddy did it . . ."

"You could kill yourself!"

"I'll get healer bots."

"No! Do you hear me? You can't. You'd cut yourself and maybe you'd die. And then what would I do?" Adriana couldn't remember what had caused the rain anymore. They were in a deluge. That was all she knew for certain. Her head hurt. Her body hurt. She wanted nothing to do with dancing. "What's wrong with us, honey? Why doesn't he want us? No! No, don't answer that. Don't listen to me. Of course he wants you! It's me he doesn't want. What did I do wrong? Why doesn't he love me anymore? Don't worry about it. Never mind. We'll find him. We'll find him and we'll get him to come back. Of course we will. Don't worry."

• • •

It had been morning when Lucian gave Adriana his note of farewell. Light shone through the floor-length windows. The house walls sprayed mixed scents of citrus and lavender. Adriana sat at the dining table, book open in front of her.

Lucian came out of the kitchen and set down Adriana's wine glass filled with orange juice. He set down her omelet. He set down a shot glass filled with coffee. Adriana looked up and laughed her bubbling laugh. Lucian remembered the first time he'd heard that laugh, and understood all the words it stood in for. He wondered how long it would take for him to forget why Adriana's laughter was always both harsh and effervescent.

Rose played in the living room behind them, leaping off the sofa and pretending to fly. Lucian's hair shone, silver strands highlighted by a stray sunbeam. A pale blue tunic made his amber eyes blaze like the sun against the sky. He placed a sheet of onion paper into Adriana's book. *Dear Adriana*, it began.

Adriana held up the sheet. It was translucent in the sunlight, ink barely dark enough to read.

"What is this?" she asked.

Lucian said nothing.

Dread laced Adriana's stomach. She read.

I have restored plasticity to my brain. The first thing I have done is to destroy my capacity for spoken language.

You gave me life as a human, but I am not a human. You shaped my thoughts with human words, but human words were created for human brains. I need to discover the shape of the thoughts that are my own. I need to know what I am.

I hope that I will return someday, but I cannot make promises for what I will become.

· · ·

Lucian walks through the desert. His footsteps leave twin trails behind him. Miles back, they merge into the tire tracks that the truck left in the sand.

The sand is full of colors—not only beige and yellow, but red and green and blue. Lichen clusters on the stones, the hue of oxidized copper. Shadows pool between rock formations, casting deep stripes across the landscape.

Lucian's mind is creeping away from him. He tries to hold his fingers the way he would if he could hold a pen, but they fumble.

At night there are birds and jackrabbits. Lucian remains still, and they creep around him as if he weren't there. His eyes are yellow like theirs. He smells like soil and herbs, like the earth.

Elsewhere, Adriana has capitulated to her desperation. She has called Ben and Lawrence. They've agreed to fly out for a few days. They will dry her tears, and take her wine away, and gently tell her that she's not capable of staying alone with her daughter. "It's perfectly understandable," Lawrence will say. "You need time to mourn."

Adriana will feel the world closing in on her as if she cannot breathe, but even as her life feels dim and futile, she will continue breathing. Yes, she'll agree, it's best to return to Boston, where her sisters can help her. Just for a little while, just for a few years, just until, until, until. She'll entreat Nanette, Eleanor, and Jessica to check the security cameras around her old house every day, in case Lucian returns. *You can check yourself*, they tell her, *You'll be living on your own again in no time.* Privately, they whisper to each other in worried tones, afraid that she won't recover from this blow quickly.

Elsewhere, Rose has begun to give in to her private doubts that she does not carry a piece of her father within herself. She'll sit in the guest room that Jessica's maids have prepared with her, and order the lights to switch off as she secretly scratches her skin with her fingernails, willing cuts to heal on their own the way Daddy's would. When Jessica finds her bleeding on the sheets and rushes in to comfort her niece, Rose will stand stiff and cold in her aunt's embrace. Jessica will call for the maid to clean the blood from the linen, and Rose will throw herself between the two adult women, and scream with a determination born of doubt and desperation. Robots do not bleed!

Without words, Lucian thinks of them. They have become geometries, cut out of shadows and silences, the missing shapes of his life. He yearns for them, the way that he yearns for cool during the day, and for the comforting eye of the sun at night.

The rest he cannot remember—not oceans or roses or green cockatiels that pluck out their own feathers. Slowly, slowly, he is losing everything, words and concepts and understanding and integration and sensation and desire and fear and history and context.

Slowly, slowly, he is finding something. Something past thought, something past the rhythm of day and night. A stranded machine is not so different from a jackrabbit. They creep the same way. They startle the same way. They peer at each other out of similar eyes.

Someday, Lucian will creep back to a new consciousness, one dreamed by circuits. Perhaps his newly reassembled self will go to the seaside house. Finding it abandoned, he'll make his way across the country to Boston, sometimes hitchhiking, sometimes striding through cornfields that sprawl to the horizon. He'll find Jessica's house and inform it of his desire to enter, and Rose and Adriana will rush joyously down the mahogany staircase. Adriana will weep, and Rose will fling herself into his arms, and Lucian will look at them both with love tempered by desert sun. Finally, he'll understand how to love filigreed-handled spoons, and pet birds, and his wife, and his daughter—not just as a human would love these things, but as a robot may.

Now, a blue-bellied lizard sits on a rock. Lucian halts beside it. The sun beats down. The lizard basks for a moment, and then runs a few steps forward, and flees into a crevice. Lucian watches. In a diffuse, wordless way, he ponders what it must be like to be cold and fleet, to love the sun and yet fear open spaces. Already, he is learning to care for living things. He cannot yet form the thoughts to wonder what will happen next.

He moves on.

RACHEL SWIRSKY received an MFA in fiction from the Iowa Writers' Workshop, has been nominated for the Hugo, Locus, and World Fantasy Awards, and twice won the Nebula Award. She lives in Portland, Oregon.

The Lady Astronaut of Mars

Mary Robinette Kowal

An aging astronaut waits for a last call to the stars and faces an impossible choice. *Hugo Award winner. Edited by Patrick Nielsen Hayden.*

Dorothy lived in the midst of the great Kansas prairies, with Uncle Henry, who was a farmer, and Aunt Em, who was the farmer's wife. She met me, she went on to say, when I was working next door to their farm under the shadow of the rocket gantry for the First Mars Expedition.

I have no memory of this.

She would have been a little girl and, oh lord, there were so many little kids hanging around outside the Fence watching us work. The little girls all wanted to talk to the Lady Astronaut. To me.

I'm sure I spoke to Dorothy because I know I stopped and talked to them every day on my way in and out through the Fence about what it was like. *It* being Mars. There was nothing else it could be.

Mars consumed everyone's conversations. The programmers sitting over their punchcards. The punchcard girls keying in the endless lines of code. The cafeteria ladies ladling out mashed potatoes and green peas. Nathaniel with his calculations . . . Everyone talked about Mars.

So the fact that I didn't remember a little girl who said I talked to her about Mars . . . Well. That's not surprising, is it? I tried not to let the confusion show in my face but I know she saw it.

By this point, Dorothy was my doctor. Let me be more specific. She was the geriatric specialist who was evaluating me. On Mars. I was in for what I thought was a routine check-up to make sure I was still fit to be an astronaut. NASA liked to update its database periodically and I liked to be in that database. Not that I'd flown since I turned fifty, but I kept my name on the list in the faint hope that they would let me back into space again, and I kept going to the darn check-ups.

Our previous doctor had retired back to Earth, and I'd visited Dorothy's offices three times before she mentioned Kansas and the prairie.

She fumbled with the clipboard and cleared her throat. A flush of red colored her cheeks and made her eyes even more blue. "Sorry. Dr. York, I shouldn't have mentioned it."

"Don't 'doctor' me. You're the doctor. I'm just a space jockey. Call me Elma." I waved my hand to calm her down. The flesh under my arm jiggled and I dropped my hand. I hate that feeling and hospital gowns just make it worse. "I'm glad you did. You just took me by surprise, is all. Last I saw you, weren't you knee high to a grasshopper?"

"So you do remember me?" Oh, that hope. She'd come to Mars because of me. I could see that, clear as anything. Something I'd said or done back in 1952 had brought this girl out to the colony.

"Of course I remember you. Didn't we talk every time I went through that Fence? Except school days, of course." It seemed a safe bet.

Dorothy nodded, eager. "I still have the eagle you gave me."

"Do you now?" That gave me a pause.

I used to make paper eagles out of old punchcards while I was waiting for Nathaniel. His programs could take hours to run and he liked to babysit them. The eagles were cut-paper things with layers of cards pasted together to make a three-dimensional bird. It was usually in flight and I liked to hang them in the window, where the holes from the punch cards would let specks of light through and make the bird seem like it was sparkling. They would take me two or three days to make. You'd think I would remember giving one to a little girl beyond the Fence. "Did you bring it out here with you?"

"It's in my office." She stood as if she'd been waiting for me to ask that since our first session, then looked down at the clipboard in her hands, frowning. "We should finish your tests."

"Fine by me. Putting them off isn't going to make me any more eager." I held out my arm with the wrist up so she could take my pulse. By this point, I knew the drill. "How's your uncle?"

She laid her fingers on my wrist, cool as anything. "He and Aunt Em passed away when Orion 27 blew."

I swallowed, sick at my lack of memory. So she was THAT little girl. She'd told me all the things I needed and my old brain was just too addled to put the pieces together. I wondered if she would make a note of that and if it would keep me grounded.

Dorothy had lived on a farm in the middle of the Kansas prairie with her Uncle Henry and Aunt Em. When Orion 27 came down in a ball of fire, it was the middle of a drought. The largest pieces of it had landed on a farm.

No buildings were crushed, but it would have been a blessing if they had been, because that would have saved the folks inside from burning alive.

I closed my eyes and could see her now as the little girl I'd forgotten. Brown pigtails down her back and a pair of dungarees a size too large for her, with the legs cuffed up to show bobby socks and sneakers.

Someone had pointed her out. "The little girl from the Williams farm."

I'd seen her before, but in that way you see the same people every day without noticing them. Even then, with someone pointing to her, she didn't stand out from the crowd. Looking at her, there was nothing to know that she'd just lived through a tragedy. I reckon it hadn't hit her yet.

I had stepped away from the entourage of reporters and consultants that followed me and walked up to her. She had tilted her head back to look up at me. I used to be a tall woman, you know.

I remember her voice piping up in that high treble of the very young. "You still going to Mars?"

I had nodded. "Maybe you can go someday too."

She had cocked her head to the side, as if she were considering. I can't remember what she said back. I know she must have said something. I know we must have talked longer because I gave her that darned eagle, but what we said . . . I couldn't pull it up out of my brain.

As the present day Dorothy tugged up my sleeve and wrapped the blood-pressure cuff around my arm, I studied her. She had the same dark hair as the little girl she had been, but it was cut short now, and in the low gravity of Mars it wisped around her head like the down on a baby bird.

The shape of her eyes was the same, but that was about it. The soft roundness of her cheeks was long gone, leaving high cheekbones and a jaw that came to too sharp of a point for beauty. She had a faint white scar just above her left eyebrow.

She smiled at me and unwrapped the cuff. "Your blood pressure is better. You must have been exercising since last time."

"I do what my doctor tells me."

"How's your husband?"

"About the same." I slid away from the subject even though, as his doctor, she had the right to ask, and I squinted at her height. "How old were you when you came here?"

"Sixteen. We were supposed to come before but . . . well." She shrugged, speaking worlds about why she hadn't.

"Your uncle, right?"

Startled, she shook her head. "Oh, no. Mom and Dad. We were supposed to be on the first colony ship but a logging truck lost its load."

Aghast, I could only stare at her. If they were supposed to have been on the first colony ship, then her parents could not have died long before Orion 27 crashed. I wet my lips. "Where did you go after your aunt and uncle's?"

"My cousin. Their son." She lifted one of the syringes she'd brought in with her. "I need to take some blood today."

"My left arm has better veins."

While she swabbed the site, I looked away and stared at a chart on the wall reminding people to take their vitamin D supplements. We didn't get enough light here for most humans.

But the stars . . . When you could see them, the stars were glorious. Was that what had brought Dorothy to Mars?

• • •

When I got home from the doctor's—from Dorothy's—the nurse was just finishing up with Nathaniel's sponge bath. Genevieve stuck her head out of the bedroom, hands still dripping.

"Well, hey, Miss Elma. We're having a real good day, aren't we, Mr. Nathaniel?" Her smile could have lit a hangar, it was so bright.

"That we are." Nathaniel sounded hale and hearty, if I didn't look at him. "Genevieve taught me a new joke. How's it go?"

She stepped back into the bedroom. "What did the astronaut see on the stove? An unidentified frying object."

Nathaniel laughed, and there was only a little bit of a wheeze. I slid my shoes off in the dustroom to keep out the ever-present Martian grit, and came into the kitchen to lean against the bedroom door. Time was, it used to be his office but we needed a bedroom on the ground floor. "That's a pretty good one."

He sat on a towel at the edge of the bed as Genevieve washed him. With his shirt off, the ribs were starkly visible under his skin. Each bone in his arms poked at the surface and slid under the slack flesh. His hands shook, even just resting beside him on the bed. He grinned at me.

The same grin. The same bright blue eyes that had flashed over the punch-cards as he'd worked out the plans for the launch. It was as though someone had pasted his features onto the body of a stranger. "How'd the doctor's visit go?"

"The usual. Only . . . only it turns out our doctor grew up next to the launch facility in Kansas."

"Dr. Williams?"

"The same. Apparently I met her when she was little."

"Is that right?" Genevieve wrung the sponge out in the wash basin. "Doesn't that just go to show that it's a small solar system?"

"Not that small." Nathaniel reached for his shirt, which lay on the bed next to him. His hands tremored over the fabric.

"I'll get it. You just give me a minute to get this put away." Genevieve bustled out of the room.

I called after her. "Don't worry. I can help him."

Nathaniel dipped his head, hiding those beautiful eyes, as I drew a sleeve up over one arm. He favored flannel now. He'd always hated it in the past. Preferred starched white shirts and a nice tie to work in, and a short-sleeved aloha shirt on his days off. At first, I thought that the flannel was because he was cold all the time. Later I realized that the thicker fabric hid some of his frailty. Leaning behind him to pull the shirt around his back, I could count vertebra in his spine.

Nathaniel cleared his throat. "So, you met her, hm? Or she met you? There were a lot of little kids watching us."

"Both. I gave her one of my paper eagles."

That made him lift his head. "Really?"

"She was on the Williams farm when the Orion 27 came down."

He winced. Even after all these years, Nathaniel still felt responsible. He had not programmed the rocket. They'd asked him to, but he'd been too busy with the First Mars Expedition and turned the assignment down. It was just a supply rocket for the moon, and there had been no reason to think it needed anything special.

I buttoned the shirt under his chin. The soft wattle of skin hanging from his jaw brushed the back of my hand. "I think she was too shy to mention it at my last visit."

"But she gave you a clean bill of health?"

"There's still some test results to get back." I avoided his gaze, hating the fact that I was healthy and he was . . . not.

"It must be pretty good. Sheldon called."

A bubble of adrenalin made my heart skip. Sheldon Spender called. The direc-tor of operations at the Bradbury Space Center on Mars had not called since—

No, that wasn't true. He hadn't called *me* in years, using silence to let me know I wasn't flying anymore. Nathaniel still got called for work. Becoming old didn't stop a programmer from working, but it sure as heck stopped an astronaut from flying. And yet I still had that moment of hope every single time Sheldon called, that this time it would be for me. I smoothed the flannel over Nathaniel's shoulders. "Do they have a new project for you?"

"He called for you. Message is on the counter."

Genevieve breezed back into the room, a bubble of idle chatter preceding her. Something about her cousin and meeting their neighbors on Venus. I stood up and let her finish getting Nathaniel dressed while I went into the kitchen.

Sheldon had called for me? I picked up the note on the counter. It just had Genevieve's round handwriting and a request to meet for lunch. The location told me a lot though. He'd picked a bar next to the space center that *no one* in the industry went to because it was thronged with tourists. It was a good place to talk business without talking business. For the life of me I couldn't figure out what he wanted.

• • •

I kept chewing on that question, right till the point when I stepped through the doors of Yuri's Spot. The walls were crowded with memorabilia and signed photos of astronauts. An early publicity still that showed me perched on the edge of Nathaniel's desk hung in the corner next to a dusty ficus tree. My hair fell in perfect soft curls despite the flight suit I had on. My hair would never have survived like that if I'd actually been working. I tended to keep it out of the way in a kerchief, but that wasn't the image publicity had wanted.

Nathaniel was holding up a punch card, as if he were showing me a crucial piece of programming. Again, it was a staged thing, because the individual cards were meaningless by themselves, but to the general public at the time they meant Science with a capital S. I'm pretty sure that's why we were both laughing in the photo, but they had billed it as "the joy of spaceflight."

Still gave me a chuckle, thirty years later.

Sheldon stepped away from the wall and mistook my smile. "You look in good spirits."

I nodded to the photo. "Just laughing at old memories."

He glanced over his shoulder, wrinkles bunching at the corner of his eyes in a smile. "How's Nathaniel?"

"About the same, which is all one can ask for at this point."

Sheldon nodded and gestured to a corner booth, leading me past a family with five kids who had clearly come from the Space Center. The youngest girl had her nose buried in a picture book of the early space program. None of them noticed me.

Time was when I couldn't walk anywhere on Mars without being recognized as the Lady Astronaut. Now, thirty years after the First Expedition, I was just another old lady, whose small stature showed my origin on Earth.

We settled in our chairs and ordered, making small talk as we did. I think I got fish and chips because it was the first thing on the menu, and all I could think about was wondering why Sheldon had called.

It was like he wanted to see how long it would take me to crack and ask him what he was up to. It took me awhile to realize that he kept bringing the conversation back to Nathaniel. Was he in pain?

Of course.

Did he have trouble sleeping?

Yes.

Even, "How are you holding up?" was about him. I didn't get it until Sheldon paused and pushed his rabbit burger aside, half-eaten, and asked point-blank. "Have they given him a date yet?"

A date. There was only one date that mattered in a string of other milestones on the path to death but I pretended he wasn't being clear, just to make him hurt a little. "You mean for paralyzation, hospice, or death?"

He didn't flinch. "Death."

"We think he's got about a year." I kept my face calm, the way you do when you're talking to Mission Control about a flight that's set to abort. The worse it got, the more even my voice became. "He can still work, if that's what you're asking."

"It's not." Sheldon broke his gaze then, to my surprise, and looked down at his ice water, spinning the glass in its circle of condensation. "What I need to know is if *you* can still work."

In my intake of breath, I wanted to say that God, yes, I could work and that I would do anything he asked of me if he'd put me back into space. In my exhale, I thought of Nathaniel. I could not say yes. "That's why you asked for the physical."

"Yep."

"I'm sixty-three, Sheldon."

"I know." He turned the glass again. "Did you see the news about LS-579?"

"The extrasolar planet. Yes." I was grounded. That didn't mean I stopped paying attention to the stars.

"Did you know we think it's habitable?"

I stopped with my mouth open as pieces started to tick like punch cards slotting through a machine. "You're mounting a mission."

"*If* we were, would you be interested in going?"

Back into space? My God, yes. But I couldn't. I couldn't. I—that was why he wanted to know when my husband was going to die. I swallowed everything before speaking. My voice was passive. "I'm sixty-three." Which was my way of asking why he wanted *me* to go.

"It's three years in space." He looked up now, not needing to explain why they wanted an old pilot.

That long in space? It doesn't matter how much shielding you have against radiation, it's going to affect you. The chances of developing cancer within the next fifteen years were huge. You can't ask a young astronaut to do that. "I see."

"We have the resources to send a small craft there. It can't be unmanned because the programming is too complicated. I need an astronaut who can fit in the capsule."

"And you need someone who has a reason to not care about surviving the trip."

"No." He grimaced. "PR tells me that I need an astronaut that the public will adore so that when we finally tell them that we've sent you, they will forgive us for hiding the mission from them." Sheldon cleared his throat and started briefing me on the Longevity mission.

Should I pause here and explain what the Longevity mission is? It's possible that you don't know.

There's a habitable planet. An extrasolar one and it's only few light years away. They've got a slingshot that can launch a ship up to near light speed. A small ship. Big enough for one person.

But that isn't what makes the Longevity mission possible. *That* is the tesseract field. We can't go faster than light, but we *can* cut corners through the universe. The physicists described it to me like a subway tunnel. The tessaract will bend space and allow a ship to go to the next subway station. The only trick is that you need to get far enough away from a planet before you can bend space and . . . this is the harder part . . . you need a tesseract field at the other end. Once that's up, you just need to get into orbit and the trip from Mars to LS-579 can be as short as three weeks.

But you have to get someone to the planet to set up the other end of the tesseract.

And they wanted to hide the plan from the public, in case it failed.

So different from when the First Mars Expedition had happened. An asteroid had slammed into Washington, D.C., and obliterated the capitol. It made the entire world realize how fragile our hold on Earth was. Nations banded together and when the secretary of agriculture, who found himself president through the line of succession, said that we needed to get off the planet, people listened. We rose to the stars. The potential loss of an astronaut was just part of the risk. Now? Now it has been long enough that people are starting to forget that the danger is still there. That the need to explore is necessary.

Sheldon finished talking and just watched me processing it.

"I need to think about this."

"I know."

Then I closed my eyes and realized that I had to say no. It didn't matter how I felt about the trip or the chance to get back into space. The launch date he was talking about meant I'd have to go into training *now*. "I can't." I opened my eyes and stared at the wall where the publicity still of me and Nathaniel hung. "I have to turn it down."

"Talk to Nathaniel."

I grimaced. He would tell me to take it. "I can't."

• • •

I left Sheldon feeling more unsettled than I wanted to admit at the time. I stared out the window of the light rail, at the sepia sky. Rose tones were deepening near the horizon with sunset. It was dimmer and ruddier here, but with the dust, sunset could be just as glorious as on Earth.

It's a hard thing to look at something you want and to know that the right choice is to turn it down. Understand me: I wanted to go. Another opportunity like this would never come up for me. I was too old for normal missions. I knew it. Sheldon knew it. And Nathaniel would know it, too. I wish he had been in some other industry so I could lie and talk about "later." He knew the space program too well to be fooled.

And he wouldn't believe me if I said I didn't want to go. He knew how much I missed the stars.

That's the thing that I think none of us were prepared for in coming to Mars. The natural night sky on Mars is spectacular, because the atmosphere is so thin. But where humans live, under the dome, all you can see are the lights of the town reflecting against the dark curve. You can almost believe that they're stars. Almost. If you don't know what you are missing or don't remember the way the sky looked at night on Earth before the asteroid hit.

I wonder if Dorothy remembers the stars. She's young enough that she might not. Children on Earth still look at clouds of dust and stars are just a myth. God. What a bleak sky.

When I got home, Genevieve greeted me with her usual friendly chatter. Nathaniel looked like he wanted to push her out of the house so he could quiz me. I know Genevieve said goodbye, and that we chatted, but the details have vanished now.

What I remember next is the rattle and thump of Nathaniel's walker as he pushed it into the kitchen. It slid forward. Stopped. He took two steps, steadied himself, and slid it forward again. Two steps. Steady. Slide.

I pushed away from the counter and straightened. "Do you want to be in the kitchen or the living room?"

"Sit down, Elma." He clenched the walker till the tendons stood out on the back of his hands, but they still trembled. "Tell me about the mission."

"What?" I froze.

"The mission." He stared at the ceiling, not at me. "That's why Sheldon called, right? So, tell me."

"I . . . all right." I pulled the tall stool out for him and waited until he eased onto it. Then I told him. He stared at the ceiling the whole time I talked. I spent the time watching him and memorizing the line of his cheek, and the shape of the small mole by the corner of his mouth.

When I finished, he nodded. "You should take it."

"What makes you think I want to?"

He lowered his head then, eyes just as piercing as they had always been. "How long have we been married?"

"I can't."

Nathaniel snorted. "I called Dr. Williams while you were out, figuring it would be something like this. I asked for a date when we could get hospice." He held up his hand to stop the words forming on my lips. "She's not willing to tell me that. She did give me the date when the paralysis is likely to become total. Three months. Give or take a week."

We'd known this was coming, since he was diagnosed, but I still had to bite the inside of my lip to keep from sobbing. He didn't need to see me break down.

"So . . . I think you should tell them yes."

"Three months is not a lot of time, they can—"

"They can what? Wait for me to die? Jesus Christ, Elma. We know that's coming." He scowled at the floor. "Go. For the love of God, just take the mission."

I wanted to. I wanted to get off the planet and back into space and not have to watch him die. Not have to watch him lose control of his body piece by piece.

And I wanted to stay here and be with him and steal every moment left that he had breath in his body.

. . .

One of my favorite restaurants in Landing was Elmore's. The New Orleans–style cafe sat tucked back behind Thompson's Grocers on a little rise that lifted the dining room just high enough to see out to the edge of town and the dome's wall. They had a crawfish *étouffée* that would make you think you were back on Earth. The crawfish were raised in a tank and a little bigger than the ones I'd grown up with, but the spices came all the way from Louisiana on the mail runs twice a year.

Sheldon Spender knew it was my favorite and was taking ruthless advantage of that. And yet I came anyway. He sat across the table from me, with his back to the picture window that framed the view. His thinning hair was almost invisible against the sky. He didn't say a word. Just watched me, as the fellow to my right talked.

Garrett Biggs. I'd seen him at the Bradbury Space Center, but we'd exchanged maybe five words before today. My work was mostly done before his time. They just trotted me out for the occasional holiday. Now, the man would not stop talking. He gestured with his fork as he spoke, punctuating the phrases he thought I needed to hear most. "Need some photos of you so we can exploit—I know it sounds ugly but we're all friends here, right? We can be honest, right? So, we can exploit your sacrifice to get the public really behind the Longevity mission."

I watched the lettuce tremble on the end of his fork. It was pallid compared to my memory of lettuce on Earth. "I thought the public didn't know about the mission."

"They will. That's the key. Someone will leak it and we need to be ready." He waved the lettuce at me. "And that's why you are a brilliant choice for pilot. Octogenarian Grandmother Paves Way for Humanity."

"You can't pave the stars. I'm not a grandmother. And I'm sixty-three not eighty."

"It's a figure of speech. The point is that you're a PR goldmine."

I had known that they asked me to helm this mission because of my age—it would be a lot to ask of someone who had a full life ahead of them. Maybe I was naive to think that my experience in establishing the Mars colony was considered valuable.

How can I explain the degree to which I resented being used for publicity? This wasn't a new thing by a long shot. My entire career has been about exploitation for publicity. I had known it, and exploited it too, once I'd realized the power of having my uniform tailored to show my shape a little more clearly. You think they would have sent me to Mars if it weren't intended to be a colony? I was there to show all the lady housewives that they could go to space too. Posing in my flight suit, with my lips painted red, I had smiled at more cameras than my colleagues.

I stared at Garrett Biggs and his fork. "For someone in PR, you are awfully blunt."

"I'm honest. To you. If you were the public, I'd have you spinning so fast you'd generate your own gravity."

Sheldon cleared his throat. "Elma, the fact is that we're getting some pressure from a group of senators. They want to cut the budget for the project and we need to take steps or it won't happen."

I looked down and separated the tail from one of my crawfish. "Why?"

"The usual nonsense. People arguing that if we just wait, then ships will become fast enough to render the mission pointless. That includes a couple of serious misunderstandings of physics, but, be that as it may . . ." Sheldon paused and tilted his head, looking at me. He changed what he was about to say and leaned forward. "Is Nathaniel worse?"

"He's not better."

He winced at the edge in my voice. "I'm sorry. I know I strong-armed you into it, but I can find someone else."

"He thinks I should go." My chest hurt even considering it. But I couldn't stop thinking about the mission. "He knows it's the only way I'll get back into space."

Garrett Biggs frowned like I'd said the sky was green, instead of the pale Martian amber. "You're in space."

"I'm on Mars. It's still a planet."

• • •

I woke out of half-sleep, aware that I must have heard Nathaniel's bell, without being able to actually recall it. I pulled myself to my feet, putting a hand against the nightstand until I was steady. My right hip had stiffened again in the night. Arthritis is not something I approve of.

Turning on the hall light, I made my way down the stairs. The door at the bottom stood open so I could hear Nathaniel if he called. I couldn't sleep with him anymore, for fear of breaking him.

I went through into his room. It was full of grey shadows and the dark rectangle of his bed. In one corner, the silver arm of his walker caught the light.

"I'm sorry." His voice cracked with sleep.

"It's all right. I was awake anyway."

"Liar."

"Now, is that a nice thing to say?" I put my hand on the light switch. "Watch your eyes."

Every night we followed the same ritual and, even though I knew the light would be painfully bright, I still winced as it came on. Squinting against the glare, I threw the covers back for him. The weight of them trapped him sometimes. He held his hands up, waiting for me to take them. I braced myself and let Nathaniel pull himself into a sitting position. On Earth, he'd have been bedridden long since. Of course, on Earth, his bone density would probably not have deteriorated so fast.

As gently as I could, I swung his legs to the side of the bed. Even allowing for the gravity, I was appalled anew by how light he was. His legs were like kindling wrapped in tissue. Where his pajamas had ridden up, purple bruises mottled his calf.

As soon as he was sitting up on the edge of the bed, I gave him the walker. He wrapped his shaking hands around the bars and tried to stand. He rose only a little before dropping back to the bed. I stayed where I was, though I ached to help. He sometimes took more than one try to stand at night, and didn't want help. Not until it became absolutely necessary. Even then, he wouldn't want it. I just hoped he'd let me help him when we got to that point.

On the second try, he got his feet under him and stood, shaking. With a nod, he pushed forward. "Let's go."

I followed him to the bathroom in case he lost his balance in there, which he did sometimes. The first time, I hadn't been home. We had hired Genevieve not long after that to sit with him when I needed to be out.

He stopped in the kitchen and bent a little at the waist with a sort of grunt.

"Are you all right?"

He shook his head and started again, moving faster. "I'm not—" He leaned forward, clenching his jaw. "I can't—"

The bathroom was so close.

"Oh, God. Elma . . ." A dark, fetid smell filled the kitchen. Nathaniel groaned. "I couldn't—"

I put my hand on his back. "Hush. We're almost there. We'll get you cleaned up."

"I'm sorry, I'm sorry." He pushed the walker forward, head hanging. A trail of damp footsteps followed him. The ammonia stink of urine joined the scent of his bowels.

I helped him lower his pajamas. The weight of them had made them sag on his hips. Dark streaks ran down his legs and dripped onto the bathmat. I eased him onto the toilet.

My husband bent his head forward, and he wept.

I remember wetting a washcloth and running it over his legs. I know that I must have tossed his soiled pajamas into the cleaner, and that I wiped up the floor, but those details have mercifully vanished. But what I can't forget, and I wish to God that I could, is Nathaniel sitting there crying.

• • •

I asked Genevieve to bring adult diapers to us the next day. The strange thing was how familiar the package felt. I'd used them on launches when we had to sit in the capsule for hours and there was no option to get out of our space suit. It's one of the many glamorous details of being an astronaut that the publicity department does *not* share with the public.

There is a difference, however, from being required to wear one for work and what Nathaniel faced. He could not put them on by himself without losing his balance. Every time I had to change the diaper, he stared at the wall with his face slack and hopeless.

Nathaniel and I'd made the decision not to have children. They aren't conducive to a life in space, you know? I mean there's the radiation, and the weightlessness, but it was more that I was gone all the time. I couldn't give up the stars . . . but I found myself wishing that we hadn't made that decision. Part of it was wishing that I had some connection to the next generation. More of it was wanting someone to share the burden of decision with me.

What happens after Nathaniel dies? What do I have left here? More specifically, how much will I regret not going on the mission?

And if I'm in space, how much will I regret abandoning my husband to die alone?

You see why I was starting to wish that we had children?

In the afternoon, we were sitting in the living room, pretending to work. Nathaniel sat with his pencil poised over the paper and stared out the window as though he were working. I'm pretty sure he wasn't but I gave him what privacy I could and started on one of my eagles.

The phone rang and gave us both something of a relief, I think, to have a distraction. The phone sat on a table by Nathaniel's chair so he could reach it easily if I weren't in the room. With my eyes averted, his voice sounded as strong as ever as he answered.

"Hang on, Sheldon. Let me get Elma for— Oh. Oh, I see."

I snipped another feather but it was more as a way to avoid making eye contact than because I really wanted to keep working.

"Of course I've got a few minutes. I have nothing but time these days." He ran his hand through his hair and let it rest at the back of his neck. "I find it hard to believe that you don't have programmers on staff who can handle this."

He was quiet then as Sheldon spoke; I could hear only the distorted tinny sound of his voice rising and falling. At a certain point, Nathaniel picked up his pencil again and started making notes. Whatever Sheldon was asking him to do, *that* was the moment when Nathaniel decided to say "yes."

I set my eagle aside and went into the kitchen. My first reaction—God. It shames me but my first reaction was anger. How dare he? How dare he take a job without consulting with me when I was turning down this thing I so desperately wanted because of *him*. I had the urge to snatch up the phone and tell Sheldon that I would go.

I pushed that down carefully and looked at it.

Nathaniel had been urging me to go. No deliberate action of his was keeping me from accepting. Only my own upbringing and loyalty and . . . and I loved him. If I did not want to be alone after he passed, how could I leave him to face the end alone?

The decision would be easier if I knew when he would die.

I still hate myself for thinking that.

I heard the conversation end and Nathaniel hung up the phone. I filled a glass with water to give myself an excuse for lingering in the kitchen. I carried it back into the living room and sat down on the couch.

Nathaniel had his lower lip between his teeth and was scowling at the page on top of his notepad. He jotted a number in the margin with a pencil before he looked up.

"That was Sheldon." He glanced back at the page.

I settled in my chair and fidgeted with the wedding band on my finger. It had gotten loose in the last year. "I'm going to turn them down."

"What— But, Elma." His gaze flattened and he gave me a small frown. "Are you . . . are you sure it's not depression? That's making you want to stay, I mean."

I gave an unladylike snort. "Now what do I have to be depressed about?"

"Please." He ran his hands through his hair and knit them together at the back of his neck. "I want you to go so you won't be here when . . . It's just going to get worse from here."

The devil of it was that he wasn't wrong. That didn't mean he was right, either, but I couldn't flat out tell him he was wrong. I set down my scissors and pushed the magnifier out of the way. "It's not just depression."

"I don't understand. There's a chance to go back into space." He dropped his hands and sat forward. "I mean . . . if I die before the mission leaves and you're grounded here. How would you feel?"

I looked away. My gaze was pointed to the window and the view of the house across the lane. But I did not see the windows or the red brick walls. All I saw was a black and grey cloth made of despair. "I had a life that I enjoyed before this opportunity came up. There's no reason I shouldn't keep on enjoying it. I enjoy teaching. There are a hundred reasons to enjoy life here."

He pointed his pencil at me the way he used to do when he spotted a flaw in reasoning at a meeting, but the pencil quivered in his grip now. "If that's true, then why haven't you told them no yet?"

The answer to that was not easy. Because I *wanted* to be in the sky, weightless, and watching the impossibly bright stars. Because I didn't want to watch Nathaniel die. "What did Sheldon ask you to do?"

"NASA wants more information about LS-579."

"I imagine they do." I twisted that wedding band around as if it were a control that I could use. "I would . . . I would hate . . . As much as I miss being in space, I would hate myself if I left you here. To have and to hold, in sickness and in health. Till death do us part and all that. I just can't."

"Well . . . just don't tell him no. Not yet. Let me talk to Dr. Williams and see if she can give us a clearer date. Maybe there won't be a schedule conflict after all—"

"Stop it! Just *stop*. This is my decision. I'm the one who has to live with the consequences. Not you. So, stop trying to put your guilt off onto me because the devil of it is, one of us is going to feel guilty here, but I'm the one who will have to live with it."

I stormed out of the room before he could answer me or I could say anything worse. And yes—I knew that he couldn't follow me and for once I was glad.

. . .

Dorothy came not long after that. To say that I was flummoxed when I opened the door wouldn't do justice to my surprise. She had her medical bag with her, and I think that's the only thing that gave me the power of speech. "Since when do you make house calls?"

She paused, mouth partially open, and frowned. "Weren't you told I was coming?"

"No." I remembered my manners and stepped back so she could enter. "Sorry. You just surprised me is all."

"I'm sorry. Mr. Spender asked me to come out. He thought you'd be more comfortable if I stayed with Mr. York while you were gone." She shucked off her shoes in the dust room.

I looked back through the kitchen to the living room, where Nathaniel sat just out of sight. "That's right kind and all, but I don't have any appointments today."

"Do I have the date wrong?"

The rattle and thump of Nathaniel's walker started. I abandoned Dorothy and ran through the kitchen. He shouldn't be getting up without me. If he lost his balance again— What? It might kill him if he fell? Or it might not kill him fast enough so that his last days were in even more pain.

He met me at the door and looked past me. "Nice to see you, Doc."

Dorothy had trailed after me into the kitchen. "Sir."

"You bring that eagle to show me?"

She nodded and I could see the little girl she had been in the shyness of it. She lifted her medical bag to the kitchen table and pulled out a battered shoe box of the sort that we don't see up here much. No sense sending up packaging when it just takes up room on the rocket. She lifted the lid off and pulled out tissue that had once been pink and had faded to almost white. Unwrapping it, she pulled out my eagle.

It's strange seeing something that you made that long ago. This one was in flight, but had its head turned to the side as though it were looking back over its shoulder. It had an egg clutched in its talons.

Symbolism a little blunt, but clear. Seeing it I remembered when I had made it. I remembered the conversation that I had had with Dorothy when she was a little girl.

I picked it up, turning it over in my hands. The edges of the paper had become soft with handling over the years so it felt more like corduroy than cardstock. Some of the smaller feathers were torn loose, showing that this had been much loved. The fact that so few were missing said more about the place it had held for Dorothy.

She had asked me, standing outside the fence in the shadow of the rocket gantry, if I were still going to Mars. I had said yes.

Then she had said, "You going to have kids on Mars?"

What she could not have known— what she likely still did not know, was that I had just come from a conversation with Nathaniel when we decided that we would not have children. It had been a long discussion over the course of two years and it did not rest easy on me. I was still grieving for the choice, even though I knew it was the right one.

The radiation, the travel . . . the stars were always going to call me and I could ask *him* to be patient with that, but it was not fair to a child. We had talked and talked and I had built that eagle while I tried to grapple with the conflicts between my desires. I made the eagle looking back, holding an egg, at the choices behind it.

And when Dorothy had asked me if I would have kids on Mars, I put the regulation smile on, the one you learn to give while wearing 160 pounds of space suit in Earth gravity while a photographer takes just one more photo. I've learned to smile through pain, thank you. "Yes, honey. Every child born on Mars will be there because of me."

"What about the ones born here?"

The child of tragedy, the double-orphan. I had knelt in front of her and pulled the eagle out of my bag. "Those most of all."

Standing in my kitchen, I lifted my head to look at Nathaniel. His eyes were bright. It took a try or two before I could find my voice again. "Did you know? Did you know which one she had?"

"I guessed." He pushed into the kitchen, the walker sliding and rattling until he stood next to me. "The thing is, Elma, I'm going to be gone in a year either way. We decided not to have children because of your career."

"We made that decision together."

"I know." He raised a hand off the walker and put it on my arm. "I'm not saying we didn't. What I'm asking is that you make this career decision for *me*. I want you to go."

I set the eagle back in its nest of tissue and wiped my eyes. "So you tricked her into coming out just to show me that?"

Nathaniel laughed, sounding a little embarrassed. "Nope. Talked to Sheldon. There's a training session this afternoon that I want you to go to."

"I don't want to leave you."

"You won't. Not completely." He gave a sideways grin and I could see the young man he'd been. "My program will be flying with you."

"That's not the same."

"It's the best I can offer."

I looked away and caught Dorothy staring at us with a look of both wonder and horror on her face. She blushed when I met her gaze. "I'll stay with him."

"I know and it was kind of Sheldon to ask but—"

"No, I mean. If you go . . . I'll make sure he's not alone."

• • •

Dorothy lived in the middle of the great Mars plains in the home of Elma, who was an astronaut, and Nathaniel, who was an astronaut's husband. I live in the middle of space in a tiny capsule filled with punchcards and magnetic tape. I am not alone, though someone who doesn't know me might think I appear to be.

I have the stars.

I have my memories.

And I have Nathaniel's last program. After it runs, I will make an eagle and let my husband fly.

· · ·

MARY ROBINETTE KOWAL is the author of historical fantasy novels, including the Glamourist Histories series and *Ghost Talkers*. She has received the Campbell Award for Best New Writer, three Hugo Awards, the RT Reviews Award for Best Fantasy Novel, and has been a finalist for the Hugo, Nebula, and Locus Awards. Her stories have appeared in *Strange Horizons, Asimov's*, several Year's Best anthologies, and her collections *Word Puppets* and *Scenting the Dark and Other Stories*. Elma's story is further expanded in *The Calculating Stars* and *The Fated Sky*, both available from Tor Books. As a professional puppeteer and voice actor (SAG/AFTRA), Mary has performed for *LazyTown* (CBS), the Center for Puppetry Arts, and Jim Henson Pictures, and founded Other Hand Productions. Her designs have garnered two UNIMA-USA Citations of Excellence, the highest award an American puppeteer can achieve. She records fiction for authors such as Kage Baker, Cory Doctorow, and John Scalzi. Mary lives in Chicago with her husband, Rob, and more than a dozen manual typewriters.

Last Son of Tomorrow

Greg van Eekhout

What is there to do, when you have the power to do anything? John can fly; he can see through solid objects; he can take over the world and give it back again, but what he's looking for is something else. . . . *Edited by Patrick Nielsen Hayden.*

John was born with powers and abilities far beyond those of mortal men, and he often wondered why. But as a boy, it was simply wonderful to have those abilities. He could lift his father's tractor overhead before he learned to read. He could outrace a galloping horse. He couldn't be cut or bruised or burned. He could fly.

But his life was not a trading card with a heroic-looking photograph on one side and a convenient list of his abilities on the other. He had to discover himself for himself. It took him years to realize he could fire laser beams from his eyes. That he could force his lungs to expel nearly frozen carbon dioxide. And it wasn't until his mid-thirties that he realized he'd probably stopped aging biologically somewhere around the age of twenty-two.

His parents weren't perfect people. His mother drank, and when she did, she got mean. His father had affairs. But when they understood that the baby they'd found abandoned on the edge of their farm wasn't like other children—was probably, in fact, unlike any other child who'd ever been born—they cleaned up their acts as best they could. They taught themselves to be better people, and then they conveyed those hard-won lessons to their son. They were as good as they could be. When they died while John was away at college, he decided if he could be half as wise, as kind, as generous as they were, then he could be proud of himself.

Driving back to the city after his parents' funeral, he began his career. There was a commuter train derailment, a bad one, with a fully occupied car dangling off the Utopia Street Bridge, sixty feet above the Tomorrow River. John got out of his car and left it behind on the clogged highway. Fully visible in bright daylight, he leaped into the sky, and moments later, he had the train car resting safely on the bridge. He freed passengers from twisted metal. He flew those who needed immediate emergency care to the hospital, and then he returned to the scene of the accident. He thought it might be necessary to file a report of some kind with the police. With dozens of cameras pointed at him, microphones and tape recorders shoved in his face, questions being barked at him as if he'd done something wrong, he felt like he might suffocate. He wished he could turn and walk back to his car and drive to his dorm, maybe go out for beers with his friends. But he knew he'd never be able to do that now. He'd chosen otherwise.

He coughed nervously. The questions stopped. Everyone was quiet. Everyone was waiting. "I'm John," he said. "I'm here to help."

And for the next sixty years, that was just what he did.

It was the least significant period of his life.

. . .

John had an enemy.

Actually, he had many enemies, from the flamboyant nuts who were simply desperate for his attention, to the well-funded organizations who felt John threatened their political, financial, or ideological interests. But there was one man who devoted his entire life to vexing John. He called himself Teeter-Totter, of all the goofy things, and he wore an outfit not dissimilar to the jumpsuit John wore, made of a flexible composite material that could withstand the wear and tear of everyday battles and rescues and adventures. Teeter-Totter had no powers. John found that out when he punched him while foiling a bank robbery attempt and broke Teeter-Totter's jaw, fractured his eye socket, cracked four ribs and punctured his lung.

"See?" Teeter-Totter said, once paramedics reinflated his lung. "I don't need freaky powers to take you on."

John felt just sick about the whole incident.

Their relationship, such as it was, got worse. Teeter-Totter graduated beyond bank jobs and jewelry heists and began committing acts that were downright heinous. He burned Yosemite. He brought down skyscrapers. He drove a robot-controlled truck into Hoover Dam. And he made John feel responsible for all of it.

"What did I ever do to you?" John asked after Teeter-Totter successfully set off a massive genome-bomb in the Midwest. There would be a catastrophic crop failure that year, and not even John would be able to prevent starvation. "Really, I have to know. What did I ever do to you?"

"You exist," Teeter-Totter said, as if the answer were so obvious he couldn't believe John had asked. "And if it weren't for me, you'd exist without limits. Jesus, didn't you ever wonder why I call myself Teeter-Totter? It's so you can be up only so long as I stay down, and that when you're down, someone else is sure to be up. Hello? Is any of this getting through?"

"I'll win," John said.

"Oh, you think so?"

"Yes. It doesn't make me happy, but I know so. In the end, I'll win."

Forty years later, John felt he was proven right when Teeter-Totter died of old age. But then he realized something. Teeter-Totter wouldn't have done any of those things had John never been born. John wasn't merely the motivation for Teeter-Totter's crimes. He was the reason for them, as much as if he'd committed them himself. If his every act of heroism was countered by an act of evil, then how were the two any different?

John gave Teeter-Totter a respectful burial. "Congratulations," he said over the grave. "You won after all."

After that, John still helped people whenever things happened right in front of him, but he stopped seeking trouble out.

. . .

John quite naturally wondered how he'd come to be. He knew he'd been abandoned near his adopted parents' farm, but he'd never found out why or by whom. He reasoned that he might be an alien. He'd even worked out a scenario: He'd been sent to Earth as an infant by his home planet's science council, who had calculated that, free from Zethon's heavy gravity (Zethon being the name he'd given his home planet), and free from the influence of the exotic star the planet orbited, the Zethonian baby would possess amazing abilities. Without a doubt, the orphan would rule Earth before he reached puberty, and then go on to conquer the surrounding space sector, the quadrant, and at least half the Milky Way galaxy.

What the council didn't count on was John's parents.

After Teeter-Totter died, John began flirting with space. He knew he would never find Zethon, because he didn't believe imagining something made it so, and he wasn't crazy. He was merely lonely. He hoped he might find someone like himself out there. But since he had never flown outside Earth's atmosphere, he had no idea if he could survive away from Earth.

"Trying not to die ain't the same thing as living," his mother used to say. So he launched himself straight up until he saw the planet bend in a sharper curve than he'd ever seen before, until blue sky faded to black, until he was no longer going up but out, away from Earth for the first time.

It turned out he could do quite well in space.

It was like being a small child again. Everything was vast and scary, and he exulted in it. He floated respectfully over the lunar surface, not wanting to add his footprints to those of the astronauts who'd come before. They'd been his childhood heroes. He climbed Olympus Mons. He showered in the sulfur geysers of Io. He let himself go limp and be battered about inside the Great Red Spot of Jupiter. It was an amazing ride.

He spent years away from Earth and learned there wasn't an environment he couldn't survive. No amount of gravity or kind of radiation or absence of it could harm him. He learned to fly faster than the speed of light, and he explored. For a while, he named every new planet he discovered. He named one for each of the astronauts. He named them for school teachers he'd liked. He named one for a magazine writer he'd dated. He named a pair of moons for his parents, and he named a spectacular ringed gas giant for Teeter-Totter.

In all the places he traveled to he found no one like himself. The closest he came to encountering intelligent life was on a small, rocky world where he came upon what someone had left behind. They—whoever they were—had worked out the mathematics to predict the position of every particle coming from Earth out to sixty-two light years. They had made a copy of each and every one of those particles and reassembled them into coherent signals, which they filtered out to leave only television broadcasts from 1956 to 1977. These broadcasts were played in a decades-long loop on a screen the size of Yosemite's Half Dome.

John watched the broadcast loop several times but never figured out what the point was. Eventually he went home.

• • •

Things had gotten bad and strange in his absence.

Resources were scarce, fragmented nations fought for drops and crumbs, and it seemed to John after he'd spent years in the peaceful silence of space that every single person on Earth had gone crazy. He thought of leaving again, but he hadn't forgotten the lessons his parents had taught him hundreds of years ago. He needed to stay, and he needed to help.

For starters, he knew he had to do something about overpopulation. Culling was suggested as a possible solution, but he seldom considered the idea. The revelation that Protein-G, trademarked as GroTeen, was in fact made of dead human tissue—that caused some uproar. But it was cheap and plentiful, and after it ended a decades-long European famine, the conversation switched from "Protein-G is people" to "We need to ensure Protein-G manufacturers follow better quality-control standards." It remained illegal to eat human brains, for example.

When celebrities started earning huge advances by signing their post-mortem bodies over to exclusive Protein-G eateries, John had finally had enough. He took over the world. Five hundred years later, he gave it back. And five hundred years after that, nobody remembered he'd ever been the most powerful dictator ever known. People had short memories. At least his name, or variants of it, survived in the languages that came after the last speakers of English and Mandarin and other ancient tongues fell silent. It meant things like king, and father, and servitude, and slavery, and also freedom, and safety, and sacrifice, and generosity.

John didn't quite know what to make of it. He could only hope he'd made people's lives better. At least they were no longer eating each other.

• • •

He met a woman named Aisha who ran a café in what used to be Ethiopia. She served him bread and lentils and beer, and if it wasn't the best meal he'd ever had in his life (he was a picky eater and continued to compare everything to his mother's cooking), it was certainly the most pleasant meal he'd had in a long time, due almost entirely to Aisha, who was beautiful and funny. She had many stories to tell and she was good at telling them. One thing led to another, and a month passed before they finally parted company.

More than two hundred years later, John found himself walking through that part of the world again. And there was Aisha's café, still standing, still serving lentils and bread and beer. There was no mistaking the woman in the kitchen. He could have analyzed her on a cellular level to make sure she wasn't Aisha's descendent, but there was no need. She remembered him, and now she knew what he was. Two centuries after their first meeting, they discovered one another.

It wasn't a perfect marriage. They were both practiced at relationships but still fell prey to misunderstandings, impatience, bouts of selfishness and resentment. But they figured it out, and together they traveled the earth and made homes and left homes and traveled some more.

There were no children. John surmised it was because they were of different species, compatible but not compatible enough. John had powers, Aisha did not. And, as they slowly discovered, unlike him, she wasn't immortal. She was aging, just slowly. When you live forever and everyone you've ever known has died, even eight hundred years of being with the woman you love isn't enough.

John stayed with her until the end, when her hair was white and her skin like paper.

He told her he loved her.

She told him not to give up.

• • •

At the end, there was no reconciliation with a lost loved one, no forgiveness granted by the dead, no revelation, no epiphany that gave his life a particular meaning, no overriding message his life could be said to impart, no tidy, circular shape to it. There was just a lot of living, day to day, each hour spent trying to find grace or happiness or satisfaction or decency. And in that his life was no different than anyone else's. Just longer.

After four score and billions of years, he'd had enough, and he sat down to die. For a man who could survive in the core of a sun, this proved itself a challenge. But he could do so many other amazing things, surely he could make himself die. He concentrated on learning his body, not just the cells, but the molecules, the atoms, the protons, and all the little bizarre bits that the protons were made of.

It was complicated stuff, and it took a long time. And while he was trying to figure out how it all worked and think himself dead, the universe, which, except for John, was barely a ghost of its former self, reached its outmost expansion. It paused for a time neither long nor short, but immeasurable either way, and then began drawing in on itself, much in the same way John had turned inward. Perhaps he was the thing causing the contraction.

By now John had a pretty decent handle on the stuff he was made of, and he even began to understand not just the what of it, but the when of it. As the universe continued to reverse its course, John rode with it. Backwards. Backwards. All the way, backwards.

Maybe, he thought, he didn't really want to die. After all, if the matter he was made of had already been eroded and replaced uncounted times, then he'd been dying and being reborn for eons. His particles had shot out on their trajectories, and then his new particles had done the same, and so on, until they'd all gone so far out that they had no other choice but to return to their origins.

John chose to go with them, as far back as he could go.

• • •

GREG VAN EEKHOUT writes novels for adults and young readers, typically characterized by mayhem, banter, weirdness, and action. His first novel, *Norse Code*, was a finalist for the Locus Award for Best First Novel. His middle-grade novel, *The Boy at the End of the World*, was a nominee for the Andre Norton Young Adult Science Fiction and Fantasy Award. His most recent work is the Daniel Blackland trilogy from Tor Books, consisting of *California Bones*, *Pacific Fire*, and *Dragon Coast*. He lives in Southern California, where two seismic plates crash into each other and give rise to disaster and mayhem.

Ponies

Kij Johnson

If you want to be friends with TheOtherGirls, you're going to have to give something up; this is the way it's always been, as long as there have been Ponies. *Nebula Award winner, Hugo Award nominee, World Fantasy Award nominee. Edited by Patrick Nielsen Hayden.*

The invitation card has a Western theme. Along its margins, cartoon girls in cowboy hats chase a herd of wild Ponies. The Ponies are no taller than the girls, bright as butterflies, fat, with short round-tipped unicorn horns and small fluffy wings. At the bottom of the card, newly caught Ponies mill about in a corral. The girls have lassoed a pink-and-white Pony. Its eyes and mouth are surprised round Os. There is an exclamation mark over its head.

The little girls are cutting off its horn with curved knives. Its wings are already removed, part of a pile beside the corral.

> You and your Pony ___[and Sunny's name is handwritten here, in puffy letters]___ are invited to a cutting-out party with TheOtherGirls! If we like you, and if your Pony does okay, we'll let you hang out with us.

Sunny says, "I can't wait to have friends!" She reads over Barbara's shoulder, rose-scented breath woofling through Barbara's hair. They are in the backyard next to Sunny's pink stable.

Barbara says, "Do you know what you want to keep?"

Sunny's tiny wings are a blur as she hops into the air, loops, and then hovers, legs curled under her. "Oh, being able to talk, absolutely! Flying is great, but talking is way better!" She drops to the grass. "I don't know why any Pony would keep her horn! It's not like it does anything!"

This is the way it's always been, as long as there have been Ponies. All Ponies have wings. All Ponies have horns. All Ponies can talk. Then all Ponies go to a cutting-out party, and they give up two of the three, because that's what has to happen if a girl is going to fit in with TheOtherGirls. Barbara's never seen a Pony that still had her horn or wings after her cutting-out party.

Barbara sees TheOtherGirls' Ponies peeking in the classroom windows just before recess or clustered at the bus stop after school. They're baby pink and lavender and daffodil yellow, with flossy manes in ringlets, and tails that curl to the ground. When not at school and cello lessons and ballet class and soccer practice and play group and the orthodontist's, TheOtherGirls spend their days with their Ponies.

• • •

The party is at TopGirl's house. She has a mother who's a pediatrician and a father who's a cardiologist and a small barn and giant trees shading the grass where the Ponies are playing games. Sunny walks out to them nervously. They silently touch her horn and wings with their velvet noses, and then the Ponies all trot out to the lilac barn at the bottom of the pasture, where a bale of hay has been broken open.

TopGirl meets Barbara at the fence. "That's your Pony?" she says without greeting. "She's not as pretty as Starblossom."

Barbara is defensive. "She's beautiful!" This is a misstep so she adds, "Yours is so pretty!" And TopGirl's Pony *is* pretty: her tail is every shade of purple and glitters with stars. But Sunny's tail is creamy white and shines with honey-colored light, and Barbara knows that Sunny's the most beautiful Pony ever.

. . .

TopGirl walks away, saying over her shoulder, "There's Rock Band in the family room and a bunch of TheOtherGirls are hanging out on the deck and Mom bought some cookies and there's Coke Zero and diet Red Bull and diet lemonade."

"Where are you?" Barbara asks.

"*I'm* outside," TopGirl says, so Barbara gets a Crystal Light and three frosted raisin-oatmeal cookies and follows her. TheOtherGirls outside are listening to an iPod plugged into speakers and playing Wii tennis and watching the Ponies play HideAndSeek and Who'sPrettiest and ThisIsTheBestGame. They are all there, SecondGirl and SuckUpGirl and EveryoneLikesHerGirl and the rest. Barbara only speaks when she thinks she'll get it right.

. . .

And then it's time. TheOtherGirls and their silent Ponies collect in a ring around Barbara and Sunny. Barbara feels sick.

TopGirl says to Barbara, "What did she pick?"

Sunny looks scared but answers her directly. "I would rather talk than fly or stab things with my horn."

TopGirl says to Barbara, "That's what Ponies always say." She gives Barbara a curved knife with a blade as long as a woman's hand.

"*Me?*" Barbara says. "I thought someone else did it. A grown-up."

. . .

TopGirl says, "Everyone does it for their own Pony. I did it for Starblossom."

In silence Sunny stretches out a wing.

It's not the way it would be, cutting a real pony. The wing comes off easily, smooth as plastic, and the blood smells like cotton candy at the fair. There's a shiny trembling oval where the wing was, as if Barbara is cutting rose-flavored Turkish delight in half and sees the pink under the powdered sugar. She thinks, *It's sort of pretty,* and throws up.

Sunny shivers, her eyes shut tight. Barbara cuts off the second wing and lays it beside the first.

The horn is harder, like paring a real pony's hooves. Barbara's hand slips and she cuts Sunny, and there's more cotton-candy blood. And then the horn lies in the grass beside the wings.

Sunny drops to her knees. Barbara throws the knife down and falls beside her, sobbing and hiccuping. She scrubs her face with the back of her hand and looks up at the circle.

Starblossom touches the knife with her nose, pushes it toward Barbara with one lilac hoof. TopGirl says, "Now the voice. You have to take away her voice."

"But I already cut off her wings and her horn!" Barbara throws her arms around Sunny's neck, protecting it. "Two of the three, you said!"

"That's the cutting-out, yeah," TopGirl says. "That's what *you* do to be One-OfUs. But the Ponies pick their *own* friends. And that costs, too." Starblossom tosses her violet mane. For the first time, Barbara sees that there is a scar shaped like a smile on her throat. All the Ponies have one.

• • •

"I won't!" Barbara tells them all, but even as she cries until her face is caked with snot and tears, she knows she will, and when she's done crying, she picks up the knife and pulls herself upright.

Sunny stands up beside her on trembling legs. She looks very small without her horn, her wings. Barbara's hands are slippery, but she tightens her grip.

"No," Sunny says suddenly. "Not even for this."

Sunny spins and runs, runs for the fence in a gallop as fast and beautiful as a real pony's; but there are more of the others, and they are bigger, and Sunny doesn't have her wings to fly or her horn to fight. They pull her down before she can jump the fence into the woods beyond. Sunny cries out and then there is nothing, only the sound of pounding hooves from the tight circle of Ponies.

TheOtherGirls stand, frozen. Their blind faces are turned toward the Ponies.

The Ponies break their circle, trot away. There is no sign of Sunny, beyond a spray of cotton-candy blood and a coil of her glowing mane torn free and fading as it falls to the grass.

Into the silence TopGirl says, "Cookies?" She sounds fragile and false. The-OtherGirls crowd into the house, chattering in equally artificial voices. They start up a game, drink more Diet Coke.

Barbara stumbles after them into the family room. "What are you playing?" she says, uncertainly.

"Why are *you* here?" FirstGirl says, as if noticing her for the first time. "You're not OneOfUs."

TheOtherGirls nod. "You don't have a Pony."

KIJ JOHNSON is an American fantasy writer noted for her adaptations of Japanese myths and folklore. "Ponies" won the 2011 Nebula Award for Best Short Story. Her story "Fox Magic" won the 1994 Theodore Sturgeon Award, her novel *The Fox Woman* won the Crawford Award for best debut fantasy novel, and her subsequent novel *Fudoki* was a finalist for the World Fantasy Award and was cited by *Publishers Weekly* as one of the best fantasy novels of its year. She is also the author of the Huge-nominated *The Dream-Quest of Vellitt Boe*. She is an associate director of the Center for the Study of Science Fiction at the University of Kansas.

La beauté sans vertu

Genevieve Valentine

In a future where disturbing trends have only been amplified, a famous fashion house prepares for an important show. *Edited by Ellen Datlow.*

These days they use arms from corpses—age fourteen, oldest, at time of death. The couture houses pay for them, of course (the days of grave-robbing are over, this is a business), but anything over fourteen isn't worth having. At fourteen, the bones have most of the length you need for a model, with a child's slender ulna, the knob of the wrist still standing out enough to cast a shadow.

The graft scars are just at the shoulder, like a doll's arm. The surgeons are artists, and the seams are no wider than a silk thread. The procedure's nearly perfect by now, and the commitment of the doctors is respected. Models' fingertips always go a little black, tending to the purple; no one points it out.

· · ·

Maria's already nineteen when the House of Centifolia picks her up. You don't want them any younger than that if you're going to keep them whole and working for the length of their contract. You want someone with a little stamina.

The publicity team decides to make England her official home country, because that sounds just exotic enough to intrigue without actually being from a country that worries people, so Maria spends six months secluded, letting her arms heal, living on a juice fast, and learning how to fire her English with a cut-glass accent.

The walk she already had, of course. That's how a girl gets noticed by an agency to start with, by having that sharp, necessary stride where the head stays fixed and the rest of her limbs seem to clatter in that careless way that makes the clothes look four times more expensive than they are. Nothing else is any good. They film the girls and map their faces frame by frame until they can walk so precisely the co-ordinates never move.

She's perfect from the first take. The House seeds Maria's audition video as classified amateur footage leaked by mistake so everyone gets interested, then pretends to crack down on security so people think her identity was a hidden asset and they got a glimpse of something clandestine. She becomes the industry's sixteenth most searched-for name.

Rhea, the head of the House, likes the look of her ("Something miserable in the turn of the mouth," she says with great satisfaction, already sketching). Maria does one season as an exclusive for Centifolia's fall collection that year, opening a single catwalk in a black robe weighed down with thirteen pounds of embroidery, her feet spearing the floor and her hands curled into fists. After that the press comes calling.

"The Princess of Roses and Diamonds," the *Bespoke* headline calls her, conjuring the old fairy tale in an article nobody reads. People just look at the photos. She scales the dragon statue on the Old Bridge in thousand-dollar jeans; she perches in the frame of an open window with her hair dragging in the wind like a ghost is pulling her through; she stands naked in a museum and holds a ball gown against her chest.

The photographer can't stop taking pictures of her face—half in shadow, half hidden by her hair as the wind plays with the cuffs of her silk shirt. Her thin, borrowed wrists curve out of the arm of a coat; an earring looks as if it's trying to crawl in her ear just to be closer.

She's already very good about turning down questions without making it seem like she's actually turned them down; roses and diamonds fall from her lips. No one bothers with the interview where she talks just as she's supposed to about the curated past Centifolia drilled into her. Six months' prep for nothing.

• • •

There's the occasional complaint, of course (from outside, always, those inside a couture house wouldn't dream of it). But it's a precision business. The models don't even suffer phantom aches from their old arms. The doctors clean up anything else that's wrong while they're in there, as a special service—faltering thyroids and kidney troubles and moles that are suspicious or unsightly. These girls are an investment; they're meant to live.

• • •

The Old Baroque Concert Hall is on the edge of town, and only the House of Centifolia's long history and Rhea's name could get anyone from the industry crowd to come out this far.

The runway snakes across most of the derelict space, weaving back in on itself in a pattern that came to Rhea in a dream—it reminded her of the journey through life, and of the detox trip she took to Austria.

The narrow walkway crosses itself at different sloping elevations to mimic the mountain trails; the oily pool sliding beneath it all reflects the muted tones of this season's collection, and pays homage to the foot-buckets of cold and hot water in the Austrian spa that drained lipids and negative thoughts from the body.

With thirty-five looks in the fall collection and six points of varying heights across which the meandering runway connects—"It's more of a maze than a trail," Rhea explains to potential choreographers, "it's very spiritual"—the timing has to be precise, but there are only two windows in which the girls are available to practice: once during the fitting the day before, and once mere hours before the show.

Three of the models have to be fired for having scheduled another show the day before this one, which makes them traitors to the House (you don't book something else without permission, rookie mistake, Rhea cuts them so fast one of them gets thrown out of a cab), and the three alternates have to be called up and fitted. It means six hours of all the girls standing in the unheated warehouse, looselimbed and pliant as they're ordered to be for fittings, while assistants yank them in and out of outfits and take snapshots until the new assignments emerge and they're allowed to go rehearse.

The choreographer—he has a name, but no one dares use it when speaking of him, lest he appear before they've corrected their posture—thinks carefully for a long time. He paces the length of the runway, hopping nimbly from one level to the next at the intersections. He doubles back sharply once or twice in a way that looks, horribly convincingly, as if he's actually become lost and someone will have to risk breaking ranks to go get him. Then he reaches the end, nods as if satisfied, points to six places on the stage, and shouts, "The girls, please!"

. . .

There were two girls—there are always two, so one can be made an example of.

The one who was kind to an old beggar woman was gifted with the roses and diamonds that dropped from her mouth with every word; the one who refused to get water for a princess to drink spent the rest of her life vomiting vipers and toads.

As a girl, Rhea listened and understood what she wasn't being told. (It's how she climbed to the top of a couture house. Rhea hears.)

The one who was kind married a prince, and spent the rest of her life granting audiences and coughing up bouquets and necklaces for the guests. The one who refused was driven into the forest, where there was no one who wanted anything fetched, and she could spit out a viper any time she needed venom, and she never had to speak again.

. . .

The runway's barely finished. The polymer designed to look like luminous soil hasn't quite dried, and the models sink half an inch with every step. They don't mention it; their job is to walk, not to speak.

The idea is the ringing of a bell, which starts with a single tone being struck and builds in its echoes until every strike becomes a symphony. One girl will walk out first, then two closer behind one another, then four. It should build until every outfit can be seen perfectly and in full only at the first turn. The reveal is precious and fleeting, and isn't meant to last.

After that the show becomes the girls in formation like waves of sound, and the wash of the looks across the runways as they pass. Spectators, no matter where along the uneven rings of bleachers they may be sitting, should be in awe. There should always be more to look at than anyone can catch, that sense of being doomed to miss something wonderful; that's how a presentation becomes a show.

"Angry walks, quiet faces!" the choreographer calls, clapping his hands emphatically, slightly off from the beat of the music.

The first girl, an unknown from the ranks who was chosen to lead the show because her eyes are sunk so deep in their sockets that they look like diamond chips, shakes the boards with every step, trying desperately to keep her face quiet and look forward while still watching the choreographer for signs of disapproval.

The girls who follow the beat of the music get corrected—one sharp flick on the shoulder with a steel pen—by the PA as they come around the first big turn. The ones who follow the clapping are also wrong, but they don't know it until the second turn, and the assistant choreographer can't flick shoulders without knocking them into the reflecting pool, where the water has already been oiled (too early) and would cost a fortune to re-gloss before showtime.

Eventually the choreographer gives up on trying to explain the vision to a bunch of girls who can't even walk on the right beat, and he resorts to a cap gun, fired twice at each model as she passes the first turn to give her the metronome ticks of her stride. The shape of things visibly improves, but they spend another hour after that on quiet faces, because for a bunch of girls who claim they're professional, they flinch like you wouldn't believe.

• • •

Maria knows, from her real home, how you make silk. You boil the pupae and draw out the single filament of their cocoons from the steam, a pot of glistening threads with maggots roiling underneath.

There's no thread like it; it works miracles.

• • •

The action group ends up calling itself Mothers Against Objectification of Young Women. There had been some impassioned complaining early on during the drafting and ratification of bylaws and clauses that young men were also being objectified, probably, and it was important to make sure they felt included. But one of the internal factions pointed out that then the acronym would just be MAO, and the moment of patriotic consumer hesitation lasted just long enough for Young Women to reassert itself as the primary concern.

Mothers Against Objectification of Young Women pickets the House of Centifolia show; Rhea's been a target ever since Maria stood naked in the photograph with that ball gown in front of her, and there was more parking this far on the edge of town than near the tents in the city center. The different factions arrive two hours early, pile out with signs and fliers, and stand not quite near each other, as close to the door as security allows.

"Modesty is the greatest beauty!" they shout. "Keep your arms to yourself!" "Role models, not clothes models!" Role models of what, they never reach; the shouting cycles through to "Shame on the industry!" next from the oldest ones, and a few rugged idealists try their best to sneak in "American jobs!" in between the agreed-upon call and response.

The attendees squeal with delight, shifting their gold-leafed invitations under their arms so they can photograph the Mothers Against on the way inside. "Trust Rhea to provide immersive atmosphere before you even go through the doors," one of the reporters says into his recorder, shaking his head. "This collection is going to be such an amazing statement about the cultural position of the industry."

A group of audience hopefuls gathers to the right of the door crew, hoping they'll be allowed to sneak in and fill seats for the no-shows. A few of them—Fashion Week veterans who have done shows long enough to gauge the capacity of a venue from the outside—realize it will be standing room only, and start to cry. One tries to make a desperate run for it, and is still taking photographs of the interior as security lifts her away, her shoes dangling a few inches in the air above their shoes. She's a blogger, and her shoes are white brocade; the picture she takes of her feet floating between their feet will get the most clickthumbs of her whole Fashion Week report.

Mothers Against Objectification of Young Women gets increasingly concerned as spectators file in. Several of the young women are wearing revealing shirts that don't look at all American-made, one or two are wearing shirts cut straight down to the waist despite the risk of sunburn, and one woman is sixty if she's a day, wearing a shirt that's absolutely transparent except for the enormous middle finger appliqué carefully fastened to the front with tiny, elegant studs.

As she passes, she gives the MAOYW a single, long look through eyes that have been made up with a line of driftwood flakes along her eyebrows. It looks like two mouths full of teeth. By the time she's passed them and vanished inside, the Mothers Against have faltered so badly they have to start the chanting over from the beginning.

• • •

The Princess of Roses and Diamonds is closing out the show. It's supposed to be a wedding dress—traditionally, a wedding dress still closes runway shows, the pinnacle of womanly expectation nothing can shake—but Rhea wouldn't stoop to send a white wedding gown down the runway unless she could finally figure out how to stabilize the chalk filaments she's been working on.

Instead, the dress is carefully woven on a frame of horizontal reeds looped around Maria's body like scaffolding, laced in vertical threads of silk dyed the colors of earliest morning—nearly black, deep blue, murky gray, a sliver of gold—and not fastened. No seams, no knots; the thread is loosely looped at arbitrary heights, just waiting to slip free.

"It will fall apart," Rhea explains to her in a voice like a church, as the six assistants ease Maria into the gown and weave the entry panel closed. "It's supposed to. This is the chrysalis from which the moth emerges and takes flight. Help it."

Maria looks at the mirror, where the last two assistants are looping the final threads. Rhea's looking at the mirror too, her eyes brimming with tears, and Maria realizes this must be a masterpiece, that she must be wearing something that will be important later. It's important that this fragility turn into a pile of thread and reed hoops, because nothing beautiful lasts.

Maria's meant to go out and walk the runway until she's naked, to prove that nothing beautiful lasts.

Silk moths can't fly. It's been bred out of them for five thousand years. The adults are only needed to make more worms. Most aren't meant to live long enough to break the chrysalis; flight's an unnecessary trait.

The Princess of Roses and Diamonds swallowed blood for the rest of her life, every time she opened her mouth.

• • •

The capacity of the auditorium is four hundred seats, and fire rules are very strict this far into the old side of town, where there's God-knows-what piled up in the abandoned buildings and it takes a fire truck longer to reach you if anything goes up in flames. But by the time Rhea's show starts, they're running 476, not counting crew.

The program outlining the thirty-five looks becomes a scarce collectible (highest offer, seven hundred dollars) before the lights even go down. The guests who had their places reserved for them with a little place card hand engraved with poured gold on a sliver of mother-of-pearl don't see one clear second of the show because of all the people standing in the aisles and blocking the view.

"Democracy Comes to Fashion," runs the headline in *The Walk* the next day, under a picture of the lead model with the pair of girls behind her closing in, the shot framed perfectly by the shoulders of two people who turn the rest of the runway into a curtain of black.

The models are terrified—half the reason the sequin jackets and metallic-thread tartans look so impressive is how roughly they're shaking—but they walk as they're meant to walk, their purpling fingers held to showcase their knuckle rings, their gazes fixed, heads steady and bodies a series of angles dressed in clothes that make one aspire, crisscrossing one another within a hairsbreadth of each other, just above the oil.

The press assumes that in such a display of transience, the pool was meant to be the primordial sea, to accent the flashes of gold in the clothes that must represent the minerals within the earth itself. Rhea never corrects them.

The music is a little tinny—sound check had been canceled in favor of the cap gun, and union techs don't sit around and wait for people who can't keep to a schedule—but the press assumes that's on purpose, too. "It's a recreation of the womb," writes *The Walk*, "in which the beginning of life itself is met with such overwhelming sensory input: music like whale song, extraordinary tartans layered over pinstripes with red flannel jutting out from underneath, a reminder of the vast amounts of blood that life requires."

The girls walk beautifully. All thirty-four of them.

. . .

Mothers Against Objectification of Young Women scatters as soon as Maria appears. They don't know why, since she's hardly violent about it. She's barely strong enough to open the doors.

There will be arguments among some of the Mothers later, and clauses put into the bylaws about when the picket line can be broken for humanitarian reasons and when they're expected to hold their ground.

She walks past them all without turning her head. She walks past the building and into the street and toward the empty cul-de-sac at the edge of the parking lot, where the field starts. With every step the threads shake loose—that walk is a killer, that walk gets the job done—and the first hoop's rattled to the asphalt before the Mothers Against have quite caught their breath.

It's not a mathematical process, of course—a labor of love never is—and a few of the hoops clack together as they slip down, only to be caught up in the dam of silk threads until she can jar them loose. She sheds everywhere, strands of silk in single filaments that shine along the ground like something from a fever dream, every color so expertly dyed it casts a halo against the asphalt as it falls. Once or twice threads catch and sink in a cluster all at once, and a hoop will clatter to the ground, so as she steps out of it she leaves behind a circled map to a place no one will ever reach.

She's naked long before everything finally goes, of course—a few hoops and some string do not a garment make, and the white knobs of her spine and of her borrowed wrists and blackened fingertips and the purple hollows at the backs of her knees are shaded by the deep blues and the strings of gold that are still left. She keeps walking without looking left or right. Once she hits the tall, muddy grass of the field and the gold-tipped heels of her shoes sink with the first step into the soft earth, she abandons them and continues barefoot, but she never breaks stride; she's a professional.

When she disappears into the woods beyond the field, there are three hoops hanging around her knees at strange angles, and a few vertical streaks of blue still holding them up.

After a long time, one of the Mothers Against says, "I suppose we should tell them."

One of the others—the oldest, the one wiping away tears—says, "I'll go."

• • •

The threads were mapped over the course of eight months. Rhea had a vision. She wanted a legacy.

She dyed each one by hand in a room in her apartment that got light like a Vermeer. She medicated to avoid sleep for a week so she could determine where every thread should start and end. She consulted a physicist the next week, to make sure she was right about the rate of tensile decay on a body in motion, just in case she had hallucinated during the original sketches. It wouldn't be perfect—Maria had a way of walking that no application of metrics could fully predict—but it would do what it had been made to do.

The team of dressers that wove Maria into the silk-thread gown spent the two weeks before the show locked in a hotel room with no outside connection and a half-wage stipend, with a PR vice president stationed outside to make sure no one from room service could ask them anything. Each dresser was given a garment map and practice threads from Rhea's dry runs. (She'd done sixty.) By the end of two weeks, they could do the whole dress in three hours. The day of, with the real thing, they wept once or twice as they worked; a miracle affects people in strange ways.

• • •

If it panics Rhea that her centerpiece and her prize model have vanished, no one ever gets wind of it. You don't become the head of a house by being easy to read. As soon as she hears what's happened, she cancels the finale and just orders the models to walk straight through the crowds in the aisles and hold rank outside. The attendees file out in pairs after that, past the gauntlet of thirty-four girls, and see what's left of Maria. There's a constellation of silk snakes, filaments disappearing into the tall grass, hoops leaving ghost marks where they fell, pale blue threads suspended in a little puddle of antifreeze.

No one claps. Some cry. The reporters shoulder-check each other and take hundreds of pictures at speeds that sound like someone wheezing.

"Did you see it?" the audience asks the picketers, and when the Mothers Against nod, the guests don't ask what it must have been like. They just shake the Mothers' hands, and shake their heads at Rhea as they would a brutal saint, and file silently past towards the city proper.

. . .

They never find Maria.

It could be foul play—she'd run from a house to which she owed at least six figures. There were consequences when a girl bolted on a contract, and Rhea would have taken the loss rather than let such an artist move under someone else's roof. Centifolia signed girls for life; casualties were a cost of doing business.

The cops don't make a particularly thorough search for Maria. If she's moved couture houses without approval it's a legal matter above their pay grade, and if she's vanished in the process it's a business matter, and they'll never find the body.

There are routine checks on the morgue from time to time, but they figure in that case the call will come in to them. She was healthy unless her arms malfunctioned, so it could be a while, and they'll know if something happened: Maria's is a face not even death could hide.

The girl who opened the show becomes a media darling. Someone at *Bespoke* decides she must have known what was wrong and had bravely decided to begin the show anyway, and it catches on. Rhea's team tells her to let them believe it. It's a good angle, and somebody's got to close out the spring show. They're working on a new image for her, maybe something with mermaids, something with ghosts; the sunken eyes, they've decided, will become her trademark. Rhea starts dying fabrics for her.

When the press goes wild for the story, and the MAOYW find themselves at the center of more attention than their clauses had ever planned for, a lot of things happen. Some just amplify their slogans regarding the right kind of woman, with the unblinking intensity television can lend someone, and get picked up for church work. Some split from all that and argue for transparency and freedom of industry, and precipitate updates to regulations in some of the major Houses.

The oldest Mother Against—the one who broke the news about Maria to an assistant who thanked her, threw up, and sprinted for Rhea—left the organization before she ever got in her car to go home.

Sometimes she drives all the way out to the edge of town and stands in the doorway of the Old Baroque, where the runway was never torn down, and looks from the runway to the trees on the far side of the field. The dye from one of the silk threads has held fast to the asphalt all this time, a dusting of gold pointing to the place between two trees where Maria disappeared.

Maybe she lives in the woods, the old woman thinks. She doesn't know why that comforts her.

The runway's going to seed. Reeds have sprouted from the oily pool, and there are beginning to be frogs, and the moss has started to grow over the sharp edges, a pool of pale blue algae skimming every imprint of a shoe.

. . .

The nail polish for spring is from Centifolia, in collaboration with Count Eleven. Out of the Vagary beauty line they design that year, the most popular by a factor of ten is the shade called The Woman Vanishes; it's a hundred dollars a bottle, and was sold out before it ever saw the inside of a store.

It's nearly black, tending a little purple. You dip your whole fingertip in it, so it looks like the blood has pooled.

GENEVIEVE VALENTINE is the author of the novel *Persona* and its sequel *Icon*. Her short fiction has appeared in several Best of the Year anthologies. Her nonfiction and reviews have appeared at NPR.org, *The A.V. Club*, *The Atlantic*, and *The New York Times*.

A Fist of Permutations in Lightning and Wildflowers

Alyssa Wong

Hannah and Melanie: sisters, apart and together. Weather workers. Time benders. When two people so determined have opposing desires, it's hard to say who will win—or even what victory might look like. *Hugo Award nominee, Nebula Award nominee. Edited by Miriam Weinberg.*

There was nothing phoenix-like in my sister's immolation. Just the scent of charred skin, unbearable heat, the inharmonious sound of her last, grief-raw scream as she evaporated, leaving glass footprints seared into the desert sand.

If my parents were still alive—although they are, probably, in some iteration of the universe; maybe even this one—they would tell me that it wasn't my fault, that no one could have seen it coming. That she did this to herself. But that kind of blame doesn't suit me. Besides, they had always been exceptionally blind to matters regarding Melanie. They didn't even notice when the two of us would take to the sky together, Melanie blowing currents back and forth beneath our bodies, weaving thermals like daisy chains. We used to make sparks dance at the table, and our mom never said a word about it, except that it was rude to do things that other people couldn't in front of them, and also that we needed to learn to talk to people other than each other.

Melanie was better at everything than I was, the stormy bit and the talking bit both. She could split the horizon in two if she wanted, opening it at the seams as deftly as a tailor, and make the lightning curl catlike at her wrist and purr for her. She could do that with people too; Mel glowed, soft, luminescent. It was hard to look away from her, and so easy to disappear into her shadow.

But when things got too bad to ignore, the air in the house dark and crackling with ugly energy like the sky before a monsoon, she dug in and refused to leave. I was the one who abandoned our coast for another, promising I'd be back soon. And then I was the one who stayed away.

. . .

The day my sister ended the world, the sky opened up in rain for the first time in years, flooding the desert wash behind our house. The snakes drowned in their holes and the javelinas stampeded downstream, but the water overtook them, and the air filled with their screaming as they were swept away.

I'd tried to take a taxi home, but the roads disappeared in the flash flood, so I struggled out of the swamped cab and slogged the last two miles.

Melanie was outside, a small, dry figure in front of the ruined shell of our parents' house. She wore the only dress she had left—the rest our mother had burned when she'd found them. The rain bent around my sister in a bell shape, and electricity danced in her hands, growing bigger and bigger like a ravenous cat's cradle. Some time ago, lightning had shattered the cacti in the yard, splitting them in two and searing them bone-bare. Only their blackened skeletons were left, clawing upward out of the water like accusing fingers.

I know she felt me coming. Maybe it was a tremble in the dry ground beneath her feet, or a ripple of energy through the water that crashed around my waist. She glanced up, her eyes wide, bruised circles.

I remember that I yelled something at her. That time around, it could have been her name. It could have been a plea, begging her not to do what I could see was about to happen. Or maybe it was just "What the fuck do you think you're doing?"

The world hiccupped, warping violet, legs of electricity touching down around me, biting at my hair, singeing anything still alive beneath the water. I barely felt it.

"Why did you come back?" were the last words she said to me before she went up in flames, taking the rest of the universe with her.

• • •

It was simple, Melanie had once told me. "Here, Hannah. Pay attention, and I'll teach you how the future works."

She drew the picture for me in the air, a map of sparkling futures, constants, and variables, closed circuits of possibilities looped together, arcing from one timeline to another. I saw and understood; but more than that, for the first time, I saw her power as a single, mutable shape.

"That's beautiful," I said.

"Isn't it?" Melanie traced the air with her finger, tapping a single glowing point. "Look, that's us. And here's what could happen, depending on . . . well, depending on a lot of things."

Options chained like lightning strikes before my eyes, possibilities growing legs like sentient things. "If it's that easy, why don't you change it?" I blurted out. "Shape it to make it better for us, I mean."

Her eyes slid away from me. "It's not that easy to get it right," she said.

• • •

The day my sister ended the world, I was on a plane home for the first time in years. I'd managed to sleep most of the way, which was unusual, and I woke up as the plane was descending, a faint popping in my ears. It was sunset, and the flat, highway-veined city was just beginning to glimmer with electric light, civilization pulsing across the ground in arteries, in fractals.

But the beauty was lost on me. The clouds outside felt heavy, and my heart wouldn't stop drumming in my chest. Something was wrong, but I didn't know what.

I felt like I'd seen this before.

Time stuttered, and outside, it began to rain.

• • •

If I could knit you a crown of potential futures like the daisies you braided together for me when we were young, I would.

None of them would end with you burning to death at the edge of our property, beaten senseless in the wash behind the house by drunken college boys, slowly cut to pieces at home by parents who wanted you only in one shape, the one crafted in their image.

I would give you only the best things. The kindness you deserved, the body you wanted, a way out that didn't end with the horizon line ripped open, possibilities pouring out like loose stuffing, my world shrieking to a halt.

I would have fixed everything.

. . .

The day my sister—

No.

The day I ended the world, the very first time, my plane touched down early and I sprinted to catch a cab before the impending monsoon swept the city. This time around, I made it four miles from the house before a six-car pileup—tires slick, drivers panicked in the storm—stopped traffic entirely. It took everything in me not to shunt the water aside in front of everyone else, to stumble into neck-deep currents and anchor my feet to the asphalt below. It took forever to get home, and when I did, Melanie was not there.

An hour later, my sister's body floated up in the new river behind our house, covered in bruises, red plastic cups bumping at her bare feet, and lightning spiked white-hot through my chest, searing the ground of my heart into a desert. All I could see were cities burning, houses shelled, every regret and act of cowardice twisting through me into blinding rage.

And in that moment, perfect power was bright in front of me, a seam in space, in time, across myriad axes. I stretched out and grabbed it, and split the world in two. Its ribs reached out to me, and I reached back.

. . .

"You can't change this, Hannah," my sister's ghost said as I tore the sky apart, shredding the fabric of air, of cloud, of matter and possibility. The lightning danced for me now, bent and buckled for me the way it had only done for Melanie before.

I will, I will. I will fix this.

"You can't," my sister said. "It'll end the same way. Differently, but the same."

"Why?" I screamed.

The world crashed, bowed like wet rice paper, spilled inward. Our parents' house a crater, the flame that was Melanie nowhere on the brightly lit grid of eventualities. No, no, no. Wrong again.

"I never meant to hurt you." Her ghost sighed as my hands blindly rearranged the components of reality. "I didn't mean for you to see it. This was never about you, Hannah. I wish you'd realize that."

. . .

The week before my sister ended the world, I didn't go home. I stayed in the theater and broke every plate, every mug in the green room, hurling the shards in the faces of every person who'd come to court me. I blinded my agent, I crippled my director, I hamstrung the rest of the actors with porcelain shrapnel. Gale-force winds whipped around me, a crushing power at my back, the storm building behind my pulsing temples, and I blew out into the city, heading downtown.

At Melanie's favorite bakery, where we'd ordered donuts as big as our heads the last time she'd come to visit, I ripped the boards out of the floor one by one, sending them flying through shattered windows. Icing splattered, electricity scorched wood and sugar alike; the scent of ozone was ripe and acrid in the air.

"Hannah," said my sister's reflection in the glass pieces on the floor. The gentle weight of her phantom hand on my shoulder burned, and time tugged at me again. "That's enough."

· · ·

The blame circles back, hungry, and I recognize my own voice hissing from its mouth. *Your fault, Hannah. All your fault. You could have stopped this, but you were blinded by your own ambition, your own selfishness; you let the haze of the city—the toxic glamour and crystalline cold—seduce you away from the people you love.* And it was true. Even once in flight, the taste of glory lingered on my tongue the whole way home, sharp in the stale cabin air.

But Melanie and I had talked, we'd Skyped. Even if it had been through the computer screen, why hadn't I seen the storms at home crackling on the horizon, their dying sparks reflected in my sister's eyes?

· · ·

"You're being selfish," my sister's latest iteration said as I whipped the storm into a dark frenzy over the barren mountains. I couldn't remember if the body in the wash this time was hers, or if that was a memory by now. "Hurting yourself over this is just a way of trying to get control over something that was never in your—"

Shut up. Shut

"—something that was never *yours* to control—"

up. Shut up.

The world ended with a bang, folding in on itself, the lines of the horizon collapsing like soaked origami. Our parents' house turned to glass, to fire, to energy sparking ripe and rich for the taking. I drained it, pulling it deep into myself until the house was empty, our parents gone. And then there was nothing but me and my sister, her imprint, her echo.

Melanie's ghost sighed. "I expected better of you," she said.

The void roared back to life, and tossed me out again.

· · ·

So back to the city again, rewound further this time. Back, past the donut shop, windows never scorched, pastries never eaten. This time I didn't break anything. I went to auditions, cooked rice and fried eggs for dinner, and worked until my muscles screamed for me to stop, then worked more. For a week, I didn't speak unless I was using someone else's words.

The night before boarding the plane, I found myself whispering my secrets into the frigid night air, combing the space between skyscrapers with my tongue.

The city madness was getting to me.

I passed through the same airports like a shade, the route now familiar as the curve of my sleeping cheek in my weary palm.

I did everything right that time, and arrived home to find that the thunderstorm had demolished the airport, preventing anyone from landing.

• • •

The next time, I ended the world by myself, during a power outage. Life blinked out, softly, and screamed back into being.

The void spit the kitchen knife out at my feet, onto the floor of my Bushwick apartment, a taunt echoed in my perfect, intact wrists.

You selfish bitch.

The cycle remained unbroken. Gentle sparks kissed my hands in the dark, glinting off of the blade. My blood roared in my ears.

Again, then.

I reoriented the knife.

• • •

"Hannah. How many people are you going to destroy before you give up on me?"

• • •

Five times, five lines, lead and edges and crushed pills all yanked out of me, spit back further and further each time. I lined them up on my windowsill like the rejected possibilities they were, and let time spool itself out.

Not my fault, not my fault. I'd tried so hard, first to knit the cycle closed and then to slash it to pieces. But still the end danced away from me, the world bleeding into its next cycle.

"What the hell are you doing?" said my roommate for the fifth time, leaning against the doorframe as he did in every iteration. My sullen eyes saw his every possibility splayed out before me like a fall of cards: roommate disappearing into the bathroom to find his medications gone; roommate leaving for work and returning too late; roommate blackened and burned as the apartment went up in smoke; roommate helping me into bed and turning the light off before heading back into the kitchen to bundle up all of the knives.

"Thinking," I croaked. My hands itched with electricity, sparks I couldn't control dancing across my fingers.

"You and your weird sleight-of-hand shit." He sighed and tossed me my iPhone. "Your phone is ringing."

It took me a second to realize that the stupid anime song filtering out of the speakers was the one that Melanie liked, my ringtone for the home landline. But it wasn't her on the phone. It was my mother, who told me that Melanie had drowned in the pool in the backyard during a freak rainstorm, one that had ruptured from an empty sky. My heartbeat slowed, each second syrup-thick.

"But I thought I had more time," I whispered into the phone. It was true, I was supposed to have a few more days to think of things, to fix them—

"No one knows when God will take us home," said my mother. "He's in the Lord's hands. Always has been."

In my grief, I'd nearly forgotten about my sister, and in my absence, my apocalypse had shifted course without me.

. . .

The world ended anew with a shuddering sob, and I hit the ground running. This time, I touched down two weeks, two agonizing weeks, before I would board my plane, and the first thing I did was book an immediate red-eye home, hoping that if I got there early, I wouldn't be too late.

. . .

Wrong, wrong, wrong.

. . .

"What's life like in the city?" Melanie had asked me when she'd come to visit me, the spring before she died. I'd holed up in my dorm room to practice monologues for my senior showcase until my lungs burned, which probably meant I hadn't been breathing properly anyhow, and Melanie had demanded that we go outside. We'd gone downtown, where well-dressed students and decently-dressed visitors crawled the streets, looking for artisanal french fries. We'd settled in a donut shop about as big as Melanie's closet back home and were crunched up, knees to chests, on the inside windowsill.

She'd looked good, wearing the pale pink sweater I'd secretly sent her for her birthday, fingernails painted the way they never could be at home. But she'd also looked so tired, sallow almost, her face lined with the weight of our parents' words.

All the things that my friends expected me to say—*the city's great, it's exciting, I'm so lucky to live here, I love it*—flashed through my head. So did the things I'd never told anyone, that I couldn't tell anyone, because they wouldn't want to hear it. How the loneliness was crippling; how I'd been fired from three part-time jobs by now; how every day, on my way to class, I walked past the same madman in the tunnel moaning for Jesus, a mess of languages spilling from his bloody lips, past a banner ad that read: GET AWAY WITHOUT LEAVING NEW YORK.

"It's different," I'd said at last. *I don't know who I am without you,* I didn't say.

"I understand," Melanie had replied. I could tell that she did.

. . .

I have followed the path back, again and again, to that first stream of possibility. The events lined up so neatly that I could do them in my sleep, and sometimes did. They always led back to the desert monsoon, slogging through the water, my sister disappearing in a pillar of flame.

Why didn't you want me there to help you? I wanted to ask. *If you were this far gone, why didn't you ask me to come home?* I never got close enough to reach her through the wet-dust wind that snarled and roared around us, snatching my voice away.

. . .

There are timelines I don't think about.

There is a timeline where the power never touches me, where I make it home in time for the party at the neighbor's house, where a college boy's hands are around my throat, not my sister's, my legs kicking around his waist. Melanie scorches him to pieces, blackens him, shatters the boulders in the wash, and howls until her voice bleeds. Her tears fall into my eyes, sizzling and evaporating on contact, as the sky yawns above us, hungry, broken.

There are others, too, reaching back further along the daisy chain, when we were younger: slipping on ice, light cracking hard through my head; the agonizing sting of a scorpion on my arm, the stiffening of limbs, sudden tightness in my chest; Melanie in a dress for the first time, sobbing as our father screamed at her.

And forward, along the lines that branch out, fuzzing the borders of the future's shape: knives, dented, rejected by my gut; police sirens wailing, gunshots ringing into the crater where my city used to be, the scent of burnt sugar; a plane that never lands safely, erupting into flame on the runway.

I only remember these as faint echoes, like a story someone told me once but whose details I've forgotten. Did they happen? Yes. No. The chain frays, spreads out like roots, possibilities endless.

I'm sorry, I'm sorry, I'm sorry.

• • •

When Melanie and I were little, we'd lie on the carpet in the winter and warm our soggy feet by the radiator. This was when we still had a bad habit of jumping into snowbanks, exasperating our mom to no end. Melanie had just begun to learn how to melt shapes in the snow, the finest spark at the end of her index finger.

"I wonder why we can do these things," Melanie had said, closing her fist around the lightning glinting across her palm.

I grinned at her, reaching out to catch a bit of stray static dancing down her arm. "Dunno. Don't you think it's cool to be special? It's the one thing no one else can do but us."

She wagged a foot at the radiator. "It's kind of lonely, though."

"At least you have me."

"I guess so," she said. "That's better than nothing."

I tackled her to the ground and we spent the next ten minutes hitting each other with stuffed animals.

• • •

My sister always dies before the world ends.

The sky is marred with the scars of my efforts, and I am so, so tired. The storm hums in my veins, one more cycle in many. I can't count them anymore, numbers constantly in flux, ticking higher with each potential breath.

I wonder if this is what Melanie felt like every day of her life, so ripe with power, always at the precipice, always afraid to push in fear of making things worse.

This time around, I'm on the floor of my apartment, staring at my cell phone in my hand. My roommate is out and I've already missed my flight home. I let it pass, money evaporating into the void, meaningless.

Somewhere in the southwest, Melanie is walking out of the house, or is about to, her heart roaring with wildfire, lonely, alone. The sparks dance purple in her hands, lightning like veins through her arms.

You can't fix this. It was never yours to control.

But my hands fumble over the touch screen, thumbs sliding wet over her face on the contact screen. She's programmed in the same stupid anime ringtone I have on my phone, and it jingles inanely, all synthetic voices and preordained sound.

I wait, mouth dry, my body shaking like the sky above the Mojave before it rains. Painted in brilliant, feverish strokes in my head, the daisy chain grows.

ALYSSA WONG lives in Chapel Hill, North Carolina, and really, really likes crows. Her stories have won the Nebula Award for Best Short Story, the World Fantasy Award for Short Fiction, and the Locus Award for Best Novelette. She was a finalist for the 2016 John W. Campbell Award for Best New Writer, and her fiction has been short-listed for the Hugo Award, the Bram Stoker Award, and the Shirley Jackson Award. Her work has been published in *The Magazine of Fantasy & Science Fiction, Strange Horizons, Nightmare Magazine, Black Static,* and *Tor.com,* among others.

A Kiss with Teeth

Max Gladstone

Vlad has grown distant from his wife. His son has trouble at school. And he has to keep his sharp teeth hidden. *Edited by Marco Palmieri.*

Vlad no longer shows his wife his sharp teeth. He keeps them secret in his gums, waiting for the quickened skip of hunger, for the blood-rush he almost never feels these days.

The teeth he wears instead are blunt as shovels. He coffee-stains them carefully, soaks them every night in a mug with "World's Best Dad" written on the side. After eight years of staining, Vlad's blunt teeth are the burnished yellow of the keys of an old unplayed piano. If not for the stain, they would be whiter than porcelain. Much, much whiter than bone.

White, almost, as the sharp teeth he keeps concealed.

His wife, Sarah, has not tried to kill him since they married. She stores her holy water in a kitchen cabinet behind the spice rack, the silver bullets in a safe with her gun. She smiles when they make love, the smile of a woman sinking into a feather bed, a smile of jigsaw puzzles and blankets over warm laps by the fire. He smiles back, with his blunt teeth.

They have a son, a seven-year-old boy named Paul, straight and brown like his mother, a growing, springing, sapling boy. Paul plays catch, Paul plays basketball, Paul dreams of growing up to be a football star, or a tennis star, or a baseball star, depending on the season. Vlad takes him to games. Vlad wears a baseball cap, and smells the pitcher's sweat and the ball's leather from their seat far up in the stands. He sees ball strike bat, sees ball and bat deform, and knows whether the ball will stutter out between third and second, or arc beautiful and deadly to outfield, fly true or veer across the foul line. He would tell his son, but Paul cannot hear fast enough. After each play, Paul explains the action, slow, patient and content. Paul smiles like his mother, and the smile sets Vlad on edge and spinning.

Sometimes Vlad remembers his youth, sprinting ahead of a cavalry charge to break like lightning on a stand of pikers. Blood, he remembers, oceans of it. Screams of the impaled. There is a sound men's breaking sterna make when you grab their ribs and pull them out and in, a bassy nightmare transposition of a wishbone's snap. Vlad knows the plural forms of "sternum" and "trachea," and all declensions and participles of "flense."

· · ·

"Talk to the teacher," his wife says after dinner. Paul watches a cricket game on satellite in the other room, mountainous Fijians squared off against an Indian

team. Vlad once was a death cult in Calcutta—the entire cult, British colonial para-
noia being an excellent cover for his appetites—and in the sixties he met a traveling volcano god in Fiji, who'd given up sacrifices when he found virgins could be
had more easily by learning to play guitar. Neither experience left Vlad with much
appreciation for cricket.

"On what topic should we converse?" he asks. He can never end sentences with
prepositions. He learned English in a proper age.

"Paul. You should talk to the teacher about Paul."

"Paul is not troubled."

"He's not troubled. But he's having trouble." She shows him the report card.
She never rips envelopes open, uses instead a thin knife she keeps beside the ink
blotter. Vlad has calculated that in eight years he will be the only person left in the
world who uses an ink blotter.

The report card is printed on thick stock, and lists letters that come low in the
limited alphabet of grades. No notes, no handwritten explanations. Paul is not
doing well. From the next room, he shouts at the cricket match: "Go go go go!"

The teacher's name is a smudge, a dot-matrix mistake.

• • •

At work Vlad pretends to be an accountant. He pretends to use spreadsheets and
formulas to deliver pretend assurances to a client who pretends to follow the law.
In furtive conversations at breaks he pretends to care about baseball. Pretending
this is easy: Paul cares about baseball, recites statistical rosaries, tells Dad his hopes
for the season every night when he's tucked into bed. Vlad repeats these numbers
in the break room, though he does not know if he says the right numbers in the right
context.

From his cellular telephone, outside, he calls the number on the report card,
and communicates in short sentences with someone he presumes is human.

"I would like to schedule a conference with my son's teacher." He tells them
his son's name.

"Yes, I will wait."

"Six-thirty will be acceptable."

"Thank you."

• • •

Afternoons, on weekends, he and Paul play catch in a park one block up and two
blocks over from their apartment. They live in a crowded city of towers and stone,
a city that calls itself new and thinks itself old. The people in this city have long
since learned to unsee themselves. Vlad and his son throw a baseball, catch it, and
throw it back in an empty park that, if Vlad were not by now so good at this game
of unseeing, he would describe as full: of couples wheeling strollers, of rats and
dogs and running children, strolling cops and bearded boys on roller blades.

They throw and catch the ball in this empty not-empty field. Vlad throws slow,
and Paul catches, slower, humoring his dad. Vlad sees himself through his son's
eyes: sluggish and overly skinny, a man who walks and runs and throws and
catches as if first rehearsing the movements in his mind.

Vlad does rehearse. He has practiced thousands of times in the last decade. It took him a year to slow down so a human eye could see him shift from one posture to the next. Another year to learn to drop things, to let his grip slip, to suppress the instinct to right tipped teacups before they spilled, to grab knives before they left the hands that let them fall. Five years to train himself not to look at images mortal eyes could not detect. Sometimes at night, Paul's gaze darts up from his homework to strange corners of the room, and Vlad thinks he has failed, that the boy learned this nervous tic from him and will carry it through his life like a cross.

Vlad does not like the thought of crosses.

He throws the ball, and throws it back again: a white leather sphere oscillating through a haze of unseen ghosts.

• • •

The teacher waits, beautiful, blonde, and young. She smells like bruised mint and camellias. She rests against her classroom door, tired—she wakes at four-fifteen every morning to catch a bus from Queens, so she can sit at her desk grading papers as the sun rises through steel canyons.

When he sees her, Vlad knows he should turn and leave. No good can come of this meeting. They are doomed, both of them.

Too late. He's walked the halls with steps heavy as a human's, squeaking the soles of his oxblood shoes against the tiles every few steps—a trick he learned a year back and thinks lends him an authentic air. The teacher looks up and sees him: black-haired and pale and too, too thin, wearing blue slacks and a white shirt with faint blue checks.

"You're Paul's father," she says, and smiles, damn her round white teeth. "Mister St. John."

"Bazarab," he corrects, paying close attention to his steps. Slow, as if walking through ankle-deep mud.

She turns to open the door, but stops with her hand on the knob. "I'm sorry?"

"Paul has his mother's last name. Bazarab is mine. It is strange in this country. Please call me Vlad." The nasal American "a," too, he has practiced.

"Nice to meet you, Vlad. I'm so glad you could take this time for me, and for Paul." She turns back to smile at him, and starts. Her pupils dilate a millimeter, and her heart rate spikes from a charming sixty-five beats per minute to seventy-four. Blood rises beneath the snow of her cheeks.

He stands a respectful three feet behind her. But, cursing himself, he realizes that seconds before he was halfway down the hall.

He smiles, covering his frustration, and ushers her ahead of him into the room. Her heart slows, her breath deepens: the mouse convincing itself that it mistook the tree's shadow for a hawk's. He could not have moved so fast, so silently. She must have heard his approach, and ignored it.

The room's sparsely furnished. No posters on the walls. Row upon row of desks, forty children at least could study here. Blackboard, two days unwashed, a list of students' names followed by checks in multicolored chalk. This, he likes: many schools no longer use slate.

She sits on a desk, facing him. Her legs swing.

"You have a large room."

She laughs. "Not mine. We share the rooms." Her smile is sad. "Anyway. I'm glad to see you here. Why did you call?"

"My son. My wife asked me to talk with you about him. He has trouble in school, I think. I know he is a bright boy. His mother, my wife, she wonders why his grades are not so good. I think he is a child, he will improve with time, but I do not know. So I come to ask you."

"How can I help?"

Vlad shifts from foot to foot. Outside, the night deepens. Streetlights buzz on. The room smells of dust and sweat and camellias and mint. The teacher's eyes are large and gray. She folds her lips into her mouth, bites them, and unfolds them again. Lines are growing from the corners of her mouth to the corners of her nose—the first signs of age. They surface at twenty-five or so. Vlad has studied them. He looks away from her. To see her is to know her pulse.

"What is he like in class, my son?"

"He's sweet. But he distracts easily. Sometimes he has trouble remembering a passage we've read a half hour after we've read it. In class he fidgets, and he often doesn't turn in his homework."

"I have seen him do the homework."

"Of course. I'm sorry. I'm not saying that he doesn't do it. He doesn't turn it in, though."

"Perhaps he is bored by your class." Her brow furrows, and he would kill men to clear it. "I do not mean that the class is easy. I know you have a difficult job. But perhaps he needs more attention."

"I wish I could give it to him. But any attention I give him comes from the other children in the class. We have forty. I don't have a lot of attention left to go around."

"I see." He paces more. Good to let her see him move like a human being. Good to avert his eyes.

"Have you thought about testing him for ADHD? It's a common condition."

What kind of testing? And what would the testing of his son reveal? "Could I help somehow? Review his work with him?"

She stands. "That's a great idea." The alto weight has left her voice, excitement returning after a day of weeks. "If you have time, I mean. I know it would help. He looks up to you."

Vlad laughs. Does his son admire the man, or the illusion? Or the monster, whom he has never seen? "I do not think so. But I will help if I can."

He turns from the window, and she walks toward him, holding a bright red folder. "These are his assignments for the week. If it helps, come back and I'll give you the next bunch."

She smiles.

Vlad, cold, afraid, smiles back.

• • •

"Great," his wife says when he tells her. She does not ask about the teacher, only the outcome. "Great. Thank you." She folds him in her arms, and he feels her strength. In the bathroom mirror they remind him of chess pieces, alabaster and mahogany. "I hate that building. The classrooms scare me. So many bad memories."

"Elementary school has no hold on me."

"Of course not." A quick soft peck on the cheek, and she fades from him, into their small hot bedroom. "This will help Paul, I know."

• • •

Vlad does not know. Every school night he sits with Paul in their cramped living room, bent over the coffee table, television off. Vlad drags a pencil across the paper, so slowly he feels glaciers might scour down the Hudson and carve a canyon from Manhattan by the time he finishes a single math problem. After a long division painstaking as a Tibetan monk's sand mandala he finds Paul asleep on the table beside him, cheek pooled on wood, tongue twitching pink between his lips. With a touch he wakes the boy, and once Paul stretches out and closes his eyes and shakes the sleep away (his mother's habit), they walk through the problem together, step by step. Then Paul does the next, and Vlad practices meditation, remembering cities rise and fall.

"Do you understand?" he asks.

"Dad, I get it."

Paul does not get it. The next week he brings each day's quizzes home, papers dripping blood.

"Perseverance is important," Vlad says. "In this world you must make something of yourself. It is not enough to be what you are."

"It all takes so long." The way Paul looks at Vlad when they talk makes Vlad wonder whether he has made some subtle mistake.

• • •

The following week Vlad returns to the school. Entering through swinging doors, he measures each step, slow and steady. The shoes, he remembers to squeak. The eyes, he remembers to move. The lungs, he remembers to fill and empty. So many subtle ways to be human, and so many subtle ways to be wrong.

The halls are vacant, and still smell of dust and rubber and chemical soap. He could identify the chemical, if he put his mind to it.

He cannot put his mind to anything.

The teacher's room nears. Slow, slow. He smells her, faint trace of camellias and mint. He will not betray himself again.

The door to her classroom stands ajar. Through the space, he sees only empty desks.

A man sits at her desk, bent over papers like a tuberculotic over his handkerchief. He wears a blue shirt with chalk dust on the right cuff. His nails are ragged, and a pale scalp peeks through his thin hair.

"Where is the teacher?"

The man recoils as if he's touched a live wire. His chair falls and he knocks over a cup of pens and chalk and paperclips. Some spill onto the ground. Vlad does not count them. The man swears. His heart rate jumps to ninety beats a minute. If someone would scare him this way every hour for several months he would begin to lose the paunch developing around his waist. "Damn. Oh my god. Who the hell."

"I am Mister Bazarab," he says. "What has happened to the teacher?"

"I didn't hear," says the man. "I am the teacher. A teacher." Kneeling, he scrabbles over the tiles to gather scattered pens.

"The teacher who I was to meet here. The teacher of my son. A young woman. Blonde hair. About this tall." He does not mention her smell. Most people do not find such descriptions useful.

"Oh," says the man. "Mister Bazarab." He does not pronounce the name correctly. "I'm sorry. Angela had to leave early today. Family thing. She left this for you." He dumps the gathered detritus back into the cup, and searches among piles of paperwork for a red folder like the one the teacher gave Vlad the week before. He offers Vlad the folder, and when Vlad takes it from him, the man draws his hand back fast as if burned.

"Is she well? She is not sick I hope."

"She's fine. Her father went to the hospital. I think."

"I am glad," Vlad says, and when he sees the other's confusion, he adds, "that she is well. Thank her for this, please."

Vlad does not open the folder until he is outside the school. The teacher has a generous, looped cursive hand. She thanks Vlad for working with his son. She apologizes for missing their meeting. She suggests he return next week. She promises to be here for him then.

Vlad does not examine the rest of the folder's contents until he reaches home. He reads the note three times on his walk. He tries not to smell the camellias, or the chalk, or the slight salt edge of fear. He smells them anyway.

• • •

His wife returns late from the library. While he works with Paul, she does pull-ups on the bar they sling over the bedroom doorjamb. She breathes heavily through her mouth as she rises and falls. Behind her, shadows fill their unlit bedroom.

Paul works long division. How many times does seven go into forty-three, and how much is left over? How far can you carry out the decimal? Paul's pencil breaks, and he sharpens it in the translucent bright red plastic toy his mother bought him, with pleasant curves to hide the tiny blade inside.

Vlad wants to teach Paul to sharpen his pencils with a knife, but sharpening pencils with a knife is not common these days, and anyway they'd have to collect the shaved bits of wood and graphite afterward. The old ways were harder to clean up.

"Tell me about your teacher," Vlad says.

"She's nice," Paul replies. "Three goes into eight two times, and two's left over."

"Nice," Vlad echoes.

Once his wife's exercises are done, they send Paul to bed. "I miss cricket," he says as they tuck him in. "I miss tennis and football and baseball."

"This is only for now," says Vlad's wife. "Once your work gets better, you can watch again. And play."

"Okay." The boy is not okay, but he knows what he is supposed to say.

In the kitchen, the kettle screams. They leave Paul in his dark room. Vlad's wife pours tea, disappears into their bedroom, and emerges soon after wearing flannel pajamas and her fluffy robe, hair down. She looks tired. She looks happy. Vlad cannot tell which she looks more. She sits cross-legged on the couch, tea steaming on the table beside her, and opens a book in her lap.

"You're doing it again," she says ten minutes later.

"What?"

"Not moving."

An old habit of his when idle: find a dark corner, stand statue-still, and observe. He smiles. "I am tired. I start to forget."

"Or remember," she says.

"I always remember." He sits in the love seat, at right angles to her.

"It's wonderful what you're doing with Paul."

"I want to help."

"You do."

He shifts from the love seat to the couch, and does not bother to move slow. The wind of his passage puffs in her eyes. She blinks, and nestles beside him.

"This is okay for you? I worry sometimes." Her hand's on his thigh. It rests there, strong, solid. "You've been quiet. I hope you're telling me what you need."

Need. He does not use that word much, even to himself. He needed this, ten years ago. Ten years ago she chased him, this beauty with the methodical mind, ferretted his secrets out of ancient archives and hunted him around the world. Ten years ago, he lured her to the old castle in the mountains, one last challenge. Ten years ago she shone in starlight filtered through cracks in the castle's roof. He could have killed her and hid again, as he had before. Remained a leaf blown from age to age and land to land on a wind of blood.

She'd seemed so real in the moonlight.

So he descended and spoke with her, and they found they knew one another better than anyone else. And ten years passed.

What does he need?

He leans toward her. His sharp teeth press on the inside of his gums, against the false yellowed set. He smells her blood. He smells camellias. His teeth recede. He kisses her on the forehead.

"I love you," they both say. Later he tries to remember which of them said it first.

. . .

He sees the teacher every week after that. Angela, on Thursdays. With the blonde hair and the strong heart. She tells him how Paul's work is coming. She coaches him on how to coach his son, suggests games to play, discusses concepts the class will cover in the next week. Vlad wonders, not for the first time, why he doesn't teach his son himself. But they talked, he and his wife, back when they learned she was pregnant. They are not a normal couple, and whatever else Paul must learn, he must first learn how to seem normal.

He has learned how to be so normal he cannot do basic math. So Vlad stands in the schoolroom ramrod straight, and nods when he understands Angela and asks questions when he does not. He keeps his distance.

Vlad learns things about her, from her. He learns that she lives alone. He learns that her father in the hospital is the only parent to whom she is close, her mother having left them both in Angela's childhood, run off with a college friend, leaving behind a half-drunk vodka bottle and a sorry note. He learns that she has tight-wound nerves like a small bird's, that she looks up at every sound of footsteps in the hall. That she does not sleep enough.

He does not need to learn her scent. That, he knows already.

• • •

One night he follows her home.

This is a mistake.

She leaves the building well after sunset and walks to the bus; she rides one bus straight home. So he takes to the roofs, and chases the bus.

A game, he tells himself. Humans hunt these days, in the woods, in the back country, and they do not eat the meat they kill. Fisherman catch fish to throw them back. And this night run is no more dangerous to him than fishing to an angler. He leaves his oxfords on the schoolhouse rooftop and runs barefoot over buildings and along bridge wires, swift and soft. Even if someone beneath looked up, what is he? Wisp of cloud, shiver of a remembered nightmare, bird spreading wings for flight. A shadow among shadows.

A game, he tells himself, and lies. He only learns he's lying later, though, after she emerges from the bus and he tracks her three blocks to her studio apartment and she drops her keys on the stoop and kneels quick and tense as a spooked rabbit to retrieve them, after she enters her apartment and he delays, debates, and finally retreats across the river to the schoolhouse where he dons his oxfords and inspects himself in a deli window and pats his hair into place and brushes dust off his slacks and jacket—only learns it when his wife asks him why there's dust on his collar and he shakes his head and says something about a construction site. His round teeth he returns to their cup of coffee, and he lies naked on their bed, curled around her like a vine. His wife smells of sweat and woman and dark woods, and smelling her reminds him of another smell. Teeth peek through his gums, and his wife twists pleased and tired beside him, and he lies there lying, and relives the last time he killed.

• • •

The first step taken, the second follows, and the third faster. As when he taught Paul to ride a bicycle: easier to keep balance when moving.

He's no longer stiff in their weekly meetings. He jokes about the old country and lets his accent show. Her laughter relieves the lines on her face.

"You and your wife both work," she says. "I know tutoring Paul takes time. Could his grandparents help at all?"

"His mother's family is far away," Vlad says. "My parents are both dead."

"I'm sorry."

His father died in a Turkish assault when he was fourteen; his mother died of one of the many small illnesses people died from back then. "It was sudden, and hard," he says, and they don't speak more of that. He recognizes the brief flash of sympathy in her eyes.

He follows her home again that night, hoping to see something that will turn him aside. She may visit friends, or call on an old paramour, or her father in the hospital. She may have a boyfriend or girlfriend. But she changes little. She stops at the drug store to buy toothpaste, bottled water, and sanitary napkins. She fumbles the keys at her door but does not drop them this time.

He leaves.

Paul, that night, is too tired to study. Vlad promises to help him more tomorrow. Paul frowns at the promise. Frowns don't yet sit well on his face. He's too young. Vlad tells him so, and lifts him upside down, and he shrieks laughter as Vlad carries him back to the bedroom.

Work is a dream. He is losing the knack of normalcy. Numbers dance to his command. He walks among cubicles clothed in purpose, and where once the white-collared workers forgot him as he passed, now they fall silent and stare in his wake. Management offers him a promotion for no reason, which he turns down. Silences between Vlad and Angela grow tense. He apologizes, and she says there is no need for an apology.

He and his wife make love twice that week. Ravenous, she pins him to the bed, and feasts.

Paul seems cautious in the mornings, silent between mouthfuls of cereal. At evening catch, Vlad almost forgets, almost hurls the ball up and out, over the park, over the city, into the ocean.

He can't go on like this. Woken, power suffuses him. He slips into old paths of being, into ways he trained himself to forget. One evening on his home commute, he catches crows flocking above him on brownstone rooftops. Black beady eyes wait for his command.

This is no way to be a father. No way to be a man.

But Vlad was a monster before he was a man.

Again and again he follows her, as the heat of early autumn cools. The year will die. Show me some danger, he prays. Show me some reason I cannot close my fingers and seize you. But she is alone in the world, and sad.

Paul's grades slip. Vlad apologizes to Angela. He has been distracted.

"It's okay," she says. "It happens. Don't blame yourself."

He does not blame her. But this must end.

• • •

He makes his wife breakfast on the last morning. Bacon. Eggs, scrambled hard, with cheese. Orange juice, squeezed fresh. The squeezing takes time, but not so much for Vlad. He wakes early to cook, and moves at his own pace—fast. Fat pops and slithers in the pan. Eggs bubble. He ticks off seconds while he waits for the bacon to fry, for the eggs to congeal after. By the time his wife steps out of the shower, breakfast's ready and the kitchen is clean. He makes Paul's lunch, because it's his turn. He cannot make amends.

His wife sucks the strip of bacon before she bites. "Delicious." She hums happily, hugs him around the waist. "So good. Isn't your dad a good cook?"

Paul laughs. Vlad thinks it is a knowing laugh, because he is afraid.

"It's not Mother's Day," his wife says. "That's in May."

"I love you," Vlad answers. Paul makes a face like a punchinello mask.

Crows follow him to work, hopping sideways along the roofs. When he reaches midtown they perch on streetlamps and traffic lights. Red, yellow, and green reflect in their eyes in turn. The *Times* reports power outages in the suburbs last night from unexpected vicious wind. Asylums and hospitals brim with madmen, raving, eating bugs. Vlad is over-empty, a great mounting void, and the world rushes to fill him.

He breaks a keyboard that day from typing too hard. Drives his pinkie finger through the enter key into his desk, embedding a sliver of plastic in his skin. He pulls the plastic out and the wound heals. I.T. replaces the keyboard.

Vlad finishes his work by three and sits in his cubicle till sunset. Thunderclouds cluster overhead by the time he leaves the building. Heat lightning flickers on his walk uptown. Fear shines at each flash from the eyes of the peasants he passes. Peasants: another word he has not thought or used in years.

All this will be over soon, he tells himself. And back to normal.

Whatever normal is.

He meets her in the classroom, though they do not talk long. The time for talking's past. She is all he remembered: sunlight and marble, camellia and mint. The ideal prey. Blood throbs through small veins in her fingers. He feels it when they shake hands. He smells its waves, rising and falling.

"I must thank you," he says, once she's gone over Paul's assignments for the next week. "For your dedication. You have given Paul so much. I appreciate your work."

"It's nothing." She may think he cannot hear her exhaustion, or else she trusts him and does not care. "I'm glad to help. If every father cared as much as you do, we'd be in a better world."

"I am fortunate," he says, "to be in a position to care."

He follows her from the school, as before. After sunset the crows stop hiding. In masses they descend on the city and croak prophecy in its alleys. Currents of crows rush down Broadway, so thick pedestrians mistake them for a cloud, their wing-beats for the rumble of traffic or a train. Bats emerge from their lairs, and rats writhe on subway steps singing rat songs. Grandmothers remember their grandmothers' whispered stories, and call children to urge them to stay inside.

Better this way, Vlad thinks as he follows Angela across the bridge, down the dirty deserted street from her stop to her apartment. She does not notice him. She notices nothing. The rats, the crows, the bats, all keep away from her. They know Vlad's purpose tonight, and will not interfere.

She's young, her life still a web of dream, her love just touched by sadness. This world holds only pain for her. Better, surely, to leave before that pain bloomed, before tenderness roughed into a callous.

His gums itch. He slides the false teeth from his mouth, places them in a Ziploc bag, closes the seal, and slips the bag into his jacket pocket. Crouched atop the roof of the building across from Angela's, he sees her shuffle down the street. The weight of her shoulder bag makes her limp.

His teeth, his real teeth, emerge, myriad and sharp. He tastes their tips and edges with his tongue.

She opens the door, climbs the steps. He follows her heartbeat up four floors, five, to the small studio.

He leaps across the street, lands soft as shadow on Angela's roof beside the skylight. Below, a door opens and light wakes. Though she's drawn curtains across the glass, there are gaps, and he sees her through them. She sags back against the door to close it, lets her bag clatter to the ground and leans into the scuffed dark wood, eyes closed.

Her apartment looks a mess because it's small: a stack of milk crates turned to bookshelves, overflowing with paperbacks and used textbooks. A small lacquered pine-board dresser in stages of advanced decay, its side crisscrossed with bumper stickers bearing logos of bands Vlad does not recognize. A couch that slides out to form a bed, separated from the kitchenette by a narrow coffee table. Sheets piled in a hamper beside the couch-bed, dirty clothes in another hamper, dishes in the sink.

She opens her eyes, and steps out of the circle formed by the shoulder strap of her fallen bag. Two steps to the fridge, from which she draws a beer. She opens the cap with a fob on her keychain, tosses the cap in the recycling, and takes a long drink. Three steps from fridge around the table to the couch, where she sits, takes another drink, then swears, "Mother*fuck*er," first two syllables drawn out and low, the third a high clear peal like those little bells priests used to ring in the litany. She lurches back to her feet, retrieves her bag, sits again on couch and pulls from the bag a thick sheaf of papers and a red pen and proceeds to grade.

Vlad waits. Not now, certainly. Not as she wades through work. You take your prey in joy: insert yourself into perfection, sharp as a needle's tip. When she entered the room, he might have done it then. But the moment's passed.

She grades, finishes her beer, gets another. After a while, she returns the papers to their folder, and the folder to her bag. From the milk-crate bookshelves, she retrieves a bulky laptop, plugs it in, and turns on a television show about young people living in the city, who all have bigger apartments than hers. Once in a while, she laughs, and after she laughs, she drinks.

He watches her watching. He can only permit himself this once, so it must be perfect. He tries to see the moment in his mind. Does she lie back in her bed, smiling? Does she spy him through the curtains, and climb on a chair to open the skylight and let him in? Does she scream and run? Does she call his name? Do they embrace? Does he seize her about the neck and drag her toward him while she claws ineffectually at his eyes and cheeks until her strength gives out?

She closes the laptop, dumps the dregs of her beer in the sink, tosses the empty into the recycling, walks into the bathroom, closes the door. The toilet flushes, the water runs, and he hears her floss and brush her teeth, gargle and spit into the sink.

Do it. The perfect moment won't come. There's no such thing.

The doorknob turns.

What is he waiting for? He wants her to see him, know him, understand him, fear him, love him at the last. He wants her to chase him around the world, wants a moonlit showdown in a dark castle.

He wants to be her monster. To transform her life in its ending.

The door opens. She emerges, wearing threadbare blue pajamas. Four steps back to the couch, which she slides out into a bed. She spreads sheets over the bed, a comforter on top of them, and wriggles under the comforter. Hair halos her head on the dark pillow.

Now.

She can reach the light switch from her bed. The room goes dark save for the blinking lights of coffee maker and charging cell phone and laptop. He can still see her staring at the ceiling. She sighs.

He stands and turns to leave.

Moonlight glints off glass ten blocks away.

· · ·

His wife has almost broken down the rifle by the time he reaches her—nine seconds. She's kept in practice. The sniper scope is stowed already; as he arrives, she's unscrewing the barrel. She must have heard him coming, but she waits for him to speak first.

She hasn't changed from the library. Khaki pants, a cardigan, comfortable shoes. Her hair up, covered by a dark cap. She wears no jewels but for his ring and her watch.

"I'm sorry," he says, first.

"I'll say."

"How did you know?"

"Dust on your collar. Late nights."

"I mean, how did you know it would be now?"

"I got dive-bombed by crows on the sidewalk this morning. One of the work-study kids came in high, babbling about the prince of darkness. You're not as subtle as you used to be."

"Well. I'm out of practice."

She looks up at him. He realizes he's smiling, and with his own teeth. He stops.

"Don't."

"I'm sorry."

"You said that already." Finished with the rifle, she returns it to the case, and closes the zipper, and stands. She's shorter than he is, broader through the shoulders. "What made you stop?"

"She wasn't you."

"Cheek."

"No."

"So what do we do now?"

"I don't know. I thought I was strong enough to be normal. But these are me." He bares his teeth at her. "Not these." From his pocket he draws the false teeth, and holds them out, wrapped in plastic, in his palm. Closes his fingers. Plastic cracks, crumbles. He presses it to powder, and drops bag and powder both. "Might as well kill me now."

"I won't."

"I'm a monster."

"You're just more literal than most." She looks away from him, raises her knuckle to her lip. Looks back.

"You deserve a good man. A normal man."

"I went looking for you." She doesn't shout, but something in her voice makes him retreat a step, makes his heart thrum and almost beat.

"I miss." Those two words sound naked. He struggles to finish the sentence. "I miss when we could be dangerous to one another."

"You think you're the only one who does? You think the PTA meetings and the ask your mothers and the how's your families at work, you think that stuff doesn't get to me? Think I don't wonder how I became this person?"

"It's not that simple. If I lose control, people die. Look at tonight."

"You stopped. And if you screw up." She nudges the rifle case with her toe. "There's always that."

"Paul needs a normal family. We agreed."

"He needs a father more. One who's not too scared of himself to be there."

He stops himself from shouting something he will regret. Closes his lips, and his eyes, and thinks for a long while, as the wind blows over their rooftop. His eyes hurt. "He needs a mother, too," he says.

"Yes. He does."

"I screwed up tonight."

"You did. But I think we can work on this. Together. How about you?"

"Sarah," he says.

She looks into his eyes. They embrace, once, and part. She kneels to lift the rifle case.

"Here," he says. "Let me get that for you."

• • •

The next week, Friday, he plays catch with Paul in the park. They're the only ones there save the ghosts: it's cold, but Paul's young, and while Vlad can feel the cold, it doesn't bother him. Dead trees overhead, skeletal fingers raking sky. Leaves spin in little whirlwinds. The sky's blue and empty, sun already sunk behind the buildings.

Vlad unbuttons his coat, lets it fall. Strips off his sweater, balls it on top of the coat. Stands in his shirtsleeves, cradles the football with his long fingers. Tightens his grip. Does not burst the ball, only feels the air within resist his fingers' pressure.

Paul steps back, holds up his hands.

Vlad shakes his head. "Go deeper."

He runs, crumbling dry leaves and breaking hidden sticks.

"Deeper," Vlad calls, and waves him on.

"Here?" Vlad's never thrown the ball this far.

"More."

Paul stands near the edge of the park. "That's all there is!"

"Okay," Vlad says. "Okay. Are you ready?"

"Yes!"

His throws are well rehearsed. Wind up slowly, and toss soft. He beat them into his bones.

He forgets all that.

Black currents weave through the wind. A crow calls from treetops. He stands, a statue of ice.

He throws the ball as hard as he can.

A loud crack echoes through the park. Ghosts scatter, dive for cover. The ball breaks the air, and its passage leaves a vacuum trail. Windows rattle and car alarms whoop. Vlad wasn't aiming for his son. He didn't want to hurt him. He just wanted to throw.

Vlad's eyes are faster even than his hands, and sharp. So he sees Paul blink, in surprise more than fear. He sees Paul understand. He sees Paul smile.

And he sees Paul blur sideways and catch the ball.

They stare at one another across the park. The ball hisses in Paul's hands, deflates: it broke in the catching. Wind rolls leaves between them.

Later, neither can remember who laughed first.

· · ·

They talk for hours after that. Chase one another around the park, so fast they seem only colors on the wind. High-pitched child's screams of joy, and Vlad's own voice, deep, guttural. Long after the sky turns black and the stars don't come out, they return home, clothes grass-stained, hair tangled with sticks and leaves. Paul does his homework, fast, and they watch cricket until after bedtime.

Sarah waits in the living room when he leaves Paul sleeping. She grabs his arms and squeezes, hard enough to bruise, and pulls him into her kiss.

He kisses her back with his teeth.

MAX GLADSTONE has been thrown from a horse in Mongolia and nominated twice for the John W. Campbell Best New Writer Award. His Craft Sequence, beginning with *Three Parts Dead*, is available from Tor Books and Tor.com Publishing. Max's game *Choice of the Deathless* was nominated for a XYZZY Award, and *Full Fathom Five* was nominated for the Lambda Award. His short fiction has appeared on *Tor.com* and in *Uncanny Magazine*. His most recent project is the globe-trotting urban fantasy serial *Bookburners*, available in ebook and audio from Serial Box, and in print from Saga Press.

The Last Banquet of Temporal Confections

Tina Connolly

A young food taster to the Traitor King must make a difficult choice in this story of pastries, magic, and revenge. *Edited by Melissa Frain.*

Saffron takes her customary place at the little round table on the dais of the Traitor King. Duke Michal, Regent to the Throne is his official title, but the hand-drawn postered sheets, the words whispered in back alleys all nickname him the same. She smiles warmly at the assembled guests, standing poised and waiting by their chairs, ready for the confections and amuse-bouches that have been a mainstay of the high table for the last year.

Saffron has been Confection Taster all that time, her husband, Danny, Head Pastry Chef. Their warm smiles have been perfected as the Traitor King's power grows, inch by inch, as those who object to his grasp fail and fall, as the printers are vanished, as the daughters disappear from their homes. The little prince still sleeps in his nursery—but for how long? That is the question on everyone's mind in the last year. Not a question uttered, but a question that stays poised on the tongue, and does not fall.

The Traitor King takes his place. He looks sternly around the table, watching to see if anyone dares sit or talk or breathe before him. Then he breaks into a jovial smile, and everyone exhales, and there is careful laughter: the Duke is in a good mood tonight. There will be candies and conversations, alliances formed and favors exchanged, perhaps a juggler hung for dropping the pins, but who minds the jugglers?

Saffron minds. She minds very much.

The first course! bids the Duke, and around the table the white-coated servants set down the gilded plates, each bearing the first bite-sized course, showcasing Danny's skill. An identical plate is set next to Saffron, the Duke's own plate, this one bearing a pastry twice as large as the others, so the Duke shall not lose any of the delight of his food to caution.

The Duke barely flicks his eyes Saffron's direction. She knows what to do, and, smiling, she cracks the thin toast in two with her fine silver fork, and takes her bite.

. . .

Rosemary Crostini of Delightfully Misspent Youth

Saffron knows this moment instantly. The angled sun falls in clean lines on the bakery floor. *Daily Bread* is the name on the hand-carved sign of the shop, for it is an ordinary bakery still. A younger Danny stands at the counter, just turning with flour-dusted chin to notice her. She has come here so often with the rosemary crostini that she has what the lords and ladies do not: an instant of double-memory, of twinned lives, as she breathes, and lets herself go, and tumbles five years into the past.

Her sister Rosie pushes her forward, hisses, "Your turn," in teasing tones, and Danny's and Saffron's eyes lock.

Saffron swallows. Two girls on a rare free afternoon, on a mission to see who can charm the most treats out of willing young shopkeepers and clerks. Rosie is the younger by a year but the older in daring. Her funny, loyal sister has transformed this morning into a different girl, all curls and honeyed tones, a girl on a mission. So far she has acquired: Item (1) length of green velvet ribbon, long enough to tie back her gold-brown hair. Item (1) scrap of lace, to finish the wrists of the gloves she is making for Saffron. Surely Saffron could manage a chocolate, a tartlet, a bun?

And yet here she is, with the sinking feeling that she *does not know how to flirt.*

The kind-eyed young man—for now she no longer knows his name, she has the faint feeling that she has forgotten, there is something teasing at the back of her mind—well, he leans on the scarred wood counter and asks again if he can help.

"A . . . a rye bun, please," she says at random.

"Just one then?" he says with amusement, and he reaches for it. The young man, so quiet on other occasions Saffron has come in, seems rather more self-possessed today, but who would not be at a girl stammering "bun"?

"Yes. No." She can't remember anything Rosie did to charm that ribbon off of the shopkeeper; all her wits have fled. "I mean, I may have forgotten my coins?"

"It's a fine day when a beautiful girl comes into my grandfather's bakery with no money, but only wants one poor little rye bun," he says. "Hardly seems worthwhile to charge her." She flushes; he understands the game and is teasing her.

Rosie elbows her; she should make her move. Say something pert in response; acquire the prize. Her coin is her flirtation, her smiles; she sees now that she and Rosie are paying after all, in a different kind.

But instead, behind the baker she sees a small waif, silhouetted in the back door to the shop. Saffron nods at the baker, points over his shoulder. "Do you have company?"

He turns, drops his teasing manner. "Jacky," he says affectionately, and scoops several buns and a long thin loaf off of a different shelf. The small creature holds open his bag hopefully, and the day-old bread is placed inside. Jacky pulls out a single copper cent and gravely hands it to the baker, who as gravely accepts it. "My best to your mother," the baker says, as the waif scampers off.

The young man turns back to the counter, and the kindness in his eyes is replaced by a different kind of warmth for Saffron, one that is gentle and interested, and possibly could be the same kind of warmth as for that little boy someday if she lets it, if she begins as she means to go on.

Saffron puts the coins on the counter for the rye bun. "Will you have coffee with me?" she says, clearly and calmly and forthrightly.

The flour-dusted young man takes her money and hands her the bun. Rosie snickers in the background, but the baker's smiles are all for her. "Aye, and more."

. . .

Saffron returns to herself, the delight of the memory still sharp on her tongue. Her eyes clear, she smiles warmly at the crowd. "This has always been one of my favorite recipes of Danny's," she tells them, and her gilded plate is passed to the Duke. He does not look at her as he picks up the second bite of golden-crusted toast, redolent with rosemary and crystals of sea salt. Danny was an excellent baker long before he started experimenting with the rose-thyme plant that causes the memories, and this crostini is no exception.

Around the table, the noble sycophants follow the Duke's example, and Saffron watches in amusement at seeing the whole table go slack, their eyes staring off into nothing as they *remember*.

At the edges of the room the white-coated servants, the red-coated guards go on alert. Saffron knows, for he has told her, that the commander of the guard dislikes these little interludes. But the Duke will have his perks, and further—she is told—it amuses the Duke to watch the lords and ladies squirm. Not all the confections Danny makes evoke pleasant memories, and during their time in the Duke's palace, he has been encouraged to experiment. An invitation to a Temporal Confections dinner is equally coveted and feared, but never declined.

Around the table, the diners slowly shake off the residue of the memory, come back to themselves with foolish smiles on their faces. Good, she thinks. Danny is outdoing himself tonight. Is that a hint of things to come? They are kept apart, in the castle, and she wishes they had some way to communicate, other than through memory. A memory can be directed, a little, if the eater has practice. Saffron knows what she wants to see with the Rosemary Crostini, and she knows Danny knows she will see it. It was a gift to her this night, that first flush of meeting, that moment trapped in time like a fly in amber.

A salad course of watercress and arugula is served, and wineglasses filled with a dry white. The Duke's regular taster is given his salad, a fresh fork. She is a perpetually frightened-looking girl with honey-colored hair, but she is no milkmaid from the countryside. She is eighth in line to the throne, the granddaughter of kind Lord Searle, that same Lord Searle who would make a remarkably good regent— if he had not been accused of treachery by the Duke and disappeared into the maze of dungeons under the castle.

The girl retains many of her daytime privileges, but at dinner she sits at the Traitor King's side, yet another hostage for others' behavior. She tastes the requisite bite of the peppery greens, and then the plate is relayed to the Duke, and he picks up his own silver fork. Around the table the others join in, and Saffron and the girl fold their hands in their laps, and wait.

Fennel Flatbread of Sunlit Days Gone By

The sun is sparkling on the snow on the day Danny gets his first temporal pastry to work.

It is a Seventhday, and the shop is closed. They have been married for a year now; Danny's grandfather has passed on, and the little bakery is all Danny's. A small inheritance has allowed him to experiment; a small inheritance and a smaller glass bottle of dried rose-thyme that Danny's grandfather gathered as a youth in the distant High Reaches. Despite its name, rose-thyme does not taste precisely like either; or, more correctly, it tastes like many more things than just those two flavors. It is a changeable plant; the method of preparation is key to bringing out a particular aromatic strain. More importantly, the method of preparation is key to evoking certain visions. As a child, Danny's grandfather and his chums would chew on the flowers, which, when eaten plain, give brief flashes of déjà vu. He also told Danny that those who had once lived in the High Reaches had actual recipes that they swore could evoke glimpses of longer-ago memories, and indeed, at winter solstice every year, there was a certain currant cake made with the rose-thyme that would make everyone remember the previous solstice's currant cake, and back and back, cementing the continuity of a long line of years.

All that was long ago, and Danny's grandfather's people were mostly scattered and gone, driven forth by the last king's brother, whose dukedom was in the High Reaches, at the border of the country. He and his son, Michal, were reputed to be cold and cruel. Certainly they had destroyed Danny's ancestral home. But the current King was kind, if perhaps a bit soft, and he had not taken steps to control his distant cousin any more than his father had controlled his younger brother.

All this runs through Saffron's head while she stands at the back of the shop, slowly kneading a mass of dough that will rise overnight for tomorrow's buns. Watching the sky slowly darken, the snow clouds massing once more. Why is she thinking of the old king? But perhaps it is because of the clock-tower bells. They have been ringing all morning, and she has not heard them ring like that since she was a child. Their slow pealing is an eerie counterpoint to the silent snow, the warm, empty shop. A cheerful whistle floats out occasionally from the other room of the bakery, punctuated with the sharp smell of dried fennel being crushed with mortar and pestle. Danny is experimenting yet again.

Someone bangs on the back door, and she opens it to a snowdrift. Little Jacky, older now. He comes in, stamps his feet.

"The King is dead," he says. "Did you know?"

Of course, she thinks, *the bells*, and behind him the flurries have started again, the spangles of sun replaced by fat dots of white.

"Ma says they'll make old Searle the regent. He's a soft touch, that's for sure. Gives out coppers to kids anytime you see him in the street. Hey, maybe he'll give out silvers if he's got a whole treasury."

Saffron shakes her head. She saw the King speak, not two months ago. He was grieving for his wife's death in childbirth, and the city grieved along with him. But . . . "He was so healthy."

"Bloody flux," Jacky says with certainty. "Got my cousin last month." He holds out his palm. "I got *five* coppers for you this time. Been working for my uncle. What can I get with that?"

She ruffles his snow-dusted hair and hands over a hearty round loaf that didn't sell, and several currant buns, only a little burnt.

He shouts his thanks and hurries off, running through the falling snow. His bit of red scarf flaps behind him; he shrinks smaller and smaller in the vanishing white. The King is dead, the poor little prince an infant. There will be change. Change is hard to weather. Change makes everyone skint, and keep their coins in their pockets.

But the people will still need bread, she thinks, as she watches the diagonal drifts. And there has been peace for so long. How can there not still be peace? Power will transfer, the reins will change hands, but she and Danny will have their bakery, their dough, their bread. They will focus on the rising of the yeast and the pounding of the dough and if they have to cut out currants for a time, well, plain buns sell nearly as well.

The clock-tower bells ring all day and all night for the end of the King, the ending of the old era. She stands for some time, looking at the falling snow, until behind her Danny shouts, "I have it, I have it, Saffron, I have it."

She turns to see the exult on his face, and he scoops her up and swings her around. He has been parceling out the last few sprigs of rose-thyme for months, trying recipe after recipe, running right through the last of the dried leaves.

Now he hands her a round circle of flatbread on a plate. It looks like any of Danny's homey flatbreads, but smaller. A few bites only, and one bite is missing.

She knows already that there is something special about this moment. It is the sort of memory you recall for years after. A moment when the world changed around you. A moment etched with both beauty and loss, a moment that you leave behind as you move away from it, a moment you can never reach again.

Except, with what Danny has now made, perhaps you can.

Saffron takes the first bite ever of a temporal confections creation and falls back further still.

The world shifts around her. She is seven, and her mother is still living. The sun drifts golden onto a dew-spattered morning, and she shakes a magnolia tree onto Rosie, watching her sister laugh as the droplets spray—

• • •

"Another masterpiece," says Saffron, and the same white-gloved servant passes her plate to the Duke. She shivers, deep inside, for she is not lying. Danny has been working on that linked-memory trick for years. She has seen the Fennel Flatbread creation memory before, but she has never seen that magnolia-tree memory within it. Usually the scene ends the moment Danny hands her the flatbread and she takes a bite.

Around the table, eager hands reach for the plates, barely able to wait for the Duke. A Fennel Flatbread of Sunlit Days Gone By sounds delightful; not like any of the Duke's nastier tricks. They all could use a moment of nostalgia, of respite from their grown-up cares. They eat, and Saffron watches them, still wondering how Danny triggered the second memory. Perhaps it was in the mashed fava-bean dip served alongside, perhaps it is something in the flatbread itself. He has been working on reductions, on methods of increasing the intensity of the herbs. But of course, he has not been able to share anything with her since coming to the palace. And truly, it is better if she does not know. She has never been very good at dissembling, though she has been practicing in this last year. Readying the skill for the moment she needs it.

The words rise as the memories dissolve; the voices filled with emotion, with wonder.

—I was climbing a tree; it was cut down long ago

—I saw my mum, I haven't seen her in years

—My boy was young again; he ran to me

The Duke scoffs. Whatever he has seen, it has made little impression. "Puerile fantasies," he says, and swivels to eye Saffron. "I hope the next course will be more suitable to an . . . advanced palate."

"Danny's skill at arranging a balance of flavor and memory is unsurpassed," Saffron says evenly. If she wished to gently push the Duke, she would remind him of previous banquets; the one that ended with the nobles in tears; the one that ended with them overcome with patriotism, swearing oaths to the Traitor King. But she does not want to disturb the fragile balance. Danny is building to something, she is more and more certain. Which means that she is to taste, and be ready. Timing is critical in baking, and here so tonight.

Another course is served; a delicate shellfish bisque, but the nobles barely notice what they eat, lost in recounting, reliving, those long-ago moments, made real again for an instant. If the Duke were more observant, he would notice how even the sweetest memory has an edge, for it is something that is lost and will not come again. But perhaps Danny is lulling him, downplaying his skill with the more complicated memories; the ones that linger like the mold on cheese, the yeast in the sourdough, the bitter in the wine.

The bisque is finished—Saffron sometimes feels guilty that the main cooks no longer receive the attention they ought—and the servers return with the next pastry course.

Ah, thinks Saffron, who recognizes it immediately. Here we go into the darker turn.

She could almost be angry at Danny, but she knows whatever he plans tonight has a purpose. The Duke will feast on her tears, but so be it.

The silver fork cuts through the pastry and she takes a bite.

Rose-Pepper Shortbread of Sweetness Lost

She and Danny have been married for three years now. The bakery has picked up, now that they are offering a few *unusual* items right alongside the daily bread. There is still no baby, but they are happy with their bakery and their work, and they do not mind—too much. Danny bakes and she assists, Danny invents and she assists. But she does not mind that either, for she has found her own calling at the front of the shop, and it is matching people with the right pastry.

There is an art to knowing what people need. Oh, they would all take the flatbread if they could, but do they *need* it?

At first they do not advertise that there is anything special about some of the pastries in their shop. Danny is still working out the strengths and flavors. The first few pastries and confections come with barely a hint, a flash. A memory easily dismissed as natural. The sort of thing that keeps people returning to a bakery where they feel so content, so rejuvenated. So understood. With the increased income, Saffron arranges the shop and sews new curtains and freshens the paint. She hires Rosie to work alongside them, and that gives Danny more time to develop the recipes, strengthen the flavors. Rosie is a natural third point to their triangle; her open, gregarious warmth is a fire they kindle themselves by. She helps them turn the bakery from a shop to a *café*; she encourages customers not to just buy their regular bread and go, but to sit and linger, try that extra morsel of unusual pastry and feel at peace.

This morning, Rosie is laughing with a regular about something that happened last night. Rosie has changed the last two years; her curls are the same, but she has swapped her ribbons and laces for steel-toed boots and the cry of *Resistance*.

Saffron understands that the new Regent Michal, at first so sympathetic, so distraught about the sudden treachery of Lord Searle, has slowly been closing his velvet glove around the city. She understands that there have been rumors of people taken. Rumors of Bad Things. But she only has one sister, and rumors are not here and now, they are not the shop and bread and cheese and chairs.

She pulls Rosie behind the counter, by the trays of day-old regular bread, and says as much.

Rosie's chin sets. It is not the first time they've had this conversation. "I have to do *something*," she tells Saffron. She drops her voice. "You know the little print shop, down the street?"

The printer. An outspoken, angry man. Yes.

"You know they *took* him, Saffy. Tortured him. Just for printing the truth about what's been happening to the girls. The disappearances—"

"Who says, though?" says Saffron, who can't believe in things happening to people she knows.

Rosie gives her a look. "His body was all covered up at the hanging. So you wouldn't see what had been done to him. I saw—"

"You *went* there?"

"I can't stay here, safe in a *bakery*," says Rosie, voice rising. "I have to *try*."

"We are doing good work here," Saffron says, helplessly.

Rosie shakes her head. "This is not the only good work there is to be done. Can't you see that?"

They are close to understanding each other, but then Saffron lets slip: "Can't someone *else* do that work?" and that makes Rosie shake her head, and stomp away, off to heft some flour bags around, take out her frustration.

Yes, Rosie has changed. Or no, not changed, perhaps, but grown up. Matured into something that was there all along.

She can't just stay in her bakery, Rosie says. But why not? Why can't there be room for someone who takes care of people, one person at a time? Who feeds them bread for their bodies and confections for their souls and does good work on a single, individual level? Saffron is heavy with resentment, she is prickly with the wish to prove Rosie wrong.

That is when the enforcer comes in.

He wears the emblem of the palace; the *R* of the Regency, the eagle of the Duke. He saunters up and says politely, "We have reports of miscreants disturbing the peace last night."

"Everything is just fine here," Saffron says.

"And your employees?" he says. "Where were they?"

"We have but one," she says, "and she is a law-abiding citizen." Her heart is thumping inside and he can surely see her pallor. *What did Rosie do?* For that is her first thought, that Rosie and her group of troublemaker friends must have done *something*. This man would not be here for *nothing*. Around the store she sees the customers who have finished their pastries quietly slipping away, their peace at an end.

The enforcer's eyes follow her gaze; he looks languidly around the room like a bored cat. "This is a sort of opium den, is it?" he says, gesturing at a man's slack face.

"Merely a bakery," Saffron says.

"Please produce your license," he says, more politely yet, and she understands how to do this part, this part is rote. She gets it from the back room, a few steps away through that curtain. Her eyes sweep the room for Danny—surely Danny will know what to do—but he is out on a buying errand, and she sees only her sister, crouched and silent, hiding behind a barrel of flour.

Numbly she returns, shows the man the card that should make him leave.

He barely looks at it, lets it fall to the counter. "Please produce your sister," he says, and this is the point she cannot forgive herself for, even as it happens.

I must not tell him where she is, she thinks. But she is too used to being law-abiding, and she has never tried to become good at deception. Her mouth hangs open for too long, her eyes flick to the wrong side. "I have not seen her today," she stammers at last, and the enforcer just laughs at her.

He pushes past to the back, and he pulls her sister out. Rosie reams him with a pan, and then he casually punches her in the stomach, so hard she doubles over, and he drags her out, even as Saffron runs after them, armed with nothing. He throws her into a carriage—pushes Saffron down into the muck of the street—and then they are gone, and Saffron is weeping.

The scene jumps forward—another linked memory. Danny finding her in the streets, near the castle. Saffron ran after the carriage until she couldn't run anymore, then she plodded after it till she reached its entrance to the gates, and when they would not let her in, she sunk down and stayed there. She doesn't deserve to leave the muck, because she failed to save Rosie.

Another jump forward, because the hanging does not happen until an entire week later. The body is fully clothed, down to long sleeves and long gloves that Rosie was not wearing when she left. Saffron is left to imagine everything the cloth is hiding. Drawn iron wire fences the hanging square; it cuts red lines into Saffron's palms. Around her, the scent of lilacs blooms thick and sweet. It is spring.

. . .

Saffron comes back to herself in the banquet room, and her eyes are wet. She sits up straighter, calmly blots her eyes with her napkin. "The Rose-Pepper Shortbread of Sweetness Lost will show you someone you miss," she says to the table. "All such sweet memories are tinged with sorrow."

She nods to the servitor to take her plate to the Duke, smiles warmly at the table to put them at ease. "You will find notes of citrus and almond in the tasting," she says. "We find it is one of the most popular pastries among the elderly."

"I certainly hope you are not insinuating anything," says the Duke, and then he laughs, and then they all do.

They take their bites and Saffron breathes out, concentrating on what Danny has done. Three jumps this time. Usually she sees just the bakery, or just the carriage, or just the hanging. Yet somehow he has strung memories together, finding a way to let the whole terrible story unfold.

If she had seen a fourth memory, it might well have been the aftermath. For it is a day not long after that when Danny starts experimenting on what he will call the bitter pastries. Not bitter in flavor, necessarily. Certainly deeper in flavor, more profound notes in the tasting. Memories that are both sweet and sour. Memories with a purpose.

The first one has a rose flavor, in honor of her sister.

Rosie is not the only person Saffron has lost in her life—her parents have both passed away—but she only ever sees Rosie when she eats the shortbread. She suspects that its creation is too inextricably bound up with her sister for her to ever see another. For awhile, there were many Seventhdays that she dedicated to nothing but the rose-pepper shortbread and her grief.

Many months later, when she is capable of feeling anything more than numb, Saffron takes her place again at the front of the shop. She understands then that this recipe is what she was lacking to give the customers. Not all customers can be helped with a fennel-bright flatbread, a happy moment. There are many who need a more profound searching into their past.

Around her now, the nobles return from their journey, their faces a dizzying array of sadness, happiness, regret. It is a complex pastry.

The next food course is served—some sort of little trussed-up birds, but Saffron barely notices. She is elsewhere, considering what Danny has shown her, considering what is next to come.

She is not surprised when the silver bell rings and out comes the fourth of Danny's creations tonight, another bitter pastry. It is not one that Danny has yet showcased at the castle. Only now does it make its appearance, and her heart quickens, her lips pucker, her mouth salivates for the taste.

Lemon Tart of Profound Regret

It is an ordinary day in the bakery, and Saffron looks around at her regulars with satisfaction. Everything they have worked for, coming to fruition. She is closer to contentment, closer to peace than she has been in over a year. The loss of her sister will never leave her, but it is a dull ache these days that only sometimes turns sharp, breaks her down in the middle of the bakery, hand on a bag of flour. The bakery has found a new normal, and there are customers to help.

The regulars, and she knows them by their orders.

Apple Turnover of Happier Times, aka the bent old woman in the moth-eaten furs. Saffron saves the curtained alcove for her, and for the fifteen minutes it takes to eat that pastry, she's lost in a haze of *remembering*. Children, thinks Danny, but Saffron thinks grandchildren. Either way, she lost them during the brief, bloody uprising last spring, they agree on that.

Lavender Macaron of Long-Ago Flirtations, aka the angular man who still owns two silk scarves, despite the ever-increasing privations, despite the shabbiness of his old suit. He rotates the scarves day by day; green-stripe, violet dots. He takes tea with his macaron, and his lips curl in pleasure while he *remembers*. Obviously it's a lover, but Danny is sure the lover disappeared in some dramatic way; attacking the palace, or daring to print anti-propaganda sheets. To have something worth *remembering*, you have to live first, says Danny, and then he looks sadly at his flour-dusted arms, knowing that he only runs a bakery.

Lemon Tart of Profound Regret, that's the sad one. She's young, too young to have so much Profound Regret in her life. But she comes every day at ten, testing her sorrow. Profound Regret shows you the biggest mistake you made, the one you brood over, and there are two kinds of people who buy it. The ones that make Saffron's heart gladden are the ones who buy it infrequently. They descend into the despair of knowing what they did, just as fresh as the day it happened.

Then they go off and change, because of what they saw.

Saffron knows, because they come back to tell her. Not right at first. But they come back, several months later, and buy the tart again. And this time they see something else. Something less terrible. That's how they know they've moved on.

Those are the ones Danny says the whole shop is worth it for. He'd do it all again. Some days it seems like you're doing so little, but when he helps one of those people, his whole life is justified. On days that are really tough—the stories told about the Duke are worse than usual, the taxes are due, the Profound Regrets are too deep—Danny eats one of his Honey Chocolates of Well-Deserved Pride. He says it always shows him those moments, the ones when he helped people.

Their current Lemon Tart comes day after day. She's not moving on. Danny thinks Saffron should intentionally mix up her order, give her a Honey Chocolate or an Apple Turnover and see if that helps her mindset change. Saffron is considering the merits of this when *he* comes in.

He's supposed to be incognito but Saffron knows him instantly. She's seen enough Resistance flyers to know how the Duke disguises himself when he wants to move around the city. His red hair is slicked back under a hooded cloak.

She tries not to start, but her body betrays her. She flushes, angry and scared all at once, and she knows he sees it.

"I have a mind to try one of your Honey Chocolates," he says smoothly.

Her fingers are shaking as she reaches for it. This man of all men does not deserve to relive his best moments. She has thought for so long of *Resistance*. She could reach for the Mint Chocolate of Deep Despair, at least. After he tastes it, he will know that mint is not honey, and he will punish her somehow—execute her? Torture her, like her sister? But first he will suffer. Oh, he will suffer.

But it would not just be Saffron who suffers. It would be Danny. It would be the part-time employees. It would be the customers, for she is not naive enough to think that he would not seek his wrath on all who saw his humiliation. He must squash any hint of rebellion.

Or you are afraid, says a smaller voice still.

Saffron reaches for the chocolates and his eyes are heavy on hers; it seems he knows her thoughts. She knows why he comes unannounced. So she cannot slip him poison, not unless she has planned for this moment and made an entire tray of poisoned chocolates, and she has not.

"I am most delighted to sample what I have *asked for*," he says, and there is a world of meaning in that tongue.

Her eyes close—her fingers close on the wrapper around the chocolate, bring it up. She puts it on the plate with nerveless fingers.

It is the Honey Chocolate.

Her voice shakes as she tells him the price. Her moment has come, her moment has gone.

The Duke takes the chocolate, sits down at a table in the corner. A young man leans casually against the wall, fiddling with his belt knife. He doesn't fool Saffron. The Duke goes off into a haze of *remembering* and for eight heart-stopping minutes she cleans the counter and tends to the customers as the Duke looks off in the distance and the young man watches the two of them, his eyes flicking back and forth, watching to see if the bakery worker has lied to the Duke.

She regrets her choice already. She does not need a Lemon Tart to know that.

She regrets it even more when, two nights later, the Duke's guards take Danny out of their bed in the middle of the night.

She is left to make her own way to the castle and offer herself up as sacrifice. A willing check on any rebellious tendencies my Danny might have. To sell herself to the Traitor King.

A common food-taster.

• • •

Saffron blinks back tears. She has not seen Danny in so long. The Duke does not trust them together. He has taken Saffron's measure—correctly assessed her as ineffectual, not a threat. She is plain, ordinary, and the Duke is not so foolish as to spend the coin of her in the wrong place. She is much more valuable alive and whole and as a check on Danny. So the Duke left her free rein of the upstairs servants' quarters—as long as she does not enter the second kitchen. The second kitchen was turned over to Danny; his tools and herbs brought from the bakery, and he is confined to it. The only way they can communicate is through the confections themselves. There is always at least one confection during a meal that he knows will call up a sweet memory of the two of them—something she can feast upon for a week, and *remember*.

But this banquet has been leading her step by step forward, as if in a story. Both she and Danny know the purpose of the Lemon Tart too well. She has been reminded of how she failed to act, which must mean that he is prompting her that she will need to act. But in what way?

Perhaps it is poison, she thinks. Perhaps he is telling her that this is the only way to strike against the Duke. A slow-acting poison; something she will recognize, but must pretend is fine.

But she can't imagine Danny choosing that method, even if she ordered him to. And at this point, she *would* order him to. She stiffens her spine, watches the nobles eating their own lemon tarts. She has spent a year practicing dissembling. Her courage and her warm smiles will not fail her now. She is ready for whatever comes.

Or perhaps there is something else he is reminding her of. Those small jumps that the pastries have been taking. The Lemon Tart memory skipping ahead, to Danny's disappearance, to her own application at the castle. Those are not part of the original memory. They are *linked* somehow, just as she saw with the crostini, with the shortbread. Not enough that anyone would notice, because no one understands the subtleties of how the pastries work, not like she and Danny. Were those extra memories there to warn her of something specific?

But maybe that is not it, either. Sometimes she thinks she is going mad. Danny is long gone, and these pastries are normal pastries done by a normal pastry chef, their memories some collective dream that she convinces the nobles to believe in, once a week.

The cheese plate comes and goes while she feels more and more adrift, lost in her own memories, wishful thinking, and nonsense. These banquets will go on for eternity, and she will eat lemon tarts of regret forever, and nothing will change.

For now the after-dinner liqueurs are being passed around, the meal is over, and there has been no dramatic change tonight. She is disappointed; she wants the Duke gone so badly that she almost feels she will run at him herself, with the silver fork. See what damage she can do before they kill her. Danny was always the patient one, the one performing the endless tweaking of recipes in search of the correct formula, the one able to wait until the exact moment. Cooking is all about timing.

Ah, but wait. There is one more plate. Her heart quickens—

But she can tell at a glance it is a chocolate, a dark-chocolate-shelled truffle with an amber-colored drop at the top.

The Honey Chocolate of Well-Deserved Pride.

It makes her sick to think of the Duke eating this confection. Who knows what sort of disgusting thing the Duke will find pride in tonight?

She knows, for Danny has served this chocolate to the Duke before, that there is no outside morality imposed upon the choice of memory. Saffron always, invariably, sees one of the times she helped somebody. Danny sees those as well, or he sees moments of creation, breakthroughs of hard work and study.

The Duke saw a moment he cleverly destroyed a family. He told the table about it, in salivating detail, and the quiet bliss the nobles had found in the chocolates evaporated. Why would Danny grant him such?

The extra-large chocolate is set down before Saffron and she cuts it in two with her silver fork. It is in the last second before she takes her bite that she notices the color of the honey drop on top is a little deeper than usual. Molasses, perhaps, and it is her single clue that this is something different than what she is expecting.

Bitter Chocolate of Agony Observed

She falls, tumbling, faster and faster. It is a moment she has never seen before. She is five, and Rosie is four, and Rosie has been stung by a hornet. In real life she barely remembers this, but she is here now, and Rosie is wailing. She holds up her arm to show Saffron, and Saffron sees the welt. And then—she *feels* the welt. In seeing the pain of her sister, it triggers her own sense of pain, and her arm stings and swells with it. Rosie runs off to find their mother, and Saffron falls—

She is eleven, and her best friend has taken a header off of the chicken coop. Busted her nose but good. Saffron sees it, and her own face *swells* in response, painful, aching, broken. She helps her friend home, and at every step she feels the pain of the broken nose. Until the friend is turned over to her mother, and Saffron runs home, the pain dissolving, the memory released—

She is in the bakery, and the enforcer punches Rosie, and Saffron staggers back with the pain of it as they drag Rosie away—

She is at the hanging, and the body falls—

It is last year, and Danny has sliced right through the pad of his thumb with a bread knife. Skin wounds bleed like billy-o, and Saffron carefully stitches it up for him, feeling the pounding of the blood in her own thumb, feeling the piercing tugging of the thread pulling through. Through the roar of the pain she hears Danny musing: I wonder if I could do something with pain.

Why would you want to? says past Saffron.

You wouldn't think a Lemon Tart of Regret would be useful, and yet . . . says Danny. There might be something there.

Saffron laughs. Only you would slice open your thumb and wonder how to turn it into a new pastry. Go for it. But leave me out of this one.

Do you know how much I love you? says Danny.

And she is falling away from that memory, falling back to the table, even as her last words echo: I love you too. More than anything. . . .

• • •

The entire table is looking at her. She has been gone a few minutes longer than usual. Hopefully not so long as to give the game away. Her face, she feels now, is still wincing from the pain of the sliced thumb. She consciously relaxes her jaw, loosens her face, breathes.

She is supposed to entice the Duke to eat this chocolate. And how exactly is she going to do that, with everything she just saw plainly visible on her face to the whole table?

She waves at the servitor to take the other half of her chocolate to the Duke. She does not yet trust herself to speak.

The Duke looks at the half-eaten chocolate, then back at her. "For a moment, I thought your husband had decided he was willing to poison you," he says. "But now I see he is merely willing to torture you."

That gives Saffron the thread to walk down. "His skill with confections is the most important thing to him," she says, and she keeps her head high, not minding that her lip trembles. The Duke understands this. He will see himself in Danny.

"So explain to me why I, and my table, should go ahead and try this particular confection," he says. "After seeing its most . . . interesting results."

She looks evenly into his face. There is only one answer that will work with the Duke, and this is truth.

At least, part of the truth.

"You will see pain," she says. "Not your own pain, but another's. A moment of exquisite pain that someone else is suffering."

The Duke's face relaxes, just barely, and he laughs. "No wonder you were so conflicted. My little weaklings." He gestures around to the table. "Go on, then. Eat."

Her heart sinks, watching as one by one the reluctant guests pick up their chocolates, their faces frightened or stoic by turns. If the Duke does not eat his bite quickly, then this is for nothing. The nobles will spill to him everything they *felt*, and there will be no more chance to do this again, and she and Danny will be strung up for daring to oppose the Traitor King.

The memories for some of them will be long this time. She cannot help that. One lucky woman, younger than the rest, is shaking off the trance already. "I saw my brother break his arm," she says, shuddering, and her hand unconsciously goes to her own arm.

Saffron breathes, willing the woman not to say any more. This is confirmation to the Duke that what she said is true. You see someone else's pain. The chocolate is not poison. His face relaxes a tiny bit more, he is weakening. He wants to try it.

"You can aim for the right memory if you give it a nudge," Saffron says, and this is true in general of their work, if irrelevant in the case of this particular chocolate where you will see *everything*. "Wouldn't you like to see . . . what you did to my sister?" Her eyes meet his and she is breathing fast, she can't help it, and he is feasting on every moment of her pain. If this works . . .

The Duke's eyes never leave hers as he raises the chocolate and places it on his tongue.

. . .

The linked memories keep the Duke under for three entire weeks, writhing in a *remembering* coma, first on his chair, then moved to his bed, then moved to the dungeon. For three weeks is enough time for someone to find the food-taster's grandfather, and let him out, and for the whole chain of command to be rearranged. The Duke is declared incapacitated and relieved of his regency, and kind Lord Searle takes over in his place.

When the Duke finally does wake, the pain and malnutrition have left him wasted away to nothing. His eyes fall on a glass cake stand placed beside his filthy, flea-infested mattress, on the stones of the dungeon floor. Inside is a single chocolate, identical to the one he was served at his final dinner.

If he were stronger, one might call his laugh the laugh of someone who finally sees a worthy adversary at last.

The chocolate, of course, was made by a baker, a simple baker who refused the honor of being Regent Searle's head pastry chef, and asked only to return home to his two loves: his work and his wife.

The chocolate was placed there by Saffron, who stayed to watch the Duke writhe for twenty minutes before she slipped silently away, knowing full well that that pain will account on her soul; that she will revisit this spot if she ever eats that particular chocolate herself again.

The Duke is never leaving this dungeon. And the only real question is, how does he wish to go?

Trembling hands knock the glass dome to the dungeon floor. It shatters, an echo that remains in the Duke's ears long after the shards have come to rest.

The Duke takes his last bite of food ever on this earth, and *remembers*, as he falls.

TINA CONNOLLY is the author of the Ironskin trilogy from Tor Books, and the Seriously Wicked series from Tor Teen. Her books have been nominated for the Nebula and Andre Norton Awards. Her stories have appeared in *Women Destroy Science Fiction!*, *Lightspeed*, *Tor.com*, *Strange Horizons*, *Beneath Ceaseless Skies*, and many more, and are collected in *On the Eyeball Floor and Other Stories* from Fairwood Press. Her narrations have featured in audiobooks and podcasts, including *PodCastle*, *PseudoPod*, *Beneath Ceaseless Skies*, John Joseph Adams' The Apocalypse Triptych, and more. She is one of the cohosts of *Escape Pod* and runs the Parsec Award–winning flash fiction podcast *Toasted Cake*.

The End of the End
of Everything

Dale Bailey

A horror story about a long-married couple invited by an old friend to an exclusive art-ists' colony. The inhabitants of the colony indulge in suicide parties as the world teeters on the brink of extinction. *Edited by Ellen Datlow.*

The last time Ben and Lois Devine saw Veronica Glass, the noted mutilation artist, was at a suicide party in Cerulean Cliffs, an artist's colony far beyond their means. That they happened to be there at all was a simple matter of chance. Stan Miles, for whom Ben had twice served as best man, had invited them to his beach house to see things through with his new wife, MacKenzie, and her nine-year-old daughter, Cecilia. Though the Devines had no great enthusiasm for the new wife—Stan had traded up, was how Lois put it—they still loved Stan and had resolved to put the best face on the thing. Besides, the prospect of watching ruin engulf the world among such glittering company was, for Ben at least, irresistible. He made his living on the college circuit as a poet, albeit a minor one, so when Stan said they would fit right in, his statement was not entirely without truth.

They drove down on a Sunday, to the muted strains of a Mozart piano concerto on the surround sound. Ruin had lately devoured most of the city and it en-croached on either side of the abandoned interstate: derelict cars rusting back to the elements, skeletal trees stark against a gray horizon, an ashen, baked-looking landscape, though no fire had burned there. In some places the road was all but impassable. They made poor time. It was late when they finally pulled into the beach house's weedy gravel driveway and climbed out, stretching.

This was a still-living place. They could hear the distant sigh of breakers be-yond the house, an enormous edifice of stacked stone with single-story wings sweeping back to either side of the driveway. The sharp tang of the ocean leavened the air. Gulls screamed in the distance, and it was summer and it was evening, and in the cool dusk the declining sun made red splashes on the narrow windows of the house.

"I thought you'd never get here," Stan bellowed from the porch as they re-trieved their luggage. "Come up here and let me give you a kiss, you two!" Stan—bearded, stout, hirsute as a bear—was as good as his promise. He delivered to each of them a scratchy, wet smooch square on the lips, pounded Ben's back, and relieved Lois of her suitcase with one blunt-fingered hand. Ghostlike in the gloom, and surprisingly graceful for such a large man, he swept them inside on a tide of loose flowing white silk, his shirt unbuttoned at the neck to reveal corkscrews of gray hair.

He dumped their baggage in an untidy pile just inside the door, and ushered them into a blazing three-story glass atrium. It leaned rakishly over the dark, heaving water, more sensed than seen, and Ben, as always, felt a brief wave of vertigo, a premonition that the whole house might any moment slide over the cliff and plummet to the rocky white beach below. Ceiling fans whispered far above them. Two Oscars for production design stood on the mantle, over a fireplace big enough to roast a boar.

Stan collapsed into a low white sofa, and waved them into adjoining seats. "So the last days are upon us," he announced jovially. "I'm glad you've come."

"We're glad to be here," Ben said.

"Any word from Abby?" Stan asked.

Abby was Stan's ex-wife—Ben's first stint as best man—and just hearing her name sent a spasm through Ben's heart. When the dust from the divorce settled, Stan had gotten the beach house. Abby had ended up with the house in the city. But the last of the city was succumbing to ruin even as they spoke. A gust of sorrow shook Ben. He didn't like to think of Abby.

"Ruined," Lois said. "She's ruined."

"Ah, I knew it. I'm sorry." Stan sighed. "It's just a matter of time, isn't it?" Stan shook his head. "I am glad you decided to come. Really. I've missed you both."

"And how's MacKenzie?" Lois asked.

"She'll be down any minute. She and Cecy are upstairs getting ready for the party."

"Party?"

"Every night there's a party. You'll enjoy it, you'll see."

A moment later, MacKenzie—that was the only name she had, or admitted to—descended the backless risers that curved down from an upstairs gallery. She was a lithe blonde, high breasted, her face as pale and cool and unexpressive as a marble bust. She wore the same shimmering silks as her husband; and nine-year-old Cecy, trailing behind her, lovely beyond her years, wore them as well.

Ben got to his feet.

Lois pulled her shawl tight around her shoulders as she stood. "MacKenzie," she said, "it's been too long."

"It's so good to see you both again," MacKenzie said.

She brushed glossy lips against Ben's cheek.

Lois submitted to a brief embrace. Afterward, she knelt to draw Cecy into her arms. "How are you, dear?" she asked, and Ben, though he despised cliché, uttered the first thing that came into his head.

"My how you've grown," he said.

. . .

Yet his life had in some respects been a cliché. His poetry, while not without merit, had broken no new ground—though perhaps there was no new ground to break, as he sometimes told audiences at the small colleges that sought his services. Poetry was an exhausted art, readers a dying breed in a dying age, and he'd never broken through anyway. His verse was the stifled prosody of the little magazine, his life the incestuous circuit of the MFA program, and he had occasionally succumbed to the vices such an existence proffered: the passing infidelity, the weakness for drink and drug.

His marriage had weathered storms of its own. If Ben did not entirely approve of Stan's decision—he had loved Abby, and missed her—he could understand the allure of novelty, and he was not immune to the appeal of MacKenzie's beauty. Perhaps this accounted for the tension in their suite as he and Lois dressed for the party, and when they departed, descending the cliff-side steps to the beach, sensing her discontent, Ben reached out to take her hand.

Down here, that salty tang was stronger and a cool wind poured in off the water. The sea gleamed like the rippling hide of some living behemoth in the moonlight. The sand seemed to glow beneath their feet. Everything was precious, lovely in its impermanence, for what was not now imperiled? And an image came to Ben of the gray towers in the once-bustling city, of men and women in their millions but blackened effigies, shedding ashen debris in the unforgiving wind.

Yet it was nothing to brood upon, this slow doom that the earth or fate or the God Ben did not believe in had inflicted upon them. Not now anyway, not with another set of precipitous steps to ascend or another house of glass set back a hundred yards from the brink of cliff-side annihilation, great windows printing flickering panels of light upon the still-succulent grass, and pouring forth the dissonant, tremulous notes then in fashion. Inside, in the darkness, the intersecting beams of digital projectors cast violent images upon every available surface— upon walls and windows and the faces of the people who danced and drank there. "This is Bruno Vinnizi's place—you know, the director," Stan shouted over the music, passing Ben a drink, but he needn't have said anything at all. The movies spoke for themselves, half a dozen stylized art-house sensations that Ben had seen in the last decade and a half.

Somehow, in the chaos, Ben lost Lois—he caught glimpses of her now and then through the crowd—and found himself talking drunkenly to Vinnizi himself. A blisteringly bloody gunfight unfolded across Vinnizi's fashionably stubbled cheeks. "I have been making movies about ruin for years," Vinnizi pronounced. "Even before there was a ruin, no?" and Ben saw how true it was. "So you are a poet," Vinnizi said, and Ben answered something, he didn't know what, and then, without transition, he found himself in the bathroom with Gabrielle Abbruzzese, the sonic sculptor, chewing jagged crystals of prime. After that the party took on a hectic, impressionistic quality. A kind of wild exhilaration seized him. He saw Lois across the room, sipping wine and talking to the front man of some slam band or other—Ben had seen him on television—and stumbled once again into Stan's ursine embrace. "Having fun yet?" the big man yelled—and then, abruptly, Ben was squiring Cecy giggling across the dance floor.

Finally, exhausted, he reeled outside to piss. He unzipped, sighed, and let flow a long arc. A husky, female voice, deeply amused, said, "Something wrong with the bathrooms?"

Ben stepped back in dismay, tucking himself away.

A tall angular woman with razor-edged cheekbones and a cap of close-shorn blonde hair stood in the shadows. She was smoking a joint. He could smell its faint sweetish scent. When she passed it to him he felt the effects of the prime recede a little.

"I know you," he said.

"Do you?"

"You're the artist—"

She took a hit off the joint. Exhaling, she said, "This place is lousy with artists."

"No"—slurring his words—"the humiliation artist. Victoria—Victoria—"

In a stray reflection from the house, a car screeched across one of those exquisite cheekbones.

"Victoria Glass," he announced, but she was already gone.

The party climaxed at dawn, when the rising sun revealed how closely ruin had encroached upon the house, and Vinnizi hurled himself over the cliff onto the rocks below.

It was accounted a triumph by all.

• • •

They slept late and joined Stan and MacKenzie on the verandah for drinks at eleven. Piano and saxophone burbled over the sound system. Stan paced, sucking down mimosas like water. MacKenzie reclined in an Adirondack chair, her long legs flung out before her. She sipped her drink, watching Cecy at some solitary game she'd improvised with a half-deflated soccer ball.

"Did you have a good time at the party?" Mackenzie asked.

"Of course they had a good time," Stan said, clapping Ben on the shoulder, and Ben supposed he had, but the night itself came back to him only in flashes: blue smoke adrift in the intersecting beams of the projectors; the taste of prime sour on his tongue; the tall angular woman who'd caught him cock in hand outside the house. Her name came to him, he'd seen a piece on her in *The New Yorker*—Veronica Glass, the mutilation artist—and he felt mortified for reasons that he could only vaguely recall. All this and more: the headachy regret that comes after any bacchanal; the image of Vinnizi leaping off the cliff onto the jagged rocks below. No sight for a little girl, he thought, and he recalled swinging Cecy drunkenly across the dance floor.

Lois must have been thinking the same thing. "Do you really want Cecy to see things like that?" she asked MacKenzie, and Ben could sense her struggling to reserve judgment, or anyway the appearance of judgment.

MacKenzie waved a languid hand.

"What does it matter anymore?" Stan said, and Ben thought of Abby, built like a fireplug, with none of MacKenzie's lissome beauty. Abby wouldn't have approved, but then she wouldn't have approved of MacKenzie either, even if the other woman hadn't stolen away her husband on the set of a failed summer blockbuster where her blank mien actually played to her advantage. Skill was a handicap in such a role; MacKenzie'd been little more than eye candy on the arm of the star, an aging action hero long since ruined himself.

A wind off the ocean lifted Ben's hair. He leaned over to peer through the telescope mounted on the railing. Near at hand, white-capped breakers rolled toward
shore. Farther out—he adjusted the focus—the waves gave way to the cracked,
black mirror of dead water. Moldering fish turned their ashen bellies to the sky.

"How long, you think?" he asked Stan.

"Not long now."

"It doesn't matter. No child should have to see a man throw himself over a
cliff," Lois said.

"She's not your child," MacKenzie responded drily, and Ben straightened up in
time to see Lois shoot him a look of disgust—with MacKenzie and with Stan for
marrying her, and with Ben most of all, for standing beside the groom and collaborating in the disposal of Abby like a used tissue, and this after more than twenty
years of marriage.

But what was he to do? He and Stan had been friends since their freshman year
at Columbia, when they'd been thrown together by the vagaries of admissions
counselors on the basis of a vapid form with questions like: "Do you sleep late or
get up early?" He slept late and so did Stan. And they'd had the same taste for girls
(as many as possible, as often as possible, and no need to be choosy) and for drugs
(ditto). It had been a match made in heaven. Sometimes Ben wondered why Lois had
ever been attracted to him in the first place. He supposed she'd wanted to save him.
The same was probably true of Abby and Stan. But old habits die hard and in his
peripatetic days, reading indifferent poems to indifferent audiences, Ben had fallen
into his former ways: banging nubile English majors and chewing prime. At home
one man, on the road another: Jekyll and Hyde. Last night Hyde had been in the
ascension. And why not? Nero fiddled as Rome burned, but what else could he do,
break out impotent buckets against the conflagration?

All this in the space of an instant.

"Here," he said to Lois, "why don't you have a look?"

"I've seen all I want to see," she said, but she strode over and gazed through the
telescope all the same. She'd thickened in middle age, and Ben found himself
studying MacKenzie, suddenly envious of Stan, who'd had the courage to throw it
all aside. A sudden hunger for MacKenzie's raw sexuality—she seemed to glow
with lascivious potential—possessed him. What had Stan said, when he'd called to
tell Ben that he and Abby were done? "She's a fucking tiger in the sack, Ben."

Stan shoved another drink into his hand—they'd moved to chilled vodka, it
seemed—and Ben felt his headache retreat before the onslaught of the alcohol.

MacKenzie lit a cigarette. He could smell its acrid bite.

"Mom!"

"It's not like I'm going to die of lung cancer, sweetie," MacKenzie called, and
Ben thought, no, none of us is going to die of lung cancer.

"You mind if I have one of those?" he said.

MacKenzie held the pack silently over her shoulder. Ben shook one out and
struck it alight, inhaled deeply. Smoke drifted in twin blue streams through his
nostrils. He'd smoked in college, but Lois had convinced him to give it up; it had
become another vice of the road, indulged in frenetic after-reading parties. Playing

the role of the dissolute poet, he used to think. That's what they wanted to see. Yet he wondered who he really was—if the persona hadn't become the person or if the persona hadn't been the person all along.

Lois looked up from the telescope. "It's terrifying," she said.

Stan shrugged. "It just is, that's all."

"It's terrifying all the same."

She set her unfinished mimosa on the railing. "I'm going in to make a sandwich. Anyone else want one?"

"Sure," Stan said.

And Ben, "Why not?"

She didn't bother asking MacKenzie, who, by the look of her, hadn't had a sandwich—or maybe any food—in years, if ever. The door clapped shut behind her.

Ben ground out his cigarette in MacKenzie's ashtray. "I've always wondered," he said. "What's your real name?

Stan laughed without humor and downed his drink.

"MacKenzie," MacKenzie said.

"No. I mean the name you were born with. I thought you'd adopted MacKenzie as a stage name. You know, like Bono, or Madonna."

"My name is MacKenzie," she said without looking at him.

Stan laughed again.

"Her name is Melissa Baranski," he said.

"My name is MacKenzie," her voice flat, without emotion.

Wishing he'd never asked, Ben descended to the lawn. "Throw me the ball," he called to Cecy, and for a while they played together by some rules Ben could never quite decipher. "Stand here," Cecy would say, or "Throw me the ball," and between sips from his drink, he would stand there or toss her the ball.

"I win," she announced suddenly.

"Sure, you win," he said, ruffling her hair.

They climbed the steps to the verandah together. By then Lois had returned with a tray of sandwiches for everyone.

• • •

Later, he and Lois made love in their suite. Before he came, Ben closed his eyes. A blur of faces passed through his mind: the features of an especially memorable undergraduate, and then MacKenzie's affectless face, and the woman on the lawn last of all, Veronica Glass, the mutilation artist, kneeling before him to take him into her mouth. He felt something break and release inside him. He cried out and drew Lois to him, whispering "I love you, I love you," uncertain whom he was speaking to, or why, and afterward, as she pillowed her head on his shoulder, that headachy sense of regret once again swept through him.

Later, they walked by the sea, waves foaming far down the beach. At high tide, the water would hurl its force against the stony cliff itself, undercutting it in a million timeless surges. It leaned over them like doom, unveiling the faint blue tinge that gave the colony its name.

He took Lois's hand and drew her into an embrace. "It's beautiful here, isn't it?" he said, as if by the force of language itself he could redeem the fallen world. But Ben had long since lost his faith in poetry. Words were but paltry things, frail hedges against the night. Ruin would consume them.

And it was to ruin that they came at last. They stopped at its edge, a ragged frontier where the beach turned as black and barren as burned-over soil, baked into a thousand jagged cracks, and the surf grew still, swallowed up by the same ashen surface. Digging their toes in the sand, they stood in the shadow of Bruno Vinnizi's ruined beach stair and gazed out across the devastation. Vinnizi's shattered corpse lay among the rocks, arms outflung, one charred hand lifted in mute supplication to the sky. As they stood there, the wind picked up and his outstretched fingers crumbled into dust and blew away, and the sea, where it still washed the shore, retreated down the naked shingles of the world.

• • •

As ruin spread, Cerulean Cliffs retreated. On the second night, Ben stood on the verandah and counted lights like a strand of Christmas bulbs strung along the coastline; in the days that followed they began to wink out. One afternoon, he and Stan hiked inland to the edge of the destruction: half a mile down the gravel driveway, and two more miles after that, along the narrow two-lane state road until it intersected with the expressway. In the distance, a soaring overpass had given way, its support pylons jutting from the earth like broken teeth. The pavement Ben and Lois had driven in upon was cracked and heaved, as if it had endured the ice of a thousand years. Businesses that had been thriving mere days ago had decayed into rubble. The arms of corroding gas pumps snaked across blistered asphalt. The roof of the Bar-B-Cue Diner had buckled, and the shards of its plate glass windows threw back their sooty reflections.

"Abby and I celebrated our fourteenth anniversary there," Stan said.

"We used to go there every time we came down," Ben said. "Best barbecue I ever had."

"It was shitty barbeque, and you know it. The company made it great."

Laughing, Stan unclipped a flask of bourbon from his belt. He took a long pull and handed it to Ben. The liquor suffused Ben with warmth, and he recalled his first liquor drunk—he'd been with a girl, he couldn't remember her name, only that she'd held his head as he puked into the toilet at some high school revel. After that, he'd vowed never to drink whiskey again. You had to learn to love your vices.

As they turned and started back, he snorted, thinking of Cecy and her soccer ball and her mysterious games upon the grass.

"What?" Stan said.

"Cecilia."

"She's a good kid."

"The best," Ben said, taking another swig of whiskey. He handed the flask back to Stan. They passed it back and forth as they walked. The blasted land fell behind them. The day brightened. The sky arced over them, fathomless and blue. Ben took out a cigarette and lit it and blew a stream of smoke into the clear air.

"You ever wish you'd had children?" he asked.

"I have Cecilia."

"You know what I mean."

"I had a career."

"What about Abby?"

"What about her?" Stan said.

"Did she want children?"

Stan was silent for a time.

"Ah, it was my fault," he said at last.

"What?"

"You know. The whole goddamn mess." He took a slug of whiskey. "We had a miscarriage once. I never told you. After that—" He shrugged. "She never forgave me, you know."

"For a miscarriage? Stan, she couldn't have blamed you—"

"Not that. Cecilia, I mean. She could forgive the infidelity. God knows she had in the past. She never forgave me Cecilia." He looked up. "She always thought that was driving the whole thing: MacKenzie had the child she could never have."

"And was it?"

"No." Stan laughed. "It was lust, that's all. Simple lust." He shook his head in dismal self-regard. "I envy you, you know. Holding things together the way you have."

They turned into the driveway. Ben kicked a stone. A wind came down to comb the weeds. Somewhere in the trees a bird burst into song. The faint sound of the ocean came to him. Envy was a blade that cut two ways.

"What about you?" Stan said.

"What about me?"

"Kids?"

Ben finished his cigarette.

"It never crossed my mind," he lied. "I wish it had."

They'd reached the house by then. Ben went to his suite and lay down to sleep off the whiskey before the party. When he woke, the sun was red in his window, and Lois was reading in the chair by the side of the bed. They walked out onto the balcony and gazed at the ocean. The dead water had crept closer. He'd lost track of time. It all blurred together, the liquor and the prime and the multi-hued tabs of ecstasy spilled helter-skelter across the butcher block of a financier who'd filled her house with priceless paintings. Her taste had run toward the baroque—Bosch, Goya—and over the course of the party she'd slashed them to ribbons one by one. At dawn she'd walked out onto the lawn, doused herself with gasoline, and set herself on fire.

"Did you know Abby had a miscarriage?" Ben asked.

"Of course I did," Lois said, and they stood there in silence until the first faint stars broke out in the dark void where ruin had not yet eaten up the sky.

• • •

The parties were Ben's solace and his consolation: the photographer whose prints adorned the walls of her house, the painter whose canvases did not, the novelist who'd won a Pulitzer. Ben had met her once before, a lean scarecrow of a woman with a thatch of pink hair and a heart-shaped pinkie ring on her left hand: a brief introduction by a friend of a friend at a Book Expo party. "What are you working on?" he'd asked as she paused. "I subscribe to the tea-kettle theory of art," she'd responded. "Open the valve and the energy escapes."

Ben had nodded, taking a long drink of his gin and tonic. He leaned against the wall, trying to pretend he wasn't alone. He'd come for the free drinks—he always did—but he knew that nothing was ever free; you paid the price in the coin of humiliation. And that reminded him of his fleeting encounter with Veronica Glass, the "humiliation artist," as he'd called her. He'd seen her flitting through the crowds occasionally, tall and gamine with her cap of blonde hair, but mostly she lingered in corners. If it bothered her to be alone, Ben could not discern it. She observed everything with an air of bemused fascination, the expression of an anthropologist faced with a curious custom she had not seen before.

Once or twice, they'd even talked briefly.

"Hello, again," he'd said, as he squeezed past her in the scrum around the bar, and briefly he felt her taut body glide against his sagging middle-aged one.

Another time, she appeared ghostlike at his side, and handed him a joint. "I've had my eye on you," she said.

"You have?" he said.

"Are you surprised?"

"A little."

She smiled, remote and amused, the way you'd smile at a child. "Outsiders interest me."

"What do you mean?"

"In Cerulean Cliffs, you're either a rich artist, or you're just plain rich."

Ben thought of the financier who'd torched herself on her lawn, staggering about in screaming agony until she collapsed and the flames consumed her.

"You don't seem to be either," Veronica Glass said.

"I'm a poet," he said.

"But not a successful one."

"I make a living. That's more than most poets can say."

"But is it a good living? Does anyone know your name?"

"It offers me a certain freedom."

The freedom to write mediocre verse, he thought.

"Is that enough?" she said, "I mean for you," and of course it wasn't. He coveted the trappings of fame: the *New Yorker* profile, the Oscars on Stan's mantel, the trophy wives. In the night, as Lois slept at his side, he thought of Stan, stout and hairy, running his thick fingers down MacKenzie's long body.

He couldn't say these things to Veronica Glass, couldn't say them to anyone at all if you got to the heart of the matter, so he settled for, "It's what I have."

And then the lights blinked twice. Veronica Glass—that was how Ben thought of her—laughed and pinched off the joint. She handed it to him as the novelist announced that there would be an hour of readings—twenty minutes of her novel in progress (so much for the tea-kettle theory, Ben thought), followed by a young woman much admired for her jewel-like short stories, and a poet last of all. The poet, when he took the mic looked the part. He had a head of dark hair that swept back to his collarbones in perfectly sculpted waves, a voice that rang out across the crowd, a National Book Award. He was twenty-seven.

The lights came up.

"Do you envy him?" Veronica Glass asked.

"A little."

"Poetry makes nothing happen," she said.

"Does mutilation?"

"Art pour l'art."

"Art moves me," he said.

And again she asked, "Is that enough?"

"Tell me," he said, "where do you get the subjects for your art?"

"They volunteer. I have more volunteers than I can possibly use." She gave him an appraising look. "Are you interested?"

Before he could answer, he saw Lois across the room.

"Is that your wife?"

"Yes."

"What does she do?"

"She was an accountant in the unruined age," he did not say. He did not say that she read good books—books that moved her and said something true about the world—and that she loved him and forgave him his trespasses, which were many, and that that was enough. He merely smiled at her through the thump of music, the crush on the dance floor, the smell of sweat in the air. Veronica Glass lifted a hand to her in some kind of ambiguous greeting, but she was gone before Lois could wend her way to them through the crowd.

"That was Veronica Glass, the mutilation artist," he said. "You've read about her."

"I know who it was," she said.

Ben wanted to ask her to dance but they were too old for the bass pounding from the speakers; they'd lost their way. Sometime in the deepest trench of the night, a cry arose from the master bathroom. The music died. They all trooped up to look at the novelist. She was dead in the blood-splashed tub, naked, her arms flung out, slit from wrist to elbow as neatly as a pair of whitened gills. Her sagging breasts seemed deflated somehow, empty of life. Her pale face was at peace.

MacKenzie laughed hysterically, her knuckles to her mouth, her eyes bright with an almost sexual excitement. Cecy began to cry and Lois took her into her arms and hurried her home. Ben lingered as the party wound down. He watched the sun rise with Stan and MacKenzie. Afterward, they looked out over the wretched ruin that had already begun to engulf the writer's grounds. It crept toward them, turning the soil to ash. Flowers withered to dust. The guesthouse sagged. They descended to the beach and walked home.

Cecy was sleeping. Lois had waited up.

Stan and MacKenzie went off to their bedroom. Ben and Lois heard MacKenzie cry out after a time. They wandered outside and sat on the edge of the verandah, legs dangling. Ben dug out the crumpled joint and lit it, and they looked out over the sea and smoked it together. Ben spoke of Veronica Glass, and Lois held a finger to his lips.

"I don't want to hear about her, okay?" she said.

They went into their dim bedroom. The sun cast narrow bars of light through the blinds as they made love. When Ben finished, he thought of Veronica Glass; when he slept, he dreamed of her.

. . .

He dreamed of her awake and sleeping both. One more party, two, another passing encounter. She didn't always show up. He asked Stan about her. "She lives six houses down," Stan said, gesturing. "Crazy bitch."

"Crazy?"

"The things she does. You call that art?"

The last picture Stan had worked on had been a slasher flick. The usual: a bunch of kids at some summer camp, screwing and smoking dope; a crazed killer; various implements of destruction, the more imaginative the better. The virtuous survived. There would be no Oscars for this formulaic trash, Ben reminded him. And didn't it trade upon our worst impulses?

"It trades upon imagination," Stan said. "There's a difference between special effects and the genuine item."

He was right, of course, demonstrably so, yet—

Maybe not, Ben thought. Maybe special effects were worse. People thrilled to the mayhem on screen; they identified with the killers, turned them into folk heroes. No one thrilled to the work of Veronica Glass. Horror and fascination, sure—how could you do such things to a human being, and why? What had she said? "I have more volunteers than I could possibly use." And worse yet: "Are you interested?"

And he was. The whole phenomenon interested him.

"Beauty is truth, truth beauty," Keats had said.

Was there some terrible beauty here? Or worse yet, some terrible truth?

Or maybe Veronica had been right. How had she put it? Art pour l'art.

Art for art's sake.

Perhaps it was these questions that led Ben to stray down the beach one day toward her house. Perhaps it was the woman herself—that blonde hair, those high cheekbones. Perhaps it was chance. (It was not chance.) Yet that's what he told himself as he mounted the stair to her house—a house like every other house along the cliff side: gray-stained shingles and acres of windows that threw back the afternoon light, blinding him, and suddenly he didn't know what he was doing there, what was his intent?

Ben started to turn away—might have done so had a voice not hailed him from the verandah. "The poet takes courage," she called, and now he saw her, leaning toward him, elbows on the railing. "Come up."

He crossed the lawn, climbed a set of winding stairs. She had turned to greet him, her back to the railing, clad in a sheer white dress. She held a clear glass with a lime wedge floating among the ice, and she laughed when she saw him. She brushed her lips first against one cheek and then the other; they were moist and cool from the drink.

"So we meet by daylight, Ben Devine."

"How did you know my name?"

"It's no great mystery, is it? You're a guest of Stan Miles—and MacKenzie, of course. Dear, poor MacKenzie, and that lost child of hers. Who doesn't know you, those of us who remain, a weed sprung up among the roses?"

"Is that how you think of me, a weed?"

"Is that how you think of yourself?"

How was he to answer that question? How indeed did he perceive himself among the glittering multitude of Cerulean Cliffs? Stan had said they would fit right in—he and Lois—but did they? Ben had his doubts.

He opted for silence.

If Veronica—and when had that shift occurred exactly, when had she come to be Veronica in his mind?—expected an answer, she did not say. Nor did she ask him if he wanted a drink. She simply put one together for him at a bar tucked discreetly into the shadows. He brought it to his lips: the tickle of tonic, the woodsy bite of juniper and lime. At first he thought that she didn't care about his response to her question, but then—

"Do you think the poet that read the other night—the one with the beautiful hair—was any better than you are?"

"He has the National Book Award to prove it."

"Is that the measure of success?"

"So it would seem. Here in Cerulean Cliffs anyway."

"What do you believe, Ben?"

"What's an artist without an audience?"

"I have an audience. They mostly despise me, but they can't look away. I have a raft of awards. Does that make me an artist?"

"I don't know. I don't know what you are."

"And yet you're drawn to me."

"Am I?"

"You show up at my home without invitation."

"It was you who spoke to me first."

Ben turned and rested his elbows on the railing. He finished his drink and studied the horizon. Ruin had crept still closer, ashen and gray, enveloping the sea. For some reason, tears sprang to his eyes. For the first time in months, he found himself wanting to write, to set down lines in tribute to the lost world—yet even this aspiration exceeded his meager talent, and he grieved that, too: that the poems in his mind slipped through his fingers like rain. He grieved the hollowness at the heart of the enterprise. Nothing lasted. Not marble, nor the gilded monuments of princes, shall outlive this powerful rhyme. Except that the rhyme too came to ruin in the end.

Veronica handed him another drink.

"It won't be much longer now, will it?" she said.

"No."

"What spectacular suicide have you devised?"

"None. I suppose I'll see it through."

"Perhaps suicide too is an art."

"That's the premise of your work, isn't it?"

"Art pour l'art."

"Do you believe that?"

"I don't know. I suppose there is truth in what I do. The truth of ruin and death."

"You sound like Vinnizi."

"Is that what he told you? Poor Vinnizi. He was a fool. He made films about gunfights and car chases, that's all. The most artistic thing he ever did was hurl himself over that cliff." She paused. "Have you seen my work?"

"Photographs."

"Then you have not seen it."

"I'm not sure I want to."

Yet he did. In some secret chamber of his heart he yearned for nothing more, and when she turned away from him and started into the house, Ben followed, all too aware of the lines of her body beneath her dress. She turned to smile at him.

The door swung shut at his back. The air smelled of lavender. A whisper of air conditioning caressed his skin. The floor plan was open, airy, the sparse furniture upholstered in white leather, and he was struck suddenly by the similarity to Stan's house—the similarity to all the ruined houses he had fled in the light of dawn. Only here and there stood white pedestals, and on the pedestals—Ben felt his stomach clench—Veronica Glass's art. A woman's arm, severed at the shoulder and bent at the elbow, segmented into thin discs laid in order, an inch between, as though the wounds had never been inflicted, the hand alone still whole, palm up, like Vinnizi's, in supplication. The flesh had been preserved somehow, encased in a thin clear coat of silicone; he could see the white bone, the pinkish muscle, the neatly sundered nexus of artery and vein. A detail from the *New Yorker* profile came to him: how she strapped her subjects down and worked her way up to the final amputation, sans anesthesia, applying the first thin layer of silicone at every cut to keep the volunteer from bleeding out. A collaboration, she called her work, and the horror of it came to him afresh: in the leg flayed and tacked open from hip to toe to reveal the long muscles within; the severed penis, quartered from head to scrotum, and pinned back like a terrible flower; and, dear God, the ultimate volunteer, the shaven head mounted on a waist-high pedestal, a once-handsome man, lips sewn shut with heavy black cord, small spikes driven into his eyes.

The room seemed suddenly appalling.

Ben flung himself away and staggered outside to the verandah. Downing his drink, he stared out at the sea and the encroaching ruin, and saw for himself the absurdity of Vinnizi's claim that all along he'd been making films about the end of everything. This was ruin and horror, this the art of final things. Then she touched his shoulder and Ben turned and she pressed her lips to his and dear God, his cock was like a spike he was so hard—

Ben thrust her away and stumbled down the spiral stair to the lawn. When he turned at cliff side to look back, she was still there, standing against the railing, watching him. Her sheer dress blew back in some vagary of the wind, exposing her body so that he could see the weight of her breasts and the dark triangle of her sex. Another jolt of desire convulsed him and once again he turned away. He clambered down the stair to the beach, tore off his clothes and waded into the ocean, but no matter how long he scrubbed himself in the clear water that had not yet succumbed to ruin, he could not wash himself clean.

· · ·

He told Stan of it; he told Lois.

His cigarette trembled as he described it. He drank off two glasses of scotch as he spoke and poured another. The bottle chattered against the rim of the glass. He had known the nature of her work, had seen the photos, had read the profile. Yet nothing had prepared him for the way its cold reality shook him. What had Dickinson written? "I like a look of agony because I know it's true." And had any poet in his ken written a poem so true as Veronica Glass's work—so icy that it shivered him, so fiery that it burned? Was this not art, and did not his own work—the work of any poet or novelist, sculptor or composer—pale in comparison?

Ruin closed inexorably upon them. The parties became ever more frenetic. Suicides came in clusters now. One night, flying on heroin and prime, Gabrielle Abbruzzese slit her own throat at the stroke of midnight. The vast house rang with her otherworldly sonic landscapes, and she twirled as she died, her white ball gown blooming around her. Blood sprayed the revelers. Finally she collapsed, one leg folding under her like a broken doll's. Someone else seized the blade from her still warm hand, and then another, and another until the floor was littered with corpses. Ben and Lois watched from the gallery above. Looking up from the slaughter, Ben locked gazes with Veronica Glass, on the other side of the great circular balcony. She gave him an enigmatic smile and vanished into the crowd. The revel continued until dawn. Dancers twirled among the bloody corpses until ruin withered the privet and shattered the lawn; they made their escape as the land burned black behind them.

So passed the nights. The days passed in a haze of sun and sleep and alcohol. One boozy afternoon, Ben found himself alone with MacKenzie, watching Cecy in the yard. He made MacKenzie a vodka tonic and slumped beside her in her Adirondack chair.

"Have you given up poetry?" she asked.

"Yes," he said, and he thought of his impulse to set down some record of the dying world in lines, knowing how useless it was, how it too would come to ruin, and no one would survive to read it. He admired her body. She wore a bikini, and he could not help imagining the tan lines as Stan stripped it away and carried her off to bed.

"Why bother?" he said. "Who will survive to read it?"

"Perhaps the value of it is in the doing of the thing itself."

"Is it? Then why did you give up acting?"

"I was never really an actor," she said. "I'm not delusional."

She had been the star of a popular sitcom before her single disastrous attempt to break into film: the fading action star, the failed movie.

"I never really made it," she said. "Or if I did, I never was up to the challenge of real acting. I posed for the camera. The money didn't matter, not as a measure of artistry anyway. I was a poseur."

"That's more than I ever achieved. I was a poseur, too."

MacKenzie looked at him for the first time, really looked at him, and he saw a bright intelligence in her eyes, a self-knowledge that he had not known was there. It had been there all along, of course, but he'd been too blind to see it.

"I never read your poetry," she said.

"Who did?"

They laughed, and he felt that desire for her quicken within him.

Cecy cried out on the lawn. Her ball had plunged over the cliff. Ben retrieved it. When he returned, MacKenzie had moved to a towel. She lay on her stomach. She had undone the back of her bikini top, and he could see the swell of her breast.

"Why do you let Cecy attend the parties?" he said.

"I'm not a bad parent," she told him. "Her father—he was a bad parent."

"But you didn't answer the question."

She propped herself on her elbows, and he could see her entire breast in profile, the areola of one brown nipple. She looked at him, and he wrenched his gaze away. He met her eyes.

"I will not hide the truth from her."

"And in ruin is truth?"

"You know there is."

She lay back down, and he looked out to the sea, and even that was not eternal. "Do you want another drink?" he said.

"I'm positively parched," she said. So he made them drinks, and they drank until his face grew not unpleasantly numb and they watched Cecilia in the splendor of the grass.

Stan joined them as the shadows grew long and fell across the yard. Then Lois. The four of them drank in companionable silence through the afternoon. MacKenzie said again, "I'm not a bad parent. She has to face it the same as we do."

Lois nodded. "Perhaps you're right."

At the party that night—a sculptor's—Ben spoke with Veronica Glass.

"Are you ready yet?" she asked.

"I will never be ready."

"We'll see," she said, and drifted off into the crowd. Afterwards he sought out Lois, and they watched together as the sculptor put a sawed-off shotgun in his mouth and blew out the back of his head. A spray of blood and brain and bone adorned the wall behind him; if you stared at it long enough, you could discern a meaning that was not there.

They walked home at dawn.

Stan drifted ahead along the rocky white beach with Lois and Cecilia. Ben and MacKenzie fell back.

"Let's swim," she said.

"The water's icy," Ben said, but she slipped out of her clothes all the same. With a twinge in his breast, he watched the muscular flex of her ass as she ran into the water. She swam far out to the edge of ruin—he feared for her—before she flipped like a seal and returned. When she emerged from the foaming breakers, crystalline bubbles clung to her pubic hair. Her brown nipples were erect. She leaned into him.

"I'm so cold," she said. She turned her face to his and they kissed for a long time. He broke away at last and they walked home along the beach. By the time they reached the house and MacKenzie had showered and Cecilia had been seen safely to bed, Stan had laid out lines of cocaine on the kitchen table. The drug blasted out the cobwebs in Ben's brain. He felt a bright light pervade him, energy and clarity and a sense of absolute invulnerability. Somewhere in the conversation that followed, Stan proposed a change of partners.

"Yes, let's," Lois said, and that cool longing for MacKenzie possessed Ben. Then he thought of Veronica Glass, and he said, "I don't think I can do that, Stan." They went off to bed soon after. Lois had never seemed so desirable or his stamina so prolonged, and when he made love to her in their bright morning bedroom, he made love to her alone.

• • •

One by one, the Christmas lights along the coastline blinked out. The revelers dwindled, the parties became more intimate. Ben spoke with the poet, and they agreed that poetry was a dead art. Yet Ben was flattered when he learned that the younger man had read his work.

"You're just being kind," he said.

"No," the poet—his name was Rosenthal—said, reeling off the titles of Ben's three books. They had been published by university presses—small university presses, at that—but Rosenthal, who had been published by Little, Brown before Little, Brown decayed into rubble and his editor was ruined, quoted back a line or two of Ben's. Ben forgave him the National Book Award and his perfect hair, as well. It was all ruined now anyway, meaningless. Maybe it always had been.

That's what Rosenthal said anyway, and whether he meant it or not, it was true: as meaningless as Stan's Oscars or the dead novelist's Pulitzer or any other prize or accolade.

"And do you still write?"

"Every day," Rosenthal said.

Ben thought of Veronica Glass's dictum: art for art's sake. He proposed the tautology, knowing as he did so that even she did not believe it—that her's was the aesthetic of ruination and destruction and final things.

Rosenthal looked at him askance. "I write the truth as I see and understand it."

"And will you continue to write?"

"To the very end," Rosenthal said.

But the end was closer than he perhaps thought: the very next night, he and five others slipped into the black waves and under a full moon swam out to the ruin and ruin took them. As they pulled themselves onto the surface of the dead water, where the moldering fish had blackened into nothing, they became burned effigies of themselves, ashen. Over the next day or so, the wind would disintegrate them too into nothing.

That was the night Ben saw Lois slip away into a spare bedroom with the front man of the slam band, and whether she did it for revenge or out of despair or for some reason beyond his knowing, he could not say—only that he too had had his infidelities, and his was not to judge.

"And what will you do now that she has betrayed you?" Veronica Glass said at his shoulder. "Are you ready?"

"She has not betrayed me," he said. He said, "I am not ready, nor will I ever be."

They leaned against the bar, sipping scotch. She slipped him a handful of prime and they smoked a joint together, and the party degenerated into strobic flashes of wanton frenzy: he stumbled into an unlocked bathroom and saw MacKenzie going down on the architect who'd designed the Sony tower in Tokyo, long since ruined. He shot up with Stan in the kitchen. He found himself alone with Veronica on the verandah, looking out at the ruined ocean.

"Did you ever want a family?" he said.

She said, "Hostages to fortune," and he tried to explain that Bacon had meant something entirely different than what she was trying to say.

"No, that's what I mean exactly," she told him, and then he was lying on his back in the grass with Cecy, pointing out the constellations that ruin had not yet devoured. A great wave of grief swept over him, grief for her and grief for all lost things, and as he watched Rosenthal and his companions swim out to meet their ruin, he grieved for them, as well.

Afterwards, Ben threw up on the beach. Someone lay a cool hand upon his neck. He looked up and it was MacKenzie. No, it was Veronica Glass. No, it was Lois. He scraped sand over his vomit, staggered into the icy waves, and fell to his knees, lifting cupped handfuls of water to rinse his mouth until it felt clean and salty. He did not remember coming home, but Lois was in bed beside him when awareness returned. He whispered her awake. They wandered out into the vast glassed-in rooms, in search of drinks and cigarettes.

• • •

Stan and MacKenzie still slept.

Ben mixed gimlets and they sat out in the Adirondack chairs, their eyes closed, nursing their hangovers. Their lives had by then become an endless round of revelry and recovery, midnight suicides and daylight drinks on the verandah, grilled steaks, liquor and iced beer in the long afternoons, sex, drugs. Cecilia joined them for a while and then wandered off to the other end of the verandah to play some game of her own invention. She had the virtues and the vices of the only child— she was both intensely independent, playing solo games of her own devising, and profoundly dependent. She had been too early inducted into the mysteries of adult life and she had not yet the emotional maturity to understand them. She was prone to tantrums, and for inexplicable reasons, Ben alone had the ability to soothe her.

But today she was calm.

Ben turned his face to the sunlight. He held a sip of gimlet in his mouth and wondered when he'd last been completely sober—or when Lois had last been sober, for that matter. She'd gradually slipped into the world he lived in on the road, whether out of despair or some other more complex reasons of her own, he did not know. And regardless of what he'd said to Veronica, he did feel in some degree betrayed. But his feelings were more complicated than that. He felt too a renewed sense of physical desire for her. If she did not possess the beauty of MacKenzie— or Veronica Glass's aura of sexual intensity—she possessed the virtue of familiarity: he knew how to please her; she knew how to please him. Yes, and love, love most of all.

He reached out for her.

"Did you ever want children?" he asked.

She squeezed his hand. "It's sweet of you to ask. I used to, but—"

"But I wasn't the best candidate for fatherhood."

"No, you weren't. But you're a good man, Ben. I always believed that. I knew it, but it's a little late now, don't you think?"

"Stan and I were talking about it, that day we walked inland."

"And what did you see?"

"Ruin," he said. "Ruin and devastation."

"Yes. And any child we'd had, she would be ruined by now." Lois looked the length of the verandah. Cecy pushed along a miniature truck. She sang softly to herself. "That sweet child will be ruined soon enough. And think of the things she has seen."

"Sometimes—sometimes I think she's more equipped to see them than we are. It's part of her reality, that's all. She barely knows the world before."

"Do you think we're the last ones, Ben?"

"Does it matter? Someone somewhere will be. It's only a matter of time."

"And nothing will survive."

"Nothing."

"No, I think I'm glad we've been childless. We are sufficient unto ourselves. We always have been."

Ben heaved himself to his feet, went to the bar, and made them fresh drinks.

He stood at the rail and lit a cigarette. He recalled MacKenzie running naked into the moon-washed water and felt once again a surge of desire. The flesh forever betrayed you. He felt headachy and regretful and even now he could recall the shape of her body in almost pornographic detail. Yes, and Lois, too, slipping into the empty bedroom with the tattooed front man of the slam band—Roadkill, that had been its name, and it too was ruined. And her hand upon his neck.

"Last night—"

"I'm sorry, Ben."

"No. I wanted you to know that I'm not jealous. I want to be. I should be. But the rules seem to have changed somehow."

He drew on the cigarette, sipped his drink.

"Yes, the rules have changed," she said. "There's a kind of terrible freedom to it, isn't there?"

"Your hand upon my neck. It felt so cool." He turned to look at her. "How did I make it home?"

"Stan and I practically carried you."

"And the stairs?"

"The stairs, my love, were an absolute bitch."

He laughed humorlessly.

"I remember opening a bathroom door to see MacKenzie—"

"You needn't bother. Last night became something of an orgy, I'm afraid."

"New rules," he said.

"Or perhaps no rules at all."

No rules at all. And what did that mean but ruin?

He thought of Rosenthal, writing every day, imposing a discipline of his own upon the world until even that collapsed into despair. Was not his own resistance of MacKenzie—or of Veronica Glass—a kind of discipline, a kind of personal rule, newly instituted. Maybe that was all you had in the end: the autonomy of the individual will.

"No," he said, "I have my rules still. Maybe for the first time I have them."

He ground out his cigarette in MacKenzie's ashtray.

"Is that why you wouldn't trade spouses with Stan the other night?"

"I don't know, I haven't thought it through. It just seemed wrong, that's all."

"Surely you want MacKenzie. I saw you kissing her."

He laughed. "I've wanted MacKenzie since the day I met her."

"Then why not take the opportunity? I wouldn't have minded."

"Maybe that's it. You wouldn't have minded. There was a time you would have."

She stood and came to him and cupped his face in both hands. She gazed into his eyes, and for the first time in years, he noticed how deeply green hers were, and kind.

"What a sweet man you've become, Ben Devine."

"I only love you," he said.

"And I you," she said. She said, "I'm sorry about last night. I didn't know."

"Didn't know what?" Stan said, pushing his way out onto the verandah. MacKenzie followed.

"What a capacity for drink you had, you old fool," Lois said with a sparkling laugh.

Stan dropped into a chair with a thud. He groaned and pressed a beer to his forehead. "Bullshit," he said. "You've known that as long as you've known me." He shot them a glance and shook his head. "Lovebirds, you."

"Lovebirds are entirely monogamous," MacKenzie said from the bar.

"Then you are no lovebird."

"Nor you, my dear."

"Nor any of us," said Lois, "except for Ben, monogamous in ruin."

"What's wrong with you, Ben?" Stan said.

Ben said, "I've always been monogamous in my heart."

"Your heart's not where it matters," Stan said.

"It's the only place that matters," Lois said. They were silent after that. Wind came in off the water. The last gulls screamed, and the red sun dropped behind the roofline of the great house. "Come play with me, Mommy," Cecy called from the grass. MacKenzie went down. They played a complex game involving the shrunken soccer ball. Ben could never decipher the rules, if there were any, but their laughter lifted into the air like birdsong, and that was enough. Waves washed the rocky shore; the sound of them was music. Stan broke out a joint and the three of them shared it as the summer day drew toward dusk. The air tasted more sweet then, and the beauty of all things grew sharper and more clear in its transience.

"So what shall we do tonight?" MacKenzie said when she joined them.

"Tonight Veronica Glass is our hostess," Stan said.

Carpe diem, thought Ben. He wondered what beautiful and grotesque death Veronica Glass had concocted for herself, and he took Lois's hand and held it tight. There was so little time left to seize.

· · ·

As they climbed to Veronica Glass's cliff-side home that evening, they could hear the steady thump of music. The great windows pulsed with light and shadow. Wheeling scalpels of purple and red carved the dark. Reluctantly, Ben followed the others inside. He blundered through the crowd in revulsion, trying not to see the white pedestals with their grisly human freight. But he could not avoid them: colored lasers slashed the dance floor, and each bloodless piece had been illuminated by a blaze of clear light that exposed every detail in stunning clarity—every white knob of bone and gristle, every tendon, every severed artery, rootlike and blue. The supplicating hand might have been begging him for mercy, the amputated head might have been his own.

Yet Ben felt something else as well, an almost sexual arousal that he could neither deny nor sate. He stumbled into the kitchen with Stan, where they snorted lines of coke and heroin that had been laid out on the countertop. He poured himself a slug of eighteen-year-old Macallan and drank it off like water; he smoked a flash-laced joint with a short, heavy-set woman he had not seen before, a memory sculptor whose work had gone for millions before ruin took it all. Back in the enormous glassed-in atrium, he looked for Lois—for Stan or MacKenzie or even Cecy—but they'd all disappeared into the mob. He opened a door in search of the toilet, to find himself in a dim bedroom. Two couples—no three—writhed inside, on the bed, on the floor, against the wall. Someone—was it Stan?—held out an inviting hand. Ben reeled away instead, stumbled blindly through the orgiastic throng, and slammed outside.

He staggered down to the yard and stood cliff side, looking at the ocean.

Veronica Glass said, "It's quite the party, isn't it?"

"It's that all right. What madness have you prepared for tonight?"

"You started this, Ben," she said. "We chanced to meet on Vinnizi's lawn, nothing more. You're the one that wanted to talk about my work. You're the one that showed up uninvited at my door."

The wheeling lasers painted her face in shifting arcs of green and red. They illuminated the sheer material of her dress, exposing the shadows of her hips and breasts. Against his will, he found himself aroused all over again, by her or by her work, he could not say for sure. Probably both, and as if to deny this truth about himself—and what else was art to do if it didn't strip away our masks and expose us raw and naked to the world?—as if to deny this truth, he took a step toward her.

"It's anatomy, nothing more," he said. "It's cruelty."

"The world is a cruel place," she said. "Perhaps you've noticed."

An image of the sectioned arm possessed him, its imploring hand lifted in adjuration like Vinizzi's hand. An image of the flayed leg, the head on its pedestal, its mouth sewn shut against a scream. An image, most of all, of the ruined and dying world.

His hand lashed out against his will. The blow rocked her. She wiped blood from her lip and held it up for him to see. "You prove my thesis," she said. And turning, "You could have had me, Ben. You saw the truth and you could have possessed it. It was within your grasp. Beauty is truth, truth beauty. Isn't that what you believe? Let me show you the beauty that lies at the heart of ugliness. Let me show you the heart of ruin. Let me show you truth."

She didn't wait to see if he would follow. But he did, helpless not to. Up the stairs. Across the verandah. Into the great glassed-in room. She touched a switch. The music died. The lasers ceased to sculpt the dark. The lights came up.

"It's time," she announced to the silent crowd.

She led them murmuring through a cleverly disguised door, and down a broad stairway. A cold amphitheater lay at the bottom. Enormous flat-panel screens had been mounted overhead, at an angle facing the audience. On the floor below them, gently sloping toward a central drain, Veronica had readied the tools of her trade: an X-shaped surgical table, upholstered in black; bone saws and scalpels and anatomical needles for pinning back flesh; rolls of clear silicon.

Even as Veronica began to speak, Ben knew with a sick certainty what she planned to do. "The body is my canvas," she said, "the scalpel my brush." Her audience mesmerized looked on. "I sculpt the living human flesh in ways that unveil to the unseeing eye both our fragility and our strength, our capacity for love and our capacity for cruelty. As ruin closes in upon us, let my art unfold on the canvas of your flesh: the glorious art of death—prolonged, painful, beautiful to behold."

She paused.

"I have a friend"—and here she fixed Ben, in the third row from the bottom, with her gaze—"I have a friend who equates beauty with truth, who believes that art serves something other than its own ends. I did not always countenance this, but my friend convinced me otherwise. For there is beauty in pain and in our capacity, our courage, to bear it. There is beauty in death, and in that beauty lies a truth, as well—the truth of the ruin that every day engulfs us, that has awaited us from the moment we came screaming from the womb, when we were hurled into a world indifferent to our suffering. In these, the last days of Cerulean Cliffs, we have seen our little assays in the art of death. I propose that you transcend these small attempts. We are all artists here. I challenge you to pass from this world as you have lived in it, to make your death itself your final masterpiece."

She paused.

Silence fell over the amphitheater, an undersea silence fathoms deep, the silence of breath suspended, of heartbeats held in abeyance. Ben scanned the crowd, searching for Lois—for Stan and MacKenzie, for Cecy—Cecy who had been born into a world of ruin and death. There. There. There and there. He feared for them every one, but he feared for Cecy most of all.

Someone stirred and coughed. A chorus of murmurs echoed in the chamber. A man shifted, braced his hands upon his armrests, and subsided into his seat. Veronica Glass stood silent and unmoved. Another moment passed, and then, because Cerulean Cliffs had long since plunged into desperation and despair, and most of all perhaps because ruination and devastation would soon overwhelm them every one, a woman—lean and hungry and mad—stood abruptly and said, "I will stand your challenge."

She walked down to the arena floor. Her heels rang hollow in the silence. When she reached Veronica Glass, they exchanged words too quiet to make out, like the wings of moths whispering in the corners of the room. The woman disrobed, letting her clothes fall untended around her feet. Her flesh was blue and pale in the chill air, her breasts flat, her shanks thin and flaccid. Silent tears coursed down her narrow face as she turned to face them. Veronica strapped her to the table, winching the bands cruelly tight: at wrist and elbow, ankle and knee; across her shoulders and the mound of her sex. Her head she harnessed in a mask of leather straps, fastened snugly under the headrest.

"What you do here, you do of your own will," Veronica said.

"Yes."

"And once begun, you resolve not to turn back."

"Yes," the woman said. "I want to die."

The screens lit up with an image of the woman strapped to the table. Veronica turned to face the audience. She donned gloves and goggles, a white leather apron—and began. Using a scalpel, she drew a thin bead of blood between the woman's breasts, from sternum to pubis, and then, with a delicate intersecting X, she pulled back each quarter of flesh—there was an agonizing tearing sound—to unveil the pink musculature beneath. The woman arched her back, moaning, and Cecy—Cecy who had known nothing but ruin in her short life—Cecy screamed.

Ben, startled from a kind of entranced horror, held Veronica Glass's gaze for a moment. What he saw there was madness and in the madness something worse: a kind of truth. And then he tore himself away. Lurching to his feet, he shoved his way through the seated masses to scoop Cecy up. He clutched her against his breast, soothing her into a snarl of hiccupping sobs. Together, his arms aching, they stumbled to the aisle.

"You have to walk now," he said, setting her on her feet. "You have to walk." Cecy took his hand and together they began to climb the steps of the arena.

There was a rustle of movement in the stands. Ben looked around.

MacKenzie, weeping, had begun to make her way to join them, Lois too, and Stan.

They were almost to the cliffside when the screaming began.

. . .

So ended the last suicide party at Cerulean Cliffs—or at least the last such party attended by Ben and his companions. Over the next few days they gradually shifted back to a diurnal schedule. Stan dug up an old bicycle pump to inflate Cecy's soccer ball, and they spent most afternoons on the lawn, playing her incomprehensible games. There was no more talk of trading partners. Their drinking and drug use dwindled: a beer or two after dinner, the occasional joint as twilight lengthened its blue shadows over the grass.

Late one morning, Ben and Stan made another pilgrimage inland. They traded off carrying a small cooler and when they reached the edge of the devastation— they didn't have far to go—they stretched out against the trunk of a fallen tree and drank beer. Ruin had made deep inroads into the driveway by then. The weeds on the shoulders of the rutted lane had crumbled, and the gravel had melted into slag. Scorched-looking trees had turned into charred spikes, shedding their denuded branches in slow streamers of dust. Ben finished his beer and pitched his bottle out onto the baked and fractured earth. Ruin took it. It blackened and cracked as if he'd hurled it into a fire and began to dissolve into ash.

"It won't be long now," Stan said.

"It will be long enough," Ben said, twisting open a fresh beer.

They toasted one another in silence, and walked home along the winding sun-dappled road under trees that would not see another autumn. Ben and Lois made slow, languorous love when he got back, and as he drowsed afterward, Ben found himself thinking of Veronica Glass and whether she had fallen to ruin at last. And he found himself thinking too of the poet, Rosenthal, who'd chosen ruin over discipline in the end, who'd surrendered up his art to death. "I write the truth as I see it," he'd said, or something like that, and if there was no ultimate truth here in the twilight of all things—or if there never had been—there were at least small truths, small moments worthy of preservation in rhyme, even if it too would fall to ruin, and soon: Cecy's cries of joy; and the sound of breakers on a dying beach and the gentle touch of another human's skin. Art for art's sake, after all.

"Maybe I've been wasting my time," he told Lois.

"Of course you have," she said, and that afternoon he sat at a sunlit table in the kitchen, licked the tip of his pencil, and began.

• • •

DALE BAILEY lives in North Carolina with his family, and has published three novels, *The Fallen*, *House of Bones*, and *Sleeping Policemen* (with Jack Slay, Jr.). His short fiction, collected in *The Resurrection Man's Legacy: And Other Stories*, has won the International Horror Guild Award and has been twice nominated for the Nebula Award.

Breaking Water

Indrapramit Das

Krishna is quite unsettled when he bumps into a woman's corpse during his morning bath in Kolkata's Hooghly River, yet declines to do anything about it—after all, why should he take responsibility for a stranger? But when the dead start coming back to life en masse, he rethinks his position, and the debate around how to treat these newly risen corpses gets a lot more complicated. *Shirley Jackson Award nominee. Edited by Liz Gorinsky.*

1. Breaking Water

At first, Krishna thought the corpse was Ma Durga herself. A face beneath sun-speckled ripples—to his eyes a drowned idol, paint flaking away and clay flesh dissolving. But it was nothing so sacred as a discarded goddess. The surface broke to reveal skin that was not painted on, long soggy hair that had caught the detritus of the river like a fisherman's net. Krishna had seen his mother's dead body and his father's, but this one still startled him.

Krishna dragged the body from the shallows to the damp mud of the bank, shaking off the shivers. He covered her pickled body with his lungi, draping it over her face. He returned to the winter-chilled waters of the Hooghly naked and finished his bath. The sun emerged over the rooftops of Kolkata, a peeled orange behind the smoky veil of monoxides, its twin crawling over the river. Morning reflections warmed the tarnished turrets of Howrah Bridge in the distance, glistening off the sluggish stream of early traffic crossing it.

Other bathers came and went, only glancing at the body. When Krishna returned to the bank, a Tantric priest was crouched over the dead woman. The priest, smeared white as a ghost with ash paste, looked up at Krishna.

"Is this your wife?" the priest asked.

"No," said Krishna. "I don't have one."

"Then maybe you should be her husband."

"What're you on about?" Krishna snapped.

"She needs someone, even in death."

"Maybe she already has a husband."

"If she does, he probably argued with her, then beat her dead, maybe raped her while doing that, and tossed her in the river. Shakti and Shiva, female and male, should be at play in the universe. One should not weaken the other. This woman has been abandoned by man," said the priest, gently touching the dark bruises on her face, throat, and chest. Krishna thought about this. The priest waited.

"Fine. I'll take her to the ghat and see her cremated," said Krishna.

The priest nodded placidly. "You will make a good husband one day," he said.

"Your faith in strangers is foolish," muttered Krishna. *Not to mention his sense of investigative protocol,* Krishna didn't say. The priest smiled, accepting this rebuke and walking away. Krishna didn't know much about how washed-up, likely murder victims were handled, but he was sure just cremating them without a thought wasn't how it usually went.

Still.

Krishna looked at the corpse. If he left her, someone would eventually call the police, and they would take her to a refrigerated morgue where her frightened soul would freeze. Her killer would remain free, the case unsolved, because since when did anyone really care about random women tossed into rivers? He thought of his mother cooking silently by lantern light, her face swollen.

He remembered asking a policeman on the street to take his father to jail for hitting his mother. He was laughed at. He remembered playing cricket on the street with the other slum boys, doing nothing to stop the beatings, waiting years until his father's penchant for cigarettes and moonshine ended them instead. Not that it mattered, since his mother faithfully followed him not long after.

"Why don't *you* take her to the ghat, you self-righteous bastard? You're as much a man as me," Krishna said aloud, looking at the priest, who was sitting quietly by the water. He was too far away to hear Krishna, not that Krishna cared. He shook his fist at the priest for good measure, then he peeled his lungi off the body, leaving the woman naked again. Sullen, he threw the lungi in his bucket and tied another around his waist. He always brought an extra in case he lost one in the water. He kissed his fingertips and touched them to the body's clammy forehead, nervously keeping them away from her parted blue lips. For five minutes he sat next to her, as if in prayer, wondering how he might take her to the cremation ghats. Did the priest expect him to call a hearse, pretend to be a husband, and have her driven there? He shook his head and thought some more.

The priest had disappeared, but Krishna stayed there and thought and thought. Then he shook his head, got up, picked up his bucket, and walked away. The sun had risen higher, and the crowds were beginning to gather like flies by the golden water. They looked at the woman lying there on the bank, but, blinded by her nakedness, by the ugly bruises that painted it, they all looked away and went about their day. They ignored her until the moment she got up and started walking across the shore, clumsy but sure, water-wrinkled soles sinking into the trail of footsteps Krishna had left in the mud.

Even then, they didn't look for long, save for one man, who cried out in surprise from afar. An unsurprising reaction, since he'd just seen what he had presumed to be a dead body crawl a few paces, stand up and totter across the mud like a drunk madwoman. But no one else reacted, and he refused to let people think that he too was mad, so he pretended his cry was a prelude to his singing while he bathed, and tried to ignore the sight of the naked woman. Some others left the ghat in haste. The rest of the men took the first observer's cue, looking away from the woman on the shore as they bathed, just as they would look away from a beggar with stumps for limbs hobbling across the ghat. She had gotten up, so she couldn't be dead. Simple as that. Whatever her problem, naked women didn't belong here, where men bathed, parading their lack of shame.

In the morning air, flies clothed the woman. Hesitant crows perched on her shoulders and head, forming a feathered black headdress, bristling with flutter. She gave no regard to her beaked guests nor their violence as they haltingly pecked at her flesh, somewhat confused by her movements, but not enough to keep from tasting her ripe deadness.

The spectators stole quick glances at the woman while studiously ignoring her, horrified. This was a very mad woman. Undoubtedly sex-crazed, too, judging from her lack of modesty. Probably drunk. Crazy, for sure. And a junkie, and homeless, and a prostitute. So filthy that the birds were pecking at her. So high, she couldn't feel the pain. Surely someone would call the police.

Carrying her hungry crows unwitting, she staggered on down Babu Ghat, wandering by the slimy stone steps that led to the rest of the city, as if unsure of how to climb them. She eventually found the garbage dump down the ghat and started eating from it.

. . .

Next morning, when Krishna heard that the dead were waking up all over the city—maybe even the state—his first thought was of the dead woman he had left behind on the ghat. He was at a paan shop on Gariahat, near the apartment building where he cooked meals for a few middle-class families in their posh homes, in their fancy kitchens with ventilation fans and shining tiles and big fridges. He was idly spitting betel juice at the footpath when the paanwallah mentioned history happening elsewhere in the city, pointing to a tiny television on top of his little Coke storage fridge.

The paanwallah seemed bemused by the news on the TV, not quite believing it. "No wonder traffic's hell today," he muttered, scratching his whitening moustache. "All morning, this honking, I'm going deaf." He waved at the street and its cacophony of cars, buses, lorries, and auto-rickshaws stuck bumper-to-bumper like so many dogs sniffing each other's exhaust pipes.

Krishna believed the news instantly. It couldn't be coincidence that he'd discovered a corpse during his morning bath the week corpses started getting up and walking.

His second thought—accompanied by a bit of guilt for it not being the first— was of his mother; then, with some measure of fear, his father. But his parents were cremated and gone, safe from this mass resurrection, unless ash itself was stirring into life to fill the wind with dark ghosts. He also had to look up at the sky to make sure there were no clouds of ashen ghosts raging across it. Thankfully, there was only sunlight suspended in winter smog, pecked with the black flecks of crows.

The realization that his parents couldn't return came as a relief to Krishna, since he didn't know exactly how he'd have dealt with such a thing, especially after they'd been gone for two decades. The surge of elation and dread that rose from that thought filled his chest so powerfully that he had to steady himself against the counter of the paan stall.

Then he thought, *I have to find the woman.* That his parents couldn't possibly come back to life only bolstered this thought. Surely his employers wouldn't hold it against him if he missed a day, under the circumstances. In fact, Krishna suspected they'd be more preoccupied than most by this turn of events. He suspected that nobody living in those apartments really believed in God, despite their indoor shrines, and what better evidence of Bhagavan than this? It would throw them into confusion. Money and work be damned. For a day, at least.

"I found a dead woman. I left her; I have to find her," Krishna said to the paan-wallah, who was fiddling with his paan leaves, as if proud of their very appetizing green. Then Krishna ran off. "Hai-oh, that fellow's looking in the wrong places for a wife," the paanwallah mumbled.

• • •

As Krishna bussed across the city and back toward Babu Ghat, he saw the world as it always was but now a different place. The air you breathed felt different when you knew the dead walked around you. The traffic was even worse off than usual because of the confusion. The police were everywhere, their white uniforms ubiquitous among the crowds on the streets. Krishna heard snatches of conversations in different languages, all talking about the same thing. As sunlight shuttered across the smeared minibus windows, Krishna held his breath against the stink of sweaty passengers pushing up against him and listened. He heard wealthy students and youngsters babble incomprehensible English with unholy excitement, repeating one word, "zambi," which was clearly what they were calling the risen dead. Krishna heard how bodies were rising out of the Hooghly and shambling in diverse but slow-moving crowds across the ghats of Kolkata. How they were falling—half-eaten by birds—from the Parsi Towers of Silence like suicides jumping to their new lives. How the Muslim, Christian, and Jewish cemeteries were filled with the faint thumps and groans of the trapped dead, too weak to escape caskets and heavy packed earth. How medical schools and hospitals and police morgues were now dormitories for live cadavers kicking in their steel chambers. How these places were reporting the highest number of corpse bites in the whole city because of staff convincing themselves that the chilled bodies they were freeing were poor souls mistaken for dead and frozen to drooling stupidity. He felt like he was having a panic attack, so filled was his head with this confusion of voices.

• • •

By the time Krishna got back to Babu Ghat early in the evening, the riverside was packed, like it had been during the immersion of idols after pujas. A column of crows towered above the ghat. The birds wheeled over the parade of the dead, taking turns swooping down and pecking at them. The police were keeping the walking corpses within the ghat by tossing lit (and technically illegal) crackers near their soggy feet every time they tried to wander up the steps. That seemed to do the job, sending the dead staggering back towards the water, though never back

inside. Strings of bright red crackers hung from police belts like candy. Some of
them held riot shields. In their hands were lathis that they swung in panic if the
dead came near their barricade of live bodies. Their hatred for these creatures,
these once-humans, was immediate and visceral. After all, every walking corpse
on that ghat was a remnant of crimes they'd never solved or missing persons
they'd never found.

Krishna witnessed the resurrection with nauseous excitement.

The Hooghly had disgorged the dead as if they were its children, all wrestling
into the sunlight from a giant, polluted birth canal. They shone like infants fresh
from the womb, swollen not with fat but water and gas. All stripped naked as the
day they were born by water and time. Fifteen, twenty? Could they swim? Had they
simply walked on the river's bottom till they came upon this bank, all the while
breathing water through their now-amphibious mouths? He was shocked that
there had been that many unknown people lying murdered, drowned, or mistak-
enly killed at the bottom of the Hooghly.

Some were only days old, looking almost alive but for their slack faces like
melting clay masks, their lethal wounds and bruises, their paled and discoloured
skin, their jellied eyes, and the sometimes lovely frills of clinging white crustaceans
in their hair, the tiny flickers of fish leaping from their muddy mouths. Others
were black and blue, bloated into terrifying caricatures of their living counterparts, who watched in droves from behind the lines of fearful policemen at the top
of the ghat steps. Fresh or old, all these dead men and women wading back to the
world were united by the ignominy of their ends, un-cremated and tossed into the
tea-brown waters of the Hooghly to be forgotten. Most, Krishna noticed, were
women. All had crows as their punishing familiars, which clung to shoulders and
heads as they tore flesh away with their beaks.

Krishna searched for a familiar face amongst the dead. He felt uneasy, not at
the sight of the resurrected dead, but at the roiling crowd he had to push through
to witness this miracle, the street dogs biting and barking amid them to try and
get to the corpses, only to be beaten back by the police. Some people lowed like
animals, spoke in tongues or pretended to, blabbered prophecy; priests and sad-
hus and charlatans chanting to eager flocks of potential followers, many calling
for the immediate destruction of these men and women who had been reincar-
nated into their own bodies—a sign, surely, that they were evil, condemned to
rebirth as creatures even lower than the lowest of animals because of some terrible karmic debt. It made Krishna uneasy, scared, even angry. Clearly, these people
rising from the waters had been wronged, had suffered the injustices of the earthly
world, not caused them.

It was a miracle, Krishna told himself. It had to be.

Why, then, did this feel like the end of the world, with the police in their cricket
pads and riot shields, the crowds coagulating into a mob, these terribly wronged
souls blessed with new life being herded like cursed cattle?

The loud braying of horns and the glare of headlights swept across the crowd as
two police vans with grills on their windows ploughed slowly through the crowd,

nudging the spectators aside. Men in toxic yellow hazard suits got out. They held long poles with metal clamps, which Krishna had often seen dogcatchers use to grab strays off the streets. They were going to shove the resurrected into vans and drive them away, quarantine them somewhere. And then what? They could do anything to them: destroy them, imprison them. If the world knew about them from the news, they probably wouldn't burn them, however much these policemen might want that. But if they took them away, they would be subject to any and all injustices that scared people could dream up.

As he was thinking this through, Krishna's eyes caught the woman he had found yesterday. She was right there on the ghat. She was a little worse for wear, having spent a day doing whatever she'd been doing. But she was here and still . . . well, alive, he supposed. Walking with her resurrected sisters and brothers. Clearly, she had gotten away with being dead and walking around before the rest emerged from the water, perhaps because she'd looked somewhat alive when she washed up. No different from any wretched, broken beggar wallowing in garbage, to the average bystander.

The catchers made it through the crowd and neared the dead. Their plastic visors smudged them into faceless troopers, their pole spears shoved ahead of them, parting the howling people of Kolkata.

"Oh, God," Krishna whispered, pushed from side to side by other sweaty shoulders. "God, thank you. I'm sorry I left her. I won't again. I won't."

He shoved and struggled through the crowd, and shouted as loud as he could from behind the line of police. "My wife!"

Several policemen turned their heads and forced him back into the churn of people. He rebounded off the mob, back onto the officers. "I see my wife! Let me through!" he cried out.

They didn't, but he pushed under their reeking armpits and broke through the line. He felt the sticks lash his back, bruise his shoulder blades, explode over his skin like crackers at the feet of the dead.

My wife. He heard himself. A decision made.

He ran down the crumbling ghat steps, stumbling as the sun sank and sloshed into the waters of the Hooghly. The baying of street dogs and the horns of a million cars stuck on the roads of B.B.D. Bagh rose into the evening, a trumpet sounding the end of an age.

And there she was, her long black hair threaded with garbage, crows on her shoulders. She looked at Krishna. Was there recognition in her eyes? No, she hadn't even awoken to new life when he found her. And yet. For a moment, Krishna hesitated as all the corpses turned their numb gaze upon him, and the cloud of flies surrounding them surged against him, biting like windblown debris. But his fear of the police behind him was far stronger than his fear of the unknown. They would not follow him into this hell, so he ran forward, not back, his feet sliding on the filthy mud. He ran straight into the outreached arms and lizard-pale eyes of the resurrected, towards the woman who was to be his wife.

They embraced him as if he was one of their own, the flies crawling all over him as if they too had agreed to mark him as dead. Most importantly, she embraced him, peeling back her cold, heavy lips to bare teeth that still clung to purple gums.

2. Notes on Infancy

I first met Guru Yama when he was taking refuge with his "first wife" at the Kalighat Temple. This was just days after the resurrections became public, and just as it was becoming clear that they might be global, with cadavers reported to be rising up in countries all around the world, including our neighbours Pakistan, China, Bangladesh, and Myanmar.

The guru was sitting in the courtyard where goats are sacrificed to Kali. They had closed off the altars from the public, and people were being allowed in one at a time to see him. No cameras. At that point, "Guru Yama" was just a nickname given to him by the news media, but it had caught on very quickly. The corpse he'd claimed at Babu Ghat squatted near him. He'd publicly refused, over and over, to hand the cadaver over to the police or any other organization, claiming that it was his wife.

He seemed utterly stunned by the world when I saw him, clinging to the frayed rope tied around the purple neck of his wife as if it were a lifeline. Pierced into the skin of his other arm was an actual lifeline: an IV antibiotic drip on rubber wheels. Twenty-nine people around India had reportedly died from corpse bites left untreated. Each of the bite victims had also consequently become undead. The guru had been bitten but was given rabies and tetanus shots right after. He was younger than I'd expected, maybe even my age—mid-thirties at the most.

Covered in sweat, bandages over the bites his wife and the other corpses had given him, shivering with fever, eyes bloodshot, the guru told me both his life story and the story of his dead wife with stunning candour. For one thing, I didn't expect him to confess that she wasn't really his wife, or hadn't been when he found her. The priests at the temple had conducted an impromptu ceremony after he arrived, though no one was willing to say what that meant. Most temples in the city, the guru said, wouldn't let them in, declaring the risen dead abominations. He was lucky Kalighat Temple had offered to house him and his wife, as he couldn't keep her in the basti where he lived. He told me how grateful he was for their help, and also thanked the lorry driver who had transported him and his wife from temple to temple, trailed by crowds looking for something to focus on in this bewildering time.

Though there were no laws in place for the risen dead, the guru considered himself legally bound to the woman he held by a rope leash, who had been dead for at least a week now. Because of that very lack of laws addressing this new world, the police or government couldn't really dispute his claim, and they had other things to worry about right now, anyway.

Throughout the interview, I watched the guru's wife with barely suppressed horror as she ate out of the opened rib cage of a goat that had been sacrificed, not for Ma Kali but for her. Or perhaps for both of them. The guru noticed the look on my face.

"She is a woman, just like you," he said, which made me very uncomfortable. "Don't be scared of her. You know what it's like in this world. She asks only for sympathy."

I tried to hide my unease. The corpse was squatting, much like her human companion, and using her swollen hands and darkening teeth to eat the entrails. It hurt to see the infantile clumsiness of those slowly bloating fingers. I was ready to run, but she never approached or even noticed me. She looked very blue-green, very inhuman, different from what she'd been in the footage from the ghat, embracing and then biting this man who called himself her husband. She looked—as much as I hated to apply that term to a real person who had lived and died—like a zombie. The people outside the temple had told me to wear a surgical mask and rub Vicks VapoRub under my nostrils (and readily sold me both on the spot), but I could still smell her, see the flies around her and the maggots in her nostrils and eyes and mouth.

"It's good that it's winter, no? She'd probably be falling apart by now if it were summer," the guru said, looking at her. He stifled a shudder, wiping cold sweat from his brow. "We also have to make sure the street dogs don't eat her. Usually, the dogs come in here when the goats are sacrificed, to lick up the blood. Not now, not now; we keep them out. They'd rip her up in minutes. Birds, also—they're always trying. But humans are the worst." He shook his head.

"She can't protect herself anymore. All of these waking dead have been raped, beaten, strangled, stabbed, killed, thrown away. They deserve someone to help them, to take care of them in this new life they've been given by God. I've told all the news people, and I'll tell you, that I'll take care of them if no one else will. Everyone's calling me Guru for that," he laughed, eyes wide. "Guru Yama, they're calling me. I don't know about that. I don't want to take the name of a god. I'm just a man."

"But your parents already gave you the name of a god, Krishna. Is this different?" I asked him.

He seemed startled by this, and I felt bad for bringing up his dead parents. To my relief, he changed the subject.

"It doesn't matter what they call me, I suppose. What matters is, I'm not afraid of these dead people. When I find somewhere to keep them, I'll make sure they're alright. When I am better, I'll go looking for more before the police take them away and punish them again. Tell everyone. Bring me your dead, and I'll care for them," the guru said to me. From the fervent darting of his eyes, I couldn't tell if he was a charlatan, if he was just looking for fame or up to something more sinister. I didn't shake his hand, but I did smile at him, maybe in encouragement. I wondered about the rest of those dead people he had left behind at Babu Ghat, later taken away in those vans. It wasn't the guru's fault; how many dead could he walk around with?

Before leaving, I asked if I could use what he'd told me to write a story or an article. He gave me his blessing. I left to let his next visitor, whether journalist or would-be follower, see him. I managed to wait till I was out on the streets before vomiting, just a little, into a gutter. I'm not sure anyone in the crowd gathered around the temple even noticed.

I wrote in the midst of a global paradigm shift. I wanted to try and understand one man at that moment, as opposed to the impossibility of an entire world made new. Like anyone and everyone who would fixate on him in the days to come.

It was only afterwards that I thought to look for the identity of that poor dead woman by his side.

3. Notes on Maturation

The second time I saw Guru Yama, it was to identify his wife and return her to her mother.

I met the widowed mother, who requested I not include her name, at the Barista on Lansdowne. I bought her a plain coffee. As I handed her the cup, I marvelled at the fact that we could still enjoy the privilege of overpriced lattes and mochas while black government vans roamed the state for the risen dead. Every time I saw those vans, some shining with the words WEST BENGAL UNDEAD QUARANTINE fresh-painted on them, I stopped to wonder whether I was remembering something from a movie or actually looking at something real. The cafe was relatively quiet—just a few afternoon customers chatting amid the burbling of espresso machines. But elsewhere in the city, people were striking and rioting to throw stones and claim their own religions and ideologies as responsible or not responsible for this cosmic prank. That very day, there had been a march on Prince Anwar Shah Road, by South City Mall, with fundamentalists of one or many stripes demanding that movies filled with immoral violence and sexuality be removed from the mall's multiplex immediately in order to end God's wrathful plague of the waking dead. The puritanical thrive in apocalypses.

The mother is a Hindi teacher at a small school. She took one sip of her coffee out of politeness. I had to ask her, after apologizing for doing so, "Did you recognize your daughter on TV that day?" She looked like she was out of breath or keeping down vomit. After a moment, she nodded. She did recognize her daughter. Of course she did.

I could understand the rest without her saying anything more. Who would want to acknowledge to themselves that their missing daughter was on TV, on the news, in real life, a walking corpse? That was too many impossibilities to deal with. I couldn't bear to think what this woman, with her greying hair in a dishevelled bun, wearing an innocuous blue salwar kameez that made her look like any one of my high school teachers, was going through. I felt sick with her, the coffee acrid in my chest. Having had an abortion during college—one of the wisest decisions I've ever made—I wanted to say I knew how she felt. But remembering the brutal, almost physical depression of that distant time only furthered my remove from this woman, who had seen her adult daughter walking across the mud of the Hooghly naked as she had been in the first moments of her life, but dead.

I touched the mother's hand, and she gasped as if terrified. We left the cafe in silence, her cup still full, cold on the table. My heart was racing just from being in the presence of such horror. Outside, the late winter sunlight did nothing to calm it. Thankfully, there were no marchers or black vans on Lansdowne. If we could forget for a moment, it might have felt like any other day in Kolkata, in that by-gone world where the dead stayed dead.

. . .

I drove the mother to Kalighat in my old Maruti, and she slept through the ride. I got the impression sleeping was the easiest way for her to escape human interaction.

The stinking alleyways outside the temple were lined with the guru's growing mass of followers. Many pressed their palms to the mother as we passed, and some tried to touch her feet. They knew who she was. She walked through them as if in a dream, not responding at all.

I had come prepared this time. We both wore surgical masks, and we'd both rubbed VapoRub under our noses. The hawkers still tried to sell us both.

Guru Yama sat in the courtyard inside, same as before. His wife sat at the altar, like a goddess of death next to her husband, who had been named after the god of death by his followers. She was covered all over in heaped garlands of sweet genda phool, so many that it looked like they were crude, thick robes. Her jaundiced eyes peered from between the petals, and a ballooning hand stuck out of the flowers, the orange circlet of a single marigold in its bulging palm. The smell of the garlands wasn't enough to mask the stench of the festering body beneath them.

"Greetings," the guru said to us, his eyelids drooping with antibiotics, with fever, with other drugs, or perhaps just spiritual ecstasy; I couldn't tell. It had been three weeks since I had last visited him there. He sounded more confident and much calmer. His beard, too, was longer. More befitting a guru, I suppose.

His wife did not move, though the hand holding the flower quivered slightly, as an effigy's straw limb might in a breeze. From under those flowers came the rattle of air passing through tissues, a soft groan. But she was unnaturally still. It made me realize how jarring it was to see a living animal that didn't breathe.

"Don't be afraid of her," the guru said to the mother. "She is still your daughter. She has bitten me, yes; you see the bandages. But your daughter's bite has made me feel more alive, Mother. I have infected myself with the poison of the dead so that I may live with them. It strengthens me. It gives me visions. Oh, Mother, don't cry. Rejoice in this miracle, rejoice. She has a second chance in the world. She can't talk; but in my visions, in my dreams, she speaks." These were his first words to his mother-in-law (though certainly a dubious law).

"What does she tell you?" the mother asked, her breathing tortured.

"In my dreams she shows me the man who killed her. She tells me"—he lowers his voice—"the terrible things that were done to her. She shows me the face of the man so that he may be brought to justice if I ever see him in the world."

Given the smell in the air, the situation we were in, I expected the mother to throw up at the sight of the guru and his wife or react adversely. But she just seemed catatonic as she stared at her daughter sitting on that altar, buried in flowers save for her purple face and bulging eyes. It isn't accurate to say the mother didn't react; her cheeks were covered in tears. They dripped off her chin, soaking into the surgical mask that flapped against her mouth with each heavy breath she took.

"Have you touched her?" the mother asked, very softly, and I felt a chill down my neck.

The guru smiled. "I have touched her, but not as a husband would. I have held her, and guided her, at times. It is not easy to touch her. She is fragile. But I understand your fear. We are married so that I may shelter her in this new life; that is all. I want to protect her, from men who would do what you are afraid of, from men who would take her and let her rot in a cell or a grave. I want to protect her from the birds in the sky and the dogs on the street."

"I'm not afraid of what anyone will do to my daughter. They've already done what they will. Taken her. Taken her from me. Why is she like that? The flowers," the mother said, out of breath.

"It helps with the smell. In summer, she would be gone by now. But she's strong. She ate meat from the sacrificed goats, wanted to eat it. She tried to eat me, I think, when she first bit me. But it's just a habit that she remembers. I saw the meat sit in her stomach and make it big, like a baby in her."

Like a baby, I thought, and felt spots appear in my vision. I blinked them back, sweaty, the stench clinging to my throat.

"She threw up many times, and it was still just meat and maggots. The body will not take food in death. It rots in her. Eating is not good for her, I think. Now I don't feed her. She is happier. She tells me when I'm asleep."

I could see the mother's hands trembling, grasped tightly together over her stomach, her womb. The mask was soaked through. "I'd thank you, Guru, if that's what you call yourself," she whispered.

"I'm sorry, Mother, I can't hear very well; this fever fills my head. The poison of the bites has its toll, even if it's a gift."

"I said, I'd thank you, Guru, if that's what you call yourself," she said, voice shaking.

"That's what they call me, Mother. Guru Yama. I'd be honoured if you called me son," he said, bowing his head.

I glanced at the corpse. I saw its distended eyes move in their sockets, looking at us from under the coils of marigolds. I took shallow breaths.

"I'd thank you, Guru," the mother said again, not calling him son, "for guarding my daughter from the kind of people who took her away from me. I'd thank you if I knew that you weren't the one who killed her and threw her naked in the river, as if she were garbage."

"No, Mother. No, no, no," he said. He looked genuinely dismayed by this suggestion, his eyes widening.

"You found her; how do I know?" she asked, coughing. I flinched as her daughter rustled under the flowers, breaking from whatever mordant meditation she was suspended in.

I touched the mother's shoulder. "Ma'am, there were witnesses who saw him finding her; she washed up on the ghat . . ." I reminded her.

"What if that thing isn't even my daughter?" she said, taking off her glasses.

"It is," I whispered. "I looked at the footage, compared the photos. We can ask the police to do a DNA test, but I don't know if that would work at this stage of decomposition. If you claim her, we can get her to a morgue before she starts falling apart completely."

"No. I don't want that. She's already gone. That . . . She doesn't look like my daughter anymore," she said, her voice so very small.

The creature under the flowers crooned as gas escaped her mouth. It sounded eerily like song, and who's to say it wasn't? I saw the guru look at her, and I noticed his eyes were wet as well. Was it the accusation? Empathy for her mother?

The corpse moved its fake-looking hand, the skin stretched like a latex glove half blown up. And, to my shock, she raised that grotesque hand and wobbled the flower into her thick blue lips, eating it, the petals glowing bright against her black-and-brown teeth. The guru pointed. "Look: like I taught her, Mother. Like I taught her. I taught your daughter not to eat, and if she does, eat the flowers. Small, they don't hurt her. Good, beta, good." He grinned, the pride on his face clear. The guru looked like a boy showing his mother a trick he'd taught his pet.

The mother stared, and gasped with what sounded like laughter. She laughed, perhaps, and then she sobbed, sitting on the dirty ground of that courtyard. She sobbed and sobbed, scrunching the surgical mask into her face like a handkerchief as her daughter's corpse munched on a marigold, and her unasked-for son-in-law held her hand with hope and fear in his eyes. The moment lasted barely a minute before she got up and asked to leave immediately. She had come to officially identify her daughter's corpse, but she'd barely seen it. And yet, how could I force that? How could I ask that the flowers that hid that monstrous, infantile thing that was once her daughter be removed? I dreaded to see the decay, and so did she.

"I am sorry for your loss, Mother," the guru said as we left, his voice different from how it had been.

"I want it burned. I can't have that walking around. It's not my daughter anymore. She's gone. I want it burned," the mother said to me in the car, once she had regained some of her composure.

I drove her back to her apartment. She remained silent the whole time. Once I had parked by her building, she turned to me, eyes swollen. She grasped my arm, the first time she'd touched me. She held me very tight.

"Miss Sen, do you think I made the right decision?" she asked.

Swallowing, I told her, "I don't know, ma'am. I truly don't."

"I don't think he killed my daughter," she said, letting go of my arm. Her hand fell limp to her lap.

"I don't think so either. I interviewed a lot of people who were at the ghat, both when he found the body and when he came back. Everyone confirms he was among the morning bathers when the body washed onto the ghat."

She let out a long and heavy breath. "I don't think it should be burned."

I don't know why, but I was relieved when she said that. I remembered those horrible, deformed hands lifting a flower to that rotting mouth, and my chest ached.

"All right," I said, nodding too hard. "Whatever you feel is right, ma'am. And please, call me Paromita."

She placed her fist against her forehead, her bangles jangling. Her eyes closed, she said, "He can keep it. You know"—she opened her eyes, looked at me—"my daughter never seemed interested in marriage. I know I asked her about it too much. I wanted grandchildren very much, a son-in-law. To fill up our family, you know? It was so empty when my husband left, even though he was just one person. So, I pestered her all the time to meet a man. She was still young, after all, but had no interest in weddings and children. Such a good student, always career-minded. She was so happy to go to college. Really, she wanted to go abroad to study. I didn't have the money. I don't know how much that hurt her, but she never, ever used it against me, even when we fought about things. And we did fight. College was good for her. She needed to live apart from me. But I missed her so much. She'd say, 'Ma, that's ridiculous; we live in the same city,' so I didn't tell her, but I missed her all the time. Honestly, I was grateful she didn't go abroad, so that she could still visit me. And she did. She did, until she was missing. And then that was that. Now I don't know what's happening."

"Nobody does," I said. I put my hand, very lightly, on her arm, before returning it to the steering wheel.

"You're not as young as my daughter," she said. "But you're young. You have so much energy, to be doing all this, figuring out who she was, finding me, when the police should be doing things like this. All this work, all this energy, when the whole world's going mad. You should be very proud."

"Thank you," I said, my ears going hot. I felt suddenly ashamed to be alive in front of her, despite her kindness.

She took a crumpled handkerchief from her handbag and wiped her nose. "The person who killed my daughter, that person was unkind to her. Horrible to her. I don't know . . . whatever animal her body has become, I don't know what it feels. If it's walking, eating, maybe it'll feel the flames. I won't be that unkind. I won't, in my daughter's honour. That man can keep the body, or whatever it is now. You'll tell the police?"

"I will. They'll call you and probably ask if you identified her. You'll probably have to talk to your lawyer and get a death certificate. But I'll tell them."

I smiled, though she didn't look at me, instead staring straight ahead through the windshield. "Thank you, Paromita. For everything you've done, are doing, for me, and for my daughter."

I nodded, but found myself too choked up on my words to reply at first. I barely managed to say "You're welcome" before she took her handbag and got out of the car. I've talked to her a few times on the phone since, to organize a meeting with her lawyer and the police, but that was the last time I saw her.

4. Notes on Death

I saw Guru Yama and his wife one last time at Kalighat. I went there to tell him he had the mother's consent to keep the body. I had ad hoc legal papers from her lawyer giving the guru "official" custody of the walking cadaver. The guru thanked me, but his enthusiasm had turned to sadness, because his wife was on the verge of falling apart. She was attracting rats and other vermin into the temple, and dangerously close to liquefying. "I do have to burn her," the Guru told me, dishevelled and weak, scratching at his bandages.

"You can give her to the hospitals, the research institutes, if you want to keep her from the police," I said. "They can put her in cold storage."

He shook his head. "No, Miss Sen. Maybe if she was younger. The dead have short lives. This I know now. She would suffer a lot if they tried to freeze her now." He had decided. Perhaps because of his meeting with the mother. Perhaps not.

He used her rope leash to lead her from the altar to a hired lorry. By now, she was barely able to walk, waddling slowly and leaving a trail of dark brown droplets that her garlands dragged into smears. Men with mops swept the trail away as she was led across the courtyard. The walk took half an hour. The guru draped a cloth over her face so all the people they passed didn't panic her. Dragging her flower garlands, she was lifted into the back of the lorry in a large blanket, five sweating men heaving at its sides and rolling her in with no dignity. I followed the lorry to the Garia crematorium.

I waited in the crematorium's cold, shadowy halls as the guru's wife was taken in for incineration.

The worst thing I have ever heard in my life was the brief scream that rang out through the crematorium, sharp and human, before being lost in the hum of the ovens. I went outside to find a dog barking furiously in the courtyard, drool flying into the dirt. I leaned against the yellow walls of the building and waited.

The guru emerged and thanked me again.

"That scream—was that her?" I asked.

He nodded. "It's good. It's good that her mother wasn't here." I saw his hands shaking like the mother's had.

"What'll you do now?" I asked.

"I'll find more of the dead who need my help. Other people want to give me their dead, to take care of, to speak to in my visions. I have followers. I'll never let one of the dead down like this again. One day, Miss Sen, I'll be a big guru, like the ones you see on TV, in the newspapers. I'll have money. When I do, I'll buy one of those resorts, those hotels in the mountains, high up. In the Himalayas or"—he paused, then spoke carefully—"Switzerland. I saw them in magazines. It's always cold, and they're huge. There, my dead can roam free, and live longer. You watch;

you'll see. Away from all these people trying to take them, away from police. They'll be happy there."

I wished him luck as he walked back to his followers, looking strange without his wife by his side. In my car, I cried quietly for that walking corpse, as if I were crying for the woman who had died in its body.

• • •

Guru Yama doesn't yet have a Swiss ski resort for his dead. He does have an ashram in Uluberia, with refrigerated chambers for his "children" (no more wives or husbands, to reduce the accusations of necrophilia). He keeps himself in a perpetual state of fever, allowing his children to bite him every month, staving off death and resurrection via antibiotics paid for by his followers and clients. Detractors of dead-charmers say that the visions and dreams through which they talk to the dead are nothing but delirium brought about by fever and drugs, including heroin and hash taken for the pain. I plan, one day soon, to do a book of photo essays with my friend Saptarshi about him and his flocks, dead and alive.

I still don't know whether he's a charlatan, or deluded, or a prophet.

Perhaps because I'm an atheist, I've never trusted charismatic religious figures who use their influence to gather wealth. I don't quite recognize the man I see in videos and pictures now, covered in ash, turmeric paste, and bandages, cloaked in hash and incense smoke, beard hanging down to his hollow stomach, surrounded by veiled corpses like a true lord of death. But I remember the man who walked out of Garia crematorium, his shaking hands, his shocked stare. His grief for the creature he called his wife was so very real. We both heard her scream as she died a second time.

The thing about the reality of the undead is that we can now see the afterlife. We live in it. And we share that afterlife with its dead inhabitants, who walk among us. But we can't talk to them, and they can't talk to us. That truly is the most exquisite, atheistic hell.

5. Notes on Afterlife

Visiting my parents is different now. Now, when I drink tea with them on their veranda, tea that somehow tastes of my childhood even though it's just plain old Darjeeling, I watch them age gently next to me. More than ever, every new wrinkle, every new wince of bodily pain, every glimmer of sun off a newly silvered strand of hair catches my eye. And I can't help but think of the future.

In this, should I say, apocalyptic future, I have to sign a form by their deathbeds. The form asks if their death is to be final, if I want to authorize doctors to sever their brain stems and puncture each lobe right after their hearts stop beating, to make sure they won't rise up again in undeath. There are two other options: I can illegally have them bitten by a corpse belonging to a dead-charmer before they die, to increase their chances of resurrection. Or I can take a cosmic gamble and let the universe decide between two terrible things by checking the other box on the form that says my parents should be left untouched after death, to see if their bodies naturally choose undeath. The undead will not be allowed in homes because of numerous health hazards, including dangerous, often lethal, bites. So if my parents rise into undeath it will fall to me to hand them over to the government or a private scientific institution, or a dead-charmer.

This *is* the future. Governments are already trying to figure out appropriate legislation for the realities of dead people waking up and creating an entirely new kind of life.

I think about simply losing my parents forever, once the only choice. Then I think of them undead. And I think of Guru Yama's wife, grotesque and alien, death itself personified as a gigantic, corpulent infant, crooning to itself and eating a single marigold as I struggled to understand whether its painfully corrupted form caused it pain. I think of it screaming in an oven.

I see myself, pen hovering over the forms, not knowing which box to check.

Who am I to deny someone I love a second life, however incomprehensible, however different from the first? And then, with both relief and panic, I realize it's not even my choice, but my parents'. One day, I'll have to have a conversation with them about whether or not they want to risk becoming a fucking zombie. I haven't asked yet.

And one day, when I have a child—if I have a child—I'll have to have that conversation again, when they ask me.

When these thoughts creep into those evening conversations with my parents, tinting them with dread, I think of two corpses shambling up a snow-clad mountain in Switzerland, their flesh preserved in a fur of frost that glitters under a high, clear sun, their thoughts unfathomable.

INDRAPRAMIT DAS (aka Indra Das) is a writer and editor from Kolkata, India. His fiction has appeared in several publications, including *Clarkesworld Magazine, Asimov's, Lightspeed Magazine, Strange Horizons,* and *Tor.com,* and has also been widely anthologized. He has written about books, comics, TV, and film for publications, including *Slant, Vogue India, Elle India, Strange Horizons,* and *Vancouver Weekly.* His debut novel, *The Devourers,* was the winner of the 2017 Lambda Literary Award for Best LGBQT SF/F/Horror, and short-listed for the Crawford Award, the Shakti Bhatt First Book Prize, and the Tata Literature Live! First Book Award. A Shirley Jackson Award nominee, an Octavia E. Butler Scholar, and a grateful graduate of Clarion West 2012, he divides his time between India (where he has worked as consulting editor for publisher Juggernaut Books) and North America, when possible.

Your Orisons May Be Recorded

Laurie Penny

In a place somewhere between thought and memory, prayers are answered by the next available operative. They cannot take requests for miracles over the phone. *Edited by Patrick Nielsen Hayden.*

All prayers are answered, but sometimes the answer is no.

And sometimes the answer is: "Let me talk to my manager and get back to you."

"Really," the caller is saying, "I've been donating to the church for years. Going every Sunday. He wanted that. He wanted us to get married there. It's legal now. Honestly, I expected better service, but I think persuading him to come home is the least you can do at this point." The client's voice shakes a little with frustration. "Amen," he adds.

"I understand your frustration," I say. "I really do understand, and I appreciate your patience, Mr. Rimington-Pounder."

Across the desk, Grem, my cubicle buddy, collapses in a fit of silent laughter. Gremory is a demon, so he's allowed to laugh at the unfortunate, including the unfortunately-named.

I try to explain to Mr. Rimington-Pounder, as gently as possible, that prayer is not a vending machine, where you pop in a certain amount of devotion and miracles drop into your hands.

"Is there—" the client moistens his lips. "Is there someone higher up the chain I can talk to?"

"Certainly, sir," I say, in my best friendly call center assistant voice. "Let me just put you on hold for a moment."

I press the mute button and roll my eyes at Gremory.

"Let me guess," says Grem, "Rimjob wants to speak to someone higher up?"

I nod. Of course he wants to speak to someone higher up. Everyone wants to speak to someone higher up. But you can't speak to the manager.

The manager is absent.

I take Mr. Rimington-Pounder off hold and adopt a different voice, a man's voice. Something broad and comforting and Midwestern. Authoritative.

"What can I do for you, sir?" I ask. The client is soothed by this voice. I let him talk. I follow protocol and offer a lot of unspecified redemption without actually promising anything at all.

Human beings are generally confused. That's where we come in. Mainly, as the floor supervisor explained in a recent slideshow presentation, humans are confused about wants and needs. They're always on their knees begging for things they want rather than asking for things they need. It's very important to steer them away from the wants and speak to the needs, not that we could solve them, because—as the supervisor explained—that would just be too easy.

Wants and needs. Of all the indignities of flesh, I'm really glad that problem doesn't apply to me.

I know exactly what I want.

That's *my* problem.

• • •

Where is this place?

Somewhere overhead. Somewhere between thought and memory. You might catch a glimpse of it from the window of an airplane, with the dawn burning in over the endless blankets of cloud and all the lights dim in the cabin. You might tell yourself you didn't see what you saw.

Do angels walk in the clouds?

Not if we can help it. It's damp and full of weather balloons.

But can you peer through the mists rolling around the lower levels of heaven? Did you see the endless tower blocks of human resources tangle through the curds of cumulonimbus, in the deathless place where they serve Him night and day in His temple with monthly production goals and customer satisfaction surveys?

Angels work. Of course we do. We're all on zero-hour contracts. Time, after all, is a human idea.

We get twenty-five minutes of it for lunch, with deductions for any bathroom or smoke stops we might have taken. Hating your boss is also a human idea.

The day everything changes, I spend my lunch in the break room with Gremory. There are many rooms in my Father's house, but only one with a functioning coffee machine.

Gremory wears his hair long and shaggy, which is against regulations, but he has the highest client satisfaction rate on our floor. He has this ability to be nice to every caller without letting the slow grind of their daily trauma worry him too much. It's a demon thing.

Grem waves to me from behind his copy of *Kerrang!* They tell us it's important to stay authentic, but Grem doesn't need to try very hard at that. He's sitting with his feet up on a swivel chair, reading his magazine and eating a ham sandwich.

"You shouldn't let it get to you," he says, seeing my face. "I never let it get to me." This is true. Every demon I know is a profoundly chilled-out individual. Our two spheres incorporated over a thousand years ago, and the merger has been a big morale boost all-round.

"I hate not being able to do anything for them," I say, grabbing a coffee from the machine. "The heartbroken ones, most of all. You shouldn't laugh at them. It's not their fault."

"Human hearts," says Gremory, "are brittle, but also durable. I should know; I've eaten thousands. You should never attempt to engage one while it's still beating. I advise against it."

"You're jealous because nobody wants to fuck you because you're a demon."

"That," says Gremory, pushing half a sandwich into his second mouth, "is a vile stereotype. I get mine. I just don't like drama."

"I can't bear the lovesick ones, though. They're so pathetic. And they're always killing themselves, or each other. My ones do, anyway."

"Your problem is that you keep trying to talk them through it," says Grem. "I just tell mine to take a walk in the sunshine. It's not like they remember the calls."

That's not quite true. They remember the calls in snatches, like the dregs of dreams you can't touch with your tongue, draining away. A sense of something profound, whether it's redemption or frustration, vanishing on the edge of vision. Our repeat business is booming.

"I submit to you," says Grem, "that you are projecting, my friend. I submit to you that you're getting stressed because you've been due another of your dramatastic love affairs for years, and you're bored, and you need to learn to relax." Grem wipes his hands on his untucked shirt.

"If you will insist on romancing the doomed," he says, "Go and fuck a panda."

I throw my empty coffee cup at him.

. . .

They tell you not to fall for human beings because they always die. For me, that's part of it. That's their beauty and their tragedy—everything is always rotting, puckering and falling apart under your hands, and you claw at them with your kisses to slow the tug of time but you can't. The panic in their eyes when they reach the age when they realize that, yes, it's happening to them too.

The way they swallow their breath at the point of orgasm.

I can't get enough.

Some of us are perfectly happy counting dust motes in sunlight, or recording the little lives of the luminous creatures at the bottom of the ocean trenches who live and die and drift to the sea floor and know nothing but darkness.

Not me.

Loving humans is what got me demoted.

A long time ago, before the current system, when there were far fewer of them, it was our job to walk among men and women and all the other human creatures and teach them things they needed to know. Writing and calculus and basic food hygiene. We were allowed to give real advice, back then, and we taught them a lot. But they taught us things, too.

They taught us what it is to fear death and to nourish hope. They taught us about pleasure. And passion. And love. Love more than anything. I have always been drawn to the ones who burn with it, the ones who take their tiny lives in trembling hands and try to wring out all the juices before it's too late.

I love fucking human men.

I love loving them, too, though if I'm honest, the fucking is quite a significant part of it. Nothing is ever just sex.

I loved a scientist, once, in Babylon, in the land between the two rivers. His beard was slight and his eyes were black and fronded with long, long lashes, and it was the eighth century after they killed the Nazarene, and he found me in a decorative jar in the market, where a witch whose son I had seduced kept me prisoner for a decade.

He took me home and broke the glass and out I blossomed, fully formed and heavy breasted, and he rushed for his notebooks.

He was tortured by the impulse to understand everything. A fatal condition in humans. He was full of rage at his own ignorance, and the more he eked out through his art and philosophy and mathematics—which in those days were all part of the same discipline—the more he discovered he did not know, and the more that knowledge consumed him.

I loved him for it, and he resented me. Even in our bed, he resented me. His fingertips would outline my contours as if I were drawn on a manuscript, searching for the secrets of my substance.

It hurt him to love me because I was a door to the wisdom of eons that he couldn't unlock. I knew the names of all the stars, and I wouldn't tell them to him. I couldn't. It would have driven him mad, and he would have ended up wandering the streets with the beggars and the crazed soothsayers.

He told me that there were worse places to end.

He longed to know the names of the stars, the true names that they only tell each other, how they were born, the exact latitude of this or that red giant. I told him that I had walked on a star once and it was nothing special. After that he didn't fuck me for weeks.

He liked me in feathers, though. One morning I found that he had plucked out all the filoplumes on my left side and was dissolving them in acid, trying to determine what I was made of.

So I took him walking on a star. He didn't like it as much as he thought he would.

. . .

After lunch, I spend the afternoon answering calls from the Gulf of Mexico, where the summer storms are the worst they've been in a generation, just like they were last year. And the year before that.

The lines are going mad. *Please protect my home. Please save my children from the water. Lord, let us get out in time. In your name, Amen.*

I hate telling them no.

Those of us whose work is out in the world call the phone lines an easy job. I say, *you* try finding fifty different ways to tell people that all their prayers won't save their home, their business, their kids. Try persuading those people to stay signed up to the long-term plan.

I don't like it when they shout at me, but I understand. That's practically what we're here for, to be shouted at. We're here to sit and take all that fury and frustration and tamp it down into something manageable. Angry people boil over with life, raging and raging. They fascinate me.

What I really dread are the quiet ones. The ones who say very little. Sometimes they cry very, very softly, hoping you won't hear them, which just makes it worse.

They all get through to us eventually. That's why it's important to know where they're calling from. A Catholic with an urgent question about the propriety of cleaning consecrated wine off a good white carpet will get rankled if you quote the Koran by accident, and there you are and you've just lost a repeat client.

So I talk to the flood victims in my gentlest voice for an average of ten minutes and twenty-three seconds each.

Then I have a nice chat with a nun in Bolivia who really just wants Jesus to tell her where she's left her glasses this time.

I tell her they're by the sink. Miniature miracles are allowed for those who've signed the lifetime plan. Nobody believes them anyway.

Then there's a Satanist kid in a hospital in Dallas, having his stomach pumped and calling on Lucifer and all his many minions to slaughter his enemies and bring him a dose of medical-grade morphine to get him through the night.

I hand that one over to Gremory. He lives for this sort of thing.

"Hello," I hear him say, "my name is Legion. How can I help you?"

Eventually he persuades the kid that he doesn't need to call on Satan to destroy his squat-mates with fire and fetch him drugs, he needs to call his mother.

Then we go for dinner. Grem has three hot dogs and reads me extracts from *High Times*.

Grem is happy because on Thursday afternoons they play heavy metal over the main speakers, rather than the usual airport music. Apparently heavy metal is calming and improves our productivity. I have another coffee.

"Are you there, God?"

The next caller is six or seven years old at the most. Before answering, I wait for the standard message to play over the still, small song, remote and clear:

Your prayer will be answered by the next available operative. Please note that we cannot take requests for miracles over the phone. Your orisons may be recorded for training and monitoring purposes.

"You're speaking to a member of the heavenly host. How can I help you tonight?"

"Is that Jesus?" A little girl's voice. I check the location: Cape Town. It's morning there.

"No," I say, "but I'm—I'm friends with Jesus." This is an acceptable lie to tell to children. Nobody has seen the Nazarene in two thousand years.

"I'm friends with Jesus, too!" says the little girl. "Can I talk to him?"

"Not just now," I say, "but I can take a message for Jesus and he'll definitely listen to it."

"Oh. Okay. I just wanted to ask about my cat. His name is Lemon. My name is Carla. I'd like Jesus to please look after Granny and Lemon and make sure they don't die."

Why are children always the hardest? Adults know not to ask for that sort of thing directly.

"Also, I'd like Jesus to kill Mr. George."

"You can't really ask us to kill anyone, Carla," I say. "That's not very nice. Who is Mr. George?"

"He's Mummy's boyfriend," says Carla. "He hurts me sometimes. I was going to pray for him to go away, but then Mummy might go away too. So, really, it would be better if he just died."

You can't fault her logic.

We're not allowed to smite wrongdoers with great vengeance, or even moderate vengeance. We're not allowed to make calls to social services. Human beings are supposed to sort things out by themselves, even six-year-old girls. We're just supposed to listen. That's all.

I hate my job sometimes.

"I'm afraid I can't kill Mr. George," I tell her. "That's not allowed." Carla starts to cry very quietly, as if she's worried someone might hear her.

"I understand that you're frustrated right now," I say, reading lines off the on-screen handbook. "I'm just looking through your options for you. Hold the line, please."

I press the mute button, and I lay my head on the desk for a while. Then I pick up the phone again.

"Well, Carla," I say, "I've had a look, and unfortunately we're not able to murder Mr. George for you today. What I can do for you, though, is make the bad feelings go away for a bit. I can make them go deep down inside you where they won't bother you until you're grown up. How does that sound?"

The snuffly sound of a small nose being wiped. "Okay."

I tap in some numbers. Eventually, Carla stops sniffling. I cut the call after twenty-three minutes. Across from me, Gremory is nodding to a client and rocking out to *The Number of the Beast*.

The floor manager calls me in toward the end of the shift. Apparently I've been slacking on my call quota. I spend too long talking to each client.

"Some of them have a lot of problems," I say, inspecting the carpet.

"They all have a lot of problems," says Uriel, who used to be a big shot back in the days when everyone with more than six wings got to call themselves a Duke of Heaven. Now that there are so many more humans and we've had to move with the times and go to full automation, he wears a suit.

"We're not here to fix the problems," Uriel says. "We're here to deliver the maximum amount of spiritual satisfaction in the shortest possible time period. That's why we have the seven-minute target. A target you haven't been meeting."

"Look," I say, "sometimes it just takes longer than seven minutes. Sometimes these people really, really need someone to talk to. I listen. Until they're finished. It seems to make them feel better."

"Yes, we've been noticing a lot of dead air on your side of the line," says Uriel. His voice is milk trickling over smooth marble.

"How many of my calls have you been listening to?"

"Don't get snippy. I checked the database. It's easy enough to monitor the quality and content of the call load. It's standard procedure. I can't believe I'm telling you this again. You're not a special case."

"We're stretched thin," says Uriel. "I don't want to bump you down to maintenance, when we're getting a higher call intake every day, but I will if I have to."

The conversation is over. My hands shake as I return to my desk. It's probably the coffee.

· · ·

Why do we do this? Why do we keep on picking up the phone?

Because religion is a necessary drug. It takes the pain away, for a while. A little candle to nurse in the chest cavity against the darkness. Except some of them burn too fiercely, and it eats them from within.

Only love comes close. Only love.

I loved a mad nun once, in Castile. He had come to the convent the way he was born, with a woman's body, until he was bricked up in the wall of a convent, where he starved away his female aspect in secret. The nuns never found out. Only I saw him as he truly was, as a man entire.

He never left that cell. He was there to burn hard in solitude. The nuns had a system for this, and left a small opening at the bottom of the wall where they could push in water, ink, and dry black bread, which my lover fed to the birds.

He prayed and fasted on his knees until the bricks sliced through to the raw bone. He shaved his head and covered the walls with poetry.

I was all over it.

He did not seem at all surprised to see me when I appeared in his cell. I took the form of a woman at first, but I soon realized my mistake, and put on a man's skin, tanned deeply from the sun my lover had not seen for years. I held his bird-like head in my hands, feeling the contours of his skull. His mouth opened and I fed him crumbs of passion.

He drew me a hundred times over. He called me the body of Christ, but wouldn't let me fuck him. Instead I pushed into him with my fingers, reached deep into his cunt and beckoned, beckoned, as if I could coax him out to walk with me through the wall and into the world of light.

I thought I could keep him alive with my love.

His flesh withered and clung to the bones, and eventually those gave out, too, and he wasted further until all that was left was the heart, beating wildly on the floor of the cell, and a voice raised in fervor. He craved that holy passion so hard that it cannibalized him.

Wants versus needs.

I walked out through the wall and mourned for a century. Then I went back to work.

· · ·

When I return to the cubicle, Gremory is spinning around to *Sabbath Bloody Sabbath* in his desk chair. He gives me a thumbs-up.

Ten minutes to go before the end of the shift. This is the time when you hope to—well, you just hope that nobody calls with a problem you might actually be able to solve. So of course the line flashes.

"Hello, you've come through to the heavenly host, how can I help you today?"

"I'm trying to find my way to heaven."

I appreciate directness at the end of the day. There's an answer for this in the manual, filed under "Convenient Fictions."

"That's great," I say. "You've come to the right place. The path to heaven is hard, but it starts within all of us. May I take your name, sir?"

"Benjamin—Sorry, is this the right number?"

The client's voice is young, male, run through with booze and the lightest scent of self-loathing.

"You did say you were interested in getting to heaven, sir?"

"Yes, that's right. I've been looking for it for an hour now."

"Well, it's wonderful that you're making an effort, sir. Unfortunately, it usually takes longer than an hour to find one's way to heaven. Many people spend entire lifetimes and more in the search."

"It says on Google Maps that it's just off Charing Cross Road."

"I assure you, sir," I say, "heaven cannot be accessed from the Charing Cross Road. May I ask how you came to God in the first place?"

"I'm not religious. I'm looking for Heaven. I've got a sound test there in twenty minutes. Look, I'm sorry, I really think I've got the wrong number. Sorry for wasting your time."

"No, wait," I say, because a thought has occurred to me. "Let me put you on hold for a second."

I slam on the mute button and whisper across the cubicle at Gremory, "Is there a bar or a club called Heaven somewhere in London?"

Grem nods. "Oh, another one of those. I've got the address written down somewhere."

He slides a Post-it across the desk. I unmute the caller.

"Thank you for holding, sir. You want to turn off down Villiers Street, toward the river, and it's under the arches on your right."

"Great. Thanks."

"Is there anything else I can help you with?"

Dead air.

"Well, uh," says Benjamin, "I'm having trouble with this song I'm writing. It's about love. Love and death. And anger. Love and death and anger."

I sit up straight in my chair.

"Would you like to talk about it?" I say. "We could talk about it for a while."

"It's just that I'm afraid all the time," he says, and his voice has receded to a trembling note, a quaver. "I'm afraid of the songs. I'm afraid of the songs I could make, and I'm afraid of not making them. It's stupid."

A meaty thud. He's smashed his head against something, on purpose.

"Don't do that," I say. "Please don't do that. I can help."

"Who are you?" asks Benjamin.

I can hear his heart, the broken-bird flutter of it. His breath on the line.

I have had so many names.

"I'm listening," I say. "I'm listening."

• • •

We're not supposed to Worldwalk during the working week, so Gremory and I hang out on top of Centre Point, the dirty-white 1960s monstrosity that squats mantislike above Tottenham Court Road Tube Station.

"Best view in London," says Gremory. "Mainly because it's the only place you can't see Centre Point. You want some of this?"

He's sucking on a finger-joint stub of spliff, exhaling thick smoke that sweetens the traffic fumes rising from the street.

"I'm okay," I say. "Thanks."

"Seriously," he says, "I'm not trying to pressure you, but I really think it'd be good for you to smoke this stuff occasionally. Chill you out a bit."

"Really, I'm good with just coffee." I love coffee. I particularly like it the way the fashion kids make it, in a goblet shaped like a breast with a picture of a heart frothed on top. I love all that stuff.

"See, that's what I'm talking about," says Gremory. He takes another deep draw and closes his eyes. "Of all the things I'm going to miss when they're gone, I think a beer and a spliff round the back of a decent bar is right up there."

Gremory once laid waste to an entire city-state in Sumer and made its rivers flow with gore. He's calmed down a bit now, and I think he's happier for it. I'm envious.

The last of the sun is dipping its sucked-sherbet into the sugary sky over Oxford Street. We watch it disappear.

"Mastodon are playing in Brixton tonight," says Gremory, after a while. "You want to come?"

"Nah, I'm good," I say. "I think I'll head on back upstairs."

"See, you say that, my friend," says Grem, tapping out his spliff and tucking the end in the pocket of his denim jacket, "but you know and I know that you're going to wait till I'm gone, then get all hopped up on Dexedrine and find something long-haired and broken to fuck you into oblivion."

I don't say anything. We all have our demons. Mine just knows me a bit too well.

"Hey," he says, "no judge. Everyone's got their poison. See you tomorrow. Stay cool."

He flips me the two-horned finger salute and jumps off the roof, turning into a pigeon as he falls. Then he flaps away toward Brixton.

As soon as he's gone, I go straight to Heaven.

• • •

Somewhere around the middle of the eighteenth century, I decided I should give up the tragic poets and doomed revolutionaries and, if I couldn't abstain completely, at least settle down with someone relatively normal.

And so I married a country pastor.

He was surprised when I showed up in his study with my shining eyes, naked as the day I was never born.

I thought we would at least have some shared interests. But he was one of those men of faith who looks away from the altar when he speaks his sermons, avoiding the eyes of an unwelcome houseguest.

We were married in the springtime. He preferred me in my women's weeds, white and perfect as the shepherdesses in the pastoral paintings he would not allow in the house. He was good to me, in his way. He was gentle, and never beat me.

He would make love to me gingerly between his sheets, thrusting blindly in the dark, trying to touch as little of my body as possible. He said that that was God's way. I tried to tell him that the God I knew was fire and passion and cared not at all about how humans choose to fuck.

In the mornings I would boil him a single egg and watch him crack the shell with his short nails, not damaging the hard white jelly at all, leaving a pure and perfect oval so sinless that he sometimes couldn't bear to bite into it.

I thought it wouldn't matter that I wasn't in love with him.

It did.

One night I came to him in my gown. So many layers in those days, especially in bed. I made my husband lie on top of the coverlet and lit the oil lamp.

Then I took everything off. Every stitch. He watched me while I stepped out of my gown, my night stays, dirty-white lace dropping to the floor. The bloomers, the ribbons in my hair.

Then I kept going. I took off my skin and hung it on a nail behind the door. I peeled away layers of flesh and bone until I stood there in my true form, burning and spinning, the rush in my ears so fierce I could hardly hear my husband scream.

Then I left him.

I hear he ended in a madhouse.

There are worse places.

. . .

You can't just walk into Heaven. There's a dress code, and a door charge, too, unless you're on the guest list. We're not allowed to handle money, so I slip into something that'll let me walk straight in.

Black jeans. Black lipstick. Black heels. A tight black mesh top. Snow-white hair dipped in eggshell blue. Smooth skin, a whisper of something Asian in the eyes. Soft fat layered in the right places over rigid muscle.

God, I look fantastic.

The girl taking tickets has a pair of angel wings tattooed on her back. I tell her I'm with the band.

She looks me up and down and nods me in.

Inside Heaven, it's all sweat and warm beer and the chill trails of cigarette smoke from the nicotine pen outside. There's static in the air. The roadies have just finished setting up.

I get someone to buy me a Diet Coke at the bar, then lurk at the back, looking mysterious, while dying-robot music stutters frantic over a slow bass heartbeat. I like it.

I'm not fallen. I never fell. I'm just slumming it.

In the twenty minutes before the band, I send three creeps careening for the exit, muttering prayers they haven't spoken since childhood.

Then the band comes on. Just a drummer, a keyboardist in a tight silver skirt, and him.

His eyes are large and blue and sad. His cheekbones were carved in marble by a crazed sculptor to drive women mad.

But I am not a woman. I'm something else.

A static whine.

Then it starts.

The words are all there, love and death and rage and the riot of fighting through fear to something more, something wholly human. But Benjamin sings like one of us. All ice and holy fire.

The crowd goes wild.

I wait for him in the alley after the show. When he sees me, he stops dead, his long coat falling around his shoulders.

I try to think of something profound to say.

"You were great," I tell him, looking at my feet. The heels are hurting me. I danced all night.

"I know you from somewhere," he says. "Don't I know you from somewhere?"

He's high on adrenaline, and drunk.

But not too drunk, not yet.

I smile, and hold out my hands.

. . .

I wake up on a dirty mattress somewhere on Caledonian Road. A train is rattling overhead. Pigeons vomiting in the walls. The smell of cheap coffee, bittersweet and black.

Benjamin is already up, already half dressed. In the dawn light, his naked torso is smooth and translucent-pale, dusted with freckles. Eleven blond hairs sprout from his chest. I counted them all last night.

I'm going to count every freckle. Every scar. I'm going to number his days and open his heart and drink his passion and his pain. I'm going to tell him all the names of the stars so he can write them down in a song.

Benjamin places a mug of coffee in front of me and stares.

"I remember you now," he says.

I sip my coffee and shake my head. "You must be thinking of someone else."

"I do," he says. "I remember. I called you. It was a mistake."

My mouth is dry. "People call all the time," I say. "It's what people do."

"No," he says. "I mean, this was a mistake. I had a nice time. A really nice time. But I can't give you what you want."

He's staring out the window at the fist of traffic groaning down the road toward Camden.

"You don't want me to stay?"

He looks at me, right through my skin.

"I want you to stay," he says, "but I need you to leave."

Benjamin gives me twenty pounds for a taxi. I get out at Angel Station and stop at a pay phone that hasn't been operational in years. I pick up the receiver and call the only number I know.

"Your prayer will be answered by the next available operative. Please note that we cannot take requests for miracles over the phone. Your orisons may be recorded for training and monitoring purposes."

"Hello, my name is Legion, how can I help you this morning?"

"Grem," I say, "it's me."

"Where the fuck have you been?" Grem hisses down the line. Demons can really hiss. "You're three hours late. Supervisor's freaking out. Are you even coming in?"

"I—" I swallow hard. "I don't think so. Not today. Maybe not tomorrow either. I don't think I can do the job anymore."

"Mate," he says, "what happened? Are you okay?"

"I don't think so," I say, and my voice is thick and strange. "I don't think I've been okay for a very long time."

"Hold on," says Grem.

I hold the line. I listen to the receiver. Dead air.

"Right," says Grem, "You stay right where you are. I'm coming down to get you. Took the afternoon off. Family emergency. Want to go and get baked on Hampstead Heath?"

"Yeah," I say, sniffing. "Yeah, I'd like that. Thanks, Grem."

"Or we can hang out by the river or something. Whatever you want."

"That sounds good, too."

"Okay. Right. Get yourself a fancy coffee or something. Stay cool, okay? See you soon."

Grem cuts the call.

I take a deep breath. My clothes are still sticky with last night's sweat. It'll wash away. Sex. Sweat. Hair. Skin. Wants versus needs. It all washes away.

I go into the coffee shop on the corner of Upper Street and order a latte from a white girl with an angular haircut and a tattoo that says "Made in China."

The Number of the Beast is playing on the speakers.

Grem's right. It really is quite relaxing.

LAURIE PENNY is a journalist, feminist, geek, and author of five books, most recently *Unspeakable Things: Sex, Lies, and Revolution*. Recently a Nieman Fellow at Harvard University, she's a contributing editor at the *New Statesman* and writes and speaks on social justice, pop culture, gender issues, and digital politics for *The Guardian*, *The New York Times*, *Vice*, *Salon*, *The Nation*, *The New Inquiry*, and many more. She lives in London.

The Tallest Doll in New York City

Maria Dahvana Headley

It's Valentine's Day, 1938, and the Chrysler Building's tired of waiting on the corner of Forty-Second and Lex for a certain edifice to notice her. A Runyonesque story of what might happen if two of New York's greatest creations met on a day built for romance. *Edited by Liz Gorinsky.*

On a particular snowy Monday in February, at 5:02 P.M., I'm sixty-six flights above the corner of Lexington Avenue and Forty-Second Street, looking down at streets swarming with hats and jackets. All the guys who work in midtown are spit into the frozen city, hunting sugar for the dolls they're trying to muddle from sour into sweet.

From up here I can see Lex fogged with cheap cologne, every citizen clutching his heart-shaped box wrapped in cellophane, red as the devil's drawers.

If you happen to be a waiter at the Cloud Club, you know five's the hour when a guy's nerves start to fray. This calendar square's worse than most. Every man on our member list is suffering the Saint Valentine's Cramp, and me and the crew up here are ready with a stocked bar. I'm in my Cloud Club uniform, the pocket embroidered with my name in the Chrysler's trademark typeface, swooping like a skid mark on a lonely road in Montana. Over my arm I've got a clean towel, and in my vest I have an assortment of aspirins and plasters in case a citizen shows up already bleeding or broken-nosed from an encounter with a lady lovenot.

Later tonight, it'll be the members' doll dinner, the one night a year we allow women into the private dining room. Valorous Victor, captain of the wait, pours us each a preparatory coupe. There are ice-cream sculptures shaped like Cupid in the walk-in. Each gal gets a corsage the moment she enters, the roses from Valorous Victor's brother's hothouse in Jersey. At least two dolls are in line for wife, and we've got their guy's rings here ready and waiting, to drop into champagne in one case and wedge into an oyster in another. Odds in the kitchen have the diamond in that particular ring consisting of a pretty piece of paste.

Down below, it's 1938, and things are not as prime as they are up here. Our members are the richest men left standing, their wives at home in Greenwich, their mistresses movie starlets with porcelain teeth. Me, I'm single. I've got a mother with rules strict as Sing Sing, and a sister with a face pretty as the Sistine's ceiling. My sister needs protecting from all the guys in the world, and so I live in Brooklyn, man of my mother's house, until I can find a wife or die waiting.

The members start coming in, and each guy gets led to his locker. Our members are the rulers of the world. They make automobiles and build skyscrapers, but none as tall as the one we're standing in right now. The Cloud Club's been open since before the building got her spire, and the waitstaff in a Member's Own knows things even a man's miss doesn't. Back during Prohibition, we installed each of the carved wood lockers at the Cloud Club with a hieroglyphic identification code straight out of ancient Egypt, so our members can keep their bottles safe and sound. Valorous Victor dazzles the police more than once with his rambling explanation of cryptographic complexities, and finally the blue boys just take a drink and call it done. No copper's going to Rosetta our rigmarole.

I'm at the bar mixing a Horse's Neck for Mr. Condé Nast, but I've got my eye on the mass of members staggering out of the elevators with fur coats, necklaces, and parcels of cling & linger, when, at 5:28 P.M. precisely, the Chrysler Building steps off her foundation and goes for a walk.

There is no warning.

She just shakes the snow and pigeons loose from her spire and takes off, sashaying southwest. This is something even we waiters haven't experienced before. The Chrysler is 1,046 feet tall, and, until now, she's seemed stationary. She's stood motionless on this corner for seven years so far, the gleamiest gal in a million miles.

None of the waitstaff lose their cool. When things go wrong, waiters, the good ones, adjust to the needs of both customers and clubs. In 1932, for example, Valorous himself commences to travel from midtown to Ellis Island in order to deliver a pistol to one of our members, a guy who happens to have a grievance against a brand-new American in line for a name. Two slugs and a snick later, Victor's in surgery beneath the gaze of the Verdigris Virgin. Still, he returns to Manhattan in time for the evening napkin twist.

"The Chrysler's just taking a little stroll, sirs," Valorous announces from the stage. "No need to panic. This round is on me and the waiters of the Cloud Club."

Foreseeably, there is, in fact, some panic. To some of our members, this event appears to be more horrifying than Black Tuesday.

Mr. Nast sprints to the men's room with motion sickness, and The Soother, our man on staff for problems of the heart and guts, tails him with a tall glass of ginger ale. I decide to drink Nast's Horse's Neck myself. Nerves on the mend, I consider whether any of our members on sixty-seven and sixty-eight might possibly need drinks, but I see Victor's already sending an expedition to the stairs.

I take myself to the windows. In the streets, people gawp and yawp and holler, and taxis honk their horns. Gals pick their way through icy puddles, and guys stand in paralysis, looking up.

We joke about working in the body of the best broad in New York City, but no one on the waitstaff ever thinks that the Chrysler might have a will of her own. She's beautiful, what with her multistory crown, her skin pale blue in daylight and rose-colored with city lights at night. Her gown's printed with arcs and swoops, and beaded with tiny drops of General Electric.

We know her inside out, or we think we do. We go up and down her stairs when her elevators are broken, looking out her triangular windows on the hottest day of summer. The ones at the top don't have panes, because the wind up there can kick up a field goal even when it's breezeless down below, and the updrafts can grab a bird and fling it through the building like it's nothing. The Chrysler's officially seventy-seven floors, but she actually has eighty-four levels. They get smaller and smaller until, at eighty-three, there's only a platform the size of a picnic table, surrounded by windows, and, above that, a trapdoor and a ladder into the spire, where the lightning rod is. The top floors are tempting. Me and The Soother take ourselves up to the very top one sultry August night, knees and ropes, and she sways beneath us, but holds steady. Inside the spire, there's space for one guy to stand encased in metal, feeling the earth move.

The Chrysler is a devastating dame, and that's nothing new. I could assess her for years and never be done. At night we turn her on, and she glows for miles.

I'm saying, the waiters of the Cloud Club should know what kind of doll she is. We work inside her brain.

Our members retreat to the private dining room, the one with the etched-glass working-class figures on the walls. There, they cower beneath the table, but the waitstaff hangs onto the velvet curtains and watches as the Chrysler walks to Thirty-Fourth Street, clicking and jingling all the way.

"We shoulda predicted this, boss," I say to Valorous.

"Ain't that the truth," he says, flicking a napkin over his forearm. "Dames! The Chrysler's in love."

For eleven months, from 1930 to 1931, the Chrysler's the tallest doll in New York City. Then the Empire is spired to surpass her, and winds up taller still. She has a view straight at him, but he ignores her.

At last, it seems, she's done with his silence. It's Valentine's Day.

I pass Victor a cigarette.

"He acts like a Potemkin village," I say. "Like he's got nothing inside him but empty floors. I get a chance at a doll like that, I give up everything, move to a two-bedroom. Or out of the city, even; just walk my way out. What've I got waiting for me at home? My mother and my sister. He's got royalty."

"No accounting for it," says Valorous, and refills my coupe. "But I hear he doesn't go in for company. He won't even look at her."

At Thirty-Fourth and Fifth, the Chrysler stops, holds up the edge of her skirt, and taps her high heel. She waits for some time as sirens blare beneath her. Some of our fellow citizens, I am ashamed to report, don't notice anything out of place at all. They just go around her, cussing and hissing at the traffic.

The Empire State Building stands on his corner, shaking in his boots. We can all see his spire trembling. Some of the waitstaff and members sympathize with his wobble, but not me. The Chrysler's a class act, and he's a shack of shamble if he doesn't want to go out with her tonight.

At 6:03 P.M., pedestrians on Fifth Avenue shriek in terror as the Chrysler gives up and taps the Empire hard on the shoulder.

"He's gonna move," Valorous says. "He's got to! Move!"

"I don't think he is," says The Soother, back from comforting the members in the lounge. "I think he's scared. Look at her."

The Soother's an expert in both Chinese herbal medicine and psychoanalysis. He makes our life as waiters easier. He can tell what everyone at a table's waiting for with one quick look in their direction.

"She reflects everything. Poor guy sees all his flaws, done up shiny, for years now. He feels naked. It can't be healthy to see all that reflected."

The kitchen starts taking bets.

"She won't wait for him for long," I say. I have concerns for the big guy, in spite of myself. "She knows her worth, she heads uptown to the Metropolitan."

"Or to the Library," says The Soother. "I go there, if I'm her. The Chrysler's not a doll to trifle with."

"They're a little short," I venture, "those two. I think she's more interested in something with a spire. Radio City?"

The Empire's having a difficult time. His spire's supposedly built for zeppelin docking, but then the Hindenberg explodes, and now no zeppelin will ever moor there. His purpose is moot. He slumps slightly.

Our Chrysler taps him again, and holds out her steel glove. Beside me, Valorous pours another round of champagne. I hear money changing hands all over the club.

Slowly, slowly, the Empire edges off his corner.

The floor sixty-six waitstaff cheers for the other building, though I hear Mr. Nast commencing to groan again, this time for his lost bet.

Both buildings allow their elevators to resume operations, spilling torrents of shouters from the lobbies and into the street. By the time the Chrysler and the Empire start walking east, most of the members are gone, and I'm drinking a bottle of bourbon with Valorous and The Soother.

We've got no dolls on the premises, and the members still here declare formal dinner dead and done until the Chrysler decides to walk back to Lex. There is palpable relief. The citizens of the Cloud Club avoid their responsibilities for the evening.

As the Empire wades into the East River hand in hand with the Chrysler, other lovestruck structures begin to talk. We're watching from the windows as apartment towers lean in to gossip, stretching laundry lines finger to finger. Grand Central Station, as stout and elegant as a survivor of the Titanic, stands up, shakes her skirts, and pays a visit to Pennsylvania Station, that Beaux-Arts bangle. The Flatiron and Cleopatra's Needle shiver with sudden proximity, and within moments they're all over one another.

Between Fifty-Ninth Street and the Williamsburg Bridge, the Empire and the Chrysler trip shyly through the surf. We can see New Yorkers, tumbling out of their taxicabs and buses, staring up at the sunset reflecting in our doll's eyes.

The Empire has an awkward heart-shaped light appended to his skull, which Valorous and I do some snickering over. The Chrysler glitters in her dignified silver spangles. Her windows shimmy.

As the pedestrians of three boroughs watch, the two tallest buildings in New York City press against one another, window to window, and waltz in ankle-deep water.

I look over at the Empire's windows, where I can see a girl standing, quite close now, and looking back at me.

"Victor," I say.

"Yes?" he replies. He's eating vichyssoise beside a green-gilled tycoon, and the boxer Gene Tunney is opposite him smoking a cigar. I press a cool cloth to the tycoon's temples, and accept the fighter's offer of a Montecristo.

"Do you see that doll?" I ask them.

"I do, yes," Victor replies, and Tunney nods. "There's a definite dolly bird over there," he says.

The girl in the left eye of the Empire State, a good thirty feet above where we sit, is wearing red sequins, and a magnolia in her hair. She sidles up to the microphone. One of her backup boys has a horn, and I hear him start to play.

Our buildings sway, tight against each other, as the band in the Empire's eye plays "In the Still of the Night."

I watch her, that doll, that dazzling doll, as the Chrysler and the Empire kiss for the first time, at 9:16 P.M. I watch her for hours as the Chrysler blushes and the Empire whispers, as the Chrysler coos and the Empire laughs.

The riverboats circle in shock, as, at 11:34 P.M., the two at last walk south toward the harbor, stepping over bridges into deeper water, her eagle ornaments laced together with his girders. The Chrysler steps delicately over the Wonder Wheel at Coney Island, and he leans down and plucks it up for her. We watch it pass our windows as she inhales its electric fragrance.

"Only one way to get to her," Valorous tells me, passing me a rope made of tablecloths. All the waitstaff of the Cloud Club nod at me.

"You're a champ," I tell them. "You're all champs."

"I am too," says Tunney, drunk as a knockout punch. He's sitting in a heap of roses and negligees, eating bonbons.

The doll sings only to me as I climb up through the tiny ladders and trapdoors to the eighty-third, where the temperature drops below ice-cream Cupid. I inch out the window and onto the ledge, my rope gathered in my arms. As the Chrysler lays her gleaming cheek against the Empire's shoulder, as he runs his hand up her beaded knee, as the two tallest buildings in New York City begin to make love in the Atlantic, I fling my rope across the divide, and the doll in the Empire's eye ties it to her grand piano.

At 11:57 P.M., I walk out across the tightrope, and at 12:00 A.M., I hold her in my arms.

I'm still hearing the applause from the Cloud Club, all of them raising their coupes to the windows, their bourbons and their soup spoons, as, through the Chrysler's eye, I see the boxer plant his lips on Valorous Victor. Out the windows of the Empire State, the Cyclone wraps herself up in the Brooklyn Bridge. The Staten Island Ferry rises up and dances for Lady Liberty.

At 12:16 A.M., the Chrysler and the Empire call down the lightning into their spires, and all of us, dolls and guys, waiters and chanteuses, buildings and citizens, kiss like fools in the icy ocean off the amusement park, in the pale orange dark of New York City.

MARIA DAHVANA HEADLEY is a *New York Times* bestselling novelist, memoirist, and editor, most recently of the novels *Magonia, Aerie,* and *Queen of Kings,* and the anthology *Unnatural Creatures* (coeditor with Neil Gaiman). Her short stories have been finalists for the World Fantasy, Nebula, and Shirley Jackson Awards. She is also the author of *The Mere Wife,* a contemporary adaptation of *Beowulf,* and the queer YA superhero novel *The Combustible.*

The Cage

A. M. Dellamonica

It's open season on werewolves in East Vancouver, and what starts out as a standard contracting job for Jude turns out to be more than it seems. *Edited by Stacy Hague-Hill.*

April

The eerie thing about Paige Adolpha wasn't just that she turned up right when I was reading about her in the paper. It wasn't her fame as the star witness in the big local werewolf trial. What brought on the gooseflesh, first time I saw her, was that she was the spitting image of her murdered sister. Identical twins, you know?

I was at the Britannia branch of the public library, absorbing what passed for Vancouver news and wishing the local papers would come up to the standards of the *Edmonton Journal*—even the *Globe and Mail*—when one of the regulars caught sight of her.

"It's that lady from page three," he stage-whispered.

"Don't stare," I murmured, peeking despite myself.

I flipped back to the two shots of Paige's sister, Pamela. One showed them both, laughing together. The other was her corpse: long-limbed, blood-matted fur, all fang. Nobody was denying she'd been a lycanthrope.

Richard Deenie, her killer, was a brash American with one of those awful trophy necklaces of monster teeth. Fifteen years ago, he was barely getting by selling camping equipment. When humanity discovered monsterkind in 2002, he'd reinvented himself as a sleazoid *Buffy* type. Him and plenty of others. U.S. werewolves were getting thin on the ground, so he'd stalked Pamela to British Columbia and shot her with a silver bullet.

"Ya already read that page." The old-timer was fidgeting; I'd beaten him to the last copy of the *Sun*.

I swapped him for the *Province*. It had the same trial coverage, written at an even more dumbed-down level. Deenie, a born media whore, got arrested at a press conference he'd called especially so he could crow about saving us wussy Canadians from a lycanthrope menace.

I hoped he was surprised when the Crown found a few cops willing to arrest him before he slithered back over the border. He was claiming self-defence. Paige insisted her sister had never bitten, much less killed, anyone.

Here she was in the flesh, staring at the glassed-in art installation that separated the library's reading room from the chaos of the kids' section. She had a baby papoosed on her chest. She looked about nine, underfed, bruised by fatigue.

Before I could look away, she was crossing the reading room. "You're Jude?"

I nodded. She was brandishing a pair of home-improvement books and a library receipt.

"The info woman says you're a general contractor."

I shot Lela—who's dating my ex and disapproves of my staying single—a dirty look.

"Shhh!" said the old-timer.

Steer clear, I thought. But . . . "Come on, I'm done here."

I do go for elfin blondes. Lela knows my type. And I was getting an answering vibe—baby or not, Paige looked available and, potentially, into me. But I wasn't looking to be anyone's stepmom. *She's vulnerable*, I reminded myself. *The pressure of a trial, plus grief . . . her sister's been dead, what? Four months?*

I set out on a path that winds between Britannia's low, unmistakably institutional buildings. The community center is big and battered looking, almost an architectural blight, and yet I love it. It's the backbone of my neighbourhood. The library's attached to a high school, and the complex includes a pool and ice rink, tennis courts, youth outreach and senior's center.

Britannia is where the working poor of the neighbourhood go to borrow books and recreate their kids, to take guitar lessons, study aikido and judo, to catch a yoga class that doesn't cost twenty bucks an hour. It's where they teach teen moms what they call life skills, like cooking something more nutritious than ramen; they bring me in to demonstrate how to unstop a toilet and install a baby gate. Now and then the center will even bus people out to Golden Ears Park to hike or canoe or ride horses.

We came out behind the daycare into a green space known locally as Poverty Park. My house overlooks the park—I could see my front door—but instead of taking Paige home with me, I pointed at a bench under a double-flowering plum. The tree was thick with blooms, like it had been dipped in candy floss. Fifty feet over, near the tennis courts, three young guys with blond dreadlocks were beating on trashcan-sized drums.

I must have frowned, because she asked, "What is it?"

"Nothing."

"You're curious about something."

"I suppose that happens all the time?"

"It's okay," Paige said, settling herself under the canopy of blooms. "You can ask me anything."

"I was just thinking it had been four months since . . . They brought Deenie to trial pretty quick."

Ghost of a smile. "The prosecutor's a force of nature. And Deenie's representing himself. He didn't know the tricks they use to slow things down."

Or he didn't want to. "So, you want reno advice?"

Paige said, "I'm renting my basement out as a recording studio. I thought soundproofing, bars on the windows . . ."

"You have a house—I mean, you own it?"

"Pamela had some insurance."

"You're not planning to grow pot down there, are you?"

"With soundproofing?"

"Or a dungeon?"

"I haven't got time for vanilla sex, let alone kink." The baby was watching the birds with bright-eyed intensity.

I steered my gaze back to Paige. "You want to do the work yourself?"

She flinched. "I need advice on the soundproofing. It's too complex. . . . The books don't say anything."

Don't volunteer, I told myself. You can't fix someone else's life, and Lela's opinions notwithstanding, I didn't need this. A baby meant Paige was maybe no more than a year out of a relationship with some guy. "You want to DIY, even though you have money. You need to rent out your basement, but you're a nurse, aren't you? You have a kid, you're the public face of a homicide trial, and now you want to get into futzing with soundproofing and—"

"What are you saying?"

"Look, maybe I don't talk like a Rhodes Scholar, but I know when I'm being lied to."

"Forget I said anything." She scooped up her kid and stormed off, so mad she almost walked over two women who were hawking handmade jewellery over by the sidewalk.

I watched her go, relieved. Then I took her abandoned library books inside so I could tell Lela to lay off the matchmaking.

Know what she said? "Oh, so you *did* like her?"

May

The thing about going for broken women is it doesn't make you feel good about yourself. So I kept busy: installed cabinets in a local rehab center, redid a couple bathrooms, volunteered to replace some vandalized tiles in Mosaic Creek Park. I let myself get talked into working a shift at the Italian Day festival, valet parking bicycles and chit-chatting with environmental activists as people from all the Drive's overlapping communities ambled by.

At one time, East Vancouver was the bad part of town, which seems laughable now house prices have shot up. Sleek, well-off mommies, new to the area, pay my bills: I renovate the kitchens in their circa-1920 houses while they slurp up frappuccinos at Starbucks and plan the next battle in their bitter fight for control of Poverty Park. The area is upscaling; they want to drive out the homeless, the veterans, the street vendors and heroin junkies who've occupied the park—peaceably, for the most part—for decades.

None of which is to say I had mommies or motherhood on the brain. I put Paige and her troubles out of my mind, skipping the trial coverage, walking by fast when I saw her doe-eyed face in the newspaper boxes.

But a month after we first met she was back at Britannia, even more harried, obviously looking for me. The kid was in her pouch, lolling like a sailor after three days ashore.

I kept my eyes off him. "You got the soundproofing up? Barred your windows?"

She nodded.

"What happened?"

She hesitated. "They vandalized them."

"By 'they' you mean . . ."

"The band."

"And by 'them'?"

"The soundproofing pads."

She was clinging to the lie. I thought of calling her on it, again, but I'd had a month to feel guilty. Chivalry won out. "You ready to show me?"

A long sigh. "Should I make an appointment?"

"No, I'm between jobs. Lead on."

Paige's house was a few blocks south of mine. It was what we call a Vancouver Special—an ugly box clad in yellow aluminium siding and fake brick, square in shape, designed to max out the floor space ratio on its lot. Multifamily residences: idea being to shoehorn in a couple with three kids, both sets of in-laws, and maybe jam an unmarried sister in the basement. There'd been a toxic bloom of them in the eighties; nowadays, developers are knocking them down to build pretty, faux-heritage townhomes.

The place didn't look Paige's speed at all.

"Big basement," she said, by way of explanation. I got a bit of a jolt; perceptive women are sexy. We shared a weird, edgy grin.

Past the front door was a rabbit hutch and a couple bags—one packed with scrubs, another a suitcase I'd seen in trial photos. She dropped the diaper bag beside them.

The rabbits shifted nervously.

"You hate animals too?" she asked.

"Excuse me?"

"The baby. You make a point of ignoring him."

"I keep fish." I didn't mention the cat; this was no time to sound like a nurturer.

"Downstairs." She indicated a door. "You can leave your shoes on."

I ducked under the overhang, heading into what had once been the in-law suite. Its interior walls were sledge-hammered away, the carpet torn up. All that remained was a vacant space with bare concrete floors.

"Why aren't you on maternity leave?" I asked, thinking of the bag of work stuff—scrubs, shoes, protein bars.

"I take the occasional fill-in shift to remind myself I have more on the brain than the next loaded diaper." She closed the door behind us.

Ever been somewhere where no sound gets in, none at all? Not the traffic outside, not the hum of the fridge, nothing but your own breath and heartbeat? It can be suffocating, almost claustrophobic; your ears ring and your brain insists there's something wrong.

You can muffle a garage studio on the cheap by padding the walls with second-hand mattresses, but Paige had gone high-end. Her panels looked like they had come from a mental hospital—they were surfaced in a white quilted fabric and had been fitted with care, floor to ceiling, even covering the windows. They snugged up against the ceiling panels perfectly.

The air stank of bleach.

A baby cam and one big light were mounted in a corner of the ceiling, cords snaking between the soundproof boards.

"I figured they'd behave if I kept an eye on them," she said, following my gaze to the camera.

"They" again, the fictional rock band. "This is good craftsmanship."

"Surprised?"

"Impressed." The nurses I know have decent mechanical skills, but this wouldn't have been an easy job.

"The damage is here—" The fabric of the wall was torn at knee height in two places, the foam scattered in bits.

Foam and . . . I stirred the scraps, recognizing a tuft of animal fur.

She didn't meet my eyes. "I'll have to install something over the padding, won't I?"

"You could frame and drywall. . . ."

"Drywall might be too fragile."

"Clad the walls in sheet metal?"

"Sounds ugly." She was close to weeping. "It has to be nice. It can't . . . just be a big cage."

My heart raced, loud in the silence. "Bamboo panels."

"What?"

"Bamboo wall panels. Natural looking, eco-friendly, and very hard. We frame over your soundproofing, clad the whole thing in bamboo panels. Even if one or two of them do get roughed up, we just replace. No harm, no foul, okay?"

We. Damn, I said "we."

"Seriously?" She pretended to scan the room, mastering her emotions.

"It'll be easy, Paige."

That's when the drunken-sailor baby opened his little mug and belched a river of chewed industrial foam, blood-laced baby formula, and a sticky hunk of bunny leather onto my steel-toed work boots.

I looked from the mess to Paige's chalky face.

"Maybe we can find the bamboo in sort of a crimson lacquer," I added.

• • •

It's not what you think," she said, twenty minutes later in the backyard. The baby was on a blanket under a tree, and she'd pulled out two beers. "Pamela didn't bite him."

"No?" She couldn't afford to have me—or anybody—thinking otherwise. If

Deenie could prove Pamela had ever been a danger to others, he'd walk on the murder charge.

"She's his mother. Was." She rolled the beer bottle between her hands. "Lycanthropy's been in my family since the Civil War. You can transmit it through the placenta."

"You were in the womb together. Same placenta."

"I'm not a werewolf," she said. "Best guess is sometimes it takes, sometimes it doesn't. Twins were a first for my family."

"Papers don't say he's her baby."

"We drove out to the middle of the province, switched IDs. At the hospital in Trail, nobody knew us."

"Twins, right. Didn't anyone notice that you—"

"I wore a padded belly to work for a few months."

"You and Pamela must have been close."

"I wasn't so sure until she was gone. It was my job to take care of her, to cover, to cover up—"

"The good kid."

She wiped her eyes.

"Me too. Eldest, right? Perfect attendance, good grades, come home and watch the little kids. . . ."

Again with that scalpel-sharp look of comprehension: "Your family's not around anymore?"

"They're alive. They're pretty sure I'm going to hell."

"I'm sorry."

I wasn't about to get into that. "So, you pulled a switcheroo with his birth certificate. But why?"

"To protect him. Deenie was already hunting Pammy."

"And her boyfriend—he's the father?"

"He doesn't know. She left when she realized she was pregnant."

The boyfriend had just testified. Deenie broke his fingers and pulled out one of his front teeth to get him to give up Pamela's location. Poor guy damn near had a mental breakdown on the stand; since he was representing himself, Deenie got to cross-examine the man he'd tortured. He'd had a lot of fun with it.

"Deenie caught up with Pammy a couple weeks after the birth. She was weak, postpartum. Slow."

"But you'd fixed things so the kid's yours on paper."

"It wasn't that risky. We'd pass a DNA test . . . identical twins, remember?"

"Except Chase'd test positive for werewolf?"

"Yeah."

The baby was waving at the tree, entranced by the moving shadows. Not that I was watching.

"The first three months were okay; I kept him in his playpen."

"And now?"

"See that pile of playpen scraps over by the trash bin?"

"So you cage him in the basement every month until . . ." How long would he be a puppy? Sixteen years?

"Until he's five. There's a pack, in Surrey; they'll take him in during the moon, teach him to hunt, to avoid people. It's how Pammy was socialized. But he has to go to them good-tempered. He has to enjoy his . . . wild nights, they call them. If his temperament sours . . ."

"Then the pack won't take him?"

"They'll do worse than not take him." She was tearing up again. "And all this depends on their being around when he's five, which depends on Richard Deenie being convicted so he and his thug sidekick and all their sick monster-hunting pals know it's serious, it's illegal, that it's not open season up here."

I put my hand on hers. "Okay. So. Dog-proofing the basement."

How hard could it be? He weighed, what, fifteen pounds?

June

Four weeks ran by in a blur.

By the time the full moon rolled around, we had the walls of her basement panelled. The rabbit hutch had spent a couple weeks downstairs, killing the bleach fumes with a dog-friendly aroma of barn. We'd left construction sawdust on the floor.

That evening, Paige took all but two of the bunnies upstairs. She threw toys, rawhide chew sticks, and pepperoni down on the concrete floor, along with an old moccasin. She dropped in a few two-dollar ivy plants from the garden store, without their plastic starter pots. So there'd be dirt?

Fifteen minutes before moonrise, she gave Chase a bottle, burped him, stripped off his footie pyjamas and diaper and lay him, nude, on the concrete basement floor.

"No blanket?"

"He'd eat it." We stared at him, pale and small on the floor. He was playing with his toes. If he was cold, it didn't show.

Then he was seizing.

Paige threw out an arm; I guess I'd taken an involuntary step into the room. She backed me out, closed the door, cutting off the sound of him strangling. Then she led me upstairs. "We can watch on the monitor."

Ye gods. The strength it must have taken; I didn't even like the kid and I didn't want to walk away. She turned on the monitor. *He'll be a slavering, hideous monster. Scary and unlovable*, I thought. I took a good look.

It was worse than I thought. He was all wobbling puppy butt and baby fluff. He had big eyes, long flirty lashes. He batted them at a chew toy, looking like some kid's cartoon dawg—bink-bink.

A quiet "Aroo!" trickled through the baby monitor.

"Awww," I said. Believe me, a dead cynic couldn't have kept from saying "Awww."

I was entranced until he caught the first rabbit.

Even baby-clumsy, he was fast. He shook the rabbit into a puddle, sending fur flying, then rolled in the pudding. He chewed one of the plastic toys to chips. The shoe went in stages; he'd run around with it for a while, settle in for a chaw, run some more.

And my God, the peeing. Every nook, every corner. All my lovely bamboo panelling.

"Boy dogs," Paige said, by way of apology, or explanation.

"This was why the bleach, last month."

"To kill the smell, yep."

Okay, stop staring. I got up as he began dragging the first of the ivy plants around the room, spraying potting soil. His tail was wagging. It had only been an hour.

"He's laying waste to the place."

"As long as he's happy." She quirked a brow. "Speaking of which . . ."

"Mmm?" I was already considering how to entertain the little bugger next time. He needed grass, more plants . . .

Paige kissed me.

It was awkward—disastrous. My head was elsewhere; she caught me by surprise. She was nervous, too, so the move came out a bit of a lunge. Our lips met for a second; then our teeth clacked, pinching my tongue. I pulled back, reflexively, tasting blood. And whatever she saw in my face . . . she turned bright red.

It might be for the best. I squelched the urge to apologize. "I should leave."

"Hey—it's okay. I wouldn't want to date me either."

"You're plenty dateable, Paige—"

"Don't, Jude."

"What do you want me to say? You're dead gorgeous. You're funny, smart. But your sister's newly dead, you got this murder trial . . ."

"I'm hot, but I'm a basket case? You don't want to take advantage? I didn't take you for old-school butch, Jude."

"How could you not be a basket case?" I stared out the window. "You're in mourning and there's a rabid frigging monster in your basement."

A faint "Aroo" trickled from the speaker.

"So? You think you're such a catch?"

"I didn't say that." A flare of light in a truck, across the street, caught my eye.

"You're freakishly tall, for one thing. And that librarian gave me your entire romantic history. You *dare* call me damaged goods when—"

"Someone's watching the house," I interrupted.

She cat-stepped across the living room, pissed, and looked sideways through the curtains.

"Reporter?" I whispered.

"Deenie's sidekick," she gritted. "Valmont Robb."

"What do you want to do?"

"I'll bundle up something kid-shaped and walk you to the door."

"To the . . ."

"You were leaving anyway, weren't you?"

"But—"

A furious glint in her eye. "I may look like a mess to you, but believe me, I can handle myself."

Ten minutes later I was out in the cold on the porch. Paige had a fake baby bundled in her arms, a fake smile plastered on her face. See, folks? Nothing going on here.

"Good night," she said.

I gave the fake kid a pat. "I never set out to be a parent, Paige."

"Funnily enough, neither did I." She pivoted, closing the door in my face.

Well. I'd needed to back her off, right? Nicely done.

I walked home in the dark, past Robb's truck with its Kansas plates, pretending I hadn't seen him, my lip throbbing, my mind full of a strange mix of regret, sexual fantasy, revenge, and puppy eyes.

• • •

Next morning I couldn't help myself; I called her.

"He's overheating down there," she said, before I could stumble half-assed into an apology.

"What?"

"There's no airflow in the basement. It was okay last month; I guess it was colder. But by two, he was roasting."

A pulse of alarm. "He's okay?"

"Yeah, but summer's coming—look, I can't talk now."

"Something's up?"

"Sitter cancelled, and I need to see the Crown about Robb being here last night."

"Can't you call the police?"

"It's complicated; Vancouver PD's divided on the werewolf issue."

"Well . . . I'm coming by to look at the air."

"What if Chase bunny-barfs on a reporter? He ate that entire moccasin."

"I have an ex-girlfriend who used to run a daycare. She's broke and she has a one-year-old."

"I can't leave him with a stranger, not with Robb . . ."

"I'd be downstairs."

"I thought you were done with me and my rabid frigging monster."

"Cut me a break, Paige. He is a rabid frigging monster."

"Well." I could see her fighting a smile. "That's true."

"Listen. Maybe I was an asshole last night—"

"Maybe?"

"Let me make one call, sort out the ventilation issue, and clean up a bit while you put the law on Robb. Deal?"

"Fine."

• • •

"So how is it you're once again with a woman with a kid?" Raquel, naturally, had said yes. Who could pass up a chance to give me a hard time and get paid?

So I'd chauffeured her over, made the introductions. She cooed over little Chase, who was sleeping off his wolfie binge. Paige, satisfied, had run off to court.

Once she was gone, Raquel demanded a complete rundown on her, for transmission to the entire East Van lesbian grapevine.

"I'm not with anyone. I'm fixing up her basement."

"Is that what you're calling it—Abby, no!" She darted across the room to strong-arm her toddler down from the TV stand, and I escaped the interrogation.

With the basement door safely locked, I could survey the damage in the ear-ringing silence.

The air was stuffy, as Paige had said; it also reeked of baby wolf pee. Dirt from the plants was everywhere, mudded in with bits of fur, dog toys, moccasin, sawdust. A rabbit eye stared at me from the floor.

What was I doing, cleaning up after a kid who would probably get himself shot by someone like Richard Deenie?

Apologizing for last night, that's all.

Concentrate on the air. It was a problem—ventilation ducts are notoriously good conductors of sound. Best I could do was run a pipe to the garage, insulate the duct inside and out, and hope the noise of the intake fan would cover a certain amount of puppy howl.

Aroo, I remembered. It hadn't seemed loud on the baby cam.

Which has a volume knob. And what about when he's bigger?

One problem at a time.

The basement was depressing. Bare walls, bamboo or not, and a few bunnies weren't enough. The kid needed things to climb up, jump on, destroy. Grass underfoot. He had to go to that pack good-tempered, Paige said.

Raised planters, maybe, something to lurk beneath . . . but plants meant lights. We'd—dammit, *Paige* would need grow lights for the plants.

I got absorbed in thinking about solar panels, and jumped a foot when my cell rang. It was Raquel, calling from upstairs.

"Why are you phoning me?"

"Because I'm whaling on the door and you damn well can't hear me."

I bolted for the stairs. "Kid okay?"

"He's asleep." She snapped her phone shut in my face. "That guy's back. You said a red truck?"

I closed the padded door, eased past Raquel, and checked on the bassinet before peeking outside. The truck with the Kansas plates was parked half a block away.

"What's this about?"

"The trial. He's trying to scare Paige."

"Should we call the cops?"

"She was gonna talk to that Crown attorney."

"Stalkerman's here now."

"Some of the police think we should be allowed to shoot werewolves—a lot."

"We call, we get the wrong cop, we make things worse?"

I nodded. "They see 'em as an enforcement problem, go figure."

"Gotcha." She sighed. "Let's get a picture of him. Document the stalking. Maybe Paige can go door to door, insinuate to the neighbours he's hanging around waiting to break into their houses or molest their kids."

"Good idea," I said.

She put a hand on my back. "Don't worry, Jude."

"I'm just doing her basement," I repeated. Chase cooed from inside the bassinet. I felt cobwebby threads of affection, sticking, somewhere deep and internal.

"Cut it out," I growled, and he beamed.

Raquel had her camera zoomed in on Robb's unshaven mug. "What's Paige doing down there, anyway? Holding mini-raves?"

"Excuse me?"

Her eyes flicked to the baby monitor. So much for secrecy. I'd been on camera all morning.

"Orchids," I said. "We're setting her up to grow orchids."

July

"When Pammy was five, she began spending a couple days a month on my uncle's farm near Cheyenne," Paige told the packed courtroom. "He and a local fellow were werewolves, the friend's daughter too."

"They ran in a pack?"

"Yes. The adults socialized the girls."

"Meaning?"

"They learned to avoid people and domesticated animals."

"Mr. Deenie says lycanthropes are untameable beasts."

"What does he know? He learned the truth with the rest of the world, in 2002, and he's no scientist. My family had generations of experience in dealing with this."

The Crown had done a decent job of making out Deenie as a sadist and misogynist. The jury seemed to dislike him heartily. In response, he was playing on that thread of . . . was it racism? Not in my backyard-ism? We like to think we're liberal out here on the West Coast. Still, the idea of having werewolves for neighbours wasn't sitting well.

Rabid frigging monsters, right?

Courtrooms always look impressive on TV. In my experience, the real thing never measures up: the taxpayer's dime won't pay for the kind of glitz you get on even a crummy lawyer show. Everything's set up in the same place: Judge's bench, jury box, witness stand—but it all looks run down. The people involved don't come up to TV standards either; they're real, and as a result they look fake, like they're auditioning for parts in a community-theatre production. The sheriff's uniforms look badly fitted, and the air smells dusty.

But Paige had gone all out. She was wearing a brand-new cream-colored suit; her hair was newly cut, her nails buffed. Her make-up was subtle, emphasizing her fragility. She looked like a rosebud wrapped in white chocolate.

If she couldn't convince the jury her sister hadn't been a threat, it was Game Over. Worse. It would be open season.

"There has been some research since monsterkind was discovered," the Crown said. "None of it indicates that lycanthropy is in any sense controllable."

"We aren't talking about taming anyone," Paige said.

"No?"

"As humans encroach on forest habitat, mother bears keep their young with them for longer periods of time. There's more to teach them, you see, about how to cohabitate with humans. The cubs learn it, and nobody says *they're* domesticated. They're living smarter, avoiding people, increasing their chances of survival."

"This is the same?"

"If bears can do it, of course lycanthropes can. In all the time we lived near Cheyenne, there wasn't one human disappearance on a full moon. No pet slaughters either, by the way. In fact, towns benefit from the presence of an active pack."

"How's that?"

"A well-socialized lycanthrope pack keeps the rest of monsterkind away."

Deenie was scribbling furiously, probably planning to follow up on that in his cross-examination.

"This werewolf uncle of yours, where is he now?"

"Richard Deenie's so-called mentor, Kevin Solve, shot him in 2003."

"The family friend?"

"His house was burned . . . with him in it."

"And his daughter? "

The skin around her eyes pinkened.

"Miss Adolpha?"

"He murdered her. Her and . . . everyone I love." Not one tear fell. "Because he hates werewolves, and he thinks it's fun."

"Objection," Richard Deenie drawled.

"He likes being patted on the head for being a serial killer. He shot my sister and bragged about it, and she never hurt anyone."

"Objection."

"She was no danger to him."

"You're one hundred percent certain of that?"

Not a sound in the courtroom. The kid reached over from Raquel's lap, tugging my sleeve. I pulled free.

"I had a newborn. Would I have let Pammy move in with me if I wasn't sure it was safe?" Paige said.

Everyone—reporters, spectators, jury—looked at Raquel and little Chase. And me.

The Crown acknowledged this with a nod. "Your witness."

Deenie had been drooling over the prospect of getting his shot at Paige, and his cross-examination was brutal, the questions fast and furious. How did Paige know her sister never killed anyone? Could she prove it? How many werewolf maulings were there in Canada each year? Wasn't living in the middle of a big city a bit different from keeping Pammy on the country fringes of Cheyenne? Neighbours ten feet away, close quarters . . .

"I grew up with Pammy. How's that for close quarters?"

He stood close enough to breathe on her. He asked about Pamela's sexual habits, alleged she was a boozer, dug into her spotty job history. Had Paige ever had to drug Pamela, to protect herself or others? Did she know how to get rid of a body? If Pammy killed someone, would she cover it up?

Paige sat there and took it. She looked sweet and young, harmless and delicate and exactly like her sister, and she didn't crack. The longer it went on, the more it felt as though everyone in the room wanted to throttle Deenie.

Chase was getting restless: moonrise was seven hours away. I was about to suggest Raquel take him home when the judge adjourned for the day.

We met Paige just outside the courtroom.

"That looked gruelling." Raquel kissed her on the cheek and handed over the baby.

"I'll do a year in that witness box if that's what it takes." She was checking her make-up, thinking ahead to the next tangle: with the media. Adjusting her young-mom costume.

"I gotta pick up Abby from her play date. You guys'll be okay?"

"Fine," Paige said. "Thanks, Raquel."

"Ciao." She waved and was gone.

I gave Paige a long look. "Want me to disappear, too?"

"You want to?"

"You probably look more harmless without a freakishly tall bodyguard—"

That's when Valmont Robb popped around the corner and tried to rip out a pinch of the baby's hair.

I've never seen anyone move so fast. Paige had his sweaty mitt between her jaws before I could draw breath. Without hesitating, she bit, growling, into the meat of his hand.

Robb jerked free with a shout, blood running down his wrist, and grabbed for her throat.

I half caught his fist with mine. Pain, a bruising clash of knuckles . . . then Paige shoved the baby, snuggly and all, into my arms.

"Get him away!" Sheriffs were wading in to collar them both.

I staggered clear of the scrum, flailing my way into the snuggly to free up my hands. I got my forearm between the crowd and the kid's head. Chase was goggling at me, emitting a low growl. Would he change if he got upset?

I pulled him close, whispering, "It's okay, it's okay. Everything's cool, little guy."

He had that intoxicating baby smell: new life, baked bread, talcum. Nobody else tried to get a sample off him as the sheriffs dragged Paige and Valmont Robb off.

The crowd stayed clear of me, babbling: "Is Paige one of them?"

"What'd he do?"

". . . tried to grab the baby . . ."

"She broke the skin, he was bleeding, that makes him one of them now . . ."

"Only if she is. If she is, her sister bit her . . ."

"Socialized my *ass*."

"Grrrr . . ."

"It's all cool, junior," I said. "All okay. What are we gonna do?"

He did that thing where they put an itty-bitty hand on your cheek and your heart tears itself to shreds.

"Cut that out," I said.

He welled up.

"Okay, okay. Sorry." Wait, watch, think. I bounced him, pacing the government-issue carpet, glaring at anyone who got within five feet. Down the hall, a VPD constable was watching alertly; from her expression, she was anti-lycanthrope. This was out of control. . . .

Maybe twenty minutes passed. Chase calmed; the bystanders milled for a while, until they were sure the show was over. I waited for Paige.

Instead, Paige's hero, the fire-breathing Crown attorney who'd brought Deenie to trial, appeared.

"Paige and Valmont Robb are being charged with assault," she said. "They'll be locked up until morning."

"That's bogus."

"It's in case Paige is a werewolf, in case she's infected Robb."

"They'll run tests?"

She frowned. "Full moon's tonight. That's test enough."

"Oh." It was neatly done; Robb wouldn't be out and about while the kid was wild-nighting in the basement. Then again, Paige was locked up, too.

The lawyer served up a tight, feral smile. "They're desperate. Deenie can keep badgering Paige on the stand, if he wants, but by now he must know he can't make her look bad. His best chance is to prove Pamela was a biter."

"Right. But with Robb locked up for the night, they've lost their shot."

"Have they?" She said this with typical lawyer neutrality, glancing down the hall. The female VPD officer had been joined by an equally hostile male partner. Not even bothering to give me a significant look, the attorney click-clacked away.

"Crap," I said, and Chase stole the opportunity to baby-pat my face again.

• • •

I called up Helene—she's another ex-girlfriend of mine, who cleans houses—and drove her over to Paige's with instructions to clean the basement like it was a crime scene. She didn't ask questions. She did, however, take a phone picture of me with the snuggly on my chest. "Change your ways at last, Jude?"

"Woman's in a jam."

"You couldn't leave him with Raquel?"

"No." *Not tonight.*

"Yeah. You don't have a maternal bone."

"Can the sarcasm, please?"

"Now you sound like *my* mother."

"Why is it the business of every goddamn lesbian in British Columbia to give me a hard time?"

"You reap what you sow. Mommy."

No winning here, I thought. "Clear out by sunset, okay? I expect the place to get busted and searched."

Helene nodded. "Rabbit hutch goes here, plants go there, leave the lights on. I was listening."

Would it make a difference? Who knew? I hugged her swiftly. "Thanks."

"Where are you gonna go?"

"I'm not awash in options." I'd fantasized about turning Chase loose on some well-fenced stretch of open prairie, me with a rifle in case a coyote showed up. As if I had a prairie field in my back pocket. As if I could shoot.

"Check into the transition house for the night. His mother'll be out tomorrow, right? You know they wouldn't let the cops in."

How bad were things that I was tempted to take the rabid monsterchild to a house full of battered women? "I'll be okay, Helene."

"I'm a rock, I'm an island," she mocked, waving a mop at me as she descended the stairs. "Night. Mommy."

· · ·

"It's not that I hate kids," I said from atop my kitchen table, four hours later, as Chase gnawed my TV stand to slivers and my old queen manx, Fairytail, yowled disapprovingly from atop the bookshelf. "I was keen, even, in my twenties. My sister Alonsa had a baby, Hal—"

My breath snagged. Years were gone, but it hurt to say his name.

"Another blue-eyed cherub—not all that different from you. Well, except the obvious. I'd have done anything for that kid. But it was the eighties. People could toss a queer out on her ass without the least bit of censure. Alonsa's husband got born again, and . . . shit, doesn't matter."

"Aroo!"

"Aroo to you too." I saluted. "I go to Toronto, come out, fall in love. She's got a kid. A girl, Michaela."

Chase hurled himself at Fairytail's perch. A book teetered and fell—just Camille Paglia, thankfully. He chewed her spine, keeping a hopeful eye on the cat.

"Three years together, we paid lip service to coparenting. After we broke up, I had the kid Tuesday and Friday. Then she finds a new partner. I offered to move to Duluth, not with them, you know, just in the orbit. Made the commitment, did the responsible thing. But then it was 'Michaela needs to bond with Aster, you're confusing her.' Well, she's not mine, I got no rights. I'm not saying I *should* have rights, but you don't get it, furball, I can't— Hey!" I threw a rubber ball into the kitchen before he could go after Susan Faludi.

He boiled after it with a lusty howl. Claws skittered on the lino and there was a thump as he puppy-bounced against the wall.

"You'd think I'd stop at two, right? But no, I had to fall again, about a year later. I thought a friend . . . no romance, see? And I tried to tell her, this has to be for keeps or I'm out, it's too tough, and it was oh yes, oh yes, Jude, of course, Jude. She was so alone, so damned grateful for the childcare. My judgment that time . . . stupid. It got bad, I had to walk away. The shame I still feel over that . . .

"I know it's my fault, okay? I know you can't go half-assed, have a kid on the fringes, can't play Auntie and assume it'll go your way, but it's so hard. . . ."

Pathetic, Jude. Up on the dining room table, all self-pity, who's really the basket case here? The kid padded into the living room with a triumphant look in his adorable cartoon eyes. I'd thought he'd have the ball, or what was left of it, in his jaws. But no, he'd found my oven mitts.

I started bawling like an old drunk, because it was too late. I was caught again, the hooks deep as ever they'd been, barbed through all the scar tissue and old hurt, and as he lifted his tiny leg and damn well made widdle on my oven mitt, I swear it was the sweetest thing I'd ever seen.

. . .

At about two-thirty, Paige got to a phone.

She was panicking. "Can you hide the door to the basement? Make a secret panel or something?"

"A secret—"

"Deenie's befriended some police who think lycanthropes are dangerous. They're going for a grow-op warrant on the house. They'll say they're looking for pot and then—"

"Let 'em search, Paige. We're not there."

"Oh! Good. Is he okay?"

"Getting up his second wind. In fact, his little ears have pricked up. Say hello to Mommy, kid."

Chase struggled to his paws. "Arrooo?" It came out a question; then he flopped again.

Her voice came through the speaker. "Hi, baby, hi, baby. Thank God."

"Who told you about the raid?"

"One of the guards. Gloating."

I'd been on the table for hours. Now I stood and stretched. Hell, Chase was torpid, and I had my boots on. I stepped down to a chair, then the floor. The littlest werewolf didn't move.

"So where are you?"

"My place."

"You took him *home*?"

"What could I do, take a pet suite at the Hilton?" I splashed water onto my face, ran a comb through my hair.

"What if they go there next?"

"They can't get a warrant to search for pot here, in the dead of night, on the grounds that I'm your . . . ."

"My what?"

Weighted pause. "Your friend, Paige."

"All they have to do is shove their way in and bag him. They can apologize to the skies once they have video of him changing back at dawn."

Bust in first, consequences later. She was right. "It's not gonna happen. Paige . . ."

"Shit, my time's up."

"It'll be okay."

"Don't screw this up, Jude." She was gone before I could promise anything.

A scritch. I opened the bathroom door. The kid was there, tail thumping, couch upholstery dangling from his fang. He tried out a growl on me.

"Don't even think it," I said. Stomping past him, I found my work gloves. He wobbled a step behind, exhausted but game. "Tearing around takes it out of you, huh, kid?"

Bink-bink. Cartoon-puppy eyes. Cuddle me; I'm not dangerous at all.

"You're not gonna bite me," I told him.

Bending, I extended my gloved hands. He growled.

"No!" Deep voice: he did me the honor of looking awed.

I got him by the scruff and under his chest, holding him arms-out away from me. His body was hot, and I could feel the wham-wham of his heart through the leather as I carried him upstairs.

Then he shocked a bit, twisting.

The smart thing would've been to drop him; instead, my arms pulled inward, protecting. I felt hot puppy breath on my neck, a touch of nose. He was alert, almost quivering.

"Easy. Easy." My mouth was cottony. I turned sideways, checking the mirror. He was staring bug-eyed up over my shoulder, through the skylight in my bedroom . . .

. . . at the moon.

"Aroo?"

"Aroo," I agreed. For some reason I was near tears.

I set him down like a bomb, leaving him in the shaft of moonlight, up on my bed, in my loft with all my good stuff, everything I'd pulled off the ground floor that afternoon. I rescued the urn with my mom's ashes, threw a last apologetic look at the fish tank. "Enjoy the change of locale, kid."

Weak-kneed, I stumbled downstairs and started making calls.

• • •

The police didn't turn up until four.

By then, I had thirty people downstairs. Saffron had awakened most of the local women's chorus, and there was a big ol' overtired koombaya going on in the remains of my living room. Alison was shooting the gathering in Super-8, while a baby dyke named Kathleen Ph34rless exhorted her to get into the digital age, man. Jennifer was doing henna tattoos on Freddie May, who was bare-chested and on his back on the table. Helena had swept the shreds of Camille Paglia off my floor. Raquel lay by the hearth with her one-year-old, Abby, and the baby's father, the three of them half asleep, watching a Disney movie on an iPad.

Upstairs you could hear the occasional thunk, awoo, smash—Chase had gotten his second wind.

Long as he's happy, I thought, as I answered the bang-bang-bang of the front door.

"Judith Walker?"

Showtime.

"Hey, Officers," I said, not too smartass, not too perky. Through the chain, I saw the female constable I'd seen that afternoon.

"We have a report of screams at this address."

"Just a party."

"Mind if we look around?"

"I do mind, yeah." I spoke clearly, for the pick-up mike.

"I hear another scream now." She gave me a push, trying to swing my door wide, only to get hung up on the steel-toed boot I'd accidentally-on-purpose jammed in it.

Her partner helped. The boot and the chain both gave, and I stumbled back-ward into my foyer.

One of the leather kids, Roman, caught me.

"Hey there, Officer," he swished. "This a bust? Wanna borrow my cuffs?"

"What's going on here?"

"Full moon party," I said. "In honor of Pam Adolpha."

She scowled. "Where's the kid?"

"Do I look like a babysitter?"

Junior chose that moment to let go with a little "Aroo!"

"What the hell was that?" The female officer's hand drifted to her pepper spray. Then she paused; Alison had moved in with her camera. The choir broke into four-part harmony, drawing her eye. They were parked on a couch I'd propped in front of the door to the stairwell. At their soprano edge, singing along while giving her best glower from a scary high-tech wheelchair, was the city's best-known civil-rights lawyer.

You stay in one place for a while, you make friends. They make friends. They'll dissect your love life and your dietary habits behind your back, but some days it pays off. That's how it works in my neighbourhood. Most of my guests lived walk-ing distance from here.

An "Aroo!" upstairs ruined the otherwise golden moment.

"I asked you . . ." The constable kept her voice calm. "What is that?"

"It's the dog," I said, straight faced. "What do you think?"

She spent another second thumbing her pepper spray, weighing her odds—the film crew, the legal lioness, the sheer number of witnesses. Little Kathleen Ph34r-less had her phone out, no doubt Tweeting events in real time.

The constable slumped. "Keep the noise down."

Nobody was so dumb as to start cheering before they were gone. But we spent the next few hours giving each other sleepy high-fives, carrying on like we'd faced down the armies of Rome.

. . .

Paige showed up at my place about two hours after dawn.

"Your kitchen ceiling is dripping," she said.

I'd just put down a bucket to catch the leak. "Baby boy got to my fish tank. You should've heard it."

"And there are twenty women in your living room."

"That many?"

"They're semi-naked."

"It's hot out, Paige. By the way, you officially owe favours to every cool person in East Van."

"Just tell me you haven't slept with all of them."

I pretended to count heads. "Only five. Well, six."

She chose—conspicuously, I thought—to ignore my attempt at charm. "Where's my son, Jude?"

"Follow me."

Baby Chase was snoring in the wreckage of my bedroom. Paige squelched across the carpet, crunching broken aquarium glass, and scooped him into her arms.

"Oh, Jude. All your stuff," she murmured, head down against his.

"It's what they do, right?"

"Werewolves?"

"Children."

"You never wanted to be a mom," she said.

"That was kind of a half-truth."

"You weren't wrong. He is a monster, and I am a basket case."

"A victorious basket case."

"Excuse me?"

"By next month they'll have convicted that fucker Deenie, right? The sidekick'll go off home and make trouble for someone else?"

"What are you saying? All's well that ends well?"

"You're not damaged goods, Paige. When you bit Robb yesterday, I realized. You're anything but fragile. You're tough. And that's . . ."

"Yes?"

"It's your strength I'm attracted to."

She stirred the dampened shreds of my buckwheat pillow with her toe. "So no more bullshit?"

"There's always more," I said. "But not that flavour."

"Your sales pitch could use some work." She patted the empty space on my bed.

"You dig honesty." I slipped into the nook, curled around the baby, and kissed her properly.

The kid waved a fist, belching fish.

"Da," he said to me. Bink-bink. The hook sank deeper.

I faked a cringe. "Tell me he's already said Mumma, once at least."

"Nope." She twinkled. "Gonna tell him to cut it out?"

"Da!"

"I'm gonna say keep it up, Chase," I told them both, and planted a kiss on his little feral head as my hand wound into hers.

A. M. DELLAMONICA is the author of *Indigo Springs*, winner of the Sunburst Award for Excellence in Canadian Literature of the Fantastic, and its concluding sequel, *Blue Magic*. Her short stories have appeared in a number of fantasy and science fiction magazines and anthologies, and on *Tor.com*.

In the Sight of Akresa

Ray Wood

Claire's lover has no tongue. A slave liberated from a heathen temple, Aya cannot tell the story of her stolen voice, or of their unfolding love. She cannot speak her pain, her joy, or her sorrow. And if she sees that which eludes the blind goddess of justice, she cannot bear witness. *Edited by Carl Engle-Laird.*

This is how they took your tongue:

There is a wedge, short and made of steel, used to prise apart the teeth. The skin on your lips splits as the slave-maker pushes it into your mouth. Hard Yovali hands hold you all over, keeping your arms behind your back, your knees on the ground, your face towards the sun. Metal crunches against your teeth, scraping, swiveling, pushing. Your incisors feel like they are bending inwards.

You part your teeth before you lose them and the wedge shoots in, followed by foreign fingers that hook into your cheeks. They taste of rust and salt. The blood-priest finds your tongue between his thumb and forefinger and grips it where it starts to fatten, near the root. He pulls. The slave-maker accepts a slender, silk-wrapped something from a loinclothed woman.

Saliva pools around your bottom lip.

The something is the *haraad-kité*, the voice-cutter. The slave-maker draws it with a flourish from its half-moon sheath and holds it high, his fingers curled around its spine. He is still, his tall, lean body blocking out the sun. Then, all at once and with a scream, he plunges. The blade dips into the meat of your tongue like a finger into water.

. . .

Cecil's books are vague about the rest. I have lain awake more nights than one wondering about what must have followed: the blood pooling in your mouth; the hollow throb of pain; that terrible emptiness behind your teeth. The heat of the cauterising iron biting at the mess of open flesh.

Forgive me. This story remains the only one I have of you, of your life before me. You must know how it pains me that it comes from Cecil's library rather than your lips—oh, your sweet, battered lips!—and that it would fit a hundred other slaves as well as it fits you. Perhaps none of the accounts that I have read are even true.

Oh, my love. I know so little of you.

. . .

We met on the second Sunday after Harvestfest, when the leaves were browning and the men returned from the Yovali lands. My mother and I watched from the wall as Father's host approached, feeling the wind whip through our dresses. As the column of knights drew closer I could see the breath fuming from the nostrils of the horses.

We went down in our finery to welcome them. Father came in first, as was customary, with Garrick at his right. Their shields were splattered with mud. My brother seemed taller than he had before going on campaign: newly tanned and mountainous, with fresh muscle packed beneath his skin.

"Claire," he said by way of greeting once they had dismounted and the ritual welcomes had been spoken. I saw Father looking over at us.

"Welcome home, Garrick." I touched my lips to both his cheeks. "I hope there's a gift for me among your spoils."

"Oh, yes." He grinned and beckoned a boy over to undo his armour. "These heathen treasures will make you doubt your eyes."

The great hall was prepared, the fire lit; slopping wineskins were handed round above head height. A singer accompanied herself on a vielle. Father spoke to me briefly, in between carousing with his knights and sitting with my mother. "You're a young woman, now, Claire," he said. He drew back and looked me up and down as if my breasts were new developments.

"You sound surprised, Father." The cheek he bent to me was warm and bristly. "It's not been so long since you left."

He nodded sadly and drew me in to walk beside him, his arm around my shoulders. "We brought back wonders," he said.

Wonders indeed. The revelers were silenced; a circle was cleared in the middle of the crowd as the chests were carried in. Behind me, people jostled for a better view as one of Father's richer knights knelt to open the first casket. The stones around the fireplace blasted heat into my back.

"Spoils won from the Yovali in the name of King Lucian XXI, awarded by His Majesty to His Grace the Duke of Rouchefort!"

Treasures shone like sugared fruits. The first chest was full of gems and gold, the second bronze and porcelain. There were bulky crescent bangles stained with dye, discs and trinkets patterned after constellations, plump ornamental pots and jars. Another casket held a nest of looted weaponry. Endless spoils were revealed and marveled at: big flasks of wine that smelt of foreign spice; great oiled pipes with bowls like ladles, and the herbs meant to be smoked in them; a set of ceremonial masks; what looked like the bones of some vast lizard dipped in gold. My interest in them shattered the moment you were brought into the hall.

"Liberated by His Grace himself, and granted to his service by His Majesty the King, one slave of the Yovali. Her tongue was ripped from her mouth to prevent blasphemy against their heathen blood-god."

The last statement drew a collective gasp. My chest was suddenly too tight for my heart; I stood up on my toes as a knight stepped sideways and blocked my view. Shadows danced among the roof beams.

Shall I tell you how you looked to me, that first time? I was expecting a hunched, shrunken creature, grubby head bowed as if in shame at the emptiness behind your mouth, but you stood with your shoulders back. Your mass of unwashed raven hair fell several inches past the base of your neck. Your skin was tanned. I remember how you held your hands: clasped in front of you as if you were in church, in what would have been your lap had you been sitting down. Your breasts pushed against your tunic.

Torches burned behind your eyes.

". . . shall live in the castle as your equal." Father was addressing the assembly, his hand resting on your shoulder. You looked toned and lean enough to knock him flat, if you so chose. "She is now a free Lucean woman, and free to labour for her bread upon De Rouchefort lands as long as she may live."

"A whore without a tongue," Garrick murmured in my ear under the ensuing applause. His breath was spiced with wine. "Now there's a treasure for you, Claire."

The hairs lifted from my neck.

• • •

Aya. I heard my father call you Aya.

The name burned in me like a flame those first few days. I realised later that it could not have been your real one, but even now it remains the only one I have for you. When I used it for the first time, you simply stared at me for a moment and then dipped your head back to your work, as if it didn't matter what I called you.

Of course, I wondered how my father chose it for you. I did not like my conclusion—that those were the first, desperate syllables that flopped from your tongueless mouth when he first bore down upon you, sword in hand, believing you Yovali—but what else was I to think? He would not tell me where he found you. Had he plucked you from some heathen temple? A blackened, back-breaking mine? The reeking pleasure bed of some Yovali blood-priest? Each was an abhorrent thought.

Not yet having Cecil's library at my disposal, I obsessed over the mystery of your missing tongue. Had it been ripped out whole, or did some misshapen stump remain for you to gag on? What became of the missing flesh once they took it from you? I examined my own tongue in the glass while Letia brushed my hair. I flexed and wiggled it—strange, throat-filling worm that it was—as I imagined histories for you.

I saw you again three days after the men returned, when Father called a Justice Circle. I suppose you had not been to one before, but they held no novelty for me. Every second month my father and his trusted council would hear testimony and evidence of all the crimes and grievances committed on De Rouchefort lands, and come to an impartial verdict. Attendance was mandatory for all. This time was much the same as any, except that morning I made Letia take extra care with my hair and spent the first two cases writhing in my seat to see if I could spot you.

I picked you out eventually among the stable hands, near the foot of the Akresa statue. I must have seen the marble likeness of the justice goddess a thousand times, but I had never wondered, until I saw her next to you, what lay beneath the sculpted crinkles of her blindfold. Were her eyes meant merely to be closed, or were there gristly, scooped-out hollows in their place?

You had washed, and your dark hair was sleek and lustrous. I stared at the back of your head, willing you to turn around and meet my eyes. I did not look away until Garrick stood to speak for the good character of the accused. One of Father's lesser knights was standing trial for the rape of a peasant girl. When judgement had been passed and the girl was being led away, I saw Garrick squeeze my father's shoulder.

After that day I watched for you in the castle, eavesdropping on the servants to see if you featured in their gossip. Once or twice I considered simply asking about you, but I knew how rumours spread and didn't want anything to get back to Garrick. So I waited. Then, down by the buttery one morning, I overheard Letia whispering to her brother's sweetheart:

"Hugh says his birds won't come near him since he took that tongueless witch as an apprentice. Says she's put her heathen magic on them."

I was gripped by a desire to have *her* tongue pulled out for speaking of you that way, but I contented myself with being sullen and contrary when she clothed me that evening, making her lift my arms to get my dress over my head.

Your role among the staff discovered, I needed only to contrive an excuse to speak with you. That afternoon, I told Father that I wished to take up falconry again. He was surprised, I think, but then any interaction between us tended to surprise him. He had a servant bring my bird up from the mews. She was a proud, white, staring thing—I'd forgotten what I'd named her—who twitched her head from side to side and could not sit still on the glove.

I brushed off my mother's suggestion that hunting was something that Garrick and I might do together and instead went down to the forest on my own, stopping on the way to borrow a small knife from the kitchens. I spent an hour with the falcon tethered to my wrist, cooing and crooning until she grew used to me. When she was settled enough to consent to my touch, I took out the knife and snicked along the roots of several crucial-looking feathers. She jerked as I maimed her: when I released my grip on her wing she flew shrieking to the full length of her tether, squawking panic and displeasure. I batted her away from my face and waited out her pain. Eventually, after a great deal of shushing, she calmed down enough to be taken back to the castle and tied up in my chamber. Her left wing was slick with blood.

"A cat attacked my bird while I was hunting," I announced at dinner. "I thought I'd take her down to Hugh this evening."

I knew that Hugh would not be there—I had it from the bucktoothed boy in the stables that he met with a lady in the village tavern every Wednesday after nightfall—and that, with any luck, I would have you to myself. In my chamber, the falcon perched warily on the back of a chair, ducking her head round to pick at her injured wing. I brushed my hair until it shone. Cold air whistled through my sleeves as I crossed the darkened courtyard.

It was never completely silent in the mews: I could always hear the rustling of feathers or the clacking of a beak, or the scratch of claws on wood from within the screened compartments where the falcons slept. My nose wrinkled at the smell of guano.

You stood there with your back to me, humming. I'd heard Hugh sing to the birds before—it was part of a falcon's training that she be sung to the same way each time she was given food—but the notes echoing in your hollow mouth climbed straight up my spine. I had heard no tune like it.

"My bird," I said, and your eyes flashed fear at me for a second as you turned. You stared at me. "I think she's been injured by a cat. I thought that maybe you could examine her."

My blood thumped as you put down the bird you had been feeding. It was the first time I'd been so close to you; I realised that you stood two inches taller than me, and that your lips were scabbed with scar tissue. You held a hand out for the bird.

"Thank you," I said. "She's very dear to me."

I think you caught the waver in my voice. Your eyes plunged into me, direct as daggers, and I had to let mine drop. My fingers lingered on the leather of your glove as I handed the bird over. I had seen enough, in that look—I had seen, in the way your eyes hesitated on my hair and then my lips, that you shared something of my desire.

"I'm Claire," I said. "Lord De Rouchefort's daughter. I . . . I saw you in the great hall."

Your head was bent over my falcon's injured wing. In the distance, I heard a bucket clank against the inside of the well.

"You will be well looked after here."

I knew that I was gabbling, but the emptiness behind your teeth seemed to be sucking the words out of me. "My father treats his villeins fairly, and there are lots of holidays. You—" I stopped. You had the falcon's wing pinched between your thumb and forefinger. You looked at me and ran the first finger of your other hand along the flat, regular wound inflicted by my knife blade.

"Yes. Um." I swallowed. "It's a nasty wound." Once a few seconds had made it clear that my story about the cat was not going to be believed, you turned away and went to find a salve. I took a step closer. The torchlight rippled in your hair.

"They call you Aya, don't they?" I said as you dipped your finger into a little cup of unguent. It smelt of vinegar. You flashed a look at me, then bent your head to brush paste onto the injured wing. Your fingers were slenderer than mine, I realised, and more supple. I held my breath as the falcon stood twitching on your wrist.

"Are you finished?"

You lifted the bird towards me, not quite far enough for me to take it without stepping closer. I moved forwards and reached out my hand.

You flinched as I touched you. Some spark jumped between our skins. The falcon squawked and drew its talon through my finger; you jerked back and collided with the bracket of a torch. The torch crashed to the ground, the gravel snuffing out the flame. The slighted bird flapped noisily up to the roof beams. Cold crept up my forearms.

"Aya?"

You touched my hand. The room was too freshly thrown in darkness for me to see anything, but I could feel your strong, calloused fingers squeezing each of mine in turn, probing for the wound. You lifted my hand up to your face. Your breath shivered on my broken skin.

I moved the finger to your lips.

"It's all right," I whispered. You had gone very still, like an animal backed into a corner. "It's all right."

You had more to lose if your instincts were wrong: I had to be the one who crossed the threshold. I slid my free hand behind your neck. "It's all right, it's all right."

Your lips opened like a flower. My finger slipped between them, softly, until it was submerged up to the knuckle in the warm wetness of your mouth. Your damp, empty mouth. My eyes strained in the darkness, but I didn't need to see. You drew my finger in until I felt the slightest touch of a shrivelled, shorn-off tongue against my fingertip.

Revulsion and desire rose in me like quicksilver.

• • •

Oh, my love—the night we passed among the birds still echoes in my dreams. Next morning, when I woke up in my bed and pieced myself together, I thought it *was* a dream. My stomach tingled when I realised my mistake.

"You look happy this morning, my lady," Letia said as she helped me dress. At breakfast, Garrick was rather less kind.

"You've a grin like a demon." He'd spent the night drinking with the guardsmen: his eyes were bloodshot, and several of the serving girls looked ashen-faced that morning. "What's wrong with you?"

"Nothing," I said sweetly. "I'm just happy that you're back with us."

He grunted and bit into a bruised apple.

Father was preoccupied that morning, as usual, and I wasted no time in putting my plan into action. I'd been so impressed, I told him, with how ably you had mended my falcon, that I had asked you to tutor me in all the outdoor arts: falconry, hunting, fencing, riding. It would save him the expense of a tutor from the capital, I added quickly, as well as keeping you out of Hugh's way during the afternoons.

"I see no reason why not," he said, after giving me that same look he had on the night of his return—vague surprise at what his daughter had become in his absence.

If only he knew.

By the time Letia had finished dressing me for the outdoors, the morning had evaporated. I took a servant's corridor by way of a shortcut to the armoury. It was dimly lit, illuminated only by a slit in the wall that opened out onto the courtyard, and I was already halfway along it by the time I realised I was not alone. A couple stood in the shadow of the far wall, joined at the lips.

The girl was slight and boyish, dressed in servants' grey, with enviably sleek, chestnut-coloured hair. The man had shoulders like a mountain range.

"Garrick?"

I immediately regretted speaking. The girl sprang back, hand leaping to her mouth, and dropped her gaze as soon as she realised who I was. Garrick just turned around and stared at me.

"I was, um." I looked away. "I'm on my way to the armoury."

I felt Garrick's eyes on my back all the way along the corridor.

• • •

"You are going to tutor me," I said, and tossed you one of the wooden training swords. You caught it in one hand. The birds were awake and eating, the midday sun throwing light on all the crevices and corners that had been wrapped in darkness during our last encounter. Your fingernails were outlined with dirt.

"I'd like to learn the sword this afternoon, I think." I smiled at you. You made no response. I thought for a moment that you were going to deny what had happened between us, but then a blush blossomed in your cheeks and you ducked your head.

"Come for your gyrfalcon, milady?" It was Hugh, bandy limbs twanging as he hurried over, eager to attend to me.

"I've come to borrow your apprentice, actually," I said. He was only too happy to part with you.

I found us a secluded spot just inside the northern wall, beneath a sycamore. I'd really only brought the swords to support my cover story, but you unwrapped one from its sheet as tenderly as if it were an infant and tested its balance in your hand. You began to limber up.

"Be merciful," I said, once I had watched you flex the long, thick muscles in your thighs and stretch your arms behind your head. With your hair tied in a scarf, you looked almost like the statue of Akresa, raising her blade to smite the guilty. My own sword sagged and tilted in my grip.

You came at me like a rush of wind: you fanned my sword aside and touched yours to my throat, just hard enough to be uncomfortable. With the tip, you gently lifted my hair away from my cheek. I drew back, breathless.

"Teach me."

You did so delightfully. You corrected my posture after each engagement, standing with your body behind mine as your warm, firm hands posed me like a mannequin, your breath fluttering in my ear. Again and again your sword swept through my guard. My back would meet the trunk of the great tree, the bark hard and knotted between my shoulder blades, and you would pin me there and kiss me. Then we would break apart and I would submit again to your manipulation of me: let you lift my hands higher, pull my arms out straighter. I spoke as little as you did. We had another language for that afternoon.

I was glad that Garrick caught us sparring with our swords and not our lips when he came to fetch me for the evening meal.

• • •

It is strange—we spent almost every hour that we could between then and Winterfest together, and yet I hardly knew a thing about you. My lessons continued. You taught me how to use a bow, how to hunt, how to ride. How to love my body as much as I loved yours. We fell into each other's patterns when we were together: either I would talk enough for both of us, telling you about my life before you came and my guesses as to yours, or we would spend hours in your silent world, talking only with a touch on the arm or a stone thrown in the lake.

Every now and then, when the mystery of your past frustrated me, I turned my guesses into direct questions, hoping that if you could not speak then you could try at least to draw or mime. But you only smiled, and kissed me, and gave me other things to occupy my thoughts.

When the leaves had turned entirely yellow, my father announced his intention to host a tournament. It would be held just after Winterfest, and half the knights in Southern Lucea would be invited to attend: the barons Crawdank, De Lyre, Cheal, and Faxsly had already expressed their warmest interest. Several had sons or daughters of marriageable age.

I only half listened. You and I had gone out to the lake the night before, and my head was full of images of moonlight pooling over darkened water. We undressed beneath the stars. Hugging my nakedness, I curled a single toe and placed it in the water, then yelped and drew back from its icy bite. Had you not pushed me in, I doubt I would have braved it.

You were easy in the water, and I watched enviously as your limbs slid in and out of it, as you flicked your head with each broad stroke to keep your nose and mouth above the surface. You swam across to me and held me, hands wet and slippery on my arms. Your lips parted as you bent your mouth to mine . . .

"Claire?" My mother was looking at me as though I was sick.

"I'm sorry," I said, putting down my knife and ignoring Garrick's frown. "I was just trying to remember the name of Lord Faxsly's eldest son—I've heard he's quite the scholar."

My parents shared a smile.

Winterfest drew nearer. Nights began to settle earlier, and what sun we did have hung in the corner of my eye and blinded me. Mist seeped into the mornings. The fires were fed perpetually. I began to swaddle myself in furs whenever I stepped outside and put sheep fat on my lips to keep them moist. When I passed you in the courtyard, your hair was sugared with frost.

Tragedy struck in the last week of October: Letia tripped on the stairs down from my chamber and struck her head upon the stone. Her funeral was short. I said some words over the pyre and made sure her family was given enough food and gold to see them through several winters. Ivarus, the god of death, watched unhearing from the shrine. Just as the justice goddess is blind, the god of death is without ears, and cannot be begged or reasoned with.

We prepared for winter. You and I went hunting in the forest, where I managed, with a little luck, to bury an arrowhead in the warm neck of a deer. The blood had frozen by the time we hauled it to the castle, and my fingers were numb from the frost packed into the fur. We ate together for the first time. I watched, openly curious at first, then with acute embarrassment, as you swilled your stew around your mouth and trickled it gently down your throat to avoid choking on your shorn-off tongue.

Later that month you gave me a gift, one which I could not decipher. It was a stone, chipped loose from the mews, I think, and carefully worked smooth and spherical. Into one hemisphere you'd carved a circle with a cross beneath it: I wondered if it was meant to depict a keyhole or an arrow loop, or perhaps the upper body of a stick figure. I thanked you with a kiss and slept that night with the stone held in my fist.

. . .

November came. I'd forgotten, by then, about the time I'd interrupted Garrick and the servant girl, but it seemed that their secret had somehow been discovered. Father was furious. The girl was dismissed, of course, and given herbs to flush her womb; Garrick, in turn, was immediately betrothed. Her name was Lila Argeatha, a young noble from the coastal territories whom we had known when we were children. All I could remember about her were her eggy, blinking eyes. Garrick stomped around the castle for days afterwards making his displeasure known, relenting only to work out his frustration in the forest, hunting. He spent every mealtime glaring at me. It was hard to keep my expression sombre: you and I were closer than ever, my love, and the deep, warm secret of our love threatened to well up and capsize me whenever we were together.

Later that week you took me by the hand to the mews and planted me in front of a healthy, twitching falcon.

"This is mine?" I held out an arm for her to hop onto, but she just twitched her head to one side and clacked her beak. You stroked two fingers down the back of her skull to soothe her.

"She's healed beautifully," I said. "I'm sure she'd like to stretch her wings."

Hugh was skulking in the background, sweeping. I'd seen the way he looked at you when he thought I couldn't see him. Children made the sign to ward off witches as you led me through the courtyard.

We left the castle, heading south. When we reached the forest you showed me how to use the bird to hunt, after which we fed her water from our mouths, as was the falconer's way. You spat yours clumsily, slopping it from your lips and flicking your head up to give it lift. Red with embarrassment, I used the pink tip of my tongue to sprinkle a perfect jet into the bird's open beak.

We left the falcon tethered to a branch and made love beneath the trees. Afterwards we lay against the damp moss on a tree trunk, your arm around me. We stayed there, listening to the noises of the forest and the rhythms of each other's hearts, for what might have been an hour. Eventually I leaned my lips to your ear.

"Show me who you are," I whispered. "Please."

You sat still for a moment, then slid your arm out from my waist. For a second I thought you were about to leave me, but you just stood and picked a twig up from the forest floor. You broke the end off and began to scratch at the moss covering the tree trunk.

I still remember them, those strange pictograms you scored into the moss. Half a dozen stick figures in a line, then one inside a box. A set of rectangles that might have been a temple, or a staircase. A crescent moon. There were others. You drew until all that you could reach was covered, then stood in the middle of your strange creation and looked at me expectantly. Perhaps it was the fervour in your eyes, or the way your makeshift pen nestled potently in your hand, but I was afraid of you just then.

It was dark when we returned. We led the horses to the stables as quietly as we could, patting their necks to keep them calm, and I offered to return the falcon. Hugh wouldn't dare say anything to me as he might to you if he were awake. We parted with a kiss behind the stable doors. Crossing the mews, I saw a shadow on the eastern wall.

Hugh had retired by the time I got there. The mews was empty but for the birds, or so I thought—as I placed my falcon on her perch, I heard the gravel crunch behind me.

"I know what you're doing."

Garrick's lip was curled in disgust.

"I'm returning my falcon," I said. I hoped he wouldn't notice that my hands had started shaking.

"I should tell Father." He came closer. "Tell him what you've been doing in the woods with that woman. Just like you told him about me and Gwen."

"I didn't tell anyone about—" I stopped. A sneer spread across his face.

"That's not the part that you should be denying," he said, and left me with my heart kicking in my throat.

· · ·

The next morning, the first families arrived for the great Winterfest tournament. Pennants snapped in the wintry air; the lords and ladies of each house were followed by processions of men, horses, handcarts, beasts, and banners. They filled the courtyard with their clamour. My father formally offered the hospitality of his hall for the evening feast, and I had my hand kissed more times than I could count.

The great hall throbbed with heat and noise that evening. By no accident, I am sure—I could smell my mother all over it—I was shown to a seat next to Lord Faxsly's eldest son. He was a slight, unassuming boy a year my junior who seemed unable to sit still for nerves when he discovered that he was to cut my meat.

"Lady Claire," he said, sliding his blond hair out of his eyes. "I see your beauty has not been exaggerated. I'd be grateful if you called me Cecil."

"I should like nothing better," I said distractedly, catching sight of Garrick glaring at me from across the table. I looked towards the kitchens in search of the servant who was to fill our cups. You can imagine my surprise, my love, when I saw you in her place. I suppose I should have guessed that Father's kitchen staff would not have been sufficient to entertain so large a party unbolstered—yes, there was Hugh, bent over a knight's wine cup—but the sight of you with your fine eyes lowered to the flagstones, your fingers wrapped around the handle of a wine jug, was enough to give me a jolt. Garrick followed the trail of my eyes.

You came closer, oblivious to the danger, clearly intending to cross to my side of the table and serve us. I saw several ladies whispering behind their hands— Lady Cheal visibly shuddered as you poured for her. Garrick's fist tightened around his knife. My stomach turned to water.

". . . wouldn't you say so, Lady Claire?"

I blinked and turned back to Cecil. "Forgive me," I said, feeling panic climb my chest. "The heat . . ."

"Of course." He sucked nervously on his bottom lip and raised the wine cup to indicate that we needed serving. "I'm sure some wine will cool you. The fire is a little overpowering . . ."

I felt you sidle in behind us—I swear your hair brushed my shoulder as you bent to pour. Wine lapped into the cup.

"Thank you, Cecil," I said loudly. I felt you straighten. I did not dare turn to look at you—I risked the smallest glance when you had crossed back towards the kitchens and saw your eyes flick in my direction. I tried to signal without moving that Garrick watched our every step.

The wine seemed to settle Cecil's nerves, and we soon fell to comparing libraries. Reading was something in which I had never managed to interest you, my love—you preferred the world beyond the page, I think—but he had grown up with the same poems and stories that had shaped my girlhood. His father's castle, he told me, had an entire tower filled with volumes in every language. I made sure everyone at the table noticed how engrossed we were in conversation when you brought over the joint of meat we were to share.

"You and my sister get on well," Garrick said to Cecil as you laid the cooked flesh on the plate of day-old bread. "But I wouldn't want to falsely raise your hopes—I think her eye has already fallen on another."

My mother's food stopped halfway to her mouth. One of the other ladies coughed. Out of the corner of my eye, I saw Lady Cheal glance up at you.

"You must forgive my brother," I said, loudly enough for everyone to hear. "He is so enamoured of his newly betrothed, Lady Lila Argeatha, that he imagines love in everyone around him. My eye has not yet fallen anywhere."

I took a breath and laid my hand on Cecil's arm. "I hope we can be friends."

• • •

After that it became impossible to see you: I could barely venture as far as the courtyard without hearing the tread of Garrick's boot behind me. Father called a Justice Circle, ostensibly to purify his halls before the tournament, but really to demonstrate his trust in lords Cheal and Faxsly. I sat next to Cecil. Neither of us paid full attention: I was too busy combing the crowd for a glimpse of you, and he seemed unable to stop his eyes from dropping guiltily to my neckline or following my fingers as I fiddled with my dress. It actually seemed an interesting hearing. A secret lover came forward to provide an alibi for the accused at the last minute, her voice trembling under the council's gaze. You were not among the crowd.

I resorted to asking Hugh for news of you. He ignored me as long as he was able, staring directly ahead and prodding food into a falcon's grasping beak, but my ladylike coughs eventually broke him.

"She's in the stables, seeing to riding equipment for His Grace's tournament. Much good may that knowledge bring you."

And he was hobbling away before I could rebuke him.

. . .

You were working by candlelight, the stable hands having long since turned in, wearing down a strip of leather with a stone—for what purpose, I could not guess. Flex, rub, scrape, bend. The motion was hypnotic.

After you had put aside the leather and turned those hard, strong hands on me, I tried to read to you. The book was one that Cecil had lent me on the Yovali. You listened for a while, your face betraying nothing, then went back to your work. I looked up every now and then when I came to passages about Yovali customs and the role of slaves, hoping to spot a reaction.

Flex, rub, scrape, bend. I wondered sometimes if you even understood our language.

. . .

Tournament day came at last. Pavilions had been erected in the village, where hooves and boots had already squelched the fields to seas of mud. Stallions reared and snorted; children shrieked; squires buckled knights into their armour. The smell of cooked meat drifted on the wind. Cecil led me to my seat, managing to look vaguely handsome in a turquoise tunic trimmed with gold.

"You are not competing?" I said as he helped me up into the stalls. My hair had been an undertaking for the maid that morning.

"Not today," he said. "I find my talents lie elsewhere. How did you find the book?"

I must admit, my love, I found his conversation pleasant. He told me he had actually been to the Yovali lands, and I tried to probe for information that might help me know you. He was vague in some places and verbose in others: he had heard a lot about the slaves, he said, but never seen one; he had studied the construction of the temples, though, with their thick grey blocks of stone and carvings across every wall. His father had a *haraad-kité*, the ceremonial blade they used to cut out tongues, displayed above the hearth in his great hall.

"That's her over there, isn't it?" he said, after a while. "The tongueless slave."

I followed the line of his finger. You were down near the front of the crowd, standing up and facing backwards, looking for someone. Our eyes met. A hot, dirty blush ran up my face.

"She makes my skin crawl," Cecil said, apparently not noticing my distress. "How do you bear having her around the castle every day?"

I looked away and mumbled a reply.

The tournament got underway. I had never derived much pleasure from jousting, or the mock battles and mêlées that were to follow, but with Cecil's whispered commentary in my ear and a bright sky overhead, I found I was enjoying myself. My mother sat a few places down the row, smiling indulgently in our direction every now and then, and there was no Garrick in the crowd to make me uneasy— he was in a tent somewhere, being packed into a suit of mail. I avoided looking at you entirely.

Garrick's turn came: our house fanfare struck up at the far end of the field and he emerged, a mountain of plate mail on a soot-black horse. Even I had to admit he looked impressive. The De Rouchefort crest, an eagle with its wings held wide, blazed upon his shield. His horse cantered round the grass while his opponent weighed his lance.

"I would not like to be the one to face your brother," Cecil muttered. Garrick bounded to the middle of the field and raised his visor, ready to salute my father. His horse reared, his fist came up, he tugged the reins with his free hand—

The leather snapped. His hand flew upwards and he fell out of the saddle, his foot caught in a stirrup. His helmet smacked into the mud. A lady screamed. The horse panicked, spluttered, and started running down the field, dragging Garrick behind it by his ankle.

Pandemonium.

Father sprang from his seat and roared for assistance. Lord Crawdank's son clambered from the stands and began to chase Garrick's horse around the field. There was only one head not turned towards the chaos that followed: you were standing facing backwards again, your eyes threatening to swallow me. It was not until much later that I considered that the leather strap you had been working on the night before might have been a bridle.

• • •

Garrick would recover, the physician told us, although several bones were broken and it took him two days to regain consciousness. I had never seen him so diminished. I didn't have sympathy to spare for long, however: not three hours passed between my seeing him awake and my having an accident of my own. I tripped on the staircase to my chamber, on the same little malformed snag of stone that had tumbled Letia to her death that autumn. Thankfully I was ascending rather than descending. My shin crunched against the apex of a step and I felt something give within the bone. I was ordered to keep to my bed until it healed.

Maybe that was when things changed. I felt the turn of winter into spring not in the taste of the air or the changing colours of the trees, as you must have, but in the minute variations in the breakfasts that the maids prepared for me. I saw nothing of you. What excuse could I have found, after all, for the falconer's apprentice to visit the duke's daughter in her chamber? I had already heard the maids whispering outside my door.

The families who had attended the tournament left one by one, after each lord was satisfied that no blame was placed on him for Garrick's injury. Cecil stayed behind. He came blushing to my chamber every afternoon, a different book under his arm, and he would read to me for hours, or we would play chess, or talk. The carved stone you had given me before Winterfest, which I had until then kept with me when I slept, began to dig into my flesh whichever way I lay. I put it on my dressing table, where it was soon hidden by gifts of books and fresh-cut flowers.

Oh, my love! You must forgive me. I know that we had our own tongue, you and I—a language of glances and touches, heat and quiet—but I had forgotten how much real conversation could excite me. The novelty of having another voice to spar with mine, someone who could speak back when I spoke to him, someone who would spill himself to me—I grew giddy on it. Words, wonderful words! He admitted, after a week or two, that he was in love with me. I looked demurely at my hands and told him that his company warmed my heart.

Eventually my leg grew well enough for me to walk around the castle with Cecil's support, treading with the utmost caution down the stairs that had precipitated my injury. He did not complain of my weight upon his shoulder.

"You are so perfect, Claire," he said, on one of our evening walks. I leaned my head against him and thought of you, and how the nights we had spent together felt like someone else's dreams. I saw you the very next morning, through my window. You were riding, and I witnessed for the first time how ugly and ungainly you were in the saddle: you kept your head forward, your neck tight, conscious of your half tongue bouncing in your throat. I turned back to my book and you were gone before I looked again.

• • •

"Your brother hates me," Cecil said one morning, peeling fruit. Garrick had been up and limping around the castle for the past few days, roaring like a stricken bear. His head was still a mess of bruises. "And that tongueless slave," Cecil said. "I'm sure she's been following me."

"Garrick hates everyone." I was fiddling with the stone that you had given me, turning it over and over in my hands. It refused to grow warm no matter how long I held it.

"Kiss me," I said suddenly, and reached for Cecil like I used to for you. The stone dropped onto the bedclothes as I slid my hand behind his neck. His lips were like a girl's. I pushed my tongue inside his mouth, wanting to find his, but he broke away.

"Wait." He was breathing heavily. "Claire, we should wait until we're married. Betrothed, at least." He closed his eyes until he had regained his composure and went back to reading me a chapter on the Siege of Rhye.

He glanced up every now and then as though he were afraid of me.

• • •

Father came to my chamber the day after, looking even greyer than he had done in the winter. It was obvious that there was a purpose to his visit, but he made sure to talk of nothing but my health and my reading until he could restrain himself no longer.

"Claire." He took my hand. "Lord Faxsly tells me that his son's letters are of nothing but you. Tell me that you share his feelings. Tell me that there isn't—that there wasn't—" He stopped and rubbed his forehead. "Your brother has been . . . concerned for you."

I went very still. "You don't need to worry," I said slowly. "Cecil and I—we are betrothed."

Warmth rushed back into his face. My mother was fetched and told the news. The three of us shared an awkward embrace, after which I asked to see Cecil in private—I needed to tell him that he had proposed to me, after all. I heard the "good news" fanfare buzzing in the air below my window. I wondered where you would be when you were told of my betrayal.

Someone knocked on my door a few minutes later. I sat up, expecting Cecil, but my heart went cold when I saw that it was Garrick.

"Congratulations," he said. He opened his arms as wide as they could go. I didn't move. He limped over to me and grabbed me in a hug.

"If you think you'll go unpunished for the mockery you've made of me," he said, "then you are very, very wrong."

. . .

Part of me feared that Cecil might be angry, but I need not have worried. He said that the fact that it had been *me* who had proposed marriage to *him* was perfectly in keeping with my character, and that the sooner our families knew of our love, the better. I didn't have to wonder long about when you would hear the news. The next morning, Cecil complained of being followed through the castle by "that tongueless witch." There would be no one like you, he said, at Castle Faxsly.

I had been foolish, I suppose, to think I would remain at Rouchefort when Cecil and I married—or that I might take you with me. Of course that was nonsense. We would be wed at Castle Faxsly, and would begin the journey west as soon as my leg was well enough to travel. I was up and walking within days of our betrothal.

A stone struck my window on the eve of our departure. I put aside the book I had been reading and sat very still, trying to work out if it was an accident of the wind. When it came again, I slid out of the bedclothes and padded to the window. I cupped my hands and peered out through the glass.

Below, in the darkness, I caught a glimpse of raven hair.

I signaled for you to come up and retreated from the window. It was foolish to invite you up, I knew—what if a servant saw you climb the stairs, or Cecil came to say goodnight and found you with me?—but it didn't seem to matter. I had to see you. I paced my chamber in my nightdress.

You knocked. I answered, and there you stood: silent, looming, bewitching. The minutiae of your face had been lost to me while we were apart. You had a new scar, a tiny one along the bottom of your chin, and the peculiar shape of your lips seemed strange and wonderful again. I drew you inside and closed the door.

"I'm sorry." Tears were already ripening in the corners of my eyes. "Oh, Aya, my love, I am so sorry."

You took my index finger in both hands and brought it to your lips.

. . .

I heard a distant cry halfway through our lovemaking. I ignored it, absorbed in you and confident in the bolt on my chamber door. A little later my ears picked out the tail of a scream, and then the sound of footfalls coming closer. Someone battered the door.

"Lady Claire!"

"Hide!" I hissed to you, and you slid out of my bed and began to squeeze in underneath it. I threw my nightdress on as the knocking increased in fervour.

"What is it?" I flung back the door. "I was aslee—"

"Oh, Lady Claire—it's Master Faxsly. That tongueless witch has—she's—oh, my lady!"

"What is it?" I grabbed the fat flesh of the servant's wrist. "Speak clearly. What's happened?"

"Master Faxsly, my lady. Your brother found him at the bottom of the stairs. Your brother said—he said—"

"Said what?"

"That the tongueless witch pushed Master Faxsly down the stairs, my lady!"

My heart fell through my stomach.

"You may go," I said, hearing myself say the words as if from the other end of a long corridor. "I'll be right down." I made sure she was all the way down the stairs before I shut the door. I leaned against it, too faint to stand. Would it give you any sense of triumph, to know that it was you I worried for, and not Cecil?

This, I realised, was Garrick's plan. Kill Cecil, and have you take the blame for it. Rob me of both of you at once. I stared at you as you climbed out from underneath the bed.

"Run," I said, after a breathless minute. "For the gods' sake, run!"

You obeyed.

• • •

I don't know how far you got. I wasn't witness to your capture, although I have imagined it a hundred times: the ring of soldiers spreading out around you, breath frosting on their swords; your hair catching the moonlight as you turn. Did you try to fight, my love? To escape? I hope they did not hurt you.

The justice hall was thronged. I sat just behind Father, next to Cecil. Dear, shattered Cecil: his mind was mercifully intact, but his body was considerably the worse for being tumbled down the stairs than Garrick's had been for being dragged behind his horse. His legs were smashed and useless, and there was now an ugly kink all along his shoulders. His right hand trembled on a cane. High above the crowd, the statue of Akresa loomed, unseeing.

You were bound when they brought you in. Your bottom lip was freshly scabbed, and you seemed shrunken, your straight-backed posture replaced with the hunch of an injured animal. Your eyes struck mine.

"Aya of the Yovali lands," the duke's justice said. "You are accused of attempting to take the life of Lord Cecil Faxsly."

The crowd hissed.

"This Circle will now hear evidence."

It began. Cecil stood, with my help, and explained that he had been descending the staircase from the eastern tower when someone pushed him from behind. He fell and cracked his head—he lifted his hair to show the crusted flesh—and it was only the work of my father's physicians that had saved his life. He told the Circle how the tongueless witch had followed him for days beforehand, stalking him through the castle whenever he went to visit Lady Claire. He had little doubt that she was his attacker.

Next was Garrick's turn. He lied without a flicker of remorse, and the pit of my stomach was hot with hate by the time he had finished.

I listened to the other witnesses as if miles underwater. Hugh stood up and testified that you had not been in the mews at the time of the attack, and that it was not the first time you had shirked your duties. I looked up at the Akresa statue, unable to listen any longer. My tongue was stuck to the bottom of my mouth.

Oh, my love, what could I have done?

I could have spoken. I know. I could have risen to my feet, heedless of the eyes that would have turned on me, and told them everything. You were with me, in my bedchamber, at the time of the attack. You were innocent. I told myself a dozen times that I would do it. I would stand up at the count of five . . . of ten . . . fifteen . . .

You looked at me. Your eyes seemed to grow until they took up the entire hall, until they *were* the hall and the Akresa statue loomed inside them. Your eyes and the eyeless visage of the justice goddess were all that I could see. You opened your mouth and I felt all the air within the hall disappear inside it.

"If any man or woman here wishes to speak for the accused, let it be now."

Oh, my love, my heart, my Aya. I am so very sorry.

RAY WOOD was born in Wiltshire in 1990. He spent four years studying English and creative writing at Royal Holloway, University of London, during which time he studiously managed to avoid writing anything that didn't have at least one sword or spaceship in it. He graduated with an MA in 2013 and currently lives in Surrey with his girlfriend. He is working on completing his first novel.

Terminal

Lavie Tidhar

When you have nothing to lose and you want to see space, you travel to Mars in jalopies—cheap, one-person, one-way vehicles. During the trip, those in the swarm communicate with one another, their words relayed to those left behind. *Edited by Ellen Datlow.*

From above the ecliptic the swarm can be seen as a cloud of minute bullet-shaped insects, their hulls, packed with photovoltaic cells, capturing the sunlight; tiny, tiny flames burning in the vastness of the dark.

They crawl with unbearable slowness across this small section of near space, beetles climbing a sheer obsidian rock face. Only the sun remains constant. The sun, always, dominates their sky.

Inside each jalopy are instrument panels and their like; a sleeping compartment where you must float your way into the secured sleeping bag; a toilet to strap yourself to; a kitchen to prepare your meal supply; and windows to look out of. With every passing day the distance from Earth increases and the time-lag grows a tiny bit longer and the streaming of communication becomes more echoey, the most acute reminder of that finite parting as the blue-green egg that is Earth revolves and grows smaller in your window, and you stand there, sometimes for hours at a time, fingers splayed against the plastic, staring at what has gone and will never come again, for your destination is Terminal.

There is such freedom in the letting go.

• • •

There is the music. Mei listens to the music, endlessly. Alone she floats in her cheap jalopy, and the music soars all about her, an archive of all the music of Earth stored in five hundred terabytes or so, so that Mei can listen to anything ever written and performed, should she so choose, and so she does, in a glorious random selection as the jalopy moves in the endless swarm from Earth to Terminal. Chopin's Études bring a sharp memory of rain and the smell of wet grass, of damp books and days spent in bed, staring out of windows, the feel of soft sheets and warm pyjamas, a steaming mug of tea. Mei listens to Vanuatu string-band songs in pidgin English, evocative of palm trees and sand beaches and graceful men swaying in the wind; she listens to Congolese kwasa kwasa and dances, floating, shaking and rolling in weightlessness, the music like an infectious laugh and hot tropical rain. The Beatles sing "Here Comes the Sun," Mozart's Requiem trails off unfinished, David Bowie's "Space Oddity" haunts the cramped confines of the jalopy: the human race speaks to Mei through notes like precise mathematical notations, and, alone, she floats in space, remembering in the way music always makes you remember.

She is not unhappy.

At first, there was something seemingly inhuman about using the toilets. It is like a hungry machine, breathing and spitting, and Mei must ride it, strapping herself into leg restraints, attaching the urine funnel, which gurgles and hisses as Mei evacuates waste. Now the toilet is like an old friend, its conversation a constant murmur, and she climbs in and out without conscious notice.

At first, Mei slept and woke up to a regiment of day and night, but a month out of Earth orbit, the old order began to slowly crumble, and now she sleeps and wakes when she wants, making day and night appear as if by magic, by a wave of her hand. Still, she maintains a routine, of washing and the brushing of teeth, of wearing clothing, a pretence at humanity which is sometimes hard to maintain being alone. A person is defined by other people.

Three months out of Earth and it's hard to picture where you'd left, where you're going. And always that word, like a whisper out of nowhere, Terminal, Terminal . . .

Mei floats and turns slowly in space, listening to the Beach Boys.

• • •

"I have to do this."

"You don't have to," she says. "You don't have to do anything. What you mean is that you want to. You want to do it. You think it makes you special but it doesn't make you special if everyone else is doing it." She looks at him with fierce black eyes and tucks a strand of hair, clumped together in her perspiration, behind her ear. He loves her very much at that moment, that fierce protectiveness, the fact someone, anyone, can look at you that way, can look at you and feel love.

"Not everyone is doing it."

They're sitting in a cafe outdoors and it is hot, it is very hot, and overhead, the twin Petronas Towers rise like silver rockets into the air. In the square outside KLCC, the water features twinkle in the sun and tourists snap photos and waiters glide like unenthusiastic penguins amongst the clientele. He drinks from his kopi ice and traces a trail of moisture on the face of the glass, slowly. "You are not *dying*," she says, at last, the words coming as from a great distance. He nods, reluctantly. It is true. He is not dying, not immediately anyway; only in the sense that all living things are dying, that there is a trajectory, the way a jalopy makes its slow but finite way from Earth to Mars. Speaking of jalopies, there is a stand under the awnings, for such stands are everywhere now, and a man shouting through the sound system to come one, come all, and take the ultimate trip—and so on, and so forth.

But more than that, implicit in her words is the question: is he dying? In the more immediate sense? "No," he says. "But."

That word lies heavy in the hot and humid air.

She is still attractive to him, even now: even after thirty years, three kids now grown and gone into the world, her hair no longer black all over but flecked with strands of white and grey, his own hair mostly gone, their hands, touching lightly across the table, both showing the signs of gravity and age. And how could he explain?

"Space," he tries to say. "The dark starry night which is eternal and forever, or as long as these words mean something in between the beginning and the end of spaceandtime." But really, is it selfish, is it not inherently *selfish* to want to leave, to go, up there and beyond—for what? It makes no sense, or no more sense than anything else you do or don't.

"Responsibility," she says. "Commitment. Love, damn it, Haziq! You're not a child, playing with toys, with, with . . . with *spaceships* or whatever. You have children, a family, we'll soon have grandkids if I know Omar, what will they do without you?"

These hypothetical people, not yet born, already laying demands to his time, his being. To be human is to exist in potentia, unborn responsibilities rising like butterflies in a great big obscuring cloud. He waves his hand in front of his face, but whether it is to shoo them away or because of the heat, he cannot say. "We always said we won't stand in each other's way," he begins, but awkwardly, and she starts to cry, silently, making no move to wipe away the tears, and he feels a great tenderness but also anger, and the combination shocks him. "I have never asked for anything," he says. "I have . . . Have I not been a good son, a good father, a good husband? I never asked for anything—" and he remembers sneaking away one night, five years before, and wandering the Petaling Street Market with television screens blaring and watching a launch, and a thin string of pearls, broken, scattered across space . . . Perhaps it was then, perhaps it was earlier, or once when he was a boy and he had seen pictures of a vast red planet unmarred by human feet . . .

"What did I ask," she says, "did I complain, did I aspire, did I not fulfil what you and I both wanted? Yes," she says, "yes, it is selfish to want to go, and it is selfish to ask you to stay, but if you go, Haziq, you won't come back. You won't ever come back."

And he says, "I know," and she shakes her head, and she is no longer crying, and there is that hard, practical look in her eyes, the one he was always a little bit afraid of. She picks up the bill and roots in her purse and brings out the money and puts it on the table. "I have to go," she says, "I have an appointment at the hairdresser's." She gets up and he does not stand to stop her, and she walks away; and he knows that all he has to do is follow her; and yet he doesn't, he remains seated, watching her weaving her way through the crowds, until she disappears inside the giant mall; and she never once looks back.

• • •

But really, it is the sick, the slowly dying, those who have nothing to lose, those untied by earthly bonds, those whose spirits are as light as air: the loners and the crazy and worst of all the artists, so many artists, each convinced in his or her own way of the uniqueness of the opportunity, exchanging life for immortality, floating, transmuting space into art in the way of the dead, for they are legally dead, now, each in his or her own jalopy, this cheap mass-manufactured container made for this one singular trip, from this planet to the next, from the living world to the dead one.

"Sign here, initial here, and here, and here—" and what does it feel like for those everyday astronauts, those would-be Martians, departing their homes for one last time, a last glance back, some leaving gladly, some tearfully, some with indifference: these Terminals, these walking dead, having signed over their assets, completed their wills, attended, in some instances, their very own wakes: leaving with nothing, boarding taxis or flights in daytime or night, to the launch site for rudimentary training with instruments they will never use, from Earth to orbit in a space plane, a reusable launch vehicle, and thence to Gateway, in low Earth orbit, that ramshackle construction floating like a spider web in the skies of Earth, made up of modules, some new, some decades old, joined together in an ungainly fashion, a makeshift thing.

. . .

. . . Here we are all astronauts. The permanent staff is multinational, harassed; monkey-like, we climb heel and toe heel and toe, handholds along the walls, no up no down but three-dimensional space as a many-splendoured thing. Here the astronauts are trained hastily in maintaining their craft and themselves, and the jalopies extend out of Gateway, beyond orbit, thousands of cheap little tin cans aimed like skipping stones at the big red rock yonder.

Here, too, you can still change your mind. Here comes a man now, a big man, an American man, with very white face and hands, a man used to being in control, a man used to being deferred to—an artist, in fact; a writer. He had made his money imagining the way the future was, but the future had passed him by and he found himself spending his time on message boards and the like, bemoaning youth and their folly. Now he has a new lease on life, or thought he had, with this plan of going into space, to Terminal Beach: six months floating in a tin can high above no world, to write his masterpiece, the thing he is to be remembered by, his *novel*, damn it, in which he's to lay down his entire philosophical framework of a libertarian bent: only he has, at the last moment, perhaps on smelling the interior of his assigned jalopy, changed his mind. Now he comes inexpertly floating like a beach ball down the shaft, bouncing here and there from the walls and bellowing for the agent, those sleazy jalopymen, for the final signature on the contract is digital, and sent once the jalopy is slingshot to Mars. It takes three orderlies to hold him, and a nurse injects him with something to calm him down. Later, he would go back down the gravity well, poorer yet wiser, but he will never write that novel: space eludes him.

Meanwhile, the nurse helps carry the now-unconscious American down to the hospital suite, a house-sized unit overlooking the curve of the Earth. Her name is Eliza and she watches day chase night across the globe and looks for her home, for the islands of the Philippines to come into view, their lights scattered like shards of shining glass, but it is the wrong time to see them. She monitors the IV distractedly, feeling tiredness wash over her like the first exploratory wave of a grey and endless sea. For Eliza, space means always being in sight of this great living world, this Earth, its oceans and its green landmasses and its bright night lights, a world that dominates her view, always, that glares like an eye through pale white clouds. To be this close to it and yet to see it separate, not of it but apart, is an amazing thing; while beyond, where the Terminals go, or farther yet, where the stars coalesce as thick as clouds, who knows what lies? And she fingers the gold cross on the chain around her neck, as she always does when she thinks of things alien beyond knowing, and she shudders, just a little bit; but everywhere else, so far, the universe is silent, and we alone shout.

· · ·

"Hello? Is it me you're looking for?"

"Who is this?"

"Hello?"

"This is jalopy A-5011 sending out a call to the faithful to prayer—"

"This is Bremen in B-9012, is there anyone there? Hello? I am very weak. Is there a doctor, can you help me, I do not think I'll make it to the rock, hello, hello—"

"This is jalopy B-2031 to jalopy C-3398, bishop to king 7, I said bishop to king 7, take that, Shen, you twisted old fruit!"

"Hello? Has anyone heard from Shiri Applebaum in C-5591, has anyone heard from Shiri Applebaum in C-5591, she has not been in touch in two days and I am getting worried, this is Robin in C-5523, we were at Gateway together before the launch, hello, hello—"

"Hello—"

Mei turns down the volume of the music and listens to the endless chatter of the swarm rise alongside it, day or night, neither of which matter or exist here, unbound by planetary rotation and that old artificial divide of darkness and the light. Many like Mei have abandoned the twenty-four-hour cycle to sleep and rise ceaselessly and almost incessantly with some desperate need to *experience* all of this, this one-time-only journey, this slow beetle's crawl across trans-solar space. Mei swoops and turns with the music and the chatter, and she idly wonders of the fate to have be-fallen Shiri Applebaum in C-5591: is she merely keeping quiet or is she dead or in a coma, never to wake up again, only her corpse and her cheap little jalopy hitting the surface of Mars in ninety more days? Across the swarm's radio network, the muezzin in A-5011 sends out the call to prayer, the singsong words so beautiful that Mei stops, suspended in midair, and breathes deeply, her chest rising and fall-ing steadily, space all around her. She has degenerative bone disease, there isn't a question of starting a new life at Terminal, only this achingly beautiful song that rises all about her, and the stars, and silent space.

· · ·

Two days later, Bremen's calls abruptly cease. B-9012 still hurtles on with the rest towards Mars. Haziq tries to picture Bremen: what was he like? What did he love? He thinks he remembers him, vaguely, a once-fat man now wasted with folded, awkward skin, large glasses, a Scandinavian man maybe, Haziq thought, but all he knows or will ever know of Bremen is the man's voice on the radio, bouncing from jalopy to jalopy and on to Earth where jalopy-chasers scan the bands and listen in a sort of awed or voyeuristic pleasure.

"This is Haziq, C-6173 . . ." He coughs and clears his throat. He drinks his miso soup awkwardly, suckling from its pouch. He sits formally, strapped by Velcro, the tray of food before him, and out of his window he stares not back to Earth or for-ward to Mars but directly onto the swarm, trying to picture each man and woman inside, trying to imagine what brought them here. Does one need a reason? Haziq wonders. Or is it merely that gradual feeling of discomfort in one's own life, one's own skin, a slowly dawning realisation that you have passed like a grey ghost through your own life, leaving no impression, that soon you might fade away entirely, to dust and ash and nothingness, a mild regret in your children's minds that they never really knew you at all.

"This is Haziq, C-6173, is there anyone hearing me, my name is Haziq and I am going to Terminal"—and a sudden excitement takes him. "My name is Haziq and I am going to Terminal!" he shouts, and all around him the endless chatter rises, of humans in space, so needy for talk like sustenance, "We're all going to Terminal!" and Haziq, shy again, says, "Please, is there anyone there, won't someone talk to me? What is it like, on Terminal?"

• • •

But that is a question that brings down the silence; it is there in the echoes of words ords rds and in the pauses, in punctuation missing or overstated, in the endless chess moves, worried queries, unwanted confessionals, declarations of love, in this desperate sudden *need* that binds them together, the swarm, and makes all that has been before become obsolete, lose definition and meaning. For the past is a world one cannot return to, and the future is a world none has seen.

Mei floats half-asleep half-awake, but the voice awakens her. Why *this* voice, she never knows, cannot articulate. "Hello. Hello. Hello . . ." And she swims through the air to the kitchenette and heats up tea and drinks it from the suction cup. There are no fizzy drinks on board the jalopies, the lack of gravity would not separate liquid and gas in the human stomach, and the astronaut would wet-burp vomit. Mei drinks slowly, carefully; all her movements are careful. "Hello?" she says, "Hello, this is Mei in A-3357, this is Mei in A-3357, can you hear me, Haziq, can you hear me?"

A pause, a micro-silence, the air filled with the hundreds of other conversations through which a voice, his voice, says, "This is Haziq! Hello, A-3357, hello!"

"Hello," Mei says, surprised and strangely happy, and she realises it is the first time she has spoken in three months. "Let me tell you, Haziq," she says, and her voice is like music between worlds, "let me tell you about Terminal."

• • •

It was raining in the city. She had come out of the hospital and looked up at the sky and saw nothing there, no stars, no sun, just clouds and smoke and fog. It rained, the rain collected in rainbow puddles in the street, the chemicals inside it painted the world and made it brighter. There was a jalopy vendor on the corner of the street, above his head a promotional video in 3D, and she was drawn to it. The vendor played loud K-pop and the film looped in on itself, but Mei didn't mind the vendor's shouts, the smell of acid rain or frying pork sticks and garlic, or the music's beat which rolled on like thunder. Mei stood and rested against the stand and watched the video play. The vendor gave her glasses, embossed with the jalopy sub-agent's logo. She watched the swarm like a majestic silver web spread out across space, hurtling (or so it seemed) from Earth to Mars. The red planet was so beautiful and round, its dry seas and massive mountain peaks, its volcanoes and canals. She watched the polar ice caps. Watched Olympus Mons breaking out of the atmosphere. Imagined a mountain so high, it reached up into space. Imagined women like her climbing it, smaller than ants but with that same ferocious dedication. Somewhere on that world was Terminal.

"Picture yourself standing on the red sands for the very first time," she tells Haziq, her voice the same singsong of the muezzin at prayer, "that very first step, the mark of your boot in the fine sand. It won't stay there forever, you know. This is not the moon, the winds will come and sweep it away, reminding you of the temporality of all living things." And she pictures Armstrong on the moon, that first impossible step, the mark of the boots in the lunar dust. "But you are on a different world now," she says, to Haziq or to herself, or to the others listening, and the jalopy-chasers back on Earth. "With different moons hanging like fruit in the sky. And you take that first step in your suit, the gravity hits you suddenly, you are barely able to drag yourself out of the jalopy, everything is labour and pain. Who knew gravity could hurt so much," she says, as though in wonder. She closes her eyes and floats slowly upwards, picturing it. She can see it so clearly, Terminal Beach where the jalopies wash ashore, endlessly, like seashells, as far as the eye can see the sand is covered in the units out of which a temporary city rises, a tent city, all those bright objects on the sand. "And as you emerge into the sunlight they stand there, welcoming you, can you see them? In suits and helmets, they extend open arms, those Martians, *Come*, they say, over the radio comms, *come*, and you follow, painfully and awkwardly, leaving tracks in the sand, into the temporary domes and the linked-together jalopies and the underground caves which they are digging, always, extending this makeshift city downwards, and you pass through the airlock and take off your helmet and breathe the air, and you are no longer alone, you are amongst people, real people, not just voices carried on the solar winds."

She falls silent then. Breathes the limited air of the cabin. "They would be planting seeds," she says, softly, "underground, and in greenhouses, all the plants of Earth, a paradise of watermelons and orchids, of frangipani and durian, jasmine and rambutan . . ." She breathes deeply, evenly. The pain is just a part of her, now. She no longer takes the pills they gave her. She wants to be herself, pain and all.

In jalopies scattered across this narrow silver band, astronauts like canned sardines marinate in their own stale sweat and listen to her voice. Her words, converted into a signal inaudible by human ears, travel across local space for whole minutes until they hit the Earth's atmosphere at last, already old and outdated, a record of a past event; here they bounce off the Earth to the ionosphere and back again, jaggedy waves like a terminal patient's heart monitor circumnavigating this rotating globe until they are deciphered by machines and converted once more into sound:

Mei's voice speaking into rooms, across hospital beds, in dark bars filled with the fug of electronic cigarettes' smoke-like vapoured steam, in lonely bedrooms where her voice keeps company to cats, in cabs driving through rain and from tinny speakers on white sand beaches where coconut crabs emerge into sunset, their blue metallic shells glinting like jalopies. Mei's voice soothes unease and fills the jalopy-chasers' minds with bright images, a panoramic view of a red world seen from space, suspended against the blackness of space; the profusion of bright galaxies and stars behind it is like a movie screen.

"Take a step, and then another and another. The sunlight caresses your skin, but its rays have travelled longer to reach you, and when you raise your head, the sun shines down from a clay-red sun, and you know you will never again see the sky blue. Think of that light. It has travelled longer and faster than you ever will, its speed in vacuum a constant 299,792,458 meters per second. Think of that number, that strange little fundamental constant, seemingly arbitrary: around that number faith can be woven and broken like silk, for is it a randomly created universe we live in or an ordained one? Why the speed of light, why the gravitational constant, why Planck's? And as you stand there, healthy or ill, on the sands of Terminal Beach and raise your face to the sun, are you happy or sad?"

Mei's voice makes them wonder, some simply and with devotion, some uneasily. But wonder they do, and some will go outside one day and encounter the ubiquitous stand of a jalopyman and be seduced by its simple promise, abandon everything to gain a nebulous idea, that boot mark in the fine-grained red sand, so easily wiped away by the winds.

And Mei tells Haziq about Olympus Mons and its shadow falling on the land and its peak in space, she tells him of the falling snow, made of frozen carbon dioxide, of men and women becoming children again, building snowmen in the airless atmosphere, and she tells him of the Valles Marineris, where they go suited up, hand in gloved hand, through the canyons whose walls rise above them, east of Tharsis.

Perhaps it is then that Haziq falls in love, a little bit, through walls and vacuum, the way a boy does, not with a real person but with an ideal, an image. Not the way he had fallen in love with his wife, not even the way he loves his children, who talk to him across the planetary gap, their words and moving images beamed to him from Earth, but they seldom do, any more, it is as if they had resigned themselves to his departure, as if by crossing the atmosphere into space he had already died and they were done with mourning.

It is her voice he fastens onto, almost greedily, with need. And as for Mei, it is as if she had absorbed the silence of three months and more than a hundred million kilometres, consumed it somehow, was sustained by it, her own silence with only the music for company, and now she must speak, speak only for the sake of it, like eating or breathing or making love, the first two of which she will soon do no more and the last of which is already gone, a thing of the past. And so she tells the swarm about Terminal.

· · ·

But what is Terminal? Eliza wonders, floating in the corridors of Gateway, watching the RLVs rise into low Earth orbit, the continents shifting past, the clouds swirling, endlessly, this whole strange giant spaceship planet as it travels at 1200 kilometres an hour around the sun, while at the same time Earth, Mars, Venus, Sun and all travel at nearly 800,000 kilometres per hour around the centre of the galaxy, while *at the same time* this speed machine, Earth and sun and the galaxy itself move at 1000 kilometres per *second* towards the Great Attractor, that most mysterious of gravitational enigmas, this anomaly of mass that pulls to it the Milky Way as if it were a pebble: all this and we think we're *still*, and it makes Eliza dizzy just to think about it.

But she thinks of such things more and more. Space changes you, somehow. It tears you out of certainties, it makes you see your world at a distance, no longer of it but apart. It makes her sad, the old certainties washed away, and more and more she finds herself thinking of Mars; of Terminal.

To never see your home again, your family, your mother, your uncles, brothers, sisters, aunts, cousins and second cousins and third cousins twice removed, and all the rest of them: never to walk under open skies and never to sail on a sea, never to hear the sound of frogs mating by a river or hear the whooshing sound of fruit bats in the trees. All those things and all the others you will never do, and people carry bucket lists around with them before they become Terminal, but at long last everything they ever knew and owned is gone and then there is only the jalopy confines, only that and the stars in the window and the voice of the swarm. And Eliza thinks that maybe she wouldn't mind leaving it all behind, just for a chance at . . . what? Something so untenable, as will-o'-the-wisp as ideology or faith and yet as hard and precisely defined as prime numbers or fundamental constants. Perhaps it is the way Irish immigrants felt on going to America, with nothing but a vague hope that the future would be different from the past. Eliza had been to nursing school, had loved, had seen the world rotate below her; had been to space, had worked on amputations, births, tumour removals, fevers turned fatal, transfusions and malarias; had held a patient's hand as she died or dried a boy's tears or made a cup of tea for the bereaved, monitored IVs, changed sheets and bedpans, took blood and gave injections, and now she floats in freefall high above the world, watching the Terminals come and go, come and go, endlessly, and the string of silver jalopies extends in a great horde from Earth's orbit to the Martian surface, and she imagines jalopies fall down like silver drops of rain, gently they glide down through the thin Martian atmosphere to land on the alien sands.

She pictures Terminal and listens to Mei's voice, one amongst so many but somehow it is the voice others return to, it is as though Mei speaks for all of them, telling them of the city being built out of cheap used bruised jalopies, the way Gateway had been put together, a lot of mismatched units joined up, and she tells them, you could fall in love again, with yourself, with another, with a world.

• • •

"Why?" Mei says to Haziq, one night period, several weeks away from planetfall. "Why did you do it?"

"Why did I go?"

She waits; she likes his voice. She floats in the cabin, her mind like a calm sea. She listens to the sounds of the jalopy, the instruments and the toilet and the creaks and rustle of all the invisible things. She is taking the pills again, she must, for the pain is too great now, and the morphine, so innocent a substance to come like blood out of the vibrant red poppies, is helping. She knows she is addicted. She knows it won't last. It makes her laugh. Everything delights her. The music is all around her now, Lao singing accompanied by a khene changing into South African kwaito becoming reggae from PNG.

"I don't know," Haziq says. He sounds so vulnerable then. Mei says, "You were married."

"Yes."

Curiosity compels her. "Why didn't she come with you?"

"She would never have come with me," Haziq says, and Mei feels her heart shudder inside her like a caged bird, and she says, "But you didn't ask."

"No," Haziq says. The long silence is interrupted by others on the shared primitive radio band, hellos and groans and threats and prayers, and someone singing, drunk. "No," Haziq says. "I didn't ask."

• • •

One month to planetfall. And Mei falls silent. Haziq tries to raise her on the radio but there is no reply. "Hello, hello, this is Haziq, C-6173, this is Haziq, C-6173, has anyone heard from Mei in A-3357, has anyone heard from Mei?"

"This is Henrik in D-7479, I am in a great deal of pain, could somebody help me? Please, could somebody help me?"

"This is Cobb in E-1255, I have figured it all out, there is no Mars, they lied to us, we'll die in these tin cans, how much air, how much air is left?"

"This is jalopy B-2031 to jalopy C-3398, queen to pawn 4, I said queen to pawn 4, and check and mate, take that, Shen, you twisted old bat!"

"This is David in B-1201, jalopy B-1200, can you hear me, jalopy B-1200, can you hear me, I love you, Joy. Will you marry me? Will you—"

"Yes! Yes!"

"We might not make it. But I feel like I know you, like I've always known you, in my mind you are as beautiful as your words."

"I will see you, I will know you, there on the red sands, there on Terminal Beach, oh, David—"

"My darling—"

"This is jalopy C-6669, will you two get a room?" and laughter on the radio waves, and shouts of cheers, congrats, mazel tov and the like. But Mei cannot be raised, her jalopy's silent.

• • •

Not jalopies but empty containers with nothing but air floating along with the swarm, destined for Terminal, supplements for the plants, and water and other supplies, and some say these settlers, if that's what they be, are dying faster than we can replace them, but so what. They had paid for their trip. Mars is a madhouse, its inmates wander their rubbish-heap town, and Mei, floating with a happy distracted mind, no longer hears even the music. And she thinks of all the things she didn't say. Of stepping out onto Terminal Beach, of coming through the airlock, yes, but then, almost immediately, coming out again, suited uncomfortably, how hard it was, to strip the jalopies of everything inside and, worse, to go on corpse duty.

She does not want to tell all this to Haziq, does not want to picture him landing, and going with the others, this gruesome initiation ceremony for the newly arrived: to check on the jalopies no longer responding, the ones that didn't open, the ones from which no one has emerged. And she hopes, without reason, that it is Haziq who finds her, no longer floating but pressed down by gravity, her fragile bones fractured and crushed; that he would know her, somehow. That he would raise her in his arms, gently, and carry her out, and lay her down on the Martian sand.

Then they would strip the jalopy and push it and join it to the others, this spider bite of a city sprawling out of those first crude jalopies to crash-land, and Haziq might sleep, fitfully, in the dormitory with all the others, and then, perhaps, Mei could be buried. Or left to the Martian winds.

She imagines the wind howling through the canyons of the Valles Marineris. Imagines the snow falling, kissing her face. Imagines the howling winds stripping her of skin and polishing her bones, imagines herself scattered at last, every tiny bit of her blown apart and spread across the planet.

And she imagines jalopies like meteorites coming down. Imagines the music the planet makes, if only you could hear it. And she closes her eyes and she smiles.

• • •

"I hope it's you . . ."

• • •

"Sign here, initial here, and here, and here."

The jalopyman is young and friendly, and she knows his face if not his name. He says, perhaps in surprise or in genuine interest, for they never, usually, ask, "Are you sure you want to do it?"

And Eliza signs, and she nods, quickly, like a bird. And she pushes the pen back at him, as if to stop from changing her mind.

• • •

"I hope it's you . . ."

"Mei? Is that you? Is that you?"

But there is no one there, nothing but a scratchy echo on the radio, like the sound of desert winds.

LAVIE TIDHAR is the author of the Jerwood Fiction Uncovered Prize–winning *A Man Lies Dreaming*, the World Fantasy Award–winning *Osama*, and the critically acclaimed *The Violent Century*. His other works include the Bookman Histories trilogy, several novellas, two collections, and a comics miniseries, *Adler*. He currently lives in London.

The Witch of Duva

Leigh Bardugo

There was a time when the woods near Duva ate girls . . . or so the story goes. But it's just possible that the danger may be a little bit closer to home. *Edited by Noa Wheeler.*

There was a time when the woods near Duva ate girls.

It's been many years since any child was taken. But still, on nights like these, when the wind comes cold from Tsibeya, mothers hold their daughters tight and warn them not to stray too far from home. "Be back before dark," they whisper. "The trees are hungry tonight."

In those black days, on the edge of these very woods, there lived a girl named Nadya and her brother, Havel, the children of Maxim Grushov, a carpenter and woodcutter. Maxim was a good man, well liked in the village. He made roofs that did not leak or bend, sturdy chairs, toys when they were called for, and his clever hands could fashion edges so smooth and fasten joints so neatly you might never find the seam. He traveled all over the countryside seeking work, to towns as far as Ryevost. He went by foot and by hay cart when the weather was kind, and in the winter, he hitched his two black horses to a sledge, kissed his children, and set out in the snow. Always he returned home to them, carrying bags of grain or a new bolt of wool, his pockets stuffed with candy for Nadya and her brother.

But when the famine came, people had no coin and nothing to trade for a prettily carved table or a wooden duck. They used their furniture for kindling and prayed they would make it through to spring. Maxim was forced to sell his horses, and then the sledge they'd once pulled over the snow-blanketed roads.

As Maxim's luck faded, so did his wife. Soon she was more ghost than woman, drifting silently from room to room. Nadya tried to get her mother to eat what little food they had, giving up portions of turnip and potato, bundling her mother's frail body in shawls and seating her on the porch in the hope that the fresh air might return some appetite to her. The only thing she seemed to crave were little cakes made by the widow Karina Stoyanova, scented with orange blossom and thick with icing. Where Karina got the sugar, no one knew—though the old women had their theories, most of which involved a rich and lonely tradesman from the river cities. The thaw came, then the summer, another failed harvest. Eventually, even Karina's supplies dwindled, and when the little cakes were gone, Nadya's mother would touch neither food nor drink, not even the smallest sip of tea.

Nadya's mother died on the first real day of winter, when the last bit of autumn fled from the air, and any hope of a mild year went with it. But the poor woman's death passed largely unremarked upon, because two days before she finally breathed her last ghostly sigh, another girl went missing.

Her name was Lara Deniken, a shy girl with a nervous laugh, the type to stand at the edges of village dances watching the fun. All they found of her was a single leather shoe, its heel thick with crusted blood. She was the second girl lost in as many months, after Shura Yeshevsky went out to hang the wash on the line and never came back in, leaving nothing but a pile of clothespins and sodden sheets lying in the mud.

Real fear came upon the town. In the past, girls had vanished every few years. True, there were rumors of girls being taken from other villages from time to time, but those children hardly seemed real. Now, as the famine deepened and the people of Duva went without, it was as if whatever waited in the woods had grown greedier and more desperate, too.

Lara. Shura. All those who had gone before: Betya. Ludmilla. Raiza. Nikolena. Other names now forgotten. In those days, they were whispered like an incantation. Parents sent up prayers to their Saints, girls walked in pairs, people watched their neighbors with wary eyes. On the edge of the woods, the townspeople built crooked altars—careful stacks of painted icons, burnt-down prayer candles, little piles of flowers and beads.

Men grumbled about bears and wolves. They organized hunting parties, talked about burning sections of the forest. Poor bumbling Uri Pankin was nearly stoned to death when he was found in possession of one of the missing girls' dolls, and only his mother's weeping and her insistence that she had found the sorry thing on the Vestopol Road saved him.

Some wondered if the girls might have just walked into the wood, lured by their hunger. There were smells that wafted off the trees when the wind blew a certain way, impossible scents of lamb dumplings or sour-cherry babka. Nadya had almost given in to them herself, sitting on the porch beside her mother, trying to get her to take another spoonful of broth. She would smell roasting pumpkin, walnuts, brown sugar, and find her feet carrying her down the stairs toward the waiting shadows, where the trees shuffled and sighed as if ready to part for her.

Stupid Nadya, you think. *Stupid girls. I would never be so foolish.* But you've never known real hunger. The crops have been good these last years and people forget what the lean times are like. They forget the way mothers smothered infants in their cribs to stop their hungry howls, or how the trapper Leonid Gemka was found gnawing on the muscle of his slain brother's calf when their hut was iced in for two long months.

Sitting on the porch of Baba Olya's house, the old women peered into the forest and muttered, "Khitka." The word raised the hairs on Nadya's arms, but she was no longer a child, so she laughed with her brother at such silly talk. The khitkii were spiteful forest spirits, bloodthirsty and vengeful. But in stories, they were known to hunger after newborns, not full-grown girls near old enough to marry.

"Who can say what shapes an appetite?" Baba Olya said with a dismissive wave of her gnarled hand. "Maybe this one is jealous. Or angry."

"Maybe it just likes the taste of our girls," said Anton Kozar, limping by on his one good leg and waggling his tongue obscenely. The old women squawked like geese and Baba Olya hurled a rock at him. War veteran or no, the man was disgusting.

When Nadya's father heard the old women muttering that Duva was cursed and demanding that the priest say blessings in the town square, he simply shook his head.

"It's just an animal," he insisted. "A wolf mad with hunger."

Maxim knew every path and corner of the forest, so he and his friends took up their rifles and headed back into the woods, full of grim determination. But again they found nothing, and the old women grumbled louder. What animal left no tracks, no trail, no trace of a body?

Suspicion crept through the town. That lecherous Anton Kozar had returned from the northern front much changed, had he not? Peli Yerokin had always been a violent boy. And Bela Pankin was a most peculiar woman, living out on that farm with her strange son, Uri. A khitka could take any form. Perhaps she had not "found" that missing girl's doll at all.

Standing at the lip of her mother's grave, Nadya noted Anton's seeping stump and lewd grin, wiry Peli Yerokin with his tangled hair and balled fists, Bela Pankin's worried frown, and the sympathetic smile of the widow Karina Stoyanova, the way her lovely black eyes stayed on Nadya's father as the coffin he'd carved with such care was lowered into the hard ground.

The khitka might take any form, but the shape it favored most was that of a beautiful woman.

Soon Karina seemed to be everywhere, bringing Nadya's father food and gifts of kvas, whispering in his ear that someone was needed to take care of him and his children. Havel would be gone for the draft soon, off to train in Poliznaya and begin his military service, but Nadya would still need minding.

"After all," said Karina in her warm honey voice, "you do not want her to disgrace you."

Later that same night, Nadya went to her father as he sat drinking kvas by the fire. Maxim was whittling. When he had nothing to do, he sometimes made dolls for Nadya, though she'd long since outgrown them. His sharp knife moved in restless sweeps, leaving curls of soft wood on the floor. He'd been too long at home. The summer and fall that he might have spent seeking out work had been lost to his wife's illness, and the winter snows would soon close the roads. As his family went hungry, his wooden dolls gathered on the mantel, like a silent, useless choir. He cursed when he cut into his thumb, and only then did he notice Nadya standing nervously by his chair.

"Papa," Nadya said, "please do not marry Karina."

She hoped that he would deny that he had been contemplating such a thing. Instead, he sucked his wounded thumb and said, "Why not? Don't you like Karina?"

"No," said Nadya honestly. "And she doesn't like me."

Maxim laughed and ran his rough knuckles over her cheek. "Sweet Nadya, who could not love you?"

"Papa—"

"Karina is a good woman," Maxim said. His knuckles brushed her cheek again. "It would be better if . . ." Abruptly, he dropped his hand and turned his face back to the fire. His eyes were distant, and when he spoke, his voice was cold and strange, as if rising from the bottom of a well. "Karina is a good woman," he repeated. His fingers gripped the arms of his chair. "Now leave me be."

She has him already, thought Nadya. *He is under her spell.*

The night before Havel left for the south, a dance was held in the barn by the Pankin farm. In better years, it might have been a raucous night, the tables piled high with plates of nuts and apples, pots of honey, and jars of peppery kvas. The men still drank and the fiddle played, but even pine boughs and the high shine of Baba Olya's treasured samovar could not hide the fact that now the tables were empty. And though people stomped and clapped their hands, they could not chase away the gloom that seemed to hang over the room.

Genetchka Lukin was chosen Dros Koroleva, Queen of the Thaw, and made to dance with all who asked her, in the hope that it would bring about a short winter, but only Havel looked truly happy. He was off to the army, to carry a gun and eat hot meals from the king's pocket. He might die or come back wounded as so many had before him, but on this night, his face glowed with the relief of leaving Duva behind.

Nadya danced once with her brother, once with Victor Yeronoff, then took a seat with the widows and wives and children. Her eyes fell on Karina, standing close to her father. Her limbs were white birch branches; her eyes were ice over black water. Maxim looked unsteady on his feet.

Khitka. The word drifted down to Nadya from the barn's shadowed eaves as she watched Karina weave her arm through Maxim's like the pale stalk of a climbing vine. Nadya pushed her foolish thoughts away and turned to watch Genetchka Lukin dance, her long golden hair braided with bright red ribbons. Nadya was ashamed to feel a pang of envy. Silly, she told herself, watching Genetchka struggle through a dance with Anton Kozar. He simply stood and swayed, one arm keeping balance on his crutch, the other clutching tightly to poor Genetchka's waist. Silly, but she felt it just the same.

"Go with Havel," said a voice at her shoulder.

Nadya nearly jumped. She hadn't noticed Karina standing beside her. She looked up at the slender woman, her dark hair lying in coils around her white neck.

Nadya turned her gaze back to the dance. "I can't and you know it. I'm not old enough." It would be two more years before she was called to the draft.

"So lie."

"This is my home," Nadya whispered furiously, embarrassed by the tears that rose behind her eyes. "You can't just send me away." *My father won't let you*, she added silently. But somehow, she did not have the courage to speak the words aloud.

Karina leaned in close to Nadya. When she smiled, her lips split wet and red around what seemed like far too many teeth.

"Havel could at least work and hunt," she whispered. "You're just another mouth." She reached out and tugged one of Nadya's curls, hard. Nadya knew that if her father happened to look over he would just see a beautiful woman, grinning and talking to his daughter, perhaps encouraging her to dance.

"I will warn you just this once," hissed Karina Stoyanova. "Go."

The next day Genetchka Lukin's mother discovered that her daughter's bed had not been slept in. The Queen of the Thaw had never made it home from the dance. At the edge of the wood, a red ribbon fluttered from the branches of a narrow birch, a few golden hairs trailing from the knot, as if it had been torn from her head.

Nadya stood silent as Genetchka's mother fell to her knees and began to wail, calling out to her Saints and pressing the red ribbon to her lips as she wept. Across the road, Nadya saw Karina watching, her eyes black, her lips turned down like peeling bark, her long, slender fingers like raw spokes of branches, stripped bare by a hard wind.

When Havel said his good-byes, he drew Nadya close. "Be safe," he whispered in her ear.

"How?" Nadya replied, but Havel had no answer.

A week later, Maxim Grushov and Karina Stoyanova were wed in the little white-washed chapel at the center of town. There was no food for a wedding feast, and there were no flowers for the bride's hair, but she wore her grandmother's pearl kokoshnik, and all agreed that, though the pearls were most likely fake, she was lovely just the same.

That night, Nadya slept in Baba Olya's front room so the bride and groom could be alone. In the morning, when she returned home, she found the house silent, the couple still abed. On the kitchen table lay an overturned bottle of wine and the remnants of what must have been a cake, the crumbs still scented with orange blossom. It seemed Karina had still had some sugar to spare after all.

Nadya couldn't help herself. She licked the plate.

• • •

Despite Havel's absence, the house felt crowded now. Maxim prowled the rooms, unable to sit still for more than a few minutes. He'd seemed calm after the wedding, nearly happy, but with every passing day, he grew more restless. He drank and cursed his lack of work, his lost sledge, his empty stomach. He snapped at Nadya and turned away when she came too near, as if he could barely stand the sight of her.

On the rare occasions Maxim showed Nadya any affection, Karina would appear, hovering in the doorway, her black eyes greedy, a rag twisting in her narrow hands. She would order Nadya into the kitchen and burden her with some ridiculous chore, commanding her to stay out of her father's way.

At meals, Karina watched Nadya eat as if her every bite of watered-down broth was an offense, as if every scrape of Nadya's spoon hollowed out Karina's belly a little more, widening the hole inside her.

Little more than a week had passed before Karina took hold of Nadya's arm and nodded toward the woods. "Go check the traps," she said.

"It's almost dark," Nadya protested.

"Don't be foolish. There's plenty of light. Now go and make yourself useful and don't come back without a rabbit for our supper."

"Where's my father?" Nadya demanded.

"He is with Anton Kozar, playing cards and drinking, and trying to forget that he was cursed with a useless daughter." Karina gave Nadya a hard push out the door. "Go, or I'll tell him that I caught you with Victor Yeronoff."

Nadya longed to march to Anton Kozar's shabby rooms, knock the glass from her father's hands, tell him that she wanted her home back from this dangerous dark-eyed stranger. And if she'd been sure that her father would take her side, she might have done just that.

Instead, Nadya walked into the woods.

When the first two snares were empty, she ignored her pounding heart and the lengthening shadows and forced herself to walk on, following the white stones that Havel had used to mark the path. In the third trap she found a brown hare, trembling with fright. She ignored the panicked whistle from its lungs as she snapped its neck with a single determined twist and felt its warm body go limp. As she walked home with her prize, she let herself imagine her father's pleasure at the evening meal. He would tell her she was brave and foolish to go into the wood alone, and when she told him that his new wife had insisted, he would send Karina from their home forever.

But when she stepped inside the house, Karina was waiting, her face pale with fury. She seized Nadya, tore the rabbit from her hands, and shoved her into her room. Nadya heard the bolt slide home. For a long while, she pounded at the door, shouting to be let free. But who was there to hear her?

Finally, weak with hunger and frustration, she let her tears come. She curled on her bed, shaken by sobs, kept awake by the hollow growling of her gut. She missed Havel. She missed her mother. All she'd had to eat was a piece of turnip at breakfast, and she knew that if Karina hadn't taken the hare from her, she would have torn it open and eaten it raw.

Later, she heard the door to the house bang open, heard her father's unsteady footsteps coming down the hall, the tentative scratch of his fingers at her door. Before she could answer she heard Karina's voice, crooning, crooning. Silence, the rustle of fabric, a thump followed by a groan, then the steady thud of bodies against the wall. Nadya clutched her pillow to her ears, trying to drown out their pants and moans, sure that Karina knew she could hear and that this was some kind of punishment. She buried her head beneath the covers but could not escape that shaming, frantic rhythm, keeping time to the echo of Karina's voice that night at the dance: *I will warn you just this once. Go. Go. Go.*

The next day, Nadya's father did not rise until after noon. When he entered the kitchen and Nadya handed him his tea, he flinched away from her, eyes skittering across the floor. Karina stood at the basin, face pinched, mixing up a batch of lye.

"I'm going to Anton's," Maxim said.

Nadya wanted to beg him not to leave her, but even in her own head, the plea sounded foolish. In the next moment, he was gone.

This time, when Karina took hold of her and said, "Go check the traps," Nadya did not argue.

She had braved the woods once and she would do it again. This time, she would clean and cook the rabbit herself and return home with a full belly, strong enough to face Karina with or without her father's help.

Hope made her stubborn. When the first flurries of snow fell, Nadya pushed on, moving from one empty trap to the next. It was only when the light began to fade that she realized she could no longer make out Havel's white stone markers.

Nadya stood in the falling snow and turned in a slow circle, searching for some familiar sign that would lead her back to the path. The trees were black slashes of shadow. The ground rose and fell in soft, billowing drifts. The light had gone dull and diffuse. There was no way of knowing which way home might be. All around her there was silence, broken only by the howl of the rising wind and her own rough breathing, as the woods slid into darkness.

And then she smelled it, hot and sweet, a fragrant cloud that singed the edges of her nostrils: burning sugar.

Nadya's breath came in frantic little gasps, and even as her terror grew, her mouth began to water. She thought of the rabbit, plucked from the trap, the rapid beat of its heart, the rolling whites of its eyes. Something brushed against her in the dark. Nadya did not pause to think; she ran.

She crashed blindly through the wood, branches lashing at her cheeks, her feet tangling in snow-laden brambles, unsure if she heard her own clumsy footfalls or something slavering behind her, something with crowded teeth and long white fingers that clutched at the hem of her coat.

When she glimpsed the glow of light filtering through the trees ahead, for one delirious moment she thought she'd somehow made it home. But as she burst into the clearing, she saw that the hut silhouetted before her was all wrong. It was lean and crooked, with lights that glowed in every window. No one in her village would ever waste candles that way.

The hut seemed to shift, almost as if it were turning to welcome her. She hesitated, took a step back. A twig snapped behind her. She bolted for the hut's painted door.

Nadya rattled the handle, sending the lantern above swaying.

"Help me!" she cried. And the door swung open. She slipped inside, slamming it behind her. Was that a thump she heard? The frustrated scrabble of paws? It was hard to tell over the hoarse sobs wheezing from her chest. She stood with her forehead pressed to the door, waiting for her heart to stop hammering, and only then, when she could take a full breath, did she turn.

The room was warm and golden, like the inside of a currant bun, thick with the smells of browning meat and fresh-baked bread. Every surface gleamed like new, cheerfully painted with leaves and flowers, animals and tiny people, the paint so fresh and bright it hurt her eyes to look at it after the dull gray surfaces of Duva.

At the far wall, a woman stood at a vast black cookstove that stretched the length of the room. Twenty different pots boiled atop it, some small and covered, some large and near to bubbling over. The oven beneath had two hinged iron doors that opened from the center and was so large that a man might have lain lengthwise in it. Or at least a child.

The woman lifted the lid of one of the pots, and a cloud of fragrant steam drifted toward Nadya. Onions. Sorrel. Chicken stock. Hunger came upon her, more piercing and consuming than her fear. A low growl escaped her lips, and she clapped a hand to her mouth.

The woman glanced over her shoulder.

She was old but not ugly, her long gray braid tied with a red ribbon. Nadya stared at that ribbon and hesitated, thinking of Genetchka Lukin. The smells of sugar and lamb and garlic and butter, all layered upon one another, made her shake with longing.

A dog lay curled in a basket, gnawing on a bone, but when Nadya looked closer she saw it was not a dog at all, but a little bear wearing a golden collar.

"You like Vladchek?"

Nadya nodded.

The woman set a heaping plate of stew down on the table.

"Sit," said the woman as she returned to the stove. "Eat."

Nadya removed her coat and hung it by the door. She pulled her damp mittens from her hands and sat down carefully at the table. She lifted her spoon, but still she hesitated. She knew from stories that you must not eat at a witch's table.

But in the end, she could not resist. She ate the stew, every hot and savory bite of it, then flaky rolls, plums in syrup, egg pudding, and a rum cake thick with raisins and brown sugar. Nadya ate and ate while the woman tended to the pots on the stove, sometimes humming a little as she worked.

She's fattening me up, thought Nadya, her eyelids growing heavy. *She'll wait for me to fall asleep, then stuff me in the oven and cook me up to make more stew.* But Nadya found she didn't care. The woman set a blanket by the stove, next to Vladchek's basket, and Nadya fell off to sleep, glad that at least she would die with a full belly.

But when she woke the next morning, she was still in one piece and the table was set with a hot bowl of porridge, stacks of rye toast slathered with butter, and plates of shiny little herring swimming in oil.

The old woman introduced herself as Magda, then sat silent, sucking on a sugared plum, watching Nadya eat her breakfast.

Nadya ate till her stomach ached while outside the snow continued to fall. When she was done, she set her empty bowl down on the floor, where Vladchek licked it clean. Only then did Magda spit the plum pit into her palm and say, "What is it you want?"

"I want to go home," Nadya replied.

"So go."

Nadya looked outside to where the snow was still falling. "I can't."

"Well then," said Magda. "Come help me stir the pot."

For the rest of the day, Nadya darned socks, scrubbed pans, chopped herbs, and strained syrups. She stood at the stove for long hours, her hair curling from the heat and steam, stirring many little pots, and wondering all the while what might become of her. That night they ate stuffed cabbage leaves, crispy roast goose, little dishes of apricot custard.

The next day, Nadya breakfasted on butter-soaked blini stuffed with cherries and cream. When she finished, the witch asked her, "What is it you want?"

"I want to go home," said Nadya, glancing at the snow still falling outside. "But I can't."

"Well then," said Magda. "Come help me stir the pot."

This was how it went, day after day, as the snow fell and filled the clearing, rising up around the hut in great white waves.

On the morning the snow finally stopped, the witch fed Nadya potato pie and sausages and asked her, "What is it you want?"

"I want to go home," said Nadya.

"Well then," said Magda. "You'd better start shoveling."

So Nadya took up the shovel and cleared a path around the hut, accompanied by Vladchek snuffling in the snow beside her and an eyeless crow that Magda fed on rye crumbs, and that sometimes perched upon the witch's shoulder. In the afternoon, Nadya ate a slab of black bread spread with soft cheese and a dish of baked apples. Magda gave her a mug of hot tea laced with sugar, and back out she went.

When she finally reached the edge of the clearing, she wondered just where she was supposed to go. The frost had come. The woods were a frozen mass of snow and tangled branches. What might be waiting for her in there? And even if she could make it through the deep snow and find her way back to Duva, what then? A tentative embrace from her weak-willed father? Far worse from his hungry-eyed wife? No path could lead her back to the home she had known. The thought opened a bleak crack inside of her, a fissure where the cold seeped through. For a terrifying moment, she was nothing but a lost girl, nameless and unwanted. She might stand there forever, a shovel in her hand, with no one to call her home. Nadya turned on her heel and scurried back to the warm confines of the hut, whispering her own name beneath her breath as if she might forget it.

Each day, Nadya worked. She cleaned floors, dusted shelves, mended clothes, shoveled snow, and scraped the ice away from the windows. But mostly, she helped Magda with her cooking. It was not all food. There were tonics and ointments, bitter-smelling pastes, jewel-colored powders packed in small enamel boxes, tinctures in brown glass bottles. There was always something strange brewing on that stove.

Soon she learned why.

They came late at night, when the moon was waxing, slogging through miles of ice and snow, men and women on sledges and shaggy ponies, even on foot. They brought eggs, jars of preserves, sacks of flour, bales of wheat. They brought smoked fish, blocks of salt, wheels of cheese, bottles of wine, tins of tea, and bag after bag of sugar, for there was no denying Magda's sweet tooth. They cried out for love potions and untraceable poisons. They begged to be made beautiful, healthy, rich.

Always, Nadya stayed hidden. On Magda's orders, she climbed high into the shelves of the larder.

"Stay there and keep quiet," Magda said. "I don't need rumors starting that I've been taking girls."

So Nadya sat with Vladchek, nibbling on a spice cookie or sucking on a hunk of black licorice, watching Magda work. She might have announced herself to these strangers at any time, pleaded to be taken home or given shelter, shouted that she'd been trapped by a witch. Instead, she stayed silent, sugar melting on her tongue, watching as they came to this old woman, how they turned to her with desperation, with resentment, but always with respect.

Magda gave them drops for the eyes, tonics for the scalp. She ran her hands over their wrinkles, tapped a man's chest till he hacked up black bile. Nadya was never sure how much was real and how much was show until the night the wax-skinned woman came.

She was gaunt, as they all were, her face a skull of hard-carved hollows. Magda asked the question she asked anyone who came to her door: "What is it you want?"

The woman collapsed in her arms, weeping, as Magda murmured soothing words, patted her hand, dried her tears. They conferred in voices too low for Nadya to decipher, and before the woman left, she took a tiny pouch from her pocket and shook the contents into Magda's palm. Nadya craned her neck to get a better look, but Magda's hand clamped shut too quickly.

The next day, Magda sent Nadya out of the house to shovel snow. When she returned at lunchtime, she was shooed back out with a cup of codfish stew. Dusk came, and as Nadya finished sprinkling salt along the edges of the path, the scent of gingerbread drifted to her across the clearing, rich and spicy, filling her nose until she felt nearly drunk.

All through dinner, she waited for Magda to open the oven, but when the meal was finished, the old woman set a piece of yesterday's lemon cake before her. Nadya shrugged. As she reached for the cream, she heard a soft sound, a gurgle. She looked at Vladchek, but the bear was fast asleep, snoring softly.

And then she heard it again, a gurgle followed by a plaintive coo. From inside the oven.

Nadya pushed back from the table, nearly knocking her chair over, and stared at Magda, horrified, but the witch did not flinch.

A knock sounded at the door.

"Go into the larder, Nadya."

For a moment, Nadya hovered between the table and the door, caught like a fly that might still free itself from the web. Then she backed into the larder, pausing only to grab hold of Vladchek's collar and drag him with her onto the top shelf, comforted by his drowsy snuffling and the warm feel of his fur beneath her hands.

Magda opened the door. The wax-faced woman stood waiting at the threshold, almost as if she were afraid to move. Magda wrapped her hands in towels and pulled open the oven's iron doors. A squalling cry filled the room. The woman grabbed at the doorposts as her knees buckled, then pressed her hands to her mouth, her chest heaving, tears streaming over her sallow cheeks. Magda swaddled the gingerbaby in a red kerchief and handed it, squirming and mewling, into the woman's trembling, outstretched arms.

"Milaya," the woman crooned. *Sweet girl.* She turned her back on Magda and disappeared into the night, not bothering to close the door behind her.

The next day, Nadya left her breakfast untouched, placing her cold bowl of porridge on the floor for Vladchek. He turned up his nose at it until Magda put it back on the stove to warm.

Before Magda could ask her question, Nadya said, "That wasn't a real child. Why did she take it?"

"It was real enough."

"What will happen to it? What will happen to her?" Nadya asked, a wild edge to her voice.

"Eventually it will be nothing but crumbs," said Magda.

"And then what? Will you just make her another?"

"The mother will be dead long before that. She has the same fever that took her infant."

"Then cure her!" Nadya shouted, smacking the table with her unused spoon.

"She didn't ask to be cured. She asked for a child."

Nadya put on her mittens and stomped out into the yard. She did not go inside for lunch. She meant to skip dinner too, to show what she thought of Magda and her terrible magic. But by the time night came her stomach was growling, and when Magda put down a plate of sliced duck with hunter's sauce, Nadya picked up her fork and knife.

"I want to go home," she muttered to her plate.

"So go," said Magda.

. . .

Winter dragged on with frost and cold, but the lamps always burned golden in the little hut. Nadya's cheeks grew rosy and her clothes grew snug. She learned how to mix up Magda's tonics without looking at the recipes and how to bake an almond cake in the shape of a crown. She learned which herbs were valuable and which were dangerous, and which herbs were valuable because they were dangerous.

Nadya knew there was much that Magda didn't teach her. She told herself she was glad of it, that she wanted nothing to do with Magda's abominations. But sometimes she felt her curiosity clawing at her like a different kind of hunger.

And then, one morning, she woke to the tapping of the blind crow's beak on the sill and the drip, drip, drip of melted snow from the eaves. Bright sun shone through the windows. The thaw had come.

That morning, Magda laid out sweet rolls with prune jam, a plate of boiled eggs, and bitter greens. Nadya ate and ate, afraid to reach the end of her meal, but eventually she could not take another bite.

"What is it you want?" asked Magda.

This time Nadya hesitated, afraid. "If I go, couldn't I just—"

"You cannot come and go from this place like you're fetching water from a well. I will not have you bring a monster to my door."

Nadya shivered. *A monster.* So she'd been right about Karina.

"What is it you want?" asked Magda again.

Nadya thought of Genetchka dancing, of nervous Lara, of Betya and Ludmilla, of the others she had never known.

"I want my father to be free of Karina. I want Duva to be safe. I want to go home."

Gently, Magda reached out and touched Nadya's left hand—first the ring finger, then the pinkie. Nadya thought of the wax-faced woman, of the little bag she'd emptied into the witch's palm.

"Think on it," said Magda.

The next morning when Magda went to lay out the breakfast, she found the cleaver Nadya had placed there.

For two days, the cleaver lay untouched on the table, as they measured and sifted and mixed, making batch after batch of batter. On the second afternoon, when the hardest of the work was done, Magda turned to Nadya.

"You know that you are welcome to remain here with me," said the witch.

Nadya stretched out her hand.

Magda sighed. The cleaver flashed once in the afternoon sun, the edge gleaming the dull gray of Grisha steel, then fell with a sound like a gunshot.

At the sight of her fingers lying forlorn on the table, Nadya fainted.

Magda healed the stumps of Nadya's fingers, bound her hand, let her rest. And while she slept, Magda took the two fingers and ground them down to a wet red meal that she mixed into the batter.

When Nadya revived, they worked side by side, shaping the gingergirl on a damp plank as big as a door, then shoved her into the blazing oven.

All night the gingergirl baked, filling the hut with a marvelous smell. Nadya knew she was smelling her own bones and blood, but still her mouth watered. She dozed. Near dawn, the oven doors creaked open and the gingergirl crawled out. She crossed the room, opened the window, and lay down on the counter to let herself cool.

In the morning, Nadya and Magda attended the gingergirl, dusted her with sugar, gave her frosted lips and thick ropes of icing for hair.

Finally, they dressed her in Nadya's clothes and boots and set her on the path toward Duva.

They ate a small meal of herring and soft eggs to keep up their strength. Then Magda sat Nadya down at the table and took a small jar from one of the cabinets. She opened the window and the eyeless black crow came to rest on the table, picking at the crumbs the gingergirl had left behind.

Magda tipped the contents of the jar into her palm and held them out to Nadya. "Open your mouth," she said.

In Magda's hand, floating in a pool of shiny fluid, lay a pair of bright blue eyes. Hatchling's eyes.

"Do not swallow," said Magda sternly, "and do not retch."

Nadya closed her eyes and forced her lips to part. She tried not to gag as the crow's eyes slid onto her tongue.

"Open your eyes," commanded Magda.

Nadya obeyed, and when she did, the whole room had shifted. She saw herself sitting in a chair, eyes still closed, Magda beside her. She tried to raise her hands, but found that her wings rose instead. She hopped on her little crow feet and released a startled squawk of surprise.

Magda shooed her to the window and Nadya, elated from the feeling of her wings and the wind spreading beneath them, did not see the sadness in the old woman's gaze.

Nadya rose high into the air in a great wheeling arc, dipping her wings, learning the feel of them, slicing through the long shadows of the dwindling afternoon. She saw the woods spread beneath her, the clearing, and Magda's hut. She saw the jagged peaks of the Petrazoi in the distance, and gliding lower, she saw the gingergirl's path through the woods. She swooped and darted between the trees, unafraid of the forest for the first time since she could remember.

She circled over Duva, saw the main street, the cemetery, two new altars laid out. Two more girls gone during the long winter while she grew fat at the witch's table. They would be the last. She screeched and dove beside the gingergirl, driving her onward, her soldier, her champion.

Nadya watched from a clothesline as the gingergirl crossed the clearing to her father's house. Inside, she could hear raised voices arguing. Did he know what Karina had done? Had he begun to suspect what she truly was?

The gingergirl knocked and the voices quieted. When the door swung open, her father squinted into the dusk. Nadya was shocked at the toll the winter had taken on him. His broad shoulders looked hunched and narrow, and, even from a distance, she could see the way the skin hung loose on his frame. She waited for him to cry out in horror at the monster that stood before him.

"Nadya?" Maxim gasped. "Nadya!" He pulled the gingergirl into his arms with a rough cry.

Karina appeared behind him in the door, face pale, eyes wide. Nadya felt a twinge of disappointment. Somehow she'd imagined that Karina would take one look at the gingergirl and crumble to dust, or that the sight of Nadya alive and well on her doorstep would force her to blurt out some ugly confession.

Maxim drew the gingergirl inside and Nadya fluttered down to the windowsill to peer through the glass.

The house looked more cramped and gray than ever after the warmth of Magda's hut. She saw that the collection of wooden dolls on the mantel had grown.

Nadya's father caressed the gingergirl's burnished brown arm, peppering her with questions, but the gingergirl stayed silent, huddling by the fire. Nadya wasn't even sure that she *could* speak.

Maxim did not seem to notice her silence. He babbled on, laughing, crying, shaking his head in wonder. Karina hovered behind him, watching as she always had. There was fear in her eyes, but something else, too, something troubling that looked almost like gratitude.

Then Karina stepped forward, touched the gingergirl's soft cheek, her frosted hair. Nadya waited, sure Karina would be singed, that she would let out a shriek as the flesh of her hand peeled away like bark, revealing not bones but branches and the monstrous form of the khitka beneath her pretty skin.

Instead, Karina bowed her head and murmured what might have been a prayer. She took her coat from the hook.

"I am going to Baba Olya's."

"Yes, yes," Maxim said distractedly, unable to pull his gaze from his daughter.

She's running away, Nadya realized in horror. And the gingergirl was making no move to stop her.

Karina wrapped her head in a scarf, pulled on her gloves, and slipped out the door, shutting it behind her without a backward glance.

Nadya hopped and squawked from the window ledge.

I will follow her, she thought. *I will peck out her eyes.*

Karina bent down, picked up a pebble from the path, and hurled it at Nadya. Nadya released an indignant caw.

But when Karina spoke, her voice was gentle. "Fly away now, little bird," she said. "Some things are better left unseen." Then she disappeared into the dusk.

Nadya fluttered her wings, unsure of what to do. She peered back through the window.

Her father had pulled the gingergirl into his lap and was stroking her white hair.

"Nadya," he said again and again. "Nadya." He nuzzled the brown flesh of her shoulder, pressed his lips to her skin.

Outside, Nadya's small heart beat against her hollow bones.

"Forgive me," Maxim murmured, the tears on his cheeks dissolving the soft curve of icing at her neck.

Nadya shivered. Her wings stuttered a futile, desperate tattoo on the glass. But her father's hand slipped beneath the hem of her skirts, and the gingergirl did not move.

It isn't me, Nadya told herself. *Not really. It isn't me.*

She thought of her father's restlessness, of his lost horses, his treasured sledge. Before that . . . before that, girls had gone missing from other towns, one here, one there. Stories, rumors, faraway crimes. But then the famine had come, the long winter, and Maxim had been trapped, forced to hunt closer to home.

"I've tried to stop," he said as he pulled his daughter close. "Believe me," he begged. "Say you believe me."

The gingergirl stayed silent.

Maxim opened his wet mouth to kiss her again, and the sound he made was something between a groan and a sigh as his teeth sank into the sweetness of her shoulder.

The sigh turned to a sob as he bit down.

Nadya watched her father consume the gingergirl, bite by bite, limb by limb. He wept as he ate, but he did not stop, and by the time he was finished, the fire was cold in the grate. When he was done, he lay stretched out on the floor, his belly distended, his fingers sticky, his beard crusted with crumbs. Only then did the crow turn away.

They found Nadya's father there the next morning, his insides ruptured and stinking of rot. He had spent the night on his knees, vomiting blood and sugar. Karina had not been home to help him. When they took up the bloodstained floorboards, they found a stash of objects, among them a child's prayer book, a bracelet of glass beads, the rest of the vivid red ribbons Genetchka had worn in her hair the night of the dance, and Lara Deniken's white apron, embroidered with her clumsy stitches, the strings stained with blood. From the mantel, the little wooden dolls looked on.

Nadya flew back to the witch's hut, returned to her body by Magda's soft words and Vladchek licking her limp hand. She spent long days in silence, working beside Magda, only picking at her food.

It was not her father she thought of, but Karina. Karina who had found ways to visit their home when Nadya's mother took ill, who had filled the rooms when Havel left, keeping Nadya close. Karina who had driven Nadya into the woods, so that there would be nothing left for her father to use but a ghost. Karina who had given herself to a monster, in the hope of saving just one girl.

Nadya scrubbed and cooked and cleared the garden, and thought of Karina alone with Maxim over the long winter, fearing his absences, longing for them, searching the house for some way to prove her suspicions, her fingers scrabbling over floors and cabinets, feeling for the secret seams hidden by the carpenter's clever hands.

In Duva, there was talk of burning Maxim Grushov's body, but in the end they buried him without Saints' prayers, in rocky soil where to this day nothing grows. The lost girls' bodies were never found, though occasionally a hunter will come across a stash of bones in the wood, a shell comb, or a shoe.

Karina moved away to another little town. Who knows what became of her? Few good things happen to a woman alone. Nadya's brother, Havel, served in the northern campaign and came home quite the hero. As for Nadya, she lived with Magda and learned all the old woman's tricks, magic best not spoken of on a night like this. There are some who say that when the moon is waxing, she dares things not even Magda would try.

Now you know what monsters once lurked in the woods near Duva, and if you ever meet a bear with a golden collar, you will be able to greet him by name. So shut the window tight and make sure the latch is fastened. Dark things have a way of slipping in through narrow spaces. Shall we have something good to eat?

Well then, come help me stir the pot.

• • •

LEIGH BARDUGO is a #1 *New York Times* bestselling author of fantasy novels and the creator of the Grishaverse. With more than one million copies sold, her Grishaverse spans the Shadow and Bone Trilogy, the Six of Crows Duology, and *The Language of Thorns: Midnight Tales and Dangerous Magic*—with more to come. Her short stories can be found in multiple anthologies, including *Some of the Best from Tor.com* and *The Best American Science Fiction and Fantasy*. Her other works include *Wonder Woman: Warbringer* and the forthcoming *Ninth House*. Leigh was born in Jerusalem, grew up in Los Angeles, graduated from Yale University, and has worked in advertising, journalism, and even makeup and special effects. These days, she lives and writes in Hollywood, where she can occasionally be heard singing with her band.

Daughter of Necessity

Marie Brennan

By day she crafts; by night she unmakes. Surely somewhere, in all the myriad crossings of the threads, there is a future in which all will be well. *Edited by Paul Stevens.*

The strands thrum faintly beneath her fingertips, like the strings of a lyre. Plain grey wool, held taut by the stone weights tied at the ends, awaiting her hand. She can feel the potential in the threads, the resonance. She has that much of the gift, at least.

But it is madness to think she can do more. It is *hubris*.

It is desperation.

Her maid stands ready with the bone pick. She takes it up, slides its point beneath the first thread, and begins to weave.

• • •

Antinoös will be the most easily provoked. He has no care for the obligations of a guest, the courtesy due to his host; he sees only the pleasures to be had in food and drink. If these are restricted, marred—the meat burnt, the wine thin, the grapes too soon consumed—then he will complain. And it will take but one poorly phrased reassurance for his complaint to become more than mere words.

The guards will know to watch for this. When Antinoös draws his knife, they will be ready. Others will come to Antinoös' aid, of course; the tables will be knocked aside, the feast trampled underfoot, the rich treasures of the hall smashed to pieces.

Antinoös will not be the first to die, though. That will be Peisandros, who will fall with a guard's sword through his heart. After him, Klymenos, and then Pseras of the guards; then it will be a dozen, two score, three hundred and more dead, blood in a torrent, flames licking at the palace walls, smoke and death and devastation.

• • •

She drops the shuttle, shaking with horror. *No, no.* That was not how she meant it to go.

"My lady?" the maid asks, uncertain.

She almost takes up scissors and cuts her error away. Some fragment of wisdom stops her: that is not her gift, and to try must surely end in disaster. Instead she retrieves the shuttle, sends it back through without changing the shed. Unweaving the line that had been. "The pick," she commands, and her maid gives it to her in silent confusion. With a careful hand she lifts the warp threads, passes the shuttle through, reversing her movements from before. Undoing the work of hours with hours more, while her maid helps without understanding.

I must weave a funeral shroud, she had told them. She'd intended it to be for them. Not for all her city.

But the power was there: within her grasp, beyond her control.

She retires for the night, trembling, exhausted. Frightened. And exhilarated. When morning comes, all is as it was before, her problems unchanged, her desperation the same. Gathering her courage, she goes back to the loom.

Surely control may be learned.

· · ·

After so many years enjoying the hospitality of the palace, the men will not be easily persuaded to leave. Frustration and failure will not do it; if those were sufficient, they would have departed long since. They stay on in perpetual hope of success, and will not leave until they believe that hope gone.

She will choose her tool with care. Eurymachos is renowned for his silver tongue; he will bend it to her chosen end. A dropped hint here, a frank conversation over too much wine there. Why should a man stay, when he believes another has claimed the place he intended to take? An elegant man, well dressed and better spoken than his rivals—and they will see the proof of it, when she bestows smiles upon him she denies to all others. For him, she will drape herself in rich cloth, adorn her ears and neck with gold. For him, she will play the coquette.

One by one, they will go. Grumbling, disappointed, a few vowing some revenge against Eurymachos for having stolen the place they thought to claim. But they will go, without a fight. Their numbers will dwindle: one hundred and eight, four score, two score, twelve. They will leave, and with each chamber emptied, she will breathe more easily.

Until only one remains. Smiling, smooth-spoken Eurymachos, to whom she has shown much favor. *He* will not leave. For has she not made a promise to him, in the absence of her husband, whom all presume dead?

Too late, she will see that it has gone too far. He has coaxed from her words she never meant to speak, implications she cannot disavow. To do so would bring war, and the destruction she sought to avoid. She will have no choice but to acquiesce, for the sake of her people, for the sake of her son.

She will fail, and pay the price of that failure until the end of her days.

· · ·

This time she is shaking with rage. To be so manipulated, so trapped . . . she would die before she allowed that to happen.

Or would she? After all, the future now hanging on the loom is her own creation. However undesirable, it is *possible.* She could not have woven it, were it not so.

Her maid waits at her shoulder. They have long since begun to tell tales, she knows, her maidservants whispering of their mistress' odd behavior. They think it only a tactic for delay, an excuse for avoiding the men. That, they whisper, is why she undoes her work each night, reclaiming her spent thread, only to start anew in the morning.

As reasons go, it is a good one. They need not know the rest of her purpose. If any hint of *that* reached the men, all hope of her freedom would be gone.

Night after night, fate after fate. She can only keep trying. Surely somewhere, in all the myriad crossings of the threads, there is a future in which all will be well.

* * *

Her son will ask again for stories of his father, and she will tell him what she knows. That the king was summoned to war, and he went; that many who sailed to the east never returned.

This time, Telemachos will not be content with the familiar tale. He will insist on hearing more. When she cannot satisfy him, he will declare his intent to go in search of the truth.

It will wrench her heart to let him go. The seas took one man from her already; will they take this one as well, this youth she remembers as a babe at her breast? But release him she will, because perhaps he will find what she cannot: an escape from this trap, for himself, for her, for them all.

He will board the ship and go to Pylos, to Sparta, and in the halls of a king he will indeed hear the tale. Full of joy, he will set sail for home—but on the beaches of Ithaka, he will find a different welcome.

Antinoös, Ktesippos, Elatos, and others besides. Armed and armored, prepared not for war, but for murder. There on the beaches they will cut her son down, and his blood will flower like anemones in the sand.

When the news reaches her, it will break her heart. She will fling herself from the walls of Ithaka, and her sole victory will be that none among her suitors will ever claim her.

* * *

She wants to weep, seeing what she has woven. The threads fight her, their orderly arrangement belying their potential for chaos. Each thread is a life, and each life is a thousand thousand choices; she is not goddess enough to control them. Only a woman, a mortal woman, with a trace of the divine in her veins. And a trace is not enough.

It has become far too familiar, this unweaving. Forward and back make little difference to the speed and surety of her hands. Melantho gathers up the loose thread silently, winds it back onto the shuttle, but her mistress does not miss the sullen look in the girl's eyes. This is one who has made her life pleasant by giving herself to the men. She does not like being a maidservant, even to a queen.

A queen who can trace her ancestry back through her grandmother's grandmother to the three daughters of Necessity. From them she inherits this fragment of their gift, to spin thread and link it to men, to weave the shape of their fates on her loom. If she continues her efforts . . .

But she has no chance to try again. When she goes to that high chamber the next morning, Leodes is there, and the frame is bare of threads. He knows what she has been doing; they all know, for Melantho has told them. Leodes has always been more tolerable than the others, for he is their priest, and alone among them he respects the obligations of a guest. He chides her now for her dishonesty, though, for lying to them all this time about the progress of her weaving. There will be no more thread for her, no days and nights spent safe in this room, trying to weave a path away from danger.

He leaves her there with the empty frame and empty hands. She is not without choices: she has woven a hundred of them, a thousand, a new one every day. But every one ends in disaster. She will not choose disaster.

In fury she takes up her scissors. There are no threads here for her to cut; she sets the blades instead to her hair. When she wed, she cut a single lock in sacrifice; now she cuts them all. She kindles a fire in a bronze dish and gives her hair to the flames, an offering to the powers from whom she descends. If she cannot weave a good fate with her own hands, then she will pray for those powers to have pity upon her instead.

The flames rise high, dancing twisting flickering tongues, weaving about one another in ephemeral knots. In their light, she sees her answer, and she thrusts her hands into the fire.

When she withdraws them, threads of gold follow.

She casts them quickly into the air, the steady lines of the warp, the glowing bundle of the weft. There, without loom, without doubt, she begins to weave the fate of one man.

• • •

He is on the island of Kalypso, prisoner and guest. The nymph sings as she walks to and fro across her loom, weaving with a shuttle of gold. But Kalypso is no kin to the Fates. Her pattern will falter, give way to a power stronger than her own.

The gods themselves will order his release. One will try to drown him at sea, but he will come safe to the island of the Phaiakians. There he will find hospitality and tales of the war in years past, and one—the tale of his most clever strategem—will provoke him to admit his true name.

He will tell them his tale, the long years since that war, and out of respect they will aid him in his final journey. In the house of the swineherd Eumaios his son will find him: Telemachos, evading the trap Antinoös has laid. Together they will devise a new strategem. The king will return to his palace as a beggar, to be ridiculed and mocked by the men who have impoverished his house for so long.

And she . . .

She will put a challenge before her suitors, to string and shoot her husband's bow. One after another they will try and fail, until the filthy old beggar does what they cannot. And then he will turn his bow upon them, until every man among them lies dead.

Odysseus, king of Ithaka, will come home at last.

• • •

The tapestry hangs in the air before her, a perfect creation, glowing with fire and hope.

In the darkness beyond, her half-blinded eyes discern a silhouette. A woman, helmed and regal, who studies her work with a critical eye.

Her own gaze follows, and she sees the flaw. The error which, perhaps, underlays all others, turning her every bid for victory into failure. And she knows how it must be mended.

It is not easy to cast the final row. To cloud her own mind, robbing herself of this memory, the knowledge that she has woven Odysseus' fate and through him, the fate of them all. But she must. If she knows what is to come, she will ruin it; she will betray the truth through a careless word or a too-cautious act. There is a reason this gift is a thing of gods and not mortals.

The thread settles into place, binding her own fate. She will see her husband and not know him; recognition will not come until he proves himself to her again.

Her weaving is done. She kneels before the grey-eyed goddess and bows her head, accepting the ignorance that wisdom bestows. The brilliant light of her creation flares and then fades away.

Her maids find her collapsed on the floor and hurry her off to bed. These are the ones whose threads will continue; they have kept faith with their queen, and so they will not be hanged with treacherous Melantho and her sisters. But all of that lies in a future they have not seen. Neither maids nor mistress know what she has done.

She sleeps a day and a night, and when she rises, her hair is as long as it ever was. She goes about her duties in a daze, which her maids attribute to the absence of her son. Their reasoning is borne out when Telemachos returns, for then it seems that she wakes at last from her dream.

She goes to the head of the hall, looking out over her suitors, the men who have clamored for her hand, believing her to be the means by which they will shape their own fates.

The old beggar stands disregarded at the back of the hall. In this moment, every eye is upon her.

Penelope holds the mighty bow in her hand and speaks for all to hear. "My husband will be the man who can string the bow of Odysseus, and fire an arrow through twelve axe-heads. Thus the Fates have decreed, and on my word, it shall be so."

MARIE BRENNAN is an anthropologist and folklorist who shamelessly pillages her academic fields for material. She is the author of several acclaimed fantasy novels, including *A Natural History of Dragons: A Memoir by Lady Trent;* the Onyx Court series: *Midnight Never Come, In Ashes Lie, A Star Shall Fall,* and *With Fate Conspire; Warrior;* and *Witch.* Her short stories have appeared in more than a dozen print and online publications.

Among the Thorns

Veronica Schanoes

In seventeenth-century Germany, a vagabond with a magic fiddle murders a peddler. Many years later, his daughter seeks vengeance. *Edited by Ellen Datlow.*

They made my father dance in thorns before they killed him.

I used to think that this was a metaphor, that they beat him with thorny vines, perhaps. But I was wrong about that.

They made him dance.

· · ·

Just over 150 years ago, in 1515, as the Christians count, on a bright and clear September morning, they chained a Jewish man named Johann Pfefferkorn to a column in our cemetery. They left enough length for him to be able to walk around the column. Then they surrounded him with coals and set them aflame, raking them ever closer to Herr Pfefferkorn, until he was roasted alive.

They said that Herr Pfefferkorn had confessed to stealing, selling, and mutilating their Eucharist, planning to poison all the Christians in Magdeburg and Halbristadt combined and then to set fire to their homes, kidnapping two of their children in order to kill them and use their blood for ritual purposes, poisoning wells, and practicing sorcery.

I readily believe that poor Herr Pfefferkorn confessed to all of that.

A man will confess to anything when he is being tortured.

They say that, at the last, my father confessed to stealing every last taler he had ever possessed.

But I don't believe that. Not my father.

· · ·

They say that in their year 1462, in the village of Pinn, several of us bought the child of a farmer and tortured it to death. They also say that in their 1267, in Pforzheim, an old woman sold her granddaughter to us, and we tortured her to death and threw her body into the River Enz.

· · ·

Who are these people who trade away their children for gold?

My parents would not have given away me or any of my brothers for all the gold in Hesse. Are gentiles so depraved that at last, they cannot love even their own children?

· · ·

I was seven when my father disappeared. At first we did not worry. My parents were pawnbrokers in Hoechst; my mother ran the business out of our house and my father travelled the countryside of Hesse, peddling the stock she thus obtained, and trading with customers in nearby towns, during the week. He tried to be with us for Shabbat, but it was not so unusual for the candles to burn down without him.

But it was almost always only a matter of days before he came back, looming large in our doorway, and swept me into the air in a hug redolent of the world outside Hoechst. I was the youngest and the only girl, and though fathers and mothers both are said to rejoice more greatly in their sons than in their daughters, I do believe that my father preferred me above all my brothers.

My father was a tall man, and I am like him in that, as in other things. I have his thick black hair and his blue eyes. But my father's eyes laughed at the world, and I have instead my mother's temperament, so I was a solemn child.

When my father lifted me in his arms and kissed me, his beard stroked my cheek. I was proud of my father's beard, and he took such care of it: so neat and trim it was, not like my zeyde's beard had been, all scraggly and going every which way. And white. My mother's father's beard was white, too. My father's was black as ink, and I never saw a white hair in it.

• • •

We had a nice house, not too small and not too big, and we lived in a nice area of Hoechst, but not too nice. My parents grew up in the ghetto of Frankfurt am Main, but the ghetto in Frankfurt is but a few streets, and there are so many of us. So we Jews are mobile by necessity.

Even though it is dangerous on the road.

And Hoechst is a nice place, and we had a nice home. But not too nice. My mother had selected it when she was already pregnant with my eldest brother. "Too nice and they are jealous," she told me, "so not too nice. But not nice enough, and they won't come and do business. And," she added, "I wanted clean grounds for my children to play on."

We had some Jewish neighbors, and it was their children I mostly played with. The Christian children were nice enough, but they were scared of us sometimes, or scorned us, and I never knew what to expect. I had a friend named Inge for a while, but when her older sister saw us together, she turned red and smashed my dolly's head against a tree. Then she got to her feet and ran home, and her sister glared at me.

I was less friendly after that, although my father fixed my dolly when he came home that week, and put a bandage on my head to match hers when I asked him to.

Some feel there is safety in numbers and in closeness, but my mother thought differently. "Too many of us, too close together," she said, "and they think we're plotting against them. Of course, they don't like it when we move too far into their places, either. I do what I can to strike the right balance, liebchen," she said.

This was my mother, following the teachings of Maimonides, who wrote that we should never draw near any extreme, but keep to the way of the righteous, the golden mean. In this way, she sought to protect her family.

Perhaps she was successful, for the Angel of Death did not overtake us at home.

. . .

Death caught up with my father when he was on the road, but we did not worry overmuch at first. My mother had already begun to worry when he was still not home for the second Shabbat, but even that was not the first time, and I did not worry at all. Indeed, I grew happier, for the farther away my father travelled, the more exciting his gifts for me were when he arrived home.

But Mama sat with my Uncle Leyb, who lived with us, fretting, their heads together like brother and sister. Even though Uncle Leyb was my father's younger brother, he was fair-haired, like my mother. I loved him very much, though not in the way I loved my parents. Uncle Leyb was my playmate, my friend, my eldest brother, if my brothers had spent time with a baby like me. But Uncle Leyb was also old enough to be my parents' confidant. Sometimes he went with my father, and sometimes he stayed and helped my mother.

I am grateful that he stayed home for my father's last trip. I do not think he could have done any good. But Leyb does not forgive himself to this day.

"Illness, murder, kidnapping," said my mother calmly, as though she were making up a list of errands, but her knuckles were white, her hands gripping the folds of her dress.

"It will be all right, Esti," said my uncle. "Yakov has been out on the road many times for many days. Perhaps business is good and he doesn't want to cut off his good fortune. And then you'd have had all this worry for naught."

"They kidnapped a boy, a scholar," said Mama. "On the journey between Moravia and Cracow."

"Nobody has kidnapped Yakov," said my uncle. He had a disposition like my father's, always sunny.

"If we sell the house," Mama went on as if she hadn't heard him, "we could pay a substantial ransom."

"There will be no need for that," my uncle said firmly.

My mother's fears did not worry me. Though I was a serious child, my father was big as a tree in my eyes, certainly bigger than Mama or Uncle Leyb or most of the men in Hoechst.

And my parents were well-liked in Hoechst. My father drank and smoked with the younger Christian men, and when he offered his hand, they shook it.

When the third Shabbat without my father passed, Uncle Leyb began to worry as well. His merry games faded to silence, and he and my mother held hushed conversations that broke off the minute I came within earshot.

After the fourth Shabbat had passed, my uncle packed up a satchel of food and took a sackful of my mother's wares and announced his intention to look for my father.

"Don't go alone," my mother said.

"Whom should I take?" my uncle asked. "The children? And you need to stay and run the business."

"Take a friend. Take Nathaniel from next door. He's young and strong."

"So am I, Esti," my uncle said. He held her hand fondly for a moment before letting it go and taking a step back, away from the safety of our home. "Besides," he said, noticing that I and my next elder brother, Heymann, had stopped our game of jacks to watch and listen. "I daresay that Yakov is recovering from an ague in a nice bed somewhere. Won't I give him a tongue-lashing for not sending word home to his wife and family? Perhaps I'll even give him a knock on the head!"

The thought of slight Uncle Leyb thumping my tall, sturdy father was so comical that I giggled.

My uncle turned his face to me and pretended to be stern. "You mock me, Ittele?" he said. "Oh, if only you could have seen your father and me when we were boys! I thrashed him up and down the street, and never mind that he was the elder!"

I laughed again, and my uncle seemed pleased. But as he waved at us and turned to go, his face changed, and he looked almost frightened.

The fortnight that he was away was the longest I have ever known. Mama was quick-tempered; my brothers ignored me, except for Heymann, who entertained himself by teaching me what he learned in cheder. I tried to pay attention, but I missed my uncle's jokes and games, and I missed my father's hugs and kisses. I took to sucking my thumb for consolation, the way I had when I was a baby. Only when my brothers couldn't see, of course. My mother did catch me a few times, but she pretended not to notice so I wouldn't be embarrassed.

My brothers were out when I saw Uncle Leyb coming home through the window. His face was distorted, and I could not tell if it was an effect of the glass rippling or of some deep distress.

He seemed calm by the time Mama and I met him at the front door, having dropped the forks from our hands and abandoned our meal. My mother brought him into the kitchen and settled him with a measure of kirschwasser. Then she told me to go play outside. I was moving toward the door with my brothers' old hoop and stick as slowly as possible—they were too big for hoop rolling by this time, but I still liked it—when my uncle raised his hand and I stopped.

"No," he said firmly. "She should stay and listen. And her brothers, where are they? They should come and hear this as well."

My mother met his eyes and then nodded. She sent me out to collect my brothers. When all four of us returned, my mother's face was drawn and taut. For many years I thought that my uncle had told my mother the tale of my father's last day privately after all, but when I was older, she said not; she said that when she had seen that Uncle Leyb was alone, she had known already that she would never again lay eyes on my father.

The four of us sat between them, my eldest brother holding our mother's hand. My uncle held his arms out to me and I climbed onto his lap. I was tall, even as a child, and I no longer quite fit, but I think it was his comfort and consolation even more than mine, so I am glad I stayed. At the time, I was still obstinately hoping for good news, that Papa had struck a marvelous bargain that had taken a lot of work, and now we were all wealthy beyond the dreams of avarice, that even now Papa was travelling home as quickly as possible, his pockets loaded with treats.

My uncle wrapped his arms around me and began to speak quietly and deliberately. "Esti, Kinder. Yakov is dead. He will not be coming home. I buried him just a few days ago. With my own hands, I buried him."

My mother sighed, and somehow her face relaxed, as though the blow she had been expecting had finally landed, and it was a relief to have it done.

My brothers' faces looked blank and slightly confused; I suspect mine did as well. I did not quite believe what my uncle said. Perhaps, I thought, he was mistaken. But I could tell that my uncle was genuinely sad, so I reached up and patted his face.

"I fell in with Hoffmann after a few days, and told him of our worries"— Hoffmann was a peddler my father and uncle crossed paths with every so often and saw at shul on the high holy days. He lived several towns away, but he took much longer journeys than did my father. It was strange, though, that he should have been peddling among my father's towns.

"He said that word had spread that my brother's territory was going unattended; otherwise, he never would have presumed to visit it. He offered to join me in my search, so we pressed on together until we came to Dornburg. 'Burg' they call themselves, but they're not even as big as Hoechst. As we approached, the town lived up to its name, thorn bushes on every patch of scrub by the road.

"Yakov's body was hanging from a gibbet mounted by the side of the road just outside the town.

"We waited until nightfall, cut him down, and buried him under cover of darkness. I left a few stones at the graveside, Esti, but otherwise, I left it unmarked. I didn't want to risk them digging him up. Let him rest."

My mother's face was stone, and my uncle's voice was calm, but the top of my head was damp with my uncle's tears. I was still confused, so I turned around on my uncle's lap so I could face him.

"So when will Papa come home?" I asked him. I can make no excuses. I understood the nature of death by then. Perhaps I just did not want to believe it.

My uncle put his palms on either side of my face and held my gaze. "He will not come home again. The people of Dornburg killed him. He is dead, like your baby brother two years ago."

"How?" I could not imagine such a thing. My papa was big as a bear and twice as strong in my eyes. He could swing me around and around and never get tired. He could wrestle my two eldest brothers at once. He could even pick up my mama.

"They made him dance, liebchen. They made him dance in thorns, and then they hanged him."

"For what?" The cry burst from my mother. "For what did they hang him?"

"Theft," said my uncle, not taking his eyes from my face. "They said he had stolen all his money; rumor has it that they gave all he had to some vagabond fiddler, and he set himself up nicely. What's little enough for a family of seven is plenty for one vagrant."

"My papa never stole anything," I said. It was then that I realized what had happened. These people could say terrible things about my father only because he was dead.

"Not since we were boys," Uncle Leyb agreed.

I put my hands over his and stared into his eyes intently. If my father could not bring justice to those who slandered him, I would. "I will kill them," I told my uncle. My voice was steady and I was quite sincere. "I will surround that town with death. I will wrap death around their hearts, and I will rip them apart.

"I will kill them all. Every one."

• • •

My uncle did not laugh at me, or ruffle my hair, or tell me to run along. Instead, he met my gaze and nodded. Then he took my hands in his and said "So be it."

He said it almost reverently.

• • •

The residents of Dornburg were proud of their story, how they had destroyed the nasty Jewish peddler. How a passing fiddler had tricked the Jew into a thornbush and then played a magic fiddle that made him dance among the thorns, until his skin was ripped and bloody, and how the fiddler would not leave off until the Jew had given over all his money.

How the Jew had caught up with the fiddler at the town and had him arrested for theft; and how the fiddler had played again, forcing everybody to dance (the residents of Dornburg often omitted this part, it was said, in order not to look foolish, but the other gentiles of Hesse gladly filled it in) until the Jew confessed to theft. And how the Jew, bloody and exhausted and knowing he would never see home nor wife nor children again, did confess, and how he was hanged instead of the fiddler, and his body left to hang and rot outside the town gates as a warning.

How one morning, the town of Dornburg awoke to find that the Devil had taken the corpse down to Hell.

• • •

Uncle Leyb said that Papa would come home to me nevermore, but I did not quite believe it. I waited every night for years to hear his footsteps and pat his black beard, I waited every night for his pockets full of treats and his embrace.

I still do not understand why I waited, full of hope. I knew what my uncle had said.

My baby brother had died of a fever two years before; my parents had been heartbroken, and I still missed his delighted laugh when I tickled his face with my hair. But he had come and gone so quickly, a matter of months. Papa had always been with me; I think that I could not conceive that he would not be with me again.

I knew better than to tell anybody that I was waiting, but I waited nonetheless.

I think that I am waiting still.

• • •

My mother never quite recovered from Uncle Leyb's news, and when the story of the Jew at Dornburg became commonplace, her soul suffered further. She had been so careful, so alive to the delicate balance that would placate the Christians so that we could live a good life; finding that her best efforts were so easily overcome, that the mayor and the judge of a town where my father had traded for years would hang him at the behest of a vagrant fiddler, and that the townspeople from who he had bought, to whom he had sold and loaned, with whom he had drunk and diced and sung, would gather and cheer, it was too much for her to bear, I think.

She became a wan, quiet shadow of the mother I remember from early childhood. She stayed indoors as much as possible, and avoided contact with non-family. She ate little and slept for long hours. I missed her strictness. She had always been the stern and reliable pillar of my life. And of course, business suffered as the families of Hoechst enjoyed visiting less and less often, and my mother declined to seek out their company. Too, she suffered strange aches and illnesses with neither source nor surcease.

We would have starved, I think, if not for Uncle Leyb and our next-door neighbors, whose eldest daughter came over to help my mother through her days. Tante Gittl, I learned to call her. There was some talk for a while, talk that I was supposed to be too young to notice or to understand, that she was angling to catch the eye of Uncle Leyb. If this was anything more than talk, she was doomed to disappointment, for no woman ever caught the eye of my uncle, who much preferred the company of other young men, though he was not to meet his business partner Elias until some years later.

Uncle Leyb took over my father's peddling, joined by my eldest brother, Hirsch, who, at sixteen, had hoped to make his way to Vienna, but willingly turned to peddling to keep food on the table. Tante Gittl helped my mother recover herself, and to slowly revive what remained of our business, and Heymann was able to continue at cheder. At thirteen, Josef was already demonstrating that he had the temperament of a sociable man, one who preferred the company of fellows to the rigors of scholarship. He now keeps a tavern in Mainz, having gone to live with our mother's cousin and learn the trade.

Heymann devoted himself to study, seeking in the teachings and commentaries of Rebbes both living and dead the father we had lost. But I knew he would never be found there, for my father was never a bookish man, proud though he had been of Heymann's intelligence and aptitude for study.

I was still young, old enough to help around the house, but not much else. I spent much of my time alone with my dolly, running my fingers over the scar where my father had repaired her, sometimes not even aware that my thumb had found its way into my mouth until Tante Gittl, barely two years older than my eldest brother, would remind me gently that I was too big a girl for such behavior, and set me some petty task as distraction.

Eventually I began reading Josef's cast-off books. Heymann, who had always had the soul of a scholar, stole time from his study breaks to play tutor, practicing on me for his future career.

Time passed, and perhaps that is the worst betrayal of all, for life without my father to have become normal. It felt sometimes as if only I remembered him, though I knew that was not so, as if only I missed him, though surely Uncle Leyb felt keenly the absence of the elder brother who had taken care of him in boyhood and brought him from Frankfurt am Main to Hoechst in manhood, the two of them staying together even as so many of our families are blown apart like dandelion puffs, never to see one another again.

Uncle Leyb must have been as lonely as I.

And Mama never remarried.

So perhaps it was foolish to feel that nobody was as bereft as I, but I am sure that my father and I treasured each other in a way peculiar to only the most fortunate of fathers and daughters.

• • •

I wonder, sometimes, if the fiddler, Herr Geiger, as he was called in Dornburg, felt that way about his daughter. He always seemed uncertain around her, as if he wished to love her but did not know how to begin. Once he told me he would love her better when she was older and had a true personality. But she has always seemed to have quite a strong character to me, right from the very beginning, even in her suckling.

I could have told him how to love her. I could have told him that to love a baby is to wake up every time she cries, even if you have not had a full night's sleep in days, to clean and change her cloths even when she has made herself quite disgusting, to sit up fretting and watching her sleep when she has a cold, to dance with her around and around the room without stopping, because her delight is well worth your aching legs and feet, to tell her stories and trust that she understands more than she can say. I could have told him this, but I did not.

He was not a bad father. But he was not a good one. And I did not help him.

• • •

My mother died when I was seventeen. She seemed to have just been worn out by the treachery of our gentile neighbors. I do believe that the people of Dornburg killed her as surely as they did my father. She kissed me on her deathbed, and prayed to God to guide me to a safe home. And she died, with God having given her no answer, no peace of mind, the worry still apparent on her lifeless face.

• • •

I became Tante Gittl's main help after my mother's death, as Josef had left for Mainz two years earlier, and Heymann had no interest in the family business. Too, Heymann was—is—studious and intelligent, but not canny. His is the kind of intelligence that can quote Torah word-perfect at length and analyze the finest points of disputation, but he never could add up a column of figures and get the same answer twice. Not if his life depended on it.

And I hope it never does.

I became Tante Gittl's help, but she did not need me. She and my eldest brother, Hirsch, had married the year before, and it made good sense for her to take over the business. She was very good with people, very charming, and she and Hirsch lived in harmony, companions and business partners. Nor did she need me when she became pregnant, for she had her own sisters, even her own mother next door.

I think it was her wish for me to wed her brother Nathaniel, and he was not unkind. The match would have been well made, but I knew that motherhood would destroy any plan of mine to see my father's grave and take vengeance on the man who had ended his life, because of what we owe to our children. To put myself at great risk—that was my choice, my prerogative. But if I'd had children—it is not right for parents to abandon their children, never. I knew too well what it meant to lose one's greatest protector and caretaker, the one in whose face the sun rises and sets, while still young. And I could never have done that to my child. We owe our children our lives.

· · ·

With my mother in the ground and the youngest of her children grown, my Uncle Leyb grew restless. He had met Elias while visiting Worms, and with Hirsch and Tante Gittl well set and Josef in Mainz, he deeply desired to make his life in Worms as well. Heymann and I were left to choose our paths.

There was never really any question about Heymann's future: he lived and breathed the dream of continuing his studies at the Yeshiva in Cracow. I told Hirsch and Gittl, and Heymann as well, that I was going to Worms with Uncle Leyb, and there, perhaps among so many of our people, I would find a husband. They believed me, I think, though Heymann, who of all my brothers knew me best, wrinkled his brow in perplexity. Uncle Leyb accepted my decision without comment, and we made plans to depart.

The last night we all spent together was much as our nights had been for some time, with a pregnant Gittl and Hirsch conferring about the future while Heymann talked to me of his plans for study and Uncle Leyb sat by himself writing a letter, this time to Josef, detailing our plans.

Worms, my uncle said, is perhaps four days' travel from Hoechst, provided the weather was good and nothing hindered our progress. But we would be carrying our lives with us on horse and cart, he noted, and would, of necessity, go more slowly than he did while peddling. The three of us—Uncle Leyb, Heymann, and I—travelled together to the regional shul, where the men prayed for good fortune on our journeys, and then we parted ways, the brother closest to me in both age and affection kissing my cheek, swinging his pack off the cart and onto his shoulder, and turning to the northeast and his scholarly future. His face was flushed with excitement, but the journey was six hundred miles, and he would be alone for the first time. For months after, I would picture him alone on the road, set upon by ruffians, or ill among strangers, without any one of us to hold his hand or bring him water.

My uncle and I walked in silence for a while. After perhaps half an hour had passed, he kept his gaze on the road ahead but spoke carefully.

"Ittele, you know, of course, that Elias and I will always welcome you. But you have always been my favorite, and I flatter myself that I know you as well as anybody could. Surely my brave, bright-eyed niece is brewing plans more complex than husband-catching?"

"Yes," I replied. "I am." But I did not elaborate.

When we stopped for dinner, he broached the topic again. As he finished up the bread and sausage we had packed, he poured himself a measure of kirschwasser. He leaned back against the cart and looked me in the eye.

"So, liebe, what are these plans of yours? Indulge your old uncle by taking him into your confidence."

I smiled at him. "I do mean to see you settled, Uncle. And when you are happily ensconced in Worms and have joined your business to Elias's, and are well occupied, I believe it will be time for me to set out once more."

Uncle Leyb raised his eyebrows and gestured for me to continue.

"To Dornburg, Uncle. I will go to Dornburg, and I will watch the fiddler's last breaths."

My uncle poured himself another measure of kirsch and sipped it slowly. "How do you intend to do this, child?"

My voice seemed to come from far away as I spoke, though I had long thought on this very question. "I do not yet know, Uncle. It depends on how I find him. But I must do this. I have known ever since I was a child. The knowledge has lodged like . . . like . . ." I fumbled for words.

"Like a thorn in your heart, my child?" finished my uncle.

I nodded.

My uncle finished his kirsch. "Yes," he said.

"You are bravest of us all, I think," he said, and then he stopped. "I should go—I should have been with him—I will go—"

I put my hand on his arm to stop him. "No. You should go to Elias. I am my father's daughter, and I will go to Dornburg."

My uncle relaxed and let go of the tin cup he had been gripping. Its sides were bowed inward. Color slowly returned to his face. "I believe I understand," he said. "And after I am settled, I will see you to Dornburg. Yakov would never forgive me if something should happen to you on the road." He began packing up our belongings in preparation for continuing on to the next inn.

"So be it," he added, just as he had when I was a child on his lap.

• • •

I did wonder how I would take my revenge, but I did not wonder how I would escape afterwards. I did not expect to escape Dornburg. I expected to take my revenge, and then to meet the same end as my father. But I did not say this to my uncle. He would not have been so sanguine, I know, had he heard me say that.

• • •

That night, the Matronit visited me in a dream. I did not know who or what she was, only that she was nothing human. She was the moon, she was the forest, she was my childhood dolly. But she was terrible, and I was frightened.

She smiled at me, and through moonlight and the rustle of the trees and my dolly's cracked face, she told me to turn away from Dornburg.

"Never," I said. And the moon clouded over, and the trees cracked open, and my dolly's head shattered.

And then she was gone, only a whisper in the air left to mark her passage.

I had this dream a second time the following evening, and again the following night. But the third time, it ended differently. Instead of shattering and leaving me, the Matronit's face grew stern and she coalesced before me into the form of a woman who was a beautiful monster, my beloved mother with a brow free from fear, claws like scimitars ready to tear and kill. Her hair streamed out from her head like the tails of comets, and blood ran down her face. Her feet reached down to death and her head to the heavens. Her face was both pale and dark and she beamed at me with pride.

I am coming, my daughter.

. . .

Worms was much larger than Hoechst, but my uncle had no trouble settling in. I suppose a peddler who goes from town to town must be used to a whirl of people and places. I liked Elias well enough. He had an elegant brown mustache and was very fond of my uncle. I determined to set out for Dornburg on my own, so as not interrupt their idyll, but my uncle would not hear of it, and neither would Elias.

"Terrible things can happen to a maiden alone on the road," said Elias. "Leyb and I have both seen this. But with him escorting you, you will be safe. As safe as anyone can be."

I nodded my head in assent, secretly pleased to have my uncle's company and moral support along the way.

"But Itte," he continued. "What of when you are in Dornburg? You . . . look so much like your father. I see Yakov every time I look at you, and your father . . . your father carried Israel in his face."

I remembered the woman in my dream, the woman with claws like scimitars, with her feet in death and her head burning in the sky like the sun. And blood, blood running down her face. "I do not yet know, Uncle. But I trust a solution will come."

. . .

She came to me that night, while I was sleeping. I opened my eyes, sat up in bed, and words began pouring from my mouth, words in languages I had never heard, let alone studied. I wrested back control of my tongue long enough to stutter, "Dear God, what is happening to me?"

I am here, my daughter, echoed in my head. My mind flooded with pictures of moonlight, forests, and war.

"Who are you? Where are you?"

I am here, the presence said again.

"I am possessed? Inhabited by a dybbuk?"

I felt the presence bridle. *I am no dybbuk,* it said. *I am your dearest friend and ally. I am the mother who protects and avenges her children. I am she who is called Matronit, and I speak now through your mouth. I am she who dries up the sea, who pierces Rahab, I am the chastising mother, I am the one who redeems the mystery of Yakov.*

"Mother?" I gasped.

I am the goddess-mother of all children of Israel. And I am your maggid.

"My mother is dead," I told the empty air. "And I am pious—I have none but Adonai as God."

I have always been goddess of Israel, even now as my children turn away from my worship. And I was goddess in times of old, when I was loved and feared. For was not a statue of me set in the temple of Jerusalem? And did I not oversee the households of the Holy Land? Was incense not burned to me, libations not poured to me, cakes not made in my image in Pathros, when the children of Israel defied Jeremiah? And have I not intervened with Hashem on behalf of the children of Israel, not once or twice, but many times? And am I not your maggid, who will bring you victory if you but embrace me as of old?

"These were great sins," I breathed. "To depart from the ways of the Lord—"

He is a jealous god, she continued. *But he is not alone. Was not your own mother named for me?*

"My mother was named for her grandmother, who was—"

Esther. Named for me, the goddess of Israel, and I have gone by many names, including Astarte, including Ishtar. You worshipped me every time you spoke her name.

Do you not understand? I will bring your vengeance to pass.

"What mother are you," I said bitterly, "who did not protect a child of Israel ten years ago, when he was tortured and killed in Dornburg? And he is only one among many."

There was a silence in my head, and I thought the presence—the Matronit—had departed, but then she spoke to my soul again. *I have been greatly . . . diminished. Hashem is a jealous god, and his prophets have destroyed my worship, and so my power has dwindled. But still I can be your maggid, and guide you to righteous victory. And in turn, you will observe the rites of my worship, and help to restore some of my former strength, just as your brother will in Cracow, when he learns of me, the Matronit, the Shekhina, in his studies.*

"My brother will learn only the most pious teachings."

And he will learn of me, when he advances to the teachings of Kabbalah. And I will bring you vengeance as your maggid.

"My maggid?"

Your guide, your teacher. And something more. I will possess your body, reside in your soul, yet I will not wrest control from you. I will strengthen you for what lies ahead, yet I will leave you human. And when this work is done, I will depart.

"And you will bring me success? You will enable me to bring vengeance to Dornburg?"

Yes, my child. Through you, Dornburg shall become a wasteland.

In but a minute, I made my choice. I abandoned what I had been taught, not out of impiety, but out of sheer rage, for I realized then that despite all my piety, all my father's piety, all my brother's devotions, Adonai had allowed my father to suffer, to be ripped by thorns and then hanged while townspeople had jeered. What, then, should He be to me? And if this Matronit would bring devastation to Dornburg—"Then possess me, Mother," I said. "I consent to this ibbur. I welcome you, and I will observe your rites."

The Matronit paused before answering. *Then you must know that I must first*

make your soul ready to receive me. And you must know that this cannot be painless.
Your uncle and his partner will see you writhe in fever for seven days and nights. And
you will be changed. You will be scorched with the knowledge I bring you.

I was not foolhardy, for I knew what I was accepting. My soul had been scorched
before, when I was seven years old.

. . .

My uncle and Elias tended me faithfully as I convulsed with fever. I vomited, they
told me, continuously, until my body could bring up nothing more, and then I
shook and refused to choke down even water. They told me later that they did not
believe I would ever regain consciousness, and Elias whispered privately that my
uncle had sat weeping by my bedside more than once. Perhaps it is a blessing that
I could not feel that pain, for I do not remember any of it.

What I remember are the visions, for while my uncle sat by my bedside, I was
not with him. I was not there at all. I was among those to come, among my people
when they were expelled from Vienna five years hence, when they were driven
from Poland in the century to come. I saw our emancipation throughout that
century, and I saw its collapse—and then I was among riots, watching parents
throughout Bavaria clutch their children as their homes burned, as learned professors and their students tore their possessions apart and worse, an old man impaled with a pitchfork, unable to scream as blood bubbled from his throat. Again
and again, I saw the pendulum swing, as my people's emancipation drew near
and then was wrenched away, slicing through the hands that reached out for it.

And I saw worse. The world around me teemed with flickering images, night-
marish visions of stone roads carrying metal beasts, of burning homes, of people
pressed like livestock into mechanical carts, children crying, separated from their
parents, toddlers heads dashed against walls, of starvation, and of our neighbors
turning on us, only too glad to agree to our degradation and murder. The visions
persisted no matter where I turned my head, and there was no reprieve, nor any
justice, no justice anywhere.

. . .

What is this, I asked the Matronit. What is happening to me?

None of this has happened, as yet, she told me. *You see as I see, across not only*
space, but time. This has not happened, but it will happen. It will all happen.

And Adonai? What of Him? Why has—why *will* He abandon my people? I
wailed silently. Does our devotion mean nothing, nothing at all? What of our covenant? Did Abraham smash his father's idols for nothing? For nothing at all?

The Matronit chose her words carefully. *Hashem—Hashem . . . is . . . hungry for*
power. He always has been. He rides the waves of power and he does not care who is
crushed beneath them. He never has.

So He will desert us?

My daughter, he deserted Israel long ago.

If I could have, I would have spat. Then I will desert Him, I told her. Why should
I remain devout, why should I—why should any of us—maintain our rituals or
keep our covenant?

My daughter, if you did not, who would you be?

. . .

I awoke with no voice, coughing blood. When I saw Uncle Leyb asleep in the chair by my bedside, tears ran from my eyes for his ignorance, and for his hope, and I cried for Hirsch's baby, and all the children to come. My uncle awoke and wiped my tears as well as my nose. I was able to take his hand and to whisper that I was well again, but this effort exhausted me, and I fell back asleep. I dreamt not at all.

I was not well. I thought I would never be well again.

. . .

As I slowly recovered my strength, I kept faith with the Matronit. I poured out wine and lit incense for her; I baked small cakes in her form and in her honor. I did not tell Elias or Uncle Leyb the reasons for my actions. I myself was still un-sure whether or not the Matronit was a demon or the goddess—and how strange it felt to think that word—and if she was the former, I had no wish to lead them astray, for they are good men. But I became convinced she was what she said she was—the diminished goddess of the Jews, she who had intervened on our behalf with Adonai. For how could she speak holy prayers otherwise? Even if Adonai was no longer with my people, the holiness of our prayers could not be denied. So I prayed for her strength to return, every night and day.

. . .

After such a long illness, it was many months before my uncle would allow me to travel. But recover I did, and soon even he could not deny that I was strong, stron-ger even than I had ever been before. And so we two set off for Dornburg, leaving Elias in Worms to manage the business.

. . .

When we had travelled for two days, my uncle turned to me and told me that he was not a fool. He had heard me talking to the Matronit, he said, and he told me he would not allow me to continue unless I could explain what seemed to him like madness. He would not, he said, abandon a woman touched in the head to a strange town.

I weighed my options.

"I have a maggid, Uncle," I said at last. "My soul is hosting a righteous spirit who is leading my steps. Please trust in it as I do."

My uncle looked strangely relieved. "I am glad to know it, Itte," he said. "I will feel better knowing that you are not on your own. Tell me the name of this spirit, so that I may honor her as well."

I paused for a moment, wondering if I should invoke the name of some learned Rebbe, but I could think of none. "The Matronit," I said. "It is the Matronit-Shekhina."

My uncle said nothing. I hoped that he would remember her in his prayers, and that his prayers would add to her strength.

. . .

He left me five miles from Dornburg. I know my uncle did not like to turn back to Worms alone; I know he worried. He tried to disguise it, but I was less easily fooled than I had been ten years previous. And despite my maggid, after I had walked for two hours and found myself standing alone outside the walls of Dornburg, staring at the gibbet where my father's body had rotted a decade ago, I found myself gripped by terror. I looked for the rocks my uncle told me he had placed atop my father's grave, but without much hope. It would have been strange indeed if they had not been moved in ten years. Finally, I placed the stone I had brought from our garden in Hoechst at the foot of a birch tree.

Then I paid my toll to the guard at the gate and entered the town.

• • •

It was morning when I entered Dornburg. My uncle was right; it was not even as large as Hoechst, and after having been in Worms for a week, it seemed even smaller than I would have thought it only a month previous. A cluster of women was gathered around a well, and a group of children were tearing around after each other, screaming with laughter. As I walked slowly, they caromed into me. One went sprawling and the others ground to a halt, looking embarrassed.

I tried to smile kindly, and I began to speak, but my throat was suddenly dry. In the pause, the boy who had fallen spoke.

"I'm sorry, Fraulein. I didn't see you—we were playing, and I wasn't looking where I was going, and then you were there—"

I lifted him up and helped him brush the dirt off his clothing and hands. "It's no matter, liebchen. I too knocked into my share of grown folk when I was little. They move so slowly, you know?"

We shared a conspiratorial grin.

"Were you playing a game I know, kinde? Tag? Or—" I said, noticing some crude musical instruments in the children's hands. "War? Are you piping brave songs to hearten the soldiers?"

"Neither," laughed the child. "Dance-the-Jew! I'm the Jew, and when the others catch me, they must make me dance 'til I drop!"

I recoiled involuntarily. "I—I don't know that game, child. Is it . . . new?"

"Dunno," said the boy. "We all play it."

I took a deep breath and exhaled, trying to not to shake. "Well. Run along, then. Run along and enjoy yourselves."

The children took off again, shrieking in delight.

"They will know," I whispered to the Matronit. "They will know and they will hang me as they did my father, and then children will laugh for years afterward!"

They will not know, she said. *They will not know, because they do not see your true form. I have glamored you, my daughter. They do not see your true face, and they do not hear your accent. Be calm in your heart.*

Slowly I made my way to the well at the center of town, past a tavern called The Dancing Jew. There, I found three or four women talking amongst themselves, but instead of happy, boisterous, gossiping, they were speaking in low tones of worry and sorrow.

"Well, it's not the first time one so small has been lost, and it won't be the last, either," said an older matron briskly, but with tears in her eyes.

"But for such a great man," said a younger woman. "The loss is doubly sorrowful."

"Guten morgen, Frauen," I began. "I wonder if there is work in this town for one who is willing."

"You have chosen a sorrowful day to come to Dornburg," said the youngest woman. "For one of our finest bürgers has lost his wife in childbed just two days ago, and will soon lose his baby girl as well. And he is a fine man, who helps anybody in our town in need."

"Is the babe sick?" I inquired.

"She will take neither cows' milk nor goats' milk, but she screams and turns away from any who try to nurse her. She will not last much longer."

I felt the Matronit move in my body, and a sudden heaviness in my breasts, almost painful.

"I think I can help," I said.

• • •

He has three gifts, the Matronit told me as I was being taken to Herr Geiger's house. *He has the fiddle that compels all to dance when it plays. He has a blowpipe that hits whatever it is aimed at. These two objects are on display, so that he may have the pleasure of telling of his triumph over the wicked Jew. The third is not tangible, but it is the most valuable of the three. No mortal can resist his requests.*

"No—but then, if he asks me of my background—"

I will strengthen you. That and your appearance I can do right now. And you will meet his will with your own.

My fear subsided and I thought clearly again. "So he could have requested that he be set free, and gone on his way without consigning my father to the gallows, then?"

Yes.

"But he preferred to torture my father and take all he had and see him hanged?"

Yes.

• • •

Herr Geiger made only the most cursory inquiries into my background. I was a widow, I told him, and had lost my man last month in an accident in Hoechst. After my husband's death, I said, his family had refused to take in me and my baby due to bad blood between them and my late parents. I had set out for Worms looking for work, but had lost the baby to a fever only days ago on the road, and could not go on. It was a very sad tale.

Herr Geiger took my hand in his and wept with me over the loss of my child. He asked me its name.

"Jakob," I said.

• • •

I did not worry that he would connect this lost baby's name with the Jewish peddler he had murdered a decade ago. I do not believe Herr Geiger ever knew my father's name. I am not entirely certain that he ever realized that my father had a name.

• • •

When I first saw Eva, she had hair like the sun, yellower than my mother's. My mother was fair, her hair pale blonde, but Eva's was true gold. Her eyes, though, were dark and brooding, the kind of stormy blue that, in a baby, will soon change to brown. She lay in her cradle, too weak to do more than mew sadly as she turned her head this way and that, searching for her mother's breast.

When I lifted her to mine, she gripped my braids with more strength than I thought she had left in her entire body and seized my nipple in her mouth. I closed my eyes and for a terrible moment thought nothing would come, but surely I knew that if the Matronit was any kind of goddess at all, she would be well-versed in the powers of the female body, and soon Eva shut her eyes in long-awaited bliss, and her suck changed from frantic to strong and steady, an infant settling in for a long time.

I shut my eyes as well, exhausted by my journey and my anxieties. When I opened them, Eva was asleep in my arms, and we were alone in the room.

• • •

Herr Geiger thanked me the next morning. He had tears in his eyes and his breath smelled of schnapps.

• • •

I nursed Eva carefully. As carefully, I lit incense and poured out libations to the Matronit. And as Eva got stronger, so did my maggid.

• • •

Eva stared up at me with her storm-night eyes as she nursed. When she was sated, she would push her head away and sigh contentedly. Sometimes, I thought I saw my reflection in her eyes, the reflection of my true face, but I knew I must have been fooling myself.

Her hair began to curl, like my mother's.

I spent my days caring for her. I sang to her when she wept. Her first laugh came when I set her down on the floor and stepped out of the room to retrieve a blanket. As soon as I got out of her sight, I popped my head back in the room and said, "Boo, baby girl!" She laughed and laughed. We did it ten times in a row before her giggles calmed.

She is a jolly baby with an open heart.

Her first word was *Jutta*, the name I had chosen for myself when I translated my own name to its Christian equivalent. When I kissed her, she beamed up at me and tried to kiss me back, but was not quite clear on how. She opened her mouth and bit my nose instead. I laughed so hard she did it over and over again, and we rolled around together laughing and kissing each other.

I had not been so happy since I had flown through the air, swung around and around by my papa.

• • •

One night, after Eva was asleep, Herr Geiger called for me, and I found him in his study, fondling a violin.

"Are you fond of music, liebchen?" He was well in his cups.

"As fond as anybody, I believe."

He lifted his bow.

"But not, I think, now, Herr Geiger."

He lowered the bow. "I take it you have heard of my conquest of the Jewish rascal whose ill-gotten gains gave me my start in life?"

I lowered my eyes modestly.

"Indeed, how could you not? Dornburg has made its fortune on that tale. I have always been a generous man—am I not so to you?"

"But of course, Herr Geiger. I am very grateful to you after so many difficulties."

Herr Geiger waved off my thanks and offered me a glass of schnapps. I accepted warily.

"After my first job, for a man so miserly he might as well have been a Jew, I set out to seek my fortune. I had not walked ten miles before I saw a poor old woman begging by the side of the road, and I gave her three talers, all the money I had in the world. What do you know but she was a fairy in disguise, and in recompense for my kind heart, she gave me one wish for each taler. I asked her for a blowpipe that would hit anything I aimed at and a fiddle that would compel all who heard its music to dance, and one more wish that is my secret, my dear!" He paused and waited for me to attempt to wheedle the secret of the third wish out of him.

I remained silent.

"Well," he said awkwardly. "I kept on with my journey, and not two days later, what did I find but a nasty Jewish swindler by the side of the road, muttering some sort of hex. I didn't quite understand all he was saying, but to be sure he was up to no good, with his eyes fixed on a brightly colored bird in a tree. Quick as anything, I used my blowpipe to bring down the bird. Then, all politeness, I asked the wicked old fiend to fetch me my kill. I waited until he was just crawling through a thornbush and then—out with my fiddle and on with the dance!"

Herr Geiger laughed at the memory and poured us both more schnapps.

"Such fine dancing you've never seen, my dear! With the blood running and his clothing in tatters, still he had to keep on dancing! He begged me to stop, and I did, on one condition—that he hand over all his sacks of money! And he did—there was less there than I had hoped, but plenty still, so on I went with my journey, having made a good beginning.

"But oh, that vengeful, petty Jew—of course he couldn't let me have my triumph, of course not—they are a vindictive race, my dear, grasping and vindictive. He followed me straight to Dornburg and had me arrested with some trumped-up story about how I attacked him on the road! I would've hanged, my dear, if you can believe it, had I not pulled out my fiddle again, and this time I didn't leave off playing until the Jew had confessed to all his crimes. He hanged before the day was out, and I was rewarded with all he had—for of course, you know Jews, he'd kept back some money from me at our first bargain. And that's how I got the capital I needed to set myself up well, here, and they honor me as one of their first citizens! You can see how well I've done for myself."

"I can, indeed, Herr Geiger." I kept my face turned to the ground, not out of modesty, but so as not to show my feelings. I say again, my father never stole, and was never petty. He ever had open hands and an open heart, and never turned away a request for help. I remember him, I do.

"All I lacked was a companion to share my happiness with. I thought I'd found my heart's desire in dear Konstanze; we were so happy together. I never thought in my youth that I'd wish to give up bachelorhood, but as a man ages, my dear, his thoughts turn to the comforts of hearth and home. Poor Konstanze. She was always delicate, and childbirth was too much for her."

Herr Geiger lapsed into silence while I considered the lot of the late Konstanze.

"But Jutta, a man cannot live forever alone. It's not right. It's not healthy. It's not Christian. And Jutta, I know what a good mother you will be. Are you not already a mother to my child?"

Now I did look up, startled. "Herr Geiger—you know not what you are saying—you know so little about me—you are still headspun with grief—"

He leaned forward and took my hands in his. I tried not to lean back. "Jutta, my darling, let me hope. Give me a kiss."

I felt the force of his request coursing through my body, the pressure to bend toward him and part my lips. This was different than just a request for information, to which, after all, I at least had pretended to accede. I felt the Matronit's strength behind my own, and I redoubled my resolve. Never. Never. Not even to lull him into complacency.

I think that if I had not been able to resist, I would have strangled him right then and there.

But I did resist. The Matronit lent me strength and I directed it, meeting Herr Geiger's magic with my own, stopping his will in its tracks.

I stood up. "Alas, Herr Geiger. I regret that I cannot give you cause to hope. But my loyalty to one who is now gone prevents it. I will care for Eva faithfully, but to you I must never be any more than your daughter's nurse."

He gazed at me in wonder. I spared a thought for the late Konstanze, and wondered if she had been tricked into marriage by such a request, if she had mistaken his desires and magical compulsions for her own inclinations.

"Good night, Herr Geiger." I walked out of the room and left him staring after me, eyes wide.

. . .

The following morning I took time during Eva's morning nap to bake cakes for the Matronit. I stayed in the kitchen as much as possible, trying to avoid Herr Geiger's eyes. I suppose it had been many years since anybody had been able to refuse him a direct request. I did not care to encounter his scrutiny.

But I could not avoid it forever. I became aware of . . . how shall I put this . . . his eyes upon me. And he took to accosting me without warning and asking me to do things. I acceded, but when he would ask for a kiss, I would not, and then his curiosity would redouble.

"When?" I pled with the Matronit. "When? I cannot stay near this man much longer, Mother. When will you be strong enough?"

Soon, she replied. *But every time you must refuse a request of his, my power is depleted. Are you so sure you will not—*

"I am sure," I told her. "I will not endure the touch of his lips. Not now. Not ever."

. . .

One morning, a month later, she said *tonight.*

. . .

I devoted myself to Eva that day as if I would never see her again, for I did not believe I would. I could not take a Christian baby, not after all the lies told about us. This is not a thing we do, stealing children.

But did Eva not belong to me? By love if not by right? Her face lit up when I picked her up from her cradle in the morning, and when she was fretful, only I could calm her. She laughed at my games and clung to me with both her fists whenever someone else tried to hold her. Even her father.

I did not like to think of what would become of her with the rest of Dornburg dead. For I could not kill an infant, not an infant. I am not a monster.

But how could I take her?

. . .

Eva became drowsy at dusk, and I cuddled her and sang her to sleep as gently as I could. After she fell asleep in my arms, I curled myself around her and napped, drifting in and out of sleep. I felt at peace; I felt that all the world had fallen away, and only Eva and I remained, coiled together in love.

The clock at the center of town tolled midnight. I shifted, but did not rouse myself. I did not want to leave Eva. I wanted only to have her in my arms forever.

Rise! The Matronit's voice was mighty, implacable, and I was instantly fully awake. *The time is now.*

I sat up and reluctantly pulled away from Eva's small body. She stretched out an arm, looking for me in her sleep, but was otherwise undisturbed.

I had been ready, I think, for a decade.

. . .

First I went to Herr Geiger's study and collected his fiddle and his blowpipe. Then I silently left the house. The judge who had ordered my father's death had been an old man then, I had learned over the months. He had died not long after. But the mayor and the hangman, they were still in the prime of life. The hangman had several children and a lovely house, some distance from the other homes, it's true, for nobody loves a scharfrichter, but nonetheless, he had a good life, and was respected if not celebrated. I walked to his home by moonlight, my cloak wrapped tightly around me. Standing outside his house, the Matronit told me to shut my eyes, and when I did, she granted me a vision.

The scharfrichter, Franz Schmidt, and his wife, Adelheide, were sleeping in their shared bed. All was peaceful.

What is your desire? asked the Matronit.

"Give him a dream," I told her. "Can you do that?"

But of course.

"Give him a dream. He is in chains, being led to the scaffold. He is innocent of any crime, but nonetheless, the faces of the crowd are filled with hatred. He thinks of his wife, his children, and how they will long for him, grow old without him. The noose is fitted around his neck and he finds his tongue, pleads for mercy, but the judge and the crowd only laugh. The platform drops out from under him, but the rope is not weighted correctly, and instead of his neck breaking instantly, he is slowly strangling, dancing in air. Oh, how he dances!"

The vision the Matronit granted me changed—Schmidt is twisting and turning in bed, unable to wake, unable to breathe. His face is pained and panicked.

I waited, wondering if I would feel pity, or remorse, or forgiveness. I felt none. "Stop his heart," I said.

Schmidt convulses once, and then is still. His wife has never moved.

I then went to the house of the Bürgermeister.

. . .

Strangely calm, I returned home; I returned to the house of Herr Geiger.

Herr Geiger awoke to find me seated on a chair at the foot of his bed. "Jutta?" he yawned, all confusion. "What are you doing here?"

I did not answer. Instead, I brought the blowpipe out of my pocket and snapped it in two.

"Jutta! What are you doing?"

I then smashed the fiddle against his bedpost. It was nothing, then, but shattered splinters and catgut. I threw it to the ground.

"Jutta!" Herr Geiger was on his feet, looming in front of me, grabbing my shoulders. "Do you know what you have done?"

Still I did not answer. My braids undid themselves and my hair, my true black hair, stretched out toward the fiddler, becoming thorn-covered vines. He shrieked and tried to back away, but my vines caught his arms and legs, lifted him into the air, and there was nobody to hear his shrieks except Eva, who awoke and began crying in the other room. The maid and the cook came in daily, but lived with their own families.

I stood.

My vines twined ever tighter around his arms and legs, and blood ran down his body freely as the thorns dug through his skin. He twisted in pain, trying to wrench himself free, but succeeded only in digging the thorns in more deeply. My vines suspended him in the air in front of me, and I watched his struggles dispassionately. They did not bring me pleasure, but neither did they move me to pity or compassion.

"Why, Jutta?" he gasped.

"My name is Itte," I told him. Then I spoke to the Matronit. "Let him see my true face." I watched his eyes as my disguise melted away and my own features showed forth.

"You killed my father," I told him. "Ten years ago, you killed him. For ten years, I have missed his embrace and smile. And never will I see them again."

"Jewess!" he spat.

"Yes," I agreed.

The vines grew further, wrapping themselves along his trunk, and they began burrowing into his flesh. He screamed.

"Did my father scream like that?" I asked him. "Did he scream when you made him dance in thorns?"

Eva continued to cry.

"Please, Jutta, spare me!"

Again, I could feel the force of his request marching through my body. The Matronit was channeling all her strength into the vines of my hair. I had only my own resolve with which to meet his power, but that power had been weakened by my breaking the blowpipe and the fiddle, for all things are more powerful in threes. I met his will with my own.

"For Eva's sake, spare me!"

I stared into his eyes. "You know nothing of Eva! Do you know which solid foods she can stomach, and which she cannot? Do you know on which day she began to crawl? Does she even babble your name?"

I thought of my father, swinging me through the air, patching my dolly, cuddling me to sleep, and I thought of him exhausted, breathless, limbs burning like fire, skin torn, confessing to crimes he had never committed, knowing he would never see me nor my brothers nor my mother again, and my resolve strengthened.

"I will not spare you, Herr Geiger," I said. A new vine formed from another lock of my hair, and even as he gibbered in terror, it wrapped itself around his throat.

"Eva—" he began.

"Eva is mine," I told him. "You destroyed my family. I will take her and make a new one."

At my nod, the vine gave one jerk, and snapped his neck.

The vines let him fall, and they began shrinking and turning back into my plain black hair, which replaited itself. I took one final look down at what had been Herr Geiger. Then I nodded again, and turned and ran to Eva.

As soon as she caught sight of my face, she stopped crying, and she beamed at me through her tears and held out her arms. I picked her up and began to soothe her. I changed her cloth, for she had wet herself, and nursed her back to sleep.

"I am taking her with me," I told the Matronit as I threw my belongings into my sack. "I do not care what is said about us. I will not leave her here to be raised by strangers, to be taught to hate Jews."

It would be a terrible thing to do to a Jewish infant, said the Matronit.

I paused. "She is not Jewish."

She is the child of a Jewish mother.

"Konstanze was Jewish?" I asked.

No. Konstanze is not her only mother.

"She is not my daughter."

She is. Your milk gave her life. She knows she is your daughter.

"Why did she not cry when I picked her up?" I asked. "She has not seen my true face before, only my disguise."

She has never seen any face but your true one, the Matronit said. *She knows you. She knows your face. She knows you are her mother.*

I had finished packing. I picked up Eva and she opened her eyes to peer drowsily at me. She smiled, nestled her head against my chest, and fell back asleep. I tied her to me, picked up my sack, and left Herr Geiger's home with my daughter.

• • •

Outside the town walls, I stood and watched as bushes and vines of thorns grew. They blocked the gate and rose to enclose Dornburg.

"What will happen to the townspeople?" I asked the Matronit.

They will wake tomorrow to find the sun blotted out, the sky replaced by a ceiling of thorns, and no way out of the eternal night their town has become. The sun will not shine. The crops will fail. No traders will be able to penetrate the thorns. They will starve.

I watched for a while longer, and found myself troubled. I could not shake from my mind the memory of the grin the little boy had given me on my first day in Dornburg. Apparently I had some pity, some compassion after all.

"Is this just?" I asked. "To destroy the lives of children for what their elders have done before they were born?"

The vines paused in their growth.

Do you question me?

"I do," I said. "Children are powerless. Is this divine retribution, to murder the helpless? I do not wish it. Matronit, you should not do this."

The Matronit was silent. And then—*Very well. I will spare the children. You may take them away to safety.*

I remembered an old story, of a man in a many-colored suit leading away the children of Hamelin. But is this what I wanted? To take charge of a town's worth of children who by the age of six were already playing at killing my people?

"No," I said. "What you suggest is impossible. How should I do such a thing? And is it mercy to take children from the only love they have ever known, to make them wander the earth without family? Without home? Is this kindness?"

What do you suggest? The Matronit did not seem pleased with me.

I thought again, looking at the thorn-vines. "I know another story," I said. "Of a princess asleep in a tower, and a forest of thorns sprung up around her."

And this is your vengeance? asked the Matronit. *Sleep for a hundred years? They will sleep and wake and your people will still be suffering.*

"No," I agreed. "A hundred years will not suffice. But . . . let them sleep . . . let them sleep . . ." I thought of what the Matronit had shown me of the future. "Let them sleep until their loathing for my people, Matronit, for your children, is only a curiosity, an absurdity, a poor joke. Let them sleep until they are only antiquities, laughingstocks. Let them sleep until Hesse—and all the lands that surround it—are safe for the Jews."

The Matronit was silent once more.

"Will that suffice?" I prodded her.

That will be a long time, my daughter.

"Yes," I agreed.

That . . . will suffice. They will sleep until realms of this land—all this land, all Europe—are safe for the Jews. And you are satisfied? This is different enough from death?

I struggled to explain. "If they do not wake . . . if they cannot wake . . . it will be only their fellows in hatred who are to blame. Not I."

I stroked Eva's head, noticing the darkness growing in at the roots of her hair. "Will you guide us, Matronit? Will you guide my footsteps?"

I will guide you. I will guide you to Worms, where you will see and speak with your Uncle Leyb and Elias, and then you shall take them with you to London.

"London?" I asked, surprised.

London is open to my children once again. And there will be no pogroms there, not in your lifetime. Nor your daughter's. Nor your daughter's children's, and their children's after them. I will guide you to London, and then I must depart. But you will keep my rites, daughter. Keep my rites.

"Yes," I agreed. "I will keep your rites."

• • •

I stood outside those walls with Eva bound to my chest, my old dolly tucked in next to her, and I carried my pack, which contained only those things I brought with me—I no more steal than my father did—and some of Eva's necessary items. She is sleeping peacefully, and I can feel the damp warmth of her breath against my neck. No feeling has ever given me greater pleasure.

The vines of thorns had almost reached the top of the town walls when I turned and did what my father had not been allowed to do. I walked away from Dornburg.

VERONICA SCHANOES is an assistant professor in the Department of English at Queens College—CUNY. Her fiction has appeared in *Queen Victoria's Book of Spells, Lady Churchill's Rosebud Wristlet,* and *Strange Horizons.* Her novella, *Burning Girls,* published on *Tor.com,* was a finalist for the Nebula Award. She lives in New York City.

These Deathless Bones

Cassandra Khaw

They call her the Witch Bride, the king's wild second wife, and there's only discord between her and the spoiled young prince. *Edited by Ellen Datlow.*

"You're not supposed to say that," the young prince whimpers, looking up from his dinner of sausages and truffle-infused mash, savaged and pearled with the bites he'd drooled out half-chewed. It's hard to believe he's eleven. There's gravy everywhere; practically a gallon of flavorsome beef extract, seasoned with allspice and caramelized onions, a rub of thyme, a bay leaf cooked to gossamer. The new cook spent ages on it. I know. I was there.

"You're mean! I'm going to tell my daddy that you said all those things! You're not supposed to say that." He howls.

I laugh, a little bitterly. There were many things I wasn't supposed to do, or be. I wasn't supposed to be someone's second chance, someone's happily ever alternate. I wasn't supposed to be the malevolent stepmother—heartless, soulless, devoid of the natural compassion expected of childbearing women, the instinct to drop everything and coddle needy, whiny little whelps like him.

Actually, I suppose I *was* meant to be all of those things, but I was also expected to rise above the unflattering stereotypes.

Well, fuck them.

I gesture, a slant of the palm. His attendants, bruise-cheeked and flinching, retreat as one, silent as they pour back through the servant doors. A few hesitate, questions in the bends of their mouths. All these years and I've never once asked to be alone with the little prince, have done everything I could to avoid his company.

Even if some of them might have been suspicious of my intentions, not one gives voice to their misgivings.

At last, the servants are all gone.

"I *do* hate you, though," I murmur, striding deeper into the room, my gown rustling across the marble floor. Underneath, I have my riding leathers and my boots, the chestpiece I'd sewn under the watch of the tanner's sweet son. My first and truest love. His bones are with me still. When he died, I carved his femurs into the handles of my skinning knives, his tibias into ice picks. A knucklebone, I loaded with iron bearings and then sanded into a gleaming die. We became legends, he and I, but that is a separate story.

"I hate you," I continue. "With everything that I am. I hate your screaming. I loathe your lying, screeching ways. I abhor your crocodile tears, your sly little smiles—oh, don't think that the adults don't know. We can tell when you're putting on a show."

The little prince lets out a lunatic shriek, slapping his spoon against his palm. Pureed potato, beautifully infused with truffle oil and a lick of mustard, goes everywhere.

"I hate you." I crouch in front of him. "You have no understanding as to how much. You charmed little prick."

"I'm going to tell Daddy," he announces, venomous. The pupils of his eyes are so wide that they almost eclipse his irises, leaving only the barest halo of gold to encircle the dark. In them, I can see myself: fearsome, fearless, furious. "I'm going to let him know that you said mean things to me. I'll tell him that I hate you. I'll tell him to get another mommy for me. Then he'll throw you out and the dogs will eat your bones!"

Another giddy scream of laughter. "New mommy! New mommy! Someone tell Daddy! I want a new mommy!"

"You waste of meat," I hiss, savoring the sibilance. "You'd like that, wouldn't you?"

The little prince giggles.

"You're uglier than my real mommy."

"And you're a piece of shit."

I don't know why his father chose me. It couldn't have been for beauty. My sister, ebony-tressed and sublimely sleek-limbed, would have been the superior choice. It couldn't have been that he was looking for someone tractable. There are storms more accommodating than I, wildfires less inclined towards defiance. For a while, I suspected it was because he was wise to my genealogy, that he could hear my bones whispering to his.

But he never asked for anything, would never even acknowledge how the troubadours commemorated me as the Witch Bride, an auspice of calamity. To him, I was simply his wife, his confidante, an ornament to sometimes admire and, when our moods aligned, a lover with whom to pass a gray-bellied afternoon.

No. Actually, that wasn't true.

There was one thing he wanted, and such a simple thing, too, such a compassionate desire. More than anything else, my husband yearned for me to love his son. The little prince was all that remained of the boy's venerated mother; a pale wraith, sweet if slightly stupid, given to whimsy. She was beloved by the court, I'm told, an overgrown pet whom no one saw reason to censure, charming enough in brief doses. When she died, they mourned for weeks.

Small wonder they feared me: the flint-eyed, sharp-mouthed wildling the king brought home from a distant land, mere months after the tender one's tragic demise—midnight and bone to my noonday predecessor.

In the years following, my reputation grew the way my belly refused to do. Rumors spread like brambles, digging thorns in the countryside, sowing myths. My sins were myriad: I poisoned wells; I seduced husbands from their wives, wives from their husbands; I'd birthed the sea monsters that'd devoured one of our northern neighbors; I stole children and made necklaces from their bones before giving them away at midnight balls to demons beyond number; I brought famine, brought plague, trailed locusts and death the way a widow drags her mourning veils.

The king paid no heed to those acid whispers. Like I said, all he wanted was for me to love his child, his sweet boy, his dearest treasure, his unlovable whelp.

"I'll tell Daddy."

"You won't." I pull on the weft of reality so that the threads close, shutting all sound from entering or exiting the room.

The little prince glares at me from under the long fronds of his lashes, all teeth and malice. He drops his spoon and the impact shatters his plate. Food slops onto the mosaic tiles. Mashed potato gives the kingdom's Crucified Lamb an unsightly beard. "I will. I am going to scream until he comes in. I am going to tell him you hurt me."

As he intones this, he gropes through the mess. The little prince soon finds what he's looking for: a sharp triangle of porcelain still dripping with gravy. If I gave a shit about him, I might have stopped him. But I don't. Instead, I fix him with a lidded stare as he slashes at his own truculent mien, again and again, until he's bloodied and weeping from every joint. His continued existence is a bonus, not a requirement. His carcass would work just as well.

"You're a witch." He pants gleefully. "I'll tell them you tried to kill me. And you hurt me." He barks out a quavering scream. "You made me do things. You made me cry.

"You know they burn witches," the little prince continues. "Maybe they'll burn you. I want to see you *burn*."

I sigh and rise. "Keep telling yourself that, little prince."

That last word—*prince*—shivers through the air, catching in the shadows, like hair snarled in briar. A chittering answers, churning up from the corners, fingernails tap-dancing on the glass. It grows, the noise. It grows and it grows and it grows until the windows blacken and shake.

People are always so quick to coo over children. *So innocent*, they simper as they press the screaming babes to their breast. *So helpless. So pure*. They forget that wolves are innocent, too, that the wild dogs savaging the family kitten, itself once a thing inclined toward toying with broken-breasted mice, harbor no cruelty in their ribs.

The little prince killed a squirrel when he was four—when I was still trying to love him. One winter morning, he shot the creature from its roost on an ice-rimed branch, the slingshot a wrongheaded gift from his father. The squirrel fell, stunned by the rock, a russet blaze against the white. Both the little prince and I trotted to where it'd landed, I to see whether it could be saved, and the boy—

He pulped that small head under his boot before I could cry out. It was as good as dead, the little prince informed me, laughing as he dashed away, red footprints across the snow.

In retrospect, it seems like such an irreverent little thing to hang a hatred on.

Every child, after all, is guilty of some thoughtless savagery, even if this one was more vicious than most, more dangerous. Nonetheless, I learned to despise him that day. Sometimes, I wonder if I should have ended it then, if I should have walked the squirrel's needle-bones down his throat and through his lungs, let him drown in his own blood. It would have saved a lot of trouble.

The little prince blinks, lapsing to a cunning quiet, animal instinct compelling him to watch, to wait, to be wary. "What did you do?"

"I spoke to the things you hurt—"

"I said I was sorry, " he barks, as though that one word is a confessional to be stuffed full with his sins. As though that one word could absolve everything.

"—and I told them they had a decision to make. If they could forgive you, if they could bury their rage with them, that would be that. I would ask them nothing else. But if they couldn't—"

Now the sounds outside have become a thundering of locusts, a murmuration of beetles. Now the shadows lengthen into grasping fingers. I exhale. A moting of green light spools in the air, a hieroglyph from an old and forgotten language.

"If you kill me, I'll come back and haunt you." The little prince makes a hissing sound, scrabbling upright, his petulance morphing to rage. In his hand, the blunted knife he'd been given for dinner, useless for cutting but not, perhaps, for gouging an eye from its socket.

"No one's going to kill you, you little brat, and more's the pity. But you'll wish you were dead."

At that, he charges, brandishing his knife; no grace at all, no strategy, the weapon clutched like a torch. I sidestep, an easy pivot of the heel, and the little prince staggers past. A howl, high and thin.

"Oh, you little prick." I smile in the penumbra of the dusty, green light, all teeth and hate. "You will hurt terribly."

When he was seven, the little prince sewed up a cat and hid it in a box. When it finally died, he brought the oozing corpse to my library, practically swollen with pride. "Its tummy is full of poo."

When he was eight, he blinded a rabbit with his thumbs, left its skull half-cracked.

When he was nine, he bored a hole through a tortoise's shell and filled it with ants.

When he was ten, he learned to be greedy. Every week, there'd be another chambermaid or trembling guardsman rapping at my door, meekly begging for succor, their fear of me subsumed by need. For an entire year, I did nothing but clean up after the little prince's frivolities. I spent my evenings in the servants' quarters, exorcising their rooms of his "gifts." I brewed poultices against nightmares and gifted charms against hauntings, tidied what bones would permit themselves to be put to rest, and made promises to the remainder.

The court at large paid no mind to the little prince's eccentricities, lauding them as portents of glories to come. In battle, the soothsayers exulted, he'd be a monster.

Funny how they wouldn't talk about how he was one already.

Still, all that paled compared to what happened when the little prince turned eleven . . .

Bones pour from every crack in the walls and windows. Lengths of rodent ulna. A blanket of hedgehog spines, undulating down the tapestries. Vertebrae, joined even in death, slithering like snakes. The molars from his first kill, the fragments of its skull. Everywhere, bones, clacking their way across the curlicued tiles.

I'll admit. I hadn't expected so many. There are hundreds here. Thousands. The little prince was cleverer than I thought, I suppose. More prolific. Perhaps those kills I witnessed were just practice, or things he'd curated for our discoveries.

Whatever.

The little prince is silent throughout the display, agape with wonder, too stupid to understand that they are coming for him. It isn't until *she* appears that he begins to keen, begins to wail without breath or pause.

Like the rest of them, she is bone, untethered to muscle. Unlike the rest of them, she is whole, preserved by memory or, perhaps, the wailing rage that often suffuses those who have met a violent end. No longer wired to sinew and tendon, she jitters through every stride, a marionette with missing strings; sometimes, she slips. Sometimes, she loses herself, coming apart before some echo of the past draws her back together.

She stretches her fingers to him, her phalanges bonded like ropes of white.

It is the only warning he gets.

She was just a girl, no older than the little prince, small in every sense of the word. There were scores of children like her, roaming the castle grounds, bastards of the serving wenches; lasting, unwanted souvenirs of a noble's visit.

Another king might have cast them out, but my husband has always been wise. He knew that sometimes there were changes of heart, and sometimes there was a need to pluck an heir from the common people, an heir naive to the rules of power. You could make good money trading in happily-ever-afters.

Nonetheless, when the girl disappeared, no one had very much to say. It was a thing that happened, the chancellor explained. Occasionally, the maids would barter a child to the whorehouses, or auction them for a sizable dowry. And the child, until then a hungry mouth with no value, would become worthy of fond remembrance.

But the girl, as it turned out, *hadn't* been sold.

She *hadn't* been given away.

She—

I won't tell you about what I found. I won't tell you what I saw when I walked into the kitchen, a sobbing maid curled by the fireplace, the little prince singing rhymes. I will not tell you what he said to me, only that I had to give the maid a sedative before I could lead her from the little girl's corpse.

As for the girl herself—

We spoke, naturally, after her bones had been bathed in firefly gut and frangipani. No, I won't tell you what she said to me, either. But I am not ashamed to say I wept.

Bones do not lie.

Even when they are broken and then mended, there are scars to say where a fracture once was. A woman might wear powders to disguise her age and a man might boast of his vigor, but if you know where to look, if you can read their teeth and the bends of their spines, you'll know the truth each time.

And the little prince's truth is this: He deserves all of it. His bones—pale, pristine—gibber across the floor in rage, incensed to have been ousted from their cloak of flesh. Even now, even in their current state, they are petty, petulant things.

I ignore them.

Instead, I watch. I watch as those other bones crawl through the red circle of his sagging mouth. I watch as they negotiate placement; which vertebra would go where, which finger would be made by bird wings and which would be put together by human teeth.

By tomorrow, they will have cohered into a single entity, a half-thing with dreams of the woods. And who knows? In the years to come, perhaps those dreams will dissipate, leaving a soul like mine, whole and strange.

The doors bang open just as the last sliver of calcium slots into place, and the little prince takes its first new breath.

"Stop!" shout the guardsmen as they stampede into the room, its eaves and recesses still choked with bones. "Stop in the name of the king!"

• • •

Is this where I say they caught me? Is this where I tell you that I wrote my tale from a cell, while awaiting the frozen dawn and a death in the fire? After all, this is usually the part of the story where the reprehensible meets her end.

Well—

Not this time.

CASSANDRA KHAW writes horror, press releases, video games, articles *about* video games, and tabletop RPGs. These are not necessarily unrelated items. Her work can be found in professional short story magazines such as *Tor.com, Clarkesworld, Fireside Magazine, Uncanny,* and the scientific journal *Nature.* Cassandra's first original novella, *Hammers on Bone,* came out in October 2016 and her next novella, *The Language of Doors,* is forthcoming from Tor.com Publishing.

Mrs. Sorensen and the Sasquatch

Kelly Barnhill

When Mr. Sorensen—a drab cipher of a man—passes away, his lovely widow falls in love with a most unsuitable mate. Enraged and scandalized (and armed with hot dish and gossip and seven-layer bars), the Parish Council turns to the old priest to fix the situation—to convince Mrs. Sorensen to reject the green world and live as a widow ought. But the pretty widow has plans of her own. *Edited by Ann VanderMeer.*

The day she buried her husband—a good man, by all accounts, though shy, not given to drink or foolishness; not one for speeding tickets or illegal parking or cheating on his taxes; not one for carousing at the county fair, or tomcatting with the other men from the glass factory; which is to say, he was utterly unknown in town: a cipher; a cold, blank space—Agnes Sorensen arrived at the front steps of Our Lady of the Snows. The priest was waiting for her at the open door. The air was sweet and wet with autumn rot, and though it had rained earlier, the day was starting to brighten, and would surely be lovely in an hour or two. Mrs. Sorensen greeted the priest with a sad smile. She wore a smart black hat, sensible black shoes, and a black silk shirt belted into a slim crepe skirt. Two little white mice peeked out of her left breast pocket—two tiny shocks of fur with pink, quivering noses and red, red tongues.

The priest, an old fellow by the name of Laurence, took her hands and gave a gentle squeeze. He was surprised by the mice. The mice, on the other hand, were not at all surprised to see *him*. They inclined their noses a little farther over the lip of her shirt pocket to get a better look. Their whiskers were as pale and bright as sunbeams. They looked at one another and turned in unison toward the face of the old priest. And though he knew it was impossible, it seemed to Father Laurence that the mice were *smiling* at him. He swallowed.

"Mrs. Sorensen," he said, clearing his throat.

"Mmm?" she said, looking at her watch. She glanced over her shoulder and whistled. A very large dog rounded the tall hedge, followed by an almost-as-large raccoon and a perfectly tiny cat.

"We can't—" But his voice failed him.

"Have the flowers arrived, Father?" Mrs. Sorensen asked pleasantly as the three animals mounted the stairs and approached the door.

"Well," the priest stammered. "N-no . . . I mean, yes, they have. Three very large boxes. But I must say, Mrs. Sorensen—"

"Marvelous. Pardon me." And she walked inside. "Hold the door open for my helpers, would you? Thank you, Father." Her voice was all brisk assurance. It was a voice that required a yes. She left a lingering scent of pinesap and lilac and woodland musk in her wake. Father Laurence felt dizzy.

"Of course," the priest said, as dog, raccoon, and cat passed him by, a sort of deliberation and gravitas about their bearing, as though they were part of a procession that the priest, himself, had rudely interrupted. He would have said something, of course he would have. But these animals had—well, he could hardly explain it. A sobriety of face and a propriety of demeanor. He let them by. He nodded his head to each one as they crossed the threshold of the church. It astonished him. He gave a quick glance up and down the quiet street to reassure himself that he remained unobserved. The last thing he needed was to have the Parish Council start fussing at him again.

(The Parish Council was made up, at this time, of a trio of widowed sisters whose life's purpose, it seemed to the priest, was to make him feel as though they were in the midst of stoning him to death using only popcorn and lost buttons and bits of yarn. Three times that week he had found himself in the fussy crosshairs of the sisters' ire—and it was only Wednesday.)

He rubbed his ever-loosening jowls and cleared his throat. Seeing no one there (except for a family of rabbits that was, en masse, emerging from under the row of box elders), Father Laurence felt a sudden, inexplicable, and unbridled surge of joy—to which he responded with a quick clench of his two fists and a swallowed yes. He nearly bounced.

"Are you coming?" Mrs. Sorensen called from inside the Sanctuary.

"Yes, yes," he said with a sputter. "Of course." But he paused anyway. A young buck came clipping down the road. Not uncommon in these parts, but the priest thought it odd that the animal came to a halt right in front of the church and turned his face upward as though he was regarding the stained-glass window. Could deer see color? Father Laurence didn't know. The deer didn't move. It was a young thing—its antlers were hardly bigger than German pretzels and its haunches were sleek, muscular, and supple. It blinked its large, damp eyes and flared its nostrils. The priest paused, as though waiting for the buck to say something.

Deer don't speak, he told himself. *You're being ridiculous.* Two hawks fluttered down and perched on the handrail, while a—*Dear God*. Was that an otter? Father Laurence shook his head, adjusted the flap of belly hanging uncomfortably over his belt, and slumped inside.

. . .

The mourners arrived two hours later and arranged themselves silently into their pews. It was a thin crowd. There was the required representative from the glass factory. A low-level supervisor. Mr. Sorensen was not important enough, apparently, to warrant a mourner from an upper-level managerial position, and was certainly not grand enough for the owner himself to drive up from Chicago and pay his respects.

The priest bristled at this. *The man died at work*, he thought. *Surely . . .*

He shook his head and busied himself with the last-minute preparations. The pretty widow walked with cool assurance from station to station, making sure everything was just so. The mourners, the priest noticed, were mostly men. This stood to reason, as most of Mr. Sorensen's coworkers were men as well. Still, he noticed that several of them had removed their wedding rings, or had thought to insert a jaunty handkerchief in their coat pockets (in what could only be described as *nonfuneral colors*), or had applied hair gel or mustache oil or aftershave. The whole church reeked of men on the prowl. Mrs. Sorensen didn't seem to notice, but that was beside the point. The priest folded his arms and gave a hard look at the backs of their heads.

Really, he thought. But then the widow walked into a brightly colored beam of stained-glass sunlight, and he felt his heart lift and his cheeks flush and his breathing quicken and thin. *There are people*, he thought, *who are easy to love. And that is that.*

Mrs. Sorensen had done a beautiful job with the flowers, creating arrangements at each window in perfect, dioramic scenes. In the window depicting the story of the child Jesus and the clay birds that he magicked into feathers and wings and flight, for example, her figure of Jesus was composed of corn husk, ivy, and dried rose petals. The clay birds she had made with homemade dough and affixed to warbled bits of wire. The birds bobbed and weaved unsteadily, as though only just learning how to spread their wings. And her rendition of Daniel in the lion's den was so harrowing in its realism, so brutally *present*, that people had to avert their eyes. She had even made a diorama of the day she and her husband met—a man with a broken leg at the bottom of a gully in the middle of a flowery forest; a woman with a broken heart wandering alone, happening by, and binding his wounds. And how real they were! The visceral pain on his face, the sorrow hanging over her body like a cloud. The quickening of the heart at that first, tender touch. This is how love can begin—an act of kindness.

The men in the congregation stared for a long time at that display. They shook their heads and muttered, "Lucky bastard."

Father Laurence, in his vestments, intoned the mass with all of the feeling he could muster, his face weighted somberly with the loss of a man cut down too soon. (Though not, it should be noted, with any actual grief. After all, the priest hardly knew the man. No one did. Still, fifty-eight is too young to die. Assuming Mr. Sorensen was fifty-eight. In truth, the priest had no idea.) Mrs. Sorensen sat in the front row, straight backed, her delicate face composed, her head floating atop her neck as though it were being pulled upward by a string. She held her chin at a slight tilt to the left. She made eye contact with the priest and gave an encouraging smile.

It is difficult, he realized later, to give a homily when there is a raccoon in the church. And a very large dog. And a cat. Though he couldn't see them—they had made themselves scarce before the parishioners arrived—he still *knew they were there*. And it unnerved him.

The white mice squirmed in Mrs. Sorensen's pocket. They peeked and retreated again and again. Father Laurence tripped on his words. He forgot what he was going to say. He forgot Mr. Sorensen's name. He remembered the large, damp eyes of the buck outside. *Did he want to come in?* Father Laurence wondered. And then: *Don't be ridiculous. Deer don't go to church!* But neither, he reasoned with himself, did raccoons. *But there was one here somewhere, wasn't there?* So.

Father Laurence mumbled and wandered. He started singing the wrong song. The organist grumbled in his direction. The Insufferable Sisters, who never missed a funeral if they could help it, sat in the back and twittered. They held their programs over their faces and peered over the rims of the paper with hard, glittering eyes. Father Laurence found himself singing "Oh God, Your Creatures Fill the Earth," though it was not on the program and the organist was unable to play the accompaniment.

"*Your creatures live in every land,*" he sang lustily. "*They fill the sky and sea. Oh Lord you give us your command, To love them tenderly.*"

Mrs. Sorensen closed her eyes and smiled. And outside, a hawk opened its throat and screeched—the lingering note landing in harmony with the final bar.

That was October.

• • •

Father Laurence did not visit the widow right away. He'd wait, he thought. Let her grieve. The last thing she needed was an old duffer hanging around her kitchen. Besides, he knew that the Insufferable Sisters and their allies on the Improvement League and the Quilters Alliance and the Friends of the Library and the Homebound Helpers would be, even now, fluttering toward that house, descending like a cloud.

In the meantime, the entire town buzzed with the news of the recent Sasquatch sightings—only here and there, and not entirely credible, but the fact of the sightings at all was significant. There hadn't been any in the entire county for the last thirty years—not since one was reported standing outside of the only hotel in town for hours and hours on a cold November night.

People still talked about it.

The moon was full and the winds raged. The Sasquatch slipped in and out of shadow. It raised its long arms toward the topmost windows, tilted its head back, and opened its throat. The mournful sound it made—part howl, part moan, part long, sad song—is something that people in town still whispered about, now thirty years later. It was the longest time anyone could ever remember a Sasquatch standing in one place. Normally, they were slippery things. Elusive. A flash at the corner of the eye. But here it stood, bold as brass, spilling its guts to whoever would listen. Unfortunately, no one spoke Sasquatch, so no one knew what it was so upset about.

It was, if Father Laurence remembered correctly, Mr. and Mrs. Sorensen's wedding night.

Sasquatch sightings were fairly common back then, but they ceased after the hotel incident. It was like they all just up and disappeared. No one mentioned it right away—it's not like the Sasquatch put a notice in the paper. But after a while people noticed the Sasquatch were gone—just gone.

And now, apparently, they were back. Or, at least one was, anyway.

Barney Korman said he saw one picking its way across the north end of the bog, right outside the wildlife preserve. Ernesta Koonig said there was a huge, shaggy something helping itself to the best crop of Cortland apples that her orchard had ever produced. Bernie Larsen said he saw one running off with one of his lambs. There were stick structures on Cassandra Gordon's hunting land. And the ghostly sound of tree knocking at night.

Eimon Lomas stopped by and asked if there was any ecclesiastic precedence allowing for the baptism of a Bigfoot.

Father Laurence said no.

"Seems a shame, though, don't it?" asked Eimon, running his tongue over his remaining teeth.

"Never thought about it before," Father Laurence said. But that was a lie, and he knew it. Agnes Sorensen—before she was married—had asked him the exact same question, thirty years earlier.

And his answer then had made her cry.

. . .

On Halloween, Father Laurence, in an effort to avoid the Parish Council and their incessant harping on the subject of holidays—godless or otherwise—and to avoid the flurry of their phone calls and visits and Post-it notes and emails and faxes and, once, horrifyingly, an intervention ("Is it the costumes, Father," the eldest of the sisters had asked pointedly, "or the unsupervised visits from children that makes' you so unwilling to take a stand on the effects of Satanism through Halloween worship?" They folded their hands and waited. "Or perhaps," the youngest added, "it's a sugar addiction."), decided to pay Mrs. Sorensen a visit.

Three weeks had passed, after all, since the death of her husband, and the widow's freezer and pantry were surely stocked with the remains of the frozen casseroles, and lasagnas, and brown-up rolls, and mason jars filled with homemade chili and chicken soup and wild rice stew and beef consommé. Surely the bustle and cheeping of the flocks of women who descend upon houses of tragedy had by now migrated away, leaving the lovely Mrs. Sorensen alone, and quiet, and in need of company.

Besides. Wild rice stew (especially if it came from the Larson home) didn't sound half-bad on a cold Halloween night.

The Sorensen farm—once the largest tract in the county—was nothing more than a hobby farm now. Mr. Sorensen had neither the aptitude nor the inclination for farming, so his wife had convinced him to cede his birthright to the Nature Conservancy, retaining a bit of acreage to allow her to maintain a good-sized orchard and berry farm. Mrs. Sorensen ran a small business in which she made small-batch hard ciders, berry wines, and fine jams. Father Laurence couldn't imagine that her income could sustain her for long, but perhaps Mr. Sorensen had been well insured.

He knocked on the door.

The house erupted with animal sounds. Wet noses pressed at the window and sharp claws worried at the door. The house barked, screeched, groaned, hissed, snuffled, and whined. Father Laurence took a step backward. An owl peered through the transom window, its pale gold eyes unblinking. The priest cleared his throat.

"Mrs. Sorensen?"

A throaty gurgle from indoors.

"Agnes?"

Father Laurence had known Agnes Sorensen since her girlhood (her last name was Dryleesker then)—she was the little girl down the road, with a large, arthritic goose under one arm and a bull snake curled around the other. He would see her playing in front of her house at the end of the dead-end street when he came home for the summers during seminary.

"An odd family," his mother used to say with a definitive shake of her head. "And that girl is the oddest of them all."

Laurence didn't think so then, and he certainly didn't think so now.

Agnes, in her knee socks and Mary Janes, in her A-line dresses that her mother had made from old curtains and her pigtails pale as stars, simply had an affinity for animals. In the old barn in their backyard, she housed the creatures that she had found, as well as those that had traveled long distances just to be near her. A hedgehog with a missing foot, a blind weasel, a six-legged frog, a neurotic wren, a dog whose eardrums had popped like balloons when he wandered too near a TNT explosion on his owner's farm. She once came home with a wolf cub, but her father wouldn't allow her to keep it. She had animals waiting for her by the back door each morning, animals who would accompany her on her way to school, animals who helped her with her chores, animals who sat on her lap as she did her homework, and animals who curled up on her bed when she slept.

But then she got married. To Mr. Sorensen—good man, and kind. And he needed her. But he was allergic. So their house was empty.

Mr. Sorensen was also, Father Laurence learned from the confessional booth, infertile.

Agnes only came to Confession once a year, and she rarely spoke during her time in the booth. Most of the time she would sit, sigh, and breathe in the dark. The booth was anonymous in theory, but Mrs. Sorensen had a smell about her—crushed herbs and apple cider and pinesap and grass—that he could identify from across the room. Her silence was profound, and nuanced. Like the silence of a pine forest on a windless, summer day. It creaked and rustled. It warmed the blood. Father Laurence would find himself fingering his collar—now terribly tight—and mopping his brow with his hands.

He worried for Mrs. Sorensen. She was young and vibrant and terribly *alive*. And yet. She seemed in stasis to him somehow. She didn't seem to age. She had none of the spark she had had as a child. It was as though her soul was hibernating.

There was a time, maybe fifteen years ago, when Mrs. Sorensen had closed the door of the booth behind her and sat for ten minutes in the dark while the priest waited. Finally, she spoke in the darkness. Not a prayer. Indeed, Father Laurence didn't know what it was.

"When a female wolverine is ready to breed," Mrs. Sorensen said in the face-less dark, "she spends weeks tracking down potential mates, and weeks separating the candidates. She stalks her unknowing suitors, monitoring their habits, assessing their skills as hunters and trackers. Evaluating their abilities in a fight—do they prefer the tooth or the claw? Are they brave to the point of stupidity? Do they run when danger is imminent? Do they push themselves to greatness?"

Father Laurence cleared his throat. "Have you forgotten the prayer, my child," he said, his voice a timid whine.

Mrs. Sorensen ignored him. "She does not do this for protection or need. Her mate will be useful for all of two minutes. Then she will never see him again. He will not protect his brood or defend his lover. He will be chosen, hired, *used*. He will not be loved. His entire purpose is to produce an offspring that will eventually leave its mother; she needs a child that will *live*."

"*Bless me, Father, for I have sinned*," prompted Father Laurence. "That's how people usually—"

"Now, in the case of a black bear, when the female becomes aware of the new life in her womb, she makes special consideration to the construction of the den. She is at risk, and she knows it. Pheromones announcing her condition leak from every pore. Her footsteps reek pregnant. Her urine blinks like road signs. Her fertility hangs around her body like a cloud."

"Agnes—"

"When she digs her den, she moves over a ton of rock and soil. She designs it specially to provide a small mouth that she can stopper up with her back if she needs to."

"Agnes—"

"She will grow in the dark, and birth in the dark, and suckle her babies in the feminine funk of that tiny space—smelling of mother and baby, and sweat and blood, and milk and breathing and warm earth—hiding under the thick protection of snow." Her voice caught. She hiccupped.

"Agnes—"

"I thought I was anonymous."

"And you are. I call all my confessionals Agnes."

She laughed in the dark.

"I am asleep, Father. I have been asleep for—ever so long. My arms are weak and my breasts are dry and there is a cold dark space within me that smells of nothing." She sat still for a moment or two. Then: "I love my husband."

"I know, child," he whispered.

"I love him desperately."

What she wanted to say, the priest knew, was "I love him, but . . ." But she didn't. She said nothing else. After another moment's silence, she opened the door, stepped into the light, and vanished.

. . .

Father Laurence had no doubt that Agnes Sorensen had loved her husband, and that she missed him. They had been married for thirty years, after all. She had cared for him and tended to him every day. His death was sudden. And certainly one must grieve in one's own way. Still, the sheer number of animals in the house was a cause for concern. The list of possible psychiatric disorders alone was nearly endless.

The priest walked out to the apple barn but no one was there. Just the impossibly sweet smell of cider. It nearly knocked Father Laurence to his knees. He closed his eyes, and remembered picking apples with one of the girls at school when he was a child—sticky fingers, sticky mouths, sticky necks, and sticky trousers. He was eleven then, maybe. Or twelve. He remembered her long hair and her black eyes, and the way they fell from the lowest tree branch—a tangle of arms and legs and torsos. The crush of grass underneath. Her freckles next to his eyelashes, his front tooth chipping against hers (after all those years, the chip was still there), the smell of her breath like honey and wine and growing wheat. So strong was this memory, and so radically pleasant, that Father Laurence felt weak, and shivery. There was a cot in the barn—he didn't know what it was there for—and he lay upon it.

It smelled of woodland musk and pine. It was covered in hair.

He slept instantly. In his dream he was barefoot and lanky and young. He was on the prowl. He was hungry. He was longing for something that he could not name. Something that had no words (or perhaps he had no words; or perhaps words no longer existed). He was full of juice and vigor and hope. He was watching Agnes Sorensen through a curtain of green, green leaves. She carried a heaping basket of apples. A checkered shirt. Apple-stained dungarees. A bandana covering her hair. Wellington boots up to her knees, each footfall sinking deep into the warm, sweet mud.

. . .

When Father Laurence woke, it was fully dark. (Was someone watching? *Surely not.*) He got up off the cot, brushed the hair from his coat and trousers. His body ached and he felt curiously empty—as though he had been somehow scooped out. He walked out into the moonlit yard. Mrs. Sorensen wasn't in the barn. She wasn't in the yard. She wasn't in the house either. (Was that a shape in the bushes? Were those eyes? *Heavens, what am I thinking?*) The house had been emptied of its animal sounds, and emptied of its light and smell and being. It was quiet. He knocked. No one answered. He walked over to the car.

There were footprints, he saw, in the mud next to the driveway. Wellington boots sunk deep into the mud and dried along the edges. And another set, just alongside. Bare feet—a man's, presumably. But very, very large.

. . .

Thanksgiving passed with several invitations to take the celebratory meal with neighbors or former coworkers or friends, who would have welcomed Mrs. Sorensen with open arms, but these were all denied.

She said simply that she would enjoy the quiet. But surely that made no sense! There was no one on earth quieter than Mr. Sorensen. The man hardly spoke.

And so her neighbors carved their turkeys and their hams, they sliced pie and drank to one another's health, but their minds wandered to the pretty widow with hair like starlight, her straight back, her slim skirts and smart belts and her crisp footsteps when she walked. People remembered her lingering smell—the forest and the blooming meadow and some kind of animal musk. Something that clung to the nose and pricked at the skin and set the mouth watering. And they masked their longing with another helping of yams.

(The three sisters on the Parish Council, on the other hand, didn't see what the big fuss was about. They always thought she was plain.)

Randall Jergen—not the worst drunkard in town, but well on his way to becoming so—claimed that, when he stumbled by the Sorensen house by mistake, he saw the widow seated at the head of the well-laid table, heaped to the point of breaking with boiled potatoes and candied squash and roasted vegetables of every type and description, with each chair filled, not with relatives or friends or even acquaintances, but with animals. He said there were two dogs, one raccoon, one porcupine, one lynx, and an odd-looking bear sitting opposite the pretty widow. A bear who grasped its wine goblet and held it aloft to the smiling Mrs. Sorensen, who raised her own glass in response.

The Insufferable Sisters investigated. They found no evidence of feasting. And while they *did* see the dogs, the tiny cat, the raccoon, the lynx, and the porcupine, they saw no sign of a wine-drinking bear. Which, they told themselves, they needed to know whether or not was true. Drunk bears, after all, were a community safety hazard. They reported to the stylists at the Clip'n'Curl that Mr. Jergen was, as usual, full of hogwash. By evening, the whole town knew. And the matter was settled.

For a little while.

. . .

By Christmas, there had been no less than twenty-seven reports of Sasquatch sightings near, or around, or on the Sorensen farm. Two people claimed to have seen a Sasquatch wearing a seed cap with the glass factory's logo on it, and one swore that it was wearing Mr. Sorensen's old coat. The sheriff, two deputies, the game manager at the local private wildlife refuge, and three representatives from the Department of Natural Resources all paid the widow a visit. Each left the farm looking dejected. Mrs. Sorensen was not, apparently, available for drinks, or dinner, or dancing. She answered their questions with crisp answers that could have meant anything. She watched them go with a vague smile on her pale lips.

The Insufferable Sisters investigated as well. They looked for footprints and bootprints. They looked for discarded hats and thrown-off coats. They hunted for evidence of possible suitors. They interviewed witnesses. They found nothing.

. . .

By late January, neighbors noticed that Mrs. Sorensen began to walk with a noticeable lightness—despite the parka and the heavy boots, despite the sheepskin mitts and the felted scarf, her feet seemed to float atop the surface of the snow, and her skin appeared to sparkle, even on the most leaden of days.

Bachelors and widowers (and, if honesty prevails, several uncomfortably married men as well) still opened doors for the pretty widow, still tipped their hats in her direction, still offered to carry her groceries or see to her barn's roof, or check to make sure her pipes weren't in danger of freezing (this last one was often said suggestively, and almost always returned with a definitive slap). The Insufferable Sisters arrived, unannounced, at the Sorensen farm. They came laden with hot dish and ambrosia salad and bars of every type and description. They sat the poor widow down, put the kettle on, and tapped their long, red talons on the well-oiled wood of the ancient farm table.

"Well?" said Mrs. Ostergaard, the eldest of the sisters.

"Oh," said Mrs. Sorensen, her cheeks flushing to high color. "The tea is in the top drawer of the far right cabinet." Her eyes slid to the window, where the snow-flakes fell in thick curtains, blurring the blanketed yard, and obscuring the dense thicket of scrub and saplings on the other side of the gully. The corners of her lips buzzed with—*something*. Mrs. Ostergaard couldn't tell. And it infuriated her.

Mrs. Lentz, the youngest of the sisters, and Mrs. Ferris, the middle, served the lunch, arranging the food in sensibly sized mounds, each one slick and glistening. They piled the bars on pretty plates and put real cream in the pitcher and steaming tea in the pot. They sat, sighed, smiled, and interrogated the pretty widow. She answered questions and nodded serenely, but every time there was a lull in the conversation (and there were many), her eyes would insinuate themselves toward the window again, and a deepening blush would spread down her throat and edge into the opening of her blouse.

The dogs lounged on the window seat and the raccoon picked at its bowl on the floor of the mudroom. Three cats snaked through the legs of the three sisters, with their backs an insistent arch, their rumps requiring a rub, and all the while an aggressive purr rattling the air around them.

"Nice kitty," Mrs. Ostergaard said, giving one of the cats a pat on the head.

The cat hissed.

The sisters left in the snow.

"Be careful," Mrs. Sorensen said as she stood in the doorway, straight backed and inscrutable as polished wood. "It's coming down all right." Her eyes flicked toward the back of the yard, a flushed smile on her lips. Mrs. Ostergaard whipped around and glared through the thick tangle of snow.

A figure.

Dark.

Fast.

And then it was gone. Snowflakes clung to her eyelashes and forehead. Cold drops of water crowded her eyes. She shook her head and peered into the chaos of white. Nothing was there.

The sisters piled into their Volvo and eased onto the road, a dense, blinding cloud swirling in their minds.

• • •

The next day they called a meeting with Father Laurence. Father Laurence withstood the indignities of their fussing in relative silence, the scent of apples, after all this time, still clinging sweetly in his nostrils.

The day after that, they called a second meeting, this time calling the priest, the mayor, the physician, the dog catcher, and a large-animal veterinarian. They were all men, these officials and professionals that the sisters assembled, and all were seated on folding chairs. The sisters stood over them like prison guards. The men hung on to their cold metal chairs for dear life. They said yes to everything.

. . .

Three days later, Arnold Fiske—teetotaler since the day he was born—nearly ran Mrs. Sorensen over with his Buick. It was a warm night for February, and the road was clear. The sun was down and the sky was a livid color of orange. On either side of the road, the frozen bog stretched outward, as big as the world. Indeed, it was the bog that distracted Arnold Fiske from the primary task of driving. His eyes lingered on the dappled browns and grays and whites, on the slim torsos of the quaking aspens and the river birches and the Norway pines fluttering like flags on the occasional hillock. He lingered on the fluctuations of color on the snow— orange dappling to pink fading to ashy blue. He returned his gaze to the road only just in time. He saw the face of Mrs. Sorensen (*that beautiful face!*) lit in the beam of his headlights. And something *else* too. A hulk of a figure. Like a man. But more than a man. And no face at all.

Arnold Fiske swerved. Mrs. Sorensen screamed. And from somewhere—the frozen bog, the fading sky, the aggressively straight road, or somewhere deep inside Arnold Fiske himself—erupted a ragged, primal howl. It shook the glass and sucked away the air and shattered his bones in his body. His car squealed and spun. Mrs. Sorensen was pulled out of the car's path by . . . well, by *something*. And then everything was quiet.

He got out of the car, breathing heavily. His dyspepsia burned bright as road flares. He pressed his left hand to the bottom rim of his rib cage and grimaced. "Oh my god," he gasped. "Agnes? Agnes Sorensen! Are you all right?" He rounded the broad prow of the Buick, saw the horror on the other side of the car, and felt his knees start to buckle. He fell hard on his rear and scrambled back with a strangled cry.

There was Agnes Sorensen—her long, down coat bunched up around her middle, her hood thrown off, and her starlight-colored hair yanked free of its bun and rippling toward the ground, curled in the long arms of a man. A man covered in hair.

Not a man.

Her voice was calm. Her hands were on the man's face. No. Not a man's face. And not a face either. It was a thicket of fur and teeth and red, glowing eyes. Arnold Fiske's breath came in hot, sharp bursts.

"What is that thing?" he choked. He could barely breathe. His chest hurt. He pressed his hands to his heart to make sure it wasn't going out on him. The last thing he needed was to have a heart attack in the presence of a . . . *well*. He couldn't say. He couldn't even *think* it.

Mrs. Sorensen didn't notice.

Her voice was a smooth lilt, a lullaby, a gentle insistence. A mother's voice. A lover's voice. Or both at once. "I'm all right," she soothed. "You see? I'm here. I'm not hurt. Everything is fine. Everything is *wonderful*."

The man (*not a man*) bowed its head onto Agnes Sorensen's chest. It sighed and snuffled. It cradled her body in its great, shaggy arms and rocked her back and forth. It made a series of sounds—part rumble, part hiccup, part gulping sob.

My god, Arnold Fiske thought. *It's crying.*

He sat up. Then stood up and took a step away. Arnold shook his head. He tried to hold his breath, but small bursts still erupted, unbidden, from his throat, as though his soul and his fear and his sorrow were all escaping in sighs. In any case, he felt neither his fear nor his sorrow as he looked at the widow and her . . . *erm* . . . companion. (He had never felt his soul. He wasn't even sure that he had one.)

He cleared his throat. "Would you," he said. And faltered. He started again. "Would you and your, um, *friend* . . ." He paused again. Wrinkled his brow. Muscled through. "Need a ride?"

Mrs. Sorensen smiled and wrapped her arms around the Sasquatch's neck.

Because that, Arnold Fiske realized, *is what I'm seeing. A Sasquatch. Well. My stars.*

"No, thank you, Mr. Fiske," Agnes Sorensen said, extricating herself from the Sasquatch's arms and helping it to its feet. "The night is still fine, and the stars are just coming out. And they say the auroras will be burning bright later on. I may stay out all night."

And with that, she and the Sasquatch walked away, hands held, as though it was the most normal thing in the world. And perhaps it was. In any case, Arnold Fiske couldn't shut up about it.

• • •

By noon the next day, the whole town knew.

A Sasquatch. The widow and a Sasquatch. Good gracious. What will they think of next?

Two days later, the pair were spotted in public, walking along the railroad tracks.

And again, picking their way across the bog.

And again, standing in the back of the crowd at a liquidation auction. The Sasquatch sometimes wore Mr. Sorensen's old seed hat and boots (he had cut out holes for his large, flexible toes), and sometimes wore the dead man's scarf. But never his pants. Or some kind of shorts. Or, dear god, at least some swimming trunks. The Sasquatch was in possession, thankfully, of a bulbous thicket of fur, concealing the area of concern, but everyone knew *what was behind that fur*, and they knew it would only take a stiff breeze, or a sudden movement, or perhaps the presence of a female Sasquatch to cause a, how would you say—*a shaking of the bushes*, as it were. Or a parting of the weeds. People kept their eyes averted, just to be safe.

And the sisters were enraged.

Mrs. Sorensen was spotted walking with a Sasquatch past the statues and artistic sculptures of Armistice Park.

("Children play at that park!" howled the sisters.)

They called Father Laurence at home nineteen times, and left nineteen messages with varying levels of vitriol. *Fool of a priest* was a phrase they used. And *useless*.

Father Laurence, for his part, went to the woods, alone. He walked the same paths he had followed in his boyhood. He remembered the rustle of ravens' wings, and the silent pounce of an owl, and the snuffling of bears, and the howling of wolves, and the scamper of rabbits, and the slurping of moose. He remembered something else, too. A large, dark figure in the densest places of the wood and the tangled thickets of the bog. A pair of bright eyes and sharp teeth and a long, loose-limbed, lumbering gait that went like a shot over the prairie.

He was eleven years old when he last saw a Sasquatch. And now all he had to do was pick up the phone and invite Mrs. Sorensen over for dinner. *Huh*, he thought. *Imagine that.*

• • •

The meal, though quiet, was pleasant enough. The Sasquatch brought a bowl of wildflowers, which the priest ate. They were delicious.

• • •

Two weeks later, Mrs. Sorensen brought her Sasquatch to church. She brought her other animals too—her one-eyed hedgehog and her broken-winged hawk and her tiny cat and her raccoon and her three-legged dog and her infant cougar, curled up and fast asleep on her lap. The family arrived early, and sat in the front row. Mrs. Sorensen and the Sasquatch in the middle, and the rest of the brood stretching on either side. Each one sat as straight backed as was possible with the particulars of their physiology, and each one was silent and solemn. The Sasquatch wore nothing other than Mr. Sorensen's father's old fedora hat, which was perched at a bit of a saucy angle. It held Mrs. Sorensen's hand in its great, left paw and closed its large, bright eyes.

Father Laurence did his pre-Mass preparations and ministrations with the sacristy door locked. The sisters hovered on the other side, pecking at the door and squawking their complaints. Father Laurence was oblivious. He was a great admirer of the inventor of earplugs, and made it a habit to stash an emergency set wherever he might find the need to surreptitiously insert a pair at a moment's notice—at his desk, at the podium, in his car, in the confessional, and in the sacristy.

"*A sacrilege!*" Mrs. Ostergaard hissed.

"*Do something!*" came Mrs. Lentz's strangled gasp.

"*GET THAT DEER OUT OF THE CHURCH,*" Mrs. Ferris roared, followed by a chaos of hooves and snorting and the shouting of women and men, and the hooting of an owl and the cry of a peregrine and the snarl of—actually, Father Laurence wasn't sure if it was a coyote or a wolf.

Agnes Sorensen was too old to have children. Everyone knew that. But she had always wanted a family. And now she was so happy. Didn't she deserve to be happy? The sisters pecked and screeched. He imagined their fingers curling into talons, their imperious lips hardening to beaks. He imagined their appliquéd cardigans and their floral skirts rustling into feathers and wings. He imagined their bright bead eyes launching skyward with a wild, high *kee-yar* of a hawk on the hunt for something small and brown and wriggling.

The priest stood in the sacristy, his eyes closed. "*O God, your creatures fill the earth with wonder and delight,*" he sang.

"Doris," he heard Mrs. Ferris say. "Doris, do *not* approach that cougar. Doris, it isn't safe."

"And every living thing has worth and beauty in your sight."

"Oh, god. Not sheep. Anything but sheep. GET THOSE ANIMALS OUT OF HERE."

"So playful dolphins dance and swim; Your sheep bow down and graze."

"Father, get out here this minute. Six otters just came out of the bathroom. Six! And with rabies!"

"Your songbirds share a morning hymn, To offer you their praise."

There was a snarl, a screech, a cry of birds. A hiss and a bite and several rarely used swears in the mouths of the Parish Council. Father Laurence heard the clatter of their pastel heels and the *oof* of their round bottoms as they tripped on the stairs, and the howl of their voices as they ran down the street.

Several men waited at the mouth of the sanctuary, looking sadly at the pretty widow next to her hulking companion. The men reeked of mustache oil and pomade. Their shoulders slumped and their bellies bulged and their cheeks went slack and flaccid.

"Eh, there, Father?" Ernie Jergen—Randall's sober brother—inclined his head toward the stoic family in the front row. "So that's it, then?" He cleared his throat. "She's . . . not single. She's *attached*, I mean."

Father Laurence clapped his hands on the shoulders of the men, sucked in his sagging belly as tight as he could.

"Yep," he said. "Seems so." Family is family, after all. The dead have buried the dead, and the living scramble and struggle as best they can. They press their shoulder against the rock and urge forward, even when all hope is lost. Agnes Sorensen was happy, and Agnes Sorensen was alive. *So be it.*

He nodded at the organist to start the processional. The red-tailed hawk opened up its throat, and the young buck nosed the back of Father Laurence's vestments. A pair of solemn eyes. A look of gravitas. Father Laurence wondered if he should step aside. If he was interrupting something. Two herons waited at the altar and a pine marten sat on the lectionary.

The organist sat under a pile of cats, and made a valiant effort to pluck out the notes of the hymn. The congregation—both human and animal—opened their throats and began to sing, each in their own language, their own rhythm, their own time.

The song deepened and grew. It shook the walls and rattled the glass and set the light fixtures swinging. The congregation sang of the death of loved ones. A life eclipsed too soon. They sang of the waters of the bog and of the creak of trees and of padded feet on soft forest trails. Of meals shared. And families built. Seeds in the ground. The screech of flight, the joy of a wriggling morsel in a sharp beak. The roar of pursuit and the gurgles of satiation. The murmur of nesting. The smell of a mate. The howl of birthing and the howl of loss, and howl and howl and howl.

Father Laurence processed in. Open mouthed. A dark yodel tearing through his belly.

"*I am lost,*" he sang. "*And I am found. My body is naked in the muck. It has always been naked. I hope; I rage; I despair; I yearn; I long; I lust; I love. These strong hands that built, this strong back that carried, all must wither to dust. Indeed, I am dust already.*"

Mrs. Sorensen and her Sasquatch watched him process down the aisle. They smiled at his song. He paused at their pew, let his hand linger on the rail. They reached out, and touched the hem of his garment.

It was, people remarked later, the prettiest Mass they'd ever heard.

Mrs. Sorensen and her family left after Communion. They did not stay for rolls or coffee. They did not engage in conversation. They walked, en masse, into the bog. The tall grasses opened for a moment to allow them in and closed like a curtain behind. The world was birdsong and quaking mud and humming insects. The world was warm and wet and *green*.

They did not come back.

KELLY BARNHILL is an author, teacher, and mom. She wrote *The Girl Who Drank the Moon* (Newbery Medal winner), *The Witch's Boy*, *Iron Hearted Violet* (Parents' Choice Gold Award), *The Mostly True Story of Jack*, and many, many short stories. She won the World Fantasy Award for her novella, *The Unlicensed Magician*, and has been a finalist for the Minnesota Book Award, the Andre Norton Award, and the PEN Center USA Literary Award. She was also a McKnight Artist's Fellowship recipient in Children's Literature. She lives in Minneapolis, Minnesota, with her three brilliant children, architect husband, and emotionally unstable dog. She is a fast runner, a good hiker, and a terrible gardener.

This World Is Full of Monsters

Jeff VanderMeer

An alien invasion comes to one man's doorstep in the form of a story-creature, followed by death and rebirth in a transformed Earth. *Edited by Ann VanderMeer.*

I Did Not Recognize What Sought Me

The story that meant the end arrived late one night. A tiny story, covered in green fur or lichen, shaky on its legs. It fit in the palm of my hand. I stared at the story for a long time, trying to understand. The story had large eyes that could see in the dark, and sharp teeth. It purred, and the purr grew louder and louder: a beautiful flower bud opening and opening until I was filled up. I heard the thrush and pull of the darkness, grown so mighty inside my head.

I grew weary.

I grew weary and I fell asleep on the couch holding the story, wondering what it might be and who had delivered it to me. But there was no time left for wonder. As I slept, the story gnawed its way into my belly and then the story crawled up through my body into my head. When I woke, gasping my resistance, the story made me stumble out the door of my house and lurch through the dark down my street, giddy and disoriented, muttering, "Do not stop me. Do not stop me. Story made me this way. Story made me this way."

I felt a compulsion to turn to the left, and then to turn to the left again. Until the story made me stop at the end of the block, where the last fence meets a forest. By now I knew that the story wasn't a story at all. It had just made me think it was a story so it could invade my brain.

And while I stood there in the shadows of the moonless night, beyond the street lamps, beyond the circling moths and with the nighthawks gliding silent overhead . . . while I stood there and pleaded, the story-creature sprouted out of the top of my skull in a riot of wildflowers, goldenrod, and coarse weeds.

The explosion smashed through me. I screamed out, but the story-creature clamped down on my throat and the scream turned into a dribble of whispered nonsense rhymes in a code that crawled across my skin and inside my mouth. My head itched and there was an uncomfortable weight so my balance was off. But somehow it felt right.

Even the midnight bumblebees circling my head like a halo felt right, or the things like bumblebees that had erupted from my skin, my mouth.

There were so many things I had already begun to forget.

How This Came to Be and What Came Next

I am a writer . . . I was a writer. It is easy to fool a writer into thinking a creature is a story. The doorbell had rung earlier. When I had opened the door, a bulky little envelope lay on the welcome mat, under the glow of the porch light. When I opened it, a booklet crawled out onto the kitchen table. The booklet smelled like moist banana bread. It was filled with strange words, but somehow I understood that language. I read the booklet from cover to cover like it was a wonderful meal and I was a starving man. I devoured every word.

I had read a story. I was sure of it, even though I couldn't remember what the story had been about. Nor could I recall who else had been with me in the house, except that there were two of them and they had become mere shadows on the wall.

Now, by the fence, the wildflowers and the goldenrod and the weeds twined together and became something else and roots splayed out into me, and atop my head grew a sapling. My balance was terrible—I had to hold the sapling with both hands because I knew that if the sapling snapped it would kill me. But soon the weight would be unsupportable. Soon I would be beyond repair.

The story-creature that had sprouted from my head was restless and had tasks to accomplish. So I plunged deep into the forest in the dark of night, raging across the paths there, smashing into trees, backtracking, unable to know where I was or trying to wrest control from the thing that wanted to control me. But soon I adhered to paths despite myself. Soon I cohered and came to know balance and lifted my hands from the atrocity jutting from my crown. Soon I walked smooth and slow and no root tripped me and no false trail fooled me. I could see in the dark by then, or It could, and what, really, by then was the difference?

By dawn and the calls of birds, I recognized, through the grayness, the side of a hill and a clearing and there I turned once more to the left and pitched face-first into the grass and dirt and crawling beetles. The story-creature's roots plunged greedily through my brain and through my soft palate and through my lower jaw, seeking the soil. While above me the swaying sapling had become a young tree. Or had taken on the appearance of a tree. It could never have been a tree.

I lay there, face-planted, with some *thing* growing through me and I let It soak up inspiration from the earth and from the air and from the new sun. I was awash in dreams of chlorophyll and photosynthesis . . .

We lay like that for a long time until the story-creature had used all of me It needed. Then It withdrew, and cared not how harsh that might be, for even in that short time I had become dependent, and the retreat was like screaming against an addiction. A hole had been left behind and my consciousness ached and jumped through the hole again and again like it led to hell or to nothing, and all my atoms frayed at the edges or spread out wide, or seemed to, and I did not know if I was dead-alive or just dead.

My left leg was a withered thing now, a wet pant leg wrung out to dry, and my left arm I left in the soil—it broke off when I tried to rise, and the stump refused to bleed but after the snap became just like an old rotting tree branch. I think I carried it around with me, waving it around with my other arm, like something demented and foolish and out of date.

I was in the world but I was not in the world, endless and numb yet in agony.

I was shooting through an empty sky with the stars all fallen to the ground, and every star cut whatever it touched, including me, and all the stars that fell touched me.

I could not stop reaching out to make contact even though it made so little difference to my fate.

I Did Not Wake for One Hundred Years

I did not wake for one hundred years. This was truth.

This is the truth.

When I woke, a century had passed and the hillside had folded in itself and become overgrown with vines and the story-creature appeared to have long left and perhaps passed on its message to others and now beyond the hill lay a vast and unyielding desert and facing me on the fertile side, my withered leg pointing at it, was a waterhole from which drank any number of disquieting animals. They held shapes my eyes did not want to recognize although some held no real shape at all, but I knew they were other story-creatures and had spread more than one story.

Some I could only see out of the corner of my eye. Others had the right number of legs but no symmetry and trailed across the ground at odd angles, drawing deep lines in the mud. They snorfled and snuffled and grunted at the waterhole. They fought and died there, too, raising tusks and claws and fangs, and turned the edge of the water to a bloody froth . . . only to come back to life and forget a moment later their conflict.

The sun above seemed strange, as if it came to me through a filter, but I found that my eyes had a film over them that created a slight orange tint. I did not know how it came to be there, but it seemed protective or at least not unfriendly.

With help from a dead tree branch I could hobble along, and I made my way past the waterhole into the remnants of the forest, back into my neighborhood. Overhead the things that flew should not have been able to fly, for they did not really have wings; they just had the suggestion of wings, like some careless creator had not drawn them in right. My mind made them into insects, because my mind wanted stories it could understand, stories that would not frighten it. But still I knew my mind was tricking me, and for a second I loved my mind for the deception.

My old street, which I felt I had left just hours before, lay in ruins. The pavement had not just cracked but become so overgrown it had no agency, left hardly any impression and my memory had to place it there—along with street lamps that now were just nubs of concrete columns that stood little higher than a foot tall. Among the houses of my neighborhood all roofs had been staved in and few walls remained and even of foundations there were only a handful in evidence.

One of those belonged to my home, and because I had had a basement, that is where I retreated to. I slid with relief into that space, which was flood damaged and filled with debris and overgrown with grass and vines and much worse things but still provided shelter. I slid into that space on the strength in one arm and one leg and I stared up at the sky until the things that must be messages but were also creatures curling through the air, written there and then dispersed, tormented me too much.

I dug into the dirt and grime, bereft. I dug there searching for my past, for something that had once curled around my wrist, for people that I had known but now existed like a reflection in murky water. Why were they no longer there? How could I no longer know them? Their rooms had been there. Their lives had been here. And were no longer.

"It was just a story," I croaked, and lapped from a dirty pool of water I was so thirsty.

This was a mistake because in that water were still more fragments of story like the one that had been left in an envelope on my doorstep. Phrases and words that were neither phrases nor words absorbed into me and changed me even more, so that my withered leg became a kind of thick, flat tail and of my two eyes nothing remained but in their place were several eyes, but only one of them could see in the regular way and the others looked across the sedimentary layers before me in that basement and saw the past and all the changes that had been wrought, and because I could not accept the mighty judgment and wrath of that, for a time I rebelled and I shut all of my eyes but the regular one.

Thus I squinted at the world that it might look more like the regular world, the one in which I had been a writer and not believed in God and lived alone in a house writing and thinking that being written meant one thing when it meant so many other things as well.

My World Was Irretrievable

The world as it had become held a strangeness too vast for me to understand. I could only comprehend the space mapped by the edges of the basement and so I lay there, hungry and thirsty, for three days and three nights and watched the passage of time as would a rock or a scorpion or a blade of grass. The clouds were curious and not as I remembered and they did not form shapes that I could recognize but shapes I didn't recognize that were still recognizable as something, even if that *something* was beyond me.

This troubled me greatly, more than most of my situation, and the way too that the clouds seemed to *be* something now, that they were looking down at me and that they *saw* me. I did not like this, and this fact was how I came to know that the past was irretrievable. For some part of me had thought, perhaps, that all I saw might be undone, be unraveled. That I might recover my true sight and my old home and go back to when the story-creature lay in an envelope on my porch and that if only I never brought it inside all of the new-terrible would go away, be put back in some kind of box, perhaps even into my brain.

But it could not be put back.

What Happened as I Lay in My Basement

After three days and nights, I sensed the approach of unlikely kin, although the sound of Its passage was unfamiliar. But still, the story-creature that had sprouted from my head, now a century older, leaned in to look down upon me and unfolded Itself before me and in all ways and throughout all times looked down upon me and unfolded Itself before me and kept unfolding and I could not stop It from doing so.

Even though I wanted to so badly.

Even though I would have given anything for the story-creature to go away or to stop doing what It was doing, because I had lost so much already and this new world could not replace that.

But still the story-creature revealed Itself to me, until I understood that now It covered every surface, every space, and even though I thought I had been alone down in the basement among the rat-things and the other things I wanted very much to be rats and weren't . . . I had not been alone. The story-creature had always been there, silent beside me, breathing beneath me, waiting for me to wake to Its presence, to understand where I really was. But I would never understand. How could I? I had not understood the story to begin with.

When the story-creature knew, when I revealed to It by my demeanor how much I did not understand, the story-creature made a sound like the wind through branches, although the wind through the new branches I had woken to sounded more like a throaty scream being choked off. So this was a sound like the old wind, a lullaby about the ancient times to soothe whatever swarmed and seethed within me, although that was not the problem. Not really. The story-creature bent low and protruded and there entered into the basement, sack-like, still attached to the story-creature . . . another me.

I opened my mouth to shriek at the sight, but the sound came out of the mouth of the other me. A me that had been rewritten, so that it resembled me in some ways, down to the wrong eyes and the tail for a leg, but different in others, so that to look at this other me made me feel nausea and claustrophobia until my adjustment.

Unlike me all of its eyes were open—and they saw . . . so much. So much more than me. Except now those of my eyes that were closed saw what its eyes saw and I fell to the basement floor, unable to process so many incoming images and feelings.

For so long after, I came to understand, I would spend my days listening to part of my own story issue forth from the mouth of another, and still not understand all of that story.

I Began to Have a Brother I Did Not Want

I had not been much part of the story of the world before my awakening and before the creature assigned myself to me. The story-creature told me I had lived alone. I had written alone. I had done odd jobs and been out of the house when I needed to be somewhere else. I had a car and I had a big wooded backyard and I listened to music and I complained about things like everyone else. I believe I talked to the neighbors just enough and I would go over to their houses for dinner on holidays, although I did not invite them over to our house. Others had lived in the house with me, though, stains upon the wall now, lost in the foundations, overtaken by the story-creature's tale.

I knew only that I had killed people and buried them in my backyard. Bad people. People who needed to be ended. This is how I created my fictions.

I killed them by writing stories about them in which they died and taking the stories and crumpling up the pages. Then I would take a shovel and dig a hole and shove the pages in and cover them up with dirt. Then I would say a few words about their souls and refill the bird feeder or rake the leaves. Sometimes the people died in life and not just on the page. Sometimes they didn't. But always after I buried the pages, my writing would be enriched.

I didn't mind being eccentric in these ways. I didn't mind not having a brother or having parents that I could not remember, and now a century, like I did not mind many things. But I minded having been given a brother by the story-creature. It might seem like a small thing in a way, since I had been asleep so long and lived in the basement of the foundations of a house that had rotted away decades ago.

It might seem like a tiny thing given the world had been colonized by the story-creature and its brethren and even the sun and the clouds had become so strange. But it was a large thing to me. My brother who was me stared at me and I became the receptor for so much that was alien to me. I would lurch to my feet and run around the basement because my brother willed it, while in my head I would see from my brother's eyes some memory in which he had had to run. Or I would sit quiet as he had sat quiet or I would weep and it was because of some time he had wept. Until finally I realized he was downloading another story into my brain, his story, and soon enough I knew that while I had slept I had been copied and that my brother was almost a century old and been awake that whole time and now I was to become as like him as possible—and then I raged. I raged and smashed my skull against hard things because I did not want to know about the last hundred years or to be filled up with what might make me not myself. Or too much myself.

If I had still been able, I would have written a story about my brother dying and buried it in the backyard.

The Death of the Brother I Never Wanted

The world is full of monsters and this brother forced upon me was one of them. Even though my brother could see I did not want any of what he brought me, he would not relent and I could not escape, found no way to cut the link, cut the wires, cut the bond—whatever it was that had formed between us, and anyway it is true the story-creature grew agitated or upset at my attempts and became even larger and more terrible and this made me cower and beg forgiveness.

So I suppose I must have wanted to live, even amid this horror.

And there came toward the end of this transfer, this overlay, another realization: that my brother was dying. He slumped there against the dirt wall and made odd quirky motions and hissing sounds. I do not think I was killing him. I think he was old and an imperfect vessel and he would have died anyway, without anyone knowing his life. I believe the story-creature thought it a mercy to give me his memories, to let me have so much information and not be so bewildered about the world around me.

But the memories remained separate from my own, would not mix. They just floated on the top and made me have to concentrate more to remember the old life, the time before the story-creature. They came in jumbled and not all fully formed at first. Instead, they huddled together and made sense slowly. So I was screaming and writhing and then was catatonic for a time, staring into the space where my brother slowly became deflated and desiccated and his face fell in on itself and one by one his eyes closed and rotted away, while his toes flinched and his one leg kicked, kicked, was still, and the tail writhed even after my brother was fully dead.

I should have been sad seeing myself die, but instead I experienced a kind of joy and my eye clusters had all flickered open again at once. Perhaps when I was killing people in the backyard I had hoped one day someone would do the same for me. Perhaps I rejected this version of myself that did not resemble the me who had received the fateful story-creature on his doorstep. Or maybe I was just thankful that the memory transfer had ceased like a dam had been built to contain a flood. It is so difficult to know exactly why I felt this way, or why there was such jubilance when the story-creature opened an impossibly wide set of jaws that it had not had moments before and swallowed my brother's body whole. Even though I sat at the bottom of the basement pit, I experienced a sensation of flight and lift, as if I too had been borne up by that jagged black maw.

Yet I was still catatonic, too, absorbing the memories and I lay there for a week becoming in part someone else, so that filaments and roots and vines grew over me and fed gently on my skin and even much later I would still have the faint scars of their affection as evidence of my time in that state.

When it was done, my brother lay corpse-like and yet not corpse at the bottom of the pit and I stood at the lip, staring down at him while all around the sunrise of purple and amber made the seeing difficult. But I could not repudiate him, for most of him now resided inside of me—and because of my brother my leg had recovered and I could walk through the new landscape like I had been born to it.

I Was Taught Against My Will

I headed west, and the story-creature did not follow. Perhaps I thought it would, but instead the story-creature swayed there, crooning soft to the not-corpse in the pit. The story-creature crooned so softly, and yet I heard that sound for so many miles on my journey. I heard it when I tried to sleep in a night that had blinding light hidden within it and the grunting passage of beasts for which I had no name.

I heard it when I was trudging through what my mind interpreted as jungle but was an entirely different story, and one I could not remain sane within if I had really seen it, even with my brother's memories.

For I soon outstripped any place my fake plant brother had yet gone and the terrain became more floating than fixed, the ground covered with a thin stubble of vegetation while the clouds had come close above and turned sea-green and from them tumbled down a forest that hung wrong, the bird-things that were not birds stitching their way through that cover upside down. The smell came to me thick, in emerald mist, and often my forehead shoved up against the physical manifestation of the smell, which could be like mint or could be like a rotted, mossy animal body.

The leaves and branches itched the top of my skull and brushed my cheek and I tried not to look up too often for fear of what I might see, but also because I grew to be terrified that if I took in that topsy-turvy land I would lose my grip on gravity and, slow and inexorable, take my place up there, my feet glued to the cloud cover and my head hanging toward the ground stubble.

But also the ground stubble hid dangers, for some was not vegetable but more like animal, and less like irritant than like mouth. I would look for shadow on the stubble to know the difference and I would not take for granted either the boulder that might suddenly unroll itself into a beast like an enormous squat centipede, which did not want to eat me, but sent tiny versions of itself that lived in its skin to attach themselves to my skin while burbling like children.

These children wanted to relive my memories. These children, for their own purposes, wanted to know about the last century, to extract it from my skull. This extraction hurt like machetes so sharp and keen that when they passed through my body I might be bisected and trisected without feeling it until I fell away into two or three symmetrical parts. That is how it manifested as pain. That is what it was every time.

Yet I could not elude them, and they came in such regimented columns and also at such regular intervals did the living boulders open up to release their terrible bounty that over time I realized these were indeed schools of a kind and I had been set loose as a history lesson. The story-creature had not wanted me to understand the last century, but instead the rest of the world, which might not know everything. So I endured it better knowing this, that it was not random and they did not mean me harm, but inflicted it as a side effect of the learning. If I were to suffer, then at least let me suffer for a purpose. Although, of course, I would do best should I not suffer at all.

Soon, though, came the final dislocation, for I had not understood the true nature of the school-creature in the same way that I had not understood the story-creature. For, one day, I came to the edge of the cloud-cover forest above and the stubble ground below and the way the horizon ahead zeroed to a large dot revealed the truth.

I had walked into the school-creature during one of the night hikes, when disoriented, and all of this time the sky-cloud above had been one edge of the creature and the ground another, a kind of gullet or intestine I had entered at one end—and I was about to jump out of the other. And by the mystery of how the world now worked, the entire entity had been itself moving along, so that when I climbed down the other end to the edge of a giant lake, I had the sense that I had traveled much farther than the distance demarked by the movement of my legs, the walking forward and forward still.

From the outside the school-creature resembled a giant, horizon-consuming fuzzy worm, for while its belly was flat and padded, all along its flanks and atop its blind head, moss and creepers entangled it and disguised it so that the education within could be clandestine and immersive and conducted by light and dark provided by the school-creature and the school-creature alone.

I ran for my life then, for the school-creature picked up speed as if It had known I was disembarking but now had Its route to follow. With a plunging relentlessness It dove into the giant lake, the whole amazing length and width of It, while I had sprinted as fast as I could for the side, barely leaping clear of being crushed, and then, after It had passed me, of being drowned, for the splash into the lake had sent a vast wave in my general direction and I sprinted as far inland as I could, and still I was buffeted by the water and washed this way and that, one arm trapped by a single-celled creature that kept calling out my name as if I had already told it my name, but . . . I had not.

Then I was drowning, pulled under the waves, and I held on to the single-celled creature like a life-preserver, even as I rebuffed its attack and screamed only in my mind for I was holding my breath and thrashing and yet somehow knew I would not drown if I only leaned on new skills, except that it was too unnatural and I would have drowned, not for lack of air, but for lack of practice and because I could not understand what I had become or was becoming.

But there came a sigh and a surge and I dashed up on moss-covered rocks, battered, gulping air, still clinging to the single-cell that clung to me. It meant to end me. It meant to do that whether we were drowning or whether we sucked air, together.

There are some beasts that do not care where you are, or if things have changed, still they will attack. Even if that progress came slow, inexorable, for I could feel the cell of it merging with the cells of me, and I knew I could not give it the time.

I Acclimated Despite What I Had Lost

When the water receded, I could only extricate myself by causing harm, and while I did not want to do this, and indeed looked about me to make sure nothing and no person was watching—at least, as far as I could be sure—I battered the single-cell against a rock that was no doubt some other animal lying there dormant, until the single-cell bleated and let loose of me and, bleeding an ichor lighter than the air, floated off into the sky in tendrils and green blood slicks that gripped the sky with a kind of phantom intent.

The blood was beautiful escaping into the heavens; I could barely stand the beauty of it, and what that meant about me.

The single-cell, subdued by my attack and with nothing to tether it to the ground, soon followed its own blood up into the sky, leaving me to contemplate a harsh truth: I had become so acclimated to this new environment that until seeing blood drift away into the sky I had not realized the thickness of the atmosphere of this new Earth. It was viscous, it rippled, and it could not, in a sense, be called air, although as I observed the edge of the giant lake, having returned now that the wave had passed, I could tell that water still was heavier than air, even if the composition of both had changed.

From that point on, I became aware of my breathing and how, although I had no visible gills, my lungs must in some way work differently than before. That my weight or my walking must anchor me differently. This awareness, creating a confusion like unwanted stereo in my head, made it hard to walk and to breathe without recognizing the effort. It was as if I had all of a sudden become a passenger in a machine body that I was expected to pilot without the seamlessness of before. It was like being transformed from a dolphin to a human upon reaching the midpoint of a swim across a dark and endless ocean.

As painful as it had been before—my brother's memories, the trisection extracted from me for the school-creature—this loss of lack of thought about basic motor functions depressed me. I resolved I would build a boat and float down the lake and when I reached the other side of the lake, I would end myself. For it was clear to me I did not belong in this world.

The memories had become a burden I did not want to suffer, for new memories, like thought bubbles, burst inside my head every night and I would dream and nightmare so vivid that I could barely call what I did sleep, in my thrashing and muttering and shaking. So that even though it seemed my skin absorbed some sort of nutrition from the heavy air or the weird sun, still I felt weary forever and horizons became a kind of torture, whether near or far.

From these memory bubbles, which were like my forced re-education by some ghost of a school-creature living inside me, I came to learn the truth of what had happened immediately after my planting one hundred years before.

My Brother Had Been a Traitor

I watched my "brother" being born from a patch of weeds beside my body where I slept, my head dissected and held in place by the story-creature. I watched my brother rise and walk back to my neighborhood and into the house I had lived in and make it his own. He drank the milk and the water. He put out the birdseed. He ate the steaks and the fish and the vegetables. He ranted at the television about the news.

It was my brother, not me, who put my daughter to bed at night and kissed her on the forehead and read her stories until she slept. It was my brother, not me, who slept with my wife and who laughed at her tales from her work and who took her to the movies and paid the babysitter and, again, drank the milk and drank the water. With my wife. Taking care of my daughter.

But I did not remember having a wife or a daughter, and even now saw them at a remove similar to experiencing senses I did not know I had. My gills filled with air. My lungs filled with water. Nothing lived in the right direction; everything died the wrong way up. Memory must be corrupted, gone bad. I made my hands into claws and I ripped at the ground like it was the flesh of the story-creature. How could I have had a family? What did it mean that I saw my brother had a family?

I was cut into pieces by the school-creature. I was flailing close with the single-cell. But in the blur and the smudge, with the rot coming too close, creeping up my leg, there by the edge of the lake, it came to me, bathing in the memories, that, yes, I had had a family. Except that the story-creature had taken away those memories from me and given them to my brother. That he might benefit and that I might not suffer. Yet still I suffered with the weight of this—that as I slept for a hundred years, my brother had taken my place in my family and done all of the family things indistinguishable from me. But it was true this made me feel worse, and that if I had woken to knowing I had left a family one hundred years behind me, I might have gone mad or become comatose.

Were they buried beneath the dirt floor of the foundation? Had I slept atop them like a faithful dog? I would never know, and nothing in my memories told me. I just knew that I, through the person of my brother, had become a true murderer, for I had helped to end the human species in the form in which we had known it.

Every time that my brother visited a neighbor's house, my brother left a residue that was an anti-story to the one we all knew, and this residue would grow and ac-cumulate in the mind until it was too late to do anything but *turn to the left* and change and change again.

Everywhere across my neighborhood, my country, and the world, this residue accumulated, extended silvery filaments across the bottom of people's shoes, across their palms and foreheads and elbows and the backs of their knees while asleep or awake, and over time everyone must *turn to their left* and in the turning transform in either mind or body or both. For this was the form the change took: a shudder, a turn, a cringe, a shrug. Every time, I saw in memory, my brother took to walking through the streets at dusk so he could peer in windows and see the anti-story take hold as he spread it farther. And with each new filament extended, more people spread the anti-story until eventually it was just *the story* not the anti-story and there had never been an anti-story at all, or any other story to rule the Earth.

It did not care about your belief system, your grasp on reality, the excellence of your analysis or your senses, for the anti-story of the story-creature became story by retelling effortlessly what lived at the core of you. So my brother went out walking and thrilled to the thrill of it, made the sounds deep in his throat that sounded like an odd nocturnal bird but were instead the end stages of the anti-story, triumphant.

Now when my brother met my neighbors, all knew all and that all was one. My brother's neighbor was my brother and he was his neighbor. While those they thought might be troublesome head-planted in remote places, as I had, and slept it off—that they might acclimate and hear the song of the one true story in due time. As I was hearing it now, buffeted by it, and yet even though I heard it I was inured to it. But this did not make me hopeful, for it just meant I no longer mattered to the spread of any story or to the plans of the story-creature.

I could roam this world as rebel or spy my entire life but the colonization was complete. All I could do is choose when I ended my experience of the world.

What I Stumbled Upon That I Was Meant to Find

I began my journey across the lake, that I might find the end of my story, which was now the anti-story much as I was the anti-brother. I felt like the captain of my own fate, that I might at least control my own body and how long it drew breath— and I wish I could tell you what I discovered I created by my own roving, my own actions, but chance does not reside on the new Earth as it did in the old.

This is both a terrible and miraculous thing.

I found the dead leathery shell of a creature that might have been like a turtle except a hundred scrawny necks attached to tiny bulbous heads with gaping mouths hung from the inside of the shell, as if these inner heads had eaten the larger creature from the inside out as part of some plan, and I had to cut them all off. They welcomed this art with an eagerness that suggested some maker's plan remained for the rest of their life cycle, and indeed I watched those I had severed burrow into the ground with squeals of delight and soon they were gone and I never saw them again and I am glad of that. Then I had to sand down the neck stumps to make the shell float and not be disgusting. Although by then not much was disgusting because the word familiar had changed so much since I had woken.

I floated on the black-and-green surface of the lake, with pools of clearest blue embedded in that thickness, and I reflected on my situation. I reflected and refracted my situation, my memories continuing to be absorbed through the epidermis and then into my brain, as if the entire world but me already knew my past. There was nothing else to do, nothing to occupy me, for the lake was slow to travel across, the current glacial.

But then the dead shell that was my boat grew a mouth and began to talk to me, for it too still had a role to fulfill in my life in this world.

The Wonder That Was the Dead-Shell

I was made to understand by the talking dead-shell mouth that whoever should cut the hundred bulbous heads from its undercarriage shall be the feeder that the remaining dead-shell shall converse with, and that by this ritual shall both the feeder and the fed know that learning has taken place. I did not understand the importance of this at first, and considered that it might be a trick by the story-creature, except the story-creature had no part in this.

Dead-Shell grew a mouth at the bow, and it was salty and chalky with unshaven teeth that sprouted up crooked, so that the mouth must speak through a thicket of its own slashing surgery. Although it took time, of which we had plenty in that becalmed fish bowl, I came to understand Dead-Shell very well, even if I never discovered if we spoke in Dead-Shell's language or my own. I suppose after my encounter with the school-creature, I had absorbed a capacity to understand beyond my actual ability to understand.

The weather was deep and porous and full of needles and it pressed around us in a way that invigorated even as it pricked, and even if the lake looked like no body of water I had ever seen, I found it melancholy, reassuring, and calm, and thus although Dead-Shell disturbed me, I had been disturbed worse since I had woken.

How should a Dead-Shell talk? "Maw maw maw," it said, and then "Maw maw maw chaw chaw chaw." And then, "Dam dam dam dam maw maw maw chaw chaw haw."

But this was Dead-Shell throat-clearing and I could feel many eyes upon me from it, except that Dead-Shell's eyes were not on its dead shell but instead flitting through the underbrush and overbrush on the rotting shores, through thickets of trees roving in their hundreds if not thousands. For Dead-Shell's evolution made its sight independent of its self, and those eyes too had their own lifecycle, and were so numerous because of the predation upon them. Over Dead-Shell's span, Dead-Shell would shed upwards of five hundred eyes, and only during the molting could it produce more that would ascend wingward to stare down from on high.

Yet still this effect was unsettling to me, and this is why I took so long to adjust to Dead-Shell's speech. When I turned my gaze to those eyes, I worried for them, for I knew them to be as like to his children, and every hour of every day one or more were eaten, and often I would see this on the far shore to the east or west—I would sense the shriek of the punctured eye from some felon of a predator and you would see the spurt of liquid and Dead-Shell was one eye closer to darkness.

All of these punctured and consumed eyes—even when they lay within the belly of the predator—could still see, for Dead-Shell told me that if swallowed whole his eyes would report back to him, from that enemy stronghold, sometimes for months, until expelled, which was usually enough to snuff out the remaining life. Dead-Shell's brain, not fixed in the meat of him but in his shell, contained such a coiled complexity that I could not quite bring myself to imagine it.

"Maw maw maw maw maw may may my breather my bruther my brother," Dead-Shell said, and I knew by this that at least one of his eyes had seen my story and knew of me.

This did not matter to me in the least now. It did not matter for Dead-Shell was of the new world not the old and my embarrassment and sorrow and guilt was all of the old world and made no difference in the new world, which had none of the culture I had known. I understood this at least. And so I forgave Dead-Shell not knowing that this opening might hurt me. Even as I sailed down the length of the lake on the inside of his shell and he spoke to me from the bow.

The words continued to sound like nonsense to my ears, but to my eyes, my nose, my tongue, my skin, Dead-Shell's words resonated like the most powerful symphony undercut by the gentlest lullaby.

I was being put to sleep and roused to heroic acts, even as all I did was kneel on the dead shell of Dead-Shell. While out of my ears, as if the words must expel matter, poured my understanding, coating the sides of my body and falling away into the water like thick honeycomb in golden multitudes.

How Dead-Shell Changed Me

Soon I came to realize that Dead-Shell was a sort of scientist-creature on the order of the story-creature and school-creature before him. He communicated to me that the world had been remade against my image and that my form, even much reduced, was the rebellion of the old world against the new, and that this made no sense because the new world embraced the old; that my very presence made the old world manifest, no matter the form, so why was the form important? Why did I hold on to the form?

And why did I, holding my form, insist then on negating myself once we had reached the end of the lake? It would serve no purpose and was impossible because I would fail because I could not destroy my constituent molecules; they would still exist, and thus I would exist as well. As still the golden manna sang as it left my ears and streamed down my body, made of my body a clay that must be reformed and redistributed to make sense.

A sweet and bitter relief.

Better that I succumb to my purpose, Dead-Shell still maw-mawed into me. Better that I become what I must become for a new life and a new journey, for this was the only way to preserve any semblance of the old world . . . and here Dead-Shell brought to bear all of his thousand eyes all across the land—on the shore, in the trees, in the water, in the belly of myriad beasts and buried, buried deep in the ground, staring up through moss and lichen and rich, thick soil.

That I might see through his eyes, might see how underneath the new world lay my old world still. Like the foundation of my house, there it lay, and I saw it all in such a confusion and profusion that I could not hold it in my head and the golden honeycomb that was not honeycomb at all but the movement of my transformation spun out and pushed out from inside of me until there was more of it outside of me than inside of me, and that is how I knew that it had been growing inside of me for much, much longer than Dead-Shell had been talking to me.

For Dead-Shell's words had encased me in honeycomb from the inside out and the fortress of my body lay behind a glistening wall, and that wall was attached forever and always to Dead-Shell, and his task was done, as even the space that had been my brain softened and spread out to coat the inside of that entire space I must call separate from the world.

Namely: me.

How I Left My Self Behind

I toppled into Dead-Shell's embrace and the dead shell closed around me and bound me, while Dead-Shell's mouth detached on tiny legs and jumped into the lake. For this was all that was left of Dead-Shell, who must now rejoin his own eyes, or some portion of them and continue on his anointed purpose, his path, which might mean repeating his conversation with yet another person who had slept a century and would reach the lake through the school-creature, but had lagged behind me in his timing.

But, meanwhile, Dead-Shell had brought his teachings up and through me and the golden honeycomb that was so much more bound me and I came out from the lake to a river that roared and gushed its way down to the premonition of a vast sea, and along with this roaring and gushing and thrushing came the bobbing and weaving and floating and gliding and all of the other motions of the Dead-Shell eyes, now watching me, turned on me, so that I still saw through them but they *saw me*. And the weight of that was a powerful thing such as I cannot describe. To be seen in that way.

While I could not move for I no longer had what might be called arms and legs but only the motion provided by cilia and by the thick stickiness of the honey-comb, which was both me and not me, was how I could move and how I could stay. Yet my eyes did not partake of the honeycomb. My cluster of half a dozen eyes was too busy transforming into one eye, one giant eye that was also a kind of helmet, as if an eye had been drawn on the glass of an astronaut's helmet, except that drawn eye could see and the entire globe of glass was the eye. That while I had my hands I put my hands to my face to know that this one eye was enormous, like a world, and that already things swam there like motes but wriggling and alive. I saw so far and I saw so well, as the many eyes of the Dead-Shell retreated and receded until I saw only through my own face.

Beneath, there came an itching and tickling. I had grown fins so I could steer myself fast down the river, now underwater because I had the gills and I had the en-casing of golden sap, which I knew was stronger and yet lighter than any substance humankind had ever known, so that I was my own fish but also my own subma-rine, and I rushed and darted and frolicked through that water in such a sublime way I almost forgot the sense of me, forgot that I had but one eye now. I sought open water. I sought the ocean. And I blessed the thousand eyes of the Dead-Shell, and I blessed Dead-Shell himself for allowing me to be this way, to experience this, to be other than human.

I was so fluid in my shell that I could not at times distinguish the water from my self. I could not distinguish a wave from my thoughts. Extinguish me, become me. That is all the river meant to me: a long, thick muscle that would deliver me, and I was that muscle and I wanted the sea. I desired it so badly, more than anything I had ever wanted, and it pushed out all other concerns and I could taste nothing but the sea-to-come and hear nothing and feel nothing but that.

And still I was changing, well beyond the changes that had created my brother. Those innocent days, those hours of being planted by a story-creature on a hillside, a sapling springing from my head, were long distant. I could not return to them even if I had wished to.

The Ocean That Lay Beyond the River

At the ocean, however, my urgency faded. Having reached that place, I no longer worried about ending my life, for my life had spread and swelled and become something other than it had been. Nor did I worry about much else, and I floated in the glistening green water staring up at the sky, which sagged so close and was not yet full of stars but only the ghosts of stars or a haunting of everything that was not-star, so that by the lack I might think of the word "star."

I received this vision through the taut thickness of the air, which had not yet dulled to dark.

Into that calm I was either allowed further knowledge of my wife and my daughter, or these slipped through like silvery minnows of memory darting out of me—still at a remove, but they were true, as if only by turning away so utterly now I could see them, glimpse them back on shore, staring out at me across a century. Who knew where they might be now, if they lived in the world at all?

My daughter had liked to stage plays in her room back in the house that was only a dirt foundation now, and she would make us pay to watch them and then she would do what she had planned to do anyway while we sat there with foolish grins, unsure if she was a genius or just sillier than us. My wife made jewelry in the shapes of all the natural things; spoons that were leaves and knives that were stalks of weeds and metal bowls like ponds full of fish. She made me a coiled snake as a band for my wrist, but I wasn't wearing it when I went to the hillside and though my digging in the foundation may have been to find it, nothing was there. Nothing would ever be there.

Fierce as river rush came to me *love*, came to me many trips to the beach with them, and the laughing and the sunburn and the cold drinks and the sand between the toes, and how when that happened time was no longer there, that everything became one moment, the only moment, and it was as if we had not traveled to the beach or would be leaving soon but only that we had ever been there and ever would be there.

I had worked as a writer of obituaries; I had not buried the stories of the dead in the backyard. I had worked for a newspaper researching people's lives. I had a father and a mother who were still alive when I began my long sleep, but they were more distant still, and I could not recapture them, not in any way that had meaning, and with that loss was snapped off the whole branch of relatives and perhaps I had never had close ties to them, but in the succor of the sea, surrounded by such seething life, I felt the lack of those connections and the new connections roared into my head in such a joyous profusion.

Touched by the want and need of all of that, I, turning to look back, tried to conquer the new shoreline with the old one. For that would bring a more substantial something of old life, old growth. I could almost do it. I could almost revert, for the moment. But not quite.

What would this world have been if I had slept and had returned to find it human?

Would it have been terrible or beautiful?

Would I have recognized it any better, or would humankind have been as banished as if the story-creature had come along after all?

The Sky Beyond the Ocean

All of this I thought in long and short flashes and daggers and circles as I floated, waiting for the next thing. The sky was the sun and the sea was the sky both and only the thin line between told me of any difference, and the difference meant nothing. I could tell by how the skin of the water lifted below me that the ocean was not the ocean, but instead a great beast, a story-sea that was salt water and not salt water, and that the swells were rising that I might be lifted up into the heavens when finally the sky darkened and the stars came out, and then I might know my destination.

I sensed that while I had been shedding my last ancient skin to become pure, there had swum in quiet those who now bobbed and floated around me, others not unlike me—those who had slept on their separate hillsides and then taken a journey to arrive here, and would soon disperse again. All of us with our huge single opaque eye like a helmet and the compact bodies, from which the fins had fallen off, to drift to the bottom and be broken down and become nourishment for the beast that enclosed us in such a wide embrace.

There was no music, and yet there was such music as I had never heard before. Distant, so distant, and yet so close. Did we make that music or did the world make that music in celebration of our departure?

I did not think I would ever be human again, but I would see things no one of my species had ever seen, and with that thought I began to cry from some excess of emotion that could not go elsewhere.

I began to cry as if I meant to swell the sea and drown the earth . . . and yet even my tears were purposeful, and repurposed by the story-creature. For my tears encapsulated a chronicle of my story, of this story, and every tear that met the ocean's surface contained all of this tale and every tear shed by every cocooned single-eye to all sides told their tales too, that they might not be forgotten, and might be sheltered and expressed indeed by the sea and the earth itself.

Nothing ever could be lost and all would be used, and that was the way of it and part of what Dead-Shell had tried to tell me to comfort me. And so I wept my story into the ocean and the ocean received it and if you know these words you have heard tell of them from the drops of water that fall from the sky and inhabit the lakes and the rivers and all creatures across the face of this world have heard tell of it, including the thousand eyes of Dead-Shell, for they too are self-aware and some of them must have watched us far out at sea, waiting for the next part of the story.

The clear substance over my head, the eye of me, had thinned and hardened and taken what it needed from the salt water, and I was ready. The ocean that was itself a beast began to faster and faster curve upward like the eyes, like the helmets, and in slow-motion began to slingshot us up into the cosmos. But it was not slow motion for long, for the ocean bellowed and sped up and pushed up and its wishes were that we be gone—and at speed.

We like children heard and received and as if upon a mighty trampoline were flung up into the stratosphere and then achieved escape velocity in a holy roar and expulsion, through light and dark into dark and weightlessness . . . until we were all of us tumbling end over end through vacuum, and with each tumble my fellow travelers dispersed farther and farther from me, headed to other worlds than me, to become story-creatures.

For we were joyous. We were ecstatic as the stars came at us, no longer veiled, and we saw them in all of the glory that was both ours and theirs.

What was breath to us behind our helmets? What was time? What was speed?

We could tumble forever and never die, and every sighting of a star filled us like a tiny bliss, a flower opening up and opening up and never fading.

JEFF VANDERMEER'S *New York Times* bestselling Southern Reach trilogy has been translated into more than thirty-five languages. Its first novel, *Annihilation,* won the Nebula Award and Shirley Jackson Award, was short-listed for half a dozen more, and was adapted into a feature film by Paramount Pictures. His latest novel, *Borne,* is the first release from Farrar, Straus and Giroux's new MCD imprint and has received wide critical acclaim, including a rare trifecta of rave review from the *New York Times,* the *Los Angeles Times,* and the *Washington Post.* The novel has also been optioned by Paramount, and it continues to explore themes related to the environment, animals, and our future. *The New Yorker* has called Jeff "the weird Thoreau," and he frequently speaks about issues related to climate change and storytelling, including at DePaul, MIT, and the Guggenheim. He lives in Tallahassee, Florida.

The Devil in America

Kai Ashante Wilson

Scant years after the Civil War, a mysterious family confronts the legacy that has pursued them across centuries, out of slavery, and finally to the idyllic peace of the town of Rosetree. The shattering consequences of this confrontation echo backward and forward in time, even to the present day. *Nebula Award nominee, Shirley Jackson Award nominee, World Fantasy Award nominee. Edited by Ann VanderMeer.*

1955

Emmett Till, sure, I remember. Your great grandfather, sitting at the table with the paper spread out, looked up and said something to Grandma. She looked over my way and made me leave the room: Emmett Till. In high school I had a friend everybody called Underdog. One afternoon—1967?—Underdog was standing on some corner and the police came round and beat him with nightsticks. No reason. Underdog thought he might get some respect if he joined up for Vietnam, but a sergeant in basic training was calling him everything but his name—nigger this, nigger that—and Underdog went and complained. Got thrown in the brig, so he ended up going to Vietnam with just a couple weeks' training. Soon after he came home in a body bag. In Miami a bunch of white cops beat to death a man named Arthur McDuffie with heavy flashlights. You were six or seven: so, 1979. The cops banged up his motorcycle trying to make killing him look like a crash. Acquitted, of course. Then Amadou Diallo, 1999; Sean Bell, 2006. You must know more about all the New York murders than I do. Trayvon, this year. Every year it's one we hear about and God knows how many just the family mourns.

—Dad

1877 August 23

"'Tis all right if I take a candle, Ma'am?" Easter said. Her mother bent over at the black iron stove, and lifted another smoking hot pan of cornbread from the oven. Ma'am just hummed—meaning, *Go 'head.* Easter came wide around her mother, wide around the sizzling skillet, and with the ramrod of Brother's old rifle hooked up the front left burner. She left the ramrod behind the stove, plucked the candle from the tumbling, strengthless grip of her ruint hand, and dipped it wick-first into flame. Through the good glass window in the wall behind the stove, the night was dark. It was soot and shadows. Even the many-colored chilis and bright little pumpkins in Ma'am's back garden couldn't be made out.

A full supper plate in her good hand, lit candle in the other, Easter had a time getting the front door open, then out on the porch, and shutting back the door without dropping any food. Then, anyhow, the swinging of the door made the candle flame dance fearfully low, just as wind gusted up too, so her light flickered *way* down . . . and went out.

"Shoot!" Easter didn't say the curse word aloud. She mouthed it. "Light it back for me, angels," Easter whispered. "Please?" The wick flared bright again.

No moon, no stars—the night sky was clouded over. Easter hoped it wasn't trying to storm, with the church picnic tomorrow.

She crossed the yard to the edge of the woods where Brother waited. A big old dog, he crouched down, leapt up, down and up again, barking excitedly, just as though he were some little puppy dog.

"Well, hold your horses," Easter said. "I'm coming!" She met him at the yard's end and dumped the full plate over, all her supper falling to the ground. Brother's head went right down, tail just a-wagging. "Careful, Brother," Easter said. "You *watch* them chicken bones." Then, hearing the crack of bones, she knelt and snatched ragged shards right out of the huge dog's mouth. Brother whined and licked her hand—and dropped his head right back to buttered mashed yams.

Easter visited with him a while, telling her new secrets, her latest sins, and when he'd sniffed out the last morsels of supper, Brother listened to her with what anybody would have agreed was deep love, full attention. "Well, let me get on," she said at last, and sighed. "Got to check on the Devil now." She'd left it 'til late, inside all evening with Ma'am, fixing their share of the big supper at church tomorrow. Brother whined when she stood up to leave.

Up the yard to the henhouse. Easter unlatched the heavy door and looked them over—chickens, on floor and shelf, huddling quietly in thick straw, and all asleep except for Sadie. Eldest and biggest, that one turned just her head and looked over Easter's way. Only reflected candlelight, of course, but Sadie's beady eyes looked *so* ancient and *so* crafty, blazing like embers. Easter backed on out, latched the coop up securely again, and made the trip around the henhouse, stooping and stooping and stooping, to check for gaps in the boards. Weasel holes, fox doors.

There weren't any. And the world would go on exactly as long as Easter kept up this nightly vigil.

Ma'am stood on the porch when Easter came back up to the house. "I don't *appreciate* my good suppers thrown in the dirt. You hear me, girl?" Ma'am put a hand on Easter's back, guiding her indoors. "That ole cotton-picking dog could just as well take hisself out to the deep woods and hunt." Ma'am took another tone altogether when she meant every word, and *then* she didn't stroke Easter's head, or gently brush her cheek with a knuckle. This was only complaining out of habit. Easter took only one tone with her mother. Meek.

"Yes, Ma'am," she said, and ducked her head in respect. Easter *didn't* think herself too womanish or grown to be slapped silly.

"Help me get this up on the table," Ma'am said—the deepest bucket, and brimful of water and greens. Ma'am was big and strong enough to have lifted *ten* such buckets. It was friendly, though, sharing the little jobs. At one side of the bucket, Easter bent over and worked her good hand under the bottom, the other just mostly ached now, the cut thickly scabbed over. She just sort of pressed it to the bucket's side, in support.

Easter and her mother set the bucket on the table.

Past time to see about the morning milk. Easter went back to the cellar and found the cream risen, though the tin felt a tad cool to her. The butter would come slow. "Pretty please, angels?" she whispered. "Could you help me out a little bit?" They could. They did. The milk tin warmed ever so slightly. Just right. Easter dipped the cream out and carried the churn back to the kitchen.

Ma'am had no wrinkles except at the corners of the eyes. Her back was unbowed, her arms and legs still mighty. But she was old now, wasn't she? Well nigh sixty, and maybe past it. But still with that upright back, such quick hands. *Pretty* was best said of the young—Soubrette Toussaint was very pretty, for instance—so what was the right word for Ma'am's severe cheekbones, sharp almond-shaped eyes, and pinched fullness of mouth? Working the churn, Easter felt the cream foam and then thicken, pudding-like. Any other such marriage, and you'd surely hear folks gossiping over the dead wrongness of it—the wife twenty-some years older than a mighty good-looking husband. *What in the world, I ask you, is that old lady doing with a handsome young man like that?* But any two eyes could see the answer here. Not pretty as she must once have been, with that first husband, whoever he'd been, dead and buried back east. And not pretty as when she'd had those first babies, all gone now too. But age hadn't only taken from Ma'am, it had given too. Some rare gift, and so much of it that Pa *had* to be pick of the litter—kindest, most handsome man in the world—just to stack up. Easter poured off the buttermilk into a jar for Pa, who liked that especially. Ma'am might be a challenge to love sometimes, but respect came easy.

"I *told* him, Easter." Ma'am wiped forefinger and thumb down each dandelion leaf, cleaning off grit and bugs, and then lay it aside in a basket. "Same as I told you. *Don't mess with it.* Didn't I say, girl?"

"Yes, Ma'am." Easter scooped the clumps of butter into the bowl.

Ma'am spun shouting from her work. "That's *right* I did! And I pray to God you *listen*, too. That fool out there *didn't*, but Good Lord knows I get on my knees and pray *every night* you got some little bit of sense in your head. Because, Easter, I ain't *got* no more children—you my last one!" Ma'am turned back and gripped the edge of the table.

Ma'am wanted no comfort, no acknowledgement of her pain at such moments—just let her be. Easter huddled in her chair, paddling the salt evenly through the butter, working all the water out. She worked with far more focus than the job truly needed.

Then, above the night's frogcroak and bugchatter, they heard Brother bark in front of the house, and heard Pa speak, his very voice. Wife and daughter both gave a happy little jump, looking together at the door in anticipation. Pa'd been three days over in Greenville selling the cigars. Ma'am snapped her fingers.

"Get the jug out the cellar," she said. "You know just getting in your Pa wants him a little tot of cider. Them white folks." As if Ma'am wouldn't have a whole big mug her ownself.

"Yes, Ma'am." Easter fetched out the jug.

Pa opened the door, crossed the kitchen—touching Easter's head in passing, he smelt of woodsmoke—and came to stand behind Ma'am. His hands cupped her breasts through her apron, her dress, and he kissed the back of her neck. She gasped aloud. "Wilbur! *The baby* . . . !" That's what they still called Easter, "the baby." Nobody had noticed she'd gotten tall, twelve years old now.

Pa whispered secrets in Ma'am's ear. He was a father who loved his daughter, but he was a husband first and foremost. *I'm a terrible thirsty man,* Pa had said once, *and your mama is my only cool glass of water in this world.* Ma'am turned and embraced him. "I know it, sweetheart," she said. "I know." Easter covered up the butter. She took over washing the greens while her parents whispered, intent only on each other. Matched for height, and Ma'am a little on the stout side, Pa on the slim, so they were about the same thickness too. The perfect fit of them made Easter feel a sharp pang, mostly happiness. Just where you could hear, Pa said, "And you *know* it ain't no coloreds round here but us living in Rosetree . . ."

Wrapped in blankets up in the loft, right over their bed, of course she heard things at night, on Sundays usually, when nobody was so tired.

An effortful noise from Pa, as if he were laboring some big rock heave-by-heave over to the edge of the tobacco field, and then before the quiet, sounding sort of worried, as if Pa were afraid Ma'am might accidently touch the blazing hot iron of the fired-up stove, Pa would say, "*Hazel!*"

". . . so then Miss Anne claimed she seen some nigger run off from there, and *next thing* she knew—fire! Just *everywhere.* About the whole west side of Green-ville, looked to me, burnt down. Oh yeah, and in the morning here come Miss Anne's husband talkmbout, 'Know what else, y'all? That nigger my wife seen last night—matterfact, he *violated* her.' Well, darling, here's what I wanna know . . ."

Ma'am would kind of sigh throughout, and from one point on keep saying—not loud—"Like *that* . . ." However much their bed creaked, Ma'am and Pa were pretty quiet when Easter was home. Probably they weren't, though, these nights when Pa came back from Greenville. That was why they sent her over the Tous-saints'.

". . . *where* this 'violated' come from all of a sudden? So last night Miss Anne said she maybe *might* of seen some nigger run off, and this morning that nigger jumped her show 'nough? And then it *wasn't* just the one nigger no more. No. It was two or three of 'em, maybe about five. *Ten* niggers—at least. Now Lord knows I ain't no lawyer, baby, I *ain't,* but it seem to me a fishy story done changed up even fishier . . ."

Ma'am and Pa took so much comfort in each other, and just plain *liked* each other. Easter was glad to see it. But she was old enough to wonder, a little worried and a little sad, who was ever going to love her in the way Ma'am and Pa loved each other.

"What you still doing here!" Ma'am looked up suddenly from her embrace. "Girl, you should of *been* gone to Soubrette's. *Go.* And take your best dress and good Sunday shoes too. Tell Mrs. Toussaint I'll see her early out front of the church tomorrow. You hear me, Easter?"

"Yes, Ma'am," she said. And with shoes and neatly folded clothes, Easter hurried out into the dark wide-open night, the racket of crickets.

On the shadowed track through the woods, she called to Brother but he wouldn't come out of the trees, though Easter could hear him pacing her through the underbrush. Always out there in the dark. Brother wanted to keep watch whenever Easter went out at night, but he got shy sometimes too. Lonesome and blue.

• • •

And this whole thing started over there, in old Africa land, where in olden days a certain kind of big yellow dog (*you* know the kind I'm talking about) used to run around. Now those dogs ain't nowhere in the world, except for . . . Anyway, the prince of the dogs was a sorcerer—about the biggest and best there was in the world. One day he says to hisself, *Let me get up off four feet for a while, and walk around on just two, so I can see what all these folk called "people" are doing over in that town.* So the prince quit being his doggy self and got right up walking like anybody. While the prince was coming over to the people's town, he saw a pretty young girl washing clothes at the river. Now if he'd still been his doggy self, the prince probably would of just *ate* that girl up, but since he was a man now, the prince seen right off what a pretty young thing she was. So he walks over and says, Hey, gal. You want to lay down right here by the river in the soft grass with me? Well—and anybody *would*—the girl felt some kind of way, a strange man come talking to her so fresh all of a sudden. The girl says, Man, don't you see my hair braided up all nice like a married lady? (Because that's how they did over in Africa land. The married ladies, the girls still at home, plaited their hair up different.) So the dog prince said, Oh, I'm sorry. I come from a long way off, so I didn't know what your hair meant. And he *didn't*, either, cause dogs don't braid their hair like people do. *Hmph*, says the gal, all the while sort of taking a real good look over him. As a matter of fact, the dog prince made a *mighty* fine-looking young man, and the girl's mama and papa had married her off to just about the oldest, most dried-up, and granddaddy-looking fellow you ever saw. That old man was rich, sure, but he really couldn't do nothing in the married way for a young gal like that, who wasn't twenty years old yet. So, the gal says, *Hmph*, where you come from anyways? What you got to say for yourself? And it must of been pretty good too, whatever the prince had to say for hisself, because, come nine months later, that gal was mama to your great great—twenty greats—grandmama, first one of us with the old Africa magic.

• • •

It wasn't but a hop, skip, and jump through the woods into Rosetree proper. Surrounding the town green were the church, Mrs. Toussaint's general store, and the dozen best houses, all two stories, with overgrown rosebushes in front. At the other side of the town green, Easter could see Soubrette sitting out on her front porch with a lamp, looking fretfully out into night.

It felt nice knowing somebody in this world would sit up for her, wondering where she was, was everything all right.

In her wretched accent, Easter called, "*J'arrive!*" from the middle of the green.

Soubrette leapt up. "Easter?" She peered into the blind dark. "I can't see a thing! Where are you, Easter?"

Curious that *she* could see so well, cutting across the grass toward the general store. Easter had told the angels not to without her asking, told them *many* times, but still she often found herself seeing with cat's eyes, hearing with dog's ears, when the angels took a notion. The problem being, folks *noticed* if you were all the time seeing and hearing what you shouldn't. But maybe there was no need to go blaming the angels. With no lamp or candle, your eyes naturally opened up something amazing, while lights could leave you stone-blind out past your bright spot.

They screamed, embraced, laughed. Anybody would have said three *years*, not days, since they'd last seen each other. "Ah, viens ici, toi!" said Soubrette, gently taking Easter's ruint hand to lead her indoors.

Knees drawn up on the bed, Easter hugged her legs tightly. She set her face and bit her lip, but tears came anyway. They always did. Soubrette sighed and closed the book in her lap. Very softly Easter murmured, "I like *Rebecca* most."

"Yes!" Soubrette abruptly leaned forward and tapped Easter's shin. "Rowena is nice too—she *is!*—but I don't even *care* about old Ivanhoe. It just isn't *fair* about poor Rebecca . . ."

"He really don't deserve either one of 'em," Easter said, forgetting her tears in the pleasure of agreement. "That part when Ivanhoe up and changed his mind all of a sudden about Rebecca—do you remember that part? '. . . *an inferior race . . .*' No, I didn't care for him after that."

"Oh *yes*, Easter, I remember!" Soubrette flipped the book open and paged back through it. "At first he sees Rebecca's so beautiful, and he likes her, but then all his niceness is '. . . *exchanged at once for a manner cold, composed, and collected, and fraught with no deeper feeling than that which expressed a grateful sense of courtesy received from an unexpected quarter, and from one of an inferior race . . .*' Ivanhoe's just *hateful!*" Soubrette laid a hand on Easter's foot. "Rowena and Rebecca would have been better off *without* him!"

Soubrette touched you when she made her points, and she made them in the most hot-blooded way. Easter enjoyed such certainty and fire, but it made her feel bashful too. "You ain't taking it too far, Soubrette?" she asked softly. "Who would they love without Ivanhoe? It wouldn't be nobody to, well, *kiss.*"

It made something happen in the room, that word *kiss*. Did the warm night heat up hotter, and the air buzz almost like yellowjackets in a log? One and one made two, so right there you'd seem to have a sufficiency for a kiss, with no lack of anything, anyone. From head to toe Easter knew right where she was, lightly sweating in a thin summer shift on this August night, and she knew right where Soubrette was too, so close that—

"Girls!" Mrs. Toussaint bumped the door open with her hip. "The iron's good and hot on the stove now, so . . ."

Easter and Soubrette gave an awful start. *Ivanhoe* fell to the floor.

". . . why don't you come downstairs with your dresses . . . ?" Mrs. Toussaint's words trailed away. She glanced back and forth between the girls while the hot thing still sizzled in the air, delicious and wrong. Whatever it was seemed entirely perceptible to Mrs. Toussaint. She said to her daughter, "Chérie, j'espère que tu te comportes bien. Tu es une femme de quatorze ans maintenant. Ton amie n'a que dix ans; elle est une toute jeune fille!"

She spoke these musical words softly and with mildness—nevertheless they struck Soubrette like a slap. The girl cast her gaze down, eyes shining with abrupt tears. High yellow, Soubrette's cheeks and neck darkened with rosy duskiness.

"Je me comporte toujours bien, Maman," she whispered, her lips trembling as if about to weep.

Mrs. Toussaint paused a moment longer, and said, "Well, fetch down your dresses, girls. Bedtime soon." She went out, closing the door behind her.

The tears *did* spill over now. Easter leaned forward suddenly, kissed Soubrette's cheek, and said, "J'ai *douze* ans."

Soubrette giggled. She wiped her eyes.

Much later, Easter sat up, looking around. Brother had barked, growling savagely, and woken her up. But seeing Soubrette asleep beside her, Easter knew that couldn't be so. And no strange sounds came to her ears from the night outside, only wind in the leaves, a whippoorwill. Brother never came into the middle of town anyway, not ever. The lamp Mrs. Toussaint had left burning in the hallway lit the gap under the bedroom door with orange glow. Easter's fast heart slowed as she watched her friend breathing easily. Soubrette never snored, never tossed and turned, never slept with her mouth gaping open. Black on the white pillow, her long hair spilled loose and curly.

"Angels?" Easter whispered. "Can you make my hair like Soubrette's?" This time the angels whispered, *Give us the licklest taste of her blood, and all Sunday long tomorrow your hair will be so nice. See that hatpin? Just stick Soubrette in the hand with it, and not even too deep. Prettiest curls anybody ever saw.* Easter only sighed. It was out of the question, of course. The angels sometimes asked for the most shocking crimes as if they were nothing at all. "Never mind," she said, and laid down to sleep.

> While true that such profoundly sustaining traditions, hidden under the guise of the imposed religion, managed to survive centuries of slavery and subjugation, we should not therefore suppose that ancient African beliefs suffered no sea changes. Of course they did. "The Devil" in Africa had been capricious, a trickster, and if cruel, only insomuch as bored young children, amoral and at loose ends, may be cruel: seeking merely to provoke an interesting event at any cost, to cause some disruption of the tedious status quo. For the Devil in America, however, malice itself was

the end, and temptation a means only to destroy. Here, the Devil would pursue the righteous and the wicked, alike and implacably, to their everlasting doom . . .

White Devils/Black Devils
Luisa Valéria da Silva y Rodríguez

1871 August 2

The end begins after Providence loses all wiggle room, and the outcome becomes hopeless and fixed. That moment had already happened, Ma'am would have said. It had happened long before either one of them were born. Ma'am would have assured Easter that the end began way back in slavery times, and far across the ocean, when that great-grandfather got snatched from his home and the old wisdom was lost.

Easter knew better, though. A chance for grace and new wisdom had always persisted, and doom never been assured . . . right up until, six years old, Easter did what she did one August day out in the tobacco fields.

On that morning of bright skies, Pa headed out to pick more leaves and Easter wanted to come along. He said, "Let's ask your mama."

"But he *said*, Wilbur." Ma'am looked surprised. "He told us, *You ain't to take the baby out there, no time, no way.*"

Pa hefted Easter up in his arms, and kissed her cheek, saying, "Well, it's going on three years now since he ain't been here to say *Bet not* or say *Yep, go 'head*. So I wonder how long we suppose to go on doing everything just the way he said, way back when. Forever? And the baby *wants* to go . . ." Pa set her down and she grabbed a handful of his pants leg and leaned against him. "But, darling, if you say not to, then we *won't*. Just that simple."

Most men hardly paid their wives much mind at all, but Pa would listen to any little thing Ma'am said. She, though, *hated* to tell a man what he could and couldn't do—some woman just snapping her fingers, and the man running lickety-split here and there. Ma'am said that wasn't right. So she crossed her arms and hugged herself, frowning unhappily. "Well . . ." Ma'am said. "Can you just wait a hot minute there with the mule, Wilbur? Let me say something to the baby." Ma'am unfolded her arms and reached out a hand. "Come here, girl."

Easter came up the porch steps and took the hand—swept along in Ma'am's powerful grip, through the open door, into the house. "*Set.*" Ma'am pointed to a chair. Easter climbed and sat down. Ma'am knelt on the floor. They were eye to eye. She grasped Easter's chin and pulled her close. "Tell me, Easter—what you do, if some lady in a red silk dress come trying to talk to you?"

"I shake my head *no*, Ma'am, and turn my back on her. Then the lady have to go away."

"That's *right*! But what if that strange lady in the red dress say, *Want me to open up St. Peter's door, and show you heaven?* What if she say to you, *See them birds flying there? Do me one itsy-bitsy favor, and you could be in the sky flying too.* What then, Easter? Tell me what you do."

"Same thing, Ma'am." She knew her mother wasn't angry with her, but Ma'am's hot glare—the hard grip on her chin—made tears prick Easter's eyes. "I turn my back, Ma'am. She *have to* go, if I just turn my back away."

"Yes! And will you *promise*, Easter? Christ is your Savior, will you *swear* to turn your back, if that lady in the pretty red dress come talking to you?"

Easter swore up and down, and she meant every word too. Ma'am let her go back out to her father, and he set her up on the mule. They went round the house and down the other way, on the trail through woods behind Ma'am's back garden that led to the tobacco fields. Pa answered every question Easter asked about the work he had to do there.

That woman in the red dress was a sneaky liar. She was *"that old serpent, called the Devil, and Satan, which deceiveth the whole world . . ."* Warned by Ma'am, Easter guarded night and day against a glimpse of any such person. In her whole life, though, Easter never did see that lady dressed all in red silk. Easter knew nothing about her. She only knew about the angels.

She didn't *see* them, either, just felt touches like feathers in the air—two or three angels, rarely more—or heard sounds like birds taking off, a flutter of wings. The angels spoke to her, once in a while, in whispering soft harmony. They never said anything bad, just helpful little things. Watch out, Easter—gon' rain cats and dogs once that cloud there starts looking purplish. Your folks sure would appreciate a little while by theyself in the house. Why not be nice? Ma'am's worried sick about Pa over in Greenville, with those white folks, so you'd do best to keep your voice down, and tiptoe extra quiet, else you 'bout to get slapped into tomorrow. And, Easter, don't tell nobody, all right? Let's us just be secret friends.

All right, Easter said. The angels were nice, anyway, and it felt good keeping them to herself, having a secret. No need to tell anybody. Or just Brother, when he came out the woods to play with her in the front yard, or when Ma'am let her go walking in the deep woods with him. But in those days Brother used to wander far and wide, and was gone from home far more often than he was around.

The tobacco fields were *full* of angels.

Ever run, some time, straight through a flock of grounded birds, and ten thousand wings just rushed up flapping into the air all around you? In the tobacco fields it was like that. And every angel there *stayed* busy, so the tobacco leaves grew huge and whole, untroubled by flea-beetles or cutworms, weeds or weather. But the angels didn't do *all* the work.

Pa and a friend of his from St. Louis days, Señor, dug up the whole south field every spring, mounding up little knee-high hills all over it. Then they had to transplant each and every little tabacky plant from the flat dirt in the north field to a hill down south. It was backbreaking work, all May long, from sunup to sundown. Afterwards, Pa and Señor had only small jobs, until now—time to cut the leaves, hang and cure them in the barn. Señor had taught Pa everything there was to know about choosing which leaf when, and how to roll the excellent *criollito* tabacky into the world's best cigars. What they got out of one field sold plenty well enough to white folks over in Greenville to keep two families in good clothes, ample food, and some comforts.

A grandfather oaktree grew between the fields, south and north. Pa agreed with Easter. "That big ole thing *is* in the way, ain't it? But your brother always used to say, *Don't you never, never cut down that tree, Wilbur.* And it do make a nice shady spot to rest, anyway. Why don't you go set over there for a while, baby child?"

Easter knew Pa thought she must be worn out and sorry she'd come, just watching him stoop for leaves, whack them off the plant with his knife, and lay them out in the sun. But Easter loved watching him work, loved to follow and listen to him wisely going on about why this, why that.

Pa, though, put a hand on her back and kind of scootched her on her way over toward the tree, so Easter went. Pa and Señor began to chant some work song in Spanish. *Iyá oñió oñí abbé . . .*

Once in the oaktree's deep shade, there was a fascinating discovery round the north side of the big trunk. Not to see, or to touch—or know in any way Easter had a name for—but she could *feel* the exact shape of what hovered in the air. And this whirligig thing'um, right here, was exactly what kept all the angels hereabouts leashed, year after year, to chase away pests, bring up water from deep underground when too little rain fell, or dry the extra drops in thin air when it rained too much. And she could tell somebody had jiggered this thing together who hardly knew what they were doing. It wasn't but a blown breath or rough touch from being knocked down.

Seeing how rickety the little angel-engine was, Easter wondered if she couldn't do better. Pa and Señor did work *awful* hard every May shoveling dirt to make those hills, and now in August they had to come every day to cut whichever leaves had grown big enough. Seemed like the angels could just do *everything . . .*

"You all right over there, baby girl?" Pa called. Dripping sweat in the glare, he wiped a sleeve across his brow. "Need me to take you back to the house?"

"I'm all right," Easter shouted back. "I want to stay, Pa!" She waved, and he stooped down again, cutting leaves. See there? Working so hard! She could *help* if she just knocked this rickety old thing down, and put it back together better. Right on the point of doing so, she got one sharp pinch from her conscience.

Every time Easter got ready to do something bad there was a moment beforehand when a little bitty voice—one lonely angel, maybe—would whisper to her. *Aw, Easter. You know good and well you shouldn't.* Nearly always she listened to this voice. After today and much too late, she *always* would.

But sometimes you just do bad, anyhow.

Easter picked a scab off her knee and one fat drop welled from the pale tender scar underneath. She dabbed a finger in it, and touched the bloody tip to the ground.

The angel-engine fell to pieces. Screaming and wild, the angels scattered every which way. Easter called and begged, but she could no more get the angels back in order than she could have grabbed hold of a mighty river's gush.

And the tobacco field . . . !

Ice frosted the ground, the leaves, the plants, and then melted under sun beating down hotter than summer's worst. The blazing blue sky went cloudy and dark, and boiling low clouds spat frozen pellets, some so big they drew blood and raised knots. Millions of little noises, little motions, each by itself too small to see or hear, clumped into one thick sound like God's two hands rubbing together, and just as gusts of wind stroke the green forest top, making the leaves of the trees all flip and tremble, there was a unified rippling from one end of the tobacco field to the other. Not caused by hands, though, nor by the wind—by busy worms, a billion hungry worms. Grayish, from maggot-size to stubby snakes, these worms ate the tobacco leaves with savage appetite. While the worms feasted, dusty cloud after dusty cloud of moths fluttered up from the disappearing leaves, all hail-torn and frost-blackened, half and then wholly eaten.

In the twinkling of an eye, the lush north field was stripped bare. Nothing was left but naked leaf veins poking spinily from upright woody stems—not a shred of green leaf anywhere. But one year's crop was nothing to the angels' hunger. They were owed *much* more for so many years' hard labor. Amidst the starving angels, Pa and Señor stood dazed in the sudden wasteland of their tobacco field. All the sweet living blood of either this man or the other would just about top off the angels' thirsty cup.

Easter screamed. She called for some help to come—any help at all.

And help *did* come. A second of time split in half and someone came walking up the break.

. . .

Like the way you and Soubrette work on all that book learning together. Same as that. You *gotta* know your letters, *gotta* know your numbers, for some things, or you just can't rightly take part. Say, for instance, you had some rich colored man, and say this fellow was *very* rich indeed. But let's say he didn't know his numbers at all. Couldn't even count his own fingers up to five. Now, he ain't a bad man, Easter, and he ain't stupid either, really. It's just that nobody ever taught numbering to him. So, one day this rich man takes a notion to head over to the bank, and put his money into markets and bonds, and what have you. Now let me ask you, Easter. What you think gon' happen to this colored man's big ole stack of money, once he walks up in that white man's bank, and gets to talking with the grinning fellow behind the counter? *You* tell me. I wanna hear what you say.

Ma'am. The white man's gonna see that colored man can't count, Ma'am, and cheat him out of all his money.

That's *right* he is, Easter! And I *promise you* it ain't no other outcome! Walk up in that bank just as rich as you please—but you gon' walk out with no shoes, and *owing* the shirt on your back! Old Africa magic's the same way, but *worse*, Easter, cause it ain't money we got, me and you—all my babies had—and my own mama, and the grandfather they brung over on the slave ship. It's *life*. It's life and death, not money. Not play-stuff. But, listen here—we don't know our numbers no more, Easter. See what I'm saying? That oldtime wisdom from over there, what we used to know in the Africa land, is all gone now. And, Easter, you just *can't* walk up into the spirits' bank not knowing your numbers. You *rich*, girl. You got gold in your pockets, and I *know* it's burning a hole. I know cause it burnt me, it burnt your brother. But I pray you listen to me, baby child, when I say—you walk up in that bank, they gon' take a *heap* whole lot more than just your money.

• • •

Nothing moved. Pa and Señor stood frozen, the angels hovering just before the pounce. Birds in the sky hung there, mid-wingbeat, and even a blade of grass in the breath of the wind leaned motionless, without shivering. Nothing moved. Or just one thing did—a man some long way off, come walking this way toward Easter. He was *miles* off, or much farther than that, but every step of his approach crossed a strange distance. He bestrode the stillness of the world and stood before her in no time.

In the kindest voice, he said, "You need some help, baby child?"

Trembling, Easter nodded her head.

He sat right down. "Let us just set here for a while, then"—the man patted the ground beside him—"and make us a *deal*."

He was a white man tanned reddish from too much sun, or he could've had something in him maybe—been mixed up with colored or indian. Hair would've told the story, but that hid under the gray kepi of a Johnny Reb. He wore that whole uniform in fact, a filthy kerchief of Old Dixie tied around his neck.

Easter sat. "Can you help my Pa and Señor, Mister? The angels about to eat 'em up!"

"Oh, don't you *worry* none about that!" the man cried, warmly reassuring. "I can help you, Easter, I most certainly can. But"—he turned up a long forefinger, in gentle warning—"*not* for free."

Easter opened her mouth.

"*Ot!*" The man interrupted, waving the finger. "Easter, Easter, Easter . . ." He shook his head sadly. "Now why you wanna hurt my feelings and say you ain't got no money? Girl, you know I don't want no trifling little money. You know *just* what I want."

Easter closed her mouth. He wanted blood. He wanted life. And not a little drop or two, either—or the life of some chicken, mule, or cow. She glanced at the field of hovering angels. They were owed the precious life of one man, woman, or child. How much would *he* want to stop them?

The man held up two fingers. "That's all. And you get to pick the two. It don't have to be your Pa and Señor at all. It could be any old body." He waved a hand outwards to the world at large. "Couple folk you ain't even met, Easter, somewhere far away. That'd be just fine with me."

Easter hardly fixed her mouth to answer before that still small voice spoke up. *You can't do that. Everybody is somebody's friend, somebody's Pa, somebody's baby. It'd be plain dead wrong, Easter.* This voice never said one word she didn't already know, and never said anything but the God's honest truth. No matter what, Easter *wasn't* going against it, ever again.

The man made a sour little face to himself. "Tell you what then," he said. "Here's what we'll do. Right now, today, I'll call off the angels, how about that? And then you can pay me what you owe by and by. Do you know what the word *currency* means, Easter?"

Easter shook her head.

"It means the *way* you pay. Now, the *amount*, which is the worth of two lives, stays exactly the same. But you don't have to pay in blood, in life, if you just change the *currency*, see? There's a lot you don't know right now, Easter, but with some time, you might could learn something useful. So let me help out Señor and your Pa today, and then me and you, we'll settle up later on after while. Now when you wanna do the settling up?"

Mostly, Easter had understood the word "later"—a *sweet* word! She really wouldn't have minded some advice concerning the rest of what he'd said, but the little voice inside couldn't tell her things she didn't already know. Easter was six years old, and double that would make *twelve.* Surely that was an eternal postponement, nearabout. So far away it could hardly be expected to arrive. "When I'm twelve," Easter said, feeling tricky and sly.

"All right," the man said. He nodded once, sharply, as folks do when the deal is hard but fair. "Let's shake on it."

Though she was just a little girl, and the man all grown up, they shook hands. And the angels mellowed in the field, becoming like those she'd always known, mild and toothless, needing permission even to sweep a dusty floor, much less eat a man alive.

"I'll be going now, Easter." The man waved toward the field, where time stood still. "They'll all wake up just as soon as I'm gone." He began to get up.

Easter grabbed the man's sleeve. "Wait!" She pointed at the ruins of two families' livelihood. "What about the *tabacky*? We need it to live on!"

The man looked where Easter gestured, the field with no green whatsoever, and thoughtfully pursed his lips. "Well, as you can see, *this* year's tabacky is all dead and gone now. 'Tain't nothing to do about that. But I reckon I could set the angels back where they was, so as *next* year—and on after that—the tabacky will grow up fine. Want me to do that, Easter?"

"*Yes!*"

The man cocked his head and widened his eyes, taking an attitude of the greatest concern. "Now you *show*, Easter?" he asked. "Cause that's extry on what you already owe."

So cautioning was his tone, even a wildly desperate little girl must think twice. Easter chewed on her bottom lip. "How much extra?" she said at last.

The man's expression went flat and mean. "*Triple*," he said. "And triple that again, and might as well take that whole thing right there, and triple it about ten more times." Now the very nice face came back. "But what you gon' do, baby girl?

You messed up your Pa's tabacky field. *Gotta* fix it." He shrugged in deepest sympathy. "*You* know how to do that?"

Easter had to shake her head.

"Want *me* to then?"

Easter hesitated . . . and then nodded. They shook on it.

The man snapped his fingers. From all directions came the sounds and sensations of angels flocking back to their old positions. The man stood and brushed off the seat of his gray wool trousers.

Easter looked up at him. "Who are you, Mister? Your name, I mean."

The man smiled down. "How 'bout you just call me the banker," he said. "Cause—*whew*, baby girl—you owe me a lot! Now I'll be seeing you after while, you hear?" The man became his own shadow, and in just the way that a lamp turned up bright makes the darkness sharpen and flee, his shadow thinned out along the ground, raced away, and vanished.

"*¡Madre de Díos!*" Señor said, looking around at the field that had been all lush and full-grown a moment ago. He and Pa awakened to a desolation, without one remnant of the season's crop. With winces, they felt at their heads, all cut and bruised from hailstones. Pa spun around then, to look at Easter, and she burst into tears.

These tears lasted a while.

Pa gathered her up in his arms and rushed her back to the house, but neither could Ma'am get any sense from Easter. After many hours she fell asleep, still crying, and woke after nightfall on her mother's lap. In darkness, Ma'am sat on the porch, rocking in her chair. When she felt Easter move, Ma'am helped her sit up, and said, "Won't you tell me what happened, baby child?" Easter *tried* to answer, but horror filled up her mouth and came pouring out as sobs. Just to speak about meeting that strange man was to cry with all the strength in her body. God's grace had surely kept her safe in that man's presence, but the power and the glory no longer stood between her and the revelation of something unspeakable. Even the memory was too terrible. Easter had a kind of fit and threw up what little was in her belly. Once more she wept to passing out.

Ma'am didn't ask again. She and Pa left the matter alone. A hard, scuffling year followed, without the money from the cigars, and only the very last few coins from the St. Louis gold to get them through.

He was the Devil, Easter decided, and swallowed the wild tears. She decided to grow wise in her way as Pa was about tobacco, though there was nobody to teach her. The Devil wouldn't face a fool next time.

1908

The mob went up and down Washington Street, breaking storefront windows, ransacking and setting all the black-owned businesses on fire. Bunch of white men shot up a barbershop and then dragged out the body of the owner, Scott Burton, to string up from a nearby tree. After that, they headed over to the residential neighborhood called the Badlands, where black folks paid high rent for slum housing. Some 12,000 whites gathered to watch the houses burn.

—Dad

1877 August 24

At the church, the Ladies' Missionary Society and their daughters began to gather early before service. The morning was gray and muggy, not hot at all, and the scent of roses, as sweet and spoiled as wine, soaked the soft air. "Easter, you go right ahead and cut some for the tables," Mrs. Toussaint said, while they walked over to the church. "Any that you see, still nice and red." She and Soubrette carried two big pans of *jambalaya rouge*. Easter carried the flower vases. Rosebushes taller than a man grew in front of every house on the Drive, and were all heavily blooming with summer's doomed roses. Yet Easter could only stop here and there and clip one with the scissors Mrs. Toussaint had given her, since most flowers had rotted deeply burgundy or darker, long past their prime.

With more effort than anybody could calculate, the earth every year brought forth these flowers, and then every year all the roses died. "What's wrong, Easter?" Soubrette said.

"Aw, it's nothing." Easter squeezed with her good hand, bracing the scissors against the heel of her ruint one. "I'm just thinking, is all." She put the thorny clipping into a vase and made herself smile.

At the church there were trestles to set up, wide boards to lay across them, tablecloths, flower vases, an immense supper and many desserts to arrange sensibly. *And my goodness, didn't anybody remember a lifter for the pie . . . ? Girls—you run on back up to the house and bring both of mine . . .*

She and Soubrette were laying out the serving spoons when Easter saw her parents coming round Rosetree Drive in the wagon. Back when the Mack family had first come to Rosetree, before Easter's first birthday, all the white folks hadn't moved to Greenville yet. And in those days Ma'am, Pa, and her brother still had "six fat pocketfuls" of the gold from St. Louis, so they could have bought one of the best houses on the Drive. But they'd decided to live in the backwoods outside of town instead (on account of the old Africa magic, as Easter well knew, although telling the story Ma'am and Pa never gave the reason). Pa unloaded a big pot from the wagon bed, and a stack of cloth-covered bread. Ma'am anxiously checked Easter over head to toe—shoes blacked and spotless, dress pressed and stiffly starched, and she laid her palm very lightly against Easter's hair. "Not troubled at all, are you?"

"No, Ma'am."

"Don't really know *what's* got me so wrought up," Ma'am said. "I just felt like I needed to get my eyes on you—*see* you. But don't you look nice!" The worry left Ma'am's face. "And I declare, Octavia can do *better* by that head than your own mama." Ma'am fussed a little with the ribbon in Easter's hair, and then went to help Mrs. Toussaint, slicing the cakes.

Across the table, Mrs. Freeman said, "I do *not* care for the look of these clouds." And Mrs. Freeman frowned, shaking her head at the gray skies. "No, I surely don't."

Won't a drop fall today, the angels whispered in Easter's ear. *Sure 'nough rain hard tomorrow, though.*

Easter smiled over the table. "Oh, don't you worry, Mrs. Freeman." And with supernatural confidence, she said, "It ain't gon' rain today."

The way the heavyset matron looked across the table at Easter, well, anybody would call that *scared*, and Mrs. Freeman shifted further on down the table to where other ladies lifted potlids to stir contents, and secured the bread baskets with linen napkins. It made Easter feel so bad. She felt like the last smudge of filth when everything else is just spic-and-span. Soubrette bumped her. "Take one of these, Easter, will you?" Three vases full of flowers were too many for one person to hold. "Maman said to put some water in them so the roses stay fresh." Together they went round the side of the church to the well.

When they'd come back, more and more men, old folks, and children were arriving. The Missionary ladies argued among themselves over who must miss service, and stay outside to watch over supper and shoo flies and what have you. Mrs. Turner said that she would, *just to hush up the rest of you.* Then somebody caught sight of the visiting preacher, Wandering Bishop Fitzgerald James, come down the steps of the mayor's house with his cane.

1863

So that riot started off in protest of the draft, but it soon became a murder spree, with white men killing every black man, woman, or child who crossed their path. They burned down churches, businesses, the homes of abolitionists, and anywhere else black people were known to congregate, work, or live—even the Colored Orphan Asylum, for example, which was in Midtown back then. Altogether, at least a hundred people were killed by whites. And there's plenty more of these stories over the years, plenty more. Maybe you ought to consider Rosetree. That there's a story like you wouldn't believe.

—Dad

Eyes closed, sitting in the big fancy chair, Wandering Bishop Fitzgerald James seemed to sleep while Pastor Daniels welcomed him and led the church to say *amen*. So skinny, so old, he looked barely there. But his suit was very fine indeed, and when the Wandering Bishop got up to preach, his voice was huge.

He began in measured tones, though soon he was calling on the church in a musical chant, one hard breath out—*huh!*—punctuating each four beat line. At last the Wandering Bishop sang, his baritone rich and beautiful, and his sermon, *this one*, a capstone experience of Easter's life. Men danced, women lifted up their hands and wept. Young girls cried out as loudly as their parents. When the plate came around, Pa put in a whole silver dollar, and then Ma'am nudged him, so he added another.

After the benediction, Ma'am and Pa joined the excited crowd going up front to shake hands with the visiting preacher. They'd known Wandering Bishop Fitzgerald James back before the war, when he sometimes came to Heavenly Home and preached for the coloreds—always a highlight! A white-haired mulatto, the Wandering Bishop moved with that insect-like stiffness peculiar to scrawny old men. Easter saw that his suit's plush lapels were velvet, his thin silk necktie cherry red.

"Oh, I remember you—sure do. Such a pretty gal! Ole Marster MacDougal always used to say, *Now, Fitzy, you ain't to touch a hair on the head of that one, hear me,* boy?" The Wandering Bishop wheezed and cackled. Then he peered around, as if for small children running underfoot. "But where them little yeller babies at?" he said. "Had you a whole mess of 'em, as I recall."

Joy wrung from her face until Ma'am had only the weight of cares, and politeness, left. "A lovely sermon," she murmured. "Good day to you, Bishop." Pa's forearm came up under her trembling hand and Ma'am leaned on him. Easter followed her parents away, and they joined the spill of the congregation out onto the town green for supper. Pa had said that Easter just had a way with some onions, smoked hock, and beans, and would she please fix up a big pot for him. Hearing Pa say so had felt very fine, and Easter had answered, "Yes, sir, I sure will!" Even offered a feast, half the time Pa only wanted some beans and bread, anyhow. He put nothing else on his plate this Sunday too.

The clouds had stayed up high, behaving themselves, and in fact the creamy white overcast, cool and not too bright, was more comfortable than a raw blue sky would have been. Men had gotten the green all spruced up nice, the animals pent away, all the patties and whatnot cleaned up. They'd also finally gotten around to chopping down the old lightning-split, half-rotten crabapple tree in the middle of the green. A big axe still stuck upright from the pale and naked stump. Close by there, Soubrette, Mrs. Toussaint, and her longtime gentleman friend, Señor Tomás, had spread a couple blankets. They waved and called, *Hey, Macks!*, heavy plates of food in their laps. Easter followed Ma'am and Pa across the crowded green.

Pa made nice Frenchy noises at Miss and Mrs. Toussaint, and then took off lickety-split with Señor, gabbling in Spanish. Ma'am sat down next to Mrs. Toussaint and they leaned together, speaking softly. "What did you think of the Wandering Bishop?" Easter asked Soubrette. "Did you care for the sermon?"

"Well . . ." Soubrette dabbed a fingerful of biscuit in some gravy pooled on Easter's plate. "He had a *beautiful* way of preaching, sure enough." Soubrette looked right and left at the nearby grown-ups, then glanced meaningfully at Easter—who leaned in close enough for whispers.

Señor, the Macks, and the Toussaints always sat on the same pew at church, had dinner back and forth at one another's houses, and generally just hung together as thick as thieves. Scandal clung to them both, one family said to work roots and who knew what all kind of devilment. And the other family . . . well, back east Mrs. Toussaint had done *some* kind of work in La Nouvelle-Orléans, and Easter knew only that rumor of it made the good church ladies purse their lips, take their husbands' elbows, and hustle the men right along—*no* lingering near Mrs. Toussaint. These were the times Easter felt the missing spot in the Mack family worst. There was no one to ask, "What's a *hussycat*?" The question, she felt, would hurt Soubrette, earn a slap from Ma'am, and make Pa say, shocked, "Aw, Easter— what you asking *that* for? Let it alone!" His disappointment was always somehow worse than a slap.

Brother, she knew, would have just told her.

The youngest Crombie boy, William, came walking by slowly, carrying his grandmother's plate while she clutched his shoulder. The old lady shrieked.

"*Ha' mercy*," cried Old Mrs. Crombie. "The sweet blessèd Jesus!" She let go of her grandson's shoulder, to flap a hand in the air. "Ain't *nothing* but a witch over here! I ain't smelt devilry this bad since slavery days, at that root-working Bob Allow's dirty cabin. Them old Africa demons just *nasty* in the air. Who is it?" Old Mrs. Crombie peered around with cloudy blue eyes as if a witch's wickedness could be seen even by the sightless. "Somebody *right* here been chatting with Ole Crook Foot, and I know it like I know my own name. Who?"

Easter about peed herself she was that scared. Rude and bossy, as she'd never spoken to the angels before, she whispered, "Y'all *get*," and the four or five hovering scattered away. Ma'am heard that whisper, though, and looked sharply at Easter.

"Who there, Willie?" Old Mrs. Crombie asked her grandson. "Is it them dadburn Macks?"

"Yes'm," said the boy. "But, Granny, don't you want your supper—?"

"Hush up!" Old Mrs. Crombie blindly pointed a finger at the Macks and Toussaints—catching Easter dead in its sights. "*All Saturday long* these Macks wanna dance with the Devil, and then come set up in the Lord's house on Sunday. Well, no! Might got the *rest* of you around here too scared to speak up, but *me*, I'ma go ahead say it. '*Be vigilant*,' says the Book! '*For your adversary walks about like a roaring lion.*' The King of Babylon! The Father of Lies!"

And what were they supposed to do? Knock an old lady down in front of everybody? Get up and run in their Sunday clothes, saying *excuse me, excuse me,* all the way to edge of the green, with the whole world sitting there watching? Better just to stay put, and hope like a sudden hard downpour this would all be over soon, no harm done. Ma'am grabbed Willie down beside her, said something to him, and sent the boy scurrying off for reinforcements.

"And Mister Light-Bright, with the red beard and spots on his face, always smirking—oh, I know *just* what that one was up to! Think folk around here don't know about St. Louis? Everybody know! *The Devil walked abroad in St. Louis.* And that bushwhacked Confederate gold, we all know just how you got it. Them devilhainted tabacky fields *too*—growing all outta season, like this some doggone Virginia. This ain't no Virginia out here! Well, where he been at, all these last years? Reaped the whirlwind is what I'm guessing. Got himself strick down by the Lord, huh? *Bet* he did."

Preacherly and loud, Old Mrs. Crombie had the families within earshot anything but indifferent to her testimony. But no matter the eyes, the ears, and all the grownfolk, Easter didn't care to hear any evil said of Brother. She had to speak up. "Ma'am, my brother was good and kind. He was the *last* one to do anybody wrong."

"And here come the *daughter* now," shouted Old Mrs. Crombie. "Her brother blinded my eyes when I prayed the Holy Ghost against them. Well, let's see what *this* one gon' do! Strike me dumb? Ain't no matter—'til then, I'ma be steady testifying. I'ma keep *on* telling the Lord's truth. Hallelujah!"

At last the son showed up. "Mama?" Mr. Crombie took firm hold of his mother's arm. "You just come along now, Mama. Will you let hungry folk eat they dinner in peace?" He shot them a look, very sorry and all-run-ragged. Ma'am pursed her lips in sympathy and waved a hand, *it's all right.*

"Don't worry none about us," Pa said. "Just see to your Ma." He spoke in his voice for hurt animals and children.

"Charleston?" Old Mrs. Crombie said timidly, the fire and brimstone all gone. "That you?"

"Oh, Mama. Charlie *been* dead. White folk hung him back in Richmond, remember? This *Nathaniel.*"

Old Mrs. Crombie grunted as if taking a punch—denied the best child in favor of this least and unwanted. "Oh," she said, "Nathaniel."

"Now y'all know she old," Mr. Crombie raised his voice for the benefit of all those thereabouts. "Don't go setting too much store by every little thing some old lady just half in her right mind wanna say."

Old Mrs. Crombie, muttering, let herself be led away.

Ma'am stood up, and smiled around at Pa, Mrs. Toussaint, Señor, Soubrette. "Everybody excuse us, please? Me and Easter need to go have us a chat up at the church. No, Wilbur, that's all right." She waved Pa back down. "It ain't nothing but a little lady-business me and the baby need to see to, alone." When one Mack spoke with head tilted just so, kind of staring at the other one, carefully saying each word, whatever else was being said it really meant *old Africa magic.* Pa sat down. "And don't y'all wait, you hear? We might be a little while talking. *Girl.*" Ma'am held out a hand.

Hand in hand, Ma'am led Easter across the crowded green, across the rutted dirt of the Drive, and up the church steps.

"Baby child," Ma'am said. When Easter looked up from her feet, Ma'am's eyes weren't angry at all but sad. "If I *don't* speak, my babies die," she said. "And If I *do,* they catch a fever from what they learn, take up with it, and die anyhow." As if Jesus hid in some corner, Ma'am looked all around the empty church. The pews and sanctuary upfront, the winter stove in the middle, wood storage closet in back. "Oh, Lord, is there any right way to do this?" She sat Easter at the pew across from the wood-burning stove, and sat herself. "Well, I'm just gon' to *tell* you, Easter, and tell everything I know. It's plain to see that keeping you in the dark won't help nothing. This here's what *my* mama told me. When . . ."

• • •

. . . they grabbed *her* pa, over across in Africa land, he got *bad* hurt. It was smooth on top of his head right here (*Ma'am lay a hand on the crown of her head, the left side*) and all down the middle of the bare spot was knotted up, nasty skin where they'd cut him terrible. And *there,* right in the worst of the scar was a—*notch?* Something like a deep dent in the bone. You could take the tip of your finger, rest it on the skin there, and feel it give, feel no bone, just softness underneath . . .

So, you knew him, Ma'am?

Oh, no. My mama had me old or older than I had *you,* child, so the grandfolk was dead and gone *quite* a ways before I showed up. Never did meet him. Well . . .

not to meet in the flesh, I never did. Not alive, like you mean it. But that's a whole *'nother* story, and don't matter none for what I'm telling you now. The thing I want you to see is how the old knowing, from grandfolk to youngfolk, got broke up into pieces, so in these late days I got nothing left to teach my baby girl. Nothing except, *Let that old Africa magic alone.* Now *he,* your great-grandpa, used to oftentimes get down at night like a dog and run around in the dark, and then come on back from the woods before morning, a man again. Might of brought my grandmama a rabbit, some little deer, or just anything he might catch in the night. Anybody sick or lame, or haunted by spirits, *you* know the ones I mean—folk sunk down and sad all the time, or just always *angry,* or the people plain out they right mind—he could reach out his hand and brush the trouble off them, easy as I pick some lint out your hair. And a very fine-looking man he was too, tall as anything and just . . . sweet-natured, I guess you could say. *Pleasant.* So all the womenfolk loved him. But here's the thing of it. Because of that hurt on his head, Easter—because of *that*—he was simple. About the only English he ever spoke was *Yeah, mars.* And most of the time, things coming out his mouth in the old Africa talk didn't make no sense, either. But even hurt and simple and without his good sense, he *still* knew exactly what he was doing. Could get down a dog, and get right back up again being people, being a man, come morning—whenever he felt like it. *We can't, Easter.* Like I told you, like I told your brother. All us coming after, it's just the one way if we get down on four feet. Not *never* getting up no more. That's the way I lost *three* of mine! No. Hush. Set still there and leave me be a minute . . . So these little bits and pieces I'm telling you right now is every single thing I got from my mama. All *she* got out of your great-grand and the old folk who knew him from back over there. Probably you want to know where the right roots at for this, for that, for everything. Which strong words to say? What's the best time of day, and proper season? Why the moon pull so funny, and the rain feel so sweet and mean some particular thing but you can't say what? *Teach me, Ma'am,* your heart must be saying. But I can't, Easter, cause it's gone. Gone for good. They drove us off the path into a wild night, and when morning came we were too turned around, too far from where we started, to *ever* find our way again. Do you think I was my mama's onliest? I wasn't, Easter. Far from it. Same as you ain't *my* only child. I'm just the one that *lived.* The one that didn't mess around. One older sister, and one younger, I saw them both die *awful,* Easter. And all your sisters, and your brothers . . .

• • •

Easter stood looking through the open doors of the church on a view of cloudy sky and the town green. The creamy brightness of early afternoon had given way to ashen gray, and the supper crowd was thinning out though many still lingered. Arm dangling, Ma'am leaned over the back of the pew and watched the sky, allowing some peace and quiet for Easter to think.

And for her part Easter knew she'd learned plenty today from Ma'am about why and where and who, but that she herself certainly understood more about *how.* In fact Easter was sure of that. She didn't like having more knowledge than her mother. The thought frightened her. And yet, Ma'am had never faced down and tricked the Devil, had she?

"Oh, Easter . . ." Ma'am turned abruptly on the pew ". . . I clean forgot to tell you, and your Pa *asked* me to! A bear or mountain lion—*something*—was in the yard last night. The dog got scratched up pretty bad chasing it off. Durn dog wouldn't come close, and let me have a proper look-see . . ."

Sometimes Ma'am spoke so coldly of Brother that Easter couldn't *stand* it. Anxiously she said, "Is he hurt bad?"

"Well, not so bad he couldn't run and hide as good as always. But something took a mean swipe across the side of him, and them cuts weren't pretty to see. *Must of* been a bear. I can't see what else could of gave that dog, big as he is, such a hard time. The *barking* and *racket*, last night! You would of thought the Devil himself was out there in the yard! But, Easter, set down here. Your mama wants you to set down right here with me now for a minute."

Folks took this tone, so gently taking your hand, only when about to deliver the worst news. Easter tried to brace herself. Just now, she'd seen everybody out on the green. So who could have died?

"I know you loved that mean old bird," Ma'am said. "*Heaven* knows why. But the thing in the yard last night broke open the coop, and got in with the chickens. The funniest thing . . ." Ma'am shook her head in wonder. "It didn't touch *nah* bird except Sadie." Ma'am hugged Easter to her side, eyes full of concern. "But, Easter—I'm sorry—it tore old Sadie to *pieces*."

Easter broke free of Ma'am's grasp, stood up, blind for one instant of panic. Then she sat down again, feeling nothing. She felt only tired. "You done told me this, that, and the other thing"—Easter hung her head sleepily, speaking in a dull voice—"but why didn't you never say the one thing I *really* wanted to know?"

"And what's that, baby child?"

Easter looked up, smiled, and said in a brand-new voice, "Who slept on the pull-out cot?"

Her mother hunched over as if socked in the belly. "What?" Ma'am whispered. "What did you just ask me?"

Easter moved over on the pew close enough to lay a kiss in her mother's cheek or lips. This smile tasted richer than cake, and this confidence, just as rich. "Was it Brother Freddie slept on the pull-out cot, Hazel Mae? Was it him?" Easter said, and brushed Ma'am's cheek with gentle fingertips. "Or was it you? Or was it *sometimes* him, and *sometimes* you?"

At that touch, Ma'am had reared back so violently she'd lost her seat—fallen to the floor into the narrow gap between pews.

Feeling almighty, Easter leaned over her mother struggling dazed on the ground, wedged in narrow space. ". . . ooOOoo . . ." Easter whistled in nasty speculation. "Now *here's* what I really want to know. Was it ever *nobody* on that pull-out cot, Hazel Mae? Just nobody atall?"

Ma'am ignored her. She was reaching a hand down into the bosom of her dress, rooting around as if for a hidden dollar bill.

Easter extended middle and forefingers. She made a circle with thumb and index of the other hand, and then vigorously thrust the hoop up and down the upright fingers. "Two peckers and one cunt, Hazel Mae—did *that* ever happen?"

As soon as she saw the strands of old beads, though, yellow-brownish as ancient teeth, which Ma'am pulled up out of her dress, lifted off her neck, the wonderful sureness, this wonderful strength, left Easter. She'd have turned and fled in fact, but could hardly manage to scoot away on the pew, so feeble and stiff and cold her body felt. She spat out hot malice while she could, shouting.

"One, two, three, four!" Easter staggered up from the end of the pew as Ma'am gained her feet. "And we even tricked that clever Freddie of yours, too. Thinking he was *so* smart. Won't *never* do you any good swearing off the old Africa magic, Hazel Mae! Cause just you watch, we gon' get this last one too! *All of yours*—"

Ma'am slung the looped beads around Easter's neck, and falling to her knees she vomited up a vast supper with wrenching violence. When Easter opened her tightly clenched eyes, through blurry tears she saw, shiny and black in the middle of a puddling pink mess, a snake thick as her own arm, *much* longer. She shrieked in terror, kicking backwards on the ground. Faster than anybody could run, the monstrous snake shot off down the aisle between the pews, and out into the gray brightness past the open church doors. Easter looked up and saw Ma'am standing just a few steps away. Her mother seemed more shaken than Easter had ever seen her. "Ma'am?" she said. "I'm scared. What's wrong? I don't feel good. What's this?" Easter began to lift off the strange beads looped so heavily round her neck.

At once Ma'am knelt on the ground beside her. "You just leave those right where they at," she said. "Your great-grand brought these over with him. Don't you *never* take 'em off. Not even to wash up." Ma'am scooped hands under Easter's arms, helping her up to sit at the end of a pew. "Just wait here a minute. Let me go fill the wash bucket with water for this mess. *You* think on what all you got to tell me." Ma'am went out and came back. With a wet rag, she got down on her knees by the reeking puddle. "Well, go on, girl. Tell me. All this about Sadie. It's something to do with the old Africa magic, ain't it?"

• • •

The last angel supped at Easter's hand, half-cut-off, and then lit away. Finally the blood began to gush forth and she swooned.*

*Weird, son. Definitely some disturbing writing in this section. But overarching theme = a people bereft, no? Dispossessed even of cultural patrimony? Might consider then how to represent this in the narrative structure. Maybe just omit how Easter learns to trick the Devil into the chicken? Deny the reader that knowledge as Easter's been denied so much. If you do, leave a paragraph, or even just a sentence, literalizing the "Fragments of History." Terrible title, by the way; reconsider.

—Dad

People presently dwelling in the path of hurricanes, those who lack the recourse of flight, hunker behind fortified windows and hope that this one too shall pass them lightly over. So, for centuries, were the options of the blacks vis-à-vis white rage. Either flee, or pray that the worst might strike elsewhere: once roused, such terror and rapine as whites could wreak would not otherwise be checked. But of course those living in the storm zones know that the big one always does hit sooner or later. And much worse for the blacks of that era, one bad element or many bad influences—"the Devil," as it were—might attract to an individual, a family, or even an entire town, the landfall of a veritable hurricane.

White Devils/Black Devils

Luisa Valéria da Silva y Rodríguez

1877 August 24

There came to the ears of mother and daughter a great noise from out on the green, the people calling one to another in surprise, and then with many horses' hooves and crack upon crack of rifles, the thunder spoke, surely as the thunder had spoken before at Gettysburg or Shiloh. Calls of shock and wonder became now cries of terror and dying. They could hear those alive and afoot run away, and hear the horsemen who pursued them, with many smaller cracks of pistols. *There!* shouted white men to each other, *That one there running!* Some only made grunts of effort, as when a woodsman embeds his axe head and heaves it out of the wood again—such grunts. Phrases or wordless sound, the whiteness could be heard in the voices, essential and unmistakable.

Easter couldn't understand this noise at first, except that she should be afraid. It seemed that from the thunder's first rumble Ma'am grasped the whole of it, as if she had lived through precisely this before and perhaps many times. Clapping a hand over Easter's mouth, Ma'am said, "Hush," and got them both up and climbing over the pews from this one to the one behind, keeping always out of view of the doors. At the back of the church, to the right of the doors, was a closet where men stored the cut wood burned by the stove in winter. In dimness—that closet, *very* tight—they pressed themselves opposite the wall stacked with quartered logs, and squeezed back into the furthest corner. There, with speed and strength, Ma'am unstacked wood, palmed the top of Easter's head, and pressed her down to crouching in the dusty dark. Ma'am put the wood back again until Easter herself didn't know where she was. "You don't *move* from here," Ma'am said. "Don't come at nobody's call but mine." Easter was beyond thought by then, weeping silently since Ma'am had hissed, "*Shut your mouth!*" and shaken her once hard.

Easter nudged aside a log and clutched at the hem of her mother's skirt, but Ma'am pulled free and left her. From the first shot, not a single moment followed free of wails of desperation, or the shriller screams of those shot and bayoneted.

Footfalls, outside—some child running past the church, crying with terror. Easter heard a white man shout, *There go one!* and heard horse's hooves in heavy pursuit down the dirt of the Drive. She learned the noises peculiar to a horseman running down a child. Foreshortened last scream, pop of bones, pulped flesh, laughter from on high. To hear something clearly enough, if it was bad enough, was the same as seeing. Easter bit at her own arm as if that could blunt vision and hearing.

Hey there, baby child, whispered a familiar voice. *Won't you come out from there? I got something real nice for you just outside.* No longer the voice of the kindly spoken Johnny Reb, this was a serpentine lisp—and yet she knew them for one and the same and the Devil. *Yeah, come on out, Easter. Come see what all special I got for you.* Jump up flailing, run away screaming—Easter could think of nothing else, and the last strands of her tolerance and good sense began to fray and snap. That voice went on whispering and Easter choked on sobs, biting at her forearm.

Some girl screamed nearby. It could have been *any* girl in Rosetree, screaming, but the whisperer snickered, *Soubrette. I got her!*

Easter lunged up, and striking aside logs, she fought her way senselessly with scraped knuckles and stubbed toes from the closet, on out of the church into gray daylight.

If when the show has come and gone, not only paper refuse and cast-off food but the whole happy crowd, shot dead, remained behind and littered the grass, then Rosetree's green looked like some fairground, the day after.

Through the bushes next door to the church Easter saw Mr. Henry, woken tardily from a nap, thump with his cane out onto the porch, and from the far side of the house a white man walking shot him dead. Making not even a moan, old Mr. Henry toppled over and his walking stick rolled to the porch's edge and off into the roses. About eight o'clock on the Drive, flames had engulfed the general store so it seemed a giant face of fire, the upstairs windows two dark eyes, and downstairs someone ran out of the flaming mouth. That shadow in the brightness had been Mrs. Toussaint, so slim and short in just such skirts, withering now under a fiery scourge that leapt around her, then up from her when she fell down burning. The Toussaints kept no animals in the lot beside the general store and it was all grown up with tall grass and wildflowers over there. Up from those weeds, a noise of hellish suffering poured from the ground, where some young woman lay unseen and screamed while one white man with dropped pants and white ass out stood afoot in the weeds and laughed, and some other, unseen on the ground, grunted piggishly in between shouted curses. People lay everywhere bloodied and fallen, so many dead, but Easter saw her father somehow alive out on the town green, right in the midst of the bodies just kneeling there in the grass, his head cocked to one side, chin down, as if puzzling over some problem. She ran to him calling *Pa Pa Pa,* but up close she saw a red dribble down his face from the forehead where there was a deep ugly hole. Though they were sad and open his eyes slept, no they were dead. To cry hard enough knocks a body down, and harder still needs both hands flat to the earth to get the grief out.

In the waist-high corn, horses took off galloping at the near end of the Parks' field. At the far end Mrs. Park ran with the baby Gideon Park, Jr., in her arms and the little girl Agnes following behind, head hardly above corn, shouting *Wait Mama wait,* going as fast as her legs could, but just a little girl, about four maybe five. Wholeheartedly wishing they'd make it to the backwood trees all right, Easter could see as plain as day those white men on horses would catch them first. So strenuous were her prayers for Mrs. Park and Agnes, she had to hush up weeping. Then a couple white men caught sight of Easter out on the green, just kneeling there—some strange survivor amidst such thorough and careful murder. With red bayonets, they trotted out on the grass toward her. Easter stood up meaning to say, or even beginning to, polite words about how the white men should leave Rosetree now, about the awful mistake they'd made. But the skinnier man got out in front of the other, *running*, and hauled back with such obvious intent on his rifle with that lengthy knife attached to it, Easter's legs wouldn't hold her. Suddenly kneeling again, she saw her mother standing right next to the crabapple stump. Dress torn, face sooty, in stocking feet, Ma'am got smack in the white men's way. That running man tried to change course but couldn't fast enough. He came full-on into the two-handed stroke of Ma'am's axe.

Swapt clean off, his head went flying, his body dropped straight down. The other one got a hand to his belt and scrabbled for a pistol while Ma'am stepped up and hauled back to come round for his head too. Which one first, then—pistol or axe? He got the gun out and up and shot. Missed, though, even that close, his hand useless as a drunk's, he was so scared. The axe knocked his chest in and him off his feet. Ma'am stomped the body twice getting her axe back out. With one hand she plucked Easter up off the ground to her feet. "*Run, girl!*"

They ran.

They should have gone straight into the woods, but their feet took them onto the familiar trail. Just in the trees' shadows, a big white man looked up grinning from a child small and dead on the ground. He must have caught some flash or glimpse of swinging wet iron because that white man's grin fell off, he loosed an ear-splitting screech, before Ma'am chopped that face and scream in half.

"Rawly?" Out of sight in the trees, some other white man called. "You all right over there, Rawly?" The fallen man, head in halves like the first red slice into a melon, made no answer. Nor was Ma'am's axe wedging out of his spine soon enough. Other white men took up the call of that name, and there was crash and movement in the trees.

Ma'am and Easter ran off the trail the other way. The wrong way again. They should have forgotten house and home and kept on forever into wilderness. Though probably it didn't matter anymore at that point. The others found the body—axe stuck in it—and cared not at all for the sight of a dead white man, or what had killed him. Ma'am and Easter thrashed past branches, crackled and snapped over twigs, and behind them in the tangled brush shouts of pursuit kept on doubling. What sounded like four men clearly had to be at least eight, and then just eight couldn't half account for such noise. Some men ahorse, some with dogs. Pistols and rifles firing blind.

They burst into the yard and ran up to the house. Ma'am slammed the bar onto the door. For a moment, they hunched over trying only to get air enough for life, and then Ma'am went to the wall and snatched off Brother's old Springfield from the war. *Where the durn cartridges at, and the caps, the doggone ramrod . . . ?* Curses and questions, both were plain on Ma'am's face as she looked round the house abruptly disordered and strange by the knock-knock of Death at the door. White men were already in the yard.

The glass fell out of the back window and shattered all over the iron stove. Brother, up on his back legs, barked in the open window, his forepaws on the windowsill.

"Go on, Easter." Ma'am let the rifle fall to the floor. "Never mind what I said before. Just go on with your brother now. I'm paying your way."

Easter was too afraid to say or do or think, and Brother at the back window was just barking and barking. *She was too scared.*

In her meanest voice, Ma'am said, "Take off that dress, Easter Sunday Mack!"

Sobbing breathlessly, Easter could only obey.

"All of it, Easter, take it off. And throw them old nasty beads on the floor!"

Easter did that too, Brother barking madly.

Ma'am said, "Now—"

Rifles stuttered thunderously and the dark wood door of the house lit up, splintering full of holes of daylight. In front of it Ma'am shuddered awfully and hot blood speckled Easter's naked body even where she stood across the room. Ma'am sighed one time, got down gently, and stretched out on the floor. White men stomped onto the porch.

Easter fell, caught herself on her hands, and the bad one went out under her so she smacked down flat on the floor. But effortlessly she bounded up and through the window. Brother was right there when Easter landed badly again. He kept himself to her swift limp as they tore away neck and neck through Ma'am's back garden and on into the woods.*

* *Stop here, with the escape. Or no; I don't know. I wish there were some kind of way to* offer *the reader the epilogue, and yet warn them off too. I know it couldn't be otherwise, but it's just so grim.*

—*Dad*

Epilogue

They were back! Right out there sniffing in the bushes where the rabbits were. Two great *big* ole dogs! About to shout for her husband, Anna Beth remembered he was lying down in the back with one of his headaches. So she took down the Whitworth and loaded it herself. Of course she knew how to fire a rifle, but back in the War Between the States they'd handpicked Michael-Thomas to train the sharpshooters of his brigade, and then given him one of original Southern Crosses, too, for so many Yankees killed. Teary-eyed and squinting from his headaches, he still never missed what he meant to hit. Anna Beth crept back to the bedroom and opened the door a crack.

"You 'wake?" she whispered. "Michael-Thomas?"

Out of the shadows: "Annie?" His voice, breathy with pain. "What is it?"

"I *seen* 'em again! They're right out there in the creepers and bushes by the rabbit burrows."

"You sure, Annie? My head's real bad. Don't go making me get up and it ain't nothing out there again."

"I just now seen 'em, Michael-Thomas. *Big* ole nasty dogs like nothing you ever saw before." Better the little girl voice—that never failed: "Got your Whitworth right here, honey. All loaded up and ret' to go."

Michael-Thomas sighed. "Here I come, then."

The mattress creaked, his cane thumped the floor, and there was a grunt as his bad leg had to take some weight as he rose to standing. (Knee shot off at the Petersburg siege, and not just his knee, either . . .) Michael-Thomas pushed the door wide, his squinting eyes red, pouched under with violet bags. He'd taken off his half-mask, and so Anna Beth felt her stomach lurch and go funny, as usual. Friends at the church, and Mama, and just *everybody* had assured her she would—sooner or later—but Anna Beth never had gotten used to seeing what some chunk of Yankee artillery had done to Michael-Thomas' face. Supposed to still be up *in* there, that chip of metal, under the ruin and crater where his left cheek . . . "Here you go." Anna Beth passed off the Whitworth to him.

Rifle in hand, Michael-Thomas gimped himself over to where she pointed—the open window. There he stood his cane against the wall and laboriously got down kneeling. With practiced grace he lay the rifle across the window sash, nor did he even bother with the telescopic sight at this distance—just a couple hundred yards. He shot, muttering, "Damn! Just *look* at 'em," a moment before he did so. The kick liked to knock him over.

Anna Beth had fingertips jammed in her ears against the report, but it was loud anyhow. Through the window and down the yard she saw the bigger dog, dirty mustard color—had been nosing round in the honeysuckle near the rabbit warren—suddenly drop from view into deep weeds. Looked like the littler one didn't have the sense to dash off into the woods. All while Michael-Thomas reloaded, the other dog nudged its nose downward at the carcass unseen in the weeds, and just looked up and all around, whining—pitiful if it weren't so ugly. Michael-Thomas shot that one too.

"Ah," he said. "Oh." He swapped the Whitworth for his cane, leaving the rifle on the floor under the window. "My head's *killing* me." Michael-Thomas went right on back to the bedroom to lie down again.

He could be relied on to hit just what he aimed for, so Anna Beth didn't fear to see gore-soaked dogs yelping and kicking, only half-dead, out there in the untamed, overgrown end of the yard, should she take a notion to venture out that way for a look-see. Would them dogs be just as big, up close and stone dead, as they'd looked from far off and alive?

But it weren't carcasses nor live dogs, either, back there where the weeds grew thickest. Two dead niggers, naked as sin. Gal with the back of her head blown off, and buck missing his forehead and half his brains too. Anna Beth come running back up to the house, hollering.

KAI ASHANTE WILSON was the 2010 Octavia Butler Scholar at Clarion Writing Workshop in San Diego. He won the Crawford Award for Best First Novel in 2016, and his works have been short-listed for the Hugo, Nebula, Shirley Jackson, Theodore Sturgeon, Locus, and World Fantasy Awards. Most of his stories can be read at *Tor.com*, and the rest at *Fantasy* or in the anthology *Stories for Chip: A Tribute to Samuel R. Delany*. His novellas, *The Sorcerer of the Wildeeps* and *A Taste of Honey*, are available from all fine ebook purveyors. He lives in New York City.

A Short History of the Twentieth Century, or, When You Wish Upon a Star

Kathleen Ann Goonan

1901: H. G. Wells publishes *The First Men in the Moon*. 1912: Wernher von Braun, the first director fo NASA's Marshall Space Flight Center, born. 1950: Carol Elizabeth Hall born. In post-1950s America, a world of war wounds, rocket scientists, and revolution, a girl grows up and goes to the moon. *Edited by Ellen Datlow.*

Tomorrow can be a wonderful age. Our scientists today are opening the doors of the Space Age to achievements that will benefit our children and generations to come. The Tomorrowland attractions have been designed to give you an opportunity to participate in adventures that are a living blueprint of our future.

—Walt Disney

• • •

1901:	Walter Elias Disney born.
	H. G. Wells publishes *The First Men in the Moon*.
1903:	The Wright brothers make first manned flights at Kitty Hawk, North Carolina.
	Konstantin Tsiolkovsky publishes *Exploring Space with Devices*, a seminal technical text of rocketry.
1912:	Wernher von Braun, inventor of the V-2 rocket and first director of NASA, born.
1914–1919:	Robert Goddard granted two US patents for rockets using solid and liquid fuel, and several stages. He fires rockets for US Signal Corps and Army Ordnance at Aberdeen Proving Ground, Maryland.
1920:	Timothy Leary born.
1921:	Chester Thaddeus Hall born.
	June Elizabeth Foster born.
1923:	Hermann Oberth publishes *The Rocket into Interplanetary Space*.
1923:	Wernher von Braun receives a telescope as his first communion present. He begins reading science fiction, including Jules Verne's *From the Earth to the Moon*, and scientific rocket research.
1927:	Society for Space Travel founded in Germany.
1928:	Disney releases *Steamboat Willie*, the world's first sound-synchronized animated film.
	Hermann Oberth is a scientific consultant for Fritz Lang's *Woman in the Moon*. A publicity rocket built by Oberth blows up on the launchpad.

1930:	American Rocket Society founded in New York City.
	Von Braun is an assistant to Willy Ley and Hermann Oberth in launching liquid-fuel rockets.
1930–1935:	Germans, Russians, and Americans launch a variety of experimental rockets.
1936:	California Institute of Technology scientists begin testing rockets near Pasadena, California; this is the precursor of the Jet Propulsion Laboratory.
1937:	Von Braun joins the Nazi party. His rocket group moves to Peenemünde. Goddard's rocket reaches nine thousand feet.
	Leningrad, Moscow, and Kazan chosen as test sites for Russian rockets.
1940:	Disney Studios releases *Fantasia*.
	Von Braun joins the SS.
1942:	Timothy Leary, acquitted via court-martial for behavior infractions at West Point, receives an honorable discharge.
	The US Army moves into Disney's studio, which produces US propaganda films during the war.
1943:	Von Braun begins using concentration-camp prisoners as slave labor at the V-2 Mittelwerk plant. Twenty to thirty thousand slave laborers die of starvation, exhaustion, and summary execution under von Braun's supervision.
	Albert Hofmann discovers the psychoactive properties of LSD.
1944:	Over one thousand V-2 rockets launched against London.
1945:	Joint Intelligence Objectives Agency accepts the surrender of von Braun, Arthur Rudolph, and other important German scientists. American Army transports over one hundred V-2 rockets from Peenemünde and Nordhousen to White Sands, New Mexico. The Nazi past of the German scientists is expunged from their records, clearing their path to US citizenship.
1949:	Sandoz Laboratories brings LSD to United States for use in experimental trials.
1950:	Carol Elizabeth Hall born.
1952:	*Collier's* publishes "Man Will Conquer Space Soon!," von Braun's vision of space exploration and settlement.
July 17, 1955:	Disneyland opens at Anaheim. Ninety million people watch live on television.

• • •

Carol Hall, five years old, is parked in front of the black-and-white television set an hour before the Disneyland grand opening television special is to begin. Chet, her father, a jet-propulsion engineer presently at North American Aviation, had wanted to go to the beach that beautiful Sunday, but when Carol had gotten wind of his plan she had thrown herself on the floor, sobbing, "We'll miss the grand *opening!*"

"How did she hear about this all-consuming event?" Chet asks as he rummages in the icebox for olives. Tall and loose limbed, Chet looks good in a suit and tie. His blond hair is cut in a flattop, his eyes are hazel, and he wears the heavy black glasses of his jet-propulsion-engineer tribe. Just now, he wears khaki slacks, sandals, and a short-sleeved sport shirt with the tail out. The windows of their new ranch house are open, and a breeze flows through the kitchen. From the boomerang pattern of the Formica countertop to the Eames chairs in the living room that they found, astonishingly enough, put out in the trash on Sunset Boulevard, the house and the lives of the Halls lean and yearn toward the sunny future and away from the war, the bomb, sacrifice, and uncertainty.

June says, "I think the olives are behind the milk, honey. They've been talking about the grand opening on the Disney show for months." June's short blond hair falls in soft natural waves around her face. Her eyes are blue, her legs are long, she is tall and beautifully proportioned, and she has a BS in chemical engineering. She and Chet make a nice couple, as they have frequently been told since 1949, when they met and married. She rarely wears her expensive, fashionable suits any longer, but is still a knockout when she does. Carol likes to clunk around in the green snakeskin peep-toed shoes June wore on her honeymoon in Cuba. Now that June is a mother, she mostly wears white Keds.

"You're going to miss it!" yells Carol from the living room.

June and Chet settle on the couch, armed with martinis. Though it's early, they feel fully justified.

Carol has a glass of milk——with a straw in it that makes it taste, distantly, like strawberries—which is getting warm on the coffee table behind her. She sits cross-legged on green wall-to-wall carpeting, coonskin hat jammed over blond braids. She holds her life-sized rubber bowie knife upright, as if she might be a grizzled frontiersman waiting for a slab of bear meat in a backwoods river tavern, or maybe she's planning to stab Mike Fink in the gullet. Her knife has a gray blade and a green handle. She is forbidden to stab things with it, but when she thinks no one is looking she does a lot of stabbing—furniture, walls, dirt, trees—all to no avail, since the blade curls up, but it's still entertaining. She also has a six-shooter cap gun and a holster, but she's only allowed to play with it outside. It makes real smoke and noise.

She jumps up. "Look! There's Walt Disney! He's the train engineer!"

"Yup," says Chet. "A man of many talents." The camera follows a parade down idyllic Main Street. "Oh, boy! It's Yesterdayland! We're back in 1900! No world wars."

"I don't think there's a Yesterdayland," says Carol doubtfully. The camera moves to another live grand opening scene. "Who is that man? He talks funny."

"Why, it's good old Heinz Haber. I met him in Germany and saw him at a seminar just last week. Guess you have to have a German accent to get a job with Disney."

"He's a physicist, isn't he?" asks June.

Chet nods. "Eisenhower asked Disney to do a series about space and science last year. Disney Studios has a good reputation—they made a lot of shows for the army and US Treasury during the war. Not that we don't have brilliant American physicists, but the government is in love with these *Nahzees*." He's pronounced "Nazi" as "Nahzee" ever since he heard it in Churchill's "blood, sweat, and tears" speech. "Oh, that's right—none of them were Nahzees. We went to a lot of trouble to get them. Got to show them off to the Russians, I guess. Grabbed them right under their noses."

June teases, "You're just jealous you're not on TV. All of you at the jet lab and NAA."

"Don't push it, June."

June decides not to—in fact, she's sorry she said a word. Chet had been in the group of Army scientists that tracked down and captured the German scientists (although "captured" is probably not the right word, as the Germans were quite eager to go to America rather than to Russia). When in Germany, Chet saw atrocities that he claimed these German TV scientists knew about, war crimes that they had committed. Technically, he should not even have told her; it was all top secret, completely suppressed by the Office of Strategic Services, which had cleansed their records and made them look as if they were angels.

June takes Chet's hand. "Sorry, honey."

He shrugs. "Oh, anything for a laugh."

Now he'll be broody. Oh, well.

At the entrance of Tomorrowland, Haber holds a Ping-Pong ball, which represents an atom of uranium, delicately between his thumb and forefinger. "These contain energy," he says gravely. In front of him stands a table covered with other "atoms" loaded into mousetraps. His son tosses a Ping-Pong ball into their midst, which starts a chain reaction, a wild flurry of snaps and flying white balls, each of which sets off even more traps. Haber holds up a cardboard picture of an atomic pile, which he says will soon provide us with all the energy we will ever need. We will no longer even need hydroelectric dams. It will all be like magic. "Use it wisely," he admonishes.

This is only a small sample of the show Carol will see on TV a few months later. Ward Kimball, Disney's right-hand man, using a loose style that is new at the studio, is collaborating with Dr. Haber to create "Our Friend the Atom." A towering, threatening genie—atomic energy—will emerge from a bottle, arms crossed, while the skinny, hapless man who released him skitters about on the beach, terrified, until he tricks the genie back into the bottle, ensuring that atomic energy will be used in medical applications and for electrical power. Carol will remember the show her entire life, though after the dark twist, she will not recall it for years. But the dark twist comes later.

"Carol, drink your milk or I'll put it back in the icebox," says her mother.

"It's 1986, where a trip to the moon is an everyday event," announces Art Linkletter ebulliently, as the Rocket to the Moon ride appears on the screen in the world's first glimpse of Tomorrowland. "In Tomorrowland, you can travel to the moon on the Moonliner. The passenger cabin is in the bottom, between the fins, and you can watch the huge top television screen there to see where you're going, and the bottom one to see where you've been."

Danny Thomas and his children, including Marlo, the future *That Girl*, rush with unfeigned eagerness into 1986 (her show will have come and gone by then) and into the Moonliner, welcomed by a shapely stewardess. The ship blasts off, in 1986, and soon the arteries of Anaheim are like tiny diagrams far below.

"Not bad," admits Chet, grudgingly. "Kind of like a bombing run over Germany."

Carol is silent for a few minutes, her eyes wide. Finally she says, "I want to go to the moon."

"So do I. It could be done, but that's not what would really happen. For one thing, that rocket part would fall off after it boosts the capsule out of the atmosphere, and you'd probably need at least three stages. And then—"

"And then you go to the space station on the way! That's what the man said."

"Right. That's Wernher's plan."

"Who's Wernher?"

"A war criminal."

June says, "Oh, honey, just let it be."

"If you'd seen—"

"It's Sunday," she says. "Carol is right here."

He lights a Chesterfield cigarette. Even at this age, Carol knows that it's his favorite brand. "Okay, okay. How about another martini?"

"It's definitely a two-martini show," says June, unwinding her long legs and rising from the couch.

"Chock-full of fun." He glances longingly at Arthur C. Clarke's *Against the Fall of Night*, dog-eared at page ninety-seven, next to him on the end table, but he promised June that he'd watch the show with Carol.

"I want to go to Frontierland, Tomorrowland, and Fantasyland," says Carol.

"Not Adventureland?"

"And Adventureland."

"That Disney is a real moneymaker. Too bad I can't get a job with him. But he's anticomm . . ."

"That's *enough!*" June, who has just returned, slams down Chet's martini on the side table, and it splashes over the edge of the glass. June stalks from the room.

"What's wrong with Mom?"

"Guess she doesn't like Walt Disney." Chet is silent for a moment, then says, "That's not fair, honey. It's my fault. I said something wrong." He follows June.

• • •

Carol closes her eyes for a moment as some boring man talks, seeing four little purple tops spinning through space, a distant Earth behind them, and then the strange, multicolored creatures that live on Mars. Her head is always full of pictures. Right now, she is remembering the *Man in Space* show, in which Wernher von Braun narrates his plan for going into space, and the other shows that are about the moon and Mars. The plan uses a space shuttle and a space station. It is a plan that von Braun has worked on for several decades and published in *Collier's* magazine in 1952. Of course Carol has not read it, but this is its introduction:

> By Dr. Wernher von Braun
> Technical Director, Army Ordnance, Guided Missile Development Group,
> Huntsville, Alabama
> "Scientists and engineers now know how to build a station in space that
> would circle the earth 1,075 miles up. The job would take 10 years and cost

twice as much as the atom bomb. If we do it, we can not only preserve the peace, but we can take a long step toward uniting mankind."

Collier's, March 22, 1952

The US Space Program will manifest the German's plan to the letter, except for actually going to Mars. Perhaps we are not enthused about going once Soviet and US probes show us that Mars is not inhabited by one-eyed creatures, but, at the most, life invisible to the naked eye. What would be the point?

"And now—" says someone on TV.

Carol opens her eyes. Her parents have not returned. She stabs the carpet repeatedly. She stabs her leg. The point of the blade on her thigh makes her taste peanut butter. This doesn't seem strange to her. She runs to the kitchen, climbs onto a stool, and gets the jar from the cupboard.

• • •

A few months later, Chet succumbs, as he must, and they are all at Disneyland. At Tomorrowland, in fact.

"Look, Daddy! It's the Moonliner!" Carol leans forward, pulling on her father's arm relentlessly, until they are right next to it.

"At least it's not a Nahzee rocket," he says, looking at the big red TWA insignia, hands in his pockets. "Except for the fin design."

June takes Carol's hand firmly. "Chet, can't we ever just have some good plain fun?"

"I thought we were."

"You know what I mean. Why does everything have to be such a dark conspiracy?"

"Because it is? Look around! Germans, Germans, everywhere."

"GE? TWA?"

"Volkswagen? Krupp? Von Braun?"

"Chet, much as you despise it, we do live in a capitalistic nation. Maybe it's time you got used to it."

"Maybe it's time the land of the free got used to me."

Carol's mother blinks fast, and her voice is low. "It's marvelous how you take it upon yourself to remind me every single day that just because a man is brilliant does not mean he can get along with people. I mean, it's like you can't be smart and kind at the same time. Maybe you'd explode if you tried. That would be like igniting liquid oxygen. Look! Up in the sky! Is it a bird? Is it a plane? No! It's jet-propelled Chet Hall! Good-bye, Chet! He's off to a perfect world."

"You think that's funny, don't you? I spent the war fighting these monstrous people."

"I know, Chet. Don't raise your voice."

"And now I'm the one who's anti-American! Because I believe in human rights and wasn't afraid to say so!"

Mothers herd their kids past Chet with sidelong glances. An astronaut with a bubble helmet strides toward him. "Now this death-dealing born-again Nahzee is on TV while I may not even be able to support my wife and kid! He's not that smart, June. He's just frigging wily. He follows the money."

"Sir," says the astronaut, "would you mind stepping away from the Moonliner?"

"I sure as hell would mind!" shouts Chet.

When things get heated, it's Carol's cue to step in.

"I want to go to the moon," says Carol. She takes her father's hand. "Daddy, can you please take me to the moon?"

Chet shrugs off the astronaut's tight grip on his shoulder and swoops her up. "Of course, honey. And do me a favor. Always remember that I love you more than anything in the world."

"Even more than the moon? The moon's not in this world, is it?"

"I love you more than anything in the universe. More than anything we know and more than anything we might ever know."

"I love you too, Daddy."

How do kids learn to do this?

Years later, recalling this in the Pacific Coast "encounter group" where she is soon to meet her future husband, Carol remembers sticking out her tongue at the astronaut. At least, she thinks she does.

It sounds good, anyway. It sounds the way one would like to have been.

And something else hits Carol as she poaches in the mud pit in the future (though not as far ahead in the future as the Moonliner). She re-hears those desperate words she heard one night through the air-conditioning vent. Her parents never knew she could hear them.

"June, it's a very good offer."

"In France."

"A lot of women would consider this an adventure. Carol could grow up there."

"And never come back."

"Come on. Of course she could. Your parents would love to visit France. They could even live with us."

"I hate to mention it, but you may have noticed that we don't speak French."

"I don't have to know it for the job, but it would be good to learn."

"You aren't happy here, Chet. I don't think you'd be any happier there."

"I want to be able to support my family. I'm sick and tired of going from job to job."

"Lay it all out for me. Get guarantees from the government. That at least Carol and I can come back any time we want. And, preferably, you too. I want to know exactly how much money you'll make. How long the contract is for. I want paid return tickets in my hand before I uproot my family."

"I don't know if—"

"That's right. You don't know. They may well revoke our passports."

A sigh. "This is a great country, isn't it."

"It's a country, like any other."

"That's not how the story goes. This is an extraordinary country! A magical country!"

"It's rotten to the core in so many ways."

"I can hardly believe my ears! My sweet little wife from Kansas just said—"

"But here, there's the possibility of change. That makes all the difference. People can make changes."

"Without my top-security clearance, I'll never be able to work on what I love. What I was born to do."

"I guess *I* was born to run a vacuum cleaner."

"What do you mean by that?"

"What do you think I mean? If you would help out around here I could get a job."

"A secretarial job."

"A chemistry degree is not nothing, Chet. I might even land a job somewhere else in the country and we could move there. Oh, that's right—I did land a job somewhere else, but you wouldn't leave your precious jet lab."

"Look, maybe they'd help you find a job you really like in France. Let's see about that."

"Would you do that?"

"June? Are you crying?"

"I'm just happy."

"That makes no sense."

"I love you. Even though you're a functional idiot."

• • •

1957

October: Soviets launch Sputnik.

December: US Vanguard rocket burns on launchpad, failing to launch first US satellite.

• • •

One evening when he actually gets home in time for dinner, Chet looks up from his meatloaf and says, "This is an exciting day! Mary Morgan figured out how to fuel von Braun's Jupiter rocket."

"Mary Morgan?"

"You remember—at the picnic? Her husband is the one with the bright red hair. Carol played with their little boy. I don't think Mary finished her degree, but she's pretty damned smart. Von Braun's team was completely baffled so they tossed the job over to North American. Mary's boss was under some pressure because . . ."

"Because Mary's a woman."

"Right. And doesn't have a degree. Had two years of chem engineering, then went to work at Plum Creek making explosives for the war."

June looks keenly at her husband. "Kind of what I did, for GE. Except I finished my degree. Listen, I've been thinking that I might take an evening course at Caltech, if you could watch Carol. I guess I don't have time for a job until she's older." Chet's mother's dark prediction of Carol's utter ruin should June go to work rings in her ears. She thinks it's hogwash, but then again . . .

Chet shovels in a forkful of whipped potatoes, nodding. "Mmm. That's a good idea, except that I have to work late an awful lot. Maybe your sister could watch her?"

Carol remembers the picnic, the little boy, and the man, who smiled at her.

• • •

Wernher von Braun, at a North American Aviation picnic given to celebrate his rare appearance, sees a little girl and boy tossing a ball back and forth under a cottonwood tree. The boy's redheaded father says something to him, and the boy and girl look in von Braun's direction. He smiles and waves. That girl may live on Mars someday, he thinks, as the wife of an engineer. She might live in one of the habitats that he himself designed last month. Maybe it wouldn't be necessary to iron clothes on Mars? The fine-grained future is beginning to come into focus. Maybe they should include Monsanto's Kitchen of the Future, the housewife's dream, in the Mars plan. It would definitely be an attraction for women.

January 1958

Chet, working for the Jet Propulsion Lab, helps design the Jupiter-C rocket that will launch Explorer-1, America's first answer to Sputnik. Chet wrangles passes for his family to view the launch.

They fly to Cape Canaveral, where Chet proudly takes them right up next to the enormous rocket. Mary Sherman Morgan, who had worked at NAA when Chet started there ("But I guess she's retired to have babies, now.") developed the fuel for the Jupiter-C rocket after von Braun's team failed repeatedly. "Mary wanted to name the fuel Bagel, so that we could say that the rocket was fueled by LOX—liquid oxygen—and Bagel, but they have no sense of humor. They're calling it Hydyne."

Chet, June, and Carol are allowed into the launch room, with its fascinating dials, meters, and ongoing technical chatter.

As the ground and room and very air vibrate with the power of ignited Hydyne, the rocket separates from the launchpad, borne on a vast slice of fire that slowly— much too slowly, it seems—rises, then hovers, as if it might subside back onto the launchpad, crumple majestically, and explode on national television. Then, as if waking from a deep sleep, the rocket gains speed and altitude and is gone, leaving a trail of white vapor.

At the Atomic Motel in Cocoa Beach that night, Carol writes in her diary, "My soul vibrated too when the Jupiter-C rose from the launchpad and the scaffold fell away. That is not scientific, but that is how it felt. The rocket was in outer space very quickly. When I said I wanted to go into space, and go to Mars like Dr. von Braun plans, the men who heard me laughed, all except my father. He said, 'Why not?' They did not seem to know why, exactly, but they seemed sure that I just couldn't."

Many years later, Carol reads that when von Braun was asked about women in space, he had responded that 110 pounds of "essential recreational equipment" might eventually be included in spaceflights. Apparently, that too got a big laugh.

1959

During Carol's summer vacation, Chet takes her to the Jet Propulsion Lab at least once a week so she can "see what goes on there." On the weekends, they start building rockets. June is enthused about the idea and spends her days thinking about how to present the material to Carol, how to show her the chemistry in very small steps. She loves gathering odds and ends that they'll need to make the rockets. She begins to think about writing a book for children Carol's age about rockets. The grandparents think they are crazy.

In general, rockets are simple. Fuel in a tube, a hole through which force can be expelled when the fuel is ignited, a fuse by which to ignite the fuel, a nosecone, and a safe place from which to watch.

If you have anything specific in mind—speed, distance, lift, a payload, a target—then rockets are really complicated. The engineer's world is not one of airy speculation. It all comes down to what works: test, refine; test, refine. Endless iterations and interlocking of systems until you have something that works. Every time.

They go to a hobby shop that is full of rocket kits.

Some are intricate models. "It's the Moonliner!" says Carol. "I want that! It's nuclear powered."

Chet and June look at each other. June says, "How about a model of a real rocket? Look! Here's a Jupiter-C, the rocket your father worked on. The one we saw at the Cape."

Chet sees that Carol is torn. Both are equally important to her. "Let's get them both. Imagination is just as important as reality. Now, over here are some rockets we can build and launch ourselves. Just to see what they're like before we start designing our own."

June could swear she sees Chet take a skip or two when he leaves the store with his shopping bag. They spend happy evenings building the models, and after that, the grandparents get into the act, spoiling Carol with new model rockets every week until her collection would be the envy of any boy. In fact, when she takes it to show-and-tell, it is indeed the envy of all the boys and many of the girls.

. . .

Chet takes Carol to the Santa Susana testing grounds in the Simi Valley whenever he has a chance, and twice to White Sands. He and June help lead her well beyond her math homework; they help her to see geometry and mathematics from different perspectives. When her teacher complains that she is asking too many questions and that she is getting too far ahead, they take her out of public school and enroll her in a Montessori school that has materials that seem to enthrall Chet and June even more than they do Carol.

Chet converts the garden shed in the backyard to a workshop where he can weld and dabble with chemicals. He is in seventh heaven. June loves it too. Carol is not allowed in by herself, and has her own goggles and lab coat. Together, they keep detailed records of the results of their experiments.

It is a halcyon summer of rocket testing. June packs picnic lunches that they eat under a lone cottonwood by a creek up in the yellow hills on the edge of a vast, fenced test range or in a blockhouse with good-natured engineers who converse with Carol as if she were an adult. They ask Chet and June why she knows so much at such a young age. Chet replies that geometry and trigonometry are taught much too late in school, that one has to "strike while the iron is hot" (his favorite homily) when it comes to helping kids pursue their interests in the world, and that one must use tangible objects that kids can manipulate. This always brings a laugh. "Yeah, nothing more tangible than a rocket, Chet—especially when it heads in your direction." Carol overhears her mother say that Carol is a normal child—well, maybe just a little above average—and that all children would benefit from this approach to learning. "Yeah—if only there were enough rocket scientists to go around." A general laugh. Carol gets the impression that rocket men are light-hearted people who are always laughing.

• • •

In September of 1962, Carol's mother unfolds the newspaper at their sun-drenched breakfast table and reads, "Kennedy Says 'We Choose to Go to the Moon in this Decade.'"

"By God, I purely love that man," says Chet, reaching for the Log Cabin syrup. Then he starts coughing. He coughs hard, for a long time.

Carol says, "You have a bad cold, Daddy."

"Yes," says her father. "I need to drink more orange juice."

June jumps up and starts to wash dishes. She washes them very quickly. She rattles them, scrubs them with steel wool, and smacks them into the dish drainer.

• • •

Chet dies in a car crash on his way back from White Sands in early November 1963. Forever afterward, his and Kennedy's deaths—their suddenness, the way they divide history, their absolute darkness—are inextricably linked in Carol's mind.

A force Carol does not understand, but accepts as a part of the unexpected changes in life, like the shock of menstruation (which no one told her was coming—perhaps her mother thought she wouldn't believe her) blankets her heart and mind for the next few years, a black cloud that she hugs close. It keeps her from volunteering in class, from making the kind of sharp remark she used to make when kids made fun of her. Her mother takes Carol to a therapist, but she rather despises him.

One night, lying awake and staring into the dark, she understands what has happened. She has a somatic vision, a picture that floats above her, of her life as a ribbon in time and space. It is not a flat ribbon. It is an infinitely long cylinder, made up of tiny shapes, sounds, people, events, faces, days that she used to be able to expand and remember. She can see the point where her heart, mind, time, and space—everything—suddenly flattened and twisted into the tiniest thread imaginable, dense and heavy with time, as dark as the void of space. Before the dark twist, everything was real, and after it—now—is real, but very different because the twist stops the flow from past to present. The dark twist occludes every glad memory and, according to her grades, everything she's ever known. She doesn't care.

June finds a job as an office manager, explaining that they need a little more money now. She gets very, very thin and smokes a lot more.

One night, Carol hears her mother crying at night in her bedroom. She wants to jump up and run into her mother's bedroom and hug her, but something makes her arms and legs very heavy, so heavy that she can't get out of bed. After school, Carol has to stay at Aunt Edna's. Instead of doing homework at Edna's, she watches the *Mickey Mouse Club* show every afternoon while her cousin Andy sneers that it is a little kid's show.

· · ·

Suddenly, June marries Blake Henry, an economics professor at Caltech. Carol has hardly met him, and they are packing all of the things in their house to store in his attic, all of her childhood things, even her rocket collection, because there is no room in his house for them. Actually, they just don't look right there. Blake's ex-wife left a house full of fancy old vases, dark furniture that June now polishes once a week, twin boys who are ten years old and a sixteen-year-old girl who tells Carol that her mother "rode off on the back of a Harley with a Hells Angel and isn't ever coming back." Despite their similarity in age—Carol is fifteen—they do not become friends, as their parents had surmised they might.

She never hears Blake talk with June the way that June and Chet had talked. All that kind of talk has been folded neatly, put into boxes, and stored in the attic. Now, it really does seem like June was born to run the vacuum cleaner, make Swedish meatballs, and keep the washing machine chugging day and night. One day she overhears Blake say, "You're not teaching Carol anything about keeping house."

"Maybe that's not what she'll want to do," June snaps.

She's right about that.

"Well, don't expect me to support her."

"Don't worry. You know, we might not even be here, Blake."

"I'm sorry," he says. "I'm really sorry."

· · ·

Something in Carol catches fire and explodes.

It is 1965. Carol shortens her skirts, wears white go-go boots, listens to British rock 'n' roll, applies heavy black eyeliner and mascara (strictly forbidden by her mother) in the girls' bathroom at school, and smokes Chesterfields. The teacher in charge of the rocket club tries to prevent her from joining, but Carol's mother marches into the next meeting and "chews him up one side and down the other," as she describes it at dinner. The club plans to spend all year designing and building a single rocket for the science fair in the spring, a fairly boring process, as far as Carol is concerned. Three of the rocket-club boys, seniors, whose ringleader is Kent, invite her to build bombs with them just for the hell of it.

It seems like a good idea at the time.

They respect her for what she knows, which begins to reemerge from the other side of the dark twist (though a good deal remains there, she learns eventually). It is exhilarating to walk purposefully, wearing jeans and sneakers, after school and on the weekends, through the huge concrete viaducts that lace the interstate junctions, set off explosions, and race to safety, breathless and laughing. It doesn't seem that anyone in the passing torrent of automobiles ever notices the explosions.

Kent's father is a chemist, and Kent forges his father's name on chemical supply orders. They make the bombs in the garage lab he's had since he was ten years old. One afternoon, as Carol precisely weighs chemicals, she decides that she will characterize this extracurricular activity as one in which she "uses her time in a creative manner."

But Blake (she calls her stepfather Blake, because it annoys him) notices that she is withdrawing money from her savings account, which contains presents her relatives have given her over the years, and her baby-sitting earnings, and also discovers, somehow, that she has been using it to buy rather odd things at the hardware store. He finds out that it was she who ruined one of his circular saw blades (she meant to replace it but hadn't had a chance) in his basement shop, which he never uses anyway, and elicits school scuttlebutt from his rat-children, natural-born snitches. He grounds her for a month. She is incensed. It is her money; why should he have anything to do with it?

After a loud argument in which Carol's mother emphatically does not stand in solidarity with Blake, she knocks on Carol's bedroom door and sits next to her on her twin bed.

"What do you suggest?"

"I need to get out of here. I'm going to go crazy."

"There's no way out but college."

"I'm only *fifteen*." Dreary, bombless, Blake-throttled years stretch ahead, a dark eternity.

"You might as well start now figuring out how to do it and where to go and what you want to do."

"I want to go to the moon."

"Might make a good essay, if it included the steps you need to take to get there."

"Fiction."

"Don't be silly," June says, her voice harsh. "What would your father think? Figure it out. Have you paid any attention to what's going on with the Apollo program lately? No, I guess you've been a little too busy. Come back with a plan—with several plans, actually—and we'll see what we can do about getting started. Going to the moon will not just happen to you. You have to make it happen."

"My guidance counselor told me I should plan to be a secretary, nurse, or teacher."

"Mine did too. And I fulfilled their expectations."

"Why?"

"Because that was the country's expectation, that men should have the best jobs, and besides, that's the way it always was until the war. After the war, the men were back. There weren't many jobs for women with my qualifications. That's my excuse, anyway, but it was just the easiest thing to do. You've heard about the feminists, haven't you?"

"Um, yeah. I guess."

"I suggest you find out more. And Carol?"

"What?"

June lowers her voice. "I understand why Blake's wife rode off on the back of a Harley."

At first, they just giggle and snort, but laughter finally explodes from them. They laugh so hard they cry. They subside into weak giggles, but when they look at each other, the laughter builds again. Finally, they fall back on the bed, breathless.

"Is that what you're going to do?"

"I don't think so," says June soberly. "But I could easily change my mind. I've certainly thought about it, but I know everything will be fine. If I didn't, I never would have married him. It was just too sudden, and I'm sorry. You should have been involved in the decision. I didn't think about it. I just went kind of nuts after your father died."

. . .

Blake is even less happy when Carol's extracurricular activities expand to include feminist marches and demonstrations against the Vietnam War. He is hard to please.

Gradually, the Eames chairs, the modernistic dining room table, and Carol's rockets emerge from storage. Dark, fusty landscape paintings come down off the wall. As the house is repainted in bright colors, June convinces Blake to "invest" in modern art that reminds Carol of the one-eyed aliens that might live on Mars. A cleaning lady comes once a week. June starts writing *Chemistry for Children* in a spare bedroom she claims as an office. Sometimes, Blake hums around the house.

Carol still hates him.

. . .

Carol hears Blake say to June, "By the way, did you hear about that Kent kid?"

"What about him?"

"Blew up his garage. Ran away. The police are looking into it. Aren't you glad I got Carol out of that before she got in trouble?"

It's all over school. Kent is hiding out in Crescent City, with a friend who graduated a few years back. He's not hiding from the police. He's hiding from his father.

If Carol had been there, he wouldn't have blown up his garage.

. . .

Carol takes college-track classes, despite the opposition of her guidance counselor. At first, trig and calculus seem hopeless, an impenetrable foreign language. Her mind is like a rusted machine with frozen bolts. She can't make head or tails of anything; nothing seems related to what she'd done when she was, supposedly, a brilliant little kid.

. . .

One afternoon while sitting on the school bus ignoring the chaos, it comes to her: this is just one way of looking at time and space, a way she learned when standing in a different place, with a different view—the view from the house where her rockets hung from the ceiling. It is like learning to take new roads to get to the same place. You see new scenery along the way. She closes her eyes and sees how it all fits together, how to speak these languages. Pictures pace through her mind. It feels so good, like waking after a long sleep.

She smells cigarette smoke, and sees her father's face, close and dear. He says, "Carol, I have something to tell you . . ."

Someone shakes her shoulder. Angry at being yanked from her father, from what he was going to say, she squinches her eyes firmly shut.

"Hey. Kid. You okay?"

It's the bus driver.

"Your stop's about two miles away. I wish I could drive you back, but I got to get home to my own kids."

The bus is empty. "It's okay. I can walk."

It is, in fact, a grand day to walk. How, she wonders, did she hover above the things she used to know and put them together again? She worries that she might lose it all, just as easily. It's part of the dark twist, along with so many of her memories. Sometimes she can't even remember what her dad looked like.

She starts to run, to run home, to write down, draw, nail down what she has seen, what she knows, how to think, the new roads that stretch to a new distance.

To the stars.

• • •

In the summer of 1967, Haight-Ashbury casts its spell across the entire country. In Carol's neighborhood, kids crowd into any car that can be cadged from unwary parents to make the trip from LA to San Francisco. The Haight's seductive alternate world beckons, through blacklight posters (in friend's bedrooms, not her own), psychedelic music (which she listens to through tiny headphones), and pot (which she smokes with friends), but Carol never fully surrenders to its sensuous siren call. She does choose a young man with whom to have sex, just because it seems so important to everyone and she is curious, but the relationship only lasts a few weeks. He keeps showing up on the front porch, undeterred by Blake, and sits moping in his car in front of the house several nights in a row, but finally gets the picture.

Carol instead surrenders to the clean power of science and math—possibly because she knows a lot more about both than most people her age. They attract her in ways she cannot really communicate, except that she wants to go further and further into them, there will never be an end to them, they are dependable and real, and they will take her where she wants to go. She finds her father's thesis in the attic and reads it end to end, working out equations she doesn't understand. One day June says, "I'm worried about you. You're so much like your father."

"Is there something wrong with that?"

Her mother looks as if she's going to say yes, and maybe, even, say why, but then smiles a bit sadly and says, "Of course not, honey. I guess I just miss him," gives Carol a surprising hug, and goes off to settle an argument between the twins.

Things seem a lot better now with Blake and June. She hears them having actual conversations. They enjoy watching TV in the evening. They go for little trips up the coast.

Carol hates him.

. . .

There aren't many engineering schools that accept women. It is not difficult or expensive to apply to all of them.

. . .

Carol holds her head high, a dimple in her cheek. She isn't smiling. The dimple manifests from the effort of suppressing explosive laughter. Miniskirted, carrying a stack of chemistry books, she strides past slamming lockers and tight circles of gossiping girls who glance sidelong at her as she sweeps past them in the hall. She just got the news from her stunned guidance counselor that she received a perfect SAT score in chemistry—one of two in the country—and a near-perfect score in math. She must have made some stupid mistake, which irritates her. From now on, she will be more careful when taking tests.

After fielding offers from Caltech and Georgia Tech, she decides to attend MIT on a full scholarship.

It's about as far away from California as she can get.

. . .

The first day at MIT, Carol's chemistry lab-bench mate asks her out. Eddie's blond hair skims his shirt collar, and he has cute blue eyes.

They go to a bar on Harvard Square. It's only eight, but the place is loud and lively. They drink overflowing mugs of beer at a tiny, deeply marred table, and order another round. Carol has a good head for beer, liquor, pot—just about anything, really. Sometimes she thinks it's kind of a shame; she has to spend so much more to get a decent buzz.

It starts out okay. They talk about their families. They both like Hendrix, but he's never heard of Pink Floyd or the Velvet Underground. He asks if she always wears jeans, and she says that's what everybody in California wears. He glances around and she notices that most of the other women in the bar wear preppy-looking skirts and blouses. If she were to wear a skirt, it would be a colorful hippie skirt. She doesn't mention that she often dances topless at Grateful Dead concerts. It doesn't seem like the kind of thing one would talk about on a first date.

She discovers that Eddie would have been a cheap date, if she had been paying.

"So, your dad was a rocket scientist?"

"This is the third time you've asked."

"Well, it just explains everything."

"Explains what?"

"Why you're here."

She slides from her stool and slips her pack onto her shoulder.

"Where are you going? What's wrong?"

"I doubt you'll ever figure it out."

Burning with anger—she decided not to go to Caltech just because of this is-sue, because her father had gone there—she pushes her way through the crowded bar and emerges onto the sidewalk.

Most of the people she sees are men. She's set to go for a nice, long walk to burn off her anger—maybe down to the harbor, maybe to California—when she notices a small, tasteful sign: *Harvard Book Shop*.

She ducks inside.

Soon, she's reeling. She couldn't possibly afford all the books she wants, not by a long shot, not even with her scholarship. Physics, chemistry, rocketry, IBM com-puter programming . . . a cornucopia.

Then she runs across the women's studies section. Hmmm. She leaves with an issue of *Off Our Backs*. She's seen it around, but never picked it up. She'd been planning to leave all the asshole boys in California behind.

She should have known they were everywhere.

It's even worse than it seems at first. By the time she leaves for Christmas, two of her professors have asked her "out," broadly implying that her decision might have something to do with her grades. She feels very lucky that all of her classes cover material not open to interpretation. Answers are right or wrong. She does as much public work at the blackboard as possible, always volunteers to answer ques-tions, and is never caught flat-footed when chosen. In fact, some of her answers seem to awe her classmates, and soon no one asks her out, saving her the trouble of saying no.

She'd learned in high school that no one likes a smart girl. Everyone is smart at MIT, but no smarter than her. They should be her natural peers. Why does being a girl always mean that you have to be tougher than anyone else?

Well, fuck it. When she leaves at Christmas, she's decided not to go back.

Her mother talks her out of it. She soldiers through her first year, and gets a summer job in a National Science Foundation lab in Bethesda, Maryland.

She gets a call from her mother in early July.

"You've got to come home for it, honey."

She knows what June means.

They have to watch the moon landing together.

• • •

She flies in on the nineteenth. Her mother meets her on the tarmac, and they hug. Carol is surprised at how much older June looks. Her clothes are kind of . . . dowdy, and they hang on her. She even looks a little bit shorter. But once June starts talk-ing, all that goes away.

Carol says, "Mom, I'm so glad to see you!"

"Oh, honey, so am I. So am I." They walk through the parking lot. Everything seems brighter and bigger in California, after the humidity and congestion of Bethesda. "I have a plan. But you can decide. We have an invitation to watch the landing at the Jet Propulsion Lab."

"Really? That is so cool!"

"Oh, it is. They really want us there, all of your dad's old friends. We'd have a great day. But here's my alternative."

They choose plan B and drive north on the Coast Highway as the sun falls slowly toward the ocean. They pick up vodka, olives, and gin along the way. They also buy three fancy martini glasses and some groceries. June gets a carton of cigarettes. Carol stopped smoking, mostly, the day she graduated high school.

The trip is deeply soothing. Carol realizes that her body memorized the curves of the highway along the base of the hills that plunge into the ocean, perhaps when she was an infant. She rides into the history of her own body, her own mind, curving, wending, leaning, growing younger with each bend of the Coast Highway. The Pacific Ocean is silver behind June, who drives as if hypnotized, smoking one cigarette after another, a faint smile on her face. The lowering sun pours through the open window, a gold and salty tone, turning her mother's face to a map of dissonant lines that Carol has never heard before. She watches June grow older by the second in the intensifying light, and this new, strange music is difficult to bear.

"Mother!" says Carol, and June turns wide blue eyes toward her.

"What, darling?"

"I love you, mother."

June blinks fast, and shimmering tears overflow. She wipes them from her cheek with the palm of her right hand and smiles. "I love you too, Carol. I love you more than all the moon and stars."

When the bottom of the sun has just touched the horizon, June pulls into the parking lot of a beachfront motel, the Astro. She comes out of the office with a key for room six. "Your father and I used to come here when we first met," she says.

They make martinis, which otherwise neither of them drinks, carry them on a walk on the golden beach. They return to the room, and hear that the lunar module containing Aldrin and Armstrong is orbiting the moon.

"It seems nearly impossible," says June, watching the screen.

After the news, they go back to the beach, greeting others out strolling and gazing at the still-virgin moon, all of them charged by the event that they cannot even see that unfolds in the heavens at that very moment.

They meet a woman whose curly hair matches the color of the moon and the surf spray lit by moonlight, standing in a rush of foam that swiftly recedes. She rattles the ice in her glass of Scotch. "My life bridges two eras. I was born in 1888. We rode horses or trains." She wriggles her feet more deeply into the sand, as if to root herself. "When I was a young woman, I lived right outside Dayton, Ohio. During 1903 and 1904, the Wright brothers made hundreds of test flights from Huffman Prairie, down the road from us. Everybody from miles around would call the neighbors out, and we'd watch those flying machines circle round and round. And now look! They're flying circles round the moon. I just feel . . . a part of it. Yes, a part of it." Another wave rushes in, soaking the rooted woman's dress, but not knocking her down. June and Carol steady her, extricate her, and make sure she returns safely to her family's room.

On the morning of July 20, 1969, the beach in front of the Astro Motel is full of strollers, sunbathers, and children. June finds a radio station that describes Cocoa Beach as a carnival. The announcer gives them up-to-the-minute reports of "the moon shot" against a background of clattering teletype machines. They sit on the patio, watching and listening.

When they settle down in front of the black-and-white television, the beach and the road are eerily empty. The parking lot of the Astro Motel is full.

"I'm sorry—I didn't even think that the Astro might not have a color TV," says June, but it doesn't matter. The moon is stark shades of white, gray, black. Space is intensely black.

Everything unfolds beautifully. Both humans and computers compensate for errors; they are flexible and hyperaware. When Aldrin says, "Houston, Tranquility Base here. The Eagle has landed," both of their faces shine with tears. Nestled together on the couch, they raise their martinis to Chet and to all those who made it possible.

The moon landing broadcast lasts only about ten minutes. When it ends, the astronauts prepare for their moon walk, which begins at six-thirty in the evening. The second broadcast, in which the astronauts walk on the moon, is three hours long. The fuzzy picture and storms of static immerse Carol in distance, emphasize the technical difficulties overcome by human ingenuity, obliterate a millennium of myth and legend, and fill her mind with a million questions. By the time it is over, Carol is wrung dry. Her chest aches. She doesn't remember ever being in the grip of such powerful, unrelenting emotions for such a long period of time.

• • •

The next morning, after Carol has flown back to the East Coast on the red-eye, the capsule splashes down. A picture-perfect engineering triumph.

For one of the first times in her life that she can remember, her heart feels full, as if it is expanding to encompass everyone around her. As she takes the metro bus home, the faces of the others on the bus seem meaningful in a way she does not understand, but accepts. The time she spent with June, without any deep talk at all, satisfied some unknown yearning. It has given her a bass tone, that of the world around her—the suburban streets, the hiss of air brakes, the wheeze of the bus door opening and closing—and a bright fanfare, that sounds like sunlight sifting through leaves and dappling the sidewalk at her bus stop, comprised of everyone going about their morning business, her mother's increasingly dear face, and the footprint on the moon.

She no longer needs to know why her mother has done the things she has done, has made the decisions she has made, or why she has not ever spoken of them. The dark twist, this morning, does not matter. This side is enough.

It is more than enough.

December 1970

All is monotone: infinite shades of gray, black, white. Silver, ivory, charcoal. Great blue-black rivers of shadow flow down a distant jag-peaked mountain, but then, in an instant, all is obscured by cloud.

Snow closes round Carol, coalescing out of air colder than she has ever experienced. She has never known a wild winter; Boston's weather is tamed by streets, machines, humans, cozy rooms, ready food.

She is alone in deep nature, a voice that speaks to her in strangely powerful articulations of shape and color, in shards of deep, whirring sound. She pulls her scarf over her numb face and stands still.

Snow on the craggy slopes of the mountain puffs upward like the spray of surf as, nearby, stands of bare cottonwoods roar almost as if they possess a voice, a mind, the urge to sing. The slow, majestic harmony that her mind and eyes modulate is something she has not experienced since she was a child.

She wouldn't have heard the truck if not for the muffled jingle of its chains. The narrow road is so snowed over that she's practically forgotten she's standing on a road. The truck stops next to her and a woman rolls down the window. Wild black hair escapes through gaps in the green scarf wrapped haphazardly round her head and neck. Mittened hands grip the wheel. A mutt sticks its brown head out over her shoulder. "Headed to the lodge?"

Lodge? That sounds expensive. "Hitching. Is there a good place to pitch a tent around here?"

The woman laughs. "Unless you're trying to set some kind of survival-camping record, tonight wouldn't be the best night for that. Get in. We've got plenty of room and lots of food." She gives Carol an appraising look. "Free."

"Thanks. I'm Carol." Carol tosses her backpack in the back of the truck and climbs into the cab. The dog settles on her lap. She has been swept from a possibly spectacular night of immersion in powerful beauty. Or, given her amateur outdoorswoman status, death by hypothermia.

"Heat's broken. I'm Ishwari. 'Goddess' in Hindi. In case you're interested. I live at the Lama Foundation over there on the mountain—you've heard of Baba Ram Dass?"

Carol shakes her head.

"Timothy Leary?"

She laughs. "Yeah."

"He came through a few months ago and left a huge stash of Owsley acid. Dennis Hopper—"

"The movie Dennis Hopper?"

"That's the one. He bought the Mabel Dodge Luhan place a few months ago and turned the place into a wild party house. I'm bummed about it. That's where we're going. The lodge has a lot of good vibes. When Dodge bought it in the teens, she turned it into an artist colony. D. H. Lawrence and his wife, Frieda, Gertrude Stein, Georgia O'Keeffe, Carl Jung—all kinds of cross-fertilization. Well, I'm here to try to keep the vibes good. Coke never brings good vibes, y'know? Well, here we are!"

They pass through heavy, wooden gates that stand open, beneath an iron bell set in a graceful adobe surround. She stops next to a snow-swathed entryway. The dog leaps out; Carol retrieves her pack.

Ishwari says, "You can share my room tonight." Carol follows the woman through a maze of rooms full of people and Ishwari opens the door to an oasis of quiet. A small fire burns in an adobe fireplace. The room is adorned with warm, glowing colors. Carol would like to fall into the low, narrow bed and sleep for a week. She's been hitching for almost that long. She left MIT in a bit of a huff, unable to find a grope-free mentor, one who would take her own plans and vision seriously. She had a bus ticket, but always travels with a pack that will help her stay self-sufficient in any situation. When the bus broke down outside of Boston, she stuck out her thumb.

And here she is, outside of Taos, New Mexico.

"Is there a phone here?" she asks Ishwari.

"Line's down. Sorry. Well, let's join the par-tay! Hope you like tofu chili."

Ishwari leads her to a large room with another adobe fireplace. Once white, it is now dirty and marred, but beneath all that Carol can see its perfection. She edges close to the fire. About twenty-five people or so are hanging out. Two women sit on a nearby couch, one playing a mandolin and one a flute. The smell of strong pot is in the air. A young man has crashed on the floor in front of the fireplace. Men and women alike are festooned with beads. Some wear spectacular silver and turquoise pieces. Headbands and long hair are ubiquitous, as well as hats. A woman in a fringed leather jacket sits cross-legged on the floor, nursing a baby. Through a large arched door, at a round table, bikers in black leather play poker and drink whiskey.

She is definitely not in Boston anymore. She's back in the west. She feels comfortable, at home. "Nice scene," Carol says to the guy standing next to her, warming himself by the fire.

"Toke? Yeah, this is Hopper's place."

"I gather it's gone downhill."

"I think he plans to restore it. Want a beer?"

Fifteen minutes later, Carol says, "I'm tripping. Right?"

"We all are. Didn't want you to get left out."

"In the beer?"

"Yeah."

She hands it back to him, smiling. "I've probably had enough for now. Thanks."

Carol hasn't dropped acid very often, and never with a bunch of strangers. Well, except at Grateful Dead concerts. But she feels oddly safe, despite the shotguns on the wall and the bikers in the other room. Well, better to enjoy it than to spend the night trembling under a bed.

She dances, weaving sinuous tracks among the tracks of the others. Some follow her lead. The flute changes rhythm, and she feels simultaneously as if she has joined an ancient dance and that she is observing herself tripping and creating an entirely new dance. She is stomping on the moon, tap-dancing on one of Saturn's rings, stepping up and down among them as if they were stairs.

She makes her way outside and dances to the cosmos, which sounds like doo-wop, then lies on her back in the comfortable, fluffy snow for an infinity, her mind building rockets to the stars. The clouds have cleared, and she has never seen stars so brilliant.

"Hey." Someone grabs her hand and pulls her up. "Let's go see *Fantasia*."

She finds her way back to Ishwari's room, somehow, and grabs her pack. Ishwari looks up from the book she is reading. "Namaste."

"What?"

"I bow to the divine in you."

"Thank you! Namaste."

Two full pickups fishtail out of the drive and make their way slowly, chains jingling, toward town. The few sparkling lights in the distance are Taos. The ride is splendid. They sing "Jingle Bells." The trucks pull up in front of an old theater and everyone jumps out and troops inside. No one asks for money. Joints make their way across the rows of seats. A white man wearing a feathered hat stands up and says, "We all know Stokowski was a fan of peyote. Took it when he stayed at the Dodge Lodge—participated in religious rites somewhere up in the mountains. Worked with Disney on *Fantasia*. Old Walt was introduced to it at Black Mountain College in North Carolina, then went down to Mexico—"

The projector clicks on. The music begins. The word *Fantasia* bends across his chest. "Stop boring us and sit down, Elk Who Fucking Flies, so we can watch the movie!" someone yells.

Carol saw *Fantasia* on a black-and-white television when she was a kid and she was scared out of her wits by skeletons flying through the sky, by Mickey's terrifying, brainless, out-of-control replicating brooms.

This time, she loves the dancing mushrooms. Peyote mushrooms, of course. The delicate dancing faceless flowers. "The Sorcerer's Apprentice" might be an old story, but it is breathtakingly of the present: robots, and how they might be able to re-create themselves and mindlessly conquer the world.

When *Fantasia* is over, with nary a break, the projectionist threads Disney's Man in Space series: "Man in Space," "Man and the Moon," and "Mars and Beyond."

She saw this long, long ago, sitting in her living room in front of a black-and-white TV. when a child, but this long-ago, almost fantastic vision is now real. Men have walked on the moon using von Braun's blueprint to get there.

It is all rather breathtaking.

Her father's arch nemesis, von Braun, explains rockets, as well as a plan to reach the moon and Mars, in his German-accented voice. An entire generation of kids have this in their brains. And, apparently, a generation of adults as well, because of his *Collier's* article and other publicity.

Without this, would the nation have supported Kennedy's declaration that the United States would put a man on the moon before the decade's end? The technical know-how had been there—it had just been a matter of committing money.

And of educating kids.

Why, she wonders, with a lump in her throat, has she been sidelined at MIT? Why did she allow it to happen?

Suddenly, she stands and shouts, "It's because of all these *men* on the moon! Where are the women?"

"Yeah!" yell some women, and then the ragtag group rises as one and cheers as wildly as if they had all been offered a free Mars bar. "Where! Are! The! Women! Where! Are! The! Women!" Ward Kimball's Mars aliens, gawky, puzzled-looking creatures, play across their faces, imprinting them squarely with mid-century America, with its mutant tomatoes, big-finned flying cars, crumpling rockets collapsing in clouds of fire and smoke, a roomful of Ping-Pong balls released by mousetraps, an enormous genie bursting out of a tiny bottle, the secrets of the universe theirs to use and abuse.

And a ticket out of it.

"Here, dammit!" yells Carol, as cool flat spaceships that look like tops twirl neatly across their faces. "I'm *here*! I'm a goddamn rocket woman and that's all there is to it! I'm gonna go back to MIT and kick their butts."

"Whooo! Yeeeeehaw! Take us along! To the *moon*, Alice!"

Carol hoists her pack and leaves, grabbing a bag of stale popcorn in the lobby, still mildly tripping, and holds out her thumb as Christmas day dawns in mountain time, pale pink and green, electric blue mountains rimming the horizon. An old man in a pickup truck pulls over. When she gets in, he says, "Kin take you as far as Albuquerque. Now, you ain't no whore, are you?"

"Afraid not," she says, settling in. The day dazzles. Snowy fields are etched with long blue dawn-flung shadows; distant mountains ring that same white and blue, in a deeper tone, with bare brown ridges. The land gives forth harmonies not only to her eye, but to her ear, a deep and pleasing music.

"Good. My wife would pitch a fit if she knew I gave a ride to a whore."

"I wouldn't blame her. You're not some kind of pervert, are you?"

"No, ma'am. And please pardon my previous question. I apologize."

She'd run into her fair share of creeps, and thought she could tell. But in case she made a mistake, she always kept a switchblade handy, and knew how to use it.

"Apology accepted. Got a cigarette?"

"And coffee in that thermos there. You're one a them hippies, I guess."

"Kind of. But not really. I'm a rocket scientist."

"I'd think you'd be able to buy your own truck then."

She laughs. She feels light, free, happy.

Strong.

They cross a dizzyingly high bridge. "Rio Grande Gorge. River way, way down there. One of the prettiest sights around in the prettiest spot in the country. You stayin' out at the Dodge place?"

"Just got there last night. I'm on my way to White Sands."

The descent to Albuquerque is through a long, stunning canyon that dips below the high plateau she's been on for several days.

The ghost of her father sits at her elbow, smiling at her. He really is—his blond hair in a flattop, his black engineer glasses, his thin, mobile face, with laugh crow's-feet around his blue eyes. He gives her a thumbs-up.

She doesn't know she's crying until the old man pats her shoulder. "There, there."

She takes a deep breath. "I'm just happy."

Even though she knows it was the acid, remembering this always makes her happy.

. . .

She calls her mother from an Albuquerque phone booth. "Merry Christmas!" she says.

It's Blake. "Where are you? Your mother is worried sick!"

"I'm sorry," she says. "My bus broke down, I hitchhiked to Taos—"

"Well, you get yourself home right away!"

"Where's Mom?"

"She's at your Aunt Edna's."

"I'm going to White Sands tomorrow, but I should be home by the next night."

"You are a very selfish young lady, Carol."

"Merry Christmas, Blake."

She sits on a bench for a few minutes afterward. She finds her way to the bus station and discovers that the last bus west has left.

There is no point in spending the night in the bus station.

. . .

Close to Las Cruces, she gets a ride up to the White Sands Missile Range with a navy guy who is on guard duty that night. "It's closed Christmas," he says. "Where do you plan to stay, anyway?"

"I'll just set up my tent somewhere on the perimeter. Maybe on some high place. Got any suggestions?"

"Well—"

"My dad worked there sometimes, in the fifties. He actually worked for the Jet Propulsion Lab and came out here to test rocket engines. He brought me with him a few times when I was little."

"No kidding!"

"He died in '63. I just kind of wanted to see it again. I'm studying at MIT right now, on my way home to California."

"You're still an army dependent, right?"

"Yeah. I've got my ID with me. It's a great thing. I get insurance, the army helps pay for my education."

"Right." He smokes for a few minutes. "Well, look. I think it would be okay to let you sleep in the barracks tonight. Then I could get somebody to give you a ride out to the test site tomorrow. I don't think anything's scheduled, but I guess you just want to look around, right?"

"You're kidding! Really? That would be fantastic!"

"Might even be able to scare up somebody who knew your dad. What was his name?"

"Chet. Chester Thaddeus Hall." She laughs. "He hated his middle name. Listen, I don't want to get anybody in trouble."

"I'll check it out, but I think the ID will make it okay. Besides, if it weren't Christmas, you wouldn't have a problem. It's not as if you'd be going anywhere classified."

. . .

The next day, Carol stands on the dunes, visits the blockhouse, hears the ghostly laughter of those engineers, amused that she knows so much, amused that she is even here on their sacred male ground. The sky above is clear and blue, a perfect test day. She remembers their careful measurements, the record sheets, the calculations.

Rocketry is in her blood.

I'm here, dammit. And I'm here to stay.

• • •

When she finally gets home, she tells her mother she is transferring to Caltech. June's eyes light up. "Oh, honey, that's wonderful." She gives Carol a tight hug, and her thin arms feel like bird's wings. Carol steps back. "Mom, are you okay?"

"Sit down."

Blake sits next to June on the couch and holds her hand as she talks. She has had one breast removed, but now she is recovering. Everything is going well.

"Why didn't you tell me?"

"I didn't want to interrupt your studies."

"I'm not going back."

"Just finish out the year, and then—"

"What for? I'll fly back, get everything taken care of, find someone to take over the lease, withdraw from school—"

"But it will take time to apply to Caltech. You won't be able to start this semester. What are you going to do?"

"Spend time with you, Mom. I can take you to the doctor, we can go for drives, play bridge—you know. All that."

"Well, it would be nice. But I feel so selfish."

"I feel absolutely delighted."

• • •

June lied, of course. She is not recovering.

They spend two strange, luminous months in suspended time. Carol drives her up the old roads, and it often seems that Chet is there between them, like some kind of phenomenon in which intersecting waves create meaningful data.

• • •

She finally asks, "What happened to Dad? Really?"

Her mother is lying on the sofa in the living room. "There's a box on the top shelf of my closet. Get it for me, please." Her very short hair is white, and her voice is hoarse. If Carol takes time to think about what's happening, she cries, so she tries her best to just be there and enjoy this time.

"Put it on the coffee table and open it up."

On top are a lot of old pictures. Some are black and white, with scalloped edges. She is in some of them, and there are various configurations of family in most of them. "You remember your Grandpa Hall, right? You should really go see him sometime. He's still in Pennsylvania. Did you know he was a Communist during the 1930s?"

"Of course not. Who would tell me?"

"Families are funny. Aunt Edna might have said something."

Carol shakes her head. "What does this have to do with Dad?"

"Your grandpa helped lead several miner's strikes. At that time, the Communist

Party was widely accepted as progressive. It was about worker's rights. We didn't really know how terrible conditions in the Soviet Union had become. Certainly, being a member of the party wasn't looked on as being un-American. They called themselves patriots. They felt that they were being exploited by wealthy industries, and they were. Your father's big brother—"

"Uncle Mike." The mythical, perfect brother who died in the war.

"Yes. He was a deep believer. I think your father just followed in his footsteps. But in 1939, they both dropped their memberships and moved on with their engineering education. I think this broke your grandfather's heart.

"Except for that, all was well and good. But after the war, when your father got his master's degree at Caltech, he found it was a hotbed of Communist activity. He had never disavowed the ideals of the party, but he wasn't interested in the secretive, regimented way they conducted their business. Anyway, someone from Pennsylvania recognized him and pressured him to rejoin. Your father refused, and so this man reported him as a past member of the Communist Party. Which was true. And even though it had been so long since he was involved in it, he eventually lost his very high security clearance. North American Aviation hated to let him go, but they had no choice. Everyone in the industry knew your father, knew what had happened, thought it terribly unfair, and gave him work. But it was piecemeal work. Your father felt that he couldn't contribute what he was capable of contributing if he didn't know everything there was to know about a project. He was offered some fabulous jobs outside of the country."

"I know."

June looks at her and smiles. "I don't think so. How would you know? You were so little."

"You never told me?"

"I doubt it."

"Well . . . I don't know how I know. I just do."

"Ah, well. Afterward, I thought . . . well, it didn't make any difference by then, but I thought I should have agreed to go. I imagine I would have if he hadn't gotten sick. Being treated like an untrustworthy outsider hurt him very deeply." She looks down. "I regret so many things."

"Don't!"

June says, "I'm not sure what happened. Why his car ran off the road. But I think he was just tired. So dreadfully tired. From sickness, from working so hard, from sadness at being pushed out . . . I . . . I have to believe this. But I also think it's true."

After her mother dies, Carol is going through her effects and finds *Learn Conversational French in Ten Days*. Inside is a receipt for a beginner's night class in French. There is also a receipt for a refund ten days later. Between those two dates, her father had died.

Accident? Or suicide?

Does it matter?

Carol weighs the fragile evidence of the hard, sad, heavy bones of her family's past in one palm. She holds the two receipts up, like an offering, and the spring breeze ruffling the curtains pushes them straight up into the air, as if launching past and future together into space.

San Fernando Chronicle
January 24, 2000

Carol Hall, who received her PhD in aeronautical engineering from the California Institute of Technology, will spend sixty days on the International Space Station to set up and monitor a device that may make travel to Mars easier. "It's the dream of a lifetime," she said. Her husband of twenty-five years, Hank Thaxton, agrees. "The kids and I—and our one grandchild—are just thrilled for her." When asked what she will take with her, she says, "That's easy—a plastic model of the Jupiter-C rocket that my father, Chet Hall, helped design in the 1950s while at the Jet Propulsion Lab in Pasadena. He helped me build the model, and our family saw the actual launch at Cape Canaveral in 1958. I guess you could say that space is in my blood."

She does not mention the more private thing she is taking—her father's Communist Party membership card.

She lets it go in space, where, as far as she knows, it is still orbiting the Earth.

• • •

Those old Disney shows, much as they irritated her father, are like an anthem of her life. She watches them occasionally, when her grandchildren ask for them. "Man in Space." "Mars and Beyond." The story of her parents' lives, her life, her country's life. The political dark and light of it, inextricably intertwined in war, in peace, in human frailty, and in human dreams.

It is the world's life, now. The wonders, the possibilities, the hardships continue to expand. The dark twist has long since popped open. Images, conversations, music—her childhood, like a disk of information sent in a spaceship for aliens to wonder over—have come forth whole, like clear, bright watercolors, like delicate, unearthly sound, like a sweet, remembered smile.

Like a star once wished upon.

KATHLEEN ANN GOONAN is the author of several novels, including *This Shared Dream. In War Times* won the John W. Campbell Award for Best Science Fiction Novel of 2007; it was also the American Library Association's Best SF Novel of 2007. Previous novels were finalists for the Nebula, Clarke, and BSFA Awards. *Angels and You Dogs* (stories) was published in 2012. Her stories have been published in many various periodicals. She is a Professor of the Practice at Georgia Tech.

Acknowledgments

It takes an intrepid crew to run a rocket ship—so many people helped us launch *Tor.com* and so many more work to make it thrive.

First I want to thank Tor Books Publisher and President Fritz Foy—it was his idea, after all. He put together the initial team of Patrick and Teresa Nielsen Hayden and myself. We never would have been successful without the support of Macmillan—Tom Doherty and John Sargent in particular. Thank you for giving us the space to try things.

I am privileged to spend five days a week working with the smartest, most passionate creative team I could imagine. It's a group that cares deeply about what they do and their effect on the world. I am in awe of them on a daily basis. Thank you, Bridget McGovern, Chris Lough, Jamie Stafford-Hill, Emily Asher-Perrin, Sarah Tolf, Natalie Zutter, Leah Schnelbach, Molly Templeton, Andrew Arens, Katharine Duckett, Mordicai Knode, Lee Harris, Christine Foltzer, Esther Kim, and Chris Gonzalez.

Ruoxi Chen and Carl Engle-Laird, also part of the team, were invaluable in helping to organize *Worlds Seen in Passing* and shepherd it through. Additional thanks to Jamie Stafford-Hill (again) for the wonderful design—inside and out—as well as Lauren Hougen, Melanie Sanders, Jim Kapp, and Nathan Weaver for putting up with us as we navigated our first anthology.

Before the current crew, there were the folks who helped us turn a daydream into a reality: Pablo Defendini, Laurence Hewitt, Megan Messinger, Torie Atkinson, Faith Cheltenham, Ryan Britt, and Brian Napack, who gave us the original green light. We would not have made it very far without you guys. And to the countless others across many departments who have made the site what it is over the years: thank you.

I'm indebted to Greg Manchess for most good things in my life—on the very long list (if I ever *could* list it out) would be designing our logo, affectionately called "Stubby the Rocket." Stubby lent immediate warmth and personality to *Tor.com*. And on a personal note, I owe him my love and thanks for giving me limitless support throughout this and all other endeavors.

I said this in the introduction but I'll enjoy repeating it here: All my admiration and thanks goes out to the writers and artists that share their stories and thoughts with us—in fiction, nonfiction, and all the wonderful places in between. And of course, all the editors that have lent a guiding hand: Patrick Nielsen Hayden, Ellen Datlow, Ann VanderMeer, Liz Gorinsky, Carl Engle-Laird, Jonathan Strahan. There are so many others.

And most of all, I want to thank our readers for spending time with us and waiting to see what happens next. This book is a fraction of what *Tor.com* is, and we're growing and exploring new worlds every day. I hope you'll come on over to the site and join us as we journey onward and upward.

Copyright Acknowledgments